Radio

Radio

Tõnu Õnnepalu

Translated by
Adam Cullen

DALKEY ARCHIVE PRESS
CHAMPAIGN / LONDON / DUBLIN

Originally published in Estonian as *Raadio* by Eesti Keele Sihtasutus, Tallinn, 2002

Copyright © 2002 Tõnu Õnnepalu
Translation and translator's notes © 2013 by Adam Cullen

First edition, 2014

A catalog record for this book is available from the Library of Congress.
978-1-62897-008-1

This publication is partially supported by the National Endowment for the Arts,
a federal agency; the Illinois Arts Council, a state agency; and
the University of Illinois at Urbana-Champaign.

Supported by the Estonian Ministry of Culture and the
Cultural Endowment of Estonia

www.dalkeyarchive.com

Cover: design and composition Mikhail Iliatov

Printed on permanent/durable acid-free paper

Table of Contents

A bus ticket from Tallinn to Tartu costs twenty Estonian kroons. The kroon is pegged to the euro at an exchange rate of 15.6466 kroons to one euro: as such, the trip (189 km from the northwest to the southeast) costs about 1.30 euros, which means—so that I myself might have a better conception of it—about eight francs; thus, the price of a Paris Métro ticket. I still haven't gotten used to thinking in euros, although I have become accustomed to counting (*compter*) in them. Such obduracy is most likely due to age (thirty-nine), and perhaps also aversion to those bland notes, whose portraits of historical figures have been replaced by empty door-, window-, and bridgescapes. Especially dear to me were the portraits on the older notes, the ones before last—those of Blaise Pascal on the five hundred, and of Michel de Montaigne (he was perhaps on the two hundred). Those old, large, appealing bank notes are already starting to fade from memory; still, I earned my first real money in them. It was in January of 1991 that I met Liza Franz eye-to-eye for the first time. And so began our relationship, which I will try to document here, in the hopes of reaching an answer to the secret of Liz Franz's disappearance.

Currently portrayed on Estonian bank notes, which upon this country's future accession to the European Union will naturally also be exchanged for euros, are still historic figures: Lydia Koidula (a nineteenth-century poetess, on the one hundred kroon note), Carl Robert Jakobson (a promoter of the national awakening, agricultural theoretician, publicist, and contemporary of Koidula, on the five hundred kroon bill), and others. None of them have played even a marginal role in European history and culture, and therefore there would also be no grounds for their continued use on euro notes. Counting in francs is also convenient in the sense that it allows one to compare prices with greater ease. The franc's exchange rate was about 2.4 to the kroon, and prices for consumer goods and regular services in Estonia (belonging to the so-called Eastern- and Central-European transitional economic zone) are, for the most part, exactly the same as they are in France—numerically, I mean, and not when calculating prices in euros, but rather in francs. As such, a public transport ticket costs seven kroons in Tallinn when buying a pack of ten, etc. If a price in kroons is more or less comparable to the price in francs of an equivalent item in France, then one can estimate that it is neither a cheap nor expensive offer. Although, the cost of living in Estonia is increasing rapidly. I no longer have the feeling of being as rich as Croesus when I arrive from France, where I undoubtedly belong to the very lowest income deciles by way of my revenue, which moreover is of the intermittent sort (and it has become especially intermittent since Liz Franz's disappearance, at least from my radar).

Michel Houellebecq, a contemporary French writer and author of the national (although not international) bestseller *The Elementary Particles*, writes that his country is slowly but immutably slipping down to join the "middle-poor" states. I am interested, in the case of this analysis, by the question of which countries are still listed among the rich- and middle-rich. I certainly agree, however, that the world is growing poorer as a whole, that we are moving towards ever-greater impoverishment, and most likely also towards a new, refreshing, and rejuvenating war. Global economic growth is a systematic bluff determined by certain assumed flaws. No one will be able to conceal it infinitely, and it will only be the ritual destruction of the wealthy in the flames of war that will allow valuations to once again be brought into accordance with reality. Fictitious wealth will then be written off and vanish along with the actual wealth that will go up as smoke in chimneys; its owners will be switched as the game is played. Of course, this entire civilization of ours could also be written off in the thrill of play.

Yet right now, it is still valid along with its fictitious and actual currencies, and France is still fairy-tale rich in comparison with my native Estonia. Even if there are also ever more of those now discretely called "the marginal" (*les marginaux*), also "the excluded" (*les exclus*). People used to simply say: the poor, also: *les humbles* (the humble, impoverished). I have noticed the latter term flashing through French journalism once again. *Les humbles.*

If Tallinn (450,000 residents) and Tartu (one hundred thousand) were towns in France, then I would most likely cross the 117 miles separating the two in a sufficiently comfortable and well-ventilated train that would travel at a speed of at least seventy-five to ninety miles per hour; if, however, those towns happened to be located on a TGV track, then at as much as 185–215 mph. That ticket would cost about one hundred francs, or even up to half the amount in the event of SNCF sales offers. For example, the "two-for-one" sales campaign, which I have indeed never used—for who would that other person be? Yet, in any case, that ticket would not cost twenty francs. Twenty kroons for a Tallinn–Tartu bus ticket is likely a "dumping" price that one bus company uses to drive another off the market. A bus departs on that route every quarter-hour on Sunday morning between seven and eight o'clock. Estonia has, by the way, a very liberal economy.

I didn't go by train, however, because firstly they only run twice per day, and secondly they traverse the same distance in about three and a half hours, while the bus takes only two hours and fifteen minutes.

The bus was second-hand, as they all are, between ten and twenty years old and probably originating from one of the Nordic countries or Germany, with which Estonia has the closest economic ties. Nevertheless, they were fit for driving and presumably completely safe. The ventilation system being out of order and lack of air conditioning is not a problem in Estonia at this time of year. On the early morning of April 20th, the thermometer showed two degrees in Tallinn and two degrees below zero in Tartu according to the Celsius system. The climate in Tartu is more continental. There is always a specific aroma in those buses that is composed of diesel fuel emissions (minimally, not to an irritating extent), the stench of burnt rubber and old seats, as well as what is most likely the smell of the passengers' old clothes and the scent of beer wafting from their mouths. This is because there are, for the most part, one or two younger male passengers who have consumed beer or are consuming it over the course of the trip. Beer is a very popular beverage in Estonia, just as it is in Germany. One young male traveler had the bus driver stop when we were halfway there, and urinated right next to the vehicle. An expanse of fields surrounded us, and he had nowhere to go for cover. Not that it was really much to see. When someone urinates, it's neither interesting nor impolite; nor is it a pleasant sight.

The fields were still gray, mostly from the flattened weeds of last year. Under conditions of the transitional economy, about 30 percent of Estonia's farmland has been left to pasture (*en friche*), because the relatively unfavorable climatic conditions do not allow the country's agriculture to compete with the European Union's strongly subsidized peasants (*paysans*). In various places, the grayness of the landscape also signified gray dirt: there, where cultivation of the land still continued.

Spring had been dry, cold, and sunny for a long time. A "cold and sunny spring" is not a contradiction of terms. At this latitude, it is rather a logical consequence of global warming. The apparent beginning of spring has been shifted to an earlier time. Specifically, the snow was supposedly already melting in mid-February this year. Back in my childhood, during the 60s and

70s of the twentieth century, not to mention in the nineteeth century and during the so-called "Little Ice Age" that preceded it (between the sixteenth and eighteenth centuries, when even the Seine froze over, just as did the canals in the Netherlands, whose ice-skaters are so familiar to us from the works of famous Dutch masters), the snow on the fields of Estonia and Livonia lasted just about until St. George's Day according to the Gregorian calendar—that is, until today. St. George's Day according to the Julian calendar is moving day for peasants; thus, it must have fallen at the time of the snow melting and the beginning of field work. Yet as everyone knows, climate change does not change the Sun's visible arc across the sky. This process likewise still hasn't affected the seasonal dynamic of air masses to a significant extent, and primarily Arctic winds blow across these areas along the Baltic Sea in March–April. At the same time, the angle at which the sun shines is not yet adequate for warming the ground, and especially sea- and lake-water. Grayish strips of snow could be found in the shade of the forests along the highway. The sight of them spurred an alien feeling, as if they had been left there since the Ice Age, and a mammoth tusk or the bones of a saber-toothed tiger might melt out of them.

My favorite book during childhood was *Sannikov Land, a.k.a. The Last Onkilons*. It is the science fiction work of Russian Soviet author Vladimir Obruchev that is set somewhere in the waters off the shore of Northern Siberia, more precisely on a legendary lost island, on which was preserved the fauna that inhabited Europe—Southern France, for example—during the Great Ice Age and in its wake, as the ice receded. In addition to mammoths and other species, a so-called "primitive human" (*l'Homme primitif*) population was preserved on Sannikov Land. They were the ones called "Onkilons." I believed that such a land did still exist (at the end of the book, it is destroyed with the inhabitants in a natural catastrophe; the expedition, as far as I can remember, escapes, but no one believes their stories) and that when I was to become a naturalist in the future, I would discover it.

However, the material making up those roadside fields with dried mud that I watched through my black Fila sunglasses in the bright morning sunshine—and where the vegetative period somehow still refused to begin in mid-April—is composed mainly of rocky ground up by the continental icecap, and sediment formed as the ice melted and the glaciers moved. In some places, those ridges and heaps of sediment stretch two hundred, and even three hundred meters above the current sea level. In Estonia, these places are called "mountains" (*montagnes*).

The large areas between the "mountains" are, however, recessed and poorly drained. As yearly precipitation is significantly greater than yearly evaporation, the areas have become marshy (*marécageux*), comprising about 20 percent of Estonia's surface area. Water shortage in itself will never become a problem here, but a short-term drought (*sécheresse*) may indeed quickly dry out sandy and loamy soils; and if the drought falls, for example, during the sowing period (and the melted snow has already long sunk into deeper layers), as we have now, or during the growth period, then it can cause extensive harvest losses. In former times (lastly during just the nineteenth century), a spring such as the one this year could have caused famine (*famine*) and a catastrophic death rate primarily among the peasant population.

As such, a combination of very unfavorable climatic conditions (cold), epidemics of plague, and the Great Northern War in the beginning of the eighteenth century wiped out at least 30 percent of the population in Estonia and Livonia. The territories fell from the Kingdom of Sweden's possession into that of the Russian Empire following the Great Northern War. The import of peasants from neighboring regions and even Western and Southern Europe was employed to re-colonize the lands. Despite this, the nation that is called Estonians has maintained its distinct non-Indo-European language, and even certain recognizable "ethnic attributes" that in truth very much resemble the racial types prevalent in Northern Germany and in the Netherlands. Yet, that isn't significant. Anthropology's "racial" field of research (race as "ethnicity, tribe") has been out of favor since World War II. Yours truly is nonetheless familiar with the works of Juhan Aul, who achieved pan-European renown in the 1930s, and when looking in the mirror, may classify himself as a member of the so-called "Eastern Baltic race" (a wide eye distance; a relatively flat nose; somewhat pronounced cheekbones; light, but not quite blond hair; bluish-gray eyes, etc.). Still, significant Germanic elements can also be discerned in his face, and he is frequently regarded as a German at Parisian department stores and cafés.

I don't know why I suddenly started speaking of myself in the third person. Almost the same (from an ethnic standpoint) could be said about Liz Franz. Still, there is (was) something genuinely Asian in the slant of her eyes; in her posture, however, there was something akin to a Russian Jew. And at the same time, she was a true Livonian farm girl—in a certain sense. What sense exactly, I will discuss sometime later—that's a longer story.

I'm unable to describe her particular appearance all that well, just as is the case with people's appearances in general. I don't know what people are like. What further inhibits me in the case of Liz Franz is the fact that I have been in close contact with her over the course of nearly eleven years, during which her very discrete (in every sense) beauty operations (*chirurgie ésthéthique*) were done in Rome. She also constantly and carefully dyed her hair throughout that entire period of time. It was black, and the roots of the other color were sometimes just hardly visible; at least that goes for those times that we met. I don't know her true hair-color. I don't know whether she has gray in her hair at fifty-five years of age, and if she does, how much.

There was one period at the beginning of our acquaintance, during which I suspected that Liz Franz wore a wig; so lifeless had her hair become from constant dyeing when viewed closely. On stage—where I had indeed seen her only one single time, because the beginning of our relationship and the end of her active singing career coincided—Liz Franz's dyed hair appeared lively and impressive: a harsh, black, young and timeless bob. Nevertheless, it seemed to me that a little bit of gray would suit her quite well. It would have made her more homely, more secure. Yet, Liz Franz abstained from aging, and she never again did that, from which she had once decided to abstain. Or: from which she simply **had** abstained, in terms of which she lived in a state of abstinence.

In using the past tense, I don't mean that Liz Franz is no longer among the living (*en vie*). I'm simply deriving from the fact that she was (is) capable of switching her convictions and her abstentions, doing so with the same kind of force, with which she adhered to them. So, strictly speaking, I only know what she *was* like, and not what she *is* like. Nevertheless, over the course of our close acquaintanceship, she did not change to a significant extent, aside of the aforementioned beauty operations and the quite significant bodily aging in spite of them (subtle wrinkles on her neck, wrists, the back of her hands), which did not go unnoticed by me. However, I cannot claim anything regarding the given moment. This even more so due to the fact that if she is alive and at the same time has disappeared for me, then that in itself is already a very great and fundamental change.

Back when I believed that she wore a wig, I would have liked to rip it off of her head, revealing her light, Nordic, Germanically poor-quality hair flattened against her scalp; the kind that I had seen on my primary school teacher when she came to the spring class field trip without her wig. Those strikingly "artificial" ash-blond wigs were a regular style during the 70s. The teacher—

Ms. Valter (Krista Valter), who back then might have been somewhere close to thirty-five to forty years old, and thus twenty to twenty-five years older than I, who was a tall, muscular woman with straight, pronounced, in my mind very delicate and kingly (specifically kingly, not queenly) facial features—I was, now that I think about it, probably in love with her. I brought her books to read that I myself was thrilled by; for example, the political thriller *The Quiller Memorandum*, in which I was appalled and aroused by the question posed to the hero by the Nazis torturing him: "Do you like boys or girls?" I wondered whether I would be able to keep secret that I liked boys—their bulging, strong chests; not like the ugly, flat one that I saw in the mirror. Afterward, I impatiently awaited Ms. Valter's reply, her opinion. She often probably couldn't actually be bothered to read those books, but instead lied, saying she had read it and it was interesting. Her wigless, smoothed-down head in the bus on the way to the spring field trip aroused a feeling of sympathy and even greater love within me. She became very close to me in my mind.

But Liz Franz didn't wear a wig. That emerged when we had already become very much close physically as well, not only in my mind. Yet initially, I truly believed those unexpectedly soft hairs that tickled as they moved across my stomach, across my thighs, were not her own, but rather those of someone else. I don't know whose hair is used for making wigs.

2

Liz Franz never visited Tartu; at least she hasn't set foot there over the last eleven years, as far as I know. Most likely not even over the last two decades. Still, that is where she had her beginning— just like everyone here in the country (but that's a longer story). She told me every time that I went to Tartu—because I visited the town practically every year that I was living in Estonia, driven by God-knows-what next bout of nostalgia; and in reality just to irritate her, too—she said, albeit with laughter:

"Don't go to Tartu, the Devil lives there."

And I believed it—in a certain sense—because in a certain sense, I believed everything that Liz Franz told me, and what's more—I intentionally denied her affirmations and her warnings, I ignored them, I defied them (the verb "to defy" in Estonian is *trotsima*, a German loan word: *trotzen*—to flout, to be recalcitrant, close to *défier*; about 30 percent of Estonian vocabulary is made up of all kinds of Germanic and primarily Low-German loan words, which doesn't mean that knowing German would help one to understand spoken or even written Estonian language; Estonians' German proficiency has also nearly disappeared from the population over the last few decades.) And so, I also believed in some ever-so-dusky way that the Devil lives in Tartu, and in my unconscious fantasies, I pinpointed his whereabouts to somewhere in the vaulted caverns of the Gunpowder Cellar.

Thanks to an advertising brochure that I received from the re-opened restaurant there and was likely composed with the help of university historians, I now have a fairly detailed overview of the Gunpowder Cellar's (*Cave au poudre*) history. By command of Tsarina Catherine II (the Great) in 1763, work begins on refortifying Tartu, which had fallen to Russia in the Great

Northern War and been completely demolished. In 1768, Field Marshal Villebois's squad of engineers begins constructing the vaulted cellar in a former castle moat below Toome Hill. Ten years later, the cellar—with eleven-foot-five-inch-thick walls rising to converge in a sharp arch thirty-six feet high, forming what could easily be an enormous underground church—is finished and used for stocking gunpowder. In 1800, Tsar Paul I gifts Toome Hill and all its fortifications to the University of Tartu, which is reopened as the Imperial University of Dorpat (in German) after two years. The defense fortifications have already outlived their time by then. The university uses the cellar as a storehouse, and then rents it out for a long period of time to brewers to be used as a beer cellar. The brewery owned by one J. R. Schramm rents the Gunpowder Cellar for an entire sixty-nine years. Beer drinking is one favored pastime of Tartu's German university students.

Yet the lovely, positivistic and industrial nineteenth century is setting in. People are starting to intuit the unrest ahead, are starting to become interested in magnetism, in hypnosis, and other shadowy, inexplicable forces. By the initiative of one Professor Lewitzky, a laboratory operates in the Gunpowder Cellar, researching earthquakes and magnetic phenomena using a horizontal pendulum from 1896 up until the evacuation during World War I (1915). Unfortunately, I lack any information on whether Professor Lewitzky—who was most likely evacuated along with the rest of his laboratory—discovered an anomaly in the cellar that might point to the Devil's presence. It isn't impossible that my fantasy of the Gunpowder Cellar as the Devil's whereabouts has been subliminally tapped from the collective Tartu subconscious, which was once fed by now long-forgotten rumors of Professor Lewitzky's dealings with Beelzebub. In any case, the Gunpowder Cellar was used as a root cellar from then on. It was only in 1982, towards the end of Leonid Brezhnev's time in power, that the old cellar acquired a new rather function: it was restored and turned into a modern café/restaurant.

The end of the Brezhnev era, which is now called "stagnation," stood out for its conservative, even restorationist spirit. Greater attention was turned towards heritage protection (*protection de la Patrimoine nationale*) and restoring historic and architectural memorials. True, those memorials were often in very poor condition, had crumbled into ruins or were in the process of doing so. During the same period, a national movement that likewise bore a strong nostalgic and restorationist stamp was born in Estonia, and no doubt in the other Baltic republics as well. By that time, Liz Franz had long since wiped the dust of Tartu from her feet and lived mainly in Moscow. I, however, was studying genetics at the University of Tartu at that very time. The brand-new Gunpowder Cellar was a popular locale, especially due to the fact that it was located underground. A show-program, called a "variety" in the French fashion, was also performed there each evening.

As the downfall of the socialist planned economy was reaching its terminal phase, the phenomenon called "deficit" was ever more sharply perceptible. However, this did not mean budgetary deficit—truth be told, budgetary deficit is exactly what it meant, now that I think back; so *déficit* was an absolutely fitting term, even though it wasn't analyzed as such during that time, at least in the popular or even official consciousness. Popular analysis was based on the words "everything is out of stock." This meant something close to only being able to acquire consumer goods and services in a limited quantity using the rubles one earned deservedly or undeservedly. In other words: although the state budget was always formally balanced (and, interestingly enough, such balance has also become the idol of transitional-economy theoreticians), the country constantly printed additional, uncovered money; prices were moreover administratively pegged, because it wasn't permitted that a rise in the cost of living transpire in the Soviet Union. Interestingly, this hidden inflation elicited the same sorts of social phenomena as overt inflation did in Germany during the 1920s. The common name for these occurrences can be read as a certain form of hedonism: day-to-day living (*vivre de jour au jour*), a part of which was also spending money in cafés and restaurants. There was almost continually a line (*la queue*, literally "tail," which in English is never used to mean a man's genitals) at the door of the Gunpowder Cellar, and the doorman would let in whomever he wanted, whenever he wanted to do so, often in exchange for drinking money (*pourboire*)—a bribe (*pot-de-vin*) in reality, because the doorman was, strictly speaking, a state official who had to ensure the equal honoring of civic rights.

For me, drinking "martinis" (it was actually a mix of Hungarian vermouth and local juniper-berry spirits—exceptionally sweet and not very strong) in the Gunpowder Cellar was the first synonym for luxury. For freedom, also. It's truly interesting to note that luxury and freedom went hand in hand in my fantasies, and that those fantasies were able to blossom exceptionally well in the half-light of underground brick caverns.

Yet, I don't want to wander off too far into the past, even more so because that past has no concrete connection with Liz Franz. Which, at the same time, is debatable. For weren't those popular Liz Franz songs of the time—popular despite the fact that the nationalist-minded university students criticized her for her Moscow career and scant dissident nature—weren't those very songs a certain soundtrack or refrain to my slightly drunken dreams of freedom and luxury? Especially that song "Date":

> *The city lights up lamps and passersby's faces,*
> *the café is still empty, and I wait . . .*

Da-rai-da-rai-da-daa . . . When "Date" happened to play through the bar's speakers just as I had just finished off half of my "martini" and the first light ripple of tipsiness had caused the kind of sensation within my central nervous system that is interpreted as a certain euphoria in terms of mood, actually a sense of omnipotence (*sentiment de l'omnipotence*): "So can I . . . it can happen to me, too . . ."—by then, it had reached ten o'clock in the evening (because it was always subjectively "evening" beneath those arches, a sensual time, although it could have objectively been midday outside), offering a certain sensual counterpoint, even a catharsis.

I think that not a single other artistic phenomenon over the course of my lifetime has summarily offered as many catharses as Liz Franz's song repertoire. Yet, I never openly displayed what those songs meant to me. This was, on one hand, due to the aforementioned conformist critique (although in my heart, I despised those comfortable "dissidents"—actual conformists) of Liz Franz that people had begun to make at the time; on the other hand, it was because those songs and the catharsis they offered me were, in my mind, too simple. I should have had catharses from Bach, Beckett, Pasolini. And I did, too; I can't deny that either. Especially from Pasolini's *Teorema* and the appearance of the young Redeemer (played by Terence Stamp) in the bedroom of the family's sexually-repressed son; his beautiful hand, which slid across the poor boy (I don't remember what part it was over—his back? shoulder? the back of his neck?). It seemed unbelievable that such a thing was shown in the Soviet Union (although in a "closed" cinema club), and after that scene, I looked around uneasily—no one realized, did they? My excitement? No one seemed to understand. It was as if the audience was frozen in an all-comprehending, culturally open-minded pose. Afterwards, people discussed the "aesthetics" of Pasolini. I have to say that every time someone starts to discuss something about aesthetics,

I prefer to be in a different room, in a different company, and even in a different time. It is truly excruciating.

But I certainly must apologize now (interesting—to whom? Are you already imagining an **audience** for yourself, you poor thing?) for that truly uninteresting and furthermore long-winded "analytic" digression triggered by Liz Franz's words about the Devil. Nevertheless, it should be noted that in Estonian folklore, and most likely in our national collective subconscious, the Devil is even more ambivalent, or, let's say, contrastingly ambivalent than in Catholic lands. True—*le pauvre diable* is indeed something like "a poor little guy," and so a synonym for a somewhat simple folk, an ordinary sinner. In Estonian, the Devil is also called by the name "Old Pagan" (*le Vieux Païen*), and maybe that direct translation isn't so absurd. As "pagan" (Latin *paganus*, "rustic") in Christian terms means an unbaptized person, a non-Christian, but originally likely a non-Jew, a believer of a different faith, a barbarian, it is understandable why "Old Pagan" has become a relatively positive hero in Estonian folklore—a collective national alter ego.

Anton Hansen (pseudonym "Tammsaare"), who was Estonia's most outstanding twentieth-century novelist (nineteenth-century novelists were still lacking), eternalizes the nature of Old Pagan with this very definition in his last, allegorical and testamentary novel, *The New Devil of Hellsbottom* (something like: *Le nouveau Diable de Fond-des-Enfers*). Unfortunately, that work published in 1939 has never been translated into French, and it would hardly be of great interest to anyone anymore.

The epic series of peasant novels titled "Truth and Justice," written by Tammsaare (who is depicted on the Estonian twenty-five kroon note), indeed found warm reception in France; but this was unfortunately the occupied "free" France of Marshal Pétain, in which the authorities mistakenly saw it as an illustration of the ideology presented in the Nazi *Blut und Boden* (blood and soil).

I believe that readers, on the contrary, discerned anti-ideology, subversion, sabotage, or at least ambivalence, because Hansen-Tammsaare was actually an anti-fascist, and also regarded the idealization of rusticity and "roots" critically in his works. Due to the fact that after liberation (*Libération*), there was nothing that anyone in France or elsewhere in Europe wanted to forget more than wartime and everything associated with it (apart from the myth of *Résistance*), they naturally forgot about that marginal novel as well. Especially considering that even its people (*Nation*) ceased to exist in the realpolitik (*Realpolitik*) of the Free World.

3

When I stepped off the bus at Tartu Bus Station and started walking across the bus-station square—it is located directly on the riverbank, and it's often windy there; another high-rise building has now cropped up next to it, which is not at all necessary in a town like Tartu with its low, sparse architecture; and just as all high-rises, the building causes unique aerodynamic phenomena such as the stack effect and whirlwinds in its near vicinity—a sudden dust devil threw sand in my face, so I had to stand blinking for a few moments and wait for more intense fluid from my tear ducts in order to start seeing again normally. I put on my sunglasses after that.

Those Fila sunglasses are meant for athletic events such as cycling, and do a good job of protecting the eyes not only from ultraviolet rays (special glass), but also dust and other foreign bodies. Eye damage is one of my phobias, i.e. obsessive fears (also: snakes), especially following the laser surgery that corrected my shortsightedness (*myopie*). I went for the operation most likely because I hoped to be more competitive on the sexual market, which is euphemistically called the "gay scene." Specifically, I couldn't stand wearing contact lenses (they immediately caused irritation, making my eyes red and painful)—that actually fantastic invention, thanks to which so many women, but also men, and especially homosexual men, have escaped the curse of glasses and exposed their attractive (*in spe*), moist, naked eyes.

Specifically "naked," because the eyes of a person who wears glasses appear naked when those glasses are removed. Ninety times out of a hundred, I recognize those falsely sharp eyes even before I notice the contact lenses' specific glint (you can't see it from a distance). For me, such eyes in a potential partner (and

the ratio of potential partners to actual ones on that gay "scene"
is something like 1,000:1) is more of a minus than a plus. Ha!
Just another "wannabe," just another camouflager, just another
"man"!

I believe that in the age of contact lenses, the stocks of true,
au naturel, glassesless people have rather risen relatively further,
not fallen. The entrance of good counterfeits on the market rather
boosts the value of the originals. For when consumers are allowed
to allow themselves something *almost real*, they'll soon start to
crave *the real thing*. Because the person, as they say, has gotten a
taste of it. Even now, although it's been more than a year since the
operation (having it done in Estonia was five times cheaper than
in France), sometimes, it still seems to me when I go to sleep on
occasion that I'm wearing my glasses, and should put them on the
nightstand before nodding off. Or I lift my hand to adjust glasses
on my nose.

Liz Franz has not, of course, worn glasses a single day
in her life (sunglasses—those, of course). I found out about
her shortsightedness probably only in the second year of our
acquaintanceship. Or else it was as early as during the first
summer, when our "intimacy" had reached the phase, in which
I read a book next to her in bed before falling asleep, my glasses
on my nose. She also picked up a book of solidarity, although
she otherwise never read books, nor newspapers (she occasionally
flipped through magazines), and from the way she pressed the
book nearly up against her face, it gradually began to dawn on
me that she didn't see it. She had taken her contacts out for the
night in the bathroom.

The bathroom, into which she often shut herself for hours (it
seemed like hours to me, at least), is an entire chapter in itself. I
never knew what she was doing in there. It drove me to a rage
within. That was perhaps the time, when I hated Liz Franz the
most vehemently. Perhaps. But then once, I gathered up my

courage and asked about her vision. She wasn't ashamed of her contacts at all, and soon also acquired a pair for me. But as I mentioned before, they didn't suit me, and I only put them in during trips to the bar. They're especially excruciating in a room with smoky air. It's hard to say whether or not I've gotten any sexual partner thanks to contact lenses. Definitely not thanks to laser surgery, because I haven't had a single sexual partner since then, at least in the sense given to the words. I havent had a lack of fantasy partners, of course (sometimes even they aggravate me, down to the very last), and they are often even much more effective than any actual partner. Yet strictly speaking, for the last year and a half, I've been primarily "home" and without exception "dry"; just as the Neil Tennant duo Pet Shop Boys sings on their new album, *Release*. Specifically, the ballad "Home and Dry" came on the bus driver's radio that played quietly (I sat in the front) on the way from Tallinn to Tartu. Overall, the *Release* promotion seems to be doing quite well indeed on the local radio stations. I don't believe that any radio listener or café patron (one radio station or another often plays as background music in cafés and bars, with news and advertisements broadcasting every now and then, also) would especially consider the message of that "disco hit."

Estonia, like probably all other Central and Eastern European countries, is very much a traditionalist land, especially in what concerns sexuality and the ideals of human relations. Being "home and dry" here is certainly not yet an accepted status, although statistically, it is undoubtedly an ever more widespread situation among the men and women here. Considering, for example, the single mothers and divorced women raising their child or children alone, the proportion of whom in the population doesn't cease to grow. (I can see that daft Frenchisms, i.e. Gallicisms are starting to appear in my language: "doesn't cease to grow" is undoubtedly "*ne cesse pas d'augmenter*," a simpler way to say it would be "growing incessantly"; however, I don't have any special interest in fighting their invasion—it would take up excessive attention and lead me away from the main point.)

It is, on average, more difficult for single mothers to find a regular sexual partner than it is even for men who belong to the absolute lowest income tier; men, who for some reason are not (yet) married or don't live with a "female companion." A heterosexual man is generally still a good, for which demand considerably exceeds supply; thus, an individual belonging to this category will find a female partner (which in Estonia quite accurately used to be called a "side-warmer"—*réchauffeuse?*) with relative ease, even despite the weaknesses of the man's market position, such as some milder disability (*invalidité, débilité*), ugliness, or bad habits (alcoholism). But maybe that is a somewhat outdated understanding of mine that is no longer valid to a full extent even in countries with transitional economies, where women are becoming an ever more decisive and independent consumer group, and where ever fewer are able to sacrifice their professional career in the interests of personal happiness.

Nevertheless, there seems to also be a new type of transitional marriage that has taken form in the conditions of a transitional economy, the examples of which I've encountered in my homeland, and even glaringly often among my acquaintances. I've conditionally named this type of marriage the "reclining husband."

This is an all-around normal heterosexual man who does not, however, fulfill the traditional economic role in the household (*ménage*). His wife works and ensures the family's economic subsistence, and often very successfully, at that. The husband has lost his job or has not yet found himself in the professional field. He sometimes has creative ambitions. He plans to start writing opinion pieces (*opinions*) for the newspaper, although initially limits this to participation on Internet commentary pages, where he publishes fairly politically-incorrect positions concerning "blacks" (who are practically nonexistent in Estonia), Russians (Estonia's primary minority), gays, women, politicians, as well as other social categories and phenomena. In chat rooms (*chat*), he writes under the pseudonym "X-rays" or "Mahho" (an onomatopoeia of the word "macho") and actively takes part in social discussion under this name. For this to happen, it is naturally necessary for his partner to earn well enough to enable them having a home computer and a stable Internet connection. I must say, however, that Estonia is significantly ahead of France in terms of Internetization despite the latter's recent progress, and Internet service is offered in conditions of the free competition-economy at prices that make one outright jealous (three to four times cheaper than in France).

The man described above spends a large portion of his day on the couch (hence the conjugal configuration's conditional title) consuming a varying number of liters of beer throughout the day. Stocking the refrigerator with beer bottles is his primary task in the sphere of home chores. The crates of beer are heavy, and by carrying them from the car into the apartment, he feels manly pride and satisfaction from physical activity. However, he is generally depressed precisely because of the lack of physical burden. Late in the evening, his tired, work-addict wife also plops down on the sofa in front of some popular talk show. They argue on a regular basis. The husband grumbles at his wife, and implies that there are younger and more beautiful ones out there. This conjugal model functions well, more or less; at least as long as the man's depression does not detract from his sexual potency. I myself am so familiar with its internal mechanism because in a certain sense, I have been Liz Franz's "reclining husband," also. I believe that we can in no way avoid acting out the roll-based behaviors dominant in our society, no matter what form they might take. We play the roles that are played by others around us as well.

Liz Franz's actual husband never "reclines," however. His name is Umberto Riviera, and I won't start writing about him the past tense either, although he disappeared from my radar at the same moment as Liz Franz. Although, in principle, he doesn't really need to be on my radar: I've never had his personal cell phone number or anything of the sort. We were only connected by Liz Franz, and it is natural that the cessation of that line of contact also broke off our connection. It's possible that Umberto Riviera is still living serenely somewhere in Rome or Milano, for as a businessman involved in real estate, he can always select new apartments and houses for himself directly from the pool of his own possessions. It's possible that Liz Franz is also still living with him. Or that Umberto Riviera at least knows Liz Franz's location. Or her fate.

In any case, I haven't been successful in tracking him down, despite having quite a number of leads. At the same time—as far as I know—he's not being searched for (just as Liz Franz isn't being searched for, either). It's even not impossible that Umberto Riviera is, at the current moment, in Tallinn (still, I consider it unlikely that Liz Franz is there). Specifically, he has invested here in a small way, primarily in real estate, the prices of which were humiliatingly low following the economic collapse that accompanied the breakup of the Soviet Union. He's done his business quietly, not like Ernesto Preaton, and independently of Preaton, so I wouldn't be able to find out anything through him, either.

During one of our joint dinners at their Rome apartment, where no one answers the phone anymore, Preaton came up in conversation, because what else did the three of us really have to talk about? Umberto speaks French fluently—he studied in Paris. Liz Franz's husband (I'm not completely clear on their civil relationship, but I infer that they are officially married) did not regard Preaton badly at all. He said that the man's court cases in

Italy are too confusing to decide who is in the right. Umberto Riviera, by the way, hated Italy's administration and nepotistic politics, preferring France's republican purity and especially British "fair play." He spoke of Preaton rather as a great romantic, a man crazy for the absolute, who wanted to set up his own bank in Italy. Things with the bank went badly for him, Umberto Riviera added with a chuckle—now, he's giving it a try with a country. To *make* his own country, a country according to his own vision—so I understood, more or less.

Yesterday, I read in the newspaper that Preaton is consolidating his investments here. I'm not familiar with the matter, but I have the suspicion that it is a bad sign. Does he sense political instability, or the opposite—over-stability? Some dictatorship creeping in, which would ruin his playground that has been so free up until now? It's also possible that it was merely a deceptive maneuver that he fed to the local media, planning rather some grander "takeover" at the same time.

Umberto Riviera also had a small apartment in a house built in the sixteenth century in Tallinn's Old Town, where his always-bored secretary Hedde (maybe it was Hede; I don't know her last name, and remember her appearance poorly) sat. No one answers the office phone, and I haven't managed to get into the staircase there (the entire building belongs to Riviera Holdings, but the apartments have been rented out to foreigners or something like that—no one ever goes there) to check and see if their mailbox is full or empty. I should stalk the postal worker, if he or she even goes there. Yes—I recall that they had their own PO box at the main post office. So there's no point in checking out their stairway mailbox.

Incidentally, the apartment where I am currently sitting and making these notes, Weitzenbergi Street 6–12, also belongs to Riviera Holdings; however, a local building-maintenance company handles its upkeep and billing. The apartment is rented out in Liz Franz's mother's name, but the bills—as far as I know—were paid by Liz Franz. And the bills, as I investigated, have been paid on time to this day. Liz Franz allegedly kept that apartment as her "Tallinn rear," in the military sense. One distant relative of Liz Franz has lived here mainly, no doubt as a cover (for Umberto, who was actually aware of everything, but regardless, some decent façade must be preserved in relationships). When Liz Franz or I or the both of us came to Tallinn (from different directions, of course), that relative—a university student—quietly disappeared. I've never seen her, have only spoken to her on the phone (informing her of my arrival in advance), and know that she knows nothing. I don't even know the girl's name. Liz Franz always simply called her "the girl," and aside from that, we agreed to refer to her as "Susanna" among ourselves, and to the apartment as "going to see Susanna." That conspiring was absurd in my opinion, and I despised Liz Franz for her dishonesty. Only now am I starting to understand how masterfully she had everything arranged—her entire life.

4

As I said, it has been a long time since Liz Franz last visited Tartu, not to mention lived in Tartu, because she never went **back** anywhere, and for her, Tartu was **back** *par excellence* (according to my calculations, her short but decisive Tartu period must have fallen between the years 1961–62 or 62–63; thus, sometime around the year I was born, but I'll detail that more thoroughly later on), and I therefore didn't hope to find out any information on her in Tartu. I took the Tartu bus last Sunday morning more because it's better to think when riding the bus. It's even better to think while traveling by train, but I already wrote about the situation of trains in Estonia. There's nothing wrong with the passenger seat of a car, either, but that mode still includes a certain obligation to converse with the driver. Driving a car on your own is already work. As I started driving only from the age of twenty-five, perhaps I have not sufficiently gotten used to it even up to now. I personally call the situation of sitting on a train or a bus one of "unmoving movement," and a very specific state of mind also corresponds to such a situation. On one hand, it's not possible for you to do anything (I can't read during travel, or if I can, then on a train; but I usually don't read there, either): you sit in place and know that it will last a certain duration, and in the meantime, you can't undertake anything, can't set off anywhere as it's possible to do when in your apartment, for example. On the other hand, the "situation" itself moves from one place to another, and the picture outside the window—more precisely, the image reproduced by your vision and central nervous system—transitions accordingly. At the same time, that image isn't overly interesting or obtrusive like at the cinema or on television—nothing is going on there especially, or if it is (someone is making their way along a village road, a haystack from last summer or even a house is burning somewhere, there's been an accident on the highway), then you merely see a relatively meaningless fragment of the occurrence. Maybe in order to compensate for the fragmentation, your psyche (mind, mental system) starts to develop some kind of story, some sort of longer train of thought that itself would remain fragmented in another situation. The mental condition is less agitated (*agité*), less disjunct than otherwise.

And so, I wanted to think on the way there. Not only about Liz Franz, but in general. About what would come next. I hoped I would come up with some kind of a plan. I can't say that this plan actually formed, but something did. My mental condition is less vague following my jaunt in Tartu.

There's nothing special to do in Tartu itself. One always has some sort of irrational feeling on the way there, as if there's something to do in the town, and your state of mind may remain anxious once you have arrived. Tartu itself is quiet and provincial, and particularly on a Sunday.

Tartu is probably the oldest town within the territory of present-day Estonia: there was some important castle (*lieu fort*) and trading place there already prior to the thirteenth century, when the Teutonic Knights invaded ancient Livonia and the Christianization of the eastern shore of the Baltic Sea took place. Kievan Rus' to the east had already adopted Christianity, of course; so had the Viking kingdoms on the western shores of the Baltic. The Baltic Sea is literally termed "Western Sea" (*Läänemeri*) in Estonian, and only in Estonian. Even Finns call it the "Eastern Sea" by example of their old overlords the Swedes, and it is naturally *Ostsee* to the Germans.

The road to the east indeed led across the Baltic Sea. In the thirteenth century, Europe (likely the entire globe then, also) had lived in exceptionally favorable climatic conditions for a couple of centuries: the "little" warming period achieved its apogee around the eleventh century. By the thirteenth century, the population had flourished in these favorable conditions; life had progressed. The vaults of the cathedrals in Reims, Chartres, Ulm, and Strasbourg had already been stacked up, large stained glass windows were no longer a thing of wonder. In reality, people had already started to tire of it, it began to go out of style. For it no longer offered anything new, new heights, never-before-seen dimensions. In 1284, the vault of the Beauvais Cathedral, which had been built to a height of 158 feet, caved in. Christians' last stronghold in Palestine fell. One epoch began to reach its end. And on the shore of the Baltic Sea, that epoch was just beginning. Population growth, a flourishing economy, and new warfare technologies spurred the Holy Roman Empire's sub-states to search for new escapades in the east and the north. The written history of this land (Old-, a.k.a. Great Livonia) in the Livonian Chronicle of so-called "Henry of Latvia" begins with a romantic description of these conquests (1200–1240).

Still, warming during the Middle Ages' climactic optimum was not as sudden and extensive as that, which put an end to the post-ice-age (Würm) drying about 7,500 years earlier, melting a great extent of the glaciers and most likely causing the Great Flood: the Mediterranean Sea broke through natural dams and into the Black Sea basin. At that same time, the Northern Sea permeated the place where the straits of Denmark now are, and a chain of lakes thus became what is the present Baltic Sea. During that age, in the so-called "Atlantic climate period," humans already existed on the eastern shore of that sea; however, Estonian folklore lacks a Great Flood motif, as far as I know. Perhaps the swell wasn't so dramatic here. It may also be that the heritage of the tribes at the time has been forgotten.

The first people likely moved here on the trail of reindeer herds, starting to come from perhaps somewhere around Southern France, where "all of us" (Europeans), as Estonian geneticist Andres

Metspalu loves to say, squatted during the Ice Age. Year by year, the reindeer herds in turn pushed forward a little more according to the melting of the continental glaciers and the rooting of tundra flora on bare rock deposits. It's possible that the relatively abrupt warming of the climate and the improvement of conditions for living in post-Ice Age Europe (that period, which continues now and is called Würm IV, i.e. the Holocene) also had a favorable impact on human populations, causing unexpectedly strong migratory pressure from the south. It's possible that when this "second wave" arrived about four thousand years ago (considering the fact that "jumps" in populations take place with a certain delay after an improvement in conditions for living, being able to fall only by the time that they worsen again), they assimilated the first little-demanding settlers, wiping away their culture and heritage. A culture that is more efficient technologically is also always more prestigious—along with the skills and inventions of the cultivators arrived from the south, the hunter-gatherers most likely also adopted their language, social organization, beliefs, and "fairytales," i.e. stories (*contes*).

This is just as how my mother (seventy-four) and father (eighty-one) have unnoticeably adopted something from the mental world and language (although translated) of their U.S. television shows since they began watching them night-to-night. Still, unlike some of their older- to middle-aged compatriots, who have already become genuine soap opera addicts, they regard those "films" with a certain level of criticism. My father, for example, asserts that they don't really reflect actual life. This is called cultural resistance (*résistance*). One of the political slogans of Estonian re-independence (now, it has somewhat receded from the agenda as being too romantic) was the claim that we have inhabited this land for already ten thousand years straight. President Lennart Meri, whose second and final term in office ended last spring, also loved to spread (*véhiculer, propager*) that.

I don't know who the "we" was or is meant to be in that claim. I personally only know my ancestors up until the last years of the eighteenth century of our chronology. And I practically know nothing about those "firsts" other than their names.

They were one Hans and one Ano (Anu) from Viru-Nigula Parish: manor peasants who were given a last name in 1834. Namely, this was the tsarist (Alexander I) peasant reform undertaken in Russia's Baltic governorates in the post-Napoleon spirit of renewal. In the course of the reform, peasants attained a certain level of personal freedom; i.e. independence from their manor lord, their landlord, their *seigneur*. Until then, a manor lord was able to purchase and sell them along with the real estate (land), to which they were affixed. From then on, peasants were able to independently move from one master to another. Economic independence also came gradually following this (purchasing land "for good"), and the serf became a capitalist entrepreneur—or a salaried worker.

I read those names (Ano, Hans, Liso, Marri, Jaan, Jurri—these are the Estonian equivalents to the French names Anne, (?), Elisabeth, Marie, Jean, Georges; which in turn naturally originate from either Hebrew or Latin names, etc.) at the Estonian History Archive in Tartu. Indeed, I had no intention of going there, but when walking past the archive building the next morning (I stayed at a B&B in the Supilinna district for two hundred kroons), I felt like stopping by; especially since I had planned to do so on occasion previously.

The fashion of researching one's "family tree" by way of church and revision books was also one of the new-conservative mentalities in the 1980s and early 1990s. Back then, someone from both my father's and mother's side of the family did so, and I knew about it in general, but some vague feeling that something else might perhaps come out of the archive still remained. I certainly don't know what.

The archive had been in the same building when I studied genetics at the university, and I passed it frequently. It is a redbrick building that dates back to the end of the nineteenth century or beginning of the twentieth; most likely, some imperial institution (*administration imperiale*) was located there from the very beginning. For some reason, I have a weakness for redbrick houses, which number few in Estonia. Tartu has the most of them: apparently, suitable clay for firing bricks was found in the region. To the contrary, more in Northern Estonia (Tallinn) was built from local limestone. Limestone buildings are "cold," brick buildings are warm, and this doubtlessly explains my affection for them: a certain deficiency of spiritual and physical "warmth." Brick is burned stone, and ceramic ovens are made from it, also. Limestone forms at the bottom of the sea out of the calcium-rich creatures (corals, mollusks, starfish etc.) that once lived there. Specifically, at some time before the Great Ice Age, a warm sea stretched across the surface of the globe where Estonia is currently located. Yet, fire is still warmer than the sea, regardless of whether it is a warm one.

I stepped through the door into the archive and asked the woman sitting at the reception desk how it might be possible to research the origin of some family names in the archive. It turned out to be simpler than I thought, and after a brief time, I was already sitting behind a device for viewing microfilm and studying those nineteenth-century registries written in beautiful, yet somewhat indecipherable handwriting—not the registries themselves, that is, because they are not given to profane hands, but rather photo enlargements of registry pages on the screen before me. The archive employee, a young woman, guided me at first, not that there was anything very difficult about it. The primary source is the so-called "church books," into which parish pastors recorded the births and deaths of peasants, as well as soul revision books, in which state officials recorded the souls (*âmes*) living there according to manor and family.

The manor was still the primary economic unit in the mid-nineteenth century; the large economic unit's sub-unit was the family or household, which in addition to parents and children sometimes also included servants, farmhands, grandparents, and others. The revision book's base table was printed in Russian, and every page bore the interesting inscription: Ревизионная сказка (*revizionnaya skazka*). The word сказка in modern Russian means "fairytale"; thus: "revision story." That story or list of souls written in the administrative-regulative spirit of the nineteenth century (statistics had just become high fashion) speaks primarily of the efforts made by the Russian Empire and its Baltic governorates' administration to organize, control, and perhaps also direct rural economic life. The personal lives of those Anos, Hansos, Jurris and Marris in the modern sense can only be discerned in the records to an extremely limited extent; mainly in terms of what concerns those people's—the primary material economic force of the nineteenth century—physical, i.e. biological existence (birth, reproduction, relocation from one place to another, death). One can seek more personal biographical material from oral tradition; that is, in the given case, from the memories of my parents and my grandmother (deceased). Yet, these primarily concern the people themselves and the generation that preceded them, and are undoubtedly very subjective—in terms of the subjectivity of that rememberer, not the remembered. My dead ancestors themselves did not leave any kind of handwritten self-testimony, although then, during the nineteenth century, they were most likely already all literate (although, towards the beginning of the century, this may have only been the ability to read). For certain historical reasons (which I might detail later), there is not a single private letter or anything else of the sort left of them. What do remain are notes written by my maternal grandmother on the empty page designated for these in their family Bible (an 1889 edition). Inscribed on that page in blue ink and with extremely crooked handwriting are the names and dates of birth of her seven children; she also managed to write the dates of death behind three of the names. Those notations date to the 20s–30s of the nineteenth century.

Nevertheless, my nineteenth-century ancestors have also left me a message, if you can put it that way. At least I think—rather, I like to believe—that the words poured in cast iron on two crosses were selected/spoken by those same people, whose earthly remains are buried there beneath the crosses. Logically, they should be (although the particular church book that might prove this was destroyed) the parents of my father's father's mother. I saw those crosses for the first time just recently, a couple of weeks ago, when my father and I went to survey the farmlands that are to be restituted to him.

Land reform, which includes the restitution (*restitution*) of property to its pre-war owner or their descendants, is one part of the Republic of Estonia's re-independence on the basis of continuity (*continuité*). The initial Republic of Estonia existed during the years 1918–1941. Yet, according to the articles of international law adopted in the twentieth century, not one country *de jure* ceases to exist when another country violently annexes it. The zero-point for states' existence in Europe is the year 1920 (the Treaty of Versailles), when the given principle of international law was adopted overall. As the Republic of Estonia already existed in the year 1920, it could no longer actually be destroyed; i.e. in the ideal form, it continued to exist even during the years that it was annexed by the Soviet Union, the Third Reich, and then once again by the Soviet Union (altogether fifty years).

Of course, this and that happen in the material world over the course of fifty years. For example, an oil shale mine was erected on the land belonging to my mother's family's farm during the 1970s. Oil shale (an Estonian-French dictionary only provides an odd geological term as its equivalent: *schiste bitumineux*) is a fossil fuel with a very low energy content that is mined in the northeast part of Estonia. Just as other fossil fuels, it forms from the remains of the flora that thrived on the Earth during very warm and humid climactic periods millions of years ago. It is basically solar radiation stored up in the Earth's geological (or should one say astronomical?) past: energy from nuclear processes that occurred on the Sun. Man is the first species in the history of life on Earth that has learned to use this energy stored underground for his own benefit. Up until the nineteenth century, the primary source of energy for humankind—just as for other animal species—was the plant cover in its place of living; i.e. man mainly utilized the light-energy transformed by plants into organic material by way of photosynthesis over the course of a calendar year (agricultural products) or somewhat longer (trees). Plants need land for growing, and therefore, humans' so-called "economic activities" and overall living possibilities are very closely connected to the soil. The more ground suitable for plant growth (moisture, light, warmth, the soil's chemical makeup) that a person or community was able to keep control over, the richer and potentially more reproductive that person or community could count itself. For a long period of time, the primary motive and goal of so-called "wars" waged between human communities was that very same fertile ground.

Nineteenth-century discoveries and the Industrial Revolution changed that primordial energy situation radically. The implementation of coal, oil, and—when lacking anything better—even such a poor rock as oil shale made people ever more dependent upon the Earth. My parents had moved from the country to a town already before my birth. There were specifically several different, partly tragic reasons (such as my paternal grandfather's going missing; actually his deportation and execution by Soviet forces in 1941) for that relocation. But generally, their trajectory followed the logic of mankind's history, if there is such a thing. Some kind of a design, we'll say.

My mother had already left the country and gone to school in the city (because her mother decided so) long before the mine came to their village and that ground was carted away altogether. The dominant portion of oil shale that is mined is burned in Northeast Estonia's thermal power stations. As oil shale has a low energy content, a great deal of waste is formed when it is burned. This material is shoveled into piles, into small mountains that have completely reformed the panorama of Northeast Estonia's landscape. Yet, my mother did not move from the farm to a factory—to sort oil shale, for example, which would have been a logical first step on the way towards industrialization and urbanization—but rather jumped right into the so-called "third sector," studying to become a bookkeeper and working in that field until she retired (altogether about forty-five years). She did not directly produce any material worth with her professional activities, but as a part of the system, she nevertheless participated in their production, and even in agriculture, inasmuch as the state institution for which she did bookkeeping was involved in farmland improvement, i.e. amelioration (*amélioration*).

Specifically, the industrial Soviet Union endeavored for independence from food imports, for absolute alimentary self-supply (*autosuffisance alimentaire*), which it indeed never reached because, by its nature, socialist agriculture was systemically ineffective. The drying out of Estonia's excessively moist lands (marshes), mass-collectivization of small historical patches of field, etc. were among the arsenal of food-production programs undertaken by the Communist Party of the Soviet Union (*PC Soviètique*). My father, who as my grandmother's son had been trained to head a farmstead, also worked in socialist agriculture for his entire life; although like a third-sector worker, as a so-called "specialist."

We lived in a garden suburb on the edge of Tallinn, in a small but comfortable house that my mother and father built in 1956. It was the age of technical and social optimism. During my childhood, we acquired a "Riga" refrigerator (manufactured in the city of same name, the once-capital of Livonia) and a radiola, the brand of which I don't remember, but the design of which I now know from a documentary film shown at Artes to have copied the light and cheery design of the famous Braun radios of the fifties and sixties. Back then, that type of radio with a record player on top was called a radiola. It was from that radiola that I heard Liz Franz's voice for the first time.

My parents were still involved in agriculture to a small extent in order to ensure the family's economic subsistence, growing vegetables on the patch of land set aside for them on the edge of the city. We used the harvested vegetables for food, and the excess we turned into revenue on the so-called "kolkhoz market," where prices were free-floating and therefore relatively high. Thanks to that chimeric free- and market-economy association that was the kolkhoz market, small farming was more profitable during the last decades of the Soviet time than it had ever been before in this land's history. Peasants in the territory of Old Livonia never collected such wealth, both absolute and relative (a rural resident's income surpassed that of a city resident), as they did during the 1970s and 1980s.

That was, of course, an economic anachronism. In the developed countries of today, agriculture possesses only marginal importance in creating wealth. People live primarily in cities, and their personal wealth is often not expressed by the ownership of land and its size. As far as I know, Liz Franz—for example—has never owned any real estate. Still, she cannot be counted as a poor person. And it was through her that I learned to understand what wealth was, what money was. But in the traditional sense, she had never possessed almost any kind of property, not even mobile property (a few books, records, and clothing that she has carried along on her journey from one place to another belonging rather to the category of "personal effects," in the official classification). What, then, was (or is) the basis of Liz Franz's wealth? Her voice (which, all in all, is not in any way unusual), her ability to create personal relationships, something else?

Yet, written on one side of those nineteenth-century iron crosses that I started discussing were the names and dates of birth and death of the deceased: Tõnno T. (I don't remember the year of birth, died 1880) and An T. (died 1881). Imprinted in the cast iron on the other side was, according to the wife's wishes (I assume it was her wish), a message for the future written in the Southern Estonian dialect: *kui hüiad wimati keik surnud töuske üles, siis olgo sino käsi ka mino haua küles.* On the man's cross, however, was a brief Old Testament (*vétérotestamentaire*) request: *Jehowa, ma ootan so õnnistust.*

5

The archive surprised me mostly with its simplicity and smallness. That is, the archive itself, where originals of the records are kept, is undoubtedly quite large, because it is nevertheless an extremely imposing building (four stories), but the room that housed the cupboards filled with microfilms (which in turn contained all the church and revision books; in short, all of the **lists** from the very start, so to speak), and where they could similarly be consulted (*consulter*) at corresponding devices, was about the size of a one-family living/dining room.

The microfilms fit into two quite short chests of many drawers that were no larger than those so-called "section cupboards," which came into style in the 1970s and had to be in every home that was with the times. At the same time, during the 70s, in my childhood, the construction of panel houses (*maisons préfabriquées*) achieved its apogee: the conception of these buildings (easily-transportable and ready parts that can simply be assembled on site) is the same as that of section cupboards, the dimensions of which were in turn harmonized with the typical examples given in residential construction standards.

During that time, even I dreamed of us not only having a section cupboard (which was ultimately purchased as well), but of us also living in a state-built modular building; not in a private dwelling, which was officially regarded as an anachronism, as outdated bourgeoisie. This dream did not lack its own economic logic, as a state living space built free of charge for workers (*les travailleurs*) and with rent that was merely symbolic had undoubted advantages over a private dwelling, especially given the fact that in the course of later privatization (which back then, no one certainly could have imagined), tenants were able to purchase their living space for good at a symbolic price in exchange for vouchers. The same cannot be said, for example, about my paternal grandfather's farm, which had been acquired by the father of my grandmother Marta (Martha) from the local manor lord von Wrede in installments of silver Russian rubles, at the same time paying a percentage to the bank, collected over the course of at least thirty years at the end of the nineteenth century and beginning of the twentieth century by Scheel Bank in Tallinn. After the Witte (a Russian prime minister, German) economic reforms, the imperial ruble was put onto the gold standard, and was thus a strong "hard currency." Although, a World War and the Russian Revolution made ruble-based assignats worthless, but during my childhood, we still had around ten large silver-minted tsarist rubles under handkerchiefs in our dining room linen cupboard. When necessary, people had them made into rings and silver spoons that were customary gifts for newborns. Even I should have one such spoon lying around somewhere, given to me by that grandmother Martha.

A revolution also took place in Estonia parallel to the Russian Revolution and partly against it. On the one hand, this halted Bolshevism at about the line, which historically (until 1721) divided Russian territories from the Holy Roman Empire's sphere of influence; i.e. Orthodox areas from Catholic/Lutheran ones (interesting that the "church schism" (*schisme*) truly does also divide Europe geographically with a "rift" running from top to bottom; although in the "top," i.e. in the north, the western side is left only as a very narrow strip).

On the other hand, the Estonian War of Independence took the form of a classical and, as such, quite radical civil revolution with socialist motifs. The nobleman was almost entirely expropriated, land-purchase debts were cancelled, and the nobility's manor lands were given out for free or cheaply to peasants (renters). As such, the several-year-long real estate investment made by my grandfather's wife's father and his own father did not turn out to be all that foresightful. It would have been wiser to remain a renter and wait for revolution. For the wave of revolution that began in France in 1789 finally, with more than a century's delay, also reached historical Livonia and crushed the Baltic nobility's economic-political hegemony that lasted for centuries. Yet, presumably, people were able to foresee it as little as they could the later collapse of the Soviet Union and its economic consequences. I don't believe in people's historical foresight at all, nor in the ability of societies and the political elite to guide historic processes. Singular unconscious choices made over the course of one's lifetime due to personal psycho-physiological, cultural, etc. peculiarities end up being historically successful or rewarding; others are unsuccessful or so much as catastrophic. As such, the marriage to that Martha, the representative of a large family tree and the daughter of a relatively wealthy farm family, ended up being catastrophic for my grandfather. He paid for it with his life in a Soviet Russian prison camp.

Yet Martha herself survived, as did her children; likewise am I, her grandchild, alive to this very day, although I have no heirs and although I've emigrated and have no other interest in my genealogy than a documentary, psychological one. I'm even less able to say whether my choice of residence and just-acquired French citizenship (from time to time, I anxiously clutch my breast pocket to see if my pretty passport with its reddish-gold covers is still there) will be historically rewarding choices or not. Or what might that "reward" even mean in my case? Or in anyone's case.

I had a dream last night, in which a dentist (one molar really is breaking apart, but I'm not about to go to a doctor here, because it's expensive in Estonia; in France, *Sécurité Sociale* a.k.a. *Sécu*, as everyone says, pays dental costs properly—in Estonia, it is very difficult to access a "state" doctor, although I have health insurance here at the moment, also: I receive a salary from a nonprofit film organization and have an Estonian passport as well), that dentist checked out my molar, told me that I've been hit with cancer there, and that I've been informed of it before, too, but the metastasis has now spread throughout my body and there's nothing he can do.

Upon waking from a dream, you often spend a period of time in a half-conscious state, where the dream seems fully equivalent to the reality of waking-life and becomes mixed up with it. So, I lay in bed for some time further and thought quite acquiescently (it was still dark, the "white nights" hadn't begun yet) that I guess I'll have to die then at the age of forty, just as Liz Franz predicted one time. I should only try and finish these notes beforehand. I don't know where that sort of abrupt fatalism sprang from, I haven't the slightest desire to die yet when actually awake.

But Liz Franz indeed "predicted" my year of death to me once. It might have been six or seven years ago. A certain high fashion of mysticism was probably dominant in the world at that time; believing in horoscopes had not yet become a widespread routine. Liz Franz made fun of horoscopes. During her younger days, in the 60s and 70s, she had performed on a television show that bore the name "Horoscope." It was a proper Western hit parade. I've seen either on Arte or Cinqième a historical documentary series, where they recalled the hits from those times in France, which were, by the way, often adaptations of the same British melodies as the ones sung on that Estonian television show "Horoscope." So, it was a universal phenomenon. The fact that the show's name was "Horoscope," however, points to the fact that the word had no serious association with mysticism at the time; it was, rather, an astronomical term, and only referenced the fact that "stars" performed on the show. Because officially, mysticism was regarded very disparagingly in the Soviet Union. Perhaps the show's name did foretell the arrival of the age of mysticism around ten years later, at the time when technical/social optimism subsided.

I saw my first horoscope, which was "secretly" typed up on a typewriter, probably sometime around 1985. I found out that I'm a Virgo ("*neitsi*" in Estonian—"a young woman/virgin") and it ruined my mood, because I truly was a virgin, if that means anything in a man's case (the existence or nonexistence of penetration, and which way? and of what orifice?).

But that time, when Liz Franz presented her "prediction" to me—it might have been somewhere around 1995—she made fun of horoscopes. I had just secretly begun believing in them; that is to say, I was of an undecided standpoint. Overall, I am a supporter of the scientific world-view; I am imbued by it. But in those days, such confusion dominated my psyche and understanding of life (greatly because of Liz Franz) that I was prepared to clutch any lead that somehow seemed to set it straight. I devoured weekly newspapers' weekly horoscopes, and despised myself even more for that craven and idiotic search for certainty. Liz Franz said:

"That which is coming knows it just the same, too."

She added that she knew it about herself, that she had always known (what concerns the important things), and that she knows it about me, also. Because there's allegedly no difference.

That last claim annoyed me terribly, because I personally didn't know anything about myself in advance. But I wanted to know awfully. I thought that she was gloating and exaggerating just for fun. And at the same time, I believed her. Because her personal path in life had truly been, if viewed from the side, so straight and logical, without even a single drift to the side.

I then asked her as if mockingly, but actually with great excitement, whether she knows when I will die. She said, "Of course I do." I asked when. She said she couldn't say that. I said:

"You actually don't know."

Like during childhood when my playmate Viivi claimed she knew a secret but wouldn't say it. That had an effect. Liz Franz paled (from anger that I had doubted her?) and said calmly, I remember her voice:

"In 2002."

Maybe she also said "right at the beginning of the new millennium" or something similar, I don't remember the words exactly, but I do remember her face and tone, and now, it seems to me that she said: in 2002.

I was very disappointed on that occasion. There was still so much time until then (now)! Such distant predictions didn't interest me. I didn't believe that I still had to live for so long. I was only interested in what would happen **immediately**. My interests' farthest horizon was one year. Yet, the point and goal of that prediction made by Liz Franz baffles me to this day. It's hardly likely that she remembers it herself, hardly. I'd like to ask her about it. But in order to ask her (and not only that—it would be more a sort of little point of interest, and no doubt she'd only make fun of that "prediction" made to have a poke at me), I have to locate Liz Franz. Because I haven't disappeared to her—she has my mobile number. I don't believe she's lost it (no doubt she has it memorized), because she was very careful about phone numbers, and even taught *me* that carefulness. She said you can never know when you might need some person, you can never know when you'll be in trouble, you can never know who will be able to help you and how.

As per Liz Franz's teachings, I have a three-fold system for marking down phone numbers and addresses; actually, even four-fold (two diaries—a new one and an old one, computer/Internet, cell phone). But not a single one of the phone numbers that I have written under the letter "Z" (for "conspiracy"; I don't know why—Z is simply Liz Franz's letter) picks up, and all letters are returned from the addresses marked as either "address unknown," or disappear without a reply, as if into a black hole.

In connection with that metaphor, I'm reminded of a quote by

Stephen Hawking, a British quantum physicist and cosmologist, that is likewise metaphorical: God not only casts dice, but sometimes casts them where we cannot see them, below the edge of the universe, so to speak (my own addition, as clarification for myself). I indeed only understand quantum physics and cosmology on the metaphorical level, and thus, actually the mythological level.

6

My father wanted me to come with him to visit his farm acres and help him finish surveying the property on this visit to Estonia (which is already starting to exceed the planned boundaries), no matter what. He even called me about it in Paris, which he only does when he comes up with some "idea." My mother almost never calls me there because long-distance calls are expensive. My father said something about "surveying the river," which I didn't understand very well, and especially my own function in the undertaking. I have now gone there and know what that means.

My father's farm, which he actually shares with his two sisters and the children of his younger (deceased) brother, so he owns a notional one-fourth of the land holding of about 86.5 acres—that farm, just like the majority of farms in Estonia and Livonia, is made up of several detached pieces. The existence of these detached pieces is caused by the peculiarities of traditional land usage. Specifically, as I already noted, a large portion (about 20 percent) of Estonian and Livonian territory is made up of marshes that are impossible to cultivate; at least, it was not possible using traditional technical tools (actually, an attempt to cultivate them in the fervor of the opportunities that followed the Technical Revolution turned out to be quite unresultative, and the new lands erected in the marshes have generally been left to pasture by now due to the poor composition of the dirt). And so, there was not enough land suitable for cultivating, even though the population of present-day Estonia crossed the half-a-million mark only during the nineteenth century. Crop yield was low, and the cost of maintaining the manors and the crown (*l'État, la Couronne*), whatever crown that may have been, along with the financing of wars, swallowed up the entire excess fruit of peasants' labor, leaving for them only the minimum subsistence (*minimum vital*).

Naturally, a certain amount of the minerals necessary for plant growth is removed from a field with every harvest and must be replaced if the farmer does not wish for a decline in the field's fertility. In the case of the primitive (*primitif*) farming method, which in Livonia—just as in early-Middle-Ages France—was the slash-and-burn technique, and which prevailed here for long past the end of the Middle Ages (as wars, plagues, and famines periodically reduced the population, overgrown areas suitable for slash-and-burn techniques could be found constantly), in the case of that primitive farming method, the ground is fertilized by the ash of burned trees. The trees have, however, in turn acquired minerals from deep layers of the soil, and have likewise (such as alders, *Alnus*) tied up gaseous nitrogen. Yet, slash-and-burn land is only fertile for the first couple of years: afterwards, the crop yield declines sharply. During the long peacetime that followed the Great Northern War, and which in the territories of the Estonian and Livonian provinces of the Russian Empire lasted for over two centuries, the population grew steadily and slash-and-burn fertilization had to be replaced with a different fertilization system; that is, people had to begin systematically fertilizing fields with the only well-known fertilizer available, which was manure. This, however, is nothing more than the partially broken-down remains of grasses that have passed through animals' digestive tracts. Those grasses, i.e. hay, had to have come from somewhere, however, and as mineral soils were in use as fields, it had to be acquired from the marshes.

Acquiring the quantity of grasses from marshes and meadows necessary for sustaining a herd—"haymaking"—was a farm family's main summertime work. It turns out from respective memoirs and literature that this work segment was extremely exhausting even at the beginning of the twentieth century. Haymaking began around St. John's Day (*Saint Jean d'été*), lasted until the harvest, and even continued after it—practically until the snow arrived. This was done primarily with the use of scythes (*faux*) and rakes, as marshland is uneven and it isn't even possible to implement horse-drawn mowers there. Marshland fauna itself is very low in food value; however, the most important thing wasn't actually a herd's productivity in terms of milk and meat, but rather the mass of manure that could be spread onto the fields the next year. Peasants were often forced to trek several miles away from their homes to gather hay, and given the speed and comfort of travel by horse, this was no laughing matter, either. Tied to every manor, and later to every farm, were several plots covered by marsh and forest, which were used as hayfields as well as grazing pastures (a herd was "in the woods"). Initially, during the Middle Ages, this was common law (herding law); later, the customs were formalized in cadastres. As my father said when he and I accompanied by the two surveyors—a man and a woman—were moving along a forest path towards his farm's detached riverside plot, the surveyor was such an important man during Tsarist times that the church bells were rung upon his arrival in a village.

The female surveyor then remarked that back then, a surveyor's salary was also so high that a house could be bought with the monthly wage. This was in order to deter the temptation of bribery. The surveyor was an official of the Empire. A surveyor of the Republic of Estonia apparently doesn't belong to the lowest income bracket either, because the surveyors' family company owned what I assessed to be a completely new Peugeot station wagon. Namely, the property restitution process has been very voluminous in terms of work thanks to the abundance of those historical detached plots, and the demand for surveying work significantly exceeds its supply, which enables them to ask for, as they say, a worthy fee.

I soon also found out what "surveying the river" means. Specifically, the river is one border of a detached plot—formerly a hayfield, now a sparse, marshy forest. To be honest, the waterway is a stream (*ruisseau*)—the beginning miles of Põltsamaa River, which is part of the Emajõgi River's watershed. The water in it originates from springs, is cold and clear, and does not freeze even in the most frigid cold (according to my father; winters these days no longer allow one to check that legend). During the course of the previously mentioned Soviet amelioration projects, the riverbed was deepened and its course was straightened. Because of this, the river's bends no longer correspond to those recorded on the late 1800s land-survey maps that are measured in versts and used as base material in the restitution process. As such, the river's course must be surveyed once again and recorded on new land-survey maps. Actually, the riverbed would have changed significantly as the result of natural flow erosion over the course of a hundred years, also, but I don't know how that is regarded.

The property boundary, as the female surveyor (more talkative) explained, is the river's conceptual centerline. In order to determine this, however, one has to form a dotted line from the line of both banks, determining the coordinates of points along it. As surveying has to happen on both sides of the river, which has only one footbridge in that place, three people are indeed necessary. So, I was the third. The points' coordinates are designated with "centimeter" precision, the female surveyor claimed.

As I see it, this is certainly an obvious overstatement in designating the permitted margin of error, but I didn't start telling the surveyor that. The market price of a square meter of land in that location is in the range of five euro cents. This I calculated while stretching out on the dry grass of last year next to the tripod on the riverbank. The sun warmed me. Atop the tripod was a device that connected—as they explained to me—to a satellite (an artificial body orbiting Earth). During the communication session, which was supposed to last about twenty minutes, the small device would fixate the coordinates of its locational point.

I furthermore thought about how interesting it is that a conceptual network of coordinates on the surface of the Earth has been synchronized with the shift of Earth's axis and other phenomena. Is coordinate XY always and forever precisely that sedge (*Carex leporina L.*, sedges are plants belonging to the *Cyperaceae* family of rushes and grasses, which usually grow in marshes and meadows—over seventy species that are hard to distinguish from one another can be found in Estonia; sedges made up the main part of the mass of low-food-value marsh hay) amid the sod, counting the sod's central point as unmoving in relation to the surface? That I do not know.

It was good to lie out in the sunshine; all that could be heard were the sounds of birds and the surveyors' succinct shouts across the river (yeah!—enough!). I had to wait until the connection had lasted long enough, and then carry the device to a new point. I fantasized about what it would be like to live with that male surveyor. He was namely a young, tall boy with a cute, somewhat timid smile. He somehow, it seems to me now, reminded me of my father in his younger days. He had very long legs; I said to him that the surveyor has a long pace, at which he smiled even more awkwardly. It's not at all impossible, I found, that behind that awkward smile are certain (very hidden, even subliminal) homosexual inclinations. He seemed too sensitive for a regular heterosexual man.

We would live together in one of those large, two-story farmhouses in Central Estonia (Estonia's most fertile soils are found in those parts, as my father asserts, and the population was historically wealthy; nowadays, those houses are available for a few thousand euros). The land surveyor would survey land, I would visit Tallinn every now and then, would visit Paris every now and then (we would also go there together once, but the surveyor wouldn't like Paris, and from that point onward would, jealously, not permit me to go there anymore) to run my film projects in order to preserve economic independence. I would otherwise wait for him at home like a loving husband. I'd wash and iron. The house would absolutely have to have red or dark-green ceramic stoves that would need to be heated every day in winter. It would be truly enormous. In order to maintain a decent façade in the country, a faithful lesbian pair would also live there in the same house, and we would each be formally married to one of them. They would actually live in another wing of the house. Villagers would not get to the house—it would be surrounded by thick pine hedges once planted to protect the apple trees from cold winds. The apple trees would be old and mossy, but would burst richly into bloom every spring. Our sex life would be regular, routine, and quietly satisfying for both parties. We would plant new apple trees as well, and would follow their growth from year to year, all the way to reaching fruit-bearing maturity. Maybe we would adopt a child from an orphanage. Or even several. The surveyor, I've noticed, has beautiful veiny hands with long fingers; his long legs certainly also have long, elegant toes. In short, everything is long and sensitive, but not too much. Life would go by.

I allowed this fantasy to develop freely within me and felt that I had fallen completely in love with the surveyor (whose name I didn't know, nor do I now). I felt a pleasant erotic quiver in my body warmed by the sun, an erection. When I met the surveyor on the footbridge after a quarter of an hour, I saw that he was an absolutely ordinary boy or man (albeit with a somewhat bashful smile), and even had a wedding ring on his finger. The female surveyor—an energetic woman with a short, strong build and a loud, slightly crowing voice—was his wife. No doubt they had children, too.

As for that detached plot (or main plot), on which was once located the house where my father lived until the age of twenty-five, running the farm with his mother during the last years (his father had already been deported, and actually executed as well, but where—that, they didn't know): there is nothing pretty or of worth there. A couple of middle-aged oaks and a few weathered arborvitaes allegedly planted for the children's births. The house burned down in the 60s; unfamiliar kolkhoz workers lived there. The kolkhoz set up a grain drier on one corner of the property: its four rusted cisterns or towers form the dominant element on the landscape. As a state-owned highway separates the yard from the field (thirty acres), the surveyors recommended leaving it unsurveyed entirely, because it apparently has no significant perspective, anyway. That nondescript piece of property set amid a run-down, dilapidated village containing kolkhoz structures (a livestock farm, two multi-apartment houses—one of which is already abandoned, its windows smashed in) is undoubtedly not suitable for development by either the tourism or the resort sector, and the size of the farmland far from corresponds to the a modern farm's investment needs. The field has been rented out to someone. The surveyors confirmed: survey it, and afterwards, you'll just pay land tax—you'll pay like . . . the female surveyor searched for a more apt comparison:

"You'll pay like for a dead elephant!"

My father was confused: he scratched the back of his neck, and even wiped the corner of his eye, although there wasn't a tear there. I recorded the scene on video. Then, my father came up with a saving idea: the property had a well. Specifically, there was a farm law approved in Estonia during the final years of the Soviet Union, during "perestroika," the goal of which was to restore the traditional way of life in the country. It was deemed a guarantee for national perseverance. Under the law, land was made available for those wanting it, still using the Soviet Union's great resources and the confusion dominant in the central administration, and the building of infrastructure (roads, electric lines, wells) was even arranged. Some man had indeed begun to set up a farm there, and had a 195-foot-deep well drilled, as my father had found out by looking into the matter. The restoration of farms turned out to be a fruitless burst of nostalgia in economic terms, and that man had abandoned his project as well, although the well remained. Such a well, my father said, costs a good one hundred thousand kroons. No, go ahead and survey that plot, too.

Naturally, I must add that one hundred thousand kroons may very well be the total cost for drilling a new well, which, however, does not mean that one might successfully sell said well to someone for even ten thousand kroons nowadays. Not that my father really believed this, either. Back when his father was still alive, they had a home subscription to the magazine *Economic Cycle*, and he has quite a clear picture of the laws of economics, which is extremely rare among members of his generation (having lived most of their active life under the conditions of Soviet power). The market price for their entire real property is currently a maximum of 150,000 kroons, and they plan to sell it off, because my father's sisters would like to get something out of it before they die. In the event that the farm is sold and my father divides his share of the money in the way that he has promised, I would receive from that family inheritance—on which my ancestors paid interest to Scheel Bank for thrity years to acquire, and where my grandfather left his life—about ten thousand Estonian kroons (at best), with which I would be able to pay one month's rent on my Paris apartment.

When we drove away from there and already started to reach the town, I mused that the greatest service that my ancestors have done for me, although involuntarily, their greatest "blessing," for which I must thank them, is that they have bequeathed practically nothing to me. No farm of any sort, no old house of any kind, nothing that would tie me down to this land.

*

I don't know how far back into the past it's worth going to sufficiently define a person. I have no reason to doubt the results of a study done by psychoanalysts Anne Ancelin Schützenberger and Didier Dumas, from which it turns out that we can subconsciously search for a solution in our life to some kind of an ancestral trauma (mostly one from the generation-before-last) that is lodged in us by way of a family's "silent transmission." This is very possible. Yet, even when comprehending (fathoming) a single individual, I prefer to follow the principle of Occam's razor, which orders one to eliminate the unimportant reasons in the event that the processes are obviously guided prevailingly by other, dominantly stronger factors. Figuratively speaking, it isn't necessary to designate the coordinates of objects with centimeter, or even half-yard precision in order to draw a two hundred thousand-yard map. Something along those lines.

And it isn't worth me digging too deeply into the past or digressing into all possible relevant details to define with the precision I need the coordinates (social, psychological, cultural, political etc.) of Liz Franz the person, and of myself, and of us: of Liz Franz and me (how I hated that "us" in her mouth!). Doing so, I'd never reach—even if I don't die this year (for which I definitely don't see any distinct reason; for dying this year, that is) and live for forty years more (given the longevity of my father and his mother, I may have the genetic predisposition for this, although I also might not)—I'd never reach that, which is important to me; I'd never reach the truth of who Liz Franz was to me, and who else she might be if I do manage to restore contact with her (if this is at all necessary or even desired?). In short, I should begin from a reasonable temporal distance: from not too far, but not too close, either, in which case the risk of overlooking something important would already be unreasonably great.

7

I have truly brooded a great deal over the mystery of heritage. First of all, of course, over my homosexuality as a specific inherited psycho-physiological disposition. Generally speaking, two explanations can be found for this: the first is genetic, and the second psychoanalytic.

In the first case would be the existence of a special "homosexuality gene," the discovery of which is also announced from time to time in popular literature. It can, nevertheless, hardly be just **one** gene. If it *is*, then it's some cluster of hereditary attributes, a collection of special characteristics in mankind's massive cloud of genetic variation. One edge of that cloud, a dark rim, which smoothly transitions into another cloud. It's true that a gay recognizes a gay, distinguishes him or her (or at least the assumption of the reception of his or her own body) by way of some outer parameters, by "appearance." Which in turn could point to a group of distinct somatic features accompanying homosexuality or the inclination towards it (some refer to "feminization," *efféminement*; although firstly, that is not always noticeable in the very least, and secondly, it is often a behavioral complex, an openness to society's expectations, mimicry addressed towards a potential sexual partner), which in turn seems to support the genetic hypothesis, but which in my opinion, regardless of this and until solid statistical pools are presented, remains on weak footing.

The psychoanalytical hypothesis, beginning with papa Freud, is founded, however, on the (silent) conviction that a) this is some kind of a psychological defect, a neurosis, or hysteria of some kind, and b) one must look for its roots in childhood, and foremost in the person's relationship with his or her parents. Or from early psychological traumas (the child's sexual abuse, *sévices sexuels*, by parents, caretakers, older brothers or sisters, peers, strangers).

With this, it seems to me that practically all kinds of family- and historical-developmental constellations may "bring forth" homosexuality. A strong father, a weak mother; a strong mother, a weak father; the father's absence; the mother's absence; being the older child and the caretaker of brothers or sisters; being the youngest child and being cared for; being abandoned; being cared for too strongly; etc., etc. On the other hand, in the interests of scientific rigor (*rigueur*), one must note that similar conditions, which are put forth as reasons, sometimes bring forth homosexual tendencies, and sometimes do not. Which all undoubtedly does not reduce the psychoanalysis's intrigue, and possibly also perspective in terms of making peace with oneself, of finding certain stability in one's own skin (*dans sa peau*).

Naturally, these two hypotheses (genetic and psychological) can be combined into a third, which would state that in the event of certain genetic preconditions, in the event that a child ends up in a certain growth environment, then . . . But doesn't that ultimately lead to our simply explaining every separate case by way of itself—in short, having become convinced that we posses one "consequence," we craft reasons for ourselves from that consequence?

So, it seems to me sometimes that everything can be explained by childhood, but it really explains nothing. And then, there is always a further fourth hypothesis, which would be mystical and base itself in the assumption that a deity, the Creator has created some men to love men and some women to love women for certain purposes, just as the majority of men love women and the majority of women love men. That there is some kind of secret plan about it. That everyone must bear his or her own cross, etc., etc.

I now, by the way, am indeed living in Tartu. I moved in yesterday evening—meaning I carried a couple of bags of clothes and books from the car up to the fifth floor. I rented the apartment at the address 1–11 Ülikooli through Robinson Real Estate Bureau (realtor Eero Saar), via a classified ad. It was the only apartment that I looked at, and I liked it straight away; at least I liked it enough not to search further. Renting an apartment in Estonia is certainly easy in comparison with Paris! You can so much as set your own conditions. Although, it's true that I rent a cheap apartment in Paris and an expensive one here (which by absolute worth is indeed two times cheaper): five thousand kroons per month plus "fees." This is definitely unspeakably expensive for Tartu, in my opinion, but I've learned from Liz Franz not to haggle when you need something and when you like it.

I'll speak at greater length about why I need it and why I like it here later; right now, I don't really feel like stopping on it. The thing was that first of all, I felt that I can no longer stay in the Tallinn apartment. I don't know what its status is. And I started feeling unsettled there. In the event that Liz Franz has truly disappeared, someone could ultimately start investigating the case officially; in the event that someone, such as Liz Franz's mother, launches an investigation. I can't imagine anyone else doing so, because Umberto Riviera would already have done so, and all her other friends and acquaintances are used to her disappearances and reappearances (*réapparitions*).

Because depending on the person in regards to whom, that is, for whom Liz Franz has disappeared, the time between her disappearance and her resurfacing could span several years, and as far as I know, she has truly been practically impossible to find for those people during that time; although they have, of course, known more or less where and what life she was living, according to rumor. In general, it is currently also known that she is living some kind of very withdrawn (in the sense of from her singing career as well as cultural and social activities) life with Umberto Riviera, who is a businessman of international magnitude and travels a great deal—from Tallinn to Moscow, Rome to Istanbul, Paris to New York, Rio to Cape Town.

I know, however, that it was extremely rare for Liz Franz to go along on those trips, although *during* those very same trips, she did systematically visit Paris (in the event that they did not bring Umberto to Paris) and, even more frequently, Tallinn, because we shared a single apartment in both cases.

Liz Franz managed for the most part to visit Tallinn in such a way that none of her old friends or admirers of her work would know that she was in her homeland, or if someone found out or was informed, then she deftly left the impression that her stay would be short-term, was in connection with her husband's work affairs, her mother's health, and all in all had come up quite suddenly; that she was actually flying out on the next flight back to Rome already. In short, it was strange for me to stay in that apartment rented out in Liz Franz's mother's name, located in Tallinn's Kadriorg district (*Catherinenthal*, a summer palace and garden complex planned by Peter I and finished by Catherine II that is located in eastern Tallinn; an esteemed, although partially dilapidated residential neighborhood in its vicinity) at the address 6–12 Weitzenbergi. Nothing forces me to fly back to Paris in the near future, either. And on top of it all, I'm afraid. I don't know of *what*, but if I want to be honest, then I have to admit that I am afraid. Of Liz Franz, who has disappeared. I had been so used to Liz Franz's disappearances. She could disappear to everyone, she was always there for me. And my attempts to disappear from her radar lasted, at maximum, a month and a half, and *that* was probably by her own grace.

In any case, I no longer liked the situation at all, in which Liz Franz had disappeared to me, but where I was so easily locatable for her: Weitzenbergi 6–12, Tallinn, or Place de la Porte de Champerret 6/8 (actually eighth), on the eighth (ninth, in the Estonian sense) floor, first door to the right when coming out of the elevator. It seems to me that here, in Tartu, I'm able to be relatively well-concealed. It would take "them" (I really don't suffer any delusion of being under surveillance, and neither did I fear it directly) a fair amount of time with my finding. My name didn't mean anything to anyone at the real estate bureau. I'm only well known here in specialist circles, and perhaps one middle-aged or another woman with cultural interest knows that there does exist such an obscure film documentalist, who once produced a couple of even more obscure documentary films which are long out of circulation. The last ten years in Estonia have been as long as a century; everything that was before was before the flood.

I no longer wear glasses, which I have noticed makes me unrecognizable to semi-acquaintances. In our memory, the primary details of a person's appearance are truly often glasses, hair, a beard, a moustache; even a jacket or a coat. I'd have no need for a fake beard (my facial hair is too sparse to grow a real beard; furthermore, I don't especially like men with longer beards under the age of seventy-five)—obscurity is enough for me.

And so, I was perfectly unfamiliar to real estate workers. I consciously spoke with an accent, acted an Estonian from abroad. That cost me at least one thousand kroon per month extra if not more, but fine. The main thing is to keep that quality up in the future: an accent, a certain naivety. For example, I asked the name of the "doorkeeper" (*concierge*) so that I could "signal" (*signaler*) to him that the hallway "bulb" (*ampoule*) doesn't burn. That's enough.

This, I've certainly learned well from my own meager cinematic experience: very, very little is sufficient for a very, very strong label. A little, but sharp effect. It's already difficult to change the impression made by that well-targeted effect from then onward. I don't know whether this phenomenon has to do with the fact that people watch so many films and so much television in general that they also interpret the reality of life by way of that fictive artistic language, with which an illusion of reality is conjured for them on the screens. That people therefore seek from life an illusion of reality that can be expressed in the language of film?

Ah, confounded rambling! Today, by the way, is already April 29th. The trees are gently greening. But for some reason, I sang yesterday while driving towards Tartu in my red Opel Astra (the weather was pleasantly cloudy, very much suitable for driving, the fields that are still being cultivated are, for the most part, already plowed, grassy patches are no longer gray, but mottled green)—I bayed out (I can't hold a tune, but it came out quite well yesterday, in my opinion) that Liz Franz song, which is perhaps the best-known, and is put to the words of her contemporary (they should even be from the same part of the country), the Estonian poetess Viivi Luik:

> *I long for the bosom of the rowan tree,*
> *to bury my head in its branches.*
> *I long for the bosom of the rowan tree;*
> *to rest there would be good . . .*

Many interpretations of that song have been performed, but for me, Liz Franz's rendition (radio stations unfortunately don't play it anymore) is the best, hands down. Or at least the most original. Because the song itself, the words and the melody, are somewhat sweet (*mièvre*). When its performance is also womanly/lyrical, then what comes together is a Semolina mousse (I don't know the equivalent of that food in French, it is probably a purely German recipe). Yet, Liz Franz was able put something completely different into that simple little song. Even something perverse. She sang it in an especially low voice (she is probably an alto; to tell the truth, I don't know all that much about the topic)—in a raspy, almost manly voice; in a way as if the rowan tree was a woman and she was a man. Maybe in a way as if the rowan tree was a mother and she was a boy—a large boy with an enormous voice that still wanted to nestle into his mother's "bosom" (*sein maternel*). Or as if she was an old man and the rowan tree was a young girl. Or as if she was a middle-aged man, as I am now, and the rowan tree was a young boy: a muscular, blushing boy; a redhead. I don't know, who. And baying out that song on the monotonous highway from Tallinn to Tartu (luckily, the lane heading towards Tartu was empty on that Sunday evening) in my Opel Astra, whose radio had been stolen, I felt that the rowan tree was Liz Franz.

8

But as such, the question of origin is in no way clear to me. What is significant, what is insignificant? Is childhood actually more like an extremely autonomous period, and a universal one at that, but still quite similar for everyone, and onto which we, in hindsight, project (*projeter*) the peculiarities of our lives, the facts that distinguish us from the rest of humanity? Our particularities? Or on the contrary, as psychoanalytical theory probably claims, our adult life is just a projection of our childhood: the shadows of childhood's genuine actions and feelings on the white sheet that is post-childhood-life. But, in any case, it seems logical to me that when we investigate the disappearance of a person or a phenomenon, then we must also take a look at the conditions of its appearance. For as the Lewis Hackcocks Law, which is familiar to us all, says: objects and beings have a tendency to disappear through the same opening, from which they appeared. Take mice, for example. Or as Leonhard Cohen sings on his recently-released album *Ten New Songs*:

> *It is in love that we were made;*
> *In love we disappear.*

I don't know, of course, how much Liz Franz (actually baptized Eliisabet Frants, but I'll speak of her name later) was made "in love," but I believe that at least her father was in love when he copulated with a young, very young—twenty-two years younger than himself and only sixteen—farm girl. It must have happened in late February of 1947 for the baby to have entered the world at the end of November (on the twentieth).

There was certainly still snow on the ground, tall drifts, and biting cold. Because winters were harsh then. They were especially harsh in Livonia still before and during World War II. In 1939/40, the winter took out almost all of the fruit trees that been planted on farms in the process of home-design campaigns held during Estonia's first period of independence. In retrospect, it's seen as heralding the end of the republic.

When we went surveying my father's property, he told me that he was doing an internship at Luunja Manor (it had already been a state manor for twenty years then; a pilot farm) for agricultural school during the summer of 1940. He said that there had been an old, no doubt still "baron"-era (of course, not all Baltic noblemen carried the title of baron: there were also counts (*comte*), and some domains also temporarily fell under the possession of one Russian prince or another) gardener who packed all his arbor school's (*pépinière*) young apple trees into straw for the winter. My father had gotten along well with that gardener and was able to buy himself ten young apple trees, with which he planted an orchard on their farm. The next harsh winter of 1942/43 took the majority of them, however, and the ones that continued to grow were later uprooted by the kolkhoz in order to erect their grain drier there, the rusted towers of which I've already described.

I've rested upon the topic of apple trees at such great length because Liz Franz's father was also said to have had a weakness for apple trees: he unendingly transported saplings acquired from god-knows-where in his motorcycle's sidecar (all information presented here about Liz Franz's parents and her origins originate from the statements of hers that I remember; she spoke of those things on very rare occasion).

That father, Anton Frants, originated from the Latvian side of Livonia and was born—I remember the year—in 1905, during the first year of the Russian Revolution. Ruling the Baltic governorates, where many manors were burned down that year and where afterwards, the rebellious peasant boys were whipped—although many were executed, many bound in chains and sent to Siberia in stages (*étapes*)—ruling those Baltic governorates of Estonia, Latvia and Courland (*Courlande*) during that time was, just like the rest of the entire gigantic Russian Empire (which also included the Grand Duchies of Poland and Finland), Emperor Nicholas II.

The governorate of Livonia with its capital in Riga comprised the areas of modern-day Southern Estonia and Northern Latvia. The border between the Estonian and Latvian linguistic areas was unclear and in the nineteenth century, one could discern an expansion of Estonian peasants towards the south, as the developing metropolis of Riga drew Latvian peasants unto itself. Anton Frants was born somewhere within those areas of mixed settlement, likely into an Estonian-language peasant family in Cçsise (Võnnu) County (*Kreis*). All I know about his youth is that he made it—this was already during the time of the Republic of Latvia—to the famed Riga Polytechnic Institute, where he studied to be a radio engineer. I don't know how much was left of that educational institution's erstwhile radiation (*rayonnement*), it had lost a large portion of its student body and probably also of its faculty due to new language requirements (universities transitioned from Russian to Estonian in Estonia, and to Latvian in Latvia). Yet, things in history rarely disappear suddenly and without a trace. By the way, at the end of the nineteenth century and during the "grand years" at the beginning of the twentieth, Estonia's only mysticist poet—Ernst Enno—also studied at Riga Polytechnic Institute. (He was also the only poet whom Liz Franz admired.) I have even seen written proof of the fact that Anton Frants (written Antons Frants in Latvian) truly studied there. Specifically, Liz Franz once showed me a large-format book bound in dark red (the color of the Latvian flag) buckram, which was a list of Riga Polytechnic Institute graduates (alumni); I don't remember what years it was for, but in any case, the name Antons Frants was also listed there in one column.

The anniversary collection was trilingual: Latvian, German, Russian. Until the cataclysms of World War II, Riga was a cosmopolitan city where there also happened to live a large Jewish community. Anton Frants then naturally spoke Estonian as well: thus, all four local Livonian languages. There was nothing exceptional about that in those times. I should indeed specify that the Estonian he spoke was not quite that, which was officially in circulation in the Republic of Estonia as "written language." The idiom that Anton Frants spoke at home with his parents was the so-called Southern Estonian language. As a written language, it is actually older than the standard tongue that later became dominant and is based on Northern Estonian dialects. The Southern-Estonian-language *Wastne Testament* was published already during the time of the Swedish state, in 1686—I just acquired a facsimile copy of it, finding that upon moving to Tartu, that I must also acquaint myself with "the language of the land" (people in rural areas speak it among themselves to this very day), which furthermore was also Liz Franz's home language, although there wasn't the slightest trace of it left in her speech. I don't know a single more skilled trail-loser than Liz Franz.

In addition to those four or five (because he even mastered written Estonian later on) local languages, Anton Frants had studied a small amount of English and French at the polytechnic institute; I remember having seen a French-language radio engineer textbook among Liz Franz's few books—no doubt in her father's memory.

During the thirties, young Anton Frants relocated and took Estonian citizenship (such movement was in style at the time, foretelling violent ethnic cleansings to come), removed the excessive "s" from his name, and founded a small radio sales and repair business in the small town of Viljandi: *Anton Frantsi Raadiod*. He was a bachelor (*célibataire*). The radio, which in Estonian was then called a "broadcaster" (German *Rundfunk*), had just surged in popularity, and it was important for every wealthier family both in the country and in towns to acquire—no matter if even by installments—a radio receiver. Dutch Philips was the favored brand, as the spread of German devices was hindered by a spirit of furious nationalism. "Germans," actually the local German-speaking nobility, had been our nation's oppressor for "seven hundred years."

Emphasized nationalism became the official ideology imposed with President Konstantin Päts's coup d'état during the so-called "Era of Silence" (1934—1940). It was indeed far from Hitler's extreme anti-Semitism and other such movements, but generally followed the spirit of the time—the "historical fashion," which was dominant in Europe during that epoch. The radio became a powerful device for informing the masses; i.e. for forming a collective (sub)consciousness (Latin *informâre*: "to shape, form"). Anton Frants also undertook sales trips to the countryside on his sidecar motorcycle—across the entire Estonian part of Livonia, although probably never crossing over into the side of Estonia proper, shunning the unfamiliar linguistic dialect and probably instinctively taking into account the fact that his "vulgar" manner of speaking in the "capital region" would reduce sales figures by an improvident extent. How successful or unsuccessful his business was—that, I don't know. In any case, it was nationalized by the new power in 1940. I know a little something about that. Specifically, Liz Franz once told me the story of "Two Merchants" (my own working title).

In particular, located next to Anton Frants's Radios on Viljandi's main commercial street (*rue commerciale*) was Valdur Kaasik and Sons (certainly an Estonianized name in the 30s; a Ferdinand Birkebau or something similar): "Fabrics. Ready-made Clothing. Galanterie." Along with his sons, Valdur Kaasik was a tycoon by Viljandi dimensions: his shop was located on two floors (there was still a clothing store in that building even during Soviet times, fifteen to twenty years ago, when I last visited Viljandi); however, for some reason, the Bolshevist authorities did not arrest Valdur Kaasik when the business was nationalized, and only demoted him to a simple salesperson, promoting a former sales fellow to store director. The business was renamed "Proletariat Garments." As the new director did not have a precise overview of the warehouse stocks and was also likely not especially familiar with the finer points of commercial bookkeeping, it was easy for Valdur Kaasik to stow away a few pricier rolls of fabric that he had acquired. He was said to have hidden them somewhere "between the walls" in the hopes— and justifiably so—of the new rule's imminent downfall. Alas, he didn't make it that long. A former inferior, to whom Valdur Kaasik perhaps hadn't been the most polite, apparently got wind of it and denounced (*dénoncer*) him. The wall was ripped open and the fabric rolls were yanked out in the silent presence of the store personnel (they were witnesses to the search, bystanders). Officials managed to deport Valdur Kaasik and his family just before the arrival of the Germans in the summer of 1941. In all likelihood, he perished either on the way or somewhere in a prison camp, as did his three sons. Only his wife, who had risen to that status from the position of salesgirl, returned from Siberia and even managed to work as a seller in the fabric department of the Viljandi Consumers' Cooperative Department Store before going onto her pension.

Compared with Kaasik's business, Anton Frants's radio shop was a small company; yet taking into consideration the high price of radios at that time, the value of that mobile property was still quite great at the moment of nationalization. Comprising Anton Frants's employed labor was one "boy," no doubt a young man at the time, by the name of Jaan, who had been fully trained on radios by the shopkeeper. At the time of nationalization, Anton Frants left his entire store and all the radios in the "boy's" care, refused the director's position offered to him (as the business was small, he was not declared an enemy of the state), took his bike (the motorcycle had been added to the list of nationalized assets), and pedaled his way out of Viljandi. During and after the war, he worked as a traveling (*ambulant*) radio repairman. He was repeatedly excused from military service because of a lung disease; nevertheless, the last time was thanks to him fixing some high-ranking German officer's beloved Philips, which had been located in a building that was bombed when the Russians dropped them over Tartu. In short, Anton Frants survived.

At the time that Liz Franz told me the story, I thought she was simply doing it to pass the time; just as she sometimes did by storytelling, because we would otherwise have nothing to talk about in each other's company. *I* primarily grew sullen and incriminatingly quiet. Thinking back to that sullenness now, I'm embarrassed and reminded of Stepan Trofimovich, who lounged on Varvara Petrovna's couch as an "embodied reproach" in Dostoyevsky's "Demons."

I also grasp the fact that although Liz Franz told stories to lift my mood and pass by those long evenings when we were shut into that Tallinn apartment, from which I just removed my last items, she likewise told them with a completely different motive. All of those stories were supposed to teach me something.

It's probably not even necessary to add that Liz Franz regarded her father highly and no doubt mourned him greatly, although she never spoke of it. But in 1947, Anton Franz reached that place in Viljandi County, Tänassilma Municipality, on the banks of the small Tänassilma River, which is part of the Emajõgi river basin, on his sidecar motorcycle once again. It was a German trophy bike, and I don't know how Anton Franz came to be its owner. It's possible that it was given to him by his job, which was the National Radiofication Central Administration's Viljandi Radio Fixation Point. His task was to repair the radio devices that were left in the countryside (the Soviet authorities had initially confiscated radios, as people used them to listen to prohibited Voice of America, BBC, Vatican Radio, and other Western stations) and adjust them to exclusively receive Soviet wavelengths. So that they would no longer receive anything else. He likewise installed into larger settlements (five hundred residents and up) and state institutions public radio transmission points, i.e. megaphones (*haut-parleurs*), through which the authorities attempted to inform the population more efficiently. In addition to propaganda programs, music was broadcast from the megaphones that were positioned in village squares: brisk Soviet songs that were meant to inspire people to new victories in the work of building up the post-war socialist country.

Liz Franz's grandmother, the mother of that flowering young country girl, also had an old Philips receiver left behind by her departed husband. The name of that young girl, the old woman's sole daughter, was Laine (*Vague, Onde, Flot, Lame;* Wave)—a national-romantic name, the likes of which were given during the 20s and the 30s to drive out old "Germanic" Christian names such as Tõnu (Antonius) or Liisu (Elisabeth).

Laine was born in 1928 right there in Tänassilma Municipality, right on that farm, and had probably gone through the higher primary school's six or seven classes. Forced collectivization had not yet happened in Estonia in 1947, although the Soviet authorities attempted to motivate farm workers in the just-annexed areas to enter kolkhozes by sharply increasing the tax burden. With their two cows and around ten sheep, for which they stocked up on hay from the Tänassilma marshes all summer long, Laine Saul and her mother Anne Saul made up a farmstead, likewise. They themselves, and their animals, somehow managed to stay alive. In any case, Anne Saul initially didn't even want to hear a word about fixing the radio, because she suspected it could bring along not only an expense (and money all went to pay the state taxes, it had to be kept), but also a fight. In terms of the latter, as life later showed, she indeed wasn't mistaken. But then her daughter, who otherwise humbly obeyed her mother, came out in defense of the radio with unexpected grit.

"I'm a young person," she said. "I can't attend parties, anyway; I toil and labor with you here just like an old hag! Let's at least have a *raydyo* at home—I can listen to songs every once in a while!"

That "songs" was a clever trick, because her mother Anne had been a big singer (when the circumstances were still kinder), had sung first alto in the church choir, and had even attended the Song Festival in Tallinn. When she further heard that the repair was "completely without fee," and that the jolly man with motorcycle glasses would give them a new battery to go with it on his own behalf, she threw up her hands. Fine. And so, it happened that the radio engineer Anton Franz and young Laine made love. The only mystery for me now is how he rode around on his motorcycle in winter. Maybe he didn't have the bike anyhow on that occasion of conception, and the first visit had already been earlier, during the previous summer, and that time in March, he was already coming to "check on" the radio or switch its battery or something. The greatest probability is that the conception happened somewhere altogether farther from the home, because there could have been no great opportunity for doing the deed in a farmhouse with thin walls in February, when it was cold outside, without her mother knowing (if Anne hadn't happed to leave home). I imagine that the copulation between the "old" (forty-two-year-old) Anton and young Laine could have taken place during Laine's visit to Viljandi. In that case, the egg cell, out of which the internationally famed singer Liz Franz would later grow, was fertilized in a town regardless—no matter that it was only in Viljandi.

In any case, there was a "*raydyo*" in Liz Franz's home already at her moment of birth. Anton Frants didn't abandon the girl he knocked up, but rather married her, which nearly reconciled him with old Anne as well. He still also continued to visit their home primarily to change the radio's battery—his work was still mobile and he didn't do farm work out of principle. That manner also rubbed off on little Eliisabet (the name came from Anton Frants's mother), who was called "Liisu" at home, despite her lively protests ("I am Eliisapett!"). Once, when I probed Liz Franz on how she got by at home during her childhood (by default, having in mind her present status of "dame"—that word was definitely strictly forbidden—and "diva"—she laughed at that word), she said:

"They [that is, her mother and grandmother] already knew that it was wiser to leave me alone than to stick a rake in my hand."

No one could apparently handle bearing that clamor and fracas. Truly—what Liz Franz refused, she refused.

9

Last night, the first true spring rain finally fell upon Tartu. It wasn't at all much, but the drought ended all the same. After the rain passed, the air became warm and began to carry a scent. It seems to me that the trees on the opposite bank of the Emajõgi (few houses are visible, they are shorter than the trees, it resembles a forest there) have become much greener over the course of today. The weather is basically what it was in Paris a month ago when I left. The leaves on the trees there were probably already even bigger then, but I don't remember, either. I've become used to not paying attention to spring in Paris: it comes so gradually—from January through May—that for me, it essentially doesn't exist.

In any case, it had definitely already come by then, in terms of warmth. But as soon as I reached here, Estonia, I apparently subconsciously switched immediately into "spring-waiting" mode, because when I crossed the downtown park today (before the war, there were buildings there that were bombed—the house that I live in was the only one left standing on that block and stood there oddly alone when I attended university; now, two shopping centers have been built alongside it), I sensed while sniffing the smell of opening buds that it is here now; that the wait has borne fruit. I don't think that it smells this way in Paris. There, the smell is likely spread out over a longer period of time. As such, it seemed to me when I was reading Baudelaire (what foolishness: no one speaks that language any longer!) to supplement my French during my first year in Paris—

Le Printemps adorable a perdu son odeur!

—that what he wrote of had to be the smell of Estonian spring; just as the mystical blue and pink poured by the evening in "The Death of Lovers" had to be the blue and pink of a Tartu winter evening on the snow drifts, on the river ice.

But living in these parts, the psycho-physiological "spring-waiting" mode is the primary regime in general, commanding the body and the spirit from about November up until some day such as today. Today is April 30th. As this mode is a local individual's main state—or at least was my main state when I lived here, and I lived here for the majority of my hitherto life, twenty-nine years—it is also so dogged, probably more like imperishable, and is ready to switch on immediately when the environmental conditions give it the sign to do so.

Some kind of university-student days or something of the sort began in Tartu last night—the thumping of bass notes sounded across the river. I listened to the rhythms while lying in bed. Those seemingly similar beats are actually quite different. Just as you manage to get used to one rhythm, it breaks off and a new track begins. Regardless, I soon fell asleep—I've become accustomed to noise in Paris. Still, during the night, I did hear when some boys (*jeunes gens*) walked along the street below and belted out an operetta that was likely written for soprano. (Then I laugh ah-ah-haa! etc.) It was probably meant to be a joke. Any kind of transvestism in Estonia is a joke that emphasizes your manliness, your unambiguousness.

However, crossing the park in the daytime, I was specifically heading for the market. The stew I ate yesterday at Krambambuli (a Baltic-German fraternity brothers' drinking song) Pub particularly represented the worst traditions of the local cuisine, having been mainly seasoned with a large quantity of salt, and gave me a sense of regret over the wasted thirty-nine kroons and time spent in the unpleasant racket of the music (country, disco).

I can't exactly say that my time is very valuable in monetary terms, especially now, here in Tartu, but its waste is still regrettable. And so, I decided to make a meal myself today, especially given the fact that this apartment contains a pot and the essential dishes. I went to the neighboring "Sparketi" (German?) supermarket first. I wasn't able to buy anything more there than one lemon and plastic-wrapped "chicken wings." Nothing fresh stood out—the fruit-and-vegetable counter had a very withered appearance. There weren't even old carrots or potatoes (I specifically wanted old ones—there is still a great deal of time until there are new ones here).

Then, I remembered that Tartu has a market. What's more, the classical building on the bank of the river at the other end of the park, another structure left standing after the bombing, in addition to the one where I live, can be seen from my window. However, I had viewed it from the window merely as a conceptual object, without considering the food hidden there. Now, I remembered the market building's former smell, which was a mixture of fish, smoked meat, sauerkraut, pickles, and onions; and which always made my mouth water when I was constantly undernourished during my university years (partially from an actual lack of money, partially from obsessive repression—in the hopes of silencing the cravings that tortured me). The kolkhoz market was an expensive place then. Now, the market is a cheap place. The crowd flowing in through the door of the market building left quite a miserable impression: gray (dressed in gray) pensioners. It *was* midday as well, I suppose—pensioners' hour.

But I wasn't to be disappointed by the smell. When I entered from the end of the "fish market," I was received by that same strong odor of fish: being sold there were fresh Baltic herring and several kinds of smoked fish, no doubt from Peipus (a large lake and the historical natural boundary between Livonia and Russia). And sure enough, I also found one side in the large hall, where the sellers were offering fresh lettuce (three kroons for a bunch), chives (two kr.), radishes (six kr. for about six), and all of it truly was fresh.

Such a luxury put me in an outright euphoria. I'd already gotten used to the idea that I would have to eat poor and unhealthy food in Estonia. The older woman, from whom I bought potatoes, carrots and radishes (one would be hard-pressed to find such good radishes in Paris—northern fruits and vegetables are especially delicate and juicy) enjoined me to always "prefer local Estonian" ("*eelistada eestimaist*"—it is one slogan in a campaign organized by the Ministry of Agriculture; Estonian folk-rhyme used a plethora of alliterations), because those in the country apparently won't be able to make ends meet anymore otherwise. The laws of economics are indeed mysterious. And cruel. For them, making a small country extinct is a piece of cake. But luckily, it is still living in spite of this, and I now know where I can get food during the coming days, weeks or months that I am to spend in Tartu.

The stew came out completely satisfactorily. I'm no longer dependent on the poor food of Tartu's arrogant cafés. I eat out very rarely in Paris because there is no money for it. I mostly do it only when invited, or when I have to invite someone out myself. At first, I was embarrassed before my Estonian guests because I was unable to take them anywhere "Parisian" to eat. From what I knew, those places either had very bad food or were very expensive. I hate that perverse trend of our civilization: a branch of human activity as simple and basic as making food has been turned into one of the most exclusive services that follows the rules of trend- and image-marketing. If I live to an old age, then one day, I'l get to opening up a dining establishment, where I offer my stews at a normal price. Although, I'm most likely too lazy and individualistic for feeding people. Until then, I will wage my own small battle against the market forces by enjoying my private stew alone with the plate on the windowsill, looking out across the leafing treetops and over a small town.

I am unquestionably better than Liz Franz in at least one thing, and that is cooking. Although she gave it her best, her greatest culinary achievement remained cold chicken salad. There was nothing wrong with that, either. To tell the truth, it seemed at first—that time—outright gourmet. I hadn't yet accustomed to luxury then, and subconsciously, I probably regarded eating well as a sin (*péché de la gourmandise*).

I had, however, completely forgotten that April 30th is now the so-called "Walpurgis Night" (so, Walpurgis-Day Eve?) in Estonia. It is probably a tradition associated with some kind of Germanic fertility magic. For Livonian peoples, the equivalent rituals like making bonfires, jumping over a fire, etc. were more associated with the summertime St. John's Day; however, international market forces have also globalized "national tradition," and as such, celebrations of consumer culture including Halloween, St. Valentine's and that Walpurgis—the night before the first of May, when witches were said to have held their "Sabbat" (an obvious anti-Semitic allusion!) on Blocksberg Mountain—have strongly taken root in Estonia over the last decade.

The function of Walpurgis Night is to be a part of beer and alcohol companies' marketing campaign, because it is one of those nights, when "tradition" permits and outright requires that people drink themselves dead drunk (*ivre mort*). Starting already at around six o'clock (and lasting until at least nine o'clock) was the part of the campaign consisting of creating a common or participatory feeling in the crowd. Utilized towards these ends was a sufficiently large-scale array of amplifiers installed in the vicinity of Atlantis Nightclub on the other bank of the Emajõgi River, likewise an apparently well-known radio DJ.

I'm indeed unfamiliar with the popular voices of Estonia's commercial radio stations, but from his tempo of speech and confidence as well as the fluidity of the text, which gives an impression of persuasiveness, one could surmise a popular radio voice. As my windows face the river, I had a part in that "broadcast" (*émission*) by being in the room; even closing the windows didn't help so much. Such a strongly-amplified audio background that permeates everywhere is probably supposed to give the population the feeling that it is no longer a backdrop, noise, in the background of which their everyday life passes by—but that this time, they *themselves* are swept up in the ritual of the radio (or some other mass medium), that they are on the program, are live. Luckily, on the day that I had remembered that new day of importance on the national calendar, I had bought earplugs from the pharmacy on the day. They help quite well—I was even able to doze on the couch for a short while. I was already more tolerant after that. A daytime nap is like a computer restart that organizes your files, checks your personal settings, and saves.

Listening to that incessant racket (a rowing competition was apparently also being held on the river), I mused that people are, all in all, so immensely pleased when they are shouted at. Before that, I had been unable to imagine how people consented to things such as Hitler or Stalin's rise to power, how they didn't resist at the very beginning, when it still would have been easy. Now, I realize that they didn't *want* to resist, the majority of them. And both Hitler and Stalin relied upon the majority. Ergo: the majority wants to be shouted at. When the majority is shouted at, then it namely perceives itself as "it," as one, a being, "I"-less. In any sense, the imposition of any new "fascism" (no one calls it that, of course) doesn't appear to be an art. And no doubt it will be imposed, too. Considering that, freedom still feels dear. Maybe I will one day reminisce about the time, when people were only shouted at on Walpurgis Night. Because truly: amplification equipment has developed immeasurably since the time that Anton Frants, tasked by the Radiofication Central Administration, installed his public broadcast points. Those Stalinist megaphones were still just child's play. Although, I don't know. People accustom to everything, and I accustom as well. You are shouted at, and you don't even hear it. Meaning the volume must be increased.

I walked around town some more in the evening; the streets were filled with drunken and excited young people. I felt that they are already an entirely different generation, one opaque to me. It's a strange feeling. I myself had just belonged to that generation. I had just been young: still then, when I met Liz Franz. I've grown older beside her, but she refused to age. She preferred to disappear instead. I truly felt afraid watching the boys (and girls—those were especially perverse) marching towards me in the dusk of evening (I'm not exaggerating: they formed **columns**, although not quite in rank and file), wearing various fraternity caps.

Some carried lit torches that cast a red glow onto their faces. I don't recognize the world in which I live. But those kinds of columns, I believe, are the first footings of any kind of dictatorship, the elite. If I were to say that to those young men, they wouldn't even be offended, but would instead regard such talk as hysterical ravings from a homo. Well, fine: I represent individual hysteria, they—the collective. They're right.

I would have liked to walk opposite to those columns with Liz Franz, who would have been able to make some very bitter and very funny remark about them. Such jabs were her forte. She was definitely a true diva. That, which she decided to become while there along the Tänassilma River in Viljandi County, in that long, gray (I imagine) farmhouse with a half-hip roof (shake or shingle), where there was a radio. She had never been so foolish as to want to "get in the radio." She knew immediately that no one was *in* the radio; that those people talking and singing there are elsewhere, in a town. The first town she saw was Viljandi when she was about six years old, and that had apparently left a poor impression on her. She had known for certain: she was going to Moscow. She was said to enjoy when one woman sang in a powerful, sensitive voice on the radio. Her father had apparently used the word "diva" in reference:

"*Tuu om üits uuperitiiva.*"

No doubt that father had so much as attended a Riga "*uuperin.*" From then on, Liisu (sorry, "Eliisabet") knew with even more precision: not only was she going to Moscow, but she would become a diva as well. When the old women in the village asked what she wanted to be, she always answered importantly:

"*Mina saa tiivass.*"

I don't know how much that kind of a bourgeoisie question was really posed back then and in that place. It was a rough time, as they say now (indeed Liz Franz claimed to not remember any particular roughness). Forced collectivization and the mass deportation of peasants (the so-called "*kulaks*") who were feared disloyal was complete. The remaining peasantry was basically made into serfs anew, just as they had been before the reforms of Alexander II. They had no passports; they weren't allowed to leave the kolkhoz. Salaries were not paid: a *kolkhoznik* had to support him- or herself by way of so-called "personal assistant housekeeping," which at the same time was a despised entrepreneurial form. Yet, in her book *The Seventh Spring of Peace*, that same Estonian poetess and novelist Viivi Luik—whom we mentioned once already—wrote of that period in precise detail. Estonian culture is small, and you inevitably bump into the same people, the same names all the time when you are dealing with it. (The novel has been published in French by Christian Bourgois Publishing, but the remaining copies have most likely been recycled already—the modern market-economy doesn't favor keeping small-circulation publications in print.) So, I probably envision that period through the prism of the given novel, subconsciously believing that's just how it was.

Liz Franz herself has spoken very little of those years. Her radical aversion to work was already discussed. Added to that was apparently an aversion to food that was just as radical. As there was practically no money to be had, foods grown at home were eaten primarily: meaning potatoes, rutabaga, salted pork (to a small extent), milk when the cow wasn't dry, and traditional sour black bread (*pain fermenté, azyme*) made from rye flour, the likes of which I've found among the Poulain series of bakery goods in the Monoprix supermarkets in Paris. Although, it wasn't exactly the real thing, but the color was at least the same: dark brown, as was its somewhat doughy consistency. Later, during her "diva" life, Liz Franz never ate such bread again. She didn't exactly revile it, but she didn't eat it, either. It was generally difficult for me to understand what she survived on, because she almost never ate anything at all in my presence. A few leaves of lettuce, a few figs, fresh fruits—especially those sweet, red Italian oranges; she munched on those sometimes. I really don't know—at that time, I thought that she was afraid of getting fat, for which she probably had the natural predispositions. Her body, which many men lusted for and would have lusted for even more, and which I viewed with interest, like an anatomical female teaching material, was (and no doubt still is) absolutely toned and fit, slender. In her youth, which is visible from pictures on the record covers, she had an almost boyish figure, which in spite of that didn't lack the lightly sensual buxomness that was in style during the 60s. In any case, I don't know whether her near non-eating was a habit left with her from childhood (if food wasn't to her liking, she simply didn't eat, and no force could help), a product of willpower training, or a dematerialization-obsession of a sort.

I don't know whether or not she hated her body that was loved by many. I don't know whether she might have wanted it to *be* a boy's body—not be "like," but actually be. It's possible that I'm projecting my own fantasies upon her. I still believe, however, that Liz Franz had a secret weakness for marzipan and chocolate. Specifically, chocolate had been a rare product (*denrée rare*) during her childhood in a *kolkhoz* family in the country. I certainly never saw her eating an excessive amount of sweets, but I did sometimes notice the appearance and disappearance of chocolate bars as well as marzipan bunnies, hearts, and frogs; especially in the Tallinn apartment, because she regarded the chocolate and marzipan from Tallinn's "Kalev" sweet factory to be the very best, saying they had a "genuine taste." It is true that she didn't especially shroud that weakness—maybe she even overacted it, knowing that I hated and was jealous of her independence from food. Sometimes, she would offer *me* a marzipan bunny, allowing me to "bite its head off" first, and then would devour it herself. It seemed repulsive to me.

10

This morning in Tartu is clouded and divinely quiet. A national holiday. Only street sweepers are on the move, and workers are gathering up the trash left from nighttime partiers. The bottles were already picked up during the night, it happened in an almost organized fashion. I saw them myself on Toome Hill: little boys aged seven to twelve with large black trash bags, on bicycle or on foot, the bags sometimes filled up so heavy that they tended to rip. Glass and aluminum is bought back in the framework of European trash recycling (*recyclage*) programs; I'm not up to date with the prices. I should note that in the Soviet Union, the percentage of recycling was undoubtedly even higher, because the price of a bottle often didn't differ significantly from the cost of its contents, and those bottles weren't reprocessed, but were sent to be washed and refilled (folklore back then spoke of foreign bodies, mice, and workers' fingers left in the bottles). The Soviet Union was, in this sense, very "ecological." There was little product packaging: in shops, foods were often packed into a fibrous brown paper that companies with especially green mindsets now use for printing their envelopes and stock paper. Conversely, Soviet industry and agriculture were, of course, extremely unecological, spewing large quantities of waste into nature. Just as how Western consumer society—which fights for ecological ideals, and among the possessions of which are now Old Livonia, and even Russia—still consciously or unconsciously produces a very great amount of refuse. If not at home, then there, where the things that it consumes (that we consume) are made: in the Third World (*tiers-monde*). I wonder where the Second World is at all now? Is it still here?

At any rate, the young bottle-collecting boys on the hill seemed to be the most excited and happy out of all the partiers. Every now and then, they grouped up there in the dusky park and discussed their plan of action, exchanged info. Although they are market competitors in principle, they've apparently found that certain cooperation is more beneficial in a long-term perspective. It's also possible that the gatherings are the corporate partitioning of zones of influence.

Looking out from my window in the morning, I saw in addition to the street-cleaning brigade yet another one, which was busy raising the national flags on houses. Specifically, in Estonia, the national flag is not used to the extent of a decorative element, like it is in France. Here, the flag—likely following the German tradition—is more sacred, more an element charged with mysticism. I like Estonia's national flag—so what if it lacks traditional bright flag colors like red and yellow. The Estonian flag is a tricolor comprising three bands of color layered one above the other in equal widths: royal blue, black, and white. There is something "northern" about it, and it has an especially good effect with nature as its background, as it may remain somewhat unnoticed in the more variegated environment of a city. The stripes of the Estonian tricolor belonged initially, at the end of the nineteenth century, to a Tartu fraternity. There are, however, special little pipes on the sides of buildings in towns and settlements, into which the flag must be stuck on national days of importance that are marked in the calendar. An administrative penalty (*procès-verbal*) may be administered for not raising the national flag on a designated day, although this probably isn't really done. The flag is to be raised at sunrise and lowered at sunset, and that is the reason why this brigade was already at work at already six o'clock in the morning. I'm apparently ailed by a sort of insomnia, which, of course, is not comparable to true insomnia. Liz Franz, for example, almost never slept, as far as I knew; or in any case, she slept very little. Whenever I opened my eyes next to her, she was awake and as if she was on watch, although she feigned sleeping.

Watching the national flags being raised, I wondered which I actually like more: the French or the Estonian flag. It's true that I always soften when seeing the Estonian flag in France (whether even passing by the embassy, which I generally avoid), recognizing something that is secretly my own in it (no one around there in the city knows that it is my flag, or what flag it is at all). I feel something similar in Estonia when seeing France's tricolor. No one around knows that I'm a citizen of that country.

If I was in Paris, then I would be able to go and choose between Chirac and Le Pen in the second round of elections this coming Sunday. I wouldn't go. I've never voted and probably never will, either. I don't believe in it. I certainly agree that democracy is the best of what's known etc., but I still fear that its days are numbered. Every regime endures on belief, and belief is somehow connected to fashion in turn. It passes, changes form. To tell the truth, the far right-wing Le Pen convinces me even more than that perpetual power-politician Chirac, who is already soaked through to the marrow in democracy's lies. I believe Le Pen more in the sense that I'm afraid: those like him are becoming ever more convincing; soon, they won't even especially need to make an effort. I might have wanted to go and vote if Valéry Giscard d'Estaing had run. I saw one of his television appearances when his candidacy was still undetermined. He left an astoundingly sympathetic impression. He spoke like a person who doesn't claim to know the truth. And there was something very aristocratic (that yearning for aristocracy of ours—poor Livonians left without our masters!) about him, something very dignified. Maybe it would all have disappeared if he had become an official candidate and had been tossed into the marketing wheel. Maybe he didn't really want it. Maybe I simply like his name, because when he was the president of France (I was eleven to eighteen years old then), I sometimes heard it on the radio; I was proud that I knew the name of France's president by memory, and for some reason, it was like a mantra to me—I didn't know how it was written for a good deal of time, but I frequently repeated it in my thoughts: valeriy zhiskaar destaan, valeriyzhiskaardestaan. There was something majestic about it for me. Even less did I know—I actually realized this just now—that the second half of his name sounds exactly the same as "fate" (*destin*). Maybe he also didn't run this year because he's already been President once. And because he's old. He had the wisdom of an old man. And maybe he knew that he wouldn't get it anyway, because Chirac holds the apparatus. All in all, in any case, he was dispatched securely to become some permanent chairman of a European assembly.

Yes—I would have unconditionally wanted to go and vote if I'd been able to choose my boyhood valeriyzhiskaardestaan—I would be very proud if my president were Valéry Giscard d'Estaing. Now, I don't even know of what to be proud. When visiting Tartu for the first time two weeks ago, I read in the Estonian newspaper *Postimees* (*le Facteur*, *The Courier*) of Le Pen's success in the first round. *Postimees* is indeed published in Tallinn now, but for me, it will forever remain a Tartu paper (it bore the name *Forward*, *En Avant!* during the Soviet period), and when coming to Tartu, I always buy *Postimees* for some reason—it's part of the ritual. This time, it was indeed for looking at apartment classifieds (and there that classified was). To tell the truth, I was extremely surprised by the news. Like all naive people, I had lived in the assured conviction that such a thing is not ("in our days," or something like that) possible. Of course, Le Pen will not become president: not now, nor in the future, probably. But some Chirac, who people don't know is a Le Pen, will. Simply—since politics is a good, parties' product designers will also integrate the Le Pen product's well-selling elements into their own candidates' images. And that piece of news read in *Postimees* touched me on much more of a personal level, because I was immediately reminded of the last meeting of Amid and I, which still took place on Sainte-Croix-de-la-Bretonnerie Street, very close to the Moroccan restaurant where we had dined together on very many occasions, and where we had also eaten that last time—the three of us, with Liz Franz.

I recalled Amid's face again, on which a beard had started to grow, as if he had wanted to disguise himself, to disguise himself from me, it seemed, and maybe from himself as well. Beard growth is sometimes quick and thick for Arabs (although Amid wasn't an Arab, but rather a Berber: his mother and father originated from that Kabylie, where there were disturbances last winter). But not for Amid. His familiar and dear face had nevertheless changed almost to unfamiliarity in two weeks. He didn't want to look at me directly, but he hadn't learned to completely tame his genuine nature yet, either, and a smile of recognition even flickered in the sparse black facial hair at the corners of his mouth for a moment. However, some kind of new callousness had come over his face, and even hatred. Or that's how it seemed to me. I don't know the extent to which others' faces are merely mirrors of my own feelings and fears. Nevertheless, we exchanged a few hollow sentences, and that was very painful for me. It's quite painful for me even now, painful to think about, and Amid is a longer story in general, also in connection with Liz Franz. Only upon reading that news about Le Pen I thought for the first time that maybe he, Amid, was even right to some extent.

Yesterday, on the first warm spring day (and it rained, at that—quite generous downpours; it knocked on my skylight and the metal around my ordinary windows even at night), I also took a walk in the botanical garden (*Jardin des Plantes*). I didn't study strictly genetics at university, but rather biology; genetics was a narrower field. There is probably still the traditional system in

Tartu even now—that even geneticists have to acquire extensive knowledge about classical zoology, botany, etc. I especially hated botany, that completely obsolete rote studying. The botanical labs were in the botanical garden, and are even now. I mused yesterday that it's strange I never saw during those years how beautiful and pleasant that garden is. It is erected on seventeenth- to nineteenth-century fortifications, on those bastions, which were the next step forward from the town wall, and which have provided park architects probably everywhere in Europe and especially in France with thankworthy landscape elements (those famous *remparts*, where people still go walking). Bastions were a quickly-passing fashion in strategy, which the development of offensive technology rapidly overtook. Yet, communities would never have undertaken such large-scale earthworks just for parks.

Even the systematics department with its, for the most part, still bare and signaged flowerbeds that resembled grave mounds moved me in yesterday's rainfall. The flowerbeds there make up an orderly pattern, a concentric figure, which definitely also has its own phylogenic, plant-systematic motive. I haven't seen such an old Linné-like spirit in botanical gardens anywhere since, such an eighteenth-century love for orderliness. *That* moved me. During my university days, in my youth, my spiritual agitation was so great that some things so trivial as flowerbeds barely moved me: I didn't even see them. Or snails. They'd crawled onto the stone slabs of the sidewalk with the rain, larger ones and smaller ones, and many had already been squashed by walkers. The snails grouped into squads and appeared to be communicating. Snails are, I've learned, hermaphrodites; however, they still "mate"—meaning they exchange genetic material with another, likewise androgenic, snail. I tried to step so as to not crush a single one of those tiny squads or lone snails—it was absolutely possible. Yet, when coming back along the same path later and thinking some thought of mine,

I had already forgotten about the snails, and certainly crushed quite a few to death.

I was stopped by a strange smell along the creek, a little like the smell of sweat or body odor, which seemed to be coming from a small bunch of flowers that were unfamiliar to me. Upon closer inspection and reading the sign, they turned out to be irises (*Iris aff. bucharica*, originating from Inner Asia). Truly—they smelled like that: at once pleasant and unpleasant, and at the same time, not at all strong. The hue of their petals was almost white, but delicately bluish; the lower "lip" coming from the pistil was covered in yellow fuzz. In summary, they left a very refined impression, and reminded me of the old French king's flag that was, of course, white and ornamented with gold "lily blossoms" (*fleurs de lis*, in olden times: *fleurs de lys*), which are actually iris blossoms. The iris was Liz Franz's favorite flower: she always brought them and put them in a vase, the apartment was always adorned with them, as well as with white lilies, and sometimes even smelled stiflingly strong; especially due to the fact that Liz Franz also used strong perfumes. I don't even know what scents were all together there, but there was one specific smell that I identified as Liz Franz's. It could always be sensed in my Paris apartment for weeks after Liz Franz's visit (she always left some item behind, also; I packed them into plastic bags so they would smell less), and there was still a little of that smell in the Tallinn apartment, the keys to which I threw off of the pedestrian bridge into the Emajõgi yesterday; although—at least as far as I know—Liz Franz hasn't been there for close to a year. It was always perceptible when coming in from outside.

I now went to my wardrobe and sniffed the clothes that I brought back from that apartment: no, there's nothing on those. This apartment furthermore still has the scent of fresh paint and new furniture, because it is freshly remodeled—no one has lived here before me since the big renovation. I also signed the rental contract yesterday—the landlord was, I imagined, a typical Tartu real estate businessman (we probably immediately mistakenly deem the representative of every "species" whom we first meet as "typical"): his company was registered to Filosoofi Street and he was very serious, businesslike, and spoke to me in the familiar form of speech, to which I was unaccustomed. In France, strangers and even semi-acquaintances still use the polite form and I enjoy it, because I don't feel a need for imitating close human contacts, such as with an landlord. He didn't even smile when I said I that won't carry off a single piece of furniture until the official list of items already present in the apartment is made. I don't know—maybe it *was* a bad joke, because maybe people in Tartu steal furniture from rented apartments.

My windows face the east, and the sun now rises already at five o'clock or six-thirty—I wake up then and don't fall back asleep; thoughts come to my mind. As long as there is a mix of dreams and real thoughts in my head, as long as my reasoning is dealing with some dream problem, there is still the hope of falling back to sleep; but as soon as even one single fragment of actual daytime thoughts flits into my head, my entire consciousness suddenly switches into daytime mode, lights up, and goes to work at full speed. This morning, for example, I suddenly realized that I actually don't know almost anything factological about Liz Franz's childhood and youth aside from those few shards, those few short stories that she slipped me. At the same time, I don't believe that this factology would bring clarity to the current situation. I don't believe that the factological roots of the situation stretch so far into the past, although they may indeed stretch into the past—back to the Moscow-, even Riga-period—but more about that in due time.

The early-morning state of things is odd, fresh, and nonetheless a little somnambulant. And strange things sometimes come on the radio between six and seven o'clock. This morning, for example, Terje Soots—a well-know public-radio personality who even reminds me a little of the pleasant, intimate voices of French state radio stations—spoke about the mysterious disappearance of people.

I came out of the bathroom to hear what she had to say. She had, of course, probably read about it in a magazine somewhere, and the credibility of that data was more than doubtful. I bring the data forth here only because I stood listening to her, and for about ten minutes, I was absolutely convinced that the case of Liz Franz's disappearance (and likely Umberto Riviera's as well) was the very same sort of phenomenon. The very fact that I bought and believed stories heard from Estonian public radio between the hours of six and seven in the morning in my opinion well illustrates my mental status, anxiety, and instability, the full extent of which I no doubt refuse to admit to myself.

Specifically, there have apparently been several instances registered in the world, where a person or persons disappear abruptly and under inexplicable circumstances, only to appear once again a year or two later in the same place. In addition, in these people's minds, no more than an hour or two has passed (I should mention that the number of hours they think that they have been away corresponds to the number of years, for which they have disappeared). As far as these people are aware, nothing at all special has happened.

For example: an older woman in England went for a walk in the woods with a small dog, and disappeared without a trace. She reappeared after two years and claimed she had gotten lost in the woods for a couple of hours, but luckily found the path home. In 1994, however, the small Indian passenger ship *Starfish* sailed into a storm in Indian waters and issued an SOS signal: we're sinking! When ships in the area reached the presumed site of the disaster, there was no sign of the ship there, and after the storm died down, the Indian coast guard didn't find a single drowned passenger or crew member, nor even the remains of a shipwreck. Exactly six months later, on the fifth of July in the year 2000 (I might be mistaken about the date), ships in the same area picked up the *Starfish*'s radio signal: end SOS. It should be mentioned that there hadn't been the slightest storm in the region for several weeks. To the alarmed coastguard's great astonishment, it found the *Starfish* along with its crew and passengers, only slightly battered by the storm. The captain asserted they had battled the storm for the last six hours, but finally the weather—thank God—had calmed down, and he ordered an end to their distress signal.

The most credible scientific explanation for such instances of disappearances is supposed to be a temporary collapse of space-time in some points, upon which the objects located there disappear as if into a black hole. What is interesting, in my opinion, is precisely the fact that they then appear in the place again, and completely the same as they were. It's possible that such collapses occur in very small sections of space quite regularly, but as they don't bring with them the disappearance of people, but for example only of objects, dust, or other things, they are not registered.

In general, I nevertheless believe—now that it is already seven-thirty in the morning—that Liz Franz hasn't actually disappeared at all. She might just as well be in Italy, which is quite a sizeable country (fifty-seven million inhabitants); perhaps even there in the blue hills of Umbria, as far as I'm concerned, where she always liked to visit (Umberto has a piece of property there, where he has planted a park—that park is Umberto Riviera's true passion); or, for example, in the event that she's without Umberto, then it could be in New York (fifteen?, twenty? million inhabitants) as far as I'm concerned, not just because New York is the first metropolis that popped into my head (for some reason, I don't believe she could be in Paris—2.2 million *intra muros*, approx. twelve million in the entire Île-de-France; for me, Paris is probably too homely and accustomed for that, but I actually haven't been to New York), but because there is someone in New York who Liz Franz could stay with. That photographer, that "boy" from her Riga days, what was his name now: Yuri. Yuri Katz.

I hope to get to him in my biography of Liz Franz very soon, because I want to somehow sum that matter up concisely. I feel that I won't reach it, that the level of detail I chose in the beginning is still too great even now, although in my mind, I'm only abridging.

Although, on the other hand—what's my rush? The apartment rental contract has been made for a year; although, it can be canceled with only one month's notice (in Paris, it would be three months). I'm not a farmer being hustled by spring. Yesterday, I put my bicycle on my Opel Astra (I've still kept a car in Estonia in order to "get out of town," I don't have a car in Paris; the vehicle is in my father's name, and it is my father who has it when I'm in Paris) and drove to Krüüdneri, thirty kilometers south of Tartu. The landscape there is wide open and hilly with an abundance of lakes—one can perceive that it was once one of the wealthiest, most enjoyable places in Old Livonia. There are numerous beautiful, but now dilapidated manor ensembles in the region. Most fields in the vicinity of Valgjärve are even cultivated and sown—there isn't the sort of sense of abandonment that there is in many places in Estonia. The rain showers (although in some places, it probably hadn't rained at all) have now conceivably saved the crops as well. The warm and moist air had an especially powerful effect on birds' and amphibians' (frogs') hormonal systems, causing them to vocalize intensively. This situation—that it is warm and one can speed down slopes on a bicycle wearing only a T-shirt, and that there are already greenery and blossoms everywhere—felt downright ordinary and accustomed.

In the evening, I went for a walk in town on Toome Hill and

by the riverbank; there were many drunk university students and youths in general everywhere. One young man wearing an orange shirt and a wandering gaze sat alone on a bench by the river. Obviously homosexual. But having cast a quick glance at his appearance, I didn't want to acquaint with him. In my opinion, he very much reminded me of myself twenty years ago, and I'm probably not yet ripe for meeting my twenty-years-ago self. Something of that disdain that I felt for myself then, is still left.

I was more interested by the fresh and athletic young Russian men (why haven't I had a single ethnic-Russian lover yet? It is, in fact, the second-largest ethnic group in Estonia, and the first in the entire territory of Old Livonia), but as they were there mostly in withdrawn groups numbering from four to ten, I lacked any opportunity to approach any of them. To tell the truth, I wouldn't have known how to approach any of them even if he were alone, and even if he were ready to be approached. In that sense, I haven't in any way become much smarter than the "I" of twenty years ago. Liz Franz taught me many things, but not that. Or that lesson was left unfinished.

Even the evening was warm, and although it was the first warm evening, it felt absolutely ordinary. One gets used to it being light and warm instantly; one never accustoms to it being cold and dark.

11

I asked Liz Franz once, I don't remember where or when—it was certainly on one of those excruciating evenings that we spent together and during which we had nothing to talk about, whether it was in the Weitzenbergi-Street apartment or at my place in Paris, or in Rome when Umberto was traveling; or rather when we ourselves were somewhere on one of our secret trips to some strange city, where for some reason, those evenings were *especially* excruciating—because when going to a strange city, you subconsciously believe that the person, with whom you're going there will turn out to be a completely different person once there, but he or she is still the same, the same—I asked her, more to keep up the conversation, how she learned to sing.

"From the radio," she replied sharply.

Being perpetually home alone when her mother and grandmother were working long days at the kolkhoz until it became dark, she apparently always listened to the radio. When songs came on, she began singing along with them to pass the time and to be less afraid when alone. She claimed to remember those high-spirited Soviet songs well to this day, and when she happens to hear them somewhere, she says she is reminded of the smell of their house and the accusing eyes of their dog, Rex.

Namely, she had apparently coaxed Rex into the room and then closed the door so that the dog couldn't run off any longer. The animal hadn't been especially great as company, but braver than her just the same. Rex hadn't wanted to be home alone with her—Rex had been afraid as well, and would have been happier scampering about the village than listening to the radio in a room with a little girl (Liz Franz naturally never said that in reference to herself—she was always "I," Liz Franz).

There was said to have been a great number of Forest Brothers ("*frères de la forêt*": *combattants, résistants*) in the woods at that time, and all kinds of horror stories were told about the Forest Brothers' murders, but especially about the NKVD raids. Those were also spoken of on the radio, although they never talked about blood there, but only used heroic euphemisms: they spoke of "new advances" that the kolkhoz peasants had achieved in the "fight against banditry and collusions by kulak elements," and actually, Liz Franz would have wanted to head off into the forests with the raiders, a gun in her hand, and to cry out at the mouth of a bunker:

"*Kas saate välla!*"

But she was "just a child," and that caused her much grief. Then, she would sing along with the radio until the battery ran out. It had been pure agony—that waiting for when her father would come and bring a new battery. But she never sang when her mother or grandmother could hear. One time, her grandmother walked in on her and was quite amazed, because as far as she knew, the child didn't have a singing voice at all: she refused to sing church hymns along with her grandmother from an old Estonian Lutheran Church hymnal, or she would make such a dreadful noise that her grandmother herself had to force her to shush. A number of those hymns' melodies had been quite pretty, but she hadn't liked the words in the very least, and doesn't to this day: what kinds of words are those? Just a lot of groaning and fermatas!

After her singing ability was revealed, she apparently had to sing with her grandmother on occasion; especially if she had hopes of getting something (for example, that she would be taken along somewhere). They were said to have sung duets, because her mother truly didn't have any singing talent; however, her father did sing with her when he visited home, and sang much more fun songs than her grandmother did. The likes of "tonight with friends, the wine's all left; and I'm embracing comely women now . . ." Her grandmother had indeed cocked her head at these, but she also lacked any power to enforce sanctions, because Liz Franz's father had only laughed at her grumbling.

"Eliisapett" (her father still called her that up until the end) would indeed croon along with him, and had been fiercely proud when he once said:

"*Näeh, tuu laits ju laksuta kui üits ööpik! Vii ta linna kuuli, tule tõisest viil uuperipriimadonna.*"

"Prima donna" was the next word that she committed to memory in addition to "*tiiva,*" although it sounded a little questionable. Better a diva, still. It's also the truth, I'll add here, that prima donna means nothing other than simply "first woman." But Liz Franz didn't like when people called her a "woman." I was never allowed to classify her into the category of women. A diva is, needless to say, a deity, and Liz Franz would have further preferred, I believe, one other synonym: goddess.

In the interests of auto-psychographical truth, I should also highlight an incident that was unpleasant, that caused me momentary unease, but that was trivial. As I already wrote, there is a pretty good view from my windows: practically across the entire Ülejõe (*Rive Gauche*) city district. In the evening, the orderly faces of the Annelinna panel houses (*les HLM[1]*) that make up a part of the skyline are tinged red, as if they were

1. The French adore abbreviations (Russians have apparently adopted that fashion from them), and with the word "hashshellemm," which is from a concept formed during the period of social progress in the 1950s called *habitation à loyer modéré*—a living space with modest rent, i.e. so-called "municipal housing"— they signify generally all kinds of "panel houses" and suburban "towers," because in most cases, they are built by the state for housing underpriveleged parts of the population. In Annelinn's case, HLM certainly no longer corresponds to the current social-economic reality, given that the apartments there have been privatized, and that "chalk canyon" composed of reddening faces in the evening is thus composed of small privately-owned single-occupant apartments or cells (*cellules*).

some natural pink chalk canyon. There is not a single building or window across from me. One could only see into this apartment from either the high-rise—the so-called "Flask," which primarily contains office spaces, most of which are vacant because of rental prices that do not account for the market situation—next to the previously mentioned regional bus station, or from one tall apartment building built in Ülejõe for the "rich," which is located at the symbolic address Fortuuna (fortune) 1, and where a number of the apartments are likewise standing empty to this day. Nevertheless, I don't believe that office workers or bored women in "rich men's" homes (if there should be such women) are spending their time spying on me (and they would truly have nothing to see here); likewise, I'm not sure whether anyone could see anything, whether even with binoculars. I certainly only see reflections off of the glass windows from that direction.

That was, by the way, also a reason why I took this apartment immediately: I don't like when someone across the street or a yard looks into my window from their own. I've grown accustomed to that in Paris, although even there, I see from my own roof chamber into other, lower apartments more than they see into mine. And Paris is a different matter, too. I don't know those people, whose lives I've followed for several years without particular interest— just as they have *my* life; nor will I become familiar with anyone in the future, either. They are there and I am there, but we don't even have as much contact as do two trees growing on separate banks of a river, which, en passant, are able to exchange pollen, and thus genetic material. I most certainly will never start exchanging my genetic material or any other information of crucial importance with a single one of those renters across the way (one can't even speak of an exchange in the context of humans: in principle, I would only be able to give it).

In Estonia, however, everything is too personal or can become so at any moment; therefore, it is good if no one sees into your apartment. Aside from the broad panorama that is leafing intensely with these warm days, and the ugly walls of two department stores (one must admit that since Estonia's re-independence, a new ugliness has developed in architecture that replaces the old, Soviet ugliness), I also see a small stretch of the street below. It is a pedestrian street, and has the most traffic in Tartu. As such, when I sit on the window ledge, new pedestrians constantly enter my field of vision and disappear from it again after a few seconds. Interestingly enough, I can manage to say something about each of them. Our brains are extremely fine-tuned to discern even the slightest peculiarities in our fellow species's appearance and behavior. A representative of some (intelligent, capable of reflection) foreign species would certainly see those passersby as practically identical, just as we see cows on a pasture or bees on a blossom. Because to me, even the representatives of "foreign races": blacks, Asians and even "Arabs" in Paris, initially seemed indistinguishably alike. In any case, I've indeed learned to tell "Arabs" apart on an extremely fine level, because I subconsciously and systematically observe and differentiate their population, no matter whether in the métro or on the street, in the hopes of finding among their distinguishing faces one, which is not similar to a single other: Amid's face. But I know that I'll never see him again. I simply know, although that knowledge is not based on anything. I don't know what intuition is in general. I definitely have no sort of intuition. And although I know that I will never see Amid again in my life, I scrutinize Arabs passing on the street in Paris with an instinctive, sharpened sense of attention.

Conversely, I "saw" Liz Franz here one day while hanging out by the window: it was so realistic that I so much as jerked back from the window. The woman did not look up, and, of course, I realized immediately the next moment that it wasn't Liz Franz; not even especially similar in regards to appearance. Yet, there had been something very similar about her posture for an instant.

She moved in that odd tempo, which is not rushing or strolling; a very autonomous tempo that immediately removes her from the passersby (a number of whom rush, and a number of whom stroll); likewise by way of that stance that is at once timid, even hesitating, and at the same time very upright—I would so much as say: majestic. She strides as if ever in amazement: what am **I** doing **here**, how did I get here at all? There must be an exit right away, right behind the corner! Her posture is, at the same time, strangely rigid, although it's as if her head is lightly bowed.

I've seen such a posture in one other woman—in pictures and likewise in a documentary that further strengthened the impression: that woman is (of course: was) the legendary ethnic-Greek opera star Maria Callas, especially in the picture, where she portrays the Druid priestess Norma.

In addition to that momentary mistake, Liz Franz has "appeared" to me over the last few days, but in the faces of two old women. In both cases, of course, it purely had to do with a rational mind game: specifically, I reasoned to myself while speaking with them that Liz Franz could, in principle, also be that woman; with that fate, and having become that. Both of them were about her age, and on top of that, possessed, I believe, something else that invoked such a mental digression (*divagation*).

I saw the first about two weeks ago at the Pegasus café in downtown Tallinn. The café is part of a building complex (*immeuble*) that was built by the Soviet authorities during the 1960s to house Estonian writers, and which is indeed called the Writers' House. The building is located on one of Tallinn's most prestigious streets—Harju Street—amid medieval blocks, with a view overlooking a former German church (St. Nicolas), and was built in a gap formed by Soviet bombers in March of 1943. One can't say that the structure, which embodies early 60s aesthetics, harmonizes with the Old Town's building development, but everyone has managed to accustom to it.

During the Soviet period, literature—just like other artistic activities—was under state control and custody. Whoever made it into the artistic nomenclature once could count on having certain privileges thereafter. As such, the Writers' House has roomy apartments that are in no way similar to HLM-series (called "khrushchevkas" after the then-leader of the Soviet Union) apartments that had taken root in residential construction during the time. The lower level housed the bookstore "Lugemisvara" (*Les Trésors de la lecture*), which the current Estonian Writers' Union has rented out to a shoe store, apparently deeming the book trade as too unprofitable a business; one corner of the building comprised the Writers' Union's administrative rooms and the editorial office of the official literary publication *Looming* (*La Création*) (that's now all out of date as well); while the other corner featured a café spanning three floors with massive windows—outright glass walls (*baies vitrées*).

Those glass walls, a stairway winding around a concrete post, and an abstract aluminum sculpture looming atop the post were all something unprecedented, and in Tallinn, represented the aesthetics of a new age. Pegasus became a supremely chic place in the 60s, where members of the cultural nomenclature as well as those aspiring to it (but several kinds of so-called "alternatives," also) longed to show themselves. Even Liz Franz's career, although I'm rushing ahead by saying it, began there in a certain sense. However, I did not go to Pegasus looking for any lost time that noon, two weeks ago. The old vibe has completely disappeared from it. In the 80s and especially the 90s, the café namely descended into absolute old-fashionedness (*désuétude*): it turned into a dusty and provincial den, where only all kinds of "former" stars (indeed, primarily former wannabes) still went to wet their whistles and pick fights with one another and other patrons. In particular, much darker cellar bars came into style during that period, and Pegasus wasn't able to cover up its glass walls with curtains very well at all (although it tried) in order to create the necessary sense of "coziness." That *désuétude* finally reached the point, where the café was simply closed for several years and people even forgot that anything was ever there.

The Writers' Union has now also rented *that* space out, and one of Estonia's most famous local investors, who during the transitional period founded Hansapank with a couple of friends—a bank, which has now become the largest financial institution in all of Livonia and the Baltic States in general (for some time now, it has indeed belonged mostly to a Swedish bank)—that financial genius, Rain Lõhmus, established a new, trendy restaurant there. The interior design there now constitutes cold, new, big-city minimalism; the food prices are extremely salty; and Pegasus (the name is still the same) has become rather a chic meeting place for the new elite (*les nouveaux riches*). Cultural figures probably nearly boycott the place, I don't know; in any case, there is a relatively small chance of running into any artist who might recognize me, and thus, it is quite safe to sit there. Secondly, it has truly good pastas made right there by hand, for which on some rare days, I'm prepared to even pay eighty Estonian kroons, taking into account the fact that pasta of that quality costs at least two times as much in both Paris and Rome. From time to time, one encounters odd aberrations (*abérrations*) of luxury in Tallinn among the otherwise generally expensive and bad food offered by restaurants.

I had just purchased the aforementioned *Wastne Testament* from the neighboring bookstore—a just-published facsimile edition of the Southern-Estonian-language *New Testament* printed in Riga in 1686, which was the first true book printed in Estonian (not a mini-book like catechisms, primers, calendars) and for a long period of time, also remained almost the sole one, because the Great Northern War interrupted, and the full Estonian-language Bible—by then already in Northern Estonian—only appeared fifty-three years later. When visiting Tartu, I had just thought that I'd like to read that *Wastne Testament* because all in all, by the way, it is written in Liz Franz's home language, and she claimed that they had the 1686 edition at home, although it later went missing. She had apparently learned to read from it, because its typographic design (large red capital letters with intricate embellishments at the beginning of chapters) was to her liking. Other books had appeared inferior and gray beside it.

I thus had that facsimile *Wastne Testament* under my arm when I entered the café. I have a usual seat there, although I've only been there a few times. But living abroad has taught me to form habits quickly: they make life more secure. And so, I now directed myself towards that spot, although I immediately saw that the woman sitting at the adjacent table might easily start up a conversation with me. Something elusive gave away the fact that she is the kind of woman who is not quite mentally ill outright, but the kind that is avoided. And the more she is avoided, the more she would like to make contact, and the more she'd like that, the more she's avoided, etc. She at least had the tendencies of becoming such a woman. She was dressed properly and had a glass of white wine in front of her, which costs quite a pretty sum there (a good two to three euro). And, she immediately exclaimed:

"Oh, what a nice book! Are you the author?"

I replied that that I am not, and that the book has several authors, a portion of them most likely fictitious. I've noticed that it is better to speak with such a woman than to attempt to ignore her. Because actually, she is not so crazy at all, and may even talk about something interesting. Furthermore, a normal human tone immediately winds them down a bit.

Then, she wanted to see the book, and then, she pointed to the newspaper *Postimees* that I had taken from the wall (in order to distance myself slightly from the woman), and in particular to an article speaking about a conflict that had broken out at the Estonian National Opera between the management, the head conductor, and the company. This doesn't interest me in the very least: it concerns some monetary and career conflict so characteristic of today's cultural nomenclature, the likes of which (French ones) frequently also get into French newspapers. The sums there are indeed larger, although I still read somewhat with a sense of disbelief that the head conductor of Estonia's national opera earns one hundred thousand kroons (over six thousand euros) per month, which comes out to seventeen times the average Estonian salary.

But the woman, who introduced herself by some odd name—something like Isidora or Noreida—was very much interested in the conflict. Specifically, she was apparently a choreographer, and had been submitting staging projects to the theater for several years; productions that were, however, systematically rejected by that "mafia." She came from, it turned out, Moscow, had come to Tallinn as a young dancer probably in the late 60s (I presume), and had made a career here. Her accent in Estonian was more that of an actress than of a Russian. Yet, apparently, the "circles" had not quite accepted that somewhat eccentric lady as one of their own. She further pointed to the daily horoscope ("serious" dailies also publish those in Estonia) at the end of the newspaper, placing her dark-red painted nails on Virgo.

"I'm that," she said, not mentioning, of course, the word "Virgo," and I must say I felt a certain discomfort that I am, too. I didn't say to her, of course: "But so am I!"

The daily horoscope specifically proclaimed "an imminent jump on the career ladder" for a Virgo, and that Isidora or Noreida Yevgenyevna (she translated the patronymic out: "daughter of Yevgeny") had the hope that when "that mafia" at the top is swapped out, she will also finally be able to get to work on her productions.

While conversing with her there, it suddenly came to me that she actually must have been about Liz Franz's age (although she was far from being as well-preserved), and that their fates had been parallel in some sense. But in opposite directions. That dancer/choreographer had come from Moscow to Tallinn, thus moving from a center to a province, and now had to pay a dear price for that foolishness of her youth. Liz Franz, however, always followed solely and precisely the logic of ascent in her life, moving towards ever-larger and more powerful centers of urban gravity.

It's true that even she has had to pay her own price for that ascent. But in any case, she has not become the sort of imposing "older dame," whom even her old acquaintances only tolerate with great exertion. If she is indeed crazy—and it sometimes seemed to me that she is; I was gripped by fear on those occasions: I'm at the mercy of a madwoman!—then her craziness is well hidden from the public.

I saw the second "Liz Franz" on my bike trip the day before last in the area of Krüüdneri and Valgjärve. I had coasted down the Valgjärve hillside to the end of a swimming and boat pontoon, laid my bike down on the dock, and stretched out in the sunlight. There were a couple of rowers on the lake: the splashes of their oars grew distant, as did the sounds of their voices. I was already almost dozing off when someone's footsteps caused the pontoon to sway. I could also hear the scratching of nails, from which I surmised that the source was a dog. I propped myself up to a sitting position and saw that the source was indeed a lady with a little dog. That is to say: the little dog was truly little—a meek dachshund. The lady, however, did not exactly conform to the traditional conception of a "lady." She was wearing old, faded blue dress pants, several layers of sweaters, and had a blue, likewise faded dress blouse on top of them. On her head, she wore a pink, tureen-shaped crocheted hat. On the whole, she nevertheless left a clean, and even dignified impression. She carried a hook and line as well as a black handbag, apparently for the fish.

I greeted her, and asked something along the lines of whether there was hope of anything biting today. She wasn't encroaching, but was very much welcoming towards the idea of striking up a conversation. She seemingly lived alone with her little dog: there seemed to be a very close tie between the two—the dog kept close to her and ignored me.

"*Mis ta siin võta' või . . . tulli' niisama, et pruuvi . . .*"

She said something close to that—I can't really imitate the Võru dialect that accurately. It isn't especially similar to the language (if it ever was one), with which I've become acquainted, by way of the *Wastne Testament*. Yet, I nevertheless attempted to apply my recently acquired skills and speak with the lady in her native language. I like to at least try to speak the local language everywhere (for example: Italian in Italy, which I am able to speak as little as Southern Estonian), because it seems strange to me to speak in a language that is not either conversational partner's own. It is like some meeting of Esperantists then: extremely fake and stiff, somehow. Furthermore, the most agonizing thing is to overhear an Estonian at an adjacent table speaking English with Swedes or Germans. Their conversation is always so eager, loud and devoid of content. People around the world speak, I believe, the greatest amount of nonsense in English; they imitate communication that does not function.

As such, I said *om* (plural *omma'* or *ommava*) instead of *on* ("is" in Estonian), and even attempted to imitate the stop consonant (like "h") denoted by an apostrophe at the end of words. The woman, who at first had spoken partly in standard Estonian (apparently noting my idiom by meeting me halfway), in any case transitioned into her own dialect immediately, which was absolutely comprehensible to me (people in Estonia's southeast corner already speak such a different language that it is unintelligible to Northern Estonians without special training).

It turned out that she frequently goes fishing, and catches roach and perch, those little ones, to fry. But she's also caught a large pike with a hook; she apparently doesn't have a pole. She likewise caught forty ruffs one time, all from the same spot. No one had believed that there were ruffs in that lake. Years ago, she had been a member of the Fishing Club and participated in "fish competitions" every year—but now, there are no fish competitions or anything any longer. She even also got a bite once during the course of our conversation:

"*Eks see särg, särg jah, näe sõi ussi är'. Aga mul om iks mitu ääd ussi üten.*"

Watching how she put a new worm on the end of the hook with nimble, almost invisible movements, I thought to myself: this woman, although she looks like a true village hag, probably isn't much older than Liz Franz. If Liz Franz had remained where she was from, would she also have gone to "fish competitions," have lived in her old house together with a dachshund, and wormed hooks just as deftly?

In any case, I was reminded of Liz Franz by some kind of an autonomy, an uncaring for others' opinions in that lakeside woman, who in the village is undoubtedly regarded as somewhat strange. And I recalled that Liz Franz said that as a child, she always loved to "soak worms" by the river, had even brought fish home. She learned to fish from her father, of course.

12

Strange, I thought yesterday, *that there are such days during the year at all*. It was very warm. The bird cherries had begun to blossom. Several countries' flags flapped in front of the Imperial University of Dorpat's main building on the occasion of its two hundredth anniversary (opened by an edict of Alexander I on May 3rd, 1802). The breeze was also warm. Drivers for the diplomatic corps stood near their glistening black vehicles and talked among themselves; two handsome waiters—one with black hair, the other dyed blond—loitered between the pillars, probably awaiting the start of the ceremonial reception. Or perhaps it was already over. Foreign dignitaries walked the other way on the street—not a single coat concealed the ladies' abundant and thick gold, the men's dress coats were unbuttoned.

I saw all this from the corner of my eye, from the seat of my bike; I only rode a ceremonial circle in front of the university's main building, then coasted across the pedestrian bridge and pedaled up the hill on the left riverbank. Tartu is pleasantly small—only when going by foot does it seem quite large. With a bike, you are immediately out of the city, and the fields start immediately. Everything is already green. The poplars planted along the lane leading to Luunja Manor emitted strong-smelling, ethereal oils. *Everything* had an aroma. In this land, the entire spring is concentrated into a couple of such warm days. Then, everything kicks off. In France, the process is stretched out over several weeks, a month. There, spring is a normal, fluid process. In France, everything is normal, and that is why I love France. In Livonia, everything is abnormal, and especially that spring, which bursts out from under pressure all at once—and that is why I love Livonia.

There is no longer a single bridge on the Emajõgi downstream from Luunja Bridge. Settlement there is sparse—extensive swamps fan out in the area, where the river flows into the great Lake Peipus. In fall, people travel there en masse with boats and ships to gather cranberries. These are extremely small and very sour swamp berries, although actually, their sugar content is in fact the highest out of all Estonian berries; nevertheless falling several fold below that of grapes. The summer is short and relatively cool—there is not enough time for glucose to accumulate in the berries. Only fishermen were to be seen alongside the river yesterday. Livonia's rivers were renowned for their rich fish stocks during medieval times; now, pollution, the deepening of riverbeds, and illegal fishing (with nets, dynamite, electricity) have done their work, although one is still not left empty-handed—a plastic bag near one of the fisherman's foot moved. I was interested in whether the Kavastu ferry is still there. It is an historic river-crossing site before the start of the delta marshes. The ferry was there, but no one could be seen. I debated how it works in my mind: is there some kind of a cable on the riverbed that pulls it? I was just starting to leave when a man with a long, short-legged dog emerged from behind the boathouses. The dog was accustomed to people and didn't start barking. It's been somewhat dangerous to travel by bike in Livonia in general lately: massive, angry dogs have sprung up near houses. There used to be more small yappers. People are afraid of assault and robbery. People have become very scarce in the country, overall—you don't see anyone, for the most part. Dogs are indeed usually chained-up or fenced-in, but some may also break free.

The man asked if I wanted to get across. I replied that I certainly would've liked to. That's the polite form of saying it. The man said: well, let's go. I thought he would start up the ferry, but he got into a small rowboat standing there on the shore. The bike fit nicely between us. The river is not at all wide at that point: the crossing lasted maybe a minute. I managed to ask him how the ferry works. There was supposed to be a chain on the bottom of the river that pulls it. The ferry is for cars. The ferryman had a wrinkled face burned a yellowish-brown shade that nevertheless seemed quite young; light blue eyes. I asked whether I could take his picture, and he said he had nothing against it and even, it seemed to me, blushed beneath his tan. I asked further, quite vapidly, if he'd been a ferryman for very long. He simply replied that yes, for a long time. He had a pleasant smile.

Is it so that a person's work changes his or her personality, psychological type? That if your job is to help others across a river, then you become a "helper"? If your work is to guard and ensure that prisoners don't escape their cells, then you turn into a guard? Or rather a prisoner? That reflected itself in that ferryman's face is the satisfaction felt by the people that he carries across. It'd be around twenty kilometers to go by way of the highway and Luunja Bridge. Or is it so, that a respective type of person becomes the holder of a respective position? Liz Franz became a diva. I didn't become anything. I unloaded my bike onto the riverbank, hopped after it myself, the ferryman already pushed the boat off from the shore, when I looked back and asked incredulously what I owed him for the crossing. The ferryman smiled with his odd, broad but timid smile: ferrying a car is twenty-five kroons, a person is for nothing.

Towards evening, I saw a large flock of geese above the fields—probably white-fronted geese. Their nesting grounds are located even farther north, in the tundra; Livonia's fields are their traditional feeding grounds during migration stops. Spring has apparently not come about there, in the north, yet. That seems unbelievable. The human capacity for empathy is very limited. When it is warm and mild all around you, the grass is greening, then it seems practically impossible that it could still be cold and bleak somewhere, with even snow on the ground. I understand what Liz Franz was thinking when, upon arriving in Tallinn from Rome, she was always surprised by "what it's like here." That it's cold. Or that there are white nights. I believe she was a person with an above-average ability to adapt, and "ability to adapt" is probably a synonym for "strength." Rigidity holds fast and breaks. Liz Franz was there, where she was, and when the time was up, she moved on.

I know practically nothing of her school years at Tänassilma's seven-grade school, which I'm aware was then called an "incomplete high school." The only thing she's said about it is that school was a great disappointment for her. The children were said to have been exceptionally ugly, idiotic, and mean. Many weren't even able to read yet. She had wanted nothing more than for school to one day finally be over, because she understood very well that without completing that step, she could not rise to the next. It was practically ruled out at that time. When she went to school (approximately 1954), Stalin was indeed already dead, but life in the country remained very crude. Kolkhoz peasants' forced serfdom soon ended, and the authorities began issuing passports to them, but for youth, practically the only way to escape the country was school—especially trade schools, where a group of laborers was readied for the purpose of intensive industrialization, and where students were provided for by the state. Nevertheless, the flow of migration from rural to urban areas was not enough for industrialization, especially due to the fact that the rural population had declined a fair amount during the war and deportations. The state also began bringing labor to Livonia from other parts of the Soviet Union in order to staff the new factories, as a result of which the current "ethnic composition of the population" evolved.

However, a Russian was still a great rarity in the territory of the Viljandi Rayon Tänassilma Village Soviet. Coming out of grade school, Liz Franz did not know practically a single foreign language, if one doesn't count that standard Estonian as a foreign language, which she had acquired quite properly, but which she still, as we will see later, was not able to distinguish from her native language very well yet, or to be more exact—she wasn't able to use either language in the proper situation.

Yet upon arriving at school, among children, she apparently realized that power relationships are cruel. You either dominate or allow yourself to be dominated. Even humiliated. Children came up in conversation once after Liz Franz cautiously inquired what I think of them. At the time, I didn't understand what she was meant. She said that in her opinion, small children have always been frightful. When the village women tried to shove an infant into her arms, saying—take it, hold it, see how lovely it is—she put her arms behind her back and made such a mean face that the matrons abandoned their plan. Liz Franz had no brothers or sisters. She split up with her first husband because he had begun wanting a child from her. This was possibly the reason for the second, also. It was hideous, in her mind. All the same, she did ultimately acquire a child, and quite a big one at that. Me.

I'm aware of one other story from Liz Franz's school days, which she told me once without me understanding why again. She had always come home from school with a boy; I don't know what the distance was, probably several miles. The road ran along hay fields and the edges of meadows—in fall, large haystacks stood there; winter food for livestock (in Livonia, farmers often used to pile hay into tall stacks built so that their cone-shaped tip functioned simultaneously as a hay roof—water flowed down along the surface of the haystack—and in winter, when the ground and water froze and snow was falling, the haystacks were carried off on sleds. One time, Liz Franz said to the boy: set that haystack on fire. She was only interested in whether he would do it, in what he would say, whether a person can be set in motion with a bare statement. The boy did indeed set the haystack alight.

This resulted in a huge debacle, of course; no doubt the haystack was part of the collective kolkhoz stocks, for the destruction of which strict punishments were designated (but luckily, as I said, Stalin was already dead): an investigation was arranged, the boy confessed, and cried:

"But Liisu told me to!"

This counted for nothing, naturally.

"Do you do everything that Liisu orders you to do?" the, I imagine, teachers asked.

Liz Franz didn't conceal anything, but apparently no one believed that she could have ordered such a thing. I don't know what punishment was assigned to the boy.

I also don't know exactly how old Liz Franz was when she left home. It's possible that the seven-grade school had meanwhile been made into an eight-grade one (that happened around that point in time), and she thus spent eight years there. I further recall that she was at Viljandi's hospital with pneumonia one winter. She had apparently been on the verge of death, but then decided that she wouldn't die. Her lungs have probably been weak since then, and her voice has never carried very well. She likewise came down with an ear infection practically every winter.

There is a theory of psychology, which claims that child sicknesses are a child's certain way of discovering the world (including death). And that from a different slant, they speak of his or her main difficulties. Do Liz Franz's ear infections tell of how her mother did not and does not want to hear her? To listen to her? It is also true that excessive listening has an inhibiting effect in life. For example, I always listened to what my grandmother said. As she constantly repeated that I was a good child, I *was* a good child, although I actually wasn't such good a child in the very least. Later, I listened to everything that Liz Franz said. And I remembered it. I possess a sufficiently broad amount of documentary material for drafting an accusatory synopsis. Or a defense speech.

In any case, everything is based on facts: I write here only what I definitely remember, what I have definitely heard and seen. I regard as superfluous the assumption that some part of it could have been a hallucination, something in my inner fabric, etc. Nor is it in any way possible to prove that life is entirely an illusion, just as it's not possible to prove the opposite, because we ourselves are inevitably actors in that illusion or reality—assessing from the sidelines is not possible, and judging is actually not possible, either. Yet, judgment is a part of society's stabilizing spectacle, its ritual. Liz Franz was also part of a spectacle, or rather an "audio spectacle"—at least for me, having become familiar with her through the radio. And every now and then, her part was in no way an unimportant one.

It's now midday. There is a fair down on the street below. Its name is the "Spring Fair"—I don't know what is sold there, there are some kinds of counters. However, "Jesus" is definitely being sold. That I hear. Noise appears to be this apartment's main drawback. The windows are old, too, and don't shut very well. They're singing:

"Jesus li-ives! Jesus li-ives!"

To a very plain melody. Just about anything could be sung to that melody: go-o hoo-me. Or: drive to he-ell! I must say that Liz Franz never used such plain melodies. Not such lively ones, in any case. By the way, if they weren't singing below my window, I would be much more tolerant. Even they have to sell their wares: no one gets where they do. From the hands of market forces. In today's world, Jesus is a much less widespread trademark than Coca-Cola, for example, which is even well known in "non-Christian" lands. Like Coca-Cola, Nike (whose sneakers I bought one day: quite nice-looking, and expensive), Marlboro, and other transnational brands, those importing the Jesus brand (which has a number of other sub-brands, the consumption of which is, or at least was, at the same time ruled out; no doubt the situation is changing—

product design should be simple, coherent for all, as universal as possible) have to fight foremost for the young consumer group. Speaking of which, I don't know whether Estonia is a Christian or non-Christian country. Getting Eucharist is certainly much more difficult here than, for example, getting Coca-Cola; even Diet. Churches are closed, for the most part; stores are practically always open. Estonia is a commerce paradise—that's for sure.

Now, they're singing (that vocal-instrumental ensemble, as they used to say): "God is go-od."

I don't know anything about that. Whether he's good or whether he's evil sometimes, also, sending a vocal-instrumental ensemble with a set of amplifiers to sing "God is go-od" right under your window.

I walked on Toome Hill beforehand. A powerful, dry, warm breeze is blowing. The maple blossoms are already falling: the ground beneath the trees is light green from them. I thought about which house I would like to inhabit in Tartu, for good. Or let's put it this way: if I imagine living here permanently. I believe that it still must be up on Toome Hill. After all, I like high places more than low ones. As such, the lower town is automatically out of the running. But nowadays, there aren't exactly many dwellings on Toome Hill, especially on the very top—there practically aren't any there. There is an observatory that has the lovely name Tähetorn (*Tour aux étoiles*), and which no longer functions as an observatory because these days, the city light is too interfering of an element: the stars don't shine in the city. There is the Old Anatomical Theater with its circular auditorium, where humans' internal makeup was demonstrated publicly in the nineteenth century. It was a great novelty (*nouveauté*) back then, and attending anatomy shows was fashionable. Trend-conscious ladies reserved themselves seats in rows with a good view, where it was simultaneously convenient to faint. Respective assistants would handle their revival: tall, strong university students who came from the country, from poor conditions.

Yet, I don't want to live in the anatomy building; I'm also not especially interested in my own makeup, which I suppose is very similar to that of all humans—it's no longer a novelty these days. Then, there's also the maternity building there. I've had fantasies about having a child with Liz Franz. This didn't happen when she was still at a fertile age (and she was back then, eleven years ago; I don't doubt it), but it's too late now. I don't support violent methods, and actually, it would already have been violent then. A forty-four- to forty-five-year-old woman. Especially given that she didn't want one. Or I don't know. She wanted one, but lied to herself that she didn't. Maybe she couldn't have one.

Then, there are also the ruins of the dome church on Toome Hill, of course, which date back to the sixteenth century, to the time of the Livonian War. The ruins that is, the church was built perhaps in the fourteenth century. It was Estonia's only true cathedral by its dimensions, which even now can be traced by the standing pillars and arches. It's amazing that the brick ruins have lasted for four hundred years in a way that they're none the worse for wear. The university library was built into the choir section of the ruins in the nineteenth century, and it was still there when I attended the school. Now, it is the university history museum.

Standing there on the grass between the pillars, I realized that it would be the only building where I would like to live in Tartu if I could choose. There are the kinds of windows on the top floor of the library so that one should certainly be able to live there, with a view directly down the central nave. I comprehend that this wish is unreasonable and ostentatious. But I simply applied Liz Franz's method: "want what you want." So I call her lesson, according to which you must only want what you actually want. Not that, which can realistically be acquired; not that, which is the second best. The lesson seemed unreasonable to me. Now, I understand that it has its own essence. What point is there in troubling yourself with wanting what is second best? Better to be entirely wantless. Come what may. Yes—in Tartu, I would gladly live in the cathedral at the address Toomemägi 1, third floor on the left. Is that thought ostentatious? Would it anger the Good Lord? Is he more satisfied by a museum, where no one aside of mandatory field trips and a cleaner goes, anyway?

After walking on Toome Hill, I visited the Estonian National Museum (*Musée du Peuple estonien*), which is located in a former railway workers' cultural center. Before the war, the museum was located at Raadi Manor outside of Tartu, but a military airport was erected there after the war. Large transport planes were indeed Tartu's rulers during that period in time. Now, it is quiet and abandoned; the poplars there have grown tall and smell strongly—I cycled around there on my bike one day. One small helicopter rose from the airfield; no other aviation activity could be noted.

At the Estonian National Museum, however, I wanted to see Eric Soovere's photography exhibition "Escape to the West." He photographed while himself being a refugee, and as the accompanying text mentioned, he risked being sent to a concentration camp during the war (photography was strictly forbidden). Those pictures were indeed very true to life. The very most true to life ones were, howver, his pictures from before leaving home: of his mother, father, the neighbors. That was the subject matter he knew. Apparently, it takes at least ten years—maybe twenty—to truly learn to sense a subject. I've been working on the subject of Liz Franz for eleven years. Am I starting to get the hang of it?

Yet, it is still mysterious, I thought while viewing a picture of a refugee camp's Estonian school, how many people fled Estonia to the West during the war. And how many things they were able to carry with them, how heroically they dragged their bags and suitcases through all hardships. I wonder what might have been in them? Clothing, bed sheets, dishes? I wonder what people would take along now, if they should have to flee? It seems that there are an excessive amount of things everywhere, anyway. And there are an excessive number of people. Where would one even flee?

Then I recalled, firstly, that even now, people flee from somewhere constantly—this had completely slipped my mind while looking at those wartime pictures. For example: in France, Le Pen received so many votes precisely due to the refugee problem. They come from somewhere in the Third World, and to tell the truth: I don't really want to know how poorly they live there. I don't have the capacity to know. There are professionals and humanitarian aid workers for that; they are paid for it, and not poorly, by the way. Because even humanitarian-aid contributions have to be sold, humanitarian aid as a whole has to be sold, and high-level specialists that naturally cannot be bought cheaply are needed for product design.

I further remembered that I myself have also been a DP, a political refugee; at least in the administrative sense. That had also completely slipped my mind, and I in no way associated my former (1991) status with those wartime people hunched over in front of bags and bundles on horse-drawn wagons.

I am seriously interested by whether the actual, anthropological, measurable human appearance has changed with those years. In the photographs, those people of the 1940s appear with completely different kinds of faces; from a different breed than present-day people. At the same time, when appearing in snapshots from the 1960s, those same individuals (the photographer-refugee had become a middle-class New Jersey resident in the meantime) once again seem to absolutely be 1960s people: the "sixties' breed."

Apparently, it's possible to change the human appearance powerfully by all sorts of miniscule means: clothing, haircuts, and most of all—postures. People look like those people, whom they want to look like. Appearance is a great theater. And a question of will.

13

This spring's paroxysm (explosion, tip, crisis) was indeed out yesterday, Sunday. It could be sensed beforehand: anxiety and excitement were already ramped up high. Such warmth (the air temperature rose above seventy-seven degrees) reaches this longitude only in a very strong southern air current at such an early time of the year. That strong southern air current did actually seem to muddle the mind somewhat; there was nowhere to hide from it. On Saturday evening, I drove southward from Tartu to N. Manor in Valga County, which is owned by Veiko Saarsoo—my former classmate and (platonic) love. As under no condition do I want him to receive definite proof of my love, I will not pinpoint or name him here in exact terms, indeed I am straying from these notes' general endeavor for the truth in doing so.

I'm simply embarrassed by my former feelings and exceptionally high idealization, the victim of which being precisely him, Veiko (although he didn't suffer because of them; rather the opposite). That sort of "love" (but how else to define it?), which means fixating all of your ideals and lusts on a single person, is extremely stupid, outright idiotic. It has nothing to do with actuality—at the same time, I don't know whether there exists any other kind of love. I visit Veiko from time to time, just about every other year, depending on the frequency of my visits to Estonia and the depth of my depression. The deeper the depression, the more that I want to go "back" to him; to regress into that dark schoolboy feeling, as if to drown myself in it. Which is not possible, of course; especially in the real Veiko's presence. What happens upon seeing him is specifically what I suppose they call a clash with reality. When they say: his feelings crumbled in a clash with reality. Do people say that? I'm not saying that Veiko is an ordinary or boring person, who you could just pass with a shrug of the shoulders. He is plenty unordinary. He studied in Moscow to become a film director, and is now involved in the staging of large-scale "live art" (if such a thing exists) spectacles, as which I classify his agricultural activities. Therewithal, he is even more than a director (*régisseur*, i.e. manor steward): he is, in terms of his economic position, comparable to a manor lord. As such, he has extraordinariness and a great side to him, energy etc. All of that is, however, not enough or even necessary for loving someone.

All of that is plenty indifferent and even annoying, especially because in Veiko's case, an ever-deepening egocentrism goes along with it. Men of action and despots (generally overlapping categories) tend, the older they become, to regard their actions as more and more critical. Everyone, the entire world, should take part in it or at least hold an active interest. He didn't ask even the tiniest question about me for the entire evening—actually for just those couple of hours that we were together (he still had errands and tasks to handle at first). Almost as if I had traveled from Paris to N. Manor in Valga County only in order to acquaint with his trials in the field of fisheries. I know that we generally don't get along, and the only thing that interests us is ourselves. Others in the event and inasmuch as some sentimental or material interest connects us to them. If we hope to receive something from them. Love. Money. But at some point, egocentrism still becomes sick and disturbing. By and large, I don't know how to be with crazy people. Veiko is certainly not crazy, but we actually didn't have anything to talk about, either.

His manor left an extremely depressing impression. He truly lives in the old mansion at N. Manor, which is built in the nineteenth-century romantic style with a massive tower and a frivolous veranda. The last descendant of its former owners left Livonia for Europe during the first years of the twentieth century. That Alexander von S. studied art there, and never again returned to his ancestors' land. The manor's downfall most likely began at that time, at the hand of the strange new rulers. The property went to the state after the revolution and Estonian War of Independence, and there was a so-called "state manor" there during the inter-war period; i.e. something similar to a national pilot farm. Those state farms were reorganized into sovkhozs (*sovkhoz*—an abbreviation of советское хозяйство, i.e. "Soviet farm") as Soviet power arrived. Unlike kolkhozs, which were cooperative economic units, workers at sovkhozs were paid salaries in the post-war years, also. People couldn't be exploited in the Soviet state institutions, naturally. And so, the sovkhozs drew in the laborers roaming around the country—often people who had been shooed out of areas somewhere in the Soviet Union by the war—and over time, a very diverse and multiethnic community accumulated on the farms.

A village school had been run in the N. Manor mansion during the inter-war years, and this continued during the Soviet period as well. Such a fate befell many mansions, as it were. They were undoubtedly quite impractical as schools, but nothing else had been undertaken with those deserted, oversized structures, and the desire to tread if not directly on the defeated, then at least on their parquets and marble staircases, presumably also played its own role.

As such, entire generations of Livonian peasant children have received schooling in rather seigneurial spaces. I don't know whether this also left any mark on their mentality (*mentalité*). Schools strongly transformed the interiors of the aristocratic mansions, of course. Parquets were painted over with thick layers of "floor paint"; plank partitions were built in the great halls, because they were too large for one class. Old decorated ceramic stoves were taken apart and transported elsewhere (initially to farmhouses, later to the homes of senior party members), then replaced with black steel-cased ovens. Over time, the large roofs also began to leak here and there, because no one had the power or the desire to repair them, and often, they also had an awfully difficult structure with all sorts of angles and curves.

In short, most of those mansions are now in a decrepit state; especially since even those schools were either closed down completely several years ago, or were moved to a new and more suitable building, which are sometimes built right at on the side of the old manor house. It seems unbelievable how many families were at a fertile age in the country just thirty years ago, that they were able to fill all of those schoolhouses that now frequently stand amid absolute neglect and still life. Or continue to function half-empty in large, chilly rooms, the heating of which costs a good third of the local self-government's budget.

The school had also already long since moved out of the N. Manor mansion when Veiko acquired it from the bankruptcy estate of an insolvent agricultural company, the heir to the sovkhoz. At that time, he was intensely involved in the privatization of real estate in rural areas, because the conditions for it were exceptionally favorable.

On occasion, those so-called "privatizers" are accused of dishonest enrichment—as if there were honest and dishonest paths for the initial accumulation of capital. There are simply doers and non-doers. The former reap the benefits, the others are jealous of them. He apparently acquired the bankruptcy estate at a blind auction; he was told that "an old building," a former school, was also part of it.

I must say that even now, the mansion, despite its poor condition (the roof holds up for the most part, in any event, which is actually already a very good thing), and the quite chaotic village of sovkhoz workers that formed in its vicinity and park, leaves an imposing impression. I believe that leaving an imposing impression, asserting itself (*s'imposer*), was once one of those structures' primary functions. They literally always dominate (*dominer*) on a hilltop with the most beautiful view of the surroundings, and thus, peasants always had to look up towards the "castle" from below, which even further emphasized the difference between the titan with its white pillars and their own low, gray hut. It emphasized that a social rise to such a height is as good as impossible. N. Manor is designed on the same principle. And the impression it leaves in its current decrepitude is that much more abject. Like a nobleman, who travels to the market in a coach bearing his coat of arms to sell potatoes himself. If seeing it does still recall any social-historic truth, then it is fact that a jump on the social ladder is indeed more than rare, but from time to time, the social ladder itself can be taken off the wall, made into splinters, or turned backwards.

When Veiko saw the "large old building" that landed in his lap by chance, he was not at all enthralled by it at first. It had been in winter, and cascades of ice descending from the leaking roof towered above the stoves. The mansion had been full of furniture, litter, and a stench left from the school that had closed nearly a decade earlier. Schools have a specific stench that everyone who has attended a school will recognize without fail. In my opinion, that stench is still present there now, although the rooms are indeed scrubbed clean, heated and dry. As high unemployment is prominent in the sovkhoz settlement, one can frequently observe unkempt men fighting in the park through the "mansion's" windows: men, who will probably never again see a clear day in their earthly life, because alcohol and other toxins—such as paint thinner and others, which declassed people consume in place of alcohol—have already caused irreversible and significant damage to their brains. It is difficult to guess what their worldview is like—how many various perceptions, desires, and thoughts fit into it. This social-economic situation simultaneously means that labor at the former N. Manor is extremely cheap. Thus, Veiko can afford to employ a woman to heat all twenty stoves in the mansion every day, tidy up the rooms, etc. As he is, however, a businessman and a despot, he prefers to avoid even such an expense (today, in the epoch of global impoverishment, the principle of "cut the expenses" dominates in business; this especially concerns labor) and has invited one of his former wives to live there and heat the stoves for absolutely no fee.

That wife, Mare, was once a promising and even internationally-recognized chamber singer, but what became fateful for her career was that she fell in love with a handsome, tall, and—as it seemed to her—sensitive boy a couple of years younger than she, and on top of that—as it once again mistakenly seemed to her—an artist, likewise. Observing the human wreckage that is left of Mare, I rejoice yet again in the fact that I am not a woman (how often I've even yearned for that: it's so easy for them to win men's love!) and that Veiko has thus not been able to respond to my love with the same. Not with the same, that is, but with his own love. The love between a man and a woman, as far as I understand it, is always also a battle for power. Each has their own interests, their own project that they plan to carry out by way of that relationship. Moreover, these projects are further divided into conscious and unconscious ones. Mare's main unconscious, but perhaps also conscious project was most likely to have a child with Veiko. That she received, as well: their daughter Anu is already a pubescent young woman. As Mare was, however, apparently unable to see farther than that initial project, and had also become somewhat quixotic by being involved in music and her career for her entire life, she lost control of the reins while executing her main plan. And Veiko will now probably take revenge on her his entire life for the fact that Mare "got the upper hand" one time. At least that's how it appears.

First of all, he destroyed Mare's career, telling her fairytales about their never-ending life together, about a multitude of children, Mare's average talent, the anachronistic nature of chamber singing, etc. It *is* true, by the way, that singing arias by Schubert or Tchaikovsky with piano accompaniment no longer belongs to the main branch of the entertainment industry. Yet, culture is an interesting phenomenon, offering even those involved in areas that are seemingly completely secondary and old-fashioned (*vétustes*) the opportunities to make a living. Such as I with my documentaries, for example. Mare quit concert performance and dedicated herself entirely to Veiko.

Yet *primo*, as Liz Franz taught me: never listen to what others say about your career, calling, etc. Their own interests are always at play.

And *secundo*: such a thing as dedication to one person (I don't remember Liz Franz' having taught me this, but I definitely tuned out many of her lessons, too) is a mistake, and a tragic one. Because firstly, one person is too uncertain and unpredictable to build your whole life upon. We forget that the person we love also has their own plans. An ideal may not be allowed have plans; it must be like a marble statue. And additionally, the person to whom we dedicate ourselves will soon start to feel oppressed. Men certainly want a partner to submit to them completely, but they don't wish to give up their own freedom. Veiko constantly developed other relationships with females, which in itself is a part of normal domestic life, but this under the condition that they did not turn into analogous domestic partnerships (marriages, as people used to say). They should remain affairs. Veiko, however, openly demeaned Mare with his new and younger women, up to the point where Mare took and takes care of the children spawned by Veiko and those others; quite a nice little collection has already formed (I lack an exact overview).

Going too far in self-sacrifice is counter-productive and has a ruinous effect on a personality over a length of time. Now, Mare—who has aged unbelievably over those years—is Veiko's free maid. She used the opportunity, and told me her entire sad situation hurriedly and in a half-whisper behind one of the stoves: it was summed up by there being no money. Veiko apparently doesn't even give money for laundry detergent without being asked several times, and she—Mare—has nowhere to go. Mare has lost initiative in life. I was unable to give her any advice. Her eyes were watery, as if I was her last ray of hope. I was somewhat appalled. It wasn't the first time that I've had to hear the cries for help from the wives of my (former) objects of desire. They've suddenly felt that perhaps I could have an influence on that amazing man. But if I wasn't able to do so for my *own* ends, how should I be able to do it for them? We have then turned from competitors into allies, but weak allies. Truly—it's good that they haven't loved me, those men.

The entire mansion was unbelievably bleak and uncomfortable. Veiko claims that marching from one hall to the next boosts one's state of mind, but in reality, their life has been concentrated into the tiniest attic rooms. There is only one leaking, fetid toilet filled with rusty water for the entire mansion; the kitchen has no sink, etc. I don't know why people still want to have large houses these days. They are at least as anachronistic as chamber singing, which all in all merely requires a piano and a smaller room. Large houses belong to an era, when there were no more powerful means for entertainment yet, such as radio, television, video, the Internet etc. If one traces a modern person's primary living pathway in his or her apartment, it will run from the television and/or computer to the refrigerator, the bathroom, the bedroom.

Long views spanning across several rooms, where people appear and disappear; intricate park panoramas with romantic walkers and gazebos; an abundance of paintings on the walls and statues on the terraces—all that was necessary when there were not yet better means for dispelling boredom. Large mansions were the décor for the mise-en-scène conditionally called "life." These buildings were always full of people: in addition to a large family, they were inhabited by a group of numerous servants scuttling around and flapping their tongues, guests, houseguests, other mouths to be fed, peasant men appearing at the manor lord's request, etc., etc. These days, no one cares to fuss over such a crowd of people any longer. People on television and the radio are much more convenient: they can be turned off and on. Veiko hates Mare because she can't be turned off. If Mare had stayed with her chamber singing and if her image were to appear in front of Veiko on his television, if he were to hear her beautiful and now forever-faded voice on the radio, then he would soften, would maybe love Mare even now. But Mare is hardly shown on television any longer, and she can no longer secretly listen to the sole couple of recordings that she made, which were recorded onto vinyl together with the performances of other singers, because their gramophone broke and Veiko won't repair it under the justification that it is outdated technology that no longer has any use. He apparently downloads the music that interests him from the Internet.

By the way, Mare comes from the country, just like Liz Franz, and her career also began with the promise of a rise to fame; but it was followed by a decline. Now, she has declined even further than the social position (the daughter of a rural schoolteacher), from which she once started. Maybe her initial momentum wasn't enough; maybe it seemed misleading to her that she was guaranteed a social rise, or that she didn't really need to rise.

Actually, a rise on the social ladder is always difficult and requires tremendous effort, grievous victims. It is rare. Only a very dynamic historical epoch propels (*propulse*) a large group of people to a higher rung on the social ladder all at once. Such is what happened in Europe on several occasions during the twentieth century, and especially during the 50s—during the age when societies were growing rapidly richer. My, Mare's, and Veiko's parents underwent dizzying climbs over the course of their lifetimes, turning from simple peasants into educated service-workers who were no longer required to perform difficult manual labor. As this rise swept entire social strata along with it (and in the Soviet Union, it firstly also annihilated a group of people, who hadn't the luck of getting a share in the promises of the new times), it wasn't so traumatic for individual persons. It was a collective fate. And as practically an entire class rose to a level of better well-being and social recognition, no actual social climb really took place. They, our parents, still remained in the lower-middle class, among the workers, which was simply redefined. Liz Franz's social climb, however, was individual, relative, and genuine. From the very lowest to practically the absolute highest stratum, from the deepest backwoods to the most powerful urban centers.

I brooded over these questions while lying in the guest bed at Veiko's "castle" (so he calls that old cabin). There was no electricity in the room, just as in the majority of rooms there, and he practically didn't respond to my request for a candle. In all probability, there *are* none in the house. Thus, I was unable to read.

I pondered further whether Veiko himself has risen or fallen. Given his economic status (I certainly do not know the ratio of his assets to liabilities, his properties to loans), he has risen notably higher than it was hoped he would. For as a film director, he would most likely have been significantly poorer. His net worth would plausibly have been lower. But nevertheless, he has fallen. Veiko himself has fallen, despite his entire manor mise-en-scène, back to where his parents began—the peasant class. Although, he doesn't do manual labor. But he is dependent upon the land, he is tied to the land, his wealth is in no way liquid, and he has had losses in terms of levels of freedom, which are indeed the actual indicators of social climbing. He is subject to the weather and purchase prices, over the designation of which he has no power. He complained about the drought, which is threatening to destroy the crops, and about the low milk prices, which are keeping his production at a loss.

He didn't have the courage to take the leap that he prepared for in his youth, and which was undoubtedly a leap into the unknown, something very risky. Instead, he landed back on solid ground; he regressed historically. And if he hasn't regressed psychologically and mentally as well, then he has stagnated.

It is true that the leap into the unknown, which is a precondition for a sharp social climb, may not really lead anywhere, and most of the time indeed does not. I haven't especially gone anywhere. An average, unknown, marginal documentary filmmaker, who exists only thanks to the caprices of France's cultural administration at the turn of the twenty-first century. And nonetheless, I felt with my two rented apartments and uncertainty about the future, with my secret agony over Liz Franz's disappearance—lying in that guest room, which stank of the old heating stoves' soot and the old walls' moldy plaster, I felt extraordinarily rich and free; my Tartu apartment suddenly felt extremely luxurious, and my Paris apartment like an outright shameful privilege, which I didn't dare to even think about in that place. And all in all, I wouldn't have had any of those things without Liz Franz.

Whoever is capable of carrying out an exceptionally rare social climb pulls along an entire group of other people, or at least a few. Just as how someone's fall yanks others along, also. Perhaps it is likewise so in the greater plan, in history: sometimes, many rise; sometimes, they fall. A massive social decline like the one that can be seen now, at least here in Livonia, wouldn't have been imaginable at all just ten years ago. Entire masses have slipped into hopeless impoverishment, into living from hand to mouth. And they have generally come to accept this.

Veiko replied to my second request for a candle by saying it would be light outside soon enough, anyway. And he was right.

At five-thirty, the sun started shining into the room, which had no curtains, and I was wide-awake and raring to go. No one apart from me was moving about the house yet. I brought a kettle of water from the bathroom, and made myself tea in the kitchen. The tea had a strong aroma—of barn manure, in my opinion. A fermented mixture of livestock feces and urine from the old sovkhoz barns is apparently seeping into the groundwater that now belongs to the manor lord Veiko. I tried the downstairs door; it was locked. Veiko, who seemingly didn't care about things in his youth, has developed a noticeable fear of theft. It is also true that the surrounding social environment is a fertile ground for small crimes. As such, he left the lights on in the great hall overnight so that on Saturday evening, when people in the village drink especially en masse, no one would have the impression that the house was empty. Yet, a window facing the veranda was easy to open, and I crept out through there, sat in my car, and drove away immediately, fearing that Mare might awake and come to ask what was wrong with me for leaving like that without saying goodbye. And that she would start complaining to me about her difficult fate once again.

Somewhere amid the fields, I stopped the car and sent a message to Veiko's cell phone thanking him for the lodging and excusing myself for the early departure, about which he was—I believe—actually quite indifferent.

14

The sun had already risen and a tractor rumbled on a farther-off
field, probably sowing crops. Veiko had said the farmers also sow
at night by the light of their headlights. I had heard the humming
of milking machines in my sleep already when it was still dark. A
very small number of people are still involved in food production
in the countryside; their work is unimaginably difficult and very
poorly compensated. The early morning was, however, fresh and
pleasant in itself—I had slept just a bit too little. I decided to drive
towards the east, to Setomaa, because while staring in amazement
at the crowd of people flowing out of a Russian church in Tartu on
Friday evening (primarily older women wearing black headscarves),
I remembered that May 5th is Easter according to the Eastern
Orthodox calendar. Setomaa is the historic Eastern Orthodox
region situated in the southeast corner of present-day Estonia:
the area did not belong to the Catholic-Protestant alliance of Old
Livonia, but fell under the jurisdiction of Orthodox Russia. Setos
are a tiny ethnic group (perhaps a few thousand souls) made up of
Eastern Orthodox believers speaking an idiom distantly similar to
the Estonian language. The historic territory has still retained a few
archaic patterns in its national traditions, and I've toyed with the
idea of a documentary film project about the peoples in the Baltic
States' border areas, about ethnic transition zones. There could be
a market for it in the context of of the approaching European
Union enlargement. I figured that I could collect some ideas for
the film project during Easter, which is one of the largest holidays
for the Setos, just as it is for all Orthodox believers around the
world.

Even now, the ruins of mighty Vastseliina ("*vastne liin*,"
i.e. "new fort" (stronghold)—*Châteauneuf de Livonie*) signify

the historic border of Livonia. The fortress was erected by the Teutonic Order in the thriteenth century. To the east of it lay the principalities of Novgorod, Pskov and Moscow; to the west was the political formation called the Holy Roman Empire of the German Nation. Vastseliina Castle was thus formally also the border marker of the legendary Karl V (Charles Quint), who took the throne in 1519, of the French king of Spain, and the German Empire.

Yet, that was only formally so. The German emperor didn't have the strength or the desire to interfere in Livonia's affairs. Defending that strip of coast along the Baltic Sea from the strengthening Muscovy's plans to conquer it was probably deemed too complicated. Livonia itself did not, however, develop a centralized political structure, a kingdom. Although, according to the chronicles, Grand Master of the German Order Wolter von Plettenberg managed in 1502 to assemble behind him 2,500 horsemen (*chevalier*) and an infantry of Livonian peasant boys numbering about the same, to invade from Vastseliina to the east, and to defeat the Russian force—which was several times larger—near Lake Smolin. With that victory, von Plettenberg halted Moscow's aggressive ambitions for some time and ensured sixty years of peace for Livonia. Yet the land, where power was splintered between the masters of the Order, the bishops, and autonomous Hanseatic cities, was unable to modernize politically over this period of time. Livonia did not become a country. In the era, when the foundations were laid for the formation of nation-states throughout all of Europe at the price of great pain and toil, the elite of Old Livonia slumbered peacefully away in their medieval imaginations. Falling behind historically seems to be one of the most characteristic tendencies of this land throughout history. And time and time again, the people of Livonia have had to suffer bitterly because of it. So it was in this instance as well: in the sixteenth century, at the dawn of Europe's modernity.

With the 1558 invasion of Russian Tsar Ivan the Terrible's forces up to the walls of Vastseliina begins a period of wars lasting an entire century, known as the Livonian War, and during which the land of same name ends its former relatively independent existence. In addition to Russia, also Poland, Sweden, and Denmark lay claim to Livonia. As such, Tartu belongs to the Kingdom of Poland in the meanwhile, and Catholicism is restored there: peasants happily accept the transition, as the new Lutheran teachings had remained unclear to them. Priests at least go around giving their blessings to pigs and grain, and carrying out other preventative magical acts. Jesuits publish the so-called *Agenda Parva* as a guide to counter-reformation, the Southern-Estonian-language excerpts of which are already quite colloquial, speaking about the Jesuits' good philological and political intuition. Such as the prayer for a sickbed confession: "*Isand Jesus Christus / mina ey ole ni auwus / et sina tules mino kattusse alla änne ütle ütz sena sis saâb terwes mino heng . . .*"

Finally, in 1661, in the same year that the personal and absolute rule of Louis XIV (the "Sun King") begins in France, Sweden signs a peace treaty with Russia in Kärde, Tartu County, after which Livonia is able to enjoy forty years of peace under Sweden's enlightened despotism. Peasant schools are established, literacy spreads, the first true Estonian- and Latvian-language books are printed, etc. Only with the Great Northern War, by 1710, does Russia finally execute its will under the command of Peter the Great and become the sole ruler of Old Livonia for more than the next two centuries.

Old Livonia has been split administratively (since the Swedish period) into the governorates of Estonia (Northern Estonia, with the capital in Tallinn) and Livonia (now Southern Estonia and Northern Latvia, with the capital in Riga). A certain confusion in using the name Livonia also stems from this. Old Livonia comprised the entire area of modern-day Estonia and half of the

Republic of Latvia, but the Livonian governorate only had to do with Southern Estonia and Northern Latvia.

Presumably, however, not one country or state that has existed for long enough disappears in a period as fast as a couple of centuries, and to this day, the Livonia that comprises contemporary Estonia and Northern Latvia is one recognizable historical zone by way of its specific status.

Setomaa, as I mentioned, did not historically belong to the configuration of Livonia, but rather fell under Russian areas. Setomaa was joined with Estonia only after the latter's victorious War of Independence. Pechory (Estonian *Petseri*, Russian *Пероры*—"caves") and its historic monastery went to the Republic of Estonia by way of the 1921 Tartu Peace Treaty between Estonia and Soviet Russia, and it was thanks to this that the monastery was preserved at the time, when they were being destroyed en masse in Russia.

During the Soviet period, the administrative border between the Estonian SSR and the Russian SSR was drawn somewhere in the middle, so the areas with a primarily Russian-speaking population—including the town of Pechory—once again fell onto the Russian side, while a portion of Old Setomaa was joined administratively with Estonia's Võru and Põlva *raions* (counties). Following re-independence, the Republic of Estonia attempted to restore the situation that existed at the time of the Treaty of Versailles as historic justice, but Russia refused any kind of territorial concessions, and the actual national border was erected exactly along the Soviet administrative line. Estonia officially calls this border a "control line" to this day, although it has neither the resources nor the actual interest in rejoining those economically unimportant areas.

Nevertheless, it is just about a dozen miles from the ruins of the Vastseliina bishopric to the Russian border, so one can say: over the course of seven centuries, the border of "Western Roman" lands have been nudged exactly this much towards the east here. But not the border of creed. True: that dominant creed certainly did not especially stand out in Setomaa on the morning of Easter Sunday. A great stillness held sway everywhere, not counting a few tractors working on fields still to be sown. Country folk are still connected more to the rhythm of seasons, just as they always have been, and wake up very early during the spring-summer period.

The shop in Värska (one of Setomaa's main hamlets, *bourg*) was also open surprisingly early. It opens up every day at 7:00 a.m., and Easter Sunday morning was no exception. This early start is not, however, so much in connection with servicing cultivators of the land rushing off to work, as much as it is with the phenomenon known locally as "mending one's head." Specifically, the ample consumption of vodka (often homemade and incredibly poisonous), which is very widespread in Setomaa, causes a headache and other unpleasant bodily symptoms on the morning after drinking. If, however, alcohol is administered once again, then the central nervous system is taken to a certain state of satisfaction once more, and the unpleasant symptoms disappear.

Even I was shouted at from an old car in front of the store, where several younger males were sitting. "I have the same kind of hat that you do! Come mend your head!"

I bought sausage, potato salad, kefir (a Russian fermented-dairy beverage), cookies, and a soft drink at the store, and drove on towards the border with the provisions in tow. I didn't manage to see any church celebrations, because they had taken place at night, as is customary in the Eastern Orthodox religion: at around midnight, when the priest announces Christ's rising, and concurrently also ends the fast. Fasts are indeed generally not followed these days (priests no longer have the power to control the population's eating regime), but holding an orgy of eating and drinking after midnight is still honored. Only the rudiments of tradition have been preserved, and the more pleasant ones at that.

The small gravel road leading to a village on the border was very bumpy; I only drove past one older, hunched woman on it, who was walking in the opposite direction at quite an energetic pace, holding a cane, and disappeared into the cloud of dust rising from behind the car. It's possible that she was heading to the cemetery in order to perform some kind of traditional rites. The fields along the side of the road were abandoned, for the most part; several collapsed houses stood out with old apple trees around them that were not yet in bloom, as well as bird-cherry trees in full blossom. The village itself left a pleasant and tidy impression. The road ended between yards at the bank of a body of water. From looking at the map, it turned out that it was an inlet of Lake Peipus. Peipus is a large lake that constitutes the primary natural border between Livonia and Russia. Vastseliina Fortress guarded access from Peipus in the south, Narva Fortress in the north.

That place, Podmotsa Village (Setomaa toponyms are often Russian-sounding, or a village will have two names—one Russian and one Estonian), is located on a thin neck of Lake Peipus/ Pskov; however, the bay that I saw before me was in turn just an inlet extending from that neck. A village was likewise visible on the opposite side of the bay: one with a pretty, colorful, onion-domed church; one tower was presently ringed by scaffolding. In Russia, the Eastern Orthodox Church has once again attained half-official status as the state Church, and commands extremely large financial resources. In addition to the church domes, a Russian border-guard observation tower was discernable behind the thick patches of reeds. Such towers used to be along the western shoreline of Livonia; they still stand there now, falling apart. The border has truly been nudged back.

Frogs croaked among the reeds, most likely rare natterjack toads. Barn swallows were catching insects above the water.

The sun was already very bright, and the air temperature might have been above seventy-five degrees. I sat on a car tire lying on the shore, and began to eat. I used a Hansapank (the primary financial institution in Livonia) magnetic-stripe card as a spoon for my potato salad. While doing so, I mused that my fatty food suspiciously resembled traditional Easter food; as if even I had subconsciously gone along with tradition. It's true that life in two countries with different cultures has perhaps made me more conformist than the average. I've instinctively learned to imitate local customs as closely as possible so as not to differ too greatly from my surroundings. That would be potentially dangerous.

This conformism has sometimes been associated with a person, also. I've always wanted to become similar to my lover, to identify with him even in terms of what he himself refuses to identify with, with his scorned side. In the months that I almost "lived" with Amid, I even learned a little bit of Arabic (which Amid indeed probably wasn't able to speak at that time; at least he didn't want to hear anything of it). Since that time, I've likewise—in memory of Amid, so to speak, and partly also because it's simply healthy—adhered to the Ramadan fast, more or less. Yet, I don't love the Islamic faith at all, and actually even hate that aggressive religion (Christianity has at least lost its teeth, has softened!), because to some extent, it was precisely that abstract and extremely absurd teaching that robbed me of a real person of flesh and blood, whose name was Amid. But I'll get to Amid as soon as I have finished my geographic/historical digressions, which are, of course, only for avoiding talking about the painful main issue.

I had, however, already reached the part of my 'post-fast meal" that was *Vikerkaar* (rainbow) cookies and *Lumivalgeke* (Snow White)—both items, I must confess, I bought out of pure childhood nostalgia (spring class field trips!)—when an old man emerged from the adjacent yellow-painted house. He looked in my direction and apparently weighed up whether or not to come and start up a conversation with a stranger. I wasn't exactly in his yard, directly; it might have been something akin to the village's boat harbor. I looked towards him, indicating that I had nothing against conversation. He then walked towards me and asked if I had come to cast a line. I replied that I didn't have a line with me, just driving around for pleasure. He seemed to be satisfied with that response, also. I asked him about life in those parts, and he replied readily.

As the administrative border was very serpentine and didn't actually follow any kind of logic, several villages have now fallen into the national border's cul-de-sacs; so has Podmotsa. A car ferry apparently used to depart from there to the Russian side, probably something similar to what I saw on the Emajõgi in Kavastu. There had been a great deal of traffic: five buses ran per day—two towards Russia, three towards Estonia. Now, only one runs—to the village of Räpina (as it turned out later to my surprise, Räpina is now administratively a town).

The Soviet Union was not entirely a unitary country: there were, for example, several differences between the Estonian SSR and Pskov Oblast in terms of the economy and standard of living. The product selection in shops was also somewhat different, and residents of the "border zone" took advantage of those differences in a lively manner, carrying out "shopping trips" to the other side. Even now, it is possible for residents along the border to receive a long-term visa under favored conditions. But as the closest customs checkpoint is only in Pechory, the old man—as he explained to me—has to cross fifty miles in order to travel to the village of Kulye, which was visible about a quarter-mile across the water. Nevertheless, he apparently visits the Russian side of the border regularly: there is said to be remarkably cheaper and higher-quality gasoline (among other things) than in Estonia. However, only a full tank of it plus two-and-a-half gallons may be brought over. He asked me how large my Opel Astra's tank is; I wasn't able to say specifically. He recommended that even I register for a visa and visit the Russian side from time to time, likewise. Especially when he heard that I live in the same building as the Russian Consulate in Tartu.

"Well, then, what's the problem!" he said.

He spoke with me in an idiom comparatively close to common Estonian, for which I was thankful, because it would be difficult for me to understand Seto language. I didn't attempt to imitate any *Wastse Testament* dialect with him either, because that would only have been ridiculous.

I pondered while driving away from warm and quiet Podmotsa that I truly *should* get myself a Russian visa, but not so much for going and getting gas in Pechory as for visiting Moscow, because it might even be possible for me to find one or another of Liz Franz's former acquaintances there—for example, that "boy" Konstantin Agafonofich, or whatever his name was. Maybe I could find out something from them, maybe they've even been in contact with Liz Franz, because I'm aware that until just lately, she kept in touch with a few Moscow "old guys" and "old women," as she said; but perhaps also with some Moscow "boys" or "girls," of whom she didn't speak. I don't know.

I hope to get help from the daily *Postimees*'s Moscow correspondent Kadri Liik, whom I know. The new "emigrants," who we are, make up a sort of loose brother- and sisterhood, the members of which understand one another very well in a certain sense. I no longer find the right connection with either those who have lived only in their homeland for this entire time, nor with those actual expatriate Estonians—the descendants of wartime refugees, who were born abroad. Still more with the latter than the former, although I'm connected precisely with at-home Estonians by a common childhood, by a common language up to the minute particularities (however, I lately feel that some new elements in this are imperceptible for me), etc. The best understanding I have, altogether, is still with those whose geographic fate has been parallel to my own: emigrants of the 90s, or half-emigrants. We all visit Estonia ardently, of course, and neither do we really count ourselves as citizens of a country of residence upon having its passport; nor do we regard ourselves as citizens of Estonia, in truth. I don't know whether we actually do have a country of our very own. We are also like the Setos, too. Perhaps that's the reason why the topic indeed fascinates me.

And compared with Liz Franz, we are all—perhaps not including those quite young people that have gone to the West, with whom I'm not especially familiar—pitiful immigrants. Liz Franz shifted—at first from one city to another in one large country, following her irresistible (*irrésistible*) call to rise, and then from one country to another. She wasn't interested in countries; she regarded them as secondary. Nor did she ever read newspapers, she didn't watch television, and she hardly ever listened to the radio. To me, her behavior often felt unreasonably arrogant: what was her problem, strutting around behind Umberto's back! Now, it seems to me that she indeed lived in her own time and in her own country, which was not even dependent on Umberto or his money.

15

I drove around those sandy dead-end roads that all ended in some quiet lakeside village for a while longer. The warmth rose ever high, the southern breeze strengthened, the birches were bent; large poplars were growing on the side of the road in one place, and their leaves had such a strong smell that the aroma followed me in my wake for a good quarter-mile. Estonians regard poplars as a Russian tree. In Latin, the poplar is for some reason called a people tree (*Populus*, French *peuplier*); but in Livonia, poplars are actually alien plants spread from manor gardens and Russian military bases. Over the last decade, since independence, they have been uprooted and destroyed, as if in revenge. At the same time, not one native deciduous tree in Estonia smells as good as they do; I likewise enjoy the poplar's strong phallic-shaped crown.

That unexpected heat constantly stirred up lust within me; an aimless lust. Man is a mammal, whose sexual activity lasts year-round—not only during mating season; however, the period of heat, rutting (*le rut*) still achieves its climax during the spring/summer season, probably as a memory of our natural past (as if the present wasn't natural!). About 95–99 percent of the sexual activity of a member of the modern consumer society is not directly connected to reproduction, but constitutes an infertile erotic game; sometimes also violence, but generally the consumption of pleasure (*le plaisir*). Still, certain methods for achieving reproductive satisfaction are regarded as natural (*naturel*), while others are seen as unnatural (*dénaturé*); even so much as sins against nature (*vices contre nature*). I personally lack information about Nature's intentions (*intentions*), and the secret order (*ordre*) she sets. It is difficult for me to imagine that something in nature could contradict nature; that conception would explicitly encompass an idea of Nature as Good and her enemy (which, by the way, is a part of her) as Evil. Yet, it is difficult for me to fully understand the logic of a theological worldview. At some point, it simply demands faith—then, one can move forward again as if nothing has happened: the contradiction has been, eyes closed, skipped over. Still, what I write here sounds justified.

There, however, in Setomaa on May 5th, in the strong southern breeze of Eastern Orthodox Easter, I felt nothing but lust, and thought about how to satisfy it. I needed to. I hadn't been able to satisfy it at Veiko's place. I realize now (only now!) that nothing other than an unconscious erotic attraction (*still!*) led me to him; a vague notion that this time, the lust would ultimately be satisfied. Naturally, that notion even disappeared from my subconscious (if such a thing exists) upon seeing Veiko.

And so, sitting there in my Opel Astra, which the sun had already heated to a scorching temperature, I was seriously in heat, *en rut*. In one place on the next subsequent sandy yellow road, I was passed by a moped (in Estonian, they used to be called "thigh-shakers") ridden by two boys aged about sixteen or seventeen; thus, at an age, where the body's reproductive activity is extremely high, yet opportunities for settling this by "natural means" are practically lacking—especially, I imagine, when one lives in a Setomaa village. The boy sitting in back had his arms wrapped around the waist of the one sitting in front, and was clinging strongly to his back. They laughed, flushed.

That scene flashed by me quickly, and immediately reminded me of a certain story from filmmaker Derek Jarman's autobiographical book *Human Nature* about how as a boy, he had an older friend somewhere in a working class-district, who had either a motorbike or a moped. He sat behind that older friend, with his hands in the boy's pants. The more he stroked it, the more the boy accelerated. I lack such childhood memories.

I don't know whether extreme sexual inhibition is specifically characteristic to Livonian mentalities, or if it has more in common with the German cultural space. It seems to me that one does not encounter anything of the sort in France (probably not in Great Britain, either), nor among Russians. Maybe it is something specific to small nations, and resulting from this sexual "shyness" is their very low birth rate, their smallness overall? In any case, those Seto or Russian boys seemed to feel themselves quite free with each other.

I turned the car onto a side road through the brush right there. It turned out that the road led to the lake. Bird-cherry trees were blossoming there en masse. I decided to satisfy myself right there in the car seat, but then, I became afraid that someone might come down along the road from the lake and see me. If you do a woman in the back seat of a car in the woods during springtime, your rear moving up and down on the other side of the window, then people will pass by smiling sentimentally, although looking away in embarrassment. If you do a man, then they might not understand that a man is underneath you, and will likewise pass by, smiling sentimentally. If you do yourself, however, then they could even call the police. At least that's how it seems to me. I went towards the lake to check, and sure enough, two boys came from that direction immediately, carrying a white plastic fish container between them. Who or how those village boys do, I don't know. I became somewhat horrified by the thought that they could have seen me. I greeted them and asked stupidly whether the road led to the lake (the lake wasn't visible yet). They replied seriously, however, that it did indeed. Those boys don't do each other, each masturbates on his own. It was too open and windy by the lake. I went back into the woods—in addition to the bird-cherries, the young leaves of the silver birch (*Betula pendula*) trees smelled strongly; the grass hadn't grown that high yet, last year's leaves still crunched beneath my feet. I instinctively made sure to not step on a snake. Just one frog jumped and startled me. I leaned heavily against the trunk of a birch tree. The barking of a dog in the village alarmed me and softened my erection for a moment. My orgasm wasn't fast to come, although it was powerful and one of the more satisfactory ones I've had over the recent course of my life. My sperm fell onto the brown leaves somewhere in front of me, I didn't see—my head was arched back, I saw the blue sky and flying light-green branches.

It can almost never be as good with another person—you're forced to concentrate on him. Regardless, I felt longing for another person afterward; I would have fondled him absentmindedly, chatted with him, napped at his side.

I was nonetheless stopped by the police on the way back. Luckily, it wasn't for speeding. You are constantly stressed and alert (*alerte*) on Estonian highways at possibly being stopped and given a ticket (*procès verbal*) for having moved at a speed of seventy or seventy-five miles per hour in relation to the ground. I usually don't drive any faster, either, because firstly, it truly is dangerous, and secondly, my Opel Astra starts to vibrate. I wasn't speeding on that occasion: I was driving leisurely. It was actually a roadblock (*barrière*). There was an older police officer in uniform, who waved a disc signaling for me to stop, and a further three or four men wearing bulletproof vests and black clothes without distinguishing markings, carrying short automatic weapons (*pistolet-mitrailleur*)—probably Uzis (Israeli)—on a strap over their shoulders. The road was closed with plastic orange cones. I wondered—if I were to drive through them (they would fly clattering in two directions, light, as they should be), would the men open fire on me? There is probably either some large exercise, or someone is being searched for. Then, I remembered a story I read in *Postimees* the previous day about two probable serial killers.

Specifically, several crimes bearing a similar signature have occurred over the course of months. *Postimees* printed the following list: On March 29th at nine o'clock p.m., a taxi driver in Tartu is killed by a shot to the head, and his wallet containing about two hundred kroons (twelve euros) is stolen. On March 31st at about 7 p.m., the owner of a small shop (*épicier*) is killed by a shot to the head, with the money in the spice store's register—about one thousand kroons (sixty euros)—taken as the spoils. After that, on April 11th at 2:47 p.m., a murderer critically wounds a female saleswoman at a store on Riia Road in Tartu with a shot to the head, and takes her cell phone and seven hundred kroons (forty euros) in change. After that, at around 4:30 p.m. on April 24th in the small Northeast Estonian industrial city (once a large military plant) of Sillamäe, which is primarily inhabited by ethnic Russians, a driver is killed by a shot to the head and the woman sitting next to him is injured, with the loot being a bag containing fifty thousand kroons (about three thousand euros). Finally, between the hours of 9:30 and 10:00 a.m. on May 3rd, a twenty-five-year-old salesman at a hunting weapon shop near Tallinn's regional bus station is killed by two shots to the head, a display case is smashed, and a box of rounds is taken.

In the cases that police have managed to find any witnesses, they have spoken of two young Russian-speaking men—one with light hair, the other dark. They haven't worn masks. They are also credited with a bomb explosion that happened in front of a downtown-Tallinn weapons business in March, where no one died, but police found an undetonated explosive device labeled "Predator."

I must say—the list of crimes that I read absent-mindedly yesterday morning in a small Tartu café on Kuperjanovi Street left me feeling quite indifferent. Firstly, not a single story was presented about any of the victims. For example: that one was just planning to get married, that one was supposed to fly to the US on the same day; or else that the victim's mother had talked about the his or her childhood, their dreams. That would have moved my imagination. Secondly, five killings or attempted killings over the course of a month in a country of 1.5 million residents also does not at all significantly increase the probable danger of personally falling victim to a murder-robbery. Weekly reports from Israel about suicide attacks and the Israeli army's acts of revenge are just about as moving as that murder chronicle. For certain reasons (Amid), those are personally even more moving for me; better put—they cause more anguish.

Dominating my mind in that café (in addition to me, there was a group of drunken Finnish tourists, who drank beer and vodka regardless of the early hour) on Kuperjanovi Street, which was called Heidemanni Street during the Soviet period, was the impression that the Tartu Railway Station had given me. I walked there to see whether perhaps some train might travel somewhere outside the city, with me carrying my bicycle along, etc. The front of the station was completely devoid of people: only one taxi stood there on that Saturday morning, its potential murder/robbery victim napping at the wheel in the sunlight. The front of the station was always bustling, as I remember it. The train station itself is made of wood, built in the nineteenth-century Russian romantic style (with carvings)—probably erected at the end of that century, at the same time as that same railway, which led onwards from here to Riga via Valga, and through Pechory to Russia, to Moscow. On the wall under the entranceway awning was a departure schedule, which showed that only six trains leave from Tartu Station throughout the day, with the destinations of Tallinn (twice per day), Valga (once), Elva (a town near Tartu, twice) and Orava (a village before the Russian border on the Pechory side, once).

During the Soviet period, and even just recently, there were about three to four times more of those local trains: additionally, the Pskov, Riga, Minsk, and Moscow routes. In those times, that small station was unpleasantly crowded, full of the bundles (*bagages*) brought by "goods passengers" arriving from Russia, as well as the stench of onion and garlic. Now, it already seems like a lost exotica, like some Orient Express.

The railway station itself was luxurious overall. Maybe it is opened at trains' departure times; however, there wasn't a single departure to be seen before evening. That's just what I was thinking while scanning the newspapers there in the café: how quickly things, which seemed eternal and eternally aggravating—such as the onion-stinking bustle at Tartu Railway Station—disappear, leaving not a single trace. I believe that those who live in Tartu no longer even remember well that things were once different; accustomedness to the new has already dulled the old memories in their minds.

I also can't say that I was sad to see the trains don't run any longer. At some point, I probably just ceased to feel disappointed about changes. I decided that there's no point in doing so. That decision came sometime last fall, and it's possible that it was due to Liz Franz's influence (in retrospect), because she never regretted anything. She had even done an Estonian-language version of Edith Piaf's song "No, I have no regrets," which, needless to say, has the lyrics: "I start again from emptiness" (*je recommence à zéro*), and: "with you, new is all again."

Liz Franz's interpretation was naturally quite different from Edith Piaf's emotional expressiveness. She sang it rather quietly, but with very strong inner conviction—like casting a spell, like giving testimony in court. Liz Franz's attitude in life (not in her songs) seemed callous and cruel to me on quite a number of occasions. I don't know whether or not she truly didn't regret anything.

I'd like to know, Liz Franz: if you're alive, are you sorry that you won't see me again? Or, staying strictly with that known only to me: that I won't see you? And in the case that you've nevertheless decided this, then why? For what reason? From the train schedule I could see that not a single train stops at many of the smaller stops at all anymore—at the so-called vault stations (*arrêts*). There was once astonishingly dense traffic between us, likewise—between Liz Franz and I. That station is now closed. Not even just empty, as in the song from her Moscow period, "Зал ожидания" (*Salle d'attente*), in which the "empty waiting hall" (unthinkable in the Soviet Union, where stations were even full at night—travelers slept on benches and the floor) gave one the feeling that the song was about some foreign city—some small city in France or Switzerland, where lovers, both arriving from big cities, meet in secret; or, rather, are supposed to meet, because the other never came:

> . . . всё свистят поезда . . .
> Ты будешь— некогда.

But what moved me much more than that front-page murder chronicle (it wasn't yet clear at all that it had always been the same criminals) was a story on the newspaper's second page about a thirteen-year-old boy, who had been stabbed to bits right here behind my building last night. A surgeon at the university clinic, who had stitched the young boy together the entire night, said he had never seen such a horrible sight in his entire career: there were a great deal of knife wounds in his face, his neck, his body, his legs . . . The boy was partly homeless, and his mother (this surfaced in the paper only yesterday) belonged to the "asocial" (German *Asozial*)—i.e. unemployed, alcoholic, etc.—category. The boy was supposed to be sent to an orphanage the next day. The police representative believed the incident almost certainly had to do with a settling of scores (*règlement de comptes*) among a gang of boys. The representative further added that these incidents are often especially cruel, and mangling a companion in such a way is not rare in the very least. It's possible that the boy was in debt to one of them, and now threatened to disappear off the radar. In that case, the incident was a routine economic operation calling in the payment of debts from a debtor. The boy is in the intensive care ward of the university clinic, and has not yet regained consciousness.

Such stories always affect be quite heavily, because I vividly imagine what that boy must have had to live through. They didn't kill him—not immediately, in any case. It took a very long time, and it had to have been very painful. Furthermore, it's awful when you are at the whim of a force hopelessly more powerful than you (*force majeure*), when you have absolutely no escape (*issue*).

16

Today is Ascension Day (*l'Ascension*) in France. It is here, too, of course, in the church sense, but as it isn't a national holiday, no one is really aware of it. But Paris is quiet and quite devoid of people this morning. As Ascension Day is always a Thursday, most people make the famed "Ascension bridge" (*pont de l'Ascension*) for themselves: that is, they also take Friday off and go out of town. It's almost summer already. That is the kind of Paris that I like the very best. I never travel anywhere during that time, because the city itself is almost like the country then: people go away from me, and I don't need to escape. Actually, I travel away from Paris on extremely rare occasion at other times as well. There's no money, there's no initiative, it seems as if it would require immense effort to tear myself away from that city.

Ascension Day and other holidays in the spring cycle (the last of them is Pentecost, which is on the Sunday after next, and then the French have Monday off) are, however, only a preparation for the city's summer emptying-out. That Paris— hot and empty, when many businesses' steel shutters aren't raised for weeks at a time (*Paris des canicules*)—is the closest to my heart; it is my city. From July 15th through August 15th. July 14th is a national holiday, and August 15th is *Assomption*, the Assumption of Mary—that is also a holiday, the tip of the vacation orgy; even the bakery below is closed for two or three days around that holiday. The temperature in my attic apartment constantly rises above ninety-five degrees. Any coolness can only be found beneath the trees of Monceau Park or the Luxembourg Gardens. The few people left in the city (who aren't that few at all, of course) also congregate there. It is there, in the shade of the trees, where it smells of cut and scorched grass, of the park paths' white dust—it is there that I met Amid. Or more like he met me, I suppose.

It was in August, right around the *Assomption*—I don't remember the exact date—in 1998. Might one say that in connection with the distinct thinning of the human mass in the city, the likelihood of those remaining there meeting one another rose significantly? Nevertheless, it (the likelihood of A's meeting precisely with B) remained extremely low. One could say rather that the heat increases both lust and loneliness all at once—at night, you can't sleep between the sheets that are moist from sweat, and the days are hallucinated from nighttime dreams.

I don't know why I started speaking about late-summer Paris now, when it is currently only May 9th, and I'm in Tartu. Anyway, people there in France had yet another holiday yesterday—Victory Day, specifically—thus, *pont de l'Ascension* is especially mighty and crowded this year, and Paris is practically abandoned. I've probably started to develop that, which is called homesickness. Although, I'm already used to being in Tartu, I accustom to new places very rapidly—the main thing is for there to be peace somewhere, my own corner, where no one else can go.

Recently, following the Setomaa trip, I visited Tallinn in connection with that film project on the Forest Brothers, the money from which I pay for this apartment. The film is being made by Eerik Kross, the son of famed Estonian writer Jaan Kross. Jaan Kross has primarily written historical books, the most renowned of them being *The Czar's Madman* (*Le Fou du Tsar*).

The main pathos of Jaan Kross's works is focused on proving that a prominent portion of the nobility and other Baltic Germans of Livonia and Estonia (*Estlande*), of those provinces of the Kingdom of Sweden and the Russian Empire, were of Estonian, i.e. peasant, descent. In other words: that quite a few "German" admirals, scientists or politicians that made their career at the imperial court in St. Petersburg or at the University of Tartu were actually "Estonians." Jaan Kross has attempted to lengthen and ornament our people's history by way of this. In my opinion, it would be more economical to assume that all Estonians are actually Germans—although those, who speak a very distinct dialect. The nobility has often spoken a different language than the commoners, and so much as proven its radically different origins. For example: during the eighteenth century, a theory was cultivated among the French nobles that they descended from the Franks, who once defeated the Galls (from whom the entire lower class descended). This theory cost them a great deal of blood during the revolution; just as how the Baltic nobility's arrogant and uncompromising juxtaposition from the local commoners cost them both blood and land during the Estonian Revolution (War of Independence). In that sense, their expropriation was entirely just. Rigidity is always self-destructive.

Jaan Kross's son Eerik worked for a time in the new republic's intelligence service, thus continuing his father's streak of trying to carry out subversion against the Soviet state and its ideology between the lines of his historical books. Now, he (the son) has gone even father. With his military-history film about the anti-Soviet fight for freedom, he is striving to change Estonians' historical feeling of being a victim nation into that of a fighting nation (*peuple guerrier*). This is the film that I am consulting.

I find that there is a large trend in that undertaking, yet an even greater trend is in those people who are capable of individually tearing themselves away from their nation's collective fate, of rising higher than it—in a certain sense, of cancelling its determination. I heard the calling to such a path, I now believe, from Liz Franz's songs; especially because they never possessed political or social content at that time, and they only dealt with individual problems. Sometimes, especially in the 70s, they were even quite frivolous: "If you think that I lo-ove yo-ou . . ." (tai-da-raida-taida-rai-rai-raa . . .). For me, who had curled up in the armchair next to our "radiola"—no one else was at home and I could turn the radio up as loud as it went—for me, those songs were all hymns to freedom, calls to battle. I masturbated to them sometimes. After that, they felt sad, melancholic; they could even drive me to tears. Ultimately, someone always came home, and I had to stop my orgy.

I now have nowhere to stay in Tallinn, if not with my parents in Nõmme (a Tallinn suburb, a garden suburb), but I can't bear to stand a single day there—to tell the truth, I have a horrible feeling of regression that hollows me out inside already during the first hours. I cannot stay there. On occasion, in our "visiting marriage" years, I would escape from Liz Franz in the Weitzenbergi Street apartment to my parents' place in order to affirm (*affirmer*) my autonomy to Liz Franz. But being there, Liz Franz's apartment felt like a true island of freedom, and I was often back there—in her embrace, so to speak—already by the same evening. I never held up for over one night at home. Liz Franz was never offended or angered by my abrupt departures. She knew that her lost son would not remain lost for long.

Even that time in Tallinn, after my "creative meeting" at the film producer's, I walked down Weitzenbergi Street in the daytime—I don't even know why (like a fool: like a "criminal," who always returns to the scene of the crime (*lieu du crime*))—and stared at those top-floor windows out of the corner of my eye. The curtains were exactly how they were when I left them, it seemed. No movement could be detected. The entire street was so empty of people and quiet—even the dog in the yard of the house across the street, which otherwise always barks, lay with its head on its paws, and only followed me with its gaze. I started to get an awful feeling, and I got out of there quickly. I drove back to Tartu right away in the evening. The highway was quite empty in that direction, the sun behind me. There were no longer police on the road—the trip probably only took an hour and a half, and I developed some strange sense of freedom.

"Maybe still . . . maybe still . . ."—that feeling could just about be characterized with those words. Maybe I'll still become free, also—individually, not just collectively, as the member of one nation. Maybe Liz Franz was still only one stage, maybe the most important, but . . .

But maybe she still set her "duckling" free . . . Why particularly a "duckling," I'll address later—that's a story in itself.

I felt something of the sort, pushing the gas. There was a pair of young boys with quite hopeless expressions hitchhiking on the side of the road. One trudged onward along the shoulder, as if planning to reach Tartu by foot. Specifically, the public was being warned on the radio about male individuals hitchhiking (*faire du stop*) alone, who could turn out to be the serial murderer Yuri Ustimenko. I believe that lone hitchhiking males are having an even harder time than usual these days. I didn't pick anyone up, either. I used to pick people up—hitchhiking boys in particular. But it was always a disappointment. First of all, it wasn't possible to assess their appearance from a distance, and it turned out to be shabby, for the most part. But it was already too late to say no by then. Secondly, they turned out to be exceptionally inhibited (verbally; I never did try their sexual side), frequently pimply, reeking of beer, in short—tiresome. It's better to drive alone, no one bothers you.

I fantasized about picking up a hitchhiker and him turning out to be Yuri Ustimenko: I recognize him only after he sits in the car and sticks a pistol between my ribs. I look straight at him, but as my countenance starts to radiate especially then, at that moment of peril, he—likewise driven by some sudden enlightenment—realizes that there's no point in killing me, that there's no point in killing anyone at all. He instead starts to cry like a child (according to the newspaper, he is only twenty-one years old). Indeed not over those, whom he has killed (one probably doesn't cry over them when they are strangers?), but over his killed accomplice, to whom he was tied by an unacknowledged, yet that much more powerful loving relation, over his ruined life, over fear, over the fear of death.

The thing is, in fact—I haven't said this yet, correct—that in the meantime, their trail was picked up, and when they attempted to cross the Estonian-Latvian border in Valga, they were stopped by a Latvian police patrol. They killed one police officer and wounded a private security guard (*vigile privé*). Yuri Ustimenko's accomplice Dmitri Medvedyev also died in the firefight. Left at the scene was a briefcase containing Yuri Ustimenko's diary, which included pasted newspaper cutouts of articles reporting the murders, as well as a photo camera with undeveloped film. The first photograph of Yuri Ustimenko was acquired from that same roll of film, and was immediately flung all around all of Old Livonia. Specifically, it wasn't exactly clear whether the criminal escaped back to Estonia or stayed in Latvia and attempted to enter Russia from there. Both serial killers (who are likely responsible for all the killings that were listed in the previously cited *Postimees*) were namely cadets at the St. Petersburg Peter the Great Naval Institute. The photograph, which had been made into a portrait-sized image for "wanted" ads, was published in its entirety in the next day's *Postimees*. In it, the fugitive Ustimenko, who is smaller and has bleached hair, is sitting, wrapped in the arms of now-dead Medvedyev (*медведь—l'ours*), who is chubbier and black-haired; like a child in its father's arms. Medvedyev is standing, wearing a proud expression, but Ustimenko has a happy, childish look—he is smiling in a way that shows his missing front tooth (that is, its absence). I believe that the "callousness," which one of my Tallinn acquaintances—Anne—read from that face is purely a projection. One could, however, certainly pick up a labile psychological type, which could easily dive into a fantasy world.

Pictures of Lenin and Stalin were glued into his diary; from one of his pictures, where he is standing right in front of the modern Baptist church near Weitzenbergi Street in Kadriorg, with the church's quite phallic tower as the background and the cross right above his head—from that picture, he made a collage on his own, gluing onto it the words cut out of a newspaper: МУЖЩИНА ТВОЕЙ МЕЧТЫ (*L'homme de tes rêves*).

In that picture, he has on a "tough" expression and extremely naive gangster sunglasses. But seeing that first picture of them in each other's arms, enlarged on the front page of *Postimees*, I winced on the inside. I know what many Estonians' interpretation of that "killer couple" is now: faggots! People now have their reason. By the way—they are correct in their own right, although they are mistaken in the main point. Those two military-school cadets are undoubtedly connected by a certain erotic relationship. According to my analysis, the bigger one, Medvedyev, is—was, that is—more of a ladies' man (yesterday's newspaper had already collected information on their numerous girlfriends); thus the pair's Clyde. The smaller one, Yuri, who had bleached hair that is now dyed black according to police data, although publicly a ladies' man, actually only loves Dmitri (Dima), which he most likely does not admit to himself. It's in order to impress Dima that he has constructed the fantasy character he plays—that cold-blooded murderer. He wants to be like those film heroes, whom Dima admires. And not just that: he wants for both of them to be film heroes, who are parted on the screen only by death.

The fantasy, as they say, was tragically confused with reality that time. Or luckily, however you take it.

And so, in the event that homosexuality has its own part in the psychological design of that Bonnie and Clyde pair, then it is specifically repressed, forbidden, military-school-fierce, and at the same times supremely scorned homosexuality. The murders are a sublimation of that forbidden love. That it was particularly the murders and all that stuff: that's already easy to explain by a certain ideological confusion, some aimless brainwash that might govern in that military academy. Obviously, the Russian military has been in a sharp identity crisis since the breakup of the Soviet Empire. Those naive youngsters probably lived out their "fathers'" (superiors') aggressiveness and lust for revenge by coming precisely to the "governorates" cut away from the Russian Empire in order to do their deeds, etc.

In short, Yuri would lower the barrel of the submachine gun and cry like a little child. He is now completely alone, and will be caught sooner or later. In the event that he is gotten alive, he can likely expect a lifetime jail sentence, because the death penalty has been abolished in the Baltic States and is not administered in Russia. I stop the car so that he can cry in peace and get out, if he wants. I ask what he will do now. He clings to my arm and begs me not to leave him here, for me to drive him to this place and that. I say that I won't turn him in (*dénoncer*). He believes me, because he no longer has anyone that he can believe, but a person has to believe someone. I take him to this place and that. I won't go to the police, or inform them. That is certain. I'll never give anyone up to the authorities. The authorities can certainly make do on their own; that's why they are the authorities. Even in France, the judicial system and *Code Napoléon*, which I do actually regard to be relatively honest and just, I wouldn't give anyone up to the authorities—yes, no matter what he or she might have done. A person must retain their freedom, I don't know anything else. Even the freedom to shoot oneself in the head. I know that it is a socially dangerous viewpoint, but it can't be helped. I actually hate law abidance (myself generally being, outside of my fantasies, embarrassingly law-abiding and exact about it), because law-abiding people are those, who drive others to, and themselves are taken to, the gas chambers. Or the Siberian tundra. Alas, so it is. Even less would I want to give anyone up to the authorities here in Livonia, where both the police and the court system have already traditionally, throughout history, regardless of the regime, been famed for their partiality (*partialité*) and ability to be bought off.

If the authorities should interrogate me, however, I would say—at least I hope I would (I'm generally also able to chicken out)—that no, I haven't seen such an individual. I don't remember. Not *everyone* has to read the newspapers. For example, one ethnic Russian night-kiosk vendor (*vendeuse*) in Tallinn, who was asked by a reporter whether she was afraid of the serial killer, was utterly amazed: she hadn't heard of any serial murderer! I, however, am amazed every time that people in court are able to swear when giving their testimony: yes, I saw that very person then and then, there and there. How do they remember so precisely? I often don't even recognize a person, with whom I've had a very interesting conversation for several hours. There are so many typical elements in people. An as such, someone could be found guilty simply because he or she is of a certain type.

I am more interested in one aspect of the manhunt that has broken out in Livonia. Specifically, by how difficult it still is to find a person. Even when his picture is out across the entire land, when all forces have been utilized to search for him, and when the politicians in power could make themselves a fantastic PR-event by way of his capture, whether alive or dead.

But when a person hasn't actually committed a crime? For as far as I know, Liz Franz hasn't committed a single crime that could fall under the criminal code. Which doesn't mean that she hasn't killed, at least in a certain sense; but I'll talk about that later. She isn't being sought. Officially, as far as the officials are concerned, she hasn't disappeared, and officials don't provide private individuals with information about people's locations, either (actually: they simply don't know). And she hasn't gone missing in little but heavily-forested Livonia, but rather in the entire world, in the stricter sense. Although, it would still be reasonable to limit this to just particular, more likely locations. For example—China, Asia in general, and Africa are out of the question. At least more or less. Latin America? My nose (indeed, untrustworthy) says that she actually hasn't gone so "far" at all—in the sense of far from the places that can be associated with her. But these number many as well, and altogether tens of millions of people live within them. And so: I will find her when she wants me to. When Liz Franz wants me to. (And do I want to?) Or else it is a very great chance. No matter what that last sentence might mean.

Returning to Tartu—it was already evening, that special May dusk, from which one would like to forcefully read a promise—driving past the wall of the botanical garden, glimpsing the river for a moment, I suddenly calmed down. As if I had come home. I wonder where that home really is, then? Home, "where nothing bad can happen to me."

I went to bed almost immediately, and slept deeply and at length for the first time in a great while.

17

According to my calculations, Liz Franz arrived in Tartu in 1963 or 1964. It wasn't spring then, as it is now, but probably towards the autumn end of summer, August, and in my imagination, that arrival is associated with the aforementioned song "I Long for the Bosom of the Rowan Tree . . ." Tartu wasn't a rowan tree, of course, but was more like that which is outside of the rowan tree.

All that Liz Franz has told me about her leaving home is that her mother held her hand tightly and asked her not to go. Her grandmother apparently didn't say a word, and sat mutely in front of the stove in the kitchen. Her father wasn't home. She pulled her hand free of her mother's, and started to go to catch a bus. I don't know whether the bus came directly to Tartu, or whether she had to first travel to Viljandi, and then transfer to another bus there. I also don't know where Tartu's regional bus station was at that time: the current building is more recent, in any case. But Liz Franz reminisced about the bus station. She exited the bus there, and it was the first city that she had seen in her life, aside of Viljandi. Even Tartu had apparently been a disappointment to her: the buildings were smaller than she had thought; there was a great deal of wood and openness. All of that had still reminded her too much of a rural place. However, she knew that Tartu had a music school, and that she was going there.

She had had to ask two people before she did. The first didn't know anything about a music school, and so much as claimed that Tartu *hadn't* such a thing, which had horrified Liz. I assume it was some country person who was just as smart as she was.

The second did give her directions, but the party receiving these directions got lost before arriving, because she hadn't listened attentively and haughtily thought—how hard can it be? You start heading in that direction, and the music school will meet you halfway like the Tänassilma dairy plant.

The third person that she asked—a "kind old crone," as Liz Franz characterized her, "more like the kind of lady that there still was then in Tartu"—took her by the hand and led her straight to the school; it wasn't all that far from the place.

It isn't far from right here, from where I'm sitting now, either—on the slope of Toome Hill, below Angel Bridge, right across the road from the Gunpowder Cellar. I've already spoken about Toome Hill; I just haven't mentioned the bridges. Specifically, small, compulsory bridges were also part of that nineteenth-century romantic park ensemble, which was erected on the site of the razed fortress of the German Order, the bishopric castle etc., in place of later defenses. They don't span rivers—just deep, dry valleys. Toome Hill is an extremely imposing mound with quite steep hillsides. There are two bridges—Angel Bridge and Devil Bridge. The latter lies away from present-day routes, behind the hospitals, but Angel Bridge is a beloved walking place to this day—opening up from it is a good view of the lower town and the opposite riverbank. On that bridge, one can let the mind wander in the spirit of a completely authentic, romantic central point of the nineteenth century. Many nineteenth-century customs have been preserved in Tartu, a respective atmosphere—it is, in its own way, a museum town, and what is especially interesting is that the new, incoming youth unconsciously adopt these customs again and again.

One day, I stopped and stood on Angel Bridge, and listened to someone practicing Bach, which came through the windows of the music school below—it was probably some prelude from "The Well-Tempered Clavier"; Bach, in any case. The practicing musician faltered and started again. The music sounded out onto Toome Hill unusually clearly, mingling with the spring birdsongs.

I happily listen to musical performances in such a form. You don't have to sit until the end of the concert, or at least until the intermission; you can walk away when you've had enough, and the playing itself isn't at all pretentious in its imperfection.

Liz Franz had practically no musical preparation upon reaching Tartu, if one doesn't count her radio-acquired singing ability (and even so, from her grandmother as well, I'd add), and likewise some understanding of musical annotation that she was taught by her father. There was no children's music school in their near vicinity, and no one had the money or desire to send her to Viljandi. Yet, Liz Franz was convinced that her "incomplete high school diploma" and steadfast will were quite enough to get into music school. She had, in any case, found out that auditions, entrance attempts, were held at the music school namely on that day, and she was indeed heard that evening.

The women judging the auditions were said to have been "three old crones": two of them regarded her with hostility, one with friendliness. They, of course, rolled their eyes and exchanged glances when they heard about her preparation, or unpreparedness. She felt quite badly beneath their stares, wearing a dress sewn by her grandmother. One can guess that as a young girl and in the heat of an August evening in Tartu, she didn't exactly sweat very little. The dress's armpits had certainly turned treacherously into a darker shade; maybe even white streaks had already managed to form there. Yet those "old crones" were certainly used to sweating young girls. Having heard that she wanted to learn to become a "singer," they had mercifully allowed her to sing for them, regardless.

She had prepared three different songs: two Soviet songs and "A Birch Grew in Our Yard," which is often regarded as an Estonian folk song or so much as a folk tune, but is actually a Schubert melody (there is a linden in place of the birch in the German song, of course).

The two hostile crones, those "bony" ones, had smirked when she was singing, but the friendly one, that "round" one, had smiled at her encouragingly, and that's what she sang to. Yet already after the first verse, one of the bony ones signaled that it was enough, and she fell silent halfway through a word, a hollow feeling inside. The bony ones exchanged a further glance, hadn't even looked towards the round one, and she realized with horror that the bony ones had the upper hand and didn't care one bit about the round one's opinion. Then, they said something to her about preparation courses, children's music school, even industry school, where she could initially study and then come back to try again "after two or three years." Liz Franz stood up without saying a word upon hearing that "two or three years," and marched out of the room and the building.

Outside, she didn't know where else to go other than to walk straight up the hill: those redbrick ruins of the church were there, there was a plank fence around it, but the fence was quite dilapidated and she squeezed through a gap in the planks, then sat there in the tall hay between the pillars. But she didn't cry. She was angry. She sat there in the ruins of the Cathedral of Saints Peter and Paul until it started to grow dark. Then, she began to have a dreadful feeling. She exited from the hole in the planks, but no longer remembered the direction from which she had come. Still, one light burned close by—things seemed lighter and braver beneath it, and so she sat right there on a bench beneath the lamppost. She didn't know anyone in Tartu—she had thought that if she was coming, then she would certainly also be given something to eat and a place to sleep; the music school should be happy that she, Eliisabet Frants, had wanted to come and study there. Now, she didn't know what to do next. She wouldn't go back home—that much was immediately clear to her. The August night was indeed warm, but she nevertheless started getting chilly in her cotton-print dress. She remembered that her grandmother had also stuffed a sheep's-wool sweater in her small plywood suitcase—an old radio case given to her by her father—against her will (she had been certain that no one in the town wore sweaters like that), and she now tugged the sweater out of the radio box (the familiar smell of home came form the box, and she was overcome by a momentary surge of weakness: if she were to just travel back …) and pulled it on. Now, it was warmer to continue sitting. She decided to sit until morning, supposing that her next move would show in the light. Even now, she doesn't know what would have happened if that old man hadn't come past.

The old man came up Toome Hill, where people were no longer passing through, and stopped to stare at her. She stared back at him boldly: at that time, she had no clue that she should fear some old man on Toome Hill at nighttime. And true enough, even in Rome, she still loved to wander around at night (despite Umberto Riviera's delicate remarks) in the shadiest places, about which people told horror stories (drug addicts, Yugoslavs, human trafficking). For example, she says that it smells good at night near the closed gardens at the Palatinum, and so it is—I've gone there with Liz Franz. The very strong smell of some grasses, mainly sweet vernal grass (*Anthoxanthum odoratum*), dominated there, and Liz Franz asserted that it smelled just like in her grandmother's laundry closet. But it is also true that during our walks, I noticed *quite* suspicious shadows flickering, and they weren't at all only Rome's famous cats.

That old man on Toome Hill, however, had in fact been her father's age at the time. As it turned out later, his name was Tõnis, and he worked "on stage" at Vanemuine Theater (Tartu's only theater at the time)—meaning he didn't act on the stage, but built sets; he was a carpenter or something of the sort by trade. Now, that yet nameless old man asked what she was doing there (he understood that she was a country girl and that she was in trouble; he likewise regarded such sitting under a lamppost to be a bit dangerous). Liz Franz told the old man everything straight off, and only then did she start to cry. When she heard her story coming from her own mouth, she suddenly felt dreadfully sorry for herself. One way or another, the old man Tõnis led her to his home, gave her something to eat, and made a bed for her on the floor. Tõnis had a small, cramped room somewhere in the city center, in a communal apartment, as they were at the time. (Even here in this house, where I live, the large, old upper-class apartments below were apparently made into a number of tiny one-room apartments with the help of additional partition walls, each inhabited by its own household—often an entire family; all of those households used the sole kitchen and bathroom in the apartment.) On top of that, Tõnis promised to come up with something. Liz Franz realized that Tõnis was taking care of her now, and fell soundly asleep.

In the morning, she traipsed to the theater behind Tõnis, not falling a step behind, like a dog. Tõnis had apparently not exactly invited her along, but he hadn't driven her away, either. So, Liz Franz stayed in the theater. Back then, it was the small, old theater: the art-nouveaux building of the former German Theater. The "old-timers" who worked on the sets arranged some job for her there that was something like a set painter's assistant, where she was practically given nothing to do aside from sometimes being sent to the store to buy bread and kefir. The salary was thirty rubles per month, which is indeed impossible to express in euros, but basically, one could eat off of it, given the fact that a two-pound loaf of bread cost something like fourteen kopecks, and the "old-timers"—no doubt especially that Tõnis—always offered her their lunch sandwiches as well. She was also allowed to sleep "under the table" in the set room, although it was strictly prohibited by fire code. She also registered for evening high school, probably at the behest of that very same Tõnis. Tõnis had no wife or children: there was indeed a stage boy from the country, interested in acting, who was "like a son" to Tõnis, and with whom Liz Franz initially had friction, but afterwards became friends.

Liz Franz claimed to not remember that stage boy's name, and he apparently didn't become an actor, either. He had probably started drinking instead, but that was later: Liz Franz wasn't in Tartu anymore then. That nameless boy (I highly doubt that not-remembering, Liz Franz just didn't want to tell me) had a guitar, and he taught Liz Franz to take major chords and accompany her singing in a simple way. I certainly haven't seen Liz Franz with a guitar, or with any instrument at all. The accompaniment has always been others. Yet, she accompanied herself during her first performances. The boy also taught her a newer singing repertoire—the kind that was heard from Western radio stations (Radio Luxembourg, etc.) and was already going around on under-the-counter records. That era is generally called the "Khrushchev thaw" (*dégel*). Becoming familiar with that repertoire of newer songs was perhaps even more important than memorizing guitar majors, because the songs that Liz Franz had learned previously from the radio—stations with the signatures "Here Tallinn!" and "*Говорит Москва!*"—as well as from her grandmother and father were, as even she now understood, completely old-fashioned.

The information presented here is, in a strict sense, also everything that I know about Liz Franz's Tartu period. If something else comes to mind, I'll write it down—I want my testimony to be as exhaustive as possible; at the same time, I'm not sure that acquiring additional information would add anything significant. And where to acquire it? Tõnis is, of course, long since dead, and if it's true that the nameless musical stage boy began drinking after Tõnis's death, then he may also be either dead or have slipped into the kinds of social dregs, where practically nothing is known about people in them; where a person is just as good as nonexistent. His face is distorted, bloated; his clothes stink. One way or another, he is as good as dead. One way or another, he would hardly remember anything anymore. And if he does remember, then I don't know if I even want to know it. Every person has the right to his or her life's story, and I am conveying Liz Franz's life's story here essentially in the way that she told it to me personally. I believe that to be the most important.

But I don't even know how long that Tartu period lasted—whether it was a year and a half, or two and a half. For in any case, Liz Franz left Tartu in winter—in February or early March—and in any case, she dropped out of evening high school. Thus, her only official school diploma is the certificate of graduation from Tänassilma Incomplete High school.

I also don't know whether it is possible for us to find out very much enlightening about a person from his or her life's story. This and that, of course; but how far can one go in the conclusions made on the basis of that information? Is it possible to see in a person's life such symmetry, such orderliness, that their known life that is already lived might allow us to believe something unmistakable about his or her yet-unlived life, or the one unknown to us? Does there exist in life such symmetry as that in the Bach piano piece, which I heard on Angel Bridge through the windows of the music school? Does that symmetry, order, logic (and at the same time, the emotionality hidden in it, which does not allow everything to be surmised in advance) really fascinate me? I generally don't grasp anything in music. And I hate the sort of vague expression of feelings around something, which is unfamiliar.

However, Tartu is certainly a very symmetric, orderly town, although it might not be visible at first glance. Its older section, Tartu in the narrower sense (and we have no reason to talk about the rest), is made up of two tall hillocks—one on one side of the river, the other on the other. One is the already repeatedly-mentioned Toome Hill, Tartu's beginning. Almost nothing remarkable is left of that beginning, of medieval Tartu. A stretch of the city wall near the botanical garden, and the ruins of two churches. In addition to the Cathedral of Saints Peter and Paul, St. John's Church located in the lower town also lies in ruins (since World War II), standing out by way of its terracotta statues made of red Tartu-County clay, being, as far as I know, Livonia's only church so richly decorated by statues (the apostles and all those others). A new, shining spire topped by a weathercock has now been put on St. John's Church: it is visible at several points across the city, and hampers me from recognizing the Tartu of before, of my time. The tower was still stumped then. With its spire and weathercock, the tower reminds me rather of the Tartu from old, pre-war photographs, so I have the passing feeling as though I've in fact ended up in an older town.

Tartu is purely a nineteenth-century town by its nature, and from this probably also comes the symmetry, the order, the rationality, and, at the same time, the somewhat crazy romanticism. If you think about it, then romanticism was born in buildings with *very* strict architecture. Tartu's older architecture primarily represents the aesthetics of so-called "classicism." It is nineteenth-century classicism, somewhat formal and dry, but nonetheless not without a certain provincial elegance. Tartu's provinciality is also not a modern provinciality—the standard, supermarket-like, and universal provinciality of small towns in the globalized world, such as Tallinn. Tartu has dozed off in its own nineteenth century, and so, its provinciality holds something inexplicably dignified; although at the same time, something very rotting, decadent. If I were to believe in the existence of mysticism, then I'd say there's something mystical about it. Now, I say that it holds something elusive.

And so, located on Toome Hill are the ruins of one of Livonia's larger churches, the Cathedral of Saints Peter and Paul, which has become much older now as ruins than the church itself managed to while whole. The corpses of bishops, Grand Masters of the

German Order, priests, noble men and ladies are certainly buried beneath the cathedral. Those graves were certainly all looted later on as well, but there are definitely still some material remains there, also. The bones of the deceased from St. Mary's Cemetery, which was razed during construction of the university, are buried in a valley of Toome Hill, and on the site is a small red brick memorial with bronze plaques informing passersby of those bones in the four local languages (on this occasion, they are Estonian, German, Russian and Latin). In the poverty and confusion that followed independence, someone pried the bronze tablets off and sold them as scrap metal. Estonia was a large exporter of metal during that time. They have now been replaced with new ones.

In symbolic and symmetrical terms, that "necropolis" that is on Toome Hill, in a certain sense, must serve as a counter-balance to the old Jewish graveyard on the opposite hillside. No one has been buried there since the 1930s, when a new Jewish graveyard was erected along Räpina Road outside the city. During the Soviet period, that old graveyard—a small square ringed by a concrete wall—was quite abandoned. Large trees have grown on the site, an absolute forest, in the treetops of which nest black rooks—just as in the Toome Hill trees. The old Jewish cemetery's gravestones are unique in the sense that out of the three local languages, only one can be encountered there—German, as a historical irony. A number of the stones are solely in Hebrew. Not the slightest word of Estonian can be found there. An important, although never especially large Jewish community formed in Tartu—no doubt during the nineteenth century as well, and in connection with the university. Namely, endemic anti-Semitism wasn't as sharp in Livonia as it was in many other Russian provinces (so it was again during the period of Soviet power, when quite a few Jewish instructors—among them semiotician Juri Lotman—came to Tartu from Russia), and Jews were able to live here relatively peacefully until World War II. Then, practically everyone who hadn't been able to or realized that they should flee to the east (and even many of *them* died or were killed) were exterminated, and very quickly. Yesterday, I heard that there was a Jewish prison in the cellar of this house during the war—probably some temporary detention center. As an irony of fate once again, may we recall, this building was the only one in the area left standing by the bombings; maybe for remembrance, I don't know.

The annihilation of the Jews in Estonia went that much easier for the German authorities, because the local population gladly cooperated. Specifically, the thing was that the Soviet occupation preceding German occupation had pulled off the mass deportation and killing of the local elite right on the eve of the war. Thus, the Nazi army was generally greeted as liberators. And as there were also Jews among those who had cooperated with the Soviet authorities, with the help of German propaganda, they were likely made into scapegoats (*bouc émissaires*) to some extent—just as has happened before and elsewhere in history.

The only known case of concealing a Jew in Estonia during World War II that is listed on a stone tablet in Israel's Alley of the Righteous likewise originates from Tartu. The instance had to do with Uku Masing, an Estonian philologist and mystical poet by ambition, who hid the university's instructor of the Old Testament and Hebrew language (whose name I don't remember) at his home. Uku Masing was himself also a good Hebraist—he prepared a new and somewhat unconventional translation of psalms and some prophets' books. In addition to that, he researched folklore of the world's peoples, fairytales above all, and allegedly knew several dozen languages. He wasn't directly repressed during the Soviet period, but his works were not published, either—he somehow struggled to make ends meet, giving lessons at the Institute of Theology and perhaps doing some translations. As he lacked an opportunity to be published and likewise the possibility of conversing with other people in his field, who at the same time were as good as nonexistent in Estonia, his works remained fragmented and often raw.

In terms of his philological grasp, however, he is only comparable to the very first Estonian poet, Kristian Jaak Peterson (1801–1822), who likewise was proficient in and researched, despite his extremely short life, many old and living languages. His bronze statue is located on Toome Hill, and at the foot of it is one of his better-known verses written with bronze letters, asking: *"kas siis selle maa keel laulo tules ei voi taevani toustes ülles iggavust ommale otsida."*

However, that verse by Estonia's only classical poet is quoted incorrectly: a syllable has been added, which puts the verse out-of-whack. In my opinion, that is a gross insult in the classicist's case. Specifically, *"igavikku"* is written in place of *"igavust."* *"Igavus"* in modern Estonian is *"ennui"* (boredom), while *"igavik"* is *éternité* (eternity). During Peterson's time, in the first decades of the nineteenth century, such a subtle difference was not made. Boredom was boredom—coming from the stem *"iga"* (age, length, time): *âge*, as it is used, for example, in Baudelaire's poem "The Lighthouses," in which that "fiery sob" rolls from time to time or from age to age—*roule d'âge en âge*, finally stopping only on the shore of the Lord's eternity, or *"igavus."*

Kristian Jaak Peterson was from a mixed family in Riga. His father was an Estonian serf from Viljandi County that served as a churchman at the Estonian-Swedish congregation of Riga's St. Jacob's Church. His mother was, however, the "non-Estonian" Anna Elisabet Mikhailovna of unidentified descent. His childhood's bi- or multilingualism likely set the foundations for his exceptional philological talent as well. And it was likewise probably that very "linguistic Babel," from which the understanding arose that his native tongue is **also** a tongue; not just "what everyone speaks," but a language, like German or Latin, for example—and thus a language that likewise, incidentally, may "search for boredom unto itself" in writing.

Kristian Jaak Peterson repeatedly journeyed on foot between Riga and Tartu, where the imperial university had opened less than twenty years earlier. Just as one out-of-whack syllable has been added to the verse on the foot of his monument, one out-of-whack circumstance has been removed from his official life story. Specifically, Kristian Jaak Peterson loved—as was befitting for a nineteenth-century philologist—"young, handsome men" without exception, as he admits explicitly in his preserved twenty-page *Journal*: *Loving young, handsome men very much, I took them as my friends, teaching them wisdom and goodness. Yet, strike a match and search! Truly, you will not find a cynic!*

No one knows how much reciprocal love he found from them. In order to earn money for studying and living, he gave private language lessons to young Baltic German men, and probably fell in love with a few of them—not finding, however, understanding or a kindred soul (a "cynic," as he writes in the classical spirit of his time). At the age of twenty-one, on one wintry trek from Tartu to Riga (155 miles), Kristian Jaak Peterson apparently became seriously frozen-cold—his lung disease, once again completely in the spirit of the age, took a turn for the worse, and he died there in Riga. The site of his grave in the cemetery for the poor at St. Jacob's Church in Riga is, of course, unknown.

I'm only writing about all of this at such length because I somehow don't have the courage to approach what actually interests me right now. I'm unsettled by yesterday's events. I don't know what to make of them. I don't know—I just found a "cynic," although in the cynicism often characteristic of homosexuals, there was something in that Asko that stood out to me in addition to the sensitivity, which also has, or not, I don't know at all for certain, some kind of homoerotic background—that is, it definitely does, but I don't know the extent to which it has been acknowledged. And I don't know what will happen next, not in the least. Developing some sentimental relationship in Tartu wasn't part of my plans in any way, especially since I want to remain as unnoticed as possible here. In truth, I've outright stayed away from sentimental relationships for some time already. I know that falling in love is, in some sense, a question of letting go, of will. You can, at first, take it or leave it. Afterwards, there is no way back. But do I even want for things to develop that far? It's always painful—that I know very well, in any case; come what may. It is always unequal, also; especially when one party is about seventeen years the other's junior. As Asko is mine. Because he *is* younger, despite his "ancient Estonian" name, which, by the way, is absolutely logical for the era: during that time of national awakening, parents started giving their children exactly those kinds of names. He is about as much my junior (still, let's be honest: even a year or two more) as I am Liz Franz's. I don't know if that which is unsuccessfully called love can ever really be harmonious, symmetrical, like the city of Tartu is with its Cathedral of Saints Peter and Paul, between the pillars of which Liz Franz sat down angrily in the tall hay on one August evening nearly forty years ago—with its "dome church," which is now seemingly divided into Saint Peter's and Saint Paul's churches: one built in the nineteenth century, the other in the twentieth; one on one side of the river, the other on the other, and both—I might add—built of red Tartu County bricks. What chance do those two "parties" have of meeting? None at all.

Or what chance did I have in Tartu of preserving my (relative) anonymity, my incognito? Likewise, practically none at all. The first to recognize me on the street and call out my name was Signe.

In French, *signe* means "mark" (a homonym of *cygne*, "swan"); in Estonian, it doesn't mean anything—it's just a woman's name that generally isn't given anymore. But Signe is a woman of around my age—nearly forty. We once studied in the same class and even in the same field: genetics. Signe was the class valedictorian, and was a promising young scientist. She was a very bright girl overall: she played guitar, wrote poems, and loved to discuss philosophical questions. That's probably just how that promising young poet of the time—Siim Velner, who was already a celebrity in Tartu—won her over: original expressions. Signe married Siim Velner before university was over, and they were regarded as a very chic, intelligent pair. Yet, Siim Velner suffered from a manic-depressive psychosis that had developed in steep slopes, and which he denied to acknowledge or take any medications to relieve. Instead, he projected his manias onto his wife, whom he exhausted with either manic bursts of jealousy (once, for example, he orchestrated a shouting match on the street upon catching Signe and me calmly conversing) or depressive threats of suicide. After that, they were visited regularly by her mother-in-law, Siim's mother, who accused Signe of ruining her son's life. Signe forgot both her literary experiments and her scientific perspective very quickly. She managed to divorce her husband after about five years, and then it took nearly ten years more until she was able to fight her way out of their shared apartment, which was divided into two parts after the separation, and where her ex-husband systematically went to "check" on her. Signe is now the secretary of the genetics department. A couple of years ago, a pregnancy from a casual encounter miscarried in the third month, and Signe no longer hopes to have a child. She only hopes—and unrelentingly—to find a better, better-paid job, where there might also be fewer warped relationships than those, which she claims, dominate among the university personnel.

Signe was visibly glad to see me when we met on the street. We went to Wilde Café, in front of which stands one of the world's most absurd sculptures—one of Tartu's unique symbols of provincialism. Specifically, the bronze composition depicts two writers sitting together on the same bench. One of them is the renowned Irish/British author Oscar Wilde; the other is

Eduard Vilde (also written Wilde), who is unknown globally, but wrote a nineteenth/twentieth-century novel that is mandatory in Estonian school curricula. The only thing that connects them is the homonymy of their names, because Vilde, as we know, did not demonstrate any homo**sexual** tendencies in his lifetime. It is quite difficult to find anything erotic at all, much less homoerotic, in his predominantly social realist works of prose. Nevertheless, they are sitting on the same stone bench in front of Wilde Café. Perhaps that sculptural group depicting two stiff nineteenth-century masters symbolizes the unrecognized homoerotic fantasies of Estonian men buried deep in the dark corners of oblivion, unbeknownst to its creators and those who commissioned it. Maybe by contrasting a normal man and an "invert", it also commemorates those sufferings, humiliations, and repressions that the homosexual men of this land have had to endure throughout the ages. Yet, I emphasize once more that all those possible symbols, which the sculpture perhaps conceals, are entirely subliminal for the public. For example, that same Siim, Signe's ex, who, as a poet, continually gives hope (true enough—for many, he has disappeared from the literary horizon, although there are those who keep account of that hope; Estonian culture is small—all hopes, even the slightest ones, are accounted for), is openly homophobic in terms of his views, and surfaces from time to time in the newspaper's "letters from the readers" column with contradictory statements. He personally, as it turns out, prefers women, of course; and mature, even overly mature women, at that: his latest passionate relationship, which has lasted for several years, Hilma, is said to be a full twenty years older than him—thus, somewhere in the vicinity of sixty-five.

In the café, Signe spoke about her difficult life. She earns some three thousand kroons per month after taxes (that makes less than two hundred euros), of which about one thousand kroons go towards home expenses (an apartment bought by her father in an HLM in Tartu's Annelinn district); that being said, she was almost elegantly dressed, and said that she goes swimming regularly at Tartu's new aquatic center. Truly—the financial subsistence of people here is a mystery to me.

She further told me about her ongoing plans for the future, one of which is "some day" visiting me in her dream city of Paris. I hope that the visit turns out to be sufficiently brief, so as not to shatter or smear the eidolons she has connected with that city. Namely, it is easy and natural in "nineteenth-century" Tartu to preserve a notion of Paris in its age of blossoming, which is likewise, now that I think of it, its nineteenth-century form.

To console her, I said that Tartu seems lyrical and precious to me, but she didn't believe it. She apparently wants nothing other than to move away from here, although she lacks any material means to do so. I managed to avoid giving Signe my own phone number, but I promised to definitely call her soon.

18

I should still, however, summarize the events of that Feast of the Ascension, as their (after-)effects are lasting even today (Saturday), and do not appear to be showing signs of abatement. Rather the opposite.

I was quite calm for a while yesterday. I went to the library to listen to Maria Callas. Luckily, the sound archive there has the 1958 version of La Scala's *Norma* issued on vinyl records (there are three in the case) in Leningrad by license. It is regarded as Callas's best *Norma*, vocally and dramatically, that is left on audio recording. The *Casta diva* ("Virginal goddess") is truly stirring, not to mention the flaming (pyre!) feelings of the finale.

That opera, written by Vincenzo Bellini in 1831, is generally quite intolerable, as is the greater part of nineteenth-century music. It is interesting, truly, that such exaggerated, falsely-storming music arose amidst such strict architecture. But maybe *forte* and *fortissimo* only seem false to us, and in the nineteenth century, they expressed those people's true feelings? If such feelings exist.

When coming from the library (I borrowed a biography of Maria Callas and that same record case, for which I had my own plans), however, I met Asko in the stairway. The irony lies in the fact that he lives on the same floor in the same stairwell; not quite in the neighboring apartment, of course, but still. Which makes the situation especially complicated. A "boy next door" is such a classic gay fantasy (just like a fantasy of schoolgirls) that no one believes in the actual possibility of the situation. I have to say that "boys" live in all of the apartments on the upper floor of this building. They are small, expensive apartments, and in Estonia young men are statistically the demographic age/gender group with the highest average income. I've repeatedly seen a Nordic

Apollo exiting one apartment, for example: a blond, athletic, Swedish type of Finn. He takes two leashed, classically-trimmed poodles and a white lap dog, the breed of which I'm unable to identify, out for walks. I don't know if the dogs all belong to him, or to the Russian supermodel type of Estonian girl, who, in turn, takes the Finn out for walks, if I can put it that way, although their relationship is probably founded on quite equal bases: one is handsome, very rich in Tartu terms, and a foreigner; the other is simply very beautiful.

Unlike Estonians, who will allow a door to shut right in your face without looking back, the Finnish Apollo always looks to see whether anyone is coming in through the door after him, and will hold it open as they do in the Paris Métro, so I don't know what to say to him: whether *merci!*, *aitäh!*, or *kiitos!*, which in Finnish means *merci*, but in Estonian means something like *louange* (exaltation)—I truly feel a certain awe, a need for exaltation before such a rare being.

This time, however, Asko was smoking on the stairway's upper level. I don't know why he was smoking in the hallway when he can also smoke in his own apartment, where I believe he lives alone. The stairway is full of smoke anyway, because the women working at a telemarketing company located somewhere on the fourth floor beneath me smoke in the hallway incessantly, and there are not one or two at a time, but always four or five. They are exceptionally forward sometimes, and when I walk past will declare: "oh, of course we let young men through!" (I do indeed look younger than I am); or even so much as, "we'll surround the young man, let's not let him through!"

They aren't exactly beautiful anymore, but rather have a fairly worn appearance. Telemarketing companies employ women based on their voices, not their appearances. Apparently, constant communication gives them a certain additional courage, which in a situation of direct, wireless communication may turn out to be even exaggerated and somewhat unpleasant. But for the most part they smoke quietly and only size up passersby with their eyes. Many of them certainly have their own obsessive fantasies in connection with the Finnish Apollo. Their real husbands, if they have any, are definitely not especially handsome or at all successful. And they presumably hate, despise, and are bitterly jealous of that "floozy" (*garce*)—the Finn's girl.

How simple it is to analyze others' feelings! But as I was saying, Asko was smoking on the stairway, and the record case in my hand immediately sparked an unforced conversation between us, which was a continuation to the previous day's chat about how Asko could re-record the music for me off of the vinyl record, because he has a record player. I threw away my own record player, which sat at my parents' place and was actually also broken, several years ago. The same goes for most of my records, including all of Liz Franz's old recordings. My pitiful attempts at freedom, directed against innocent objects, damaging primarily to me myself!

Over the course of the intervening night, I had practically forgotten Asko's appearance, and come to the understanding that he was an absolutely ordinary boy, over whom I wouldn't let my relative peace be broken, in any case. Maybe he is. But he has very pretty eyes. They had slipped my mind. Speaking of which, I don't even know what color they are now. Green? Brown? And what does "pretty eyes" mean? Eyes should actually be a remarkably indifferent facial element. Everyone has eyes: large, moist orbits, which move in their sockets, and only a small surface area of which shows. That corneal area constantly moistened by the tear ducts shouldn't express any feelings in and of itself, because the only change that can happen in its appearance is the contraction and expansion of the pupil, powered by the iris dilator muscle (*musculus dilatator pupillae*, which I answered on the anatomy exam), which, by the way, is not a voluntarily-directed muscle, but rather depends solely on the vegetative nervous system. The same goes for the abundance or lack of secretion in the tear ducts, which makes the surface of the cornea shinier (more brilliant) or duller. Moreover, Asko's eyes are behind glasses. But that doesn't matter. Perhaps the glasses actually enlarge his eyes, and actually highlight them. On top of that, he is probably slightly cross-eyed, which may give the impression that he is looking fixedly at his conversation partner. And it was as if all of that had been wiped clean from my memory. My body had started to fight the cause of the sickness.

That mechanism is common in the physical aspect: antibodies or phagocytes found in the blood identify the invader (a virus, bacteria), and set to destroying it, they themselves perishing in the process. If there are no corresponding antibodies or they are not sufficiently "resilient," then the virus or bacteria will manage to multiply more quickly, and the individual will fall ill. Now, he or she must undergo the entire cycle of the sickness, during which the person will defeat the cause of the illness regardless, and thus improve, or will die.

In the psychic aspect, the capacity to forget evidently plays the part of the immune system. When the infection is recurrent or too intense, then forgetting may prove to be insufficient: newer and newer aggressive and attractive details attack our psyche until it is under their control, and one must go through the entire cycle once again (love, grief).

In short, I now remember those eyes, so what that I don't know their color. I'll check next time. The next time will be when he returns *Norma*; he promised to record it onto CD. I wonder whether recording an opera seems too strange, too old-fashioned, too queer to him? I'm actually no opera queen. I told him that it's for a film project. He studies political science at the university, but dreams rather of a film career. He most likely hopes to use me as a springboard—I do still have some connections, regardless of the fact that I'm practically forgotten in Estonia. He didn't appear to know my films. And no matter what I might tell myself, it doesn't count for anything. I'm willing to unresistingly lay myself down by the edge of a pool and be a springboard for him. His young, slim body would rise into flight, and then disappear into the green water. At the same time, I'm a little angry with myself. I didn't actually consider myself to be such easy prey. A duckling. So what that I'm already an old duck.

But yes, Ascension Day, the French word for which always reminds me of Liz Franz, because the word is also used when speaking of a career, an exceptional career in particular, when we're speaking of a politician or a star that has risen very directly to a very high height: *ascension irrésistible*—a climb, which no one and no thing is capable of impeding. I simultaneously find that even in our sexualized societies, there is something pleasant in the official celebration of Church holidays. Nothing follows the temperate zone's seasons, as well as the human pheno-physiological rhythm, so closely as the Church calendar. In truth, to be exact, it is more suited to Mediterranean nature than to that here, but the rhythms of the Sun (and the Moon) are universal in the northern hemisphere.

I took my bike and rode out of the city—the wind was quite cold, and Jõgeva Road leading north from Tartu had bad traffic as it does on weekdays, which wasn't the most pleasant. The surface relief over there is mostly made up of low, elongated hills called drumlins, which constitute morainal waves left during the melting of the glaciers. They give the landscape a majestic, wide-open look. Lakes several kilometers in length are found in the basins between them. I turned off of the highway onto a smaller road, then onto an even smaller one, which attracted me by way of its apple-tree allée just bursting into bloom. Planting apple trees as an allée along a highway was a practice that was widespread in Livonia during the last century and the one before that. It probably reached here from Germany—there is something simultaneously sentimental and utilitarian about it. Estonia is situated at the northern edge of the European wild apple's (*Malus sylvestris*) habitat. The tree's fruits are tiny and terrifically sour, but in winter, having gone through the freezing cycle, they become sweeter. Before sugar became a consumer good in Livonia (the twentieth century), frozen wild apples were a rare sweet treasured by farm workers. The custom of growing fruit trees for consumer use is not at all old in these parts: it took root only in the nineteenth century, initially at manors, then at farms. For Estonians, there is something special about the apple tree, which in France is somewhat like an inferior sort of fruit tree (next to the common grape vine, the fig tree, the Seville orange, and others). Apples were the first cultivated fruits (*fruits cultivés*), with which a Livonian peasant met. Until then, peasants subsisted primarily off of grain, pork to a lesser extent, fish, and a limited selection of vegetables (*légumes*), such as beans, peas, turnips, cabbage, and rutabagas. The potato became the main cultivated food in the nineteenth century. The fact that something large, edible, and still relatively sweet grew on a tree was, and probably still is now, a nearly incomprehensible, supernatural phenomenon for people here. An Estonian instinctively and undoubtedly identified the biblical Tree of Knowledge (*l'arbre de la connaissance*), which in Estonian is called "the tree of recognizing good and evil," solely as an apple tree. So what that apple trees don't grow in Palestine.

The apple allée led to the crest of a drumlin, transitioning there into a linden allée. The lindens were old and large, and stretched to meet above the road, but were not yet fully leafed and let sunbeams through. At the beginning of the linden allée stood a sign stating that the Vasula Allée was a natural-protection site. The majority of Livonia's old allées have been destroyed in connection with the widening and straightening of highways, or simply the natural aging of the trees. These days, roadside trees are also regarded as a source of danger, because they limit drivers' field of vision. A large apple orchard began next to the road at the point, where the apple allée turned into a linden allée. The orchard is most likely a former kolkhoz market garden, the tradition of which definitely stretches back to manorial times. Unlike most apple orchards in these parts, it was not quite left neglected: a tractor was presently unloading manure into ruts plowed between the trees. One smaller section of the orchard was set aside for pears, and they were currently in full bloom. The pear tree is already quite rare in these parts: it is even more sensitive to night frost (*gélées tardives, printanières; gélées blanches*) with its early blooming, and its yield is therefore even more uncertain than that of apple trees. The apple trees weren't quite in bloom yet. The gate was open; I steered into the orchard. Spread out towards the rear were also strawberry fields, where people were at work weeding dandelions (*pissenlit, Taraxacum officinale*)—the blossoming period for which is presently at hand, and which threaten to soon start seeding. That surprisingly busy market garden had a comforting, and even promising effect, as there is generally an impression that gardening (aside from strawberry farming) is practically withering away in Livonia, as cheap imports are making it unprofitable. Old local apple species such as "Golden Reinette" (*Reinette dorée*) or "Tartu Rose" (*la Rose de Tartu*) are indeed especially flavorful (*parfumé*), yet have a delicate skin that is easy to damage, and are therefore unsuitable for merchandizing in large supermarkets. In my opinion, the apples and pears sold in those supermarkets are often the ones from the year before last, which were left over in European gas preservation warehouses. Walking past the fruit counter, I smell an unpleasant scent that comes from, I don't know—either preservatives or the fruit's own slow, anaerobic decay (putrefaction, *putréfaction*). I never buy fruit from the store in Estonia, aside from bananas.

When I biked down the drumlin on the other side of the apple orchard, my cell phone croaked in my pocket (I've put "frog" as the ringtone for my Nokia 3310)—Asko was calling. The thing was that he was supposed to come to my apartment on the previous evening, at the landlord's request, to look at the Internet connection. This house has its own Internet connection: 150 kroons (nine euros) per month is billed for a fast cable connection. And Asko handles those things in the house. The youth of his generation are often very intimately "on familiar terms," as they say, with that computer and net business, and that often provides them with nice extra earnings, as those my age and older no longer accustom to new technology very well: for us, it is an amply mystified area. He couldn't come last night, however. He'd already come to take a look at it once, and had me buy a network card for my computer. Like a pensioner, I'd had him repeat it, and even write it onto a piece of paper: network card and adapter. For some reason, they asked at the store how powerful my computer was (how many kilos or gigs, I don't know what), and when I asked how I should know that, the salesman replied that people usually do know something about their computers. I'm apparently not a person then, but I didn't say that: I avoid conflict in the commercial network, although in Paris I've learned to behave rather more arrogantly in the store to hide my fear and honor for retailers, left overfrom my Soviet childhood.

Apologizing on the phone, Asko further said something like: "We were supposed to get together yesterday."

I liked that formula. Because in the strict sense, "we" weren't the ones supposed to get together, but rather Asko and my computer.

In short, after getting that Internet thing to work, Asko invited me to come and see the roof. You can get into the attic from the hallway by his apartment, he has the key, and from there, onto the roof. The view from the roof is much wider than from this window. Toome Hill is also visible, as is the new (indeed now already old) Vanemuine Theater, etc. We sat on the ventilation chimney on the roof until we got cold. Cumulus clouds had appeared in the sky, and their shadows dashed across Tartu's roofs and treetops. We talked about all kinds of things, I don't really remember what, about our lives. Hearing about another person's life usually bores you to tears. But I didn't get bored there on the roof. I came to understand that experiences, which to me are completely routine and even tiresome, may be almost mysterious at his age and in his situation. Even the experience of Paris, which he believed is a place where everything is probably all very different. The standard of living, he added quickly and smartly. I wasn't really able to say anything in response. The standard of living—yeah, sure thing.

Afterward, we went to Tartu's best-known Chinese restaurant, Tsink Plekk Pang, whose food resembles Chinese dishes more than the name resembles the Chinese language. There are also worse Chinese restaurants in Paris. And in my mind, it's ridiculous to ruin your (and especially your companion's) mood by talking about how far one food or another is from "the real thing."

It was ten o'clock in the evening when we parted (he had come to my apartment at two-thirty). And yet, I had forgotten his face (apart from his upper lip, which has a somewhat strange shape) by the following day, and had managed to think of him as a completely ordinary university student. It is true that his ignorance surprised me, although I personally, now that I think of it, was even more ignorant at that age. You forget about such things. However, I was just as surprised by his thirst for knowledge and courage to ask questions. We rather hid our stupidity in our day. He had seen Jung on my desk, and immediately wanted to get a brief summary of Jungian psychoanalysis from me. I must say that such direct questions lead to awkwardness, but I was still able to pull myself together and formulate some standpoints.

By the way, I heard on the radio this morning that Yuri Ustimenko—that probable serial killer, with whom the highway fantasies I wrote about were associated—was caught by the Polish border guard on Tuesday. Coincidentally, he was apprehended (in the small bus station of a Polish border town) not as an internationally wanted serial killer, but rather as a routine illegal border crosser. He was also found in possession of a loaded Walther pistol with fifteen rounds, but he didn't make an attempt to shoot it. He used a false name, and it took the Polish police several days to identify him. Now, the police and court authorities of at least three countries (Estonia, Latvia and Russia) are demanding that he be turned over to them—a series of murders bearing a similar signature has begun in St. Petersburg in connection with an entire group of Peter the Great Submarine Seamen's Academy cadets.

I was satisfied that he was apprehended by the Polish police, because be what it may, the thought of vigilantism by the authorities is gruesome all the same. And the Polish police had no cause for taking vigilante action against him. In a mug shot taken by the Polish investigative organs that was published in the online version of *Postimees* early that morning, he is smiling so much as self-confidently, the wide gap between his teeth exposed. I wonder whether he still hoped to escape? As they do in films. The paper also said that Ustimenko and his companion shot in Valka, Latvia most likely came from Russia into Estonia by swimming (in November) across the Narva River. The Narva River is Estonia's widest and most water-rich river: its discharge far surpasses the summary discharge of all of Estonia's rivers, as it collects its waters from wide areas in Russia as well as in Estonia. The investigative organs (according to *Postimees*) were somehow also aware of the method by which the criminals crossed the river; a method that was exactly identical to the one used by the young hero (actor and later film director Bodrov, whose gangster films are said to have inspired the serial killings) in the joint Russian-French film *East/West*, which moved me greatly back then. There was something very archetypal about that particular escape story.

The thing in the film, in short, is that a French woman who went to the Soviet Union after the war at Stalin's invitation—following her Russian-immigrant husband—and is caught in a trap there, encourages a young swimmer, her lover, to train despite the fact that he has been thrown out of his training group. The man coats his handsome body in goose fat and swims in the icy autumn waters of the Dnepr. Later, the young man flees by swimming to a Greek ship sailing on the Black Sea, and escapes to the West.

The St. Petersburg cadets had used the same method: coating themselves with goose fat, diving in case of danger, etc. I believe there also would have been simpler paths for crossing the Estonian-Russian border, but they wouldn't be so archetypal, so true-to-film. All in all, I was satisfied that Ustimenko was apprehended, because I felt some kind of vague mutual guilt for his fugitive status in connection with my own therapeutic/redeeming fantasy that I had developed on the Tallinn–Tartu highway.

19

I finally took a trip to Viljandi yesterday. I got a call from my former schoolmate Martin, who is one of the few to have my cell phone number, and with whom I sometimes still get together when I visit Estonia. I don't even know why this is, because we are very different. This time, he came to Tartu and had to drive to Viljandi the following day for a cycling marathon, and invited me to come along (not on the marathon—he knows that I don't attend mass events), and I suddenly realized that I still hadn't taken a trip to Viljandi. Sometimes, the simplest possible solution is so within reach that you unconsciously delay trying it longer and longer doggedly attempting to take only the most difficult, distant paths.

Martin goes to the gym regularly, and has developed himself an imposing torso—in my opinion, it's been too burly for far too long. However, Martin's torso is certainly not the reason he's capable of constantly developing and maintaining at least five simultaneous relationships with women. Martin studied psychology, he was interested in theater in his school days—he was the star of our school's acting circle, and it is there that we became friends. My self-esteem was too low to have ever gotten a lead role, or even a supporting one for that matter. I considered myself to be extremely ugly, which was an understatement, now that I look at pictures from my school years. Martin never fell below a lead role. I made a film montage of a school theater production with the school's sixteen-millimeter Krasnogorsk camera, and once, we even completed a real film, or "tele-production."

It was none other than Beckett's *Happy Days*, in accordance with the spirit of the time. Martin was Willie, and one of his female admirers at the time, his future wife, was Winnie—the character who is actually always on stage (or on screen), sinking to her waist in desert sand at the beginning, later up to her neck, and continuously giving a monologue which in her mind is a dialogue, because she is addressing her husband, Willie.

At that time, the piece was being staged at Tallinn Drama Theater, and Beckett was generally very popular there during the last few years of Soviet power—no doubt that there is something about him that is exceedingly characteristic of a period of decline.

Willie spends the entire piece in a cave beneath a dune, and very rarely responds to Winnie. For example: upon Winnie's insistent questioning of what a hog is—Winnie read from her toothbrush that it was made of 100 percent pure hog's seta—Willie finally informs her: "A castrated male swine."

Willie climbs out of the cave only at the end of the play, in order to die. Regardless, Martin was able to perform that part like a star, and even shine more brightly than Eve, his future wife. I did an expressive close-up of Willie climbing out of the cave, and was in love with Martin for some time—that is, it happened in the opposite order, to be exact. The film was, of course, outrageously embarrassing and boring, but it was regarded as intellectual, and even I as the director was a star, to some extent. That climbing out of the cave scene (it was also the end, of course, and everyone was overcome with relief that the petering-out was finally over) was especially admired, and I realized that love adds some kind of an intangible gloss to art. Martin, however, apparently sensed my admiration reflected in that close-up, and we became friends—nothing more, naturally.

He is long, long since divorced from his Eve (that same Winnie)—Eve is now an independent woman, an entrepreneur. They have a son, however, whom Martin put into Tartu's old, famous Hugo Treffner Gymnasium, about which the previously-mentioned writer A. Hansen wrote the second volume of his *magnum opus*. I remember from it only one breathtaking scene, in which the old school director Maurus (obviously a boy-lover) runs to the gate after the hero (Indrek), who was thrown out of school for blasphemy, and sticks five rubles in his pocket (quite a large sum indeed, in that currency: about a month's living), saying that if a young person wants to go to war with our German (or was it Estonian?) God, then may he at least have five Russian rubles in his pocket.

Martin's son Carl Gustav has apparently taken on a part of his father's suppressed ethical unrest, because Martin says the boy has lost sleep and also almost his health during the last school year. When his father asks what he thinks about when he can't fall asleep, Carl Gustav apparently replies: "I think about why I am the way I am, and why I can't be different."

Martin pays for all of his son's schooling, and is an outstanding father in every sense. He had been involved in some consultation business for several years and, being one of the first who started it, earns a decent sum, and is also simultaneously the family man of his time. I've never understood what his consultations consist of, but it's never really interested me, either. For me, there are large dark areas in business life; or white blotches, however you put it. From time to time, I feel great, almost religious wonder at the functioning of the system—it especially envelops me in France. There is something completely irrational about its operation, although doers, like Martin, regard my wonder as a pose, as the affectation of a freeloader—although he'll never say it that way.

Regardless of all that, I am above all still amazed by his capacity to incite and manage (*gérer*) relationships with women. The secret of this is certainly not his torso or his appearance (the top of his head has long been bald, and he shaves his entire scalp, which in short is, yes, still rather sexy), if you don't count as part of his appearance the certain psychological persuasiveness, the impression of genuineness that he emits.

All women, with whom he creates and maintains relationships, incidentally correspond not only to his taste (generally rather small women; he himself is decently large)—he has different women for different facets of his taste; for his different fantasies; his different physical, psychological, and vital needs. At the same time, he spends money on them, as far as I understand it, only very moderately: they can manage financially, for the most part, and Martin prefers to support their work-based initiative, rather than inhibit it. For he also has to avoid the women's excessive clinging (*accrocher*), which would hinder the functioning of his system. He not only has one relationship in Tallinn as well as in Tartu (where he goes frequently), but has several of them in both cities.

There is one, who works as his secretary (for a decent salary, of course—Martin is not the slave-driving type); there is one, a Russian girl, who makes amazing pancakes, and at whose place Martin loves to spend the evenings from time to time. Another Russian girl (about 80 percent of his relationships are usually with Russians in the ethnic sense, or at least with women from mixed families) is, however, very spiritual and religious, sings exquisite hymns in the choir at an Orthodox church, and regularly goes on pilgrimages to the Pechory Monastery. Even now, Martin was supposed to be taking that Verochka—names are sometimes oddly suited (*вера—la foi*), or do they actually influence the course of our lives?—to the Russian border in his Toyota Landcruiser, from where the monastery's transport service takes the pilgrims onward.

Martin asked me over the phone what part of the Book of Corinthians thirteen, four through thirteen was. That reference had apparently been hanging on the wall at Vera's place, stitched onto a velvet doily with intricate golden letters in Church Slavonic. He hadn't understood what it meant, and Vera hadn't explained it to him, either. I replied that I didn't know, that I'm not familiar with the Bible, but then I remembered that I have that Tartu-language *Wastne Testament* here, and I could look it up in there. I was almost certain that it was the very same passage from the Letter to the Corinthians that is quoted always and everywhere as a certain theological justification for the romantic cult of love. I've indeed read that the Greek word used there, *agape*, doesn't mean quite the same thing as love (*amour*), but rather merciful charity (*charité*); but all in all, it's really not at all possible to define the content of such abstract concepts.

So it was: "*Pahwli I. Rahmat Korintileistille, XIII. Pähtük,*" starting from the fourth passage—I read it aloud to him on the phone as well as I could. As Martin's grandparents had lived in Southern Tartu County and he had spent his childhood summers with them, he had no difficulty understanding:

"*Arm om pikkämeelelinne / nink helde: Arm ei wehastelle. Arm ei aja Wallatust / temmä ei paiso ülles / Temmä ei peä hendä kurjaste / ei otzi omma Kaswu / temmä ei sah wehatzesz / temmä ei mötle Kurja / Temmä ei röhmusta hendä Üllekochtust / ent temmä röhmustab hendä Töttest: Temmä sallib kik / temmä ussub kik / temmä lohdab kik / temmä kannatab kik. Arm ei wässi eäle errä. Kuhlutamisse sahwa errälöpma / nink Keele sahwa errälöpma / nink Tundminne sahb errälöpma. Sest meije Tundminne om tükkilinne / nink meije Kirjaselletäminne om tükkilinne: Ent kui Täwwelinne sahb tullema / sis sahb tükkilinne errälöpma. Kui minna Latz olli / sis könneli minna kui Latz / minna olli tark kui Latz / nink mul olli Latze Mötte: Ent kui ma Mehesz saije / sis jätti minna maha / mes Latze Wihs om. Sest meije näeme nühd läbbi Warjekajetasse pimmedän Sönnan / ent sis Palgest Palgeni: Nühd tunne minna Tükki wärki / ent sis sah minna tundma / nida kui minnake olle tuttu. Ent nühd jähb Usk / Lohtus / Arm / ne kolm: Ent suhremb neist om Arm.*"

In addition to Tallinn and Tartu, Martin also has quite a number of steady relationships in Brussels and New York, where he likewise goes on business (he also advises some state offices);

plus, as I've understood it from his stories, he furthermore meets one interesting "person" or another on practically every work dispatch to Brussels or New York.

He uses such a euphemism systematically in place of the word "woman," which is apparently practical for the phone conversations that he frequently has to hold in the company of a female partner. Person (*l'homme*) doesn't mean a man in Estonian, but is a strictly genderless signifier (*être humain*). The Estonian language lacks grammatical gender (*genre*) entirely, which makes conspiracy in love affairs pleasantly simple. The Estonian third-person singular "*tema*" can be both *il* and *elle*. This, by the way, does not cause any difficulties in communication, as the French people to whom I've spoken about this linguistic peculiarity believe. On the contrary—to me, the grammatical gender seems to be a completely superficial (*superficiel*) element, the use of which I'll never really get used to. I do understand very well that *papa* is masculine and *maman* is feminine, but what gender is a chair or a table? And what difference is there between the adjectives *beau* and *belle*? Why can't it be *belle garçon, beau fille*? But it can't.

Especially when tired, I'm incapable of keeping track of the gender of the words I am saying, and conjugate them haphazardly: for me, it will forever remain cryptic, a learned discrimination. I heard from my doctor in Paris, who is, as it turns out, of Hungarian descent (a language related to Estonian, which likewise lacks *genre*), that he has the same problem. He picked up on my incorrect conjugation, and that's how it came up in conversation. Although he has lived in France since the age of five (his family emigrated after the suppression of the Hungarian Revolution in 1956) and has only attended French school, he starts to mix up the gender of words when gets tired in the evening. I must say, however, that I make this mistake less when speaking Russian, because I've bathed (*se baigner*) in that linguistic environment since childhood, to a certain extent. Martin speaks Russian perfectly, which enables him to expand both his consultation business and the fan (*éventail*) of his relationships.

Observing Martin from the sidelines, I've striven to follow how his so-called "chatting a girl up" works: that is, effectively approaching a pleasing potential sexual partner. To me, it seems extremely robust: one must simply make an approach, and that's it—it's generally unexpected by people. By the way, maybe only 20 percent of attempts to approach a person will be accompanied by success, but that is enough on the whole (*largement*), if five or more approaches are executed while walking through a city over the course of an evening.

Yet, that lesson is of no use to me. Firstly, I cannot approach nice boys—be they Estonian or Russian—in this manner. The women, with whom Martin comes into contact, may indeed reply to him mockingly or feign annoyance, but at the same time, they are also always flattered—a certain, special, queenly smile flits across their face. Boys, on the other hand, even when obvious homoerotic desires are involved, which I believe can be sniffed out (*flairer*), for the most part could not openly react to my attempt at an approach in any way other than with an attack, an insult, or something similar. I don't know; I haven't actually tried.

And I know that it's actually completely possible to use this on men as well, only that it's more complicated. I've seen—even in Estonia, not to mention Paris—fantastic chatter-uppers, who have no problem at all with the initiation (*initiation*) of a conversational situation. The main thing is not to let your desire show: you must be cool, etc. But the ability to chat someone up is apparently a talent you are born with, not an acquired skill. It is for this reason that I'm jealous of Martin, who personally doesn't even know that he has this talent, as well as for the fact that he can regard himself as a happy person, well above average in terms of the diversity and pleasantness of his sexual relations. Nevertheless, he is afflicted by regular bouts of depression, which appear to be happening if not more frequently, then for a greater duration with age. He tells me about them every time, and I'm unable to give him any advice, because what would that be? "Be less happy, less successful in love, in work"?

Maybe he'd like to be famous—a television star, for example—and hold even better access to the local female pool. By the way, he doesn't have any more than one single child, as far as I know: he's managed to even avoid the development of that potentially freedom-curbing connection. He knows that I'm homosexual, but it's not a problem for him; to tell the truth, he probably can't really imagine, how it can be that certain women's legs, or the certain rhythm of a moving bottom doesn't seem worth seeing, and still directs my attention to it on the street.

Although, crises and disappointments sometimes come up in his relationships, too. For example: in Tartu, he told me about a very pretty and spiritual girl of Russian-Tatar descent whom he had met here in town; but who—as it turned out afterwards—had "rubber breasts."

*

The Viljandi bike marathon turned out to be a veritable mass event. Already around one hundred cars were parked along the shore of the lake, cyclists were circling around everywhere, all wearing multicolored skin-tight cycling outfits and pointed, aerodynamic helmets on their heads, which made their faces, and even their bodies astonishingly uniform. For me, they were practically indistinguishable from one another, and when I later tried to pick Martin out of the others while watching the starting column sweeping across the main square, it turned out to be beyond my capacity. If there was anything erotic in that image, then it was a purely general, activity-based collective eroticism, in which there is no place for individual differentiations. Watching that column of speeding helmets, I realized that individualism is of feminine origin in the world. Men endeavor more towards group integration, towards the loss of individuality, and therefore, they (we) apparently actually fear when someone starts to love them (us) too individually. Men are weak and cowardly. I even felt a certain sense of sympathy for all the wives of those "warriors" in bicycle uniform; wives, who are forced to love an entire team in their husbands.

After watching the start of the marathon, I headed from downtown towards the outskirts to search for that house on Lille Street (number 2C): Liz Franz's mother's dwelling place.

Viljandi (Ger. Fellin) is a small town (about twenty thousand residents) located seventy-five kilometers west of Tartu, on the other side of the relatively large, but shallow Lake Võrtsjärve. In Viljandi, just as in Tartu, there has been a fortified place of settlement since ancient times, which is likewise located on a naturally well-defendable mound—even higher and steeper than Tartu's Toome Hill. In Viljandi, this mound towers (*dominer*) over an elongated lake, not a river, and some fragments of the walls of the former castle of the German Order still remain. The castle hills are a very romantic place to walk, with bird cherries, nightingales, and other such plants. At the end of the nineteenth century, a hanging bridge (*pont suspendu*) with an iron construction was erected over a deep moat there, made at some Riga factory, as one could read from the cast-iron posts. With its powerful cables, that purely romantic structure lacking any practical purpose was apparently supposed to symbolize, among other things, the technological progress, which had reached even that *kreis* town.

Once one of Livonia's most prosperous rural centers, Viljandi is now a typical sleepy small town—the population's share in the modern-day economic bloodstream is difficult to imagine, although it certainly exists. On the warm day yesterday, the streets between the picturesque wooden houses and gardens smelled of asphalt heated in the sun, and occasionally also of lilac blossoms. Lille Street was quite far from the central square. Lille Street 2C turned out to also be a small, low wooden house, painted brown and with a glass veranda, apparently built either at the end of the nineteenth century or the beginning of the twentieth.

From what I know, Anton Frants purchased it sometime during the 1960s, when their daughter had just left home. Anton retired during that time, but of course didn't wish to spend his old age at his mother-in-law's country farmstead. Old wooden houses were no doubt cheap at that time, because a construction boom of new individual domiciles had begun under the conditions of economic prosperity. Anton was not interested in homebuilding, and no doubt he also thought he wouldn't have much longer to live in that house (all the same, he actually had to for nearly twenty years). He had always joked with Liz Franz during her childhood, saying that when he retired, he would take Laine and Eliisabet, and they'd all move to a large stone building in Riga. There, they would start visiting the zoo and walking along the riverbank.

"*Kas tiaatrin ka?*" Liz Franz had pressed, because neither the river nor animals seemed interesting to her—she had seen quite enough of those in Tänassilma. She hadn't known that "walking along the river" means something completely different in the city than it does in the country. In Paris, Liz Franz and I walked along the river almost without exception. Even one apparently decisive conversation happened on the Bridge of Arts, during our last meeting. Liz Franz likewise said that she always went to sit along the Tiber in Rome, even at night. I wonder whether on occasion, she also had the urge to cast out a line there, as she once did in the Tänassilma River? There certainly are fish in the Tiber.

But in response to her theater-begging, her father had always asserted:

"*Ikka, tiaatrin ka, uuperin. Riia uuperin omma' ilusa' verevä' vaheteki'.*"

Liz Franz had taken her father's statement literally, and feverishly awaited his retirement. Every day when her father came home, Liz Franz asked whether he was retiring now. She later came to understand that her father didn't like that question; but she kept waiting indefinitely for their move to Riga. Yet, it was just her father's banter (*plaisanterie*), even though it probably expressed his subconscious dreams. People tend at a later age to regress to the sites of memories from their youth. And so, Anton and Laine Frants actually only moved to Viljandi during the sixties, although it was still to a town, because Anton Frants didn't want to die in the country. He is buried in Viljandi Cemetery, which stands out for its abundance of romantic grave monuments—especially its Baltic-German section, which has now been fixed up once again. Anton Frants is buried in the larger, Estonian section, of course, because Viljandi Cemetery doesn't have a Latvian section. Liz Franz's grandmother, whom they brought out of Tänassilma when she "grew frail," as they say, should also be buried in the same cemetery. She had lived for barely a year in Viljandi, and started to head towards Tänassilma on foot a few days before her death. The *militsiya* had brought her back.

Around the house at Lille Street 2C was a small garden enclosed by a wooden fence. Growing there were a few large apple trees, with lush lilac bushes near the garden gate and the veranda. There are very few lilacs in Paris, and in spring, I always go to smell the couple of bushes that I know, because for me the scent of lilac blossoms is associated with the arrival of spring's culmination. Liz Franz always searched for happiness (*bonheur*, not *chance*) blossoms—i.e. having five or more petals (in place of the usual four)—in the lilacs. No doubt that is also some kind of a German custom. She laughed at that search for happiness, but always found several, and right away. She always gave them all to me and, still laughing, said:

"Eat them."

That is, in order to acquire happiness, the given blossom must be eaten while wishing for something at the same time. They are mildly bitter, but do not have a bad taste and are apparently not poisonous. I did eat them, always, and was cross with Liz Franz, because by doing so, it was as if I was acknowledging that I hoped—regardless!—for some result to come out of that superstitious ritual. I was also jealous, because I almost never found happiness blossoms. Even now, I looked almost instinctively at the lush lilac bush on the other side of the fence on Lille Street, and what I immediately spotted there were, of course, two "unlucky" ones; meaning blossoms with three petals. That branch apparently had some local mutation or a somatic abnormality.

What caught my attention first of all in the yard of Lille Street 2C were five or six beehives (*ruches*) buzzing there in the shade of the apple trees, because an entire cloud of bees flew up and down above them, and the drone could already be heard beforehand—then, when I was just approaching the yard and didn't see the bees themselves yet. I stopped to watch them, and at first didn't notice the old man sitting at a table that had been brought out onto the veranda. On the table before the old man was a large geranium (*géranium*) with red blossoms, which had apparently been brought out from the room, just like the round table. The old man wasn't doing anything, just sitting there, and was looking in my direction without any particular interest when I finally noticed him. I said hello to him, and asked whether this might be Laine Frants's house.

"Sure is," the old man replied following a short pause, "but she's not home right now."

The old man spoke entirely in standard Estonian.

"Went to the store or wherever, she did—what'd you need from her, then?"

The old man wasn't hostile, but didn't appear to be especially cooperative, either. And what old man was he supposed to be, anyway? Apparently Laine Frants's partner. I hazily recalled that Liz Franz had mentioned him, but I never listened to her especially attentively when she spoke about herself or her mother. I was only interested when she talked about me, and she was able to bring the conversation around to that interesting subject very often.

Sometime after Anton's death, Laine Frants had apparently taken that "male" into her home: unlike Anton, he was "young," meaning about Laine Frants's age, and apparently kept bees. I had come in through the gate, and their swarm beneath the apple trees there was quite dense—one constantly passed by my right or my left ear, but they were apparently accustomed to people (if such a thing occurs among bees?) and showed no signs of aggressiveness.

I said that I had come because of Liz Franz (I hesitated over whether to say Eliisabet), Laine's daughter.

"You're a journalist, huh?" the old man asked. "They still come here on occasion, but it's not as if Laine tells them anything—Eliisabet doesn't allow it."

From that sentence, I grasped that her mother had indeed started calling Liisu Eliisabet, probably due to her fame. The house had a new sheet-metal roof; I believe Liz Franz had given the money for it. I said that I wasn't a journalist. And truly—who was I, then? As whom should I have presented myself? I hadn't considered it at all (the old man luckily didn't ask any more, either). Liz Franz's lover? Acquaintance? Former classmate? But her mother should know all of those. A former coworker? And what kind, then? If Liz Franz's acquaintance doesn't know where Liz Franz is, then Liz Franz consequently doesn't want him or her to know. And she apparently hadn't disappeared for those people here—the old man certainly didn't indicate anything of the sort.

I sat in the other chair at the table, next to the old man; maybe Laine had been sitting on it before—and what did the two of them do there? They were old Viennese chairs brought from inside. The old man said:

"Dunno whether it'll rain too, or what—they did say from the comin' week. All them buds bloomin' so quick, an' the blossom's empty too; birds flyin' round just the same . . ."

I realized that he was actually a Southern-Estonian speaker— he had only switched to the other idiom when speaking with me at first. The old man didn't say anything more. I almost dozed off from that monotone buzzing, and I fought it, but all the same, I startled awake from some kind of half-sleep when the garden gate creaked.

It was an old woman wearing a wool sweater over her cotton-print dress, and it was very difficult for me to recognize anything Liz-Frantzish about her facial features. Doubtless there was something. She stared at me with immediate distrust. I rose and introduced myself as a documentary filmmaker, and said we had been looking for Liz Franz, but the addresses that we had were apparently old, and asked whether she perhaps might be able to help us. The woman became even more distrusting, and asked:

"Who sent you?"

That question led me into complete confusion, and I mumbled something about how we didn't have any definite plans yet, but there was an idea to maybe make a television show about Liz Franz (I've noticed that "TV" has an effect on people); if, of course, the songstress ("songstress"—god, what a moronic word!) herself agreed.

Actually, I already knew that I wouldn't find anything out there. The woman, who had to be Liz Franz's mother, Laine, said she didn't have the right to give any information (that's how she put it)—neither an address, nor a phone.

"She doesn't want to be bothered. Contact the Estonian Radio music programs—they have her agent's information."

That's Liz Franz's old trick, that agent. Ironically, his name is Farinelli, like the famous eighteenth-century castrated singer, and he probably was truthfully Liz Franz's agent to some extent—right around the year 1991, when her CD was put out in France. Yet, Liz Franz's international career did not take shape, and neither could it last all that long. It was connected to the fight for freedom, the so-called "Singing Revolution," which happened in the Baltic States during those years, and thanks to which some interest in those countries surfaced momentarily in the West. During that time, a few more fanciful publishers and managers purchased artists, books, music, and film from the Baltic States that were fit for selling, because the market niche existed and was untouched. That niche was filled before long, and just disappeared afterwards. One retrospective album from Liz Franz—*Voice*, of which I will still speak at greater length, because it was thanks to that album that we even met—managed to get released in Paris. Liz Franz apparently met Farinelli thanks to Umberto Riviera, to whom the "songstress" was already married by then. But now, that Farinelli is actually retired, and when an inquiry is sent to his agency's fax number or e-mail, then it is answered after some time with a standard reply containing an advertisement for that album from ten years ago, which has long since dropped out of the sales network, as well as a promise to inform the artist of "your lovely (*aimable*) interest," etc., as well as to contact you again at the soonest possible opportunity (*dans les meilleurs délais*). That "opportunity" never comes, however.

I thanked Laine Frants for the information, and said goodbye. I knew for a fact that Liz Franz had enforced a very strict regime for conversing with her mother. She sent money regularly, but her mother was only allowed to call "when extremely necessary," and as the mother apparently feared Liz Franz, she practically never called and was used to her daughter calling her perhaps once per year; to her sending a birthday card. So, if Liz Franz truly has disappeared, then her mother may not have noticed it at all: for her, Liz Franz has long since as good as disappeared—for thirty years already.

Exiting from the gate, I saw that Laine Frants indeed sat down on the same Viennese chair that I had sat on, and pushed the headscarf back over her hair. It was in that movement that I finally recognized Liz Franz—there was something youthful about it. In addition to large black glasses, a silk headscarf is, of course, a common element of disguise for all sorts of "divas" and film stars; and as I found out by being at Liz Franz's side, this was not in the least only in films. They are completely effective in life, also. For the most part, Liz Franz was successful at being in Tallinn without anyone seeing her. She said:

"If you don't want to be seen, then you won't be, either."

Upon reaching the apartment, the first thing she did was to always pushed her headscarf back over her hair, untied it, threw it onto the dressing table, and took off her sunglasses. I was fascinated by this unmasking, but I actually liked the masked Liz Franz more—I would have preferred being that woman's lover if I had to. But I never dared to tell her: leave the headscarf and the glasses on.

This is just how I will now remember Laine Frants—sitting beneath white apple trees in the garden, amid the buzzing of bees, pushing her headscarf back over her hair, as if she was planning to immediately enter into lively conversation with the old man. But they barely spoke, in reality: they merely sat there at the table. A geranium with large, red clusters of blossoms on the table before them, as if it was a third person, whom they admired and watched like a child. Suddenly, I had a bizarre thought—it *was* Liz Franz.

20

I had just written that last sentence—I finished it just now, not really remembering what I meant by it anymore—when there was a knock at my door. I knew that it could only be Asko, because the people who know that I live here are not all that many, and of those there can only be one who can come knocking at my door without calling in advance: that same Asko.

He has rapidly gathered his courage—at first, he wasn't even able to speak to me on familiar terms, and mixed up his speech with the polite form all the time. Still, I was surprised by him coming like that in the morning: I wasn't ready for a visit in the very least, and was even wearing old wool socks, because the floors are cold despite the warm weather. I tore them off my feet fast—they remained lying traitorously under the table—and opened the door.

It *was* Asko: he brought back the *Norma* records along with three CDs onto which he had copied the opera. He wanted me to try and see whether it had recorded well, apologizing that it crackled and was in mono. I put one of the discs on and searched for the *Casta Diva* part. It remained the background for our further conversation. He asked whether Bellini was a good composer. I replied saying that he wasn't especially good, and much less my favorite but that he did, however, have beautiful melodies, and that I needed *Norma* because of Maria Callas, etc. Asko remarked that the thing was quite a "rage." I affirmed that it was, yes, a rage performance.

That is a new expression used by young people, to which I currently can't provide a single French equivalent of youth slang— I'm not very familiar with that slang (of course—**argot**!) at all. It's too fine a science, it's too easy to get it "ragingly" wrong and sound ridiculous. As a genuine foreigner, I speak rather that drier standard language, about which I can be more or less certain.

This time, Asko was brave enough to approach my bookshelf and look at the few volumes that were there: the Pléiade edition of Marcel Proust's *In Search of Lost Time* (real leather and gold, although he certainly didn't perceive that; "Bible paper"; 1,500 pages in pocket format) caught his attention. I explained to him that there exists only one small fragment of that super work in Estonian—*Swann's Way*, and wondered how people of his generation could read it. In some sense, that honesty and "cynicism" should be even closer to them than it was to us back in our day—we, who deceived ourselves more with romantic lies, as it seems to me.

The joy which Asko's morning visit created within me, in spite of everything, (once again, I had managed to forget his eyes in the meantime; I had also remembered him being shorter) lasted until six-thirty in the evening exactly. Specifically, we agreed that in the evening, when his seminar project was finished, he would knock or send an e-mail, and then we'd go out somewhere "to chat." To pass the time until then, I had lunch on the patio of Zum-Zum with Martin, who was still in Tartu. Zum-Zum is a café—during the Soviet period, it bore the name "Spark," and was an unlikely café in the sense that it had large windows looking out onto the street, covered only by very sheer curtains, and so it was possible to watch passersby from the table. People mainly ate "wieners with potato salad" there (the "wieners" aren't quite what Viennese sausages are, and the potato salad isn't quite what it is in France or even Germany, because in Livonia it is mixed with mayonnaise and sour cream). Among Spark's specialties were also an ice-cream cocktail, and Soviet sparkling wine that was called champagne (*шампанское*), although it had nothing to do with the Champagne region and was actually made in Riga using some clever (*ingénieux*) method.

I must say that the former Spark has now realized fully, and even beyond expectations, its potential to be a true café in the dreamy, romantic style of small-town France. It has a large patio in summer: the windows looking out towards the street are pushed open, and tables are set in the shade of lush lindens.

The day was genuinely warm: even the breeze was warm, and it was exceptionally pleasant to eat a cheap lunch beneath the lindens. I had the vague feeling that some great new life perspective was unfolding. I kept myself from thinking of Asko. Martin complained that he was troubled by systematic fears of "missing the train": that competitors are more successful than he is, that he won't get such rewarding leads anymore, etc. As my mood was lofty and generous, I was able to, I believe, give him completely adequate advice. I recommended that he try to break through a bit in New York, where he has already done this and that, and probably not unsuccessfully. His fears come from the fact that he isn't moving upwards quickly enough any longer. This might even generate a feeling of descent. If he could manage to prove himself at the next level, then he could look down on his local consultation business from above, which always gives a good platform for asking for money.

"Big invoices must be written boldly—one doesn't dare dispute boldly-written invoices," I, who am not exactly very accomplished in terms of writing big invoices, professed. However, the money thing is simpler in France, too: there exist, in the business of state culture, some quite respectable base prices, below which fees don't drop and with which I'm completely satisfied.

There was some advertisement featuring Michele Pfeiffer's picture in the window of the perfume store next to the café. Martin looked at that poster and said mournfully: "Beautiful people." I said that's the tragedy of it (having in mind the advertisement for men's cologne next to it, which featured the portrait of an unfamiliar male model): we live amid a world of pictures, which has deceitfully raised the standard of beauty to absolutely unreal heights. Such people actually don't exist; even Michele Pfeiffer exists as such only in picture, on video, to put it briefly—in art. The lie is based in the very fact that those pictures are passed off as actuality, as realism. They are a romantic fantasy. I believe that a medieval person had a somewhat different relationship with an icon: it wasn't an ideal with which the surrounding reality was to be compared. Martin admitted that yes, his standard for females has indeed risen so high that it is practically impossible to find women who correspond to it completely. However, he did really like Michele Pfeiffer in that picture. He smiled apologetically.

As there was still much time before evening and I reasoned that Asko definitely wouldn't come knocking before six o'clock (which, as I found out later, turned out to be a false calculation), at around four o'clock, I further decided to go swimming and to the sauna at Aura Aquatic Center; especially since moderate physical activity relaxes you and makes you more charismatic in communication. That aquatic center is new in Tartu, and is a very popular phenomenon. I must say that it is truly an enjoyable spot, which almost erases the feeling of disgust for public pools that I have from the Soviet period (that stench of chlorine, red eyes, the fear of getting some skin infection, the nastily chilly and echoing space). The pool has a large glass wall that faces the street; when resting at the end of the lane, one can observe passersby outside, the blossoming lilac bushes, the sky. Thunderheads were just gathering in the sky and I hoped to see lightning from the pool, but none came. In addition to that, there are, of course, attractive bodies at the pool. Heterosexual men have a fantasy, in which homos "watch" them, lust for them. I must say that fantasy is, for the most part, built on sand. About 90 percent of male individuals (not including children and the senile) are just as erotic as a wardrobe or a Zaporozhets (a certain cheap Soviet brand of car comparable to the East German Trabant). Particularly when they are naked, because clothes may preserve fantasy to some extent. I fear that gay aesthetics are even more exclusive and cruel than the aesthetics of heterosexual men and women (still, the disdain with which they speak about ugly women!). Yet, an ordinary man is often a being whose capacity for self-reflection is mightily limited, because although he regards the majority of women as ugly, he doesn't hesitate to believe he is part of the desirable category purely because he possesses male features.

At the pool, several different forms of expression of the ugliness of the human body can indeed be observed with a certain anthropological interest. This time, I only watched one young swimming coach with a somewhat erotic interest: he was clothed, and maybe aroused my curiosity rather because of the fact that he was watching me with interest. A fantasy from the film *Mon homme à moi* immediately launched in my mind, where a somewhat older swimming coach makes a young swimmer his lover. I was shocked by the frankness and doggedness of the older boy's advances in the film. At the very first opportunity, he asked the (quite wild, *farouche*, shy) swimmer: "*Tu es pédé?*" The latter swore at him in response for being out of his mind, but still ultimately left his girlfriend, etc.

The film was tragic in itself, because that older boy had AIDS (he didn't infect the younger one, of course, so as not to be too tragic) and was supposed to die soon. I, however, would never dare to pose such a question straight away. I could have asked Asko that, for example—then, a number of excessive problems wouldn't have arisen. And I also could have made conversation with that young swimming trainer: there are a thousand different methods for approaching people. I would, under no condition, in any way, however, have dared to approach that powerful, nude swimmer that I saw in the shower room. He was approached by two Swedes—albeit, without deeper intentions—and he spoke with them in poor Swedish, smiling, sparks shooting from his eyes;

he apparently belonged to some Swedish team. The purchase and sale of athletes across national borders is an extensive business. I don't believe, either, that I could ever fall in love with him or with anyone of his type. Falling in love and erotic fantasies are two separate things. Erotic fantasies are logical, standard, and predictable in a certain sense; falling in love is illogical and unpredictable.

Asko knocked on the door practically right after I got home, as if he had heard my steps or something. It later turned out that he saw on the building's local network display that I switched my computer onto the network (I wanted to see whether or not I had any mail from him). The young have their own systems. We went to Wilde Café. As the chairs and tables on the patio had been soaked by rain (the air was steamy and smelled very strong), we had to sit inside. Our conversation about film art had barely managed to begin (I inspected whether his eyes really were crossed, and was no longer so certain of it this time) when his cell phone rang. He answered in a quite reluctant, but obedient voice. He said: "I'm sitting at Wilde with . . . a house neighbor."

The caller was soon there in person. Asko introduced her: "Mailis, my girlfriend."

That's how he put it: my girlfriend. The girl had a nicely-shaped body, but not the prettiest face, and a bad complexion. I had indeed suspected the existence of such a girl in Asko's case, but had not admitted those doubts to myself. To tell the truth, the girl's arrival put me completely out of my wits: my mood fell. Because for me, it is an archetypal situation. At some point, the man conjures up a girl from somewhere, about whom not a word has been said before. The girl is instinctively jealous from the start. Her instinct to call practically right after we sat down at the table was astonishing. I've been amazed by that instinct from women before, also. They might not call you for weeks, and then call right at the moment that you are with someone, who is their competitor in a certain sense; no matter whether it's a man or a woman. Liz Franz's ability to call at the right moment was outright phenomenal. What's more—she herself was located hundreds of miles away. I suspect that at the times when she didn't call it wasn't because she had let the moment slip, but simply because she had generously decided not to call: fine, let him have some fun, we'll skip it this time. Liz Franz did not openly deprecate or interfere in a single one of my relationships; on the contrary, she so much as supported them, encouraged them. And it is because of this that I always told her everything sooner or later. She was a perpetual witness to my relationships' development and failure.

But as such, the surfacing of an "unexpected girlfriend" is classic for me, and I'm already too familiar with the complications that arise from such a triangle as to not have an interest in them. I didn't even bother to start feigning interest and striking up a conversation with that Mailis. It's generally a working channel: to ensnare your lover's (*aimé*) girlfriend, which is that much easier because those lovers are, for the most part, tired of their girlfriends, are cold towards them, and regard them more as fulfilling a custom. Asko and Mailis did not exactly resemble young lovers, either; rather, an old married couple—they spoke in a lightly annoyed tone about going to the store and making food for dinner. The scheme for making your lover's girlfriend fall in love with you is also presented well in the previously cited film, *Mon homme à moi*. Girls are more hazardous, intrepid. We paid the bill and left; I told Asko that he should e-mail me by all means, then I could send him "those things" in return. I said goodbye to him like to the most indifferent acquaintance; how men say goodbye to each other. Friendships between men are based on common boredom, for the most part.

I walked straight from the café to Toome Hill. I was angry with myself. It's already idiotic in itself to think about falling in love, and even more idiotic to arrange an unhappy falling-in-love for myself. Alas, I know no other kind. I've fallen unhappily in love, or else had someone fall unhappily in love with me. I believe, and sometimes, when the hatred from an unlived life leads me to irrational trains of thought, I so much as hope that Liz Franz was able to feel all the joys of being unhappily in love with me. If she was in love with me at all. I don't know that, strictly speaking.

I watched a pair of lovers on Toome Hill—quite young, a Russian boy and girl. They didn't know how to act at all: they stood next to each other, but in a way that twenty centimeters of air was left between them. The girl was holding a small lilac branch that the boy had apparently broken off for her right there. She held it classically, above the cleave between her breasts. Lovers' archetypes are powerful. Walking past a lilac bush, I sensed its strong smell from after the rain. I went straight up to the bush, and immediately saw one "happy" blossom. I snatched it without a moment's hesitation, stuck it in my mouth, chewed it up, and swallowed it down. I thought of Asko's name while doing so, but wasn't able to wish for anything specific. After that, I asserted to myself that I'd cast all of it out of my head (which is still completely possible), because I've promised myself never to develop such fruitless affairs (as if I had fruitful ones to choose from!) ever again in life. Asko is an ordinary boy, who is, on the whole, trying a little to build himself a career off of me. Go make dinner with your confounded Mailis, and be happy. I'm sure, by the way, that they will argue this evening. Both know the reason, and neither will say it aloud.

21

And so, Liz Franz remained in Tartu for either a year and a half, or two and a half years. I don't know for certain, but I believe she didn't sleep beneath the table in the Vanemuine Theater's set room that entire time, and instead found herself some better accommodation. She has a nose for that. She's always been capable of finding herself relatively good, even exclusive dwellings, and while doing so, paying either little or nothing at all. With that ability, she was even Umberto Riviera's business partner in real estate. From what I know, they always went to tour possible purchase projects together. Liz Franz's decisions were categorical every time: she either liked the house or apartment, or she didn't. And Umberto Riviera trusted her intuition, because it brought in quite a hefty amount of money for him. Liz Franz had once warned Umberto about a fishy placement. Umberto pulled his money out of the project, still with profits, right before a crash. After that, he apparently put a certain share (stocks or something else, I don't know for certain) in his businesses in Liz Franz's name, making her financially independent from him with that generous step. In addition, Liz Franz had independently grown her share—indeed not greatly (she is absolutely not a player), but indeed perpetually without a single loss. At least in terms of the acquisitions in Tallinn, I'm able to say that Riviera Holdings' properties are all extra-class and furthermore acquired, as far as I know, cheaply. For Liz Franz also had a definite opinion on prices, every time: either "too expensive" or "suitable."

When she came to Tallinn that early springtime in the mid-sixties, she was already aware of where she would go to live, and that place was an attic apartment located practically behind Tallinn's Town Hall. By that time, Liz Franz had already visited Tallinn

215

repeatedly, of course. I believe that her appearance and habits had gone through a great and quick change. She had learned to observe others and imitate them. She wore fashionable clothing and a fashionable hairdo, but still somehow left a mysterious, somewhat unattainable impression. I imagine that when actual spring came, she walked through a gauntlet of men's gazes down Harju Street in a miniskirt, not looking to the side a single time, her back straight, her bobbed hair arched back, an expression on her face that said she was expected by someone higher-up and more special than those common, boring Soviet Estonian men.

It's also possible that the miniskirt appeared in her wardrobe already in April, and that she indeed sacrificed her ovaries to that very fashion; in the event, of course, that she truly was infertile, as one of her former admirers (*aspirant*) once said maliciously within my hearing range. By walking around in our harsh spring in miniskirts, many young women of that time developed ovarian infections, which, needless to say, can lead to permanent infertility.

Yet, that special person expecting her somewhere ahead, where her non-seeing gaze through eyelashes thickly colored black was focused—that person perhaps *wasn't* so special, observing the situation from the sidelines. I've seen one picture of that Ando Teino in his youth: a nondescript, and even ugly man, in my opinion. But he was a poet.

Ando Teino was five years older than Liz Franz, and had just made a name for himself as a young wonder child. Such stellar success wasn't impossible for a young person during those dynamic years. He had published one thin booklet of poems, but he was known by everyone. At least by everyone that read and counted (*lire, compter*). In truth, the poems were of a quite traditional sort (although free verse, which had once again become legal at the time, could also be found among them); however, even now, they still contain some kind of freshness, lightness, which cannot be found in a single one of Ando Teino's later collections. Liz Franz likely met him in Tartu at some fashionable "underground" (held in someone's apartment) poetry reading, where numerous female philology students at the university, all with secret ambitions to become poets, stared in the poet's mouth and eyes while sitting on the floor.

Liz Franz was neither a university student, nor anyone at all, but at the end of the evening, she grabbed a guitar and performed a song that she had written to Ando Teino's words. That settled it. Their further cooperation, which, by the way, soon also became Liz Franz's first marriage, turned out to be incredibly fruitful. Liz Franz's first widely-known songs were written to Ando Teino's words, such as that *Odd Moon*:

> *I love your silence, for I know:*
> *you hold our love in secret!*

Specifically, Ando Teino rose even higher than himself in a certain sense, writing song lyrics meant especially for Liz Franz that lacked the claim to a depth of thought otherwise characteristic of his poetry. They were truly simple and captivating tunes. Often moving as well, like this: *Cry not, rain of a white summer's day . . .* They were still played frequently on the radio even then, during my younger years, when the marriage between Liz Franz and Ando Teino had long been divorced.

But Ando Teino acquired that apartment behind Town Hall, where Liz Franz moved in, like this: at the moment when he met Liz Franz in Tartu, he actually still lived with his parents on Lootuse Boulevard in the Nõmme district—i.e. in a garden suburb; a lovely, stuffy, hopeless, and certainly exceedingly bourgeois location, especially given the fact that Ando Teino's parents were "better people," so to speak. His father was an instructor at the Polytechnic Institute, and his mother was a

French philologist, a well-known translator. They indeed did not regard Liz Franz, who came from the country and hadn't finished her secondary education, as a worthy partner for their famous son, but when they started to act upon this, they discovered that they had already lost hold of the initiative.

Liz Franz never visited Ando's parents' place in Nõmme. She simply refused to go there. And by the time she came to Tallinn, they already had their own private apartment. The scheme for acquiring it was simple and genius. Namely, Liz Franz sent Ando Teino to the Writers' Union to request an apartment. I don't know what means she utilized to be able to incite so much bravado in the otherwise shy young man (who truly ignited only at his public performances) for him to undertake those unheard-of steps and go straight to the chairman himself. As the step was relatively unconventional (the Writer's Union had its own apartment waiting list), it was productive. The chairman didn't dare turn down the young, extremely popular poet. A certain instinctive groveling before youth is common during a time of changes, such as the 1960s. A just-vacated studio space in a medieval building behind Tallinn's Town Hall was thus set aside for Ando Teino. And Liz Franz (back then, she still called herself Liis Frants) moved in with him.

Ando Teino was a homosexual. I don't know how aware he was of his orientation at that time; in any case, his poetry from that period doesn't allow things to be seen either this way or that, which in itself is already an alarming fact. A normal man isn't ambivalent in his works. Living with his parents, he had hardly had any other concrete sexual experiences, and apparently regarded his fantasies as a light particularity that was characteristic of a poet. Be what it was, the texts he wrote were fantastically suited for Liz Franz to sing. In her mouth, they immediately turned into a woman's song to a man, a young lady's song to her imagined darling. But at the same time, they also could have been a boy's songs to a girl:

each was able to recognize him- or herself in those songs. They were, by the way, somehow very erotic. Ando Teino's parents had apparently later accused Liz Franz of coaxing their son onto a bad path, of making him (with her coldness) a man-lover. Those sorts of accusations are absurd, of course. I don't know a single man who might have become a man-lover because the woman he loved was cold towards him. The man then always goes to another woman to look for consolation, and that wouldn't have been any problem for the then-famous (now almost forgotten, of course) poet—he was up to his neck in admirers. One can assume that Liz Franz, who in pictures from that time had an especially boyish appearance, somehow fit with his fantasies. I've heard through third parties that years later, Ando Teino bragged while drunk that he and Liz Franz had had tremendous sex, and moaned about how he was still in love with Liz Franz. Overall, from what I know (although even they are more like rumors), he still chased boys for his entire ensuing life, and probably did so quite unsuccessfully at that, falling in love with young heterosexual men time and time again. He hung himself five years ago. It was the first time in quite a while that he had been mentioned in newspapers again—partly because of the sensational suicide, partly out of politeness for the once-renowned poet. The obituaries remarked, by the way, "many of his poems became lyrics sung into fame by the internationally renowned songstress Liz Franz." Incidentally, not a single word was mentioned about their marriage, which had in fact been official and lasted for four or five years, from what I know.

Liz Franz became famous very quickly at that time. Initially, she was spoken of as the girl, who sang Ando Teino's poems quite beautifully at closed poetry evenings. Then, they were talked about as some kind of couple's phenomenon—they made an official poetry and song program together, with which they also traveled to Tartu, Viljandi, and smaller places (I wonder whether Liz Franz's mother and father also went to hear them?).

Liz Franz began performing independently after that. She abandoned accompanying herself on guitar, and acquired a small accompanying ensemble in the spirit of her time—sometimes, she was accompanied by only a piano, and the oddest thing was that she was even capable of keeping the audience reined in *a cappella*. Her vocal material was completely untrained, and wasn't anything exceptional. However, she learned very quickly to use the microphone, and the special allure of her singing had never been in how her voice carried, but rather in its languor, its intimacy, its often spoken-like recitation, which at the same time was very musical. She never participated in a single competition for young singers. Her first radio recordings were probably made for some literature show—from there, things progressed according to their natural path. Nevertheless, her first record was released only in 1971: the mills of the national, monopolistic (for the entire Soviet Union) sound-recording company *"Melodiya"* ground slowly. It was a small record, as they were made, with three songs on each side. Four songs on it are to Ando Teino's words, the fifth is a song by a Russian composer, and the sixth is that "Rowan Tree," which was already discussed. The university library's sound archive has that record—I checked. I could listen to it, but I won't. It's in my head. Or my body.

Namely, we had that record at home; my sisters had apparently bought it. I remember its nondescript case: some abstract, pink geometric pattern in the style of the late 60s. *Melodiya* released many records in such a standard sleeve—only larger stars got their own special design. Over time, that pink and white sleeve wore down to become quite tattered, a greasy gray; it ripped open at the edges and ultimately was lost for good, because the record wouldn't stay in it anymore, anyways. That record practically couldn't be listened to any longer either, because the radiola needle only skipped from one groove to another.

But in any case, I won't go to listen to her here in the sound archive, either; much less will I have Asko make a CD copy for me. I don't want to.

By the way, there were no signs of life from Asko himself the entire day yesterday. I checked my mailbox about ten times—nothing. I don't believe that it's just nothing, the busy spring school time, etc. Given his initial eagerness and so much as longing for excuses to do things, it's strange. Of course, yes, one day. What's one day of life? Very little. I went to the market before lunch to buy ingredients for my stew, as well as radishes, lettuce, sweet milk curd, and milk. I figured that if Asko stops by during the day, then I'd ask if he was hungry. A college-student thing. And I'd offer him my stew. It's good, better than he could even guess. Those stews are very simple in and of themselves. On average.

A little bit of oil must be poured into the bottom of the pot (advisably a pot with convex, bulged sides—those are more chic for a stew) and heated, but not until it smokes, of course. Then, brown about 10.5 oz. of ground beef (ten to twelve kroons when bought from Tartu's market) or chopped liver, chicken breasts, chopped beef, etc. in it. The meat should be browned to the right degree according to taste. At the same time, peel four to five medium-sized potatoes (about 1.50 kroons per pound), three larger carrots (I buy them pre-peeled—it's very convenient and doesn't really cost anything: three kroons per pound), chop the carrots into little sections, add it to the grilling meat, and cover. Chop the potatoes into strips, pour over everything else, and cover again. Chop five or six Italian sundried tomatoes (they can probably be acquired from Primo supermarket in Tallinn, for example; I still have some from Liz Franz's reserves—she always brought them from Rome, and I took them along from the kitchen cabinet on Weitzenbergi Street). Those dried tomatoes are salty anyhow, so one practically doesn't have to add salt; in any case, be careful with it. Add those little red pieces right to the stew, and mix everything together. If it starts sticking to the bottom of the pot, add a glass of water immediately. If it doesn't, then allow it to stew without water at first—it'll come out better. Take a jar of Pataka (a British producer of Indian spices—some random selection, available at Tallinn's Stockmann department store, not sure about Tartu), whether Curry Masala (hot) or, even better, a masala with a good amount of chili—and add around a heaped teaspoon of the paste (depending on the strength and your taste) at about the same time as the water. Those masalas jarred with oil are much better than dry spices. A jar is quite expensive—a good fifty kroons, but it lasts for a long time, especially in the case of strong types; however, those have gone off sale for some reason. Stir further, and stew lightly on "one" (if it is an electric stove) until the carrots and potatoes are appropriately soft for you. Make a fresh salad at the same time: to do so, take a small clump of lettuce (four kroons), break it up into small pieces (it's recommended to tear it with your fingers or to leave it whole entirely—I chop it on a cutting board, those large leaves are bothersome), add a teaspoon of sugar, a quarter- to half-teaspoon of lemon juice, a good amount of sour cream, and a pinch of salt, and mix. Then, chop a green onion or chives (three to four kroons for a bunch), add it to the stew that you have taken off the burner. If it now seems that there isn't enough salt, then add salt; but one should account for the fact that the tomato pieces are still salty—the concentration of salt in them has not yet homogenized with that of the entire stew. That potful is enough for about three decent portions. Everything will cost maybe twenty-five to thirty kroons altogether. Preparation time including the trip to the market is about an hour. Moreover, going to the market is a way to pass the time, to some extent, and one can listen to the radio while preparing the dish.

There are primarily pensioners at the market at midday, of course: that is their hour and time to bloom. They select and inspect, form lines for milk curd, have it weighed out in a jar they brought with them, etc. One must build up a little patience. I bought ground beef from a young, flushed meat seller right by the entrance this time. He presumably eats a great deal of meat, I thought: he was outright bursting out of his white apron, but hadn't grown fat in the very least yet. They say that excessive meat consumption makes one bad-tempered (and I've periodically avoided eating meat entirely, partially also mimicking Liz Franz, who, as I've already said, ate practically nothing, at least while I was watching); that young man—who to me indeed seemed older than I am, because I apparently can't imagine that a market meat seller, if he doesn't happen to be a little boy, could be younger than I am—that young, flushed man was, on the contrary, very kind. In addition to his chubbiness, he seized my attention with the fact that while leaning across the counter, he helped an older woman hold her bag open and nestle a piece of meat into it. His ground beef also looked good (not that I make any difference between them, to be honest: some appear to be fattier, some leaner), and there was only a quarter of it left in the container. I was mainly captivated by the meat seller himself, however: there wasn't even an option that I would buy from anyone else. Still, as a "smart market customer," I asked him what ground beef it was. It was supposed to be "mixed" and "really very high quality". I asked for "just about 10.5 oz." He weighed it, it was over fourteen, and said, "oh, that sure turned out to be more!" No problem, I said generously. He also leaned across the counter for me and helped put the little plastic into my market bag, although there was no need to do so, and bid me good day. Such natural amiability and willingness to serve are rare among Livonian salespeople. If they make an effort to be kind at all, then it's done either as a formality or somehow absentmindedly. However, it was as if that hefty guy dedicated all of his flushed blond energy to me personally. I suddenly felt a strong lust for him: I said goodbye indifferently without looking in his direction. He was still in my thoughts when I arrived home. I felt that there was something in him that came from the great and unspoiled strength of those animals, whose meat he sold; something from their innocent sexuality. He suddenly seemed even more erotic to me than Asko with his thin, so much as scrawny boyishness. Even erotic fantasies can offer surprises. However, the main secret, I believe, was the fact that he had "turned" towards me. Genuine attention that is administered to me always charms me considerably beyond a sensible degree. I believe that market boy *is* very sexual, that it lies in his superfluity, and that he shares it unknowingly (symbolically) with all shoppers—even with seventy-year-old women, maybe even with old grandpas, turning towards every one like a sunflower, so that each feels like a sun. I *felt* like I was hot like the Sun. I had to take care of the situation immediately. The room was warm with the midday, the city shuffled outside, the voices and shouts of people sounded into the room, the bell on Town Hall rang twelve, and the well-known marching melody started to play ("Estonia's loveliest town is Tartu, on the Emajõõ-gi's banks!"). But no one sees here into my apartment. The orgasm came quickly, and was powerful. I did indeed remember Asko after it, and became a bit sad that he hadn't e-mailed me.

While chopping vegetables, I thought somewhat melancholically that the realization of one's erotic fantasies in life is the privilege of only very few individuals. Great and powerful rulers (emperors, popes, France's king) could allow themselves that in old times. These days, politicians are under sharpened observation in terms of such things, and aren't allowed to undertake anything bigger. It's no wonder, then, that the number of politicians is ever dropping. What interest do powerful men have in aspiring to that? To some extent, pop stars (that status is indeed much more desirable than being a head of state) and very rich individuals have still retained the privilege of carrying out their fantasies with actual people. Yet, as historical experience has shown, the opportunity to manifest sexual fantasies still doesn't make someone automatically happy. Unhappy, rather. Consequently, happiness—in the event that it exists—lies within something else. Maybe in a simple, loyal, domestic, desireless marriage. I don't know.

The day, the evening were nevertheless still long. I took my bike to head out of town; I planned on photographing Vasula Orchard in the evening light—it was supposed to be in blossom now. When I was just tugging my bike through the building's front door (the door falls shut on a spring), Asko's girlfriend— that Mailis—came from the opposite direction. I wasn't actually one-hundred-percent certain that it was Mailis, but I smiled at her apologetically (because of my bike, which was crosswise in the doorway) and said hello. She greeted me in return. In the event that it was Mailis, she had pulled her long, luxuriant hair—which had been let down last night—into a ponytail, and had probably applied some cosmetics to her face, because her skin seemed better. But it also could have seemed bad on the previous day due to annoyance, agitation. Today, she had a winner's look; at least that's how it appeared to me. Maybe they had a stormy night of sex. Mailis did everything that Asko wanted—finally satisfied his fantasies, his manias. She dominated. Was the man.

22

Two nightingales *chee-chee*-d where Jõgeva Road crosses the Amme River. Their level of reproductive hormones is currently so high that they can't even keep quiet during the day; they otherwise always sing more in the early morning and late evening. A signpost meant for tourists pointed to the left, towards the ruins of the Kärkna Monastery, and I decided to go and take a look at them. There weren't any extraordinary ruins: there was a mount and a couple of sections of wall excavated from the earth, which had been stacked using round granite stones and lime mortar. Granite was brought to Livonia by the glaciers, which had worked the stones loose from the Fennoscandian Shield (granite is visible on the surface in Finland; in Estonia, it is covered by limestone and other sedimentary rocks). Ice and the later current of large rivers of melted ice have worn them into rounded shapes, just as streams wear down pebbles. These large granite boulders pose a great obstacle in Livonian fields during cultivation, and the stones in the monastery wall also apparently came from the surrounding fields, from which farmers hauled them to one place under the monks' direction. Those same monks brought the skill of erecting walls with lime mortar to Livonia, because before that, people here were only able to stack dry walls; actually, however, all structures were made out of wood.

Kärkna (Muuge) Monastery was erected right at the beginning, when Christianity reached this land ahead of the Teutonic Order, or on its heels. It was erected by the Cistercians, the so-called White Monks (their first monastery being in Cîteaux, France). The monastery was built along the Emajõgi in order to fortify that vitally important waterway. Russian warriors destroyed the first monastery (Novgorod did not look kindly upon the occupation of its trade routes) in the thirteenth century, but it was rebuilt to be even more powerful. The location was ideal for a fortress, as the mound was bordered by rivers on three sides: delta branches of the Emajõgi and Amme (*Fleuve-Nourrice*) rivers. Yet, from the names of the rivers ("mother," "wet nurse"), it is already apparent that the place was also very important symbolically. Churches and monasteries were generally always erected upon sites associated with some significant force (*force, magie*) in the local people's beliefs. The place, where the Amme River and the Emajõgi conjoin is so "motherly"—the wet nurse flows into the child bearer—that only a monks' monastery could be built there. The White Monks were most likely those who spread the first rudimentary understandings of the Christian worldview among the local population. What those understandings were exactly, we may never know, because that monastery—and likewise the Bishop of Tartu's archives—were completely destroyed in the Livonian War (late sixteenth century)—just as the monastery itself, which was razed by the Prince's ski-borne warriors.

It is indeed known that in the fourteenth century, the monks concluded with their "own" peasants an agreement stipulating the latter's obligations to take part in the building and military defense of the monastery. In turn, the monastery, of course, also offered defense for the surrounding land; for example, from those same Russian marauders. The existence of this agreement shows that peasants initially did not belong to the monastery, but were relatively free, which topples the widespread national myth of "seven-hundred years of slavery" that followed "submission" (*soumission*). In Livonia, relations between varying religious and secular seigneurs on the one hand, and peasants on the other apparently did not differ much at all from those relations elsewhere in medieval Europe.

In addition to the use of lime mortar (which did not especially influence peasant architecture—peasant families were too poor for that, and the wooden building is also more comfortable in this climate), the monks spread other achievements of civilization at that time, such as erecting water mills, new crops (vegetables that they grew in their gardens), some basic medicine, and notices about the existence of literacy. It is possible that at some time, monks were also recruited from among the local population. This, of course, meant a great social promotion for a peasant boy. It might also have been the case that the still somewhat poor Livonian noble families did not always provide enough sons for populating the monastery (epidemics could frequently decimate (*décimer*) that community), and monks found in the surrounding area a number of boys with handsome faces and good singing voices for joining their ranks. Also accounting for the fact that quite a few boys with handsome faces and good singing voices could have been a monk's own son, for whom he had tender, fatherly feelings. Those illegitimate children (*fils naturels*) of clergy living in celibacy were a widespread phenomenon during the Middle Ages.

And so, the monastery had a water mill for grinding grain, fishing ponds for eating well during fasting, fields, and later also their very own peasants. The monks cultivated the river meadows and floodplains (higher banks, where a river has deposited rich sediments), or utilized them as hayfields and pastures. Back then, the rivers themselves were not only the primary paths for movement and trade, but were also very rich in fish stocks. Livonia's abundance of fish was proverbial in itself during the Middle Ages: only skillful Russian fishermen concerned the locals. Even now, I saw two Russian-speaking people heading towards the Amme River—a young woman with pretty facial features and a man, who could have been either her father or her husband. They split up at the riverbank: the woman climbed onto rocks making ripples in the middle of the river, while the man went downstream. They began fly-fishing, which requires great skill, and with which one can catch valuable fish such as trout (*truite*). As far as I'm aware, it should be illegal to fish right now—they did indeed watch me suspiciously at first, but then decided that I, with my bike, was apparently not a representative of state authority. They most likely resided on the farm (*ferme*) that had a quite dilapidated appearance and was erected right there amid the ruins of the monastery. A radio in the yard played some disco hits loudly, and as I could hear from the signature, it was a local Russian music station. Competing with the disco hits was a nightingale (*rossignol*) with its not-especially-multifarious melody. The strength of the nightingale's voice was outright astonishing, practically overpowering the smallish portable radio. I listened to that interesting duet for some time, and fantasized a little about former monastery life there on the old broken-down water mill's dam.

The mill is, of course, not as old as the monastery—presumably from the nineteenth century, and no doubt built out of stones from the monastery wall. Yet its location certainly dates back to the monastery period. Strong cultural-economic centers retain their spirit and specificity for hundreds of years after their decline. And in the Middle Ages Kärkna Monastery was definitely an important economic, military, political, and cultural (civilization) center. Given the monastery's vital and material functions, which were powerful to that extent, the monks also must have been quite lively, burly figures—something akin to my meat seller, from whom I'll probably still make purchases, although the fantasy about him is no longer as engrossing.

The monks' slogan was *ora et labora*, pray and work, to which the Cistercians from the late Middle Ages further added the enlightened *lectura divina*; however, especially as *labora* fell more and more under peasants' care, their lives—I believe—increasingly became the life of an idle group of men (of course, a hierarchical, organized, committed group of men). I don't know how zealously the monks in Kärkna Monastery's single-nave church fulfilled the obligation of unceasing hymns, which was supposed to keep the surrounding land under the protection of divine blessing. Did they sing in shifts, the whole night through? The Gregorian chant has been called the West's last natural music, it was taught simply by way of imitation—a new monk initially listened to the others' song, and then gradually began to rumble along. Gregorian chant has a strong meditative effect, which even leads one into a trance (*transe, hypnose*). Thus, incessant song might have been not only an obligation, but also an agreeable way to pass the time—so much as a narcotic, in a certain sense; a psychedelic activity. I wonder whether they sang mainly on the upper floor of the church or in the crypt, or if it varied according to the liturgy, the season? The Kärkna Monastery's church crypt was one of Livonia's largest.

The crypt was a church within the church (below the church, to be exact), holiness within holiness, the relic's location, Jesus' grave, and therefore a symbol of renaissance and everlasting life; dead monks were also buried in the crypt. What's also interesting is whether or not a certain stench of corpses developed in the crypt from the decay of bodies beneath the floor. Was that part of it (*memento mori!*)? It's indeed true that a church was often built with this in mind: a crypt's temperature and humidity regime are such that corpses practically mummify. A medieval church was thus—and perhaps even foremost—the burial place of privileged deceased, where cadavers awaited the "resurrection of the flesh," covered in the livings' unceasing prayers and magical acts. The local peasantry was apparently not allowed into the church, just as it was elsewhere in Europe at that time. They could merely imagine those miraculous, chilling rituals while clustered together outside the door, listening to the chant, seeing perhaps the flicker of candles or some baffling activity in the duskiness of the church.

Monks undoubtedly also had some kind of a sex life; however, there is very little information about this, because it probably wasn't regarded as being at all important during the Middle Ages. Firstly, of course, that *ehalkäimine* in the village—an old Livonian folk tradition, which set a framework around pre-wedlock sexual relations, especially during the summer period, at the height of sexual arousal: young men went to "sleep" with young women, which was that much simpler, given that during the summer, the latter slept not in the dwelling, but in auxiliary buildings—in sheds and barns; that said, they generally strove to avoid pregnancy, the consequences of which have already been discussed. Monks could, of course, have been much better and more experienced (*expérimenté*) sexual partners than the young village boys. Yet, a separate sex life undoubtedly took place within the monastery as well. There is particularly little information about *that*, however. The thing is that a certain homoerotic component is always among the forces that cement together every group of men (such as military battalions, sports teams, etc.). Although, this is not discussed within the group in any form other than denial, disdain, and snickering ridicule. It's taboo. Which, however, makes it that much more powerful in one's unconscious. An even greater taboo is to speak about it outwardly. The extent to which this eroticism is realized (in addition to innocent jostling, embraces, half-erect cocks in the group shower), to which it is acted upon (*passer à l'acte*) depends already on the unwritten rules that function in that period and within the given structure; on the overall set of customs. Usually, when it is acted upon, then these acts are practically denied, or their importance is at least diminished to something unimportant—to just like blowing one's nose.

And so, nothing is known about the love lives between Cistercians in the Kärkna Monastery, because there isn't even much known about it where archives do exist. It's also possible that no one has researched the topic. One can believe, however, that even in Kärkna, both couple-based relationships and the dramas of passion that stem from them were part of such life. Their openness or repressed nature depended in turn on the mentality, which was dominant at that point in time in the monastery and its hierarchy. Sexuality in and of itself was probably not such a restricted phenomenon in medieval monasteries as it seems it is today. Our conception of monks' "asceticism" originates firstly from the Counter Reformation, when the Church abruptly tackled that issue in a strict manner; and secondly, from our nineteenth century, which sharply condemned the sort of social organization in which a portion of men are left out of material (re)production. Our laborious (*laborieux*) epoch requires all to produce, all to participate in reproduction. The medieval monastery, however, specifically removed a portion of men from legal reproduction, and thus from sharing an inheritance; thereby ensuring that the family's estate remained sufficiently large, and avoiding a feud between inheriting brothers. It is very possible that the emergence of the monkhood was sometimes also associated with certain homosexual tendencies, which at that time were not acknowledged as such, of course. In any case, the monastery was ideal for living out those tendencies, one's love (which was, naturally, brotherly love, a love of Christ); for the blossoming of a "homosexual" personality, and in a structure recognized by society at that.

Although, many monks at the monastery were ailed by bursts of oncoming acedia—a decline in their life's momentum, boredom, and no doubt a longing for their own hearth, wife, and children. Not one social organization or formal structure guarantees happiness, especially not for the majority.

On the other hand, however, it appears that men are quite well adapted for life in mono-gender hierarchical communities (the military, universities back in olden days, etc.), and do not feel that their personal freedom is oppressed within the limits of a hierarchy inasmuch as the men of one hierarchical level are equals, and they are, in a certain sense, "brothers" along the entire length of the ladder.

It seems that such structures are much more unnatural for women. Firstly because they are biologically that determined to reproduce, and the absence of childbirth is generally a hard sacrifice for them. Liz Franz indeed categorically claimed that she never wanted a child, and that she so much as divorced Ando Teino because he had begun wanting one—that had been hideous: someone wants you to become a progenitor (*génitrice*); the vessel for a child, into which a man pours his seed! Yet, I believe that the actual reasons for the divorce lay elsewhere, and wanting a child was simply Ando Teino's ultimate (*ultime*) attempt to tie Liz Franz to him; an attempt destined for failure.

In any case, convents and all sorts of women's organizations (such as Estonia's paramilitary structure, the Women's Voluntary Defense Organization—*Les Femmes défenseuses du foyer*), women's choirs, women's schools, etc. always seem somewhat perverse to me. As women are the bearers of individuality by nature (and incidentally also the bearers of all new individualities, in the literal sense of the word), hierarchy does not suit them—it has an inhibiting effect; they are not free in it, as men may be. Such an organization is usually led by some Mother Superior (that infamous *Mère Sup.*), who is not, however, a mother, but rather a so-called woman "with balls." At the same time, she obviously does not have any eggs, and as a kind of inverse rooster, only makes sure that not one of her chicken start laying eggs. She keeps them under severe discipline towards this end. While a monk can be chubby, jovial, pleasant, bursting with life, and erotic, a nun is classically repressed and strict-faced—in short, an extinguished, written-off woman. Monks' clothing is imposing in its own way; nuns' clothing makes the women genderless haystacks. In Rome, Liz Franz showed me a special fashion shop (a small street near the Pantheon), where ecclesiastical garments are sold. The clothing there for monks and priests is often elegant to a T, while nuns are only offered various gray smocks and similar gray sweaters (perhaps only the fineness of the gray wool differs). The young women are ruddy beneath their nun's veil at first, of course; but later, that ruddiness turns either into a soured paleness or the fanatical flush of an old maid. They are all under the Mother Superior's strict and manipulative control, capable only of integrating to ensure themselves a personally and temporally better position. Although not to form more lasting unions, which might topple the despotism. Because female friendships are treacherous. Liz Franz, for example, did not have a single "girlfriend" (although there were apparently a few special female relationships, but I'll talk more of that later), and she scorned from the bottom of her heart the entire concept of girlfriend-ness, even the word. She didn't even want to be a female friend to me, but rather a friend, a companion in battle: loyal and steadfast. I didn't perceive any old maid's flush in her case. Nor a soured paleness. And still, she is gone now. And I in my manliness, in my monkliness (in the Middle Ages, I definitely would have been—if I had lucked out in life—a monk; perhaps a Cistercian of that Amme delta rich in fish, walking around in a white cloak), in my simple-mindedness am unable to solve that mystery in any way.

Just as I can't in any way explain Asko's silence towards me in a satisfactory manner. I hear footsteps in the hallway, but they do not stop outside the door to my chamber. Asko has some other winds in his head. He's under a woman's paw. And still wants to become an artist. Imbecile (*imbécile*)! Simply an imbecile. He's already starting to exasperate me.

23

Here, however, I should record the dream I had last night. Namely, I'm thinking that my occurrence—or, to be more precise, the occurrence of Liz Franz plus me—can undoubtedly be of certain clinical interest. I don't mean so much as it having a therapeutic effect for me (or for Liz Franz, if I should some day be able to give her the notes that I plan on making, in any case—if possible). It's probably too late for that, already: the damage in both cases has become somatic, irreversible. But you can never know, either. Yet, more than a personal therapeutic effect, I'm hoping for some specialist's certain educational result for the benefit of other so-called descendent generations, on the basis of these notes.

I don't especially believe in psychoanalysis (talking can undoubtedly have a comforting effect, and even a strong comforting effect), and I've never had so much money that I could go to see an analyst in Paris. I've spent time in Estonia too irregularly, however, and neither would I trust Estonian therapists: too small of a country, too little anonymity—knowing everyone and talking behind people's backs are the norm. In addition to a lack of money, I was also hindered by linguistic deficiencies in France. I would have to overly think about the sentences I form; they wouldn't come out as being that spontaneous. Thus, what I am left with is writing—become of these notes what may. However, I haven't spoken about a single dream so far because I haven't seen any; that is, I haven't remembered them, or at least nothing significant. I did indeed remember one dream meanwhile, but it was so embarrassing that I can't bear to write it down. Nor do I need to. Every confession has its natural limits.

The dream I had last night involved water, the primary reasons for which must be sought in what was occurred during the day.

First of all, I forgot both my wallet and sunglasses when riding out on my bicycle; I didn't bring a water bottle either, thinking that I would make a stop at some village store. However, I had only three kroons in my pocket, partly in coins. One can't get anything drinkable for that, not even from a village store. As it was a stifling day, however, I was plagued by thirst already after Kärkna Monastery. The body's loss of water is astonishingly quick under conditions of physical activity and high temperature, and sport physiologists recommend (Martin taught me this) starting to fight dehydration before thirst develops, adding small quantities of water to the body regularly. Consequently, it wasn't possible for me to do this.

Back in the day, even back when I was a university student, it was customary for travelers in Livonia to drink from farm wells. Asking for water, drawing it up from deep within the bowls of the Earth, and drinking it right from the cold rim of the pail with streams flowing down from the corners of your mouth were a part of a journey's ritual. Now, however, large, angry packs of dogs have sprung up on farms (a fear of burglary), and occupying the farms themselves is often only a half-deaf, terrified old woman, who might even set a dog on you herself. Farm wells, especially during the past epoch of large-scale socialist production, likewise fell victim to agricultural pollution, and one can never know whether their water is still clean, or whether it contains some microflora, to which your body is unaccustomed. As such, I didn't dare take that traditional path. It would also have been odd to go up to the stairway of some apartment building with "amenities," i.e. running water (*eau courante*), knock on the door, and ask for a drink from the tap.

The social atmosphere of those apartment buildings and their vicinity is very much repellant these days. As remnants of the former political-economic formation, the central settlements of collective farms have now fallen to the extreme margin (*marge*) of the social order, along with their inhabitants. The situation in the manorial heartlands might have been somewhat analogous following the land reform and the expropriation of said manors during the 1880s, when manors' hired hands (so-called *moonakad* in Estonian, from the word *moon* ("provisions")—they were traditionally paid in goods) were likewise left without work, and the manors' large workers' dwellings lost their purpose. Yet, during that period, the workers most likely found themselves application in the new economic structures, which constituted farms erected upon the manor lands. As agricultural production is in a downturn throughout all of Livonia right now, however, the former kolkhoz laborers often lack any sort of application, such as the opportunity or initiative to move to a city (that nevertheless requires certain start-up capital). And so, they often declass family by family. Drinking, along with several kinds of abuses of cheap toxins (the "sniffing" of easily-volatile substances, such as mineral spirits or others), are widespread among central settlements. I can't imagine what the situation might be in those places' schools, for example.

Considering the etymology of the word *moonakas*, I further realized that these days, a dominant portion of the population in our developed countries belongs to this class: salary earners. Then, however, I asked myself: was Liz Franz also a hired hand? For she generally did not own any land or means of production (yes, not counting in terms of the latter, the securities she received from Umberto). But she wasn't a salary earner, either. In her life, she only marketed her work in the form of performing and recording about thirty songs—that took up a trifling part of her time. As such, she was rather among the class of people (I grasped this while biking under a high-tension power line, upon which a row of crows sat) who are paid more for what they *are* than for what they *do*. This has always been the privilege of the nobles, the clerics, the few chosen ones. As far as I know, Liz Franz only "went" to do salaried work those couple of years, when she slept in the Vanemuine Theater's set room and brought the old men bread from the store. She was formally employed at a library at some point during her Tallinn period, although someone else did the work and received the wages. That was a widespread and mutually-beneficial system at the time: it was illegal and punishable to be unemployed, and working in several places at once was likewise restricted.

But so, I had nowhere from which to acquire water. I finally stopped at a small gas station near Kukulinna, which in addition functions as the local 24-hour alcohol store (all kinds of strong liquors and beer were the small shop's main goods), and asked the saleswoman whether they might have a water faucet. At first, she led me to the spigot outside, which was out of order (*en état de disfonctionnement*). When the saleswoman realized that I just wanted to drink, she filled up an empty bottle of mineral water from the faucet in their back room. I was extremely thankful to the woman, which probably even seemed exaggerated to her. I had another good drink of the water on the bank of Saadjärve Lake, near Kukulinna Castle. Kukulinna's "castle" is a run-down structure with ridiculous jagged wooden towers; apparently a small, romantic summer manor built sometime at the turn of the twentieth century. During the Soviet period, a pioneer camp was there, the buildings of which are still around now, as is the unpleasant atmosphere. I hate camps, having been at a sports camp only once during my childhood (I attempted fruitlessly and without any great ardor to learn how to play tennis, mainly in order to get my father to like me just a little; however, tennis didn't fit with me one tiny bit, and I got no farther than hitting the ball against a wall). Luckily, the camp is now abandoned. The castle's wooden towers were also sagging greatly.

The second instance involving water was in the evening, already at twilight, a thundercloud (the first lightning this spring) rose above Tartu: lightning flashed, lighting up the room, and it thundered quite heavily; however, the cloud didn't quite come *over* the city, and not a drop of rain fell.

And so, the dream was such: I lived with a female acquaintance, which was apparently my Swedish-Estonian female friend Linda (I'll speak about her at greater length later), at the home of a mistress—some German or Russian lady. I, however, belonged to a category of the population, which according to a state decree (it was wartime), was subject to execution by drowning. I was taken to a dim space with a low ceiling, a cellar, where there was a shallow, murky pool, and was forced to step into it. I walked in without looking back; the water was quite shallow. I lay down in order to drown, but my head still stuck out above the water; I floated like a cork. Then, I dove under the water myself and drew water into my lungs (I was afraid that they would start shooting at me, torturing me). Yet, the drowning *still* did not ensue—the water in my lungs didn't even especially bother me.

Thereafter, a fat, naked girl with very white skin—also to be exterminated—was brought there. I beckoned her to come to me in the water, saying something like that it was more sociable to be dead together, anyway—or at least to die, because I suddenly felt fear and loneliness. She cast herself on top of me, but it was unpleasant, suffocating. I said: "No, not on top! Let's just hold hands."

But drowning still did not occur—I always got more air from somewhere by secretly tricking (*tricher*) them. I finally had enough of it, heaved myself out of the pool, and went back to the house. It was starting to rain—the housewife was worried about her geraniums on the balcony, and rushed out to save them. I contemplated that she was a good person per se, but even so, would send her tenants into peril without hesitation when the law requires it. That mistress could go and turn me in. But I was still alive. I said to Linda with a deep sigh: oh, Jesus *Christ!*

Then, I started washing the car in the rain. Seeing the rivulets of water that flowed down the windshield, I suddenly felt immense happiness for being alive, and began to cry. I woke up from that crying, hearing my unnatural sobs already as I awoke. But my eyes were dry.

*

In a phenological sense (May 15th), spring has gotten to the point where the first dandelions are seeding (*se propager*)—their parachute-shaped seeds flew against me the entire way. Willows' "wool"—their seeds—drifted near the rivers. Carp (*carassin*) were smacking loudly in the pond in the botanical garden, eating the phytoplankton developing on the surface of the water. Hearing that sound, I for some reason had the desire to describe the situation in Tartu dialect, something like: "*Lämmi päiväkene om. Kogre matsutava tiigin.*"

Flowering season has begun for the early strains in the iris section. While that white and strangely-scented Bokhara iris somehow reminded me of Liz Franz—but of Liz Franz naked, I'd say—those blossoms with large, velvety, and strongly-colored petals (dark red, violet-gray with a shade of silver, dark blue) remind me, to move forward in the comparison, of Liz Franz in several kinds of performance costumes. But that is pure fantasy. The thing is that actually, I've seen her on stage only one single time—then, in Paris. That time, she was dressed from head to toe in black, which made her small and fragile—boyish once again, like in the early days. True, I also saw her on television in my childhood and youth, but we naturally had a black-and-white receiver (there weren't even shows in color yet), and I have no memory at all of her costumes back then.

The building stairway is either empty, or occupied only by the smoking telemarketing women from below, who have apparently lost interest in me, because they don't bother me anymore. Or some Russian consulate worker comes, or else it is some unfamiliar tenant. I see the Finnish Apollo and his dogs (he now only has one poodle and a white dog—I can't figure out whether I was seeing double the first time, or if the other poodle was really the model's) while looking out the window, both in the morning and the evening. But I haven't encountered Asko again, even though I saw him every day in the meanwhile—even at ten o'clock on the Sunday morning when I went to Viljandi. He came from the bus and had a sleepy expression, apparently having slept in it, broiled from the morning sun. I knew that he had gone home for Mother's Day, as he said. I had asked that time on the roof whether he was from Tallinn (being almost certain of it—he couldn't be from anywhere else with his necklace and open personality), but he replied that, no—he was from Central Estonia, from Ruunissaare; but right, yes, I've already written about that.

I know that I shouldn't call him first. Firstly, that cell phone could somehow be shared with Mailis, and anyway, Mailis certainly secretly checks the phone's call log. Secondly, by calling first, I would give the initiative away in a paradoxical manner. That, I also learned from Liz Franz. Every time a silence had lasted between us (and it was always by my initiative, during the time of my little abscondings)—it wasn't a matter of days, of course, but rather weeks; even months—I was always the one, who broke the silence. I couldn't resist (*résister*). In a relationship, you should never leave the impression that you need the other significantly more. That automatically makes the other person more uncaring (Liz Franz indeed never became more uncaring in relation to me; on the contrary, she cared lastingly and time and time again—but that was even worse). I have to be patient. At the most, I can sit on a bench in the park near the building so that when Asko comes or leaves home I can approach him without it being forced. I can't stand around in the stairway all the time or run up and down the stairs either, of course.

24

In the evening, just like last night, a black thunderhead rose up over Tartu; but this time from the south, from behind the department store. And this time, it truly started raining. I reached home just before the rain. I don't remember what I was doing there outside—probably just hanging around restlessly down by the river, watching a log caught behind a red buoy across from Atlantis Nightclub and the eddies forming around it. The Emajõgi's current is still quite rapid in Tartu. The river's downward slope is generally very low—the water's movement is barely visible in the swamps of the upper and lower course of the river. It starts from a lake, a smaller one—Võrtsjärv; and runs into a lake, a large one—Peipus. That water (I wonder which "that" water is?) ultimately reaches the sea, of course, through the aforementioned Narva River. The Narva River has rapids, and that is why it's never been possible to travel by boat from Tartu to the sea. However, boats did once go from here to Pskov. Now, they apparently want to restore the traffic. I looked towards the harbor—indeed, currently not a single riverboat was to be seen there. At one time, a few millennia ago (I don't know exactly when, and does anyone know?), the Emajõgi was said to have flown in the opposite direction. There was no watershed between the Emajõgi and the Pärnu river basin at the time, and a very large river flowed from Peipus to the Baltic Sea, diagonally from east to west. It was the primary path of trade and movement and trade for people at the time, as much as they exchanged goods. That powerful river was simultaneously the border between two linguistic zones, of which the difference between northern and southern Estonian dialects still exists as a memory to this day. They were two distinct lands. I don't know what was there at that time, on the site of Tartu; no doubt some stopping point for people, perhaps a river crossing-point. Tartu was then a frontier post (*poste frontière*). The southward land was no doubt kinder and more populous even at the time; the northward emptier and more desolate. Later, the border dividing the Estonian and Livonian Governorates ran along almost the same line, only slightly to the north. The river split into two as a result of an upheaval of the Earth's crust: specifically, the coastal rim of Western Estonia is rising over the course of time—it is inertia remaining from the cessation of the former ice masses' pressure. Yet, the waterway still remained in use for a long time—boats and goods were transported across the watershed even during the Hanseatic period. Now, it has slipped into oblivion, and one cannot travel from Tartu to the sea by ship.

Looking towards the empty and quiet river harbor, I was reminded of the Estonian word for "river tram." A river tram could run, for example, I don't know—between Tartu and Ihaste, where there are summer cabins (*datchas*). A river tram would make Tartu more metropolitan. Tallinn has an ordinary tram. Paris has a metro. A metro will never be built in Tartu. Liz Franz was boarding a river tram in the last postcard that I received from her. It came from Venice. The postcard showed a historic black-and-white picture of a *gondoliere*, or whatever they're called. The *gondoliere* in the photo was a young man with a face that corresponded to the ideals of beauty at the time, but is now too rounded for the current ideal; he is probably twenty years old, but looks thirty to the modern eye. The postcard is affixed to the wall here above my desk with double-sided tape (it will come off nicely and not leave a mark, which would annoy the landlord), next to the picture I took of the Kavastu ferryman. The ferryman is sitting and rowing, not looking at the lens; the *gondoliere* is standing up straight in his gondola, wearing wide *gondoliere* pants, his white shirt open at the chest, a brilliant but somewhat too simple-minded smile on his face, holding the pole.

Liz Franz never wrote letters, but she sent me postcards regularly—once per week on average. She repeatedly instructed me to destroy them, promptly after receipt, whether by burning them or ripping them into pieces and flushing them down the toilet—she didn't care. She didn't want to leave any traces, and I have generally seen that this is an attitude that pays off. Traces are always more harm than good. That is, the traces that you leave personally. Others' traces are indeed necessary—you can follow a person along them, stay on their heels (*les suivre*).

I have obediently fulfilled that order to destroy her correspondence, and as such, I don't have a single one of Liz Franz's postcards apart from that last, which was initially left undestroyed. My disobedience regarding the postcards was in the fact that I didn't destroy them promptly, one by one, but rather waited until a good quantity had collected, and then destroyed them all at once; in Paris, I actually just took them to a trash can, reasoning that no one there understands Estonian anyway, nor would anyone have any interest—trash is immediately compacted into a homogenous mass in the garbage truck. So, that card, which I regarded as merely one in an unending line of Liz Franz's cards, remained with me, because additional ones haven't come. On the back of the cards that Liz Franz sent was often only one sentence, a couple of words, or sometimes a longer description of her mood. For the most part, there was also something there directly about me. Some encouragement, a complement, sometimes a dream she had of me. In a certain sense, I needed those postcards—they confirmed my existence each time: that I am and can continue to be. There was nothing more on the back of that Venetian card than the following lines:

It was very quiet and light in Lido. Spring is in the air. You should visit this city sometime, but maybe in fall in particular. Then it's the right time, the canals stink. We're boarding a river tram now and going away. Be brave. Your That.

"That" was her usual signature. I don't know how she signed her cards for others; no doubt it depended on the addressee. I also don't know if she had already used that signature before—for example, during Ando Teino's time, in the event that she sent cards to him at all, which is quite unlikely, because she didn't travel much then, and when she was traveling—to Riga—then she probably didn't write "Your That" to Ando Teino any longer. Or she did, who knows. The Venice postcard bears a *Venezia* postmark with the date 02-20-01—the twentieth of January. To me, it felt that much more time has passed since then. Since when she disappeared. I definitely knew that it was January, but it seemed as if at least a year had passed already. But it is: January, February, March, April, half of May. Four to five months. By the way—looking at that date, I note that it could have been the anniversary of our meeting, although I don't quite know for sure what day it was in that January of 1991, when she was waiting for me there in the hotel foyer. Our eleventh anniversary, in that case. But why not. Liz Franz despised the decade system for anniversaries. Perhaps she had secretly set up some system based on elevens for herself. Maybe it just happened that way. "We're going" on the postcard apparently means that she was there with Umberto Riviera, who also had some kind of real estate in Venice. It wasn't the first time that they visited Venice together. "Away" meant Rome for me back then; now, I don't know. I also don't believe that the recommendation to visit Venice might mean that she actually is in Venice. From time to time, it does seem so to me, but that's just a usual system of thought: for our semiconscious, people always remain in the places, where we last saw them or last heard from them. As such, for a moment last night I had the ludicrous desire to stop by Wilde's patio, as if even now Asko would still be sitting where I left him, with his incessant Mailis. I managed to overcome that urge.

Lido was naturally "empty and light" because it was January. That it's superb to visit Venice in fall, when the canals stink, is classic, well known from literature. And the "river tram" is Liz Franz's equivalent for some Venetian water transport, which is hardly a river tram—more like a water tram, for example. A river tram (*речной трамвайчик*) is apparently a memory of hers from Moscow or from her concert trips to Leningrad at that time. I came upon this thought when I heard an Alla Pugacheva song of same name. Alla Pugacheva is Liz Franz's contemporary, but is a megastar, and continues to be a megastar in both the Russian and entire former Soviet Union's showbiz. They got along to some extent during her Moscow years—I should investigate that trace further. In any case, Liz Franz never spoke disparagingly of Alla Pugacheva. She had a certain generosity, and they didn't compete in quite the same weight category, anyway—Liz Franz's genre was undoubtedly more intimate, chamberlike, lyrical. Yet, there is also something similar about them: that sort of *ulitsa*-boyishness and fondness for homosexual men. And as such, the impression has been left somewhere in the "depths of my mind"—absolutely involuntarily and in the same way as how for me, the daily *Postimees* is still published in Tartu—that Liz Franz is still, ever boarding a water tram in Lido, Umberto is somewhat annoyed by her, as usual, is extending his hand with an apologetic smile, and the tram is just about to shove off to head to its next stop. I arrived home just in the nick of time to pull my skylight shut before the large downpour. Otherwise, there would have been a bona fide flood pouring into the room. For the rainfall was truly powerful. At first, it seemed that the clouds would disperse this time as well, would allow a few rare drops to drop into the dust, so that the ground beneath the trees remains completely dry and the sky clears up again in the evening. But then, the rainfall picked up suddenly. I opened the window and watched the lightning show. I still remember lightning from childhood in connection with panicked closing of the windows at my grandmother's direction, ripping the radio plug from the wall, shutting the stove flue (a valve that closes the smoke shaft so that heat absorbed into the oven or stove bricks does not diffuse into the atmosphere), even if there was a fire below: in that case, my grandmother threw water into the flames with a ladle, and the entire kitchen was filled with acrid smoke. I don't know—maybe in the country, in the case of singly-situated farmhouses, those measures of precaution (plus a categorical ban on being near the window during a lightning storm) have some rational justification. There should, however, be lightning rods everywhere in a city (here, starting from the church towers and Plasku shopping center), so that lightning "striking in" is practically ruled out. Interestingly, a number of the lightning bolts struck in a U-shape, as if the electrical solution was headed back into the cloud. Maybe that's just how it is—a short-circuit happens between two clouds? The water fell in a uniform white curtain; a couple of people apparently rushing to the bus station attempted to shield their heads with a portfolio or a plastic bag while keeping to beneath the trees—otherwise, the street was empty. I remembered that I had half a bottle of white wine in the refrigerator. I bought it just in case, back when Asko was supposed to come and take a look at the Internet connection. To offer him something to drink, as people do out of politeness; even to "workmen," at least in France. So if he chose wine, then all the better. He modestly chose juice, but that wasn't all the worse. On that occasion, everything still went like clockwork. I've poured myself a glass from that bottle on a couple of occasions since then. Alone. I thought of offering some to Signe during the day as well, but then I remembered that she can't take wine: she has kidney stones or something of the sort, apparently as a psychosomatic ailment.

I called Signe at the genetics department around lunchtime, and invited her to come over and eat yesterday's stew, as well as in order to have a housewarming party (in Estonian, a "bread-and-salt party"—probably a Russian tradition of offering a newcomer, a new resident, symbolic bread with salt; this corresponds to the French version of hanging a trammel in the fireplace: *pendre la crémaillère*). The thing is that a particular rigidity makes changing plans that were already set once very difficult for me. As I had planned to share that stew with someone—more specifically, with Asko—and as there hadn't been a peep out of that "someone," I had to somehow carry out my plan regardless. And so, I invited Signe. What's more, I could be certain that she wouldn't stay for longer than an hour, because the lunch break for the department chair's (*cathèdre*) secretary is strictly outlined.

And so, I poured myself a glass of white wine and sat at the window with it to watch the lightning storm. It felt like it could be celebrated—what *was* still that spring's first true rain—true **lightning** with rain. That word always reminds me of the song "Oblivion" from Liz Franz's later period:

> *Spring's lightning rains, the unthinking of youth;*
> *Now you need money, and may a roof be over your head . . .*

As soon as I had gulped down a couple of sips of wine (some time had already passed since my lunchtime stew as well, and my stomach was empty), it seemed simple and natural: to take the cell phone from the windowsill and write Asko a text message. Driven by some kind of (as I saw it) inspiration, I knew what and how to write, so that it would seem at once neutral, even indifferent, but would still have an effect on his emotions: *What a downpour! Good. Was supposed to send you reading* [we had talked about the working script and my notes for the film about the Forest Brothers, as well as one script of my own], *but haven't received your e-mail. I'm still at xy@email.ee.*

That's the sort of SMS I sent, without a period at the end, naturally. It was also possible that he had forgotten my address, or had mixed up the e-mail server with the mail server, which is in much wider use. I use that address primarily while in Estonia, because my "noos.fr" mailbox is not always accessible here (just as the e-mail server in Paris). The Internet is only as universal as they say, in terms of the idea.

That action—sending the SMS—suddenly filled me with an extraordinary sense of satisfaction. I poured myself another glass of wine. It was some Australian wine. I never buy French wines here—the selection is very bad and outrageously expensive. I'm otherwise not very demanding about wines, and don't even drink them especially. I become drunk and then sleepy very quickly; not counting the times when I've been in some especially compelling conversational situation, like when I was last with Asko at that Chinese restaurant. In that case, a little wine even makes me sharper.

Contrary to widespread opinion in Estonia, one doesn't in the least have to drink wine alone in France. Many of my Parisian acquaintances don't drink it at all. Amid, although "Muslim," even drank it—that was a part of his integration (now, he no longer drinks, of course; he abhors it, I assume), and in that sense, we were well matched for getting drunk just as quickly as the other. The French can take at least five times more than I can. But imbibing wine there at the window, Amid suddenly seemed distant to me, forgotten. He was very much in my thoughts just a couple of days ago. The mind is an exceptionally inconstant substance. I remembered instead that during one of our stairway encounters, Asko had made the proposal—completely by his own initiative—for us to go cycling together. I remembered that, and suddenly, I was certain that we would. He'd reply to me soon. Soon, the phone did beep, and the screen displayed a text message. But upon pressing the "read" button, it turned out that it was from Linda—simply: *How's it going? I'm a little depressed, but otherwise OK. Kisses. L.*

She sends such texts from time to time, completely randomly—this time, apparently as a reminiscence of our Tallinn meeting three weeks ago. Those messages don't especially mean anything. She's had an instance of loneliness, of relationship deprivation. That kind of mood. I almost got angry with Linda, and decided not to call her just yet as punishment. I went outside, instead; the rain had passed. The water had carved rather deep ruts into the slope of Toome Hill, into the gravel park paths; the downfall truly had been strong. And the sky hadn't cleared either, but remained dark blue—one could guess that it would start raining again soon. It was unusually dusky—especially beneath the lindens on the riverbank, the leafage of which has become very shady over the last few days. The lampposts lit up; their yellow lights reminded me of all sorts of other evenings. I stopped and stood on the new pedestrian bridge in the botanical garden. I suddenly felt a very great loneliness myself. A feeling of loneliness is completely irrational by nature, because realistically my situation has not changed significantly in terms of that over the last twenty-four hours, or even over the last few years. The evening was similar to 90 percent of my nights. Yes, I have tolerable company perhaps every tenth night on average, and good company maybe every fiftieth. So it has been for at least the last four or five years since Amid, viewing it with a statistical gaze, and so it was before him as well: even Amid was only an episode, an exception, which apparently confirms a rule; or rather, to stay specific, was a situation that fell under a different rule. Now, the first and primary rule is in force: you are alone.

I studied the passing couples. About 80 percent of the youth that walk here in the evening do so in pairs, mainly in mixed pairs. That seems to be the standard. Oftentimes, the pairs are apparently forced together uneasily—for lack of someone better, so as to not differ from the standard. I watched their faces, their states. It is generally asymmetrical. One wears a happy, satisfied expression; the other one is more or less indifferent, even fed up. One is glowing, the other has an ordinary complexion. One wants to walk arm-in-arm, the other is bravely tolerating that uncomfortable movement. Symmetry is a rare exception, and it has two variations in turn. The more frequent one is that both have quite fed-up looks, both expressions speak of thoughts and intentions that are connected more with something in front of them than the someone beside them. It's amazing that this matrimonial harmony of boredom is acquired at such an early stage. But practice makes perfect. Another, more rare symmetrical variation is, of course, the classic couple in love—looking directly at one another, both burning with desire, etc. Nevertheless, something that is indeed barely noticeable can almost always be identified—that for one of them, it is a force of nature, an absolute psycho-physiological inevitability; and likewise for the other, but only barely: he or she partially has to act it, to stand at the height of the role's demands. One is; the other is, **too**. By the way, the same laws of frequency also apply to same-sex couples, to friends and girlfriends. There is always one in a friendship who wants it, and the other who permits, allows it to unfold. One who waits, and another who is going out of their mind.

Such were my empirical observational results between ten and eleven o'clock in the evening in the green area along the Emajõgi in Tartu. And at that moment, I would have liked to be any one out of any of the couples walking past. Even the more fed up of the two fed-up people. I tried to call Martin, who was supposed to be in Tallinn, of course; but still, just to talk, all the same. His phone rang, then went to voicemail. He had a charismatic message recorded for it. "I await . . . [pause] your messages." He says this in an especially deep voice. For me, it has long been worn-out and annoying, even irritating. But he hasn't changed it in years—it works, apparently. Although the signature is old, its listeners are new, and every one of them believes that the statement is stated for him or her personally. Martin was most likely at the gym, and had simply left his phone in the dressing-room locker without switching it off. I didn't say anything—I hung up at the first syllable.

The next number I dialed was, regardless of my intentions to give her the silent treatment, Linda's cell. She has a Swedish number. But so what, I thought. A long-distance call might be quite expensive, and that much more pointless given that Linda herself may be in Tallinn. But she also might be in Stockholm—I don't remember what she said about her plans. The fact that I had seen her in Tallinn didn't mean anything about that given moment, strictly speaking. Linda's phone rang for some time, and then came Linda's somewhat strained, brisk voice—first in Swedish, then in Estonian: "I can't answer right now, but please leave your message; I'll call you back quickly."

I listened to it all the way through and remained silent. She'd see that I'd called, anyway. She often leaves her phone at home, or at someone's place, or in a café. Or else it is in her large, incessantly messy purse: Linda was sitting in a pub somewhere (she even goes to clubs) and couldn't hear her phone ringing because the music was loud, and on top of that, she had put it on silent sometime during the day so that it wouldn't "stress" her out.

There wasn't anyone else to call, especially: for everyone else, my call would have been too out of the ordinary to just chat for no reason. I won't call my mother or father either, of course, although I've done it at times when in a similar mood and as a last resort. It always only makes things worse. There is probably some automatic assumption that they are always awaiting your call; that they're thinking of you, etc. Actually, they've long since had their own world, in which I, of course, have some determined, quite unchanging, and also quite limited place. We have nothing to talk about. Their indifference (I'm indifferent anyway—it's natural) drives me to despair. They used to only talk about grandchildren; that is, my sister's children—now, they are in high school, and their relationships with their grandparents have apparently cooled. Neither do I watch the same television shows as my mother or father (their repertoires differ from each other greatly, and their television schedules frequently conflict—at the same time, out of some habit of doing everything together, they don't have two televisions); otherwise, we'd have an abundance of topics for conversation. My mother talks about them sometimes, and I don't really understand any of it. It is some form of living in itself—television-show characters. My father might, however, start speaking about land and forest affairs, in which I don't wish to be mixed up in the least.

I thought about Linda to pass the time while climbing up Toome Hill once again (it was already quite dim, almost dark; unaccustomed). She belongs to the second (or even third) generation of expatriate Estonians. Her parents were one of the some twenty thousand, who fled the Soviet forces across the Baltic Sea to Sweden during World War II. They were just small children then. Nevertheless, they were raised in quite a nationalist spirit. The immigrants—more appropriately, refugees (*réfugiés*), as they call themselves—initially lived in the firm belief that the Western countries would do something, even if it meant the arrival of World War III, that Estonia would become free again and welcome them with open arms. Their parents (just as Linda's grandparents, for example) did not actually adapt to Swedish society (nor did those in Canada, the US, or Australia, to where many moved). They themselves, like Linda's father, also adapted poorly because of it. They were put into a special Estonian high school, and their parents only spoke about Estonia at home—as if Sweden didn't even exist. Although Swedish citizens, they grew up into fiery Estonian patriots. They remembered Estonia itself either foggily or solely based on their parents' stories. They only married among themselves, for the most part—inter-ethnically. What nonetheless happened with Linda's father was that he fell in love with a Swedish girl, and married her. As his parents spoke Swedish poorly, they couldn't really converse with their daughter-in-law, and their daughter-in-law in turn didn't want to visit them; it was only the grandchildren who reconciled them somewhat. Their grandparents indeed strove to teach them Estonian, but they went to a Swedish school and didn't really want to speak the language. They wanted to be like the others. Linda has told me about how she hated Estonian Sunday school, Estonian girl scouts' camp; about how, with her mother and sister, they formed a silent common front against her father's baffling and anachronistic nationalism. Her father—just as the majority of Estonian emigrants—had almost extreme right-wing views and was an anti-communist anyway, but he also believed that Sweden accepted too many "foreigners"—especially blacks and Arabs. Linda started attending a communist youth club at the end of high school, and went on to study political science. She even stopped accepting money from her small-scale entrepreneur father, which the Swedish educational-support system also enabled her to do. But then came all of those singing and velvet revolutions and the freeing of Estonia: suddenly, Linda's fellow university students were interested in her heritage. She had to give speeches at the political science department, had to speak about the occupation of the Baltic States and their fight for freedom. She gathered up the ridiculed fragments of memory left over from her childhood. "I was lying so much that . . . I lied my pants off!" Linda told me, feeling proud of using of that idiomatic expression.

By then, she was already in Estonia. Namely, Linda was one of the few expatriate Estonians who, when freedom arrived, went from words to deeds and tied their fates with Estonia again to some extent. The majority of "refugees" were only interested in real estate that could perhaps possibly be made into money in the future. They formed an influential lobby group, which influenced naive homebred Estonian politicians to develop the kind of legislation that would guarantee the widest possible restitution of pre-war assets. Linda herself, however, so much as invested in Estonia's industrial sector. Around one hundred women were employed at her sock factory, which was located in a small town somewhere. Linda lastly informed me proudly that the women at that sock factory are already earning nearly 2,500 kroons (150 euros) per month. Linda herself spends at least twenty-five thousand kroons per month when in Tallinn, but that's another story.

And so, when we met, Linda worked for subsidiaries opened in Estonia by her father's company (the sock factory wasn't the only one: cheap labor could also be found elsewhere in Estonia), and was trying to study at the University of Tartu. She had been about twenty-four years old when she came to Estonia, and her main worry had actually been the fact that she was still a virgin. When we met, she was around twenty-six or twenty-seven and was no longer a virgin. I had come to Tallinn from Paris: it was for some gathering of the film community, back when I still attended them. Linda tried actively to associate with people in the arts. She had very high ideals for men, and not a single boy in Sweden had met them. We connected that night for some reason, and Linda spoke to me about her virginity for the first time right away—already in the past tense then—as well as about how she had been fed up with it. She apparently hadn't dared at all to visit a gynecologist in Estonia, because she feared that she would be looked upon as a handicapped person, as abnormal. "Estonia is *so* racist!" she complained. In the meantime, she had already developed the fantasy that as a virgin, she would have to give birth to the Son of God, and looked into the biblical lore on the topic. Then, she spoke about it to her therapist in Sweden, who had apparently seemed alarmed by it. I was interested by that topic, because I had always wanted to know how it is for women: whether there is some kind of a feeling, whether it is physically different, when you're a virgin. Linda said that there wasn't, but psychologically (her melody of speech was still Swedish-sounding, and she was never quite adopted into Estonian society; that's the reason why we got along immediately—I made nothing of it)—"Psychologically, it was constant stress!"

Finally, that last summer in Estonia, she had decided that it was enough. She had gotten to know a country boy around Midsummer's Eve on Saaremaa (Estonia's largest island), who had seemed pure, genuine and even somewhat special to her. "He had a very handsome body," Linda added, "I saw when he was swimming naked." I've always felt that Linda has some dose of gay sensibility, and she acknowledges it herself as well. She's very open-minded in terms of these things, in comparison with homebred Estonians, and it's sometimes cost her terribly.

Nothing came out of it yet on that Midsummer's Eve, because the Saaremaa village boy, Kalev, got drunk and passed out. But Linda invited him to come to Tallinn, where there was some rock festival. There, Kalev seemed to be a bit too simple, and neither of them was actually in love. They went to Tallinn Department Store, because Linda didn't go to Stockmann out of principle (so as not to support predatory foreign capital). Being a rich expatriate Estonian, Linda bought Kalev new, expensive jeans and a Calvin Klein T-shirt. She was amazed by how vain Kalev was, by how he stared at himself in the mirror and adjusted his bangs. They did "the deed," coming back from the department store, in the middle of the day. Linda was bent over a cabinet (she said that with a funny tinge of a Swedish accent, using a word learned from her Estonian grandmother), and Kalev had been behind her. "Dog-dog position," as Linda added to clarify. "Poor men," Linda reasoned, "I suppose not anyone could have

managed with that. Kalev's was really hard." Kalev had finally
shown off his bloody tip. Linda hadn't allowed him to ejaculate
his sperm into her under any condition. Despite that, she had
gotten some bacteria—probably chlamydia—and had to treat it
with antibiotics. Luckily, she now had the courage to go and see a
doctor. Kalev, however, called her after a few weeks and threatened
to sue her and demand damages because he got a disease from
Linda. Linda threw the phone down onto the receiver and cried
from anger. Then, however, she fell truly in love, and I don't know
whether it was thanks to some cultural infection she had gotten
from Estonia, but, she fell in love with a theater actor. Theater
actors are such idols in Estonia that they're renowned at a national
level even when they are still studying at our only acting school.
Their pictures are published regularly in weekly newspapers. That
actor was indeed already a mature man, actually in the decline
of his career, and the love of a young Swedish girl apparently
tickled his self-love. In my opinion, he was quite a poor actor
and an extremely ugly man, but Linda considered him handsome.
So she still didn't have that much gay sensibility, either. Linda
also allowed that actor—who was not quite the age of Linda's
father, but almost could have been her father—to ejaculate his
sperm into her. She was certain that the actor would leave his
wife and children (the man spoke all the time about how they
were constricting his creative potential), and that they would
move in together. Linda was impregnated, but the actor didn't
want to hear anything about a child, and ordered her to have an
abortion. "I didn't understand at all what it was at the time: it
was like I was in a dream," Linda said. She was apparently in a
very, very bad state afterwards. The abortion was done at a Tallinn
hospital—she was there completely alone, because her father
didn't know it was happening and the actor didn't come to see her,
of course. She cried so much that the nurses became alarmed and
started stuffing her with painkillers. Then, she vomited. In spite

of everything, their love affair somehow continued languidly for a few years more. Languidly, in terms of the infrequency of their meetings, but Linda still always got jittery when we were sitting together somewhere and she thought that the actor had walked past. "Did you see who he was with?" she asked me. But I almost don't know the Estonian theater crowd at all: I've even forgotten the ones I once knew. I haven't gone to see theater in Estonia even once during the entire time I've been in Paris. Linda started spending more time in Sweden at that time, and got work with non-profit projects involved in helping Estonian street children. But just that last time in Tallinn, Linda said to me (still in her singsong Swedish accent): "You know, I finally realized how **embarrassing** of a man he is!"

As I, in return for Linda's open-mindedness, had immediately spoken to her about my homosexuality, and as she possessed theoretical knowledge (Swedish education) about it, we never developed the kinds of tensions that otherwise always arise from women's groundless expectations. Yet, our meetings and phone calls have become rare lately. Linda has turned slightly more neurotic. In the meantime, she had a boyfriend in Sweden, of Moroccan descent, who was allegedly a good lover. Until then, Linda had believed that was what sex *was*: a man gets on top, pants, kneads your breasts painfully, twitches back and forth inside of you down there, then starts to groan, and before you can manage to feel anything, it's all over. Afterwards, the man wants a beer, to watch television, and go home. Yet, her Moroccan lover had become too expensive by and by, and on top of that it turned out that he worked as a callboy on his free evenings. That is—he worked as a callboy elsewhere, also; not only when Linda called him. Right now, Linda apparently prefers just to live alone and finish her therapy. I suppose we'll see what happens. She has learned how to satisfy herself well: her fantasies are apparently much more arousing than actual men. She doesn't know whether she even *wants* that thing so much at all anymore—to be with a man, for real. She is now a little over thirty. Her astrological sign is, by the way, also Virgo; just like mine.

I arrived back home quite late. I had purposefully made a long circle back from behind Toome Hill, had wandered around on Veski and Kastani streets. At one time, those nineteenth-century wooden buildings (with absurd little towers; occasionally very simple and classical) had seemed to be high-romantic, had lifted people's moods. They are undoubtedly Tartu's most unique districts. A Frenchman could imagine the events of Dostoyevsky's novels there. But on that evening, they had a depressing, dumpy, dark effect. I opened my mailbox immediately at home, thinking that if Asko was at his computer, then he'd see that I'd gotten back in. "No new messages." I went to bed, but couldn't get to sleep; my heart beat and even hurt—physically, I mean.

Idiot, I cursed myself. Fool. Imbecile. Cretin. You **knew** very well what you were getting yourself into. You should quit lying to yourself once and for all. How can it be that a person turns **forty** and **completely** doesn't get it (it was as if I was cursing myself with the words used by Asko or his friends). Mine is truly some kind of a **clinical** case, in which **immediate** hospitalization should be **unavoidable**; I transitioned to a different lexis. We'll medicate it at the hospital—no doubt we'll get it cleared up. Right now, he has certain difficulties telling reality and fantasies apart. That will pass. Medicines are good now.

Then I began to ready the harsh words that I'd say to Asko when we someday got together. I'd say offhandedly on the stairway, in passing: "Well, did the wife let you go for a walk, huh? Don't go far from home, you'll get lost." Or I'd say to him in a serious, fed-up voice (he'd be insignificant to me), didactically, at a café table or—even better—on a riverside bench: "You now, if you want to do something in life, something **more**—and it seemed to me that you do—then you do have to decide for **yourself**. You have to take all of it upon yourself. You always have to preserve some vital minimum autonomy, no matter how close someone might be to you. It's not like they'll do it for you. They have their own life, and they have their own plans with you in that life. It sounds cynical, but that's how it is. Women especially always have very concrete plans, and subliminal ones, at that. These aren't good or bad in and of themselves, but you can't forget that those are their plans—not yours. Maybe, of course, that *is* your path: a family, being a good working father, who sometimes still speaks about his creative ambitions behind a glass of beer, about his thought of traveling away that comes to mind some days; about going to New Zealand to make a film, because everything "here" is so small. Everything everywhere is just as big as you are. If you want to make a film, then do it. That must be first in your life, in spite of everything, somewhere in the back of your consciousness, no matter how in love you might be. It's cruel, maybe it's even lousy; but I don't believe that there's a middle road. Art *is* a very, very rough business. So, choose . . ."

Yes, I was already just about to continue (in my mind, in bed, but I **heard** my didactic monologue and saw Asko's ashamed, angry, exposed face):

"Choose—it's either her or me!"

That made me laugh. I laughed a little. Then, I turned onto my other side, and soon fell asleep.

I woke again to me crying in my sleep. This time, the reason had been my deported and killed grandfather. Specifically, he was a magnanimous revolutionary in my dream; he wanted good for humankind, but two vile women had issued complaints about him. He had to die. I was very, very sorry for him. My eyes were even moist upon waking. But I would be exaggerating if I said my pillow was wet. The pillow was dry. My heart beat darkly. It always seems to beat "darkly" when you wake up at night. It was now already halfway to morning: the time was four-thirty, and it was starting to grow light. A thick rain rattled against the tin window ledge. The windows here have very wide metal ledges: there's a sort of protrusion of the wall at the window base, and the rain makes a loud rattling against it. I should actually be used to that sound: the lower mansard-story's roofing sheets are below my windows in Paris. But those don't rattle, because the tin is fixed properly. The sheets here are old, loose, and rusted. The sound of rain should in fact make one drowsy. And it does, for the most part. I tried to avoid starting to think. If you start thinking, if that motor gets up to full speed, then don't even think about falling back asleep. One method is to direct your fantasy outwards, into that rain, into the country, for example. I thought about how that rain was falling on the fields, how they were finally being watered, how the ungerminated seeds were sprouting, how the harvests were saved. But outside in the rain—on a dusky field—it somehow seemed cold and bleak. Furthermore, I had the spiteful, pedantic thought that as a portion of the crop seeds were germinating only now, while the others had long-since sprouted, the crops would be ready unevenly in the fall. That would hinder the harvest (*moisson*), which in Livonia comes around only by August and September, when the nights are already getting lengthy and the sun rises to ever lower heights, no longer managing to dry the morning dew. If it isn't raining outright. In Livonia, farmers never could place cut grain straight into a barn: it isn't sundried. In olden days, there were special buildings for that—*rehad* (singular *rehi*), where grain was dried. In the *rehi* was an oven that resembled a large pile of stones, where a fire was made to heat up the stones. There was no chimney—smoke circulated through the room and exited by way of the door; the grain dried higher up beneath the ceiling on a special, sparse *mezzanine*. As the grains were smoked at the same time as they dried, and phenols contained in the smoke had a bactericidal and fungicidal quality, the grain had a long storage life and stood up well to sea transport. Livonian grain was even transported to France, where salt was bought in return. The Baltic Sea's salinity is too low and the sun here is not hot enough to decoct salt. However, salt was necessary for preserving meat for the long winter, and fish for the summer. Where *are* those salt fields in France—in Aquitaine? I've always wanted to go there, but haven't gone—there, to the ocean. I've lived in France for ten years, and haven't really gone anywhere. The *rehi* was initially a separate building, but as villages were burned down again and again during the Livonian War and the Great Northern War, peasants didn't have a chance to rebuild their buildings, and were moved into the *rehad*. Livestock was kept in the same building during winter to preserve warmth. Historians call this type of residence a "*rehi* dwelling," which spread only throughout the territory of Old Livonia—in modern-day Estonia and Northern Latvia. Chimneys were built on houses in the mid-nineteenth century: livestock and people were also moved apart for the winter at that time. However, the last chimneyless *rehi* dwelling was still in use in Estonia during the 1960s. It was, of course, already an oddity, an exception—the stubbornness of an old man living in the middle of the woods. One can always find marginal people who refuse to go along with the times. Yet, their heroic attempt to stand unmoving amid the flow never lasts for very long. In the given case, it lasted for a century.

When I'd reached that point in my thoughts, I told myself: stop. It's only mid-May currently. Right now, you can't think about the harvest, about fall yet. It's purely the depression of insomnia—nothing else. I implemented a second method for falling asleep: imagining warm white rooms, into which the summer sun shone through moving tree leaves; there were large glass doors divided into numerous squares between the rooms. It was patterned glass, milk glass—only light shone through it, nothing else showed.

You opened one door, went into the next room, and across from you there was another identical glowing door, etc. It's an effective method. If I think about where that fantasy originates, we had glass doors between the "dining room" and the "living room" at home. The quotation marks are because there were actually three beds in the dining room: my grandmother's bed, my bed, and my sisters' wide bed. My mother and father slept in the living room. We only ate in those rooms when we had guests or there was a birthday: then, the glass doors were opened wide. The table was set with a white cloth. On it were all kinds of foods: *rosolye* (*salade à la betterave rouge, harengue, pommes de terre*), Napoleon cake (*millefeuille*), pink currant juice in large pitchers . . . But all the same, it's better if the rooms with the glass doors are empty, white, quiet—you open the next door, and the next . . .

I indeed fell asleep once again: that fantasy works, for the most part. I woke again at six o'clock in the morning—I already felt rested, and there was no point in striving to fall back asleep anymore. The rain had passed. I made tea, just as I do every morning. I brought the tea along from Paris: I'm a frequent customer of *le Palais des Thés*; I even have a customer card, which is my only customer card. The tea is going to run out soon—I didn't intend to stay in Estonia so long. I opened the window—the garbage truck had just arrived, and rumbled below. The garbage man whistled cheerfully. He probably whistles every morning; I don't know whether by all garbage cans or not. I wanted to see what the whistler looked like—I leaned out the window, but could only see the dark tip of his head next to the truck below: he had an odd, triangular bald spot on the top of his skull. The city was wet, fresh; it had become much chillier—almost cold. Perhaps that's where those nighttime fall fantasies came from, too. Now, there was nothing wrong with my mood at all. I mused that I'd actually now like it even more if Asko didn't write, didn't show any sign of life quite so soon. Firstly, his proper response would be somewhat boring (he's a little boring already). Secondly, if he didn't write, then—I know!—I'd grow out of him, distance myself. By the end of the week, I wouldn't even know what had been wrong. I underwent the first crisis of the disease yesterday evening, last night. It's interesting that just as in books, this crisis came accompanied by rain and lightning. If I were to make feature films, then I'd certainly use lightning in the place where the falling action is resolved; so what that it's cliché. But lightning could also be used in a documentary. I should consider that. Should generally consider my unfinished film ideas—perhaps there's something there to develop.

I closed the window and opened my computer. There was one message. From Asko. Unfortunate, I thought. And I was immediately both extremely excited (my pulse quickened) and, in a certain sense, relaxed. The tension actually only gave way just now. Everything withdrew to a quite ordinary framework, to the everyday. He wrote that he didn't have time to write amid his busy schoolwork. The sentences weren't especially blunt, nor were they especially sharp. But did I write sharper sentences at that age? Certainly not. He ended the letter with a promise that we would watch his unfinished and finished projects together during the weekend. Now I know that I'm free and calm until the weekend; I'll think very little about him. Today is Thursday. I found out several things from that e-mail, however. Firstly, his last name: Lens. Secondly, following some inventiveness and the application of my right mouse-button (which I otherwise practically ignore), I also saw his e-mail address, which was zair. zah@mail.ee. Not bad for a political science student, I thought. It is apparently paraphrased, or what do you call it, from the name of Afghanistan's old king (Zair Shah); Asko probably started using it last fall. No—not bad at all. Just as the fact that now, in the meantime, during the course of this calm waiting period, I can—I hope—record Liz Franz's story up to our meeting. I wouldn't like to delay it any longer—it's all branching off too widely as it is. Actually, I don't know all that much about the meanwhile, unspoken period, either. I should quickly make it to evening with that.

25

And so, the record—although small and recorded on an ugly, rose-white disc (the round center-label was blue)—was finally released in 1971. The songstress's name was transcribed on that center (because there was no writing at all on the standard sleeve): *Лийз Франц*. Liz Franz wasn't satisfied with her name in this form, but it was already too late, and furthermore, she (her name) still didn't *have* that true and final form yet—although it was soon to come. On the other hand, she had once managed to protest against another distortion of her name. Namely, when marrying Ando Teino. Ando Teino had thought it natural that his future wife would take on his name. Teino was an old and dignified name according to the family's lineage—there was a Teino, the brother of Ando's great-grandfather, who at the end of the nineteenth century studied at St. Petersburg University and later worked as a geodesist in the Kazan Governorate (Ando Teino himself wrote about it a few years before his death in the autobiographical narration *On the Uncatchable's Trail*, in which, by the way, he doesn't mention a single word about Liz Franz, and which was published posthumously in the literary magazine *Looming*). Thus, Teino was furthermore now also the name of a young, famous Estonian poet. Liz Franz had at first, as she told me, been enchanted with changing her name. She hadn't been quite satisfied with her own name—with the 'ts' at the end, which sounded like the Estonian words for "crash" or "splash."

She told me all of this in connection with one of my hesitations. Specifically, I didn't know whether or not to follow Tarmo to Tallinn. I had bought a ticket. I didn't tell Liz Franz precisely what the matter was about, of course; but as always, she could put two and two together, anyway. The matter wasn't just sentimental, however, but also administrative. Specifically, by traveling across a border, and furthermore to Estonia, I at that moment risked losing my just-acquired refugee status, and thus my entire perspective in France. I also wasn't quite sure whether or not I was so in love with Tarmo. I had indeed invited him to Paris, even paid for his ticket—at first, he was highly elated by Paris, but then homesickness started to plague him there. I didn't have very much money either; the apartment was shabby, the weather turned scorching, and he began putting on obnoxious scenes, demanding that I buy more and more new things, and finally traveled back to Tallinn. However, he called from there and told me he missed me, apologized, etc.

And so, I had a ticket purchased, but still didn't know whether I would use it. It probably would have meant moving back to Estonia. It was then that Liz Franz told me the story about changing/not changing her name. She called from Rome and related it over the phone. About how she had changed her decision at the last minute.

It had been the evening prior to registering at the Tallinn Department of Family Status Acts, which was also known by its Russian abbreviation: ZAGS (pronounced "Saks"). When that evening arrived, she suddenly had a sick feeling about having to give her name away the next day and start bearing a name that was completely strange for her (she suddenly realized that it was completely strange). It was Ando's name, not hers. They sat in a café, excited about the events of the coming day, although neither one displayed it, because such a bourgeois formality as a marriage registration (it was supposed to happen in secret with only two trustworthy friends as witnesses) in no way needed to disrupt the usual course of their day as bohemians. At some moment, Liz Franz stood up from the table and said that she had to step out for a while. Ando was astonished, but the agreement between them—one likewise corresponding to the ideal of free-mindedness—required not looking into each other's goings excessively. Jealousy is likewise a bourgeois anachronism. Liz Franz went to ZAGS straight from that café. It was the end of the workday, and the official hadn't wanted to receive her at all. When the official further heard that she wanted to cancel her name change, he laughed right in her face. The documents are all already prepared. Do you, young lady, wish to pay a fine, or what? As luck would have it, however, the official was a male; perhaps so much as a department director. Liz Franz did not share any details about the situation, but I can imagine them very well on my own. As it was spring, she was wearing a miniskirt. She crossed her legs. She made her voice faint and hoarse. She stared pleadingly from between her eyelashes. Maybe a tear even appeared in the corner of her eye and rolled down across her cheek. Back then she wore jumpers that emphasized her womanly shape, her breasts. In short, it turned out that when the official picked up his phone and called the passport desk, the completion of their passports had miraculously been left to the next morning. They hadn't gotten to it. It was possible to reverse the process. Liz Franz filled out a corresponding notice right there on the corner of the table, and her passport was left unexchanged: only a marriage stamp was put into it the next day. She continued being Eliisabet Frants. She told me that story in order to tell me: a decision can always be changed if things haven't happened yet. It's never too late until it's too late. You decide: it's your life. You change your own decision. And that changed decision is still your decision.

I refrained from traveling to Tallinn that time, probably in 1992, although only half of the money was reimbursed for those tickets. When I saw Tarmo in Tallinn a couple of years later, I was even amazed at how I could have hesitated at all. He only stirred pity in me. He had aged unbelievably over those years, although he was much younger than I. His life had remained exactly the same, meaning it had gone downhill. He still lived with his parents in

Lasnamäe (a district of HLMs in Tallinn). He still spoke about his "old man's" ignorance and refusal to recognize his son's sexual orientation, about his mother's relative understanding—yet living with them was apparently still too much to take. But he could at least have a full belly at home. His mother worked as an assistant at a restaurant and brought leftovers home. Tarmo still hadn't finished his incomplete secondary education, or found any work either. From time to time, as I understood it, he only went to Finland, where he had some old men that took him in, bought him clothes, took him to the theater. He was actually an emotional young man, had an interest in the arts, read. But during high school, when his homosexual tendencies began to dawn on him (I am always amazed at how late they appear for some people—is human self-reflection truly so collectivist?), he had ended up in the claws of alcohol, and with a toxin addiction following that—the previously-described "sniffing." (By the way: that little boy stabbed into pieces on Vallikraavi Street regained consciousness in the hospital. There was an article about him in *Postimees*, where it turned out that he was also a "sniffer" and begged for money to buy solvents; he had otherwise been a very sincere, cheerful, sociable boy. His face will probably remain scarred for life.) Tarmo dropped out of school: he got off of his addiction to toxins, but his health and nervous system were already damaged. He had a very handsome, slender face, and emphatically masculine movements (when lighting a cigarette, holding a cigarette), but haunting behind it all was a great weakness, even helplessness. There was something about him like a lamb to the slaughter. During the years when I had been in Paris and unable to travel to Estonia, he had been severely beaten near his home on two occasions, had been robbed of a middling sum from his wallet once, and another time had a leather jacket and the lighter I gave him as a present in Paris stolen. He ended up in the hospital both times. His nasal bone had healed somewhat crookedly, his fear of life and tendency to give up were greater. To me, he seemed like a forty-five-year-old at the age of twenty-eight. His eyes only started to sparkle when he spoke about our weeks in Paris. I've now lost contact with him entirely. To tell the truth, I don't dare to call, because I fear that nothing has changed in his life, or else he has hit rock bottom. And I'm unable to help him in any way either. I tried, but was unable.

A crisis in Liz Franz's life most likely followed the release of that record, however. She has never told me about it, but I can surmise. One's first great success always brings along the first great crisis, and despite all of her strength, I don't believe that Liz Franz was an exception in these terms. In any case, a crisis followed their marriage. Specifically, Liz Franz traveled to Riga. At that time, she was already giving solo concerts in Tallinn's new intimate performance venues. A photographer—a young boy, but apparently one with good cameras—had come to one of them. Liz Franz had looked at those cameras with an immediate expression of approval; she didn't pay very much attention to the boy. That boy was Juri Katz. He had come from Riga. He had purchased the record and listened to the songs. He didn't understand the words, but her voice had somehow entranced him, and he decided to travel to Tallinn.

Juri Katz was an avant-garde photographer, who was more or less Liz Franz's age and had already made a name for himself. He had had an exhibition in Riga, and his works were published in a Latvian youth magazine. After the concert, he approached Liz Franz and asked whether he could photograph her. Liz Franz looked him in the eyes and said in her poor Russian: of course, definitely. That is the reason why she had to travel to Riga—Juri's studio was in his apartment in Riga, and he only took "actual" photographs in his studio. He had backdrops there, self-combined lighting, etc.

I don't know what Liz Franz told Ando Teino. Maybe she said it how it was. In any case, she had to go to the bus station secretly, but driven by some instinct, Ando Teino still managed to come after her. However, Ando Teino's instinct—or his decisiveness to follow it—had nonetheless not been sharp enough. When he reached the bus station by taxi, the Tallinn–Riga express bus was just pulling out of the bus stop and turning onto the street. Ando Teino ran and waved, but the bus driver didn't react. They were lords back at that time. If the bus was departing, then it was departing, and whoever was running late missed it. Ando Teino came right up next to the bus all the same; through the bus window, Liz Franz watched him running with interest, even wondering: will he make it, won't he? He made it, but the bus didn't stop. Liz Franz saw Ando Teino's face through the window, quite closely. That face, which in an instant turned as pale as death, stayed with her for her entire life. In my opinion, an echo of something from that face can be found in a rather later song, *"Прощание"* (*"L'Adieu"*). Although Liz Franz never wrote the words (or melodies) to her own songs, they all somehow spoke of her.

According to my information, Liz Franz lived in Riga during the years 1971–73. I don't know very precisely. She has never told me the address, either, and I believe that would be very difficult to find out. She never wrote a sender's address on her letters, for example. And did she write from there at all? When I asked her (I prodded her quite mercilessly about that Riga period, because I was interested in Juri Katz) how it could be that Ando Teino didn't start looking for her, Liz Franz said that she called Ando and told him the way things were. That she would never come back. She later called him regularly, but not too often: just so that Ando Teino wouldn't undertake any futile steps. She was generally thought to be in Riga in order to record a new record in the Melodiya studio there. There wasn't anything special about it, just the same as with the separation. As far as I know, not a single one of Liz Franz's songs originate from that period. It was as if Liz Franz fell silent in Riga. Her record did gain popularity at the same time (it must have sprung up in our home at that time as well; no doubt my sisters bought it), she was played on the radio, etc. I don't remember when I became conscious of Liz Franz's name, but it must have been just about then or slightly later. I don't remember when exactly I reached puberty: it's a very hazy time. But in any case, that name and those songs—listening to them, lonely afternoons in the company of the radiola—came with it.

In Riga, Liz Franz's name also acquired the orthographic form that I use here, and which has been commonly known for quite a long time; it is practically the only one that is known. Juri Katz gave her that form. Juri Katz was (is—he should be living) of Jewish heritage, as the name says. Juri (Georges) is indeed a Christian name, but at that time, many Jews in the Soviet Union gave Russian names to their children. This was especially because the Katz family had disassociated from the religion and was Russian-speaking. Which doesn't mean that they had abandoned the network of contacts and mutual assistance characteristic of the Jewish community. They had moved to Riga from Vitebsk, Belarus, where they had moved in turn from Siberia. An administrative body called the Jewish Autonomous Oblast was once formed in Siberia, incorporated with the Khabarovsk Krai along the border with China in the Far East, with its capitol in a city named Birobidzhan. That step was taken under the framework of Leninist national policy, which was ideally supposed to give the large nations of Russia the so-called right of self-determination; meaning certain cultural autonomy in the framework of the workers' state. Jews had, however, already lived for nearly two thousands years in Europe as an exterritorial nation without a homeland. Although, according to Marxist teachings, the proletariat apparently did not have a homeland either (the same went, symmetrically, for capital); such an exterritorial, cosmopolitan nation somehow did not fit—and perhaps for that very reason (unnecessary competition!)—at all with the schemes of Leninist national policy. Every nation has its own language, territory, and culture. Jews lacked the second of these, however. It is undoubtedly difficult to administrate such an ethnicity. It can always be a headache for the administration in terms of its inability to be grasped, but its simultaneous organized nature. In order to avoid the headache, that Soviet "Palestine" was formed in Siberia in 1934; at the same time that Hitler ran his own Jewish policy at the other end of Eurasia. However, probably not very many Jews relocated there voluntarily. Yet, the state always has methods of force. In spite of all these methods, Jewish territorial autonomy became a stillborn project, and never got on its feet. Jews comprised 5.4 percent of the Jewish Autonomous Oblast's population, according to data from 1980. I don't know whether such a formation can be found any longer in the present-day Russian Federation. It also might. The liquidation of countries, even relatively fictitious ones, is not so simple in the least.

Still, it is hardly likely that the Yiddish newspaper *Birobidzhaner tern* is still published in Birobidzhan; back then, the publication had, as an odd phenomenon, been delivered to the mailbox of the Katzs' apartment in Riga (Juri's mother's childhood language had still been Yiddish, that unique German dialect). In any case, after all the ups and downs, of which I know nothing, but which can be imagined on the basis of respective memoirs, the Katzs successfully landed in an apartment on the fourth story of a large stone art-nouveau building in downtown Riga. According to Liz Franz's stories, it had high ceilings—over thirteen feet; strange old furniture (it couldn't have even been brought along from Siberia, from Vitebsk, could it?); old, worn rugs; and just-as-worn velvet curtains, resulting in the apartment always being nearly pitch-black. She had supposedly liked that apartment. Only Juri's atelier was white, when he hadn't drawn the black darkening shades in order to use artificial lighting. Juri had hand-built a darkroom from plywood in one corner of that large room, had somehow even routed water into it, etc. Liz Franz told me about all of this once when we were in Rome, in their Viale Liegi apartment. She claimed that the apartment reminded her of Riga. At my request, she finally even pulled out an entire pack of pictures. There was nothing to be ashamed of about them; quite the opposite. They are the best pictures that have ever been taken of Liz Franz. There were two series of photographs: a "boy" series and a "woman" series. I believe that Juri Katz is truly a good photographer. He apparently lives in New York now—I've tried to find information about him on the Internet but haven't found anything.

Liz Franz is as boy as boy can be in that series of pictures. A brow-wrinkling gymnasium student (*lycéen*) in a dark, somewhat wide suit, a narrow black tie, and a uniform cap. A young, dreamy poet wearing a velvet barrette and holding a guitar; a turner student who has just finished industrial school, wearing new overalls and holding a wrench, her face smeared with oil; a military-academy cadet. (It seems to me that in that picture, she is looking at the lens especially expressively, or the lens is looking at her very impressionistically. It seems that Juri was the love of Liz Franz's life, if it is suitable to use such a phrase.) A gardener with a wheelbarrow, a shovel, and a rake—taken somewhere in a park in Riga—ends the series.

The "woman" series has quite a different frame of mind, of course. Liz Franz is not a girl or a young lady in those photographs, but rather a mature woman. And not just a woman: a diva. That role is unchanging throughout the entire series: the diva is just captured doing her various activities, wearing different clothing, in different places, at different times of day.

The diva, apparently a songstress, is in full costume with jewelry (no doubt Juri's mother's), a long velvet dress, and a braided wig with a diadem, ready to play the part of queen. In another picture, she has her own natural bob and is wearing a long, white "antique ruche," holding a vase with antique form in her outstretched hands. A priestess. Norma. A diva as a modern, 1970s woman in a state-of-the-art kitchen (a "Riga"-brand refrigerator and radio can be seen), netting over her head, frying eggs in a pan on the electric stove. A diva in a bathrobe, sitting in an massive old armchair under a floor lamp (her book has fallen to the rug), listening to what is apparently her own voice coming from the adjacent radio. A diva on the street—somewhere on the riverbank in Riga, which leaves a completely unbelievable European impression—wearing a white silk handkerchief over her head, large black "cat" sunglasses, a light-colored mini-suit, white shoes with high heels, carrying a small white handbag, and with a little lapdog (that had apparently been Juri's mother's as well).

I don't know where all of those clothes and accessories were conjured up from, but the photographs give a rare true-to-nature effect, simultaneously speaking of the utter cooperation between the model and the photographer. I've never seen Liz Franz being so diverse. She was generally quite uniform with me, or else presented herself in two, three, or four types, maximum. I wasn't able to stage her, or if I was, then only in my imagination. Those pictures, some of which she promised to make copies of for me, but never did, greatly excited my imagination. When Liz Franz was away and when she didn't call, then I had time to imagine her in the most different types of roles, of identities. She appeared infinite to me in that changeability, and I was deeply disappointed—even offended—every time that she appeared before me once again in her final form.

Wedding pictures were, however, the summary of the two series of photographs. It was in them that I then too saw Juri Katz's face then. But I don't believe that I would recognize him according to that memory now, nearly thirty years later. There were two variations of the wedding pictures. They were taken so that the camera was on a tripod and set with a timer, and Juri managed to position himself in the frame. Maybe that's the reason why he isn't as "natural" as Liz Franz in any of the pictures. He is a classic groom wearing a black suit in some pictures, while Liz Franz is a 1970s-style bride in a miniskirt made of stiff synthetic material ("crimplene"?) and a short, funny veil. In other pictures, Liz Franz is the groom with a *belle époque* moustache and a *chapeau méloni*, while Juri is an art-nouveau bride wearing a white dress adorned with grape vines, and a hat decorated with feathers, birds, and fruits.

They certainly never married in reality. It's probably not even necessary to add that Juri Katz was a homosexual. But I'm not sure whether just that, or Ando Teino's initial refusal to divorce was the reason that they did not marry.

Writing all of this, I'm getting some nostalgia and the desire to travel to Riga. I haven't visited that city since Liz Franz and I went there together in a compartment on the night train six or seven years ago (I lack notes—I've never kept a diary). As it was risky to go out together in Tallinn, we traveled to the nearest large city—Riga. Although Riga is on the other side of the border, no visa is necessary for going there. The train no longer runs there from Tartu; no doubt some buses do. The only thing is that today is already Friday. Asko and I were supposed to watch his videos over the weekend. I attached to the letter that I sent him yesterday the excerpts of Proust's *Time Regained* that I once translated to pass the time. I'm not a translator, nor do I know the field, but that time I wanted to talk to an Estonian friend about Proust, and as there was nothing more of his writing in Estonian than *Swann's Way*, I did a few excerpts on my own. It contains a lot of talk about "inversion," about the common "vice" of Baron de Charlus and Robert de Saint Loup. Asko had noticed the

French-language Proust on my shelf and shown an interest in it. Let him untangle those awkward sentences of mine now. If he is truly interested in that thing (that "inversion"), then no doubt he'll untangle them; I know. And I am interested in his reaction. I'm also a little worried too: perhaps it was too sharp of a start? I saw him in front of the building yesterday evening when I was coming home. It was around ten o'clock at night, dusk, and the evening was cool, almost cold. He sat on a bench on the small square here in front of the building with a boy of his age, and was having a lively conversation. He turned his head and I said hello, but I didn't slow my pace: I knew that he didn't want me to approach him under any circumstance. But I don't know, either. His face rather expressed consternation, aversion. Sometimes, especially in an especially unexpected situation, a face will show feelings contrary to what they actually are. I punched in the code to the outer door, luckily without making any mistakes, and felt their stares on my back. That bench wasn't visible from the window above—it's too close to the wall of the building, and I didn't want to bend my entire body out of the window.

But I left off explaining that change of her name's form. The thing was apparently that Juri Katz, with whom she spoke in Russian (Liz Franz's Russian became quite good over that time), refused to call her Liza (*Лиза*, a shortened version of *Елизавета*). It had reminded him of a neighbor named Yelizaveta Sergeyevna in their communal apartment in Vitebsk (the atmosphere of a communal apartment is portrayed well in the previously mentioned film *East/West*). And so, Juri Katz gave her the name: Liz. He wrote it exactly like that in the Latin alphabet (his mother had taught him a bit of German and French), also transcribing Eliisabet's last name from Cyrillic into a form similar to his own family name: Franz. Only Juri's mother, who never looked upon their relationship approvingly, although she didn't speak poorly of it or condemn it either, stubbornly continued to call her Yelizaveta

Antonovna; but nonetheless later "Liz," as well. She just had to come to terms with it.

Those photographs taken by Juri Katz, which Liz Franz initially didn't want to show me at all—even claiming that she didn't know where they had gone, but which she still showed me in the end, after changing her mind; it was in 1996 or 1997, when she repeatedly cried in my sight (or when I could hear her, in the other room; I inferred that she was mourning Ando Teino, who committed suicide, but I didn't ask)—those pictures (*images*) had a very strong effect on me. And they haunt (*hanter*) me to this very day. Firstly, I understood that Juri Katz was a very sharp documentalist with a great, natural talent—the type of which I'll never reach. With incredible ease, he saw straight away what is beneath the surface, as they say, but which is actually nowhere below it—we simply refuse to see it. One needs freedom to see it, nothing more. Consequently, I haven't been free, nor am I now. I see Liz Franz with Juri Katz's eyes—meaning deep enough, but no more, either. One more Liz Franz manifested in addition to my former radio-and-television Liz Franz, but neither of them were my own, were created by me. I had created them earlier, and still do. Those photos tortured me, made me jealous; but I didn't know for certain *of* whom and *for* whom. Juri Katz was very charming in those wedding pictures—a boy with shining black eyes, and a dreamy, but at the same time mocking, uncaring face. Together, they had some kind of a common valor. I myself would have wanted to be in Riga in 1971; to sit next to Juri Katz in the darkroom where Liz Franz, as she said, was endlessly bored, thinking about ice cream, about sitting in a café, or about her Tallinn friends. I wouldn't have felt boredom next to Juri Katz for a single moment. I would have immediately recognized the superiority of his gift to mine, but I would have learned much more from him. All in all, I've always been told that I have "vision" (not only *de la vue*, but also *de la vision*; by the way, why

are both of the words feminine in gender?), and all in all, I've
been able to operate in the documentary field in France to some
extent, which already shows something too. But Juri Katz and I
would have flown far together. We would have been like Pierre
and Gilles: I light, he dark; I taller, he shorter. There would have
been magnificent wedding pictures of **us**. In every variation,
every position. Even costumes wouldn't have been necessary—we
would have acted from pure psychology. We would have gone
to New York together, would have broken through, would have
been unbeatable. And inseparable. Unbeatable **because** we were
inseparable. If I had met Juri Katz in my youth, at the age of
twenty-four, then my life would have turned out quite differently.
I wouldn't be sitting in Tartu right now as some pointless
Parisian-Estonian expatriate (because Estonian expatriates are
all pointless), I wouldn't be troubled by a baffling angst (German
Angst) over Liz Franz's disappearance, which I have actually
yearned for the entire time (yearned for her to disappear from my
life), and I wouldn't hear footsteps in the corridor or dream with
an irresistible and, at my age, completely embarrassing passion
that they might be the footsteps of young Asko, and that they
might stop at my door. He hasn't responded to my e-mails from
yesterday. He's already thinking that he can play with me, and he's
right. People grasp instantaneously when they can start playing
with you. They have a sense for it like hunting dogs.

It's a crying shame that I was only nine years old in 1971, and
wasn't able to go to Riga. But I would still—in 1997—have liked
to go to New York and look Juri Katz up—it seemed that we
would have had much to say to each other. To me, it seemed that
he—Juri—would have been able to become for me, the person
whom Liz Franz wanted to be, but couldn't be. I didn't admit to
myself, although I knew very well, that Juri Katz was just as old
as Liz Franz at that time—so, somewhere around fifty—and I've
never felt any draw towards men who are so old. I'm at least not

looking for a father figure, I hope. I have a father, and my father is my father. All old men belong to the "father" category, and I somewhat fear them, shy away from them. I even attempted to pry Juri's coordinates out of Liz Franz, and proposed to her that we could go to New York together and find Juri Katz. However she, who otherwise seized upon my every idea inspired in a moment of weakness to go somewhere together, said that time that there was no point in it, and that New York was a city outdated and outmoded, old and nasty; a city of the sixties, but she apparently hates the sixties. When I badgered her about it, she so much as started to cry, and since I was afraid of those bouts of weeping because I wasn't able to do anything about it (console her—but how? and about what?), I didn't talk about it further.

But the fantasy of me as Juri Katz's "bride" wasn't it all. I also identified with Juri Katz and was full of bitterness against Liz Franz for her leaving me (Juri Katz), over how she hadn't been able to appreciate me. And furthermore, I was jealous because Juri Katz had known the young, impudent Liz Franz who glared mockingly and arrogantly through her thick eyelashes; the Liz Franz, whose picture ripped out of *Youth* magazine had hung on the wall of my boyhood bedroom, and whom the Liz Franz with whom I was acquainted now only symbolized, driving me into a rage with her fakeness. As far as I'm concerned, Liz Franz could have been a respectable older lady by now, who would have allowed me to kiss her hand—a hand extended from a lace cuff adorned with diamonds.

"The old bag's up to it again," I said to myself out of my incapable anger and malice as Liz Franz once again started playing a valiant boy, an arrogant young girl. At the same time, I felt very bad for calling her an "old bag" behind her back. Am I then truly an old bag's lover? Consequently.

26

Then, just before the beginning of that crying period—crying, the reason for which I assumed was Ando Teino's death, and which even now I'm unable to otherwise explain—then, those monks appeared withal. That is—*I* never saw them, but they haunted us (although strictly speaking, only Liz Franz) for an entire year or even two, I don't remember anymore when they disappeared in a single day.

One time, Liz Franz called me in Paris from Rome—she was highly agitated, even afraid; I had never heard her like that. She said she didn't know what to do, and asked me to travel to Rome right away because she had to talk to me. I was certain that it was her next ruse (*comédie*), and asked indifferently what the problem was, saying she *could* tell me about it over the phone too. But she swore that she couldn't speak about it by phone. That I was mistaken if I thought they wouldn't be listening in anymore. Everyone was listened in upon if necessary.

Now, even I became afraid: afraid that Liz Franz was going crazy, that she had developed some delusion of being followed, and I'm unable to act at all around people who suffer from insanities or delusion. I know that one should agree with them, calm them down, calmly direct their thoughts onto other paths, etc. But I start to argue, to try to prove that they're wrong. They automatically count that kind of person among their enemies, their trackers. They say simply: you don't know, you're simple-minded; and shut themselves off into their delusion.

In short, I traveled to Rome. Even by plane that time (Liz Franz paid for the flight, as always). As that trip was so clearly only in her interests, I didn't consider the flight tickets too large of a present. Otherwise, I modestly used the Paris-Rome night train. That smell, the sounds, the Italian chattering, young university students' singing at night, the rare stops at inexplicable lit platforms, which I eyed half-asleep from my second-class top (always top) bunk—I firmly remember them, the steady constant of my Paris years. I hear, see, and feel them precisely when I close my eyes now. The full lights turning on when carabineers or the French border police (before the common Schengen Area was instituted) boarded. That train was checked rarely, but sometimes all the same, and I initially had a panicked fear of them, but they usually just walked past me. They hunted other kinds of faces.

I would like to make a documentary film about that night train before it's taken out of commission or the train compositions are switched. It already no longer departs from Gare de Lyon, but rather from Bercy. It's still Roma Termini in Rome—official arrival time 09:57. Departure from Paris at 19:09. Train no. 213. The 212 back from Rome. Roma Termini at 19:35, Paris Bercy at 09:58. Interestingly, it doesn't take much more time to travel even those nine hundred-something (?) miles than the Tallinn–Tartu–Riga night train did in its own day, having many stops and managing to stretch that route (about 250 m) over eight hours. That train no longer even exists, so a documentary couldn't be made about it anymore. Liz Franz took it repeatedly over the course of her Riga years (or a year and a half). Although I said she went silent during that time, the statement isn't quite exact. From what I know, she didn't do new songs and didn't perform especially actively either; however, she still appeared in Tallinn on episodes of the television show *Horoscope* from time to time. There, she performed her already-famous songs. We watched that show with my entire family: my sisters were big Liz Franz fans (that word didn't exist in Estonia yet), although I didn't dare to show too much of my fandom, because I suspected that there was something feminine about liking Liz Franz's songs; that they were women's songs.

That only time Liz Franz and I visited Riga, we booked an entire four-person cabin for the two of us. Those train tickets still cost next to nothing in European money. The price of a Paris–Rome ticket has likewise risen somewhat, but still remained somewhere in the vicinity of five hundred francs—I think it was 570 last time. I haven't traveled to Rome since the euro. Nor do I remember how much the plane ticket cost when I flew to Rome that time to find out what had Liz Franz so out of her wits.

I stayed in a hotel on that occasion, because Umberto was home and I still hadn't met him then. The hotel was small and quite filthy, although on the surface it was even luxurious, being located on a small street near the Colosseum. If I were to go there, I'd find it again. Liz Franz appeared at the hotel in her diva disguise: wearing a light handkerchief and large sunglasses, a pantsuit and a coat. In my opinion, that disguise was ridiculous in Rome, because truly no one knew her there aside from Umberto's acquaintances and family. We didn't even go out walking in the evening that time—we only sat in the dim hotel room. It was the spring end of winter, but compared with Paris spring was already in full swing in Rome. I would rather have wanted to amble around the city in the sunlight, and to do so without Liz Franz. But I didn't know anyone else in Rome. My ability to establish and develop chance meetings is nonexistent, but I've already complained about that.

There was nothing else in the room aside from one bed, a small table, and a chair. The window looked out into a narrow courtyard, as they frequently do in single rooms. Liz Franz knew that I don't like it when she spends too much money on me and that she does so too obviously, which is why she didn't dare get a better room. I sat on the chair, she on the bed. After some time, she stood, went to the window—over which white day curtains were drawn—stood behind my chair, which I couldn't stand in the least, and put her hand on the back of my neck. I tolerated it quietly. She said she had received a call one day from a monastery (she didn't say which one) in the middle of siesta time, around two o'clock, when barely anyone calls in Rome. She had thought it was a wrong number, but they had requested her specifically. It had been some *padre* Salvatore, who had asked if they might be able to meet some day, because he had been given a mission by someone to inform Liz Franz of something; but he apparently could only do so directly, not over the phone. That had seemed suspicious to Liz Franz—she said that she was just leaving Rome, but would return in a week, and asked if *padre* Salvatore might be able to call her back then, because she wasn't certain of her schedule for the next week.

That lie angered me even despite the fact that it was all-around sensible. For it was one of Liz Franz's tricks, which she was able to employ brilliantly. "The diva's schedule is full, yes, practically full until the month after next." I had repeatedly overheard her lying over the phone like that. And she did it as if she even believed it herself. When I joked about it, she said innocently that she *didn't* have any time. She allegedly had many things going on. What things, I wondered? As far as I knew, she mostly just sat at home and did absolutely nothing at all. Because Maria, a Portuguese woman, made them meals and cleaned the rooms.

I was annoyed by that lie because she also used it with me: she always had to be aware of when we would meet again several weeks, several months in advance. My quiet sabotage consisted of rescheduling those previously designated meetings at the last minute. Then, she was indeed able to meet at the changed time, although she had to "cancel some appointments." Right now, I realize that I used the very same trick with Asko yesterday, writing to him in my e-mail that I have several plans for the weekend (simultaneously hinting that they can still be shuffled around), and asking when we'll watch those films. I'd like to know more precisely. Actually, all I need from him is confirmation that we are going to watch them—as far as I'm concerned, it could even be at five o'clock in the morning, at one o'clock after midnight. The main thing is that there be something **ahead**. Something certain. He hasn't replied.

Liz Franz had indeed wanted to ask my advice then, there in the hotel room in Rome. I believe that was the first time she had done so. To tell the truth, I was flattered. I felt like a man and that I had completely earned my flight tickets, hotel, lunches, dinners, and pocket money. What should she do? Should she go and meet with that *padre* Salvatore or not? It apparently all seemed somehow strange to her, and reminiscent of what she had heard in Moscow about KGB methods. These had been discussed a great deal in Konstantin's company: everyone had had a brush with them. I felt superiority: as a person of the new age, I was completely free of such phobias. I had never come into contact with the KGB, although I had written an entire coherent and almost intriguing story in my French asylum forms about how the KGB followed me. In short, I found that the fear was a part of her newly revealed mania of being followed. I didn't tell her that. However, I recommended that she arrange the meeting somewhere in a very public and populated place, and inform someone else about it as well, even me. What could really happen? "They" already knew where she lived anyway; and apparently, someone truly had asked them to convey something to her. So, what was strange about that? Liz Franz actually appeared to calm down. *Padre* Salvatore was supposed to call her the next day. She promised to think about it more, and made me swear not to leave Rome before it had been cleared up:

"I've never asked you for something like this,"—which wasn't quite true—"but now, I'm truly asking."

She set up the meeting with *padre* Salvatore for two days' time, at two o'clock by the cross in the Colosseum. The cross was placed in the arena in memory of the martyrs killed there. I must admit that once again, that meeting place had Liz-Franzish genius in terms of nailing life's mise-en-scènes. I wouldn't have come up with such a simple, and at the same time so dramatic solution. She asked me to wait for her in the hotel. She might also call to agree on another meeting place somewhere else. Nevertheless, she came, at about three o'clock. I think I waited and fretted there for just about an hour, no more. Despite all of my skepticism, she had managed to drag me into her mania. When she arrived, she was even more out of her wits than the first time. There had been so much as two of them: the second was *padre* Vincenzo. In her anxiety, she hadn't even been able to ask what monastery they came from, but they had worn long, white habits—the type that are common in Rome. They had been quite nice and agreeable, quite young men, almost boys (I immediately had a greater interest), and had made jokes and laughed. But this had not surprised Liz Franz: she knew that monks are often jolly guys and laugh a great deal—she had encountered a few through Umberto, because one of Umberto's brothers was a priest. Umberto himself was agnostic, but he got along well with his brother. However, the message that those "fathers" passed along to her had been more than odd, and now she apparently knew even less what to do. It had concerned a person, a person from her former life.

"Strange," she said. "You've completely forgotten a person, and then he surfaces again suddenly, as if time hadn't even gone by."

Some kind of intuition that still visits me from time to time told me straight away that the person was somehow connected with Riga, because Liz Franz had told me about her Riga life very grudgingly; had always dodged the topic. However, I had dug up a thing or two on my own initiative. So, I immediately asked: "Is it that Riga boy?"

"Yes . . ." she replied without any kind of surprise, as if she was actually thinking back to remember whether it had been in Riga, or if they had met somewhere else.

In short, that boy, whose name I actually already knew, and about whom I've also already spoken here at length—Juri Katz—was searching for her, wanted to meet. Had invited her to New York. Apparently had something important to tell her, or so much as pass along to her. What this was, those "fathers" didn't know, or didn't say. What would she do now?

"Yes, what do you think—what should I do, should I go?" she asked me.

"Of course, go!" I said spontaneously, because to me it all just seemed like an interesting story; I wanted it to have some sequel. Additionally, I hoped somehow hazily—half admittedly, half not—that there was actually still something dangerous about the whole affair. That Liz Franz wouldn't return from New York. That I would lose her. I very much wanted to mourn Liz Franz; it would have been something completely new in my life. Even at that very moment I was gripped by some great, melancholic feeling: life without Liz Franz, what would that be like? Even lonelier, even emptier . . . At the same time I hoped she would take me along to New York, that she would leave Umberto, and that there, we would start living some quite different, rather more interesting life than our routine shuttle diplomacy running in the Paris–Rome–Tallinn triangle; maybe the three of us along with that "Riga boy," Juri Katz. Romanesque elements like mysteriously-surfacing monks, and definitely stars, artists, true divas—New York divas—would have been a part of that new New York life (simultaneously truly **our** and, for the first time, truly **my** own life), and even my own career would have taken an entirely different guise there.

Yes—it seems to me that my "Of course, go!" contained just about all of that, although a part of that fantasy probably came much later, and I'm amalgamating conceptions from several different times into a single complex here.

Liz Franz, however, started crying at that "Of course, go!"

When I asked, irritated, what was wrong *now*, she replied that it was simply over-stress and a completely different thing, a different person from her former life, about whom she'd heard that . . .

True, even I had heard about it when calling an acquaintance from the hotel in Rome to pass the time (satisfied that Liz Franz would also gladly pay for that bill)—an acquaintance, who I actually can't bear: Holger, a homosexual cultural journalist, who is always up to date with all sorts of cultural gossip, and who had told me first thing about Ando Teino's suicide. I had indeed thought of Liz Franz then, but it had completely slipped my mind in the meantime, because Ando Teino didn't interest me that much, and because during that period, Liz Franz's past didn't interest me that much either. She occupied such a large part of my *present* that I didn't want to expand that area anywhere into the past yet, as if fearing that the shadows of the past could lengthen upon the future . . .

I don't know what I'm babbling about now. The thing is simply that I can only take an interest in another person to a very limited extent, and only inasmuch as it is actually within my own interests. I don't know—is it that the way with everyone?

27

The weather has turned exceptionally cold. A strong northwestern wind blows—according to the Tallinn Meteorological and Hydrological Station, at fifteen to twenty miles per hour with gusts of up to forty miles per hour on the coast. The maximum daytime air temperature in Southern Estonia will only rise to fifty-five degrees today, and will even remain below fifty on the northern coast. The weather station is, however, predicting frost in several areas at night: down to twenty degrees ground-temperature in some places. Waiting for the green light at an intersection near the bus station (the stoplight durations in Tartu are unusually long, and people generally wait very obediently, even when the street is empty), I watched with a certain sense of jealousy a small, drifter-like (although he could also have simply been poor—an old man from some run-down wooden house in Supilinn or some other similar residential district, who had let himself go) old man standing next to me, who wore an old sheepskin jacket over his other clothing. Because the wind was truly biting.

I had decided to go swimming at the aquatic center, because I wasn't able to come up with anything else. On the way there, walking through the cold wind, I thought worriedly about my financial status and about how I haven't even dealt with the Forest-Brothers film especially. They could forego my services entirely this way. Poverty suddenly seemed like an absolutely realistic perspective. In no way would I want to depend on French welfare. I know that one can nearly live off of it, and that many do; but I have the feeling that I don't have the right to do so. I'm still not quite a Frenchman. I don't want to move to Estonia either—I felt that quite sharply. Tartu is already starting to wear me out. I'm sleeping poorly and am no longer able to concentrate on anything other than these notes, which have no practical aim. And on thinking about Asko. But is the latter concentration or, on the contrary, a lack of concentration? Because my thoughts and feelings are completely uncontrollable when I think about Asko. I can think about how boring he actually is. I can forget about him entirely for half a day, and when I remember that I've thought about him, I'm embarrassed that I've allowed myself to be swept away by that fruitless fantasy. At the same time, I can lay on the couch, my heart pounding, and only hope that he comes, calls, sends an SMS, an e-mail. Nothing happens. Like always. At first, it's as if something happens, and then everything somehow disappears into the sand, leaving only an aimless inner arousal. This tires and depresses me. I truly couldn't have expected something so stupid out of Tartu. I didn't suspect that the town was capable of casting me back into such infantilism, regression. That I would fall in love. Liz Franz may have been right—symbolically, psychologically right—when she warned me, laughing, that the Devil lives in Tartu. Past, relapse. No, I came to look for peace, concentration, reflection, a refuge here.

And that's a lie. I'm lying to myself. An especially biting wind blew down bleak Turu Street, stirring up the dust—people put their hoods up as if it were winter. I'm lying to myself. I've never searched for anything *other* than that anywhere. In all cities, where I've gone. In all cities, where I've dreamed of going. In all villages, which I've seen from the window of a bus or a train, and where I've already managed to settle down in my thoughts. In all buses, all trains; especially those which travel overnight. In all the cars that I've stopped; in all the airplanes, on which I've flown; in all the ships, over the railing of which I've leaned, pretending to myself that I'm enjoying the view of the sea. In all the metro cars, where the hostile faces of metropolitan residents sway. In all the crowds that have flowed towards or past me on all streets on all evenings. In all the cafés, where I've sat. In all the libraries, where

I've been bored. In all the cinemas, where a common illusion merges strangers into one for a short amount of time. In all the apartments, where I've actually been alone. In all the hotels, all the empty places, all the shores, forests, highways, hills. In all the books, all the films, all the dreams. That is all I've searched for everywhere and all the time. Without being able to say what that **that** is. Or being able to describe, what that person would be like. It's hard for me to agree with the claim that it's sexual experience. Because actual sexual experience is always somewhat disappointing. People talk about great sexual experiences—about great sex—and maybe it exists for someone somewhere, but I still don't believe that's what it is. Sex is indeed something in that direction, somehow connected with it, good, but often tiresome as well. What I've searched for is, however, probably—I'm forced to admit it, for lack of a better word—love. From where that delusion entered my head, I don't know. I don't know whether all people are looking for love, either. Even less whether anyone has ever found it. I don't know whether for different people, there is the same, or at least a similar thing behind the same word. I don't know whether everyone is waiting for someone to recognize them, like passengers stepping off of a long-distance train onto a platform in a strange city. For someone to approach them and recognize them and take them along. I know, and I've known since I translated from Russian the words of Liz Franz's "Waiting Hall" for my own purposes, it was sometime around high school, that no one is coming. Some are met, and thanks to the exceptionally developed ability a person has for discerning his or her species' facial features, they are recognized. Most people aren't met, and many don't even expect anyone to come. They know where to go themselves.

I also put up the hood of my windbreaker: it closed me off more from the city, and was even pleasing. I wanted to be as separate as possible. May they all go to hell, and let me go to hell alone (F. Pessoa). I decided to toss that Asko out of my head before it's too late. I was suddenly very tired, I barely plodded onward. How can I have the strength to swim? Sleep, only to sleep. But if sleep doesn't come?

Luckily, it turned out at the aquatic center that the pool was closed: a competition was being held. I thought about whether or not to go back, but bought a ticket anyway—and furthermore, the more expensive one with access to all the saunas. I'll sit there in the warmth, relax. Included in the 125 kroon ticket was a separate, "more spacious" (as they said at the register) dressing room and use of the steam, aroma, and Finnish saunas, the water park (where you can go down water tubes), and usually also the pool. I naturally didn't go to the water slides, but the saunas were truly nice. There were almost no people. Some youngsters went back and forth, but they didn't interest me especially.

From place to place and time to time, one can see that life in Livonia has changed beyond recognition over the last ten years. I remember the Tartu saunas that I went to during college very well, because there was never warm water in the apartments where I lived, and that was completely normal. A sauna pass cost fifteen kopecks for a college student. Murky water flooded the floor, because the drainage pipes were plugged; no doubt from the birch leaves that floated around there, as if it was permanently fall. It's traditional to beat yourself or your companion in the sauna with birch sprays bound together (Estonian *vihad*), which are dried, but also softened in hot water. It is both a massage and a certain aromatherapy at once, because birch leaves have a nice scent. But back then, one couldn't really smell that scent in the Soviet public sauna, because it stank. The closer towards the end, the more that everything stank and clogged up in the Soviet Union. When I went to the public sauna near our home with my father as a child, it was still quite decent and clean. There was a buffet below, where soda was sold. The soda bottle was placed on top of your locker, to be opened when coming out from the sauna. I mainly awaited that moment—it was worth coming to the sauna for that. Otherwise, we usually didn't buy soda.

Initially, however, I went to the sauna with my mother, instead—to the women's sauna. Until one time, when some woman said that I was too big. I didn't understand what I was too big for, but I was very embarrassed. At first, I didn't like the men's sauna one bit—being sent there was like a punishment: all of those large, strange, ugly men. The women's sauna had been safer somehow. But I accustomed to it over time. For me, there has really never been anything erotic about the sauna. It simply doesn't belong there, and that's it. Saunas in Paris are primarily erotic meeting places—all of those hamams, massages, "saunas." In France, people probably can't even imagine such promiscuity— and completely innocent, at that—which was or still is the public sauna here, in Livonia. Dozens of naked men, strangers to one another, in a single room. I've tried those hamams and "saunas" too; but the fact that it is a sauna has strongly inhibited me. So what that everyone there is (half-)aroused. Or even more so. To me, it seemed somehow nasty, breaking taboo. One Frenchman who tried to hit on me in a hamam, even put it that way: how can you be so inhibited? I couldn't start telling him there, about my past, the public sauna, the roots of my inhibition, Estonian history. Who would care to hear about all of that, and especially in a hamam, where people are out for quite a different purpose: not strangers' recollections, in any case.

Luckily (and unfortunately at the same time, too; it's always unfortunate), no one tries to hit on you there in the Tartu Aquatic Center sauna. But on the other hand, you can surrender to your fantasies in peace. You can feel like a Roman patrician while inhaling eucalyptus vapors (it could be something finer, too; such as incense, rosehip). I don't know how Roman patricians actually felt, but I have my fantasy. And furthermore, I certainly have enough money not to worry about the senseless waste of fifty francs. You can't even get beaten up for that in Paris.

I lay there in the aromatic steam, my eyes closed, and suddenly knew that that *is* the ultimate happiness; that there's nothing more. Physical satisfaction, being undisturbed, a lack of worries. Some kind of tender nostalgia. I recited to myself the poem from Baudelaire's youth, which I love the very most. "*La vie antérieure.*" Yes, a former life. The former, of which a hazy memory remains. The next, after which there is soft nostalgia; but not that which lasts.

> *For a long time I dwelt under vast porticos,*
> *Which the ocean suns lit with a thousand colors . . .*

And especially the end, the sonnet's summary. I translated that poem into Estonian for myself one time so that it would be better for me to recite inwardly. I don't really understand poems in French.

> *It was there that I lived in voluptuous calm*
> *In splendor, between the azure and the sea*
> *And I was attended by slaves, naked, perfumed*

> *Who fanned my brow with fronds of palms*
> *And whose sole task it was to fathom*
> *The dolorous secret that made me pine away.*

Going back home, I had to tighten my hood around my face completely, because I was afraid of coming down with a cold in the icy wind—my head was still wet. I quickened my pace. However, I didn't pass up buying those red, budding paeonias (*pivoine*) and lilies of the valley, which I had seen before on a counter. Both flowers grew in our garden, and I have a picture where I'm standing with my mother in front of a paeonia bush—I'm about three years old, holding my mother's hand, and have quite a satisfied, happy, and energetic look on my face. My mother is young and blossoming, and is looking at me lovingly. I myself don't remember such a childhood and such a mother. But I certainly do remember paeonias and lilies of the valley: their blossoming time, which was simultaneously the apex of lusts and dreams, was always especially agonizing—the loneliness then, the endless, shameful masturbation. Some kind of tender nostalgia remains from even that. Completely pointless. I pushed back my hood when I reached the building's stairway, because I was afraid that Asko could walk past me. I thought that I could even hear his voice coming from the stairs above, and that startled me, cut straight into my heart. I had just managed to convince myself that it wasn't him—who would he be talking to on the stairs, anyway?—when I saw his very face from around the next flight of stairs. He looked directly at me with a serious, and at the same time somewhat dismayed expression. There was a whole group of them there—boys and girls of his age smoking or I-don't-know-what. I don't know whether or not Mailis was there too; I didn't look to the right or the left. I only looked directly at Asko for a moment, said hello quickly and impassively. He seemed to want to stop me—I halted a step higher. He said he wrote to me. I replied indifferently that I supposed I'd read it, then. I wanted nothing more at that moment than to get past there as quickly as possible. I turned my computer on immediately in my apartment. He wrote that he'd been horribly busy, but asked whether we might be able to watch the films after seven o'clock in the evening, when he'd finished working out. I replied right away that that'd be fine. I couldn't even be bothered to start explaining anything further, which would have supported my lie about weekend plans. After a while, he called me up as well, and even seemed to be somehow jittery. I think that my (involuntary) rushing-past trick worked well. His voice had a very erotic effect on me. And now, I'm waiting for this evening. But what I'm expecting from it, I really don't even know myself. Although, I do indeed. Lying has become customary for me somehow. I don't know since when.

It's now past nine o'clock and I haven't heard a peep. I'm considering whether I should say, when he either calls or comes by, that I made other plans in the meantime—we'll watch them another day. That would be very clever and useful. What's more, I'm honestly tired. It was raining before, and it seemed to me that there was some sleet mixed in as well. There was a wide stub of rainbow after the rain. Now, there are blue clouds with pink tips. The wind is dying down, the night could be truly cold. Tomorrow is Pentecost Sunday, and that means nothing to me. Simply a day, another day. If you're alive, you see it, feel, suffer, worry. If you're dead, nothing at all. Stretching out on the couch and listening to the sounds of the city echoing in from outside, I muse, all the same, that it's good to be alive. I'm actually not familiar with any other option anyway.

28

Liz Franz laid cards for me frequently in 1999. They were tarock (taro, or tarot?) cards. I hadn't seen them before, because I regarded all kinds of esoterica and mysticism with indifference before Liz Franz. And my resistance to those irrational manipulations also carried on during Liz Franz's time; incidentally, she never forced them upon me, and even poked fun at them herself, although I don't know if that was real or not. But in 1999 I no longer knew what to do at all. Following the short episode with Amid, I had lived completely alone, even without ambition or hope of altering the situation (an interesting claim: I practically lived with Liz Franz, although from a distance). I had no strength or ideas for forcing my film projects through. In reality, I didn't have any projects, either. Liz Franz paid the rent on my apartment and sent money regularly. She had honed her ability to give money to a T, so accepting it was almost a service rendered for her. She never used the word "money," but instead used only euphemisms such as "crumbs," "straw," "reeds," etc. This was partly conspiracy (in the event of phone taps, opened letters), and party, of course, a psychological measure. In short, I had slipped into lethargy and was waiting for some miracle that would pull me out of it. I slept a great deal during the day and had insomnia at night. I wandered through the city, convincing myself that I was considering film ideas. I came up with at least three or four superb ideas every day. Unfortunately, they were all films already done by someone else—I was forced to admit that to myself on the next day at the latest. I harbored the hope that something would happen at the turn of the millennium—some catastrophe, the total technology crash that people talked about, an international conflict, World War III—so that I wouldn't have to worry about my career anymore. Still, I went to bars and clubs from time to time. But I didn't even especially feel lust. I always exited with a feeling of repulsion before midnight; meaning, before the thing even began. To me, Paris's gay scene resembled a semi-military structure, where I lacked rank and my own "company" (*bataillon*). Still, practically all of the faces and bodies there had seemed desirable at the beginning, in 1991. Exoticism is a powerful erotic factor. For example, Linda always said that all the boys in Estonia have such handsome bodies—not like in Sweden. I, however, had been gripped by those Scandinavian types in Stockholm, who in Linda's opinion were fake, weak, and dull; almost like some girls, who have dressed themselves in gorgeous men's bodies. At the end of 1990 and the beginning of 1991, when I enthusiastically transferred the few francs I had earned picking Côtes du Rhône grapes (I'll never drink Côtes du Rhône wines again) onto Marais bar counters, it felt like a magical world full of fairy-tale princes. All of them had such handsome, black "sailor's" haircuts with upright bangs; such well-sculpted torsos beneath such fine, white T-shirts (which were so tight that the men were more naked with them on than off); such wonderfully and strategically filled black or light-blue jeans. I simply didn't know who to prefer. No one preferred me. Naturally so, because even if I had spent all of my savings on clothing and hair styling, I wouldn't have gained a marketable appearance. At least half a year of regularly going to the gym and tanning beds would also have been necessary. And even that, as life has shown, is still not enough. I don't have the physical requirements for meeting the standard. For example—I wouldn't attain the type of soccer-team butt, as every other man here has had since birth, even by playing soccer. I'm a bad breed. In short, wearing my cheap I-don't-know-what-brand jeans and cheap T-shirt—both bought from the C & A budget clothing store—I looked like the person that I was: an alien from behind the Iron Curtain, a potential pickpocket. I wasn't aware that not a single man who considers himself a *pédé* **ever** buys anything from C & A; or if he does, then it's the next step, some **exceptionally** fine, ultra-refined look that practically denotes saintliness, abandonment of the world's perks, enlightenment, gay communism. I didn't know that there was a "T-shirt," and then there was a "T-shirt," and that the difference between them was as great as that between the Sun and the Moon. But I fell in love with all of those disco and bar suns, at least for a fraction of a second. I just couldn't imagine how they choose between each other. Watching those identical couples, I believed they had been living together for years already. For some reason, I didn't notice that other couples were exactly the same. I didn't know that military uniformity (*uniformité*) not only has to debit the maximum amount of lust in a potential observer, but also has to ensure the perfect interchangeability (*interchangeabilité*) of objects of lust for one another, which in turn guarantees the functional cohesion (*cohésion*) of that army and gives it a certain dimension of infiniteness, of eternality; something that perhaps those thousands of clay statues of soldiers that were dug up somewhere in China, and which originated from I-don't-remember-what empire, were meant to express. All in all, the gay scene is a fantastic production of one of the most expensive gay fantasies—the military. And at the same time, it powerfully epitomizes that same fear of manly individualism, the fear of being different, of which I've already spoken. Although gays are inevitably "different" in terms of the majority, they have created for themselves a microcosm, where even they are all identical—even more identical than "normal" men are to one another. Gays just want to do everything better.

But in 1999, that production no longer aroused my fantasy. I would have liked something individual. I would have wanted Amid to not leave (for which I blamed, and still blame Liz Franz, but more about that later), I would have liked there to be someone in that whole city and outside of any kind of *scène*—in reality and not theatrically—who only I would know and who would know only me, and who would speak those magical words, which the young twenty-one-year-old Georges said to forty-five-year-old Thérèse Desqueyroux in François Mauriac's novel *The End of the Night*:

"I can't live without you,"

Exactly—without "you" in the formal, because my fantasy demanded the formal "you," which was, of course, even more theatrical than theater itself; and which on top of that is completely anachronistic. François Mauriac, a Nobel laureate (1952), is currently regarded as absolutely *démodé* in France, and is practically unreadable (*illisible*). Amid, who was actually a student of French literature, had not read a single one of his novels; nor could he bear to read them. They were boring in his opinion. I, however, have identified primarily with three unfortunate *femmes fatale*s in my fantasies: Liz Franz (during puberty), Thérèse Desqueyroux (in my twenties), and Maria Callas (during my Liz Franz period). Actually, those three fantasies are mixed and intertwined, and cannot be dated. I've probably also launched a similar scheme with Asko, but it seems to me that it doesn't work very well anymore(luckily!), even though I subconsciously utilized my entire internal artillery of tragedy and masochism to serve it.

Yesterday, Pentecost Sunday, in the café, where I invited Asko to eat a traditional French Sunday pie (Wilde's rhubarb pie was unfortunately baked on Saturday and had dried somewhat, it wasn't quite right), it was hard for me to understand what I had ever seen in him. He bored me with his talk about the Freemasons, a global Jewish conspiracy, and Umberto Eco's *The Name of the Rose*, which in his head formed some unified complex that I have already encountered among young Estonian men in one form or another. I know that a certain familiarity with such wild intellects is possible, especially because Asko is still much sharper than average; however, I'm not sure that I'm ready for that show of effort. Or that I care to constantly excuse all of his idiocies. And then incessantly convince him that he isn't gay from any point of view, to nevertheless guide him towards living out his secret desires, "into bed"; which will regardless be followed by crisis, accusations, running away from me, etc. It's all tiresome, tiresome!

Inspecting his face, I discovered that it has pimples; his eyes seemed dull and gray. It could, of course, also be that it was Asko's interest in me that had either temporarily or irreversibly declined. It could be that I'm a super-sensitive detector of interest, who reacts to the slightest ray of desire aimed in my direction. And that I'm additionally also a super-powerful amplifier of that interest, who automatically multiplies a received signal and reflects it back to the original source as its own interest and desire; thus often repelling the original source with a powerful emission. However, certain conditions are necessary in order for that detector/amplifier to turn on. The person sending the original signal cannot be just anyone. His barcode must contain a certain number, the wavelength of his desire must correspond to my range. And Asko's code had matched.

One way or another, the entire prospect that Asko had just recently embodied for me suddenly seemed so tiresome that I was happy when he had to leave. He sent me an e-mail in the evening inviting me to come to his apartment and watch some Italian film on television (he knows that I don't have one), but I was too tired and didn't go. I replied in a dispassionate tone that I had other things to do. Actually, I went to sleep. Then again, I thought, lucky that I at least hadn't gotten around to writing him a love **letter** yet. People do learn *some* things in life. Waking up in the morning, still in bed, I nevertheless couldn't stop myself from devising a fantasy, in which Asko would finally say those words to me. "I can't live without you." (He had once again accidentally addressed me in the formal case in his e-mail.) And would add, barely audibly: "I love you."

Idiocy dies hard.

But I was supposed to talk about tarot, although I no longer know why exactly tarot came to mind—and laying cards. Perhaps I would have liked Liz Franz to lay tarot for me again. On the evening before last, when I was waiting for Asko's call and looking out at where true darkness prevailed for the first time in several evenings. The astronomical white nights have indeed arrived, but dark clouds covered the sky. It appeared to me for a moment that "Asko Lens" was illuminated in neon lights on the roof of Plasku shopping center. However, "Hansapank" is written there. Staring at the glowing red light against the black sky, I felt all of a sudden—and I believe for the first time in years—a strong longing for Liz Franz. For her to call. For her to lay cards for me in Rome and report the results to me over the phone. I certainly wouldn't believe it (especially as it would be easy for her to deliver any result she pleased without seeing me), but I would calm down all the same. I must admit that some of her predictions have come true, although I can't present any credible statistics here. It's possible that I've simply forgotten her unfulfilled predictions. I also know that interpreting tarot may be both psychological manipulation and a tool of psychotherapy.

Liz Franz had apparently already become acquainted with tarot, finer horoscopes, and everything else of the sort in Moscow. The occult had been in high fashion in the circles she moved in back then, at the end of the 1970s and in the 1980s. Liz Franz's Moscow period was one of the longest in her life (about 1973–1988), and yet, I know the least about it. I can't imagine how she succeeded so well at covering her trail that there is so little information about those years in Estonia's gossip (*ragot*) culture. She apparently managed to lose anyone trailing her with that maneuver through Riga. And she has also consistently avoided having contact with any and all local cultural figures, scornfully regarding them as merely jealous and greedy circulators of the cliché. Her ability to keep her surroundings "clean" always aroused amazement in me. At the same time, even I see now that by leaving Estonia, you quite rapidly become marginal to the local folklore (because too little new information comes out and you don't converse with the inner ring), and after that, you practically vanish from circulation; you become a static legend that merely collects dust. What's more, Liz Franz wasn't forgiven for her Moscow career, and as a punishment the public began to silence her, even forget her.

One of the few documentations of her Moscow period that I know of is thus a record, which was somehow issued in 1980 as part of the cultural program for the Moscow Olympics (Liz Franz was nevertheless a "western" singer):

Лиз Франц. ЖЕЛЕЗНАЯ ДОРОГА / Liz Franz. RAILWAY

It was an LP, having room for ten songs altogether, and some instrumental interludes. Most of the songs are in Russian, but there are two in Estonian and one in German; actually, a German version of "Waiting Hall." The sleeve is designed in a certain hyperrealist style according to the fashion of the time, but nevertheless has "Russianish" exaggerations. It shows three layered, transparent photos. The overall scene depicts a passenger train departing a station, Liz Franz's portrait as the stationmaster shows through it, and the third photo is a detail—specifically, a pink rose, which blends into the signal disc held in the "stationmaster's" hand in such a way that one really can't tell whether it's a disc or a rose. The sleeve's print quality isn't exactly much to brag about, and the calligraphic design leaves a good deal to be desired. Yet, probably over 300,000 copies of that record were sold in the Soviet Union. It hadn't been any special print run. Under the conditions of a deficit economy, a print run often depended more on administrative whim than actual demand, which summarily exceeded supply anyway. I believe that other Estonian pop singers making their careers in Moscow, such as Jaak Joala and Anne Veski, also achieved similar and even better results during that time; not to mention the Soviet-wide megastar of the 50s and 60s, Georg Ots (likewise of Estonian descent). Yet in Liz Franz's genre, which was still somewhat elite, chamberlike, it was quite a statement. She had apparently had money at long last during the 1980s, and had found out what money is and what it means when you have it.

Liz Franz did speak to me about her Moscow years on occasion, but they were more like pictorial affairs that didn't especially reveal her biography or relationships. For example: about her first apartments, cockroaches, colorful apartment landladies, etc. Or about a concert at the Palace of Congresses and the line at the buffet, where she had seen several People's Artists' (a higher Soviet honor for figures in the art field) standing, wearing brown suits and a worried expression on their faces over whether they would actually get their turn in line, or if the bananas would run out before that, or if the intermission would end first and the buffet would be closed in spite of their protests, because people wouldn't go back to the auditorium otherwise.

Liz Franz herself was awarded the title of Merited Artist of the USSR for her record in that same year of 1980, and probably in the "open" Olympic spirit that was then. In terms of national awards, she further received an Estonian SSR state prize—it was already in the final phase of perestroika and generally the last prize issued under that name, in 1988 (from then on, it became the National Award of the Republic of Estonia). As Liz Franz had recorded a number of songs with patriotic and nationalist colorations at the time, the ESSR party nomenclature—having lost its head—apparently regarded honoring her as some clever move to curry favor with the new, coming powers.

Liz Franz has also, in a few words, described the absurdity of that ceremony to me. The government institution, where the award was given, was worn down: the benches wobbled and the pant-bottoms of the provincial party functionaries glistened under their overly short dress jackets. In their speeches, customary Soviet rhetoric intermixed with brown-nosing nods towards "national culture" and the ideas of Mikhail Gorbachev. By now, the young, nationalist descendents of those functionaries (sometimes also in biological terms) have developed a new and pure nationalist-European jargon. It would be interesting to see its breaking as well. And what will they have to adapt to then? Unfortunately, however, one still probably only ever manages to experience one historical juncture, when taboos and conventions become transparent for a moment. But on the other hand, it's difficult to ever take them seriously again after that experience. To become a citizen loyal to the state, a proper blind person.

In any case, what I do know is that Konstantin, a.k.a. Kostya, "took" Liz Franz to Moscow. Konstantin Agafonovich Remets was of Estonian heritage, by the way: born along the shores of Lake Peipus in the Russian Orthodox Old Believers' village of Kolkja during the first Republic of Estonia—that ephemeral state between the two wars. Hanging above the bed in Liz Franz's room in Rome was a small, old icon—the Mother of God with the baby Jesus, who was, as is frequently the way with Russian icons, simply an adult Jesus in small form; furthermore, Christ the King and not the Child Jesus—although under his mother's grace, he is visibly ruler of his mother, the God-Bearer. When I asked Liz Franz about the origin of that silver framed icon, she told me briefly about Konstantin.

Remets is a common name in villages along Lake Peipus; I saw it personally on the five-forked crosses in Kolja's cemetery. It sounds like "Reemets," but the Remetses were Russian Orthodox Old Believers. Old Believers formed after Patriarch Nikon's church reform (1653–56). The reform's goal was to modernize Orthodoxy, harmonize customs, and centralize the Church; in short—adjusting the Church to the needs of modern despotism. Those who, like the priest Avvakum, opposed recognizing the renewals and maintained the ancient rituals and ways of living, thus became the Old Believers. Out of their rebellion arose a popular movement, which the boyars additionally used to fight the emerging absolutism. And so, the wave of religious-political upheaval, which in Europe already began with the Reformation, reached Russia. Interestingly, the Russian "protestants"—those *starovery* or *raskolniky*—are those who support the old, archaic (although decentralized) Church; not the new one. Peter the Great's predecessor, Tsarina Sophia, declared them subject to persecution by way of an ukase. The Old Believers fit in even less with Peter the Great's plans for modernization and centralization, however. They were cruelly harassed, persecuted, and killed. Some of them fled to unsettled areas of Siberia, some to Estonia and Livonia. Yet, those governorates—all of Old Livonia along with Finland—were officially granted to Russia by the Kingdom of Sweden with the 1721 Treaty of Nystad; Russia became an empire in the same year, and Peter I declared himself its emperor. And so, the so-called Baltic *Landesstaat* remained in force in the governorates, which meant different kinds of laws and the preservation of the ascendancy of local German-language nobility and the Lutheran Church. Hence, the Russian Empire's newborn heterodox, its "German" periphery (although directly on the fringe of the emperor's new capital, St. Petersburg), was a suitable haven for the *raskolniky*. The desertion of the land on the banks of Lake Peipus and the Narva River following war and plague was probably also conducive to the Old Believers settling there.

I don't know the difference between the Old and the "new" believers' customs and beliefs all that well. No doubt they are trivial when observed from outside, as is always the case in theological disputes—although they are that much more important for those within the religion. No doubt there is also something fundamental about it. Furthermore, the *raskolniky* who settled in Livonia and Estonia belong to the Bespopovtsy sect, which doesn't recognize priests or any sacraments other than baptism and communion. Their spiritual leaders are the so-called *batyushki*. Old Believers lack the grandeur and flamboyance characteristic of the new Russian Church. Their music is extremely simple and—in experts' opinion—very unique, and they have their own icon-painting tradition, which, by the way, they call "writing" (*писать*)—not painting. Icons are written. Their churches are simple and their customs strict. Old Believers' villages were famed for their cleanliness and order. In Livonia, where they colonized the strip of shore along Lake Peipus, their traditional economic activity became fishing and cultivating vegetables, especially onions.

Apparently, onions weren't yet all that well known as a crop, among the local peasants; at the same time, however, a demand for new harvestable crops and herbs developed at the manors, which were quickly gaining wealth, and even at farms, following their example. The "Onion-Russians" became famous across the entire land for their golden loads. Their primary revenue base, however, probably went to the empire's rapidly growing capital, St. Petersburg. At the same time, the onion was also one of the few crops, the cultivation of which paid off in the Old Believers' areas. The land along Lake Peipus is low and sandy, and often floods. Yet, the hard-working *raskolniky* made a merit out of this shortcoming, developing a system of especially high beds with deep furrows, where the moisture from below waters the plants' roots, but the sandy surface, where the rot-prone bulb (*bulbe*) is located, is always dry. This kind of irrigation system seems to be very suitable for plants in the lily (*Liliaceae*) family, to which the common onion (*Allium cepa*) also belongs, because we also find something similar in the Dutch polder areas, where a different type of lily is grown—the tulip.

In addition to special surface conditions, one basis for the onion tradition on the shores of Peipus is a skill for preserving them: they are dried in smoke saunas, which are similar to the previously described *rehi* by way of their functional principle, but which are also used towards truly hygienic ends. And unlike the smoke-*rehad*, quite a number of smoke saunas are still in use in Livonia. The thick layer of soot covering the walls there is somewhat of a problem when washing; however, smoke has a disinfecting quality for onions, just as it does for grains. Onions from the shores of Lake Peipus preserved well over the long winter, up until the next harvest. Even now, they can be purchased from Tartu's market, although cheap imports from Poland and the European Union are generally ousting that local branch of the economy.

I visited Kolkja—which is about nineteen miles from Tartu—last Friday evening. On that village street, which winds almost unbroken along the lake shore for several miles, and which I had never seen before, I was astounded by two things. Firstly, people always speak of that region as one of Livonia's poorest and most abandoned. My impressions certainly did not confirm this. At least it hasn't been so historically. The onion-Russians apparently weren't so poor at all, because rather large redbrick houses stood side-by-side along the village street, and it all left a more wealthy and pleasant impression than many Estonian—that is, Lutheran—inland villages. It is also true that the local residents were still in an advantageous position with their horticultural skills during the Soviet period, because their second main crop—the cucumber—could be sold in an unlimited quantity, both fresh and salted, on the Leningrad market. Only now that the region's bottomless market has fallen on the other side of the customs border does poverty and abandonment haunt it. But secondly, it was interesting to see how the traditional culture doesn't want to die out at all, despite economic pressure. Furthermore, one could observe everywhere those exceptionally orderly, high-ridged onion gardens, looking as if they had been cut with a knife; as well as the headscarved women bending over them, yanking out the still miniscule weed sprouts or removing them with a hoe. Onions must reign supreme in a garden, just as Christ the King in his mother's arms.

Presumably, I pondered, Konstantin Agafon's son Remets came into the world in one of those very same redbrick houses with white window frames, because his parents (although they were Old Believers and carried old-fashioned names—Agafon and Agafya) were economically and culturally progressive people. Unlike the Old Believer families abundant in children, they for some reasons only had one descendent for a long time: that very same Konstantin. There had apparently been a piano in their Kolkja home as well, which speaks to a change in customs, because as far as I know, Old Believers do not recognize a single musical instrument. Specifically, Agafya had a brother who studied at the St. Petersburg Conservatory and supported himself in Tartu by giving piano lessons. He visited Kolkja frequently, and taught talented Konstantin how to play the piano. Kostya's uncle, mother, father, and he himself had lovely singing voices, and they sometimes all made music together. On summer evenings, Tchaikovsky's romances and Schubert's *Lieder* sounded through the open windows and far across the lake water to fishermen casting their bream nets, and maybe all the way to the Soviet border guards guarding the western edge of Stalin's country on their ships.

Liz Franz told me all of this with a somewhat vacant expression, like telling a fairytale ingrained in her mind long ago.

Konstantin—who was nearly twenty years older than her, and thus a man in the vicinity of fifty—no doubt often spoke to her about those years.

Konstantin had to be perfectly bilingual, because his parents sent him to study at Tartu's Estonian-language Hugo Treffner Gymnasium, alongside which he continued his piano studies more intensively. This all came to an end on June 14th, 1941. The Republic of Estonia had just become a part of the Soviet Union, and the border guards had disappeared from Lake Peipus. In the meantime, however, Agafya and Agafon had moved to Piirissaar for some reason. Piirissaar is a low, marshy island in Lake Peipus, where the population was likewise involved primarily in onion cultivation. Maybe they thought they would stand out less to the new authorities in that isolated and poor location. Yet, this was a false calculation. Specifically, only the Russians along Lake Peipus were deported from Piirissaar that summer—nowhere else had its turn yet. At the same time, this might have been just luck for Konstantin, as many Old Believers fell victim to repression under the next regime—German occupation. The leaders of those repressive acts were German-Estonian collaborators, who accused the Russians collectively of collaborating with Soviet powers. A number of Old Believer men were executed, and many were sentenced to forced labor on Estonian farms. But Agafon was unable to foresee all of that, of course.

On the night that the authorities came for them, Konstantin was visiting his mother and father on Piirissaar. Agafon, whose main fault (at least in the eyes of jealous neighbors—the spirit of community equality was still strong in those villages) was perhaps the ownership of a piano in his domestic household, perished quite soon after in a Siberian prison camp. The Soviet Union had been pulled into World War II in the meantime, and prisoners' living conditions became especially harsh. It might also be the case that he was murdered, as it was with many people deported from Estonia in 1941. Agafya, along with Yelizaveta—her tiny daughter, whom she miraculously gave birth to at that old age and was still nursing—and Konstantin, who was just barely still a minor, were sent to a settlement in a Western Siberian village along the large Obi River, which they reached only in autumn—just before the abrupt beginning of Siberian winter. The kolkhozniks living in the village had nothing to eat for themselves, as everything had been requisitioned by the army and the industrial cities supplying it. Now, however, yet another group of deportees utterly exhausted from the long plights across Russia's railways were put into their cabins.

Old Believers could also be found among the villagers (secretly, because Old Believers were persecuted cruelly during Stalin's time, just as they were during Peter I's), and the three Remetses were indeed placed with an Old Believer granddad. They had recognized one another by their way of doing the sign of the cross (using two fingers). However, the granddad was sick and feeble, no longer had the strength to go to work, and had absolutely nothing to eat. Agafya, who was nursing her daughter, had come down with pneumonia on the way—her breasts stopped producing milk, and she soon died. It was already winter, and no one had managed to chop a grave into the frozen ground, and especially not one for strangers. So, the kolkhoz director had the deportees dig a mass grave themselves, in which Konstantin was also supposed to take part. He wasn't used to physical labor. The old man read the appropriate funeral prayers next to the corpse, they sang Old Believer hymns softly, and Agafya was placed in the mass grave with the other deportees' help.

Konstantin also went along with the others to forage for food, digging up frozen potatoes left over beneath the snow. This was strictly forbidden, but the kolkhoz authorities looked the other way, and the rayon's party functionaries didn't come through that village, which was cut off from the world in winter. Konstantin also attempted to feed his baby sister Yelizaveta, who was still alive, with a stinking gruel made by boiling the half-rotten potatoes. The oddest thing had been how long the infant's spirit endured. She perished only just before spring. Konstantin was also amazed by how the old man ate nearly nothing, only trying the potato gruel for show and sipping from a mug of water. Despite the starvation, he didn't change in appearance all that much—he was already dried and withered before. Konstantin had also become very weak prior to spring, and no longer had the strength to go to the village to get food. Then one day, the old man went out and came back with a cup full of goat's milk and a small bag of flour. He started baking small cakes, and those saved Konstantin's life. In spring, the deportees started to eat dock and nettle leaves, roots that the locals knew to be edible, and some of them—including Konstantin—actually stayed alive. However, that old man, who only sampled his little cakes for show, died in the spring. Or, as Konstantin had told Liz Franz in Russian (otherwise, they spoke more in Estonian): *упокоился*—found peace, perished. Before doing so, he blessed Konstantin and gave him an icon that was hidden in the headboard of his bed—the same one that I saw on Liz Franz's wall in Rome.

After the war, Konstantin somehow managed to finish high school and even continue (after Stalin's death) his studies at Novosibirsk University. Indeed, he did not become the pianist he had dreamed of becoming, but as musical expert, he nevertheless found work (in Moscow, at the end of the 50s—once again, a family of Old Believers helped him to move there) at the state concert-organizing institute: Goskontsert. He never returned to Estonia again, but apparently retained some kind of nostalgia for the land where he was born, and followed the local music scene from a distance, with care. Still, he only happened to hear Liz Franz's first record a couple of years after it was released. As he remembered Estonian, those songs touched his heart; he likewise found that there was something about the young songstress, which could also be offered to the Moscow audience. He wrote to Liz Franz, and the letter circulated through state offices for a while before it reached her at the former address in Riga via Estonian Radio. Konstantin Agafonovich Remets invited Liz Franz to Moscow.

I, however, invited Asko to come and eat stew. After the pool, I visited the market hall and purchased the necessary ingredients, which also included three small, golden Piirissaar onions. For meat, I this time took prepared, sliced pieces of beef (so-called goulash—*goulache*), which was a mistake, however, because the pieces turned out to be sinewy and tough. I didn't in fact buy them from my "own" meat-seller either; he was there, but I so much as avoided him with a certain sense of embarrassment. He didn't seem interesting to me in the least this time. For extra ingredients, I also took two pickles (*concombre fermenté, salé?*), which I chopped into pieces and added at the very end, when I took the stew off the burner. This way, the pieces retain their fresh consistency and their individual taste. Namely, there is a custom of fermenting the pickles in large, wooden barrels that likewise spread to Livonia from the Russian villages along Lake Peipus: the vegetables are spiced with a good helping of pieces of horseradish (*raifort*) roots, garlic, dill, and the leaves of black currant bushes. When the stew was starting to get ready, I sent Asko an e-mail saying that he could come and eat if he was hungry, because I made my traditional "Tartu stew" and, as usual, there turned out to be a lot of it. As I was quite indifferent to whether he would come or not (but I wouldn't have anything against having the company), issuing that invitation didn't seem at all special. He wasn't at home, of course, and sent me a reply only late in the evening, regretting that he hadn't been able to come.

29

When I left the house at around eight o'clock in the evening for a walk along the river, someone whistled in the park: not with their mouth, but with the type of whistle used by swimming coaches and police officers. Those repeated short whistles instantly gave me the odd feeling that I was in Paris, near Monceau Park or the Luxembourg Gardens. When evening comes and the park watchman starts to close the gates (that hour comes either earlier or later according to the astronomic and administrative time of year), he walks along the park paths and drives people out of the gardens by blowing shortly just like that. Those whistles, which sounded from the green space between Küütri Street and the Emajõgi (where there are, of course, no fences or gates to close at night, just as with other Estonian parks), somehow hit me physically. It was such a familiar sound. But I hadn't known that it had gotten under my "skin" to such an extent. On top of that, it is a very melancholic sound for me—those brisk, short whistles. Evening has come, one idle and slow day is starting to end; Parisians rushing home from work have a sort of peace, tiredness, but also languor. Some are still sitting on a park bench, watching children playing ball on the "authorized" (*autorisé*) grass, the warm light of the summery evening sun on the treetops. The day has been suffocating, but beneath the large trees, on the watered squares of grass, moisture and coolness have still been preserved and now flow outward. The petunias and some other flowers have started to give off an aroma. One would like to stay longer in that paradise, growing dusky, but the park watchman's whistles are already sounding. I've noticed that most people don't pay any attention to them at first, and only start moving when the uniformed watchman is reaching them. They know they still

315

have the right to sit. I, however, can never continue being there peacefully when those whistles have already begun to sound. It's painful for me to hear them.

But during the evening in Tartu—the evening was very cold once again and according to the weather station, there have been strong frosts every night that are destroying potato sprouts—they reminded me rather of Paris and my life there. Viewing it from here, it seems very much unlikely. Although it is completely ordinary and concurrently my most accustomed life. I suddenly became afraid that I won't get back there again.

Going down along Ülikooli Street, those whistles still echoing in my ears, I stopped in front of the display window of a store that was already closed. All sorts of strange objects were on display there: glass balls, straw braids, dark bottles, small Buddha statues, crucifixes. The shop, which I hadn't noticed before, although I've gone past there many times, bore what in my opinion is the odd title "Esoterica and Health Goods." Looking at that window, I remembered that I'd begun to speak about how Liz Franz laid tarot cards for me in 1999; however, I digressed so far from the topic that the initial point has completely slipped my mind.

Of course, Konstantin was not the one in Moscow who taught Liz Franz that tarot or tarocchi and other "esoterica." Kostya did indeed help her out "very much," as she said, seriously.

"I'd barely be alive at all without Kostya," she added with a pathos that I somewhat distrusted.

When I asked what mouth of death it was that Kostya saved her from, she became very vague and said the mouth of death isn't always a fire or a river, from which someone fishes you out.

Liz Franz did indeed get her own Moscow apartments through Kostya, but as far as I know, they never lived together. In response to the question of whether she lived there alone, she said she was sometimes alone, and sometimes with "a girl." The girl's name was Sofya, and it was through her that Liz Franz came into contact with esoterica. Sofya conversed with the respective social circles and laid tarot cards herself, composing people's horoscopes for money. For some reason, I still believe that Liz Franz actually temporarily lived with Konstantin. It's very possible that Konstantin was simply a father figure for her. In any case, Liz Franz always spoke of him with great esteem. Konstantin became her impresario (manager) or something of the sort during those years—unofficially, of course. He had other charges as well; for example, that young pianist with a thin, romantic face and long hair—Misha, who is sitting next to Kostya in the photo that Liz Franz showed me. Misha is sitting on a Vienna chair and looking into the lens with glistening eyes while Konstantin, a gray-haired man (he had to have gone gray quite early on) with quite young and very orderly facial features, wearing an elegant suit, is standing—his hand on Misha's shoulder—and looking down upon him with the kind of loving gaze that to this very day (all in all, I only have a one-time impression from that photo), I am unable to identify as fatherly, motherly, or a lover's gaze.

Konstantin Agafonofich Remets had neither family nor children, but that does not yet prove anything about his sexual orientation. Nevertheless, I observed that Misha (whose Russian-romantic appearance was just a bit too sickly sweet for me) with a certain jealously. I would have liked to have such a loyal and wise gray-haired teacher as well. For the most part, older men have already become egocentric to the extent that they are not really teachers, despite all of the wisdom they have gained. I believe that there must be love between a teacher and a student: the teacher's self-sacrificing, non-egotistical love for the student. I don't know whether this ideal is actually realized all that often.

Misha, whose other names I don't know, and Liz Franz had apparently been "friends"; they often spent evenings all the way through early morning at Konstantin's apartment, which was located in an old Moscow building near the Patriarchs' Ponds. There were frequently other guests there as well, young and old, including someone named Maria Ivanovna—an older lady, a former songstress, Konstantin's dogged and devoted admirer, whom at first, Liz Franz didn't care for in the least, but later came to terms with her existence.

To me, that life—of which I don't really know anything—seems brilliant, fun, and interesting. I would have liked to belong to such a life as well. I often wondered bitterly why Liz Franz didn't have that sort of colorful crowd around her any longer (I fantasized about the young Russian man, whom I would have met there), why it was always just the two of us, one-on-one (I'd like to say: one-against-one) in boredom and detestation.

They had often laughed wildly on those Kostya-evenings, and Kostya was said to have especially loved to laugh. Maria Ivanovna, however, never comprehended what people were laughing about, and became offended and ultimately angry, which made them laugh even more.

"She was actually a very good-hearted woman," Liz Franz added swiftly.

During the last years of our acquaintanceship, she began to give up her quite rough evaluations of people, and everyone actually started becoming so much as "really good," "good-hearted," "smart in his/her own way," etc. To me, it always seemed that it was more of an outward pose, and that she actually continued evaluating and classifying people with that rigid, caustic derision, which I had seen flare up so often, and which I had twice personally felt upon my own skin, although muted, only for a moment, fleetingly. I must say that it was quite painful each time. But I generally remained out of the circle of those she despised. I felt only a vague fear: what would happen if some day, I fell among them because of some very great act of stupidity? I've also considered the theory that maybe Liz Franz's disappearance is her punishment: a punishment for me, for everything all at once.

So, at the time—in 1975, around my thirteenth year of life—that I became fully aware of Liz Franz's existence, she was already in Moscow, away from Estonia, and one could say—for good. Her first concerts were held there, her tours began in the endless identical provincial industrial towns, university nightclubs, and cultural centers, which were said to be horribly aggravating and tiring in general. It was at that time that her portrait appeared on the cover of the Estonian magazine *Youth*.

We had a subscription to *Youth*, but my sisters read it more often. I read *Estonian Nature*, *Horizon*, *Technology and Production*, and other serious popular-science (*vulgarisation scientifique*) publications. But that copy of *Youth*, which featured Liz Franz's portrait and had a longer story about her "creative plans" as well as her life in Moscow (back then, magazines never touched upon the more intimate aspects of someone's private life: all of those feature stories were somehow virtuous, chaste)—I hid that issue of the magazine in my desk drawer. I had already begun listening to Liz Franz's record, finding comfort from those songs in the state of depression and being closed off from the world that puberty meant for me. However, the younger of my sisters, Külli, began looking for the missing magazine and demanded that I tell her where it was. *Youth* was a deficit publication—there was no longer any hope of getting that issue from a newspaper stand. Then, I indeed stole myself a personal copy of *Youth*, my own personal picture of Liz Franz. What I did was stick that issue underneath my sweater while between the shelves of my neighborhood library, and left with it, my face as red as a beet.

But no one noticed. I had been a regular and well-behaved library visitor since the first grades of school. I always brought books back on time. But for some reason, I didn't have the courage to go and return my borrowed copies after that theft, so a library notice demanding a late fee ultimately arrived in the mailbox. Luckily, I discovered that notice myself: it was almost like a court summons. In the end, I was still forced to go to the library, because I feared they would otherwise send the militsiya to my home and find there the stolen copy of *Youth*, which contained the library's stamps.

The late fee was probably some fifteen kopecks—I paid it with a feeling of relief and never visited that library again; I began to borrow from the large collection downtown, instead. That was more chic as well. Furthermore, when downtown, I could go to Saiakäik (a café that exists even now) and get a cream pie (I was constantly, compulsively hungry) and a coffee. I would eat and drink them at the bar counter under the large window, where people walked past, and dream of a great meeting. Actually, I was so shy that I could barely even formulate what I wanted for the Saiakäik waiter. If a stranger really had spoken to me, then it wouldn't have been followed by anything other than blushing and surprised stammering. For some reason, it wasn't as good to just dream on the street as it was at Saiakäik. It was as if the café window formed a frame, inside which a film was playing. Going outside after eating the cream cake (it was always finished quickly, and I didn't dare to occupy the space for any longer; people were waiting) was awful and embarrassing, like after masturbating.

I initially kept the copy of *Youth* in the drawer, read it repeatedly, made plans to travel to Moscow to find Liz Franz: I was certain she would recognize me immediately, because she would see in me a true comprehender of her works. Then, I cut the cover, which had that quite conventional portrait (still a bob, but slightly plumper, more womanly facial features than in Riga), and the word YOUTH out of the magazine and hung them on the wall in my room. As the older one of my sisters, Velli, had just gone to the University of Tartu to study biology, I got a room to myself (the house had been extended in the meantime). That picture hung there until I went to Tartu myself. I didn't hang it up again in Tartu, and it disappeared, just like the coverless copy of *Youth* stolen from the library.

As has already come out in my writing, I grew up among four women. Maybe it's for that reason that I've never understood what people mean by womanly mysteriousness. In my opinion, there's nothing mysterious about women. More like about men. At least occasionally. Although, when I finally offered Asko my reheated stew and red wine last night, I ascertained that his eyes are green; I don't understand how I hadn't seen it before. Quite ordinary eyes. The "mystery" of their color was thus solved. The entire mystery apparently does lie in the eyes of beholder, which are clouded by lust.

The women among whom I grew up, were—in order of age— as follows: my grandmother, mother, sister Velli, and sister Külli. Both sisters are older than me: Velli six years and Külli four. My father was there as well, of course; and I can't say that he was under my mother's thumb. He was more like a classic patriarchal family head, who earned money, built a house, and approved strategic decisions concerning the family's life. Yet, he was at work almost all the time; even more than my mother, who came home at around six o'clock. The meantime was my grandmother's time to rule. And actually, that never adjourned. I now realize that my grandmother—my father's mother—was a true *reine-mère*, a queen mother. And I was her "darling son." My father may indeed have been the head of the family, but my grandmother outplayed him, had always outplayed him. Specifically, my grandmother was a great actress (*actrice*)—and at that, a *tragédienne* by way of her special sort of talent.

This I grasped only in spring of this year, a month ago, when I came from Paris: I paid my mother and father an hour-long visit (I can't withstand any longer there) and browsed through the family album for the first time in quite a while. My attention was drawn to a picture, where my grandmother is with her two first children—my father and his sister, who are still small. The picture was taken in winter—the children are wearing overcoats, scarves around their necks, and hats on their heads. Bundled up the way my grandmother did with me as well—almost impossible to move. In the photo, my grandmother is wearing great mourning (*grand deuil*), a black jacket over a black skirt, and a long, black mourning veil that falls elegantly to one side, which makes her face narrow and melancholic. The mourning had apparently been in the event of some relative's death: either her aunt or grandmother. My father claimed, however, that she wore mourning clothes practically all the time. My grandmother is a young woman in the picture: she has straight posture. It is the posture of a strong farmwoman, into which she has still managed to put I-don't-know-what weakness, trepidation, with a light tilt of her head. Her face—the way she holds her mouth, her somewhat lowered eyelashes—simultaneously expresses pride for her children, her prince and princess, as well as resignation before Death's all-powerful mystery. One hand is lightly stretched out above the head of her son, my father—her firstborn; almost as if in blessing or shrouding him. The entire composition is strictly pyramidal, an exact golden ratio. My grandfather isn't in the picture—he would also ruin the symmetry—and he hasn't played any visible role in my life, either. He was deported and killed in 1941. I had to go walking with my grandmother my entire childhood, however. I don't know where she, a country woman, acquired such a city-like and aristocratic custom as going for a stroll (*se promener*); by the way, she loved not only walking promenades, but even more that my father would take her out for a drive (*promenades en voiture*) with the purpose, for example, of visiting that same daughter, my aunt, who lived twelve miles away from us. As my father didn't have the time to stroll (*promener*) with her by car, especially during the week, I had to be the one to take my grandmother out for a stroll (*promeneur de la grand-mère*).

Specifically, walking was a health guarantee. I knew for certain that if my grandmother didn't walk, she would die. Already at the age of fifty, at the end of the 1940s, when they fled to the city in fear of deportation, she had pretty black funeral dresses sewn for both of her daughters, because a doctor told her there was something wrong with her heart. Death's mise-en-scène was supposed to be complete. Although, when she really did die, forty-four years later, those dresses were both out of style and too small for her daughters—already old, chubby women. Yet, by that time, she didn't remember this all anymore. By then she didn't remember many things anymore.

Although at the end of the 1960s and beginning of the 1970s, when Liz Franz was carrying out her rise from Tallinn to Riga and Moscow, I regularly (every day, I believe) took my grandmother walking on Vikerkaare, Rõõmu, Sõbra, and Lemmiku streets. Under no circumstances did the *reine-mère* go out without her little escort. As she repeatedly asserted to me, something could happen to her during a walk. She could fall victim to a fit of illness or a traffic accident. I imagined how I would tug at the sleeve of my grandmother collapsed on the ground, would check her pulse and respiration, would run looking for help from the nearest buildings. However, she didn't have to fall, because I held her hand (and she held a cane in the other). I supported her. During our walks, we paid visits to my grandmother's girlfriends—those that she had already managed to acquire in the garden suburb of Nõmme, although she had arrived there a complete stranger.

The women sat and talked during the visits; I was very bored—even more bored than when walking, which took place at a measured tempo in order not to speed up her heart rate too much. A doctor acquaintance came to take her blood pressure regularly.

It was only a little interesting at Mrs. Elfriide's, who lived in a small, detached courtyard house, which to me resembled that of a fairy-tale witch or fairy. The walls of Elfriide's room were covered with tapestries depicting swans, battles at sea, and deer drinking at a stream. Elfriide sewed clothes for my grandmother—dresses to wear on walks or on her birthdays, as well as on those of her children and grandchildren, at which she always crowned the end of the table, making sure that the pitchers of juice were full, that an assortment was maintained on the meat trays, wearing a festive smile. I was now able to admire the exact dose of that smile, in hindsight—there, in the family album pictures taken for the respective get-togethers. Back at that time, and in my memory up through spring of this year, my grandmother appeared to me as an old, feeble woman trodden down by life, but nevertheless fair and merciful. Actually, however, she was a diva.

My grandmother agreed to read to me in exchange for the walks. My favorite fairytale was Hans Christian Andersen's (as a smart child, I always knew the author's name, too) *The Ugly Duckling*. Obviously, Hans Christian Andersen (1805–1875) was a homosexual, and had very high literary ambitions. To his great chagrin, only his artistic fairytales became popular out of his entire extensive collection, and have been beloved reading material for many generations of children and parents. In *The Ugly Duckling*, he has staged his dearest autobiographical and erotic fantasy.

A chance farmer saves a half-frozen duckling, takes it home, and in the hopes of it becoming a proper domestic duck, a good egg-layer, or at least pretty meat fowl, puts it with a pre-existing family of farm ducks to grow up. The farmer's animals treat the duckling extremely condescendingly. It can't do anything that they can. It can't purr or shoot sparks like a cat, nor can it peck or cluck like a chicken. The mother duck nevertheless takes mercy on the duckling, and adopts it in the hope that among her fine children, the weakling will certainly still grow up to be a proper duck. But unfortunately, the foster duckling is extremely ugly, and the larger it grows, the uglier it becomes. Its plumage is ash-gray, its neck too long, its webbed feet too large, etc. It is met with only mockery and taunts from its foster brothers and sisters. Finally, the duckling runs away from home in distress. It is fall, and the duckling is in danger of dying. From a distance, he sees swans swimming in a lake. Their beauty astounds him. The duckling wants to approach them, but doesn't have the courage. They wouldn't even *look* at him, of course, and if they did, then they'd only shake their majestic heads: never in their lives had they seen something so ugly before! How could such a bastard dare to approach us at all? But fine, thinks the ugly duckling. Let them kill me. Better to die immediately, still having seen those wonderful creatures from close up even just once. He sets off towards the swans with desperate (*désespéré*) determination. Approaching them, he lowers his head in shame and humiliation, and offers his unprotected neck: may the *coup de grâce* that ends his hopeless existence come now. Doing so, however, he sees his reflection in the lake. He is just as luminous and gorgeous as they are. He has become a swan. The swans gladly accept him into their flock. They fly south together.

I had my grandmother read me *The Ugly Duckling* practically every day. If she stopped halfway through—because she had to go make dinner or a radio program that interested her came on, such as the problem-show *Of and For You* (for me, it was a single word in itself: *ofandforyou*), where radio listeners' complaint letters were answered—then I continued reading on my own. As I had the text memorized, I quickly put the letters together with the sounds and acquired the ability to recite that great, ritualistic narration to myself independently. Nonetheless, it was more powerful when my grandmother read it. Another person's voice was more convincing. Even more powerful than that, however, was when *The Ugly Duckling* was performed by actors and broadcast on the radio. The different voices of different actors played the cat, chicken, mother duck, etc. on it. The narrator was an actress. The part of the ugly duckling, including his internal monologue, was performed by a male actor with a pleasing voice. I believe that voice was connected to my first erotic fantasies. I was in love with him. The fairytale's radiophonic broadcast also had dramatic sound design that expressed grief, agitation, hope. That music blew me away completely; I would have liked to hear it over and over again. Luckily, the radio drama was broadcast more than once; it had apparently won the hearts of very many other listeners.

The younger of my sisters, Külli, was generally regarded as beautiful. On top of that, she drew well and demonstrated great talent at playing tennis. My father hoped to make her famous. Everything was allowed for her; even my grandmother couldn't really handle her. My grandmother hated Külli, I was jealous. I would have liked to be similar to her. Külli was independent. She already achieved very good results in her age group in tennis. She had pretty white tennis skirts and foreign-made rackets. I already spoke about my own tennis career—short and quickly aborted (*avorté*).

More than anything, however, I wanted to become an actor, a radio voice. I played "radio" at home all the time. My grandmother was supposed to be a listener. I broadcast the weather report, birthday and anniversary wishes, the show *Of and For You*, a tennis competition, *The Ugly Duckling*, and the show *Good Morning, Farmers!* Nevertheless, my grandmother was an impatient listener; I realized that crawling behind the armchair and making radio voices wasn't enough—I needed a true medium. It was necessary to be far away and for your voice to reach thousands of listeners through the airwaves. Then my grandmother, sisters, mother, as well as my father would all listen. To my great secret relief, however, Külli's tennis career ended tragically. She broke her arm with an unlucky fall at tennis camp, and wasn't able to fully recuperate again after that. Psychic troubles (*troubles psychiques*) began, expressed in bulimia and bouts of crying. She was treated. These days, bulimia/anorexia is so widespread among young girls that no one thinks of subjecting lighter cases to any sort of chemotherapy. At that time, those designations didn't even exist yet, at least in the Soviet Union's medicine. Külli was ahead of the times, and therefore had to suffer.

My father bought me a camera for my thirteenth birthday, which I had yearned for already for some time. Specifically, my dreams had progressed from the radio to the next stage. That was film. I certainly would have liked to act in film myself, but I had recently discovered—in connection with the changes that happen during puberty—that I was extremely ugly. I was ashamed of my body and face. I looked with wonder upon the lovely body and face of my classmate Taavet. Children in class suddenly began to make fun of me, which had never happened before. I was called a "cow" during physical education because of my timid and awkward movements, and my classmates made mooing noises. I started secretly going for runs in the woods and bought weights for myself. My athletic results improved somewhat, and the taunting luckily ceased. I did, however, continue to fear collective ball-based games forever.

I had talked to my father about the camera, a true film camera, for some time already. He deemed it expensive and reasoned that I should still learn how to film with a photo camera first. But in general, amazingly enough, he didn't oppose it either. He wasn't stingy. He had bought my sisters an Astra tape recorder. Chance also came to the rescue in terms of the camera.

*

The older of my two sisters, Velli, was generally regarded as ugly. However, she was more musical than average. She took piano lessons, and a piano was thus bought for our home. The piano teacher also began visiting our home from time to time. The teacher was a bald, middle-aged man. To me, he belonged, of course, to the category of "adults," who were all around the same age; the next category after them that merited my attention was that of women of my grandmother's age; I felt a certain sentimental weakness for them.

I now know that Velli's piano teacher was what is generally called an old pervert. I didn't know that then, but I watched him with a certain sense of disgust, and at the same time, fascination. I perceived disdain hovering around him. For some reason, I was afraid that I might become the same type of person myself; I was awfully afraid of that. I often studied him secretly through the crack in the door while he gave my sister piano lessons. He was, by the way, missing two fingers on one hand—his right hand; that was why he couldn't continue his career as a pianist or give higher piano education,. He had allegedly been very talented. I had happened to overhear my grandmother, who was visiting one of her girlfriends—Mrs. Põllu, discussing that matter of the piano teacher. The piano teacher's name was Vello Saul. According to Mrs. Põllu's version, which she had heard from Vello Saul himself, Mr. Saul's fingers had apparently been crushed by a woman wielding a brick in a fit of passion—the woman was in love with Mr. Saul, but the latter paid her no heed. That apparently also explained Mr. Saul's hatred of women. Mr. Saul sometimes carried around a film camera in a bag slung over his shoulder. Filming—my father told me—was Saul's hobby. For a long time, I only associated the word "hobby" with my sister's piano teacher, and there was something disgraceful about that. The camera was in a case. I frequently hung around at or near the piano lesson, and Mr. Saul showed me the camera one time, saying that if I wanted, I could give it a try, look through the lens. He said there wasn't any film in it, anyway.

It was a gray eight-millimeter Lantan cinefilm camera that was quite heavy for its small size; a product of the Leningrad Optical Mechanical Amalgamation (ЛОМО). On the bottom side of the camera was a handle with a trigger. Firstly, one had to wind up the spring-loaded gear "crank" (actually a flat button that came out) on the side of the camera, and then the mechanism that carried the film reel could be turned on by pressing the trigger. A unique buzzing sounded. Everything looked different through the lens view—sharper and brighter than with the naked eye. A pink, transparent frame bordered the lens view. Mr. Saul showed me how adjustable zoom (0.5–2x) works. Objects could be brought closer and taken farther with it. Thus, the Lantan's lens also functioned as a light telephoto lens. I learned these terms and others straight from *The Film Amateur's Handbook*, which Mr. Saul lent to me. And soon, I received Mr. Saul's gray Lantan for myself as well. It happened like this.

Just before my thirteenth birthday, Mr. Saul showed up at our house in the evening—outside of lesson time and very agitated. His hands were shaking. He offered to sell his camera to my father. He said that he needed money very quickly in connection with an old matter, and there was nothing he could do—he had to give the camera away cheaply. And the boy, meaning I, had an interest in filming, anyway. My father has always been a good businessman, and thus he acquired the camera—which cost probably a good couple of hundred rubles when new—for fifty rubles.

I found out what was actually behind that abrupt sale only years later, when there was a lawsuit against Mr. Saul and he was ultimately given a conditional penalty. Those proceedings were spokem about a lot, and although I was already away from home in Tartu at the time, even I heard about it. My sister Velli, who was already a young microbiologist then, told me about it.

She had actually hated piano lessons the entire time, and her going to the conservatory hadn't even come under discussion. As far as I know, she hasn't touched a piano since then. She hasn't married, either; she continues to work as a researcher at the very same institute, has defended a thesis on the metabolism of lactose bacteria, and is happiest with handling Külli's two children, to whom she is practically a mother. Those children—Raimond and Endla—are Velli's true passion. They actually live more at her place: she always drives them to somewhere on the coast for the summer, putting money from her small salary aside for it in winter. The children are nice and talented: both study at the Tallinn French Lyceum. Külli herself is an artist and does video installations, which in my opinion are uniformly neurotic and boring; but for which she regularly receives small stipends and money from funds. Nevertheless, every payday she borrows money from Velli, who never demands that she pays it back. However, I practically don't speak with my sisters and don't know all that much about their lives, just as they don't in terms of mine. I've never invited them to come visit me in Paris once, and they've been offended by it. Külli asked me once whether I was really a homo. And when I gave a positive reply, she asked if I wouldn't like to treat myself with a maharishi. The maharishi would take my pulse, put together a special diet for me, and I would be healed. Namely, Külli has always had some kind of a maharishi, priest, preacher, TM guru, sensitive masseur, or other sharer of religious or spiritual teachings, who at that moment possesses the absolute truth for Külli and heals all diseases. After that, the representative of some other teaching or sect takes the place of that "father." Külli personally doesn't see anything inconsistent in this: she is simply disappointed in the previous one. She has long been divorced, and hasn't remarried. When I asked why a maharishi should treat me, she replied, astonished, that it *was* abnormal, after all—that homo thing. I said: uh-huh.

And I haven't spoken to Külli since, only sending her birthday cards; that makes five years already.

Mr. Saul, however, was in court during the first years of the 1980s on the grounds of "satisfying sexual lust in an unnatural manner." When he was given a conditional penalty, it was accounting for the facts that firstly, he had a spotless lifestyle previously (although that satisfaction had already been his hobby for several years), and secondly, he had never in fact acted upon it (*passer à l'acte*): he had only filmed others' actions. "Little couples making love in the forest," as Velli said with extreme disapproval.

That time, however, when Mr. Saul sold his Lantan to my father (who gave it to me on the spot for my imminent thirteenth birthday), someone had come across him for the first time, and he was frightened off. Those who happened upon the situation in fact didn't call the militsiya, but the horrified Mr. Saul decided to fight his vice on his own, to estrange himself from the camera. He likewise burned all of the rolls of film in his backyard; there had allegedly been a large, black pillar of smoke. He lived with his old mother, who was luckily already dead by the time of the court proceedings in the 1980s. By then, Mr. Saul (Citizen Saul in court, of course) had acquired a new and better sixteen-millimeter camera.

Following the court case, Vello Saul lost both his camera—which was confiscated as an instrument of crime—and all of his students. He began to drink and wander, sold off his mother's house, and was found frozen to death on the street a few years later.

And so, the Lantan that I obtained from that "old pervert" was an eight-millimeter amateur camera. I never filmed anything inappropriate with it. I experimented with nature at first. Yet, the birds I recorded near the bird feeder or the birdhouse were so small that it was never in the least bit similar to the famous nature films that I'd seen. The telephoto lens was too weak. After that, Külli and I—who had become my ally after falling out of the pool of young Estonian SSR tennis hopefuls, and falling in our father's eyes—tried making a feature film. More of a documentary film came out of it. Külli spoke in front of the camera about her life and how she hated our father. The camera freed her. I realized that she was more talented than me. I abandoned filming for a long time. Külli, however, went on to study art and later turned to video, where she did achieve some level of success; although in my opinion, all of her works are repeats of that first joint film of ours.

Only in high school, when I began recording the school theater productions that I previously spoke about, did I also get a certain degree of recognition and satisfaction. However, it wasn't exactly what I would have wanted to film, nor has it ever been—to tell the truth—quite *that* to this very day.

Back then, at the age of thirteen, I nevertheless had a definite vision: I would make a film about Liz Franz. She would sing only to me, directly into the camera. Thanks to me, she would become even more famous, and I would likewise become famous. I would start to accompany her on concert tours; we would go abroad, to big cities. I would have a large, professional camera, and people would say: "Exceptional camerawork. There is some elusive philosophical grace in his author films. No one has yet been capable of opening up such psychological depths in the songstress. The visual language of the frames is perfectly in tune with the audio language of Liz Franz's songs." I had become familiar with such statements by reading the ESSR cultural newspaper *Hammer and Sickle*. However, I never had sufficient ambition for running away from home or university, going to Moscow, and following my calling. I had to wait a good number of years more before my calling found me on its own; itself indeed no longer being quite *that* anymore.

30

Today, my mood, which has become relatively peaceful (I no longer really expect to meet Asko on the stairs, to hear his knock on the door), was disturbed by one admittedly trivial incident. I was just eating boiled dumplings in the kitchen (I couldn't be bothered to go to the market and make stew) when I heard talking somewhere above my head. There is a skylight there, which I've already mentioned. It was open, and the conversation sounded as if it was right above my head; almost as if it were being spoken in this very room. Someone was apparently talking on a cell phone. At first, it seemed to me that it was Asko, because I'd been there on the roof with him at the beginning; but then, I realized that it was the voice of a young, male stranger. He spoke about this and that, and moved away from my window while talking—I heard his steps on the tin roof. I furthermore heard him say: "Yeah, he's still writing; no, nothing special . . ."

It also might have been "I'm still writing," but suddenly, I had the feeling the man was talking about me. That was definitely absolutely absurd, and I criticized myself for having such a delusional notion of being followed. Still, it was unpleasant to imagine that someone could watch me from above. However, one shouldn't really be able to see anything in the room from that skylight, which is in quite a deep shaft, and the only thing that should be visible is when I eat at the bar counter in the kitchen. One would have to use some kind of a periscope to see the rest of the room, and especially the writing desk. In short, I threw that thought out of my head, as much as thoughts *can* be thrown out of one's head. Still, I couldn't shake off the irrational feeling that I'm being followed, at least that I could be followed. By the way, the landlord can come in here, for example; he has a key.

He came here yesterday with two workers, who installed blinds in my bedroom (I can't sleep in the light, and the sun rises at four-thirty). They were two drunks, a man and a woman, and otherwise nice people; only that I had to air out the room for a while after they left. They indeed didn't poke their noses into anything or look around, and when they did glance towards the writing desk, it was with a certain awe felt before unfamiliar things (a computer, books). The landlord also isn't the type to have any interest in my life; rather, he was annoyed by the new caprices that I posed to him (the kitchen plumbing is clogged). So, all in all, I should be completely satisfied. Nevertheless, I had the desire to travel somewhere away from here for a while. Even for a day or two to air out my head, to enjoy myself (*me changer les idées*). A few pointless, compulsive steps even show that this is necessary; such as buying that pack of tarot cards (268 kroons) from the "esoterics and health goods" store. Specifically, I got the idea while going past the store again (I was now aware of it) that if I were to lay tarot for myself, I would remember what Liz Franz predicted for me that time. That I would recall what cards came up and what she wanted to tell me with them.

Back then, I had my own tarot cards as well (a present from Liz Franz, of course); however, I burned them a couple of years ago—in the winter of 2000. I did so in Estonia, at Anton's place on the island of Hiiumaa, because I don't have anywhere to start up a fire in Paris, but there is no lack of stoves and fireplaces in Anton's country home. It was even my main aim—burning the cards—when I went to visit Anton. The thing was that I had started laying cards for myself constantly, and it had already become obsessive. I did it several times a day, and never had satisfying results. The outcomes were either bad or absurd all the time. As such, I decided to destroy the cards, because every once in a while, when I was capable of seeing it more clearly, it seemed not only ridiculous, but dangerous as well. Still, I felt some strange discomfort when those Major Arcana (great secret) High Priests, High Priestesses, Deaths, Devils, Wheels of Fortune, Hermits and others—not to mention the Minor Arcana (Coins, Staves, Cups, Swords)—caught flame and turned into faceless leaves of ash there upon the glowing coals in Anton's stove. I was gripped by an irrational fear that I had done something irreversible, and that some half-deciphered secret, which affects me personally (Liz Franz and me), burned up there; a secret, which I would now never find out. I'm only speaking about all of this in order to give an idea of my mental imbalance at that time. And now.

However, I only drove to Riga. I rented a car for the Riga trip, because my Opel Astra's muffler needs to be replaced, but I didn't feel like going to a garage somewhere. (I don't know what they're called these days: still "car service"? As if the car were some living being, nearly a person, who must be serviced and loved.) And so, I called a car-rental service, and a two-door automatic 1.8-liter-engine Mercedes (I don't know what brand) was brought to me at the doors of the Barclay Hotel by eight o'clock the next morning. I ate a breakfast there, leaving the car-rental man the impression that I lived at the hotel, because I didn't want to give him my Tartu address. Such conspiracy is ridiculous, of course. I also presented myself as a French citizen with the rental—it seems to me that it made matters simpler, but perhaps my blue Crédit Lyonnais credit card counted for even more. Estonian residents don't have credit cards, for the most part: there are only debit cards, because the banks don't trust people. People indeed trust the banks, because savings are growing quickly, despite the interest rates that are falling just as quickly, and which in reality have already long been negative. Thus, the majority of Estonian residents are unable to rent a car, either, because a credit card is required for it. But they probably don't even dream of that expensive service. Everyone has his or her own vehicle.

Still, I showed my Estonian passport at the border; it will attract less attention, I thought. This was the wrong calculation, of course, because in the eyes of Estonian border officials, Estonian citizens are the most suspicious category of residents. I actually came to understand long ago at Tallinn Airport that at no time is it worth standing at the border guard booth with the sign "Estonian citizens." That line goes the very slowest.

The border checkpoint that I crossed is located on the edge of the town of Valga, and is a proper, brand new (*flambant neuf*) structure; no doubt built with aid from the European Union. There wasn't a single vehicle waiting under the awning, but there was indeed a Latvian border guard, so I drove immediately up to him. His first question was why I drove through the red light. I said I hadn't seen it—the sun was in my eyes. Actually, I didn't even look. There is the sort of system there, where they firstly have you wait at the light, and then will allow you to drive up when they're in the mood for it. Otherwise, it's apparently not sufficiently sound. After that, he had me drive the car precisely up to the stop line. I had to take out additional insurance on the vehicle, because Estonian traffic insurance is not valid in Latvia. This all took no more than perhaps fifteen minutes.

The landscape and houses on the Latvian side of Livonia don't really differ from the landscape and houses on the Estonian side, but some kind of metamorphosis still happens. For example: villages are often enhanced by water towers with pretty, romantic decorations. Such are not seen in Estonia. The greater portion of the road from Valga to Riga is lined by forest—beautiful, dry pines (the day was almost hot, and their smell even swept into the car) that stretch all the way down to Riga. The city of Riga is not built amid fertile plains like Paris is; barren dunes and heaths are its hinterland. Apparently, only its strategic location at the mouth of the Daugava (*Väina*) River became decisive during the Middle Ages.

Driving into Riga, I could sense immediately that it was a large city. There's a different kind of feeling that you can't have in Tallinn, not to mention Tartu. A large city is a place, into which you can disappear, and where something could happen to you. Some transformation happens: you enter as one person, and exit another, if you exit at all. I'd completely forgotten that feeling in the meantime, although I've only been away from Paris for a month and a half. Of course, it's a long time since I've felt that exciting sensation when in Paris, but interestingly, it hits me anew every time that I return to Paris. It was clear that I cannot stay in Tartu, nor in Estonia in general—nothing there is waiting **ahead** of me any longer, only behind me; a number of things that yank me back.

I parked my rental car somewhere on a boulevard (the drive had been truly comfortable, although I had been against driving an automatic transmission at first—I'm not used to it, but one accustoms to a good thing quickly) and paid for the parking. This didn't go so smoothly at all, because it required coins. I had exchanged money for Latvian currency (*lats*) in Tartu, but the parking meter only took coins.

Just like the Estonian kroon, the lat is fixed to the euro; thus, it likewise only constitutes a certain nationalist camouflage, which is meant to create a feeling of independence. Actually, neither country has control over any elements of independent financial policy: their national banks are merely emitters and distributors of bank notes with a handsome national design. These notes could be replaced with euros immediately, which would also be convenient, because although their exchange rate is fixed and stable, the notes cannot be converted anywhere other than domestically and in neighboring countries. Unlike the Estonian kroon, the Latvian lat's rate is fixed very high; it is somewhat like the pound sterling. As such, I needed to break the five lat note that I purchased in Tartu into coins. A post office (*Latvijas Pasts*) was located just near by, and I was certain I could get the necessary coins from it. Behind every window in the post office was a woman busy with something, and on the window in front of every woman's nose was Latvian writing that apparently meant "closed," and an arrow pointing to the next window. Moving down along those arrows, I reached a window without an arrow on it. The young woman sitting on the other side of the window was presently having a lively discussion with an older postal worker over some job related question, repeatedly pointing to a small, yellowish form in her hand.

Although there is a great deal of vocabulary in Latvian and Estonian with a common origin—whether equivalent loan words or those borrowed from German, as well as from Russian—the languages' base structures are plenty different, and it is impossible to comprehend Latvian speech on the basis of Estonian. It's somewhat easier with written text (for example, the word for "hour" in Estonian is *tund*, and in Latvian is *stunda*, etc.). I read on the young communications worker's nametag that she was Riga fifty-first Communications Hub Communications Operator, Inga. The name "Inga" was a disappointment for me, and as it turned out, my conversation with Inga did not go all that smoothly. Specifically, Inga is a Latvian name, while I would have preferred a Lyubov or an Anastassia, for example, because I've heard that Latvians fight actively for the restoration of their national language's place in state administration, in public, and in business life. Specifically, there is an even larger portion of Latvia's population that is non-Latvian-speaking than the non-Estonian-speaking portion of Estonia's population. About 40 percent, and even more in Riga. The dominant majority of those "nons" are Russian-speaking, and Russian language was a common idiom during the Soviet period; especially given the fact that it is simpler for Latvians to gain proficiency in Russian because of their greater linguistic proximity. Liz Franz had no linguistic problems during her time in Riga, because Juri initially helped her to manage affairs. After that, however, she became sufficiently proficient at Russian herself. Yet, acquired skills can become dysfunctional overnight. I naturally addressed Inga in Russian, because we probably had no other common dialects. In my opinion, it would have been ridiculous to have an English-language conversation; furthermore, my instinct told me it wouldn't have been any easier for Inga. She first replied to me in Latvian, but then nevertheless grudgingly transitioned into Russian, which she spoke much better than I do. She did so to inform me that she had little change and didn't plan to give the last of it away, because she would still need it over the course of the day.

I was truly amazed by this notice, and attempted to convince Inga that a post office really cannot function under the conditions of constant shortage of metal money (*monnaie*, Russian *монеты*); especially given that all usual means of postage cost only one hundredth of a lats, i.e. a santīms (just as it used to be in France: *centime*), considering the lats's high value. However, Inga stuck to her refusal and my argumentation made her more hostile.

Only upon leaving the post office did I realize that I could have purchased a stamp from her, because she would still have had to break my five lats note. And a stamp could be used for sending Liz Franz a postcard (which I later did), because some intuition told me that the postcard, a postcard sent from Riga, wouldn't be returned, but would reach her, no matter where she may be. But I no longer wanted to go back to Inga, because that entire *Pasts* reminded me too much of Soviet-era institutions of communication, and of institutions in general. I certainly don't feel any nostalgia for Soviet administration. I acquired coins from the Hansapank (Lithuanian *Hansabanka*, literally "Hanseatic Bank") office across the street. It is a financial institution that was founded by Estonians and now belongs primarily to Swedish capital, which has expanded across all three Baltic States. While exchanging money at the Hansapank, I felt a light sense of national pride and superiority, which of course had no basis in economic reality. I paid for parking until five o'clock, because I knew I didn't want to be in Riga for any longer than that; yet at the same time, the pre-payment would still more or less force me to stay until five.

I walked across the Old Town to the riverbank, but returned from there immediately. Old Riga is situated on one side of the river. The Daugava is quite wide where Riga lies, and bridges are apparently a rather recent phenomenon. Thus, only new districts are located on the other side of the river. As such, Riga lacks that left- and right-bank issue that exists in Paris and Tartu. It's as if Riga's bridges lead elsewhere, out of the city, to another city or another country. Only now did I understand what that song from Liz Franz's Moscow period really meant; a song, which in truth, I hadn't been able to associate with Riga up until today:

И я на мосту стою . . . Река протекает мимо . . . Но я на мосту стою . . . Всё забывается . . . Даже твоё лицо, даже твоё имя . . .[2]

Only there, looking out over the Daugava (and without mounting the bridge), did I understand that the song is about Riga and Juri Katz. That symbolic standing upon a bridge is like an eternal goodbye—both to Juri Katz and, perhaps, to her youth. At the same time, her talk of forgetting is an attempt to cast a spell and set herself free of Riga and Juri Katz. Or else it is a coming-to-terms with Juri Katz and Riga having fallen into the past, and with them actually being out of her thoughts as well, and with the fact that the yearning for them that remains is a yearning for something that truthfully has nothing to do with **them**.

2. "And I stand upon a bridge . . . The river flows past . . . But I stand upon the bridge . . . Forgetting all . . . Even your face, even your name . . ." (Russian.)

I don't know how Liz Franz left Riga, or what happened between them, or what was. I know that they nevertheless retained some connection. Whether they met after that, I don't know. Juri Katz ultimately made it abroad with his mother—years later, probably at the end of the 70s—as a part of the small limit that the Soviet Union had given its Jews for journeying to Israel. They allegedly had relatives there, also; in short—I don't know for sure. I do know, however, that Juri Katz didn't actually go to Israel, but rather to New York. His mother, who had indeed moved around a great deal during her lifetime, apparently didn't survive that change of residence and culture, because she soon died in New York. And after that Liz Franz seemingly also lost Juri Katz's trail; or rather, things had gone "as they always do": they became estranged and let each other slip from their memories. The exchange of postcards, which was infrequent already, was discontinued. Until those monks appeared: Father Vincenzo and Father Salvatore. But to this very day, I don't know whether Liz Franz actually got into contact with Juri Katz or so much as met with him during that "weeping period," which lasted for nearly a year. The Fathers' visits apparently carried on: according to her, they became almost as much as family friends at their home; in addition to Umberto's priest-brother, logically. A further third Father was quite soon added to the two—Father Serafimo, who played the flute beautifully. I dearly wanted to see those Fathers, and Liz Franz promised to get us together, but that didn't happen.

Specifically, I was giving serious thought back then to entering a monastery, because it seemed like the only right path to me, although I didn't believe in the Catholic dogmas one bit. Still, it appeared to me that I might find peace in a monastery; somehow (through spiritual exercises?) free myself and rise above my agonizing lust, sexual obsession and frustration; might once and for all sublimate my fruitless and pointless sexuality into something else, I don't know—brotherly love, selfless love for mankind, or something similar. Secondly, it seemed to me that the monastery walls could hide me from Liz Franz for good. Liz Franz even seemingly supported my monastery fantasies, and promised to talk to the fathers about me. Then, however, I met Amid, and the monastery matter was taken off the agenda. The Fathers also disappeared somewhere; at least there was no more talk of them.

That said, Father Serafimo had played the role of messenger. Specifically, he had some kind of a connection with Moscow and the Catholics there—he also frequently made personal visits to Russia, and it was he who brought Liz Franz the message about Konstantin's death. Not that Konstantin had switched religions before his death, but he was apparently somehow in contact with Catholics; perhaps via his musical acquaintances, among whom there are Roman Catholics, even in Russia, no doubt in connection with the musical culture, which is so closely associated with the Western Church. In any case, it was Father Serafimo, who brought Liz Franz that small icon from Moscow, which Konstantin Remets had bequeathed to her.

I don't know what Konstantin Agafonofich died of, but he had to have been already near the age of seventy at the time, so it was no doubt some disease. Strangely, Konstantin's death simultaneously ended Liz Franz's cycle of crying fits. And that year, now that I think about it, was also important in our relationship, in the sense that there has been no more sexual intercourse between us since then. We have been together as brother and sister, so to speak. I was satisfied that I no longer had to fulfill my unpleasant male duties, but from time to time, I also started feeling a nostalgia for our intercourse. I once even called Liz Franz and asked her to quickly fly to Paris, because I had—as I said—something very important to discuss with her. Actually, I only wanted to sleep with her; I don't know—fall asleep into her, extinguish, die. When I saw that older woman in the airport waiting hall, however, I realized that my imagination had fooled me once again. I arranged several ugly scenes for her that time, and it was then that we had the conversation on the Bridge of the Arts, during which I convinced her to let her "duckling" go— without even knowing what that "letting go" should mean (not getting money anymore?).

I pondered all of this and all kinds of other things on the patio of Nostalgija Café. That café, which has a grand early-century interior, is located along some pedestrian street in Riga's Old Town, and an unending current of people moved past there at noon. I ordered tea, dumplings, and pancakes. The waitresses were luckily Russian girls—very kind and polite, happy that they didn't have to speak with me in Latvian or in English. On top of that, the dumplings were very good. Watching the passersby, I felt that special peace that can be felt precisely, in a large city, when you step slightly to the side of that current. For some reason, I almost never sit on café patios in Paris anymore, although it could also be the case that I've already acquired a permanent sidelong-observer status there, which I no longer need a café patio to enter.

Rigans seemed significantly more diverse than people in Tallinn or Tartu. In a large city, everyone is slightlu more alone with his or her personal madness than in a small place—the individual can develop it somewhat more freely, and thus appear more the way he or she is, than the way everyone else is. Riga boys also looked more handsome and interesting, returned a glance more readily and freely, didn't immediately make a harsh or appalled, feigned expression of amazement. Although, I didn't enter into closer conversation with any of them. I remembered Asko only when driving away. I had thought to buy him something from Riga, but I hadn't gone to a single store. In truth, I also didn't know whether or not I wanted to meet him again so much. My racist allergy to stupidity turned out to be greater than I had thought. Which, of course, makes socializing with people fifteen years younger than me for longer than five hours problematic in general. Because stupidity doesn't come out over the course of five hours—only the appeal of youth works over the course of five hours, and you automatically find a thousand excuses at the speed of light to justify every thick statement (he didn't actually mean it like that; those are someone else's words that he's repeating; he's actually right in his own way; you can also see things in that perspective; at his age . . . etc.).

I was likewise the only traveler at the border checkpoint at the moment that I crossed the Estonian-Latvian border again, and the Estonian customs officials handled me with exceptional thoroughness. I don't know: maybe driving a rented car is suspicious, maybe they simply had nothing to do, maybe they somehow have a special sense for things, following recent events (the serial killers, whom I previously spoke about crossed the Estonian-Latvian border, and there was a firefight). Maybe they feel that their life is in constant danger, and simultaneously step into battle against crime at the first line of fire. I had to open all of the car's hatches and compartments to show them where the serial number (for identifying the vehicle) was; the location of which I naturally didn't know.

"So, how do you not know where the serial number is?" the customs official asked me disparagingly. "How could you even rent out a vehicle without checking? Everyone knows where the serial number of the car they're driving is located."

I noted that, already on several occasions, it's been implied in Livonia that I do not belong to the human race. But the most absurd question that angered me (they found the serial number on their own immediately—they actually knew very well where it was, and were only checking my loyalty) was formulated by the customs official in the first person plural:

"So what did we do in Latvia, then?"

At first, I was unable to respond with even an "er" or an "ah," so unexpected was that interest in "our" activities. I had never before encountered anything of the like at any border crossing. For a customs official to be interested in your personal recent past. The first time that I reached Paris, with a Soviet passport, the Roissy Airfield police officer indeed asked me what my purpose was for going to France, but I had prepared myself for that question and laid everything out nicely—telling how I would be visiting friends (my visa had been acquired on the basis of a fictitious invitation to visit) and historic sightseeing attractions, museums, the Louvre, etc.—which, however, the official was no longer even listening to; he had already stamped my passport and was waiting for me to move away from his counter.

But that Republic of Estonia customs official seemed to be taking his question completely seriously, because he continued staring straight at me and apparently expected an exhaustive reply: what had a citizen of the Republic of Estonia been doing abroad, anyway? Especially given the fact that he had brought back practically nothing (the customs official had also carefully inspected the CDs that I brought along for listening: I claimed honestly that I already had all of them prior to my trip to Latvia).

Having collected myself somewhat, I told him that I went to a museum. This past testimony was indeed just as false as the future promise given to a border police officer at Charles de Gaulle Airport eleven years ago, because just like this time in Riga, I didn't visit a single museum in Paris on that occasion. And even regardless of the fact that "that occasion" extended into a period of years. I haven't visited a single Paris museum to this day. I've never understood the unique ritual of cultural consumption that is "visiting museums and sightseeing attractions." Yet, this time as well, that cultural-conformist lie turned out to be effective, because the customs official didn't ask any more questions. I felt great relief, because I would have been at a loss for an answer to the question, "What museum?" I don't know a single museum in Riga. I was permitted to drive on, to enter my "homeland," so to speak. Small countries are somewhat perverse with their sacred and inviolable borders. But they are rarely long-term in historical terms, if they don't fit into some system of balance between large powers. The brand new Valga/Valka border checkpoint will most likely lose its function quite soon, when the areas of Old Livonia are joined with the European Union.

Actually, I did visit one historical attraction in Riga. Yet, the truth didn't immediately come to mind when I was speaking with the official. Lying is likely instinctive, because it's rare that an administration expects a true answer from you. A response must correspond more to expectations than to truth. The truth about my tourist activity was centered in the fact that I measured Riga's Dome Church with my paces, because I was interested in how much bigger it is than the one in Tartu. It did feel larger. In Tartu, however, it turned out that Riga's is indeed slightly wider (forty paces against Tartu's thirty-seven), but, on the other hand, is shorter (94:105). Furthermore, there are still two towers on Tartu's Cathedral of Saints Peter and Paul, as a proper Gothic cathedral must have, while Riga's has only one thick, centrally situated tower like that on Tallinn's Dome Church. In summary, historians' claim that in the fifteenth century, when Tartu's Dome Church was erected, the town exceeded even Riga in terms of its trade turnover due to its special relations with Novgorod, could thus be true.

Returning to Tartu from Riga, getting to my apartment, I had the pleasant feeling of arriving home. It appears that I settle in quickly; the main thing is that I have my own private apartment. I can't stand hotels. I dreamed of them during Soviet times;

however, I came to realize while traveling around with Liz Franz that I hate them. I also do not tolerate cohabitation in any form at all, nor would I likely tolerate any kind of cohabitation outside of my fantasies either.

Entering the room, I noticed the pack of cards that I purchased the day before last, and I had the immediate desire to lay cards for myself. I had already sorted the Major Arcana into a separate pack; I don't know how to lay the Minor Arcana—I haven't learned their meanings, and they aren't so interesting either. Actually, the only divination system that I remember from Liz Franz is the "small cross": four cards plus five.

Firstly, one must shuffle the cards carefully, then lift them with the left hand, then deal: right, left, up, down. Still, I didn't remember whether a card was also laid in the center, or whether it was calculated from the digit sum of the four cards' numbers. The small cross came out like this:

XIII

III (Priestess)   X (Wheel of Fortune)

XII (The Hanged Man)

A card placed in the center of the cross came out as VI (The Lovers), but by adding the digits (13+12+3+10=38, 3+8=11, 1+1=2) was II (Priestess). If I remember correctly, then the card on the left-hand side pointed to "what is for you," and the right-hand one is "what is against you." Above was "the path to an outcome," "the outcome." The middle card probably showed something like "your overall situation right now."

I don't know whether the Priestess—who is holding a scepter in one hand, a coat of arms bearing an eagle in the other, and is looking (in relation to the dealer, the observer) towards the right; thus, in the direction of reading, "into the future"—is Liz Franz in the given case. From what I know, the Priestess is something akin to "the queen of the world, who rules with her sense and ability to analyze," consciousness, wisdom, Athena. Consequently, that is "for" me.

In my Marseilles tarot deck, the Wheel of Fortune—and so, in the given position, the opposing force to the Priestess—is a crank wheel, which spinning counter-clockwise leads an animal-person up on the right-hand side, another down on the left (something like a monkey wearing a skirt), while crowning the wheel's upper tangent is a third carrying a sword, wearing a crown and a red cloak over its bat wings; the most humanlike; that, who is presently on top.

"The path leading to an outcome" is thus card number thirteen. It is traditionally a nameless card depicting a skeleton using its black scythe to cut a black land strewn with bones, hands, legs, heads. That nameless card is likewise called Death, of course, and that name is written in both French and Russian on the card I bought, because the given release was meant for distribution in areas of the former Soviet Union. Thirteen is an unlucky number, as many know; but I can't say whether it is for me as well, because it's my date of birth.

A conflict arose between Liz Franz and me over the nameless card, because she wanted to interpret it as our common card. The thing is that it is her symbol as a Scorpio, while it is also mine numerologically. Thus, Death would have united us. But I didn't like that interpretation; just as I didn't like all of her other attempts to construct some kind of "we," which she never gave up. There were things that "we" liked, others that rubbed "us" the right way. I truly hated that "we."

However, the XIII card doesn't only promise misfortune in and of itself in divination (fortune-telling). Even the opposite. The Reaper heralds "the end of the old" (this pleased Liz Franz greatly: everything old ended and something completely new began for us together, as Edith Piaf sang), similarly cutting free the path to rebirth, allowing one to enter a new stage, and all that stuff. But it can also simply mean death.

In the given instance, the outcome to which the Grim Reaper leads is thus The Hanged Man: a young man hanging by one leg from two green intersecting beams placed between two trees, his hands (bound?) behind his back. His pose is, by the way, quite casual—he doesn't appear to be suffering. The hanged man is a particular *Tagurpidi-Ants* (a person from Estonian artistic folklore, who systematically does everything backwards), a nonconformist, a rebel. His "higher" meaning, however, is something like "the abandonment of illusions; sacrifice, which leads the person to another, spiritual level."

However, due to my ignorance, I came up with two possible versions for the overall situation (the central, fifth card).

VI, a.k.a. The Lovers, depicts a young man standing between two women and unable to choose one over the other. One, on the left (still in relation to the viewer; as such, actually to the right of the young man), has dark hair and is evidently older. It symbolizes earthly, passionate love. She holds her hand possessively on the young man's shoulder. The other, on the right (to the young man's left), is blond and young; she is pointing to the young man's—likewise a blond—heart. She is meant to symbolize spiritual, heavenly love. The young man himself is looking to the left, ergo into the past; but at the same time, towards the older woman—earthly love. He is unable to choose. Yet, a choice has already been made for him. Namely, little Amor, a.k.a. Eros, is flying in front of the disc of the sun above the young man's head, and is loosing an arrow from his bow. Aiming the arrow at the young man's heart, the putto is looking to the right, towards the young woman.

The second alternative for the situation, which came out as II by addition, is the Priestess (*Papesse*).

The *Papesse* is an older woman wearing a three-tiered yellow tiara (red blossoms on the first tier, green on the second). A white veil covers her hair, there is a blue cape over her red dress. She is sitting and holding an open book in her hands, but the writing on its pages is illegible. It is said to be both the Book of Life and a kind of alchemist's handbook at once. She is looking towards the left, "into the past," just as The Lover. *Papesse* is said to be a symbol for the subconscious, and is simultaneously the priestess who guards over secrets and mysteries; a performer of initiation rites; a clairvoyant (corporally, the pineal gland; i.e. the so-called "third eye"); a great benefactress and servant of Life; the Egyptian goddess Isis, who wakens Osiris from the dead—her brother and lover, who in Plutarch's version was her twin, and with whom she already copulated in their mother's body. Namely, Osiris is ripped into fourteen pieces by Seth or Typhon. Isis gathers and rejoins all of the pieces except for one, which the fish of the Nile have gobbled up—specifically, Osiris's phallus. Yet, as a smart woman, Isis herself crafts a new phallus for Osiris, and consecrates it right then and there.

By the beginning of our historical era, Isis became the combined figure of practically all mothers, goddesses, and lovers; the consoler of the downcast and the suffering; the Sea-Star (Isis Pelagia), whose main attribute was a mystical rose, and whose many elements found reuse in the cult of the Virgin Mary.

I don't know, but I've often been interested in whether Liz Franz is (was) a virgin in the traditional sense. This is not completely ruled out in and of itself, given her sexual preferences. As our respective intercourse was limited to only fellatio, I was never able to see for myself. Yet, that question continued to gnaw at me to some extent. I resolved it for myself with the decision that every woman who has not given birth, or who at least hasn't been pregnant (although I can't confirm that Liz Franz had not been) is basically a virgin. I don't see breaking the hymen, i.e. physical deflowering, as having any significant importance here. This hypothesis of mine was also confirmed by the testimony I received from Linda, which I previously referenced. I thus believe that Liz Franz is a virgin.

31

The Eurovision Song Contest, which was held in Tallinn this year, was won by Latvia. I hadn't the slightest intention to watch Eurovision, but it just so happened that I watched it all the same, and furthermore on a large screen that was set up in the twenty-fourth floor reception room of the new Radisson SAS in Tallinn. It was an invitation only evening, and Herbert Treumann invited me to it. He is now a well-known and well-paid lawyer—his area of specialty is economic crimes. Our acquaintanceship dates back to 1987. Herbert Treumann was then a law school student in his final year, who very much wanted to make a film, and I had just been given a green light from the state film company "Tallinfilm" for making my first independent project, *The Railway Watchman's House.* I must say that the film also turned out to be my breakthrough, earning the attention of local critics with its "novel, original visual language," which I had compiled from several experimental films that are little known in Estonia. To this day, I am still amazed that not a single critic even gently alluded to my true role models and sources. Some works, which were being discussed in film circles those days, were indeed referenced. I had never seen a number of them, and I doubt whether those critics always had either. One especially fanciful analysis even made it all the way up to Fellini's *E la nave va (And the Ship Sails On).* I was proud of that comparison, although I detested Fellini. My entire film was actually only an illustration to Liz Franz's songs, and even the title, the entire idea, naturally originated from her "Railway" record. True, I have been enchanted by railways, trains, and especially railway watchmen's cabins since I was a child. Seeing them from a train window, I often imagined that I was actually the son of a railway watchman, but the watchman died in a train accident, and his wife sold me for two hundred rubles to my parents, who ergo were not really my parents. Now I know that this is a quite widespread childhood fantasy: imagining being a foundling, from a concealed, lofty lineage.

Watchmen's cabins were miniscule: they might have only had a single room and a kitchen, and were often surrounded by a garden, where cherries and apple trees blossomed, and large, colorful dahlias in the fall. The railway was a pan-Union structure during the Soviet period, and primarily Russians worked on the railway in Estonia as well. Nevertheless, I managed to find an Estonian watchman amid the forests between Kehra and Aegviidu, who held that profession for the fourth consecutive generation. No drivable road led to that cabin: the connection with the outside world still ran through the tiny Mustjõe Station, which was less than a mile away. A handcar, i.e. draisine, was also used when necessary.

Back then, the topic of heritage and national identity had just come into focus, but one wasn't quite allowed to handle it directly yet. Moscow's hegemony was symbolized most of all by long freight and passenger trains, which in the collective public awareness and subconscious was associated with both deportations and the economic system, which was regarded as extremely unfair. People especially opposed the massive export of meat under the circumstances, in which meat products weren't always available in Estonian shops, and these products' quality became ever worse. Because at the same time, trains carrying frozen swine and cattle carcasses, as well as mooing livestock, chugged along "towards Moscow." Estonia was Russia's livestock farm, although in reality, Estonia's meat output naturally constituted an insignificant portion of the entire Soviet Union's respective output. The collective fantasies of independence, which at that time spread quickly, burst into bloom, and found an ever more public expression, were indeed greatly focused on hindering that illegal meat export. The forced transport of Estonian swine and cattle to Russia had to be stopped, and pork and sausages should never be in short supply under the conditions of independence.

As Estonians can recall, the first step of that autonomy at the time, when the fight for freedom had already acquired a serious political outlet and Estonia declared its independence from Moscow (still being a part of the Soviet Union in actuality), was to enforce a so-called economic border, the primary task of which was to control the exporting of meat and butter. True—when genuine independence arrived and Russia began to block the importing of Estonia's agricultural output in turn, the nationalist fight quickly changed direction on that front, and instead accused the country's ignoble eastern neighbor of choking off its economy. Russia's restriction of meat imports was also a truly heavy blow to Estonia's agricultural sector, which had been artificially boosted by Moscow's oil money before then. A large portion of the production herd had to be taken to slaughterhouses and destroyed: there was nowhere to put the meat.

Yet, in 1987, that was all just a future scenario, with which one couldn't even frighten the party and security organs fighting against the pursuit of independence. It was popular to talk about our nation's perseverance in the face of the winds of history, and that perseverance was also reflected in my first film, *The Railway Watchman's House*, although I despised the new national rhetoric as a result of that hollowness. I actually stood no higher than it in the least, I only imagined myself to be doing so; the new ideological movement had swept *me* along entirely as well. The railway watchman's house and its fourth generation inhabitant symbolized that very same perseverance, clinging to the sod of the earth; so what that the sod quaked ever more frequently and ever more heavily to the rhythm of train wheels: in a symbolic sense, to the rhythm of those very meat trains rolling to the east, and passenger trains arriving from the east. The latter transported more and more new economic immigrants to Old Livonia, as the low local birthrate was unable to meet the labor needs of Soviet industrialization programs.

That railway watchman, Arnold Ratas, was truly quite a good find for me, because in his own way he was also a village philosopher, who gladly discussed matters of eternity while sitting in the evening sunlight on his cabin's doorstep, watching the trains speeding past. In the film, his monologues often disappear into the rumble of trains: *that* also has a symbolic effect, and at the same time, doesn't allow them to become too boring, because it wasn't as if Arnolt Ratas had anything especially original to say. What made his ramblings "philosophical" in the film were the expressively depicted evening light, old mossy apple trees just bursting into bloom, the up-and-down movement of the railroad crossties under train wheels (shot in close-up), kittens playing in the grass, and all of those other clichés that I exploited shamelessly, justifying myself with hazily-profound excuses.

Arnold Ratas and I developed quite a trusting relationship. He was a single man, an old bachelor, already nearly sixty years old, and had no children. His watchman's cabin was nevertheless fastidiously clean and orderly, just as were his white shirt and black watchman's uniform. The train schedule hung on his wall in a place of honor, along with a Russian-language certificate once received for good work. Arnold Ratas was a Virgo and a pedant of sorts; most of all, he was bothered by trains being on time ever less frequently, and that even the "high-speed" ones such as the *Estonia* (Tallinn–Moscow) and the *Chaika* ("Seagull," Tallinn–Tartu–Riga–Vilnius–Minsk) ran late ever more often. When the *Estonia* was precisely on schedule according to Arnold Ratas's watch, which he synchronized at six o'clock every morning according to the radio signal, then a satisfied smile flashed across the watchman's face, and an especially lyrical monologue could be expected of him that day. Sometimes, a rare, deep, spacious silence commanded the area around the watchman's cabin—only a woodpecker pecked in the woods, or the sound of Arnold's portable, high-reception "Ocean" radio sounded through the open door. Arnold enjoyed listening to classical music. On some summer evenings like those, Arnold's monologue could soar to such fanciful heights that the rumble of a train had to be dubbed over it right at the start. I feared at that time that the film might otherwise become too cloying, although watching it now, it is cloying all the same, and for completely different reasons. Arnold could have been shown even more, however, because actually, he was still a crazy figure.

He came to the film's test screening in his watchman's uniform, wearing a snow-white shirt and his hat, and sat erect and unmoving for the entire showing. Afterwards, everyone flocked around the cameraman (who was Herbert Treumann) and I; no one dealt with Arnold, and I didn't even notice when he disappeared. Once, I went to go see him again, but he was taciturn and only fixed his light, transparent eyes in the direction of the forest. Driven by some abrupt bout of homesickness, I sent him a postcard from Paris once, later on, but didn't receive a reply.

When Liz Franz and I traveled from Tallinn to Riga, I had an unconditional desire to see Arnold's cabin, and studied the darkness outside the window with care. I knew that Arnold would still be up at that time and listening to the radio, his "Ocean," and the light would be on in his window. But I didn't see anything. Traveling by there once more while it was still daylight—that was probably the last time that I traveled by train in Estonia—I saw that the railway watchman's cabin was no more; only the chimney was still standing. Many railway watchman points were done away with in the course of independence-era railway re-structuring: the cabins were abandoned and knocked down, ultimately set on fire. Apparently, that's what happened to Arnold Ratas's house too. As he was childless, the railway watchmen's dynasty would have ended with him anyway. I don't know whether he himself is still alive; nor have I ever wanted to find out.

But as such, I made *The Railway Watchman's House* with Herbert Treumann. Herbert was an outstandingly handsome boy—his large, dark eyes shine somehow strangely even now, although his hairline has receded somewhat; overall, however, he has aged amazingly little, as if he hadn't even been living in the interim. At the same time, he wasn't a callous and foolish knockout (in that sense, male knockouts don't differ in any way from female knockouts: both are, for the most part, hopelessly spoiled); but on top of it all, he was still sensitive, searching, and intelligent. Thus, there wasn't even an option for me to say no to him when he sought me out and offered to be my cameraman. Up until then, he had—just like me—only worked as an assistant and done amateur films, of course.

Specifically, I had worked my way into a position working with Raimond Madar, who at that time made extremely popular nature films, already during my college days. I went with him on field shoots and carried technical equipment and other gear, including beer and vodka, which Raimond Madar consumed in rather large quantities. He was an awful egocentric, a despot, and an otherwise moody person. He guarded with care to make sure that the young film careerists circling him didn't catch up too much. To me, it seems that he outright purposefully never taught anything; he only mocked you when you did something wrong. Despite this, I still learned a thing or two at his side, and maybe even quite a lot. Among other things, I also learned to sense his mental confines, and to see them in his films as well. In some sense, those popular-science films made about birds and animals, which at the same time had some poetic pretention, were all his autobiographies. He hated people. I don't know anything about his sexual orientation, because as far as I know, he didn't have either girlfriends or boyfriends in that sense. Raimond Madar was autistic in a certain way, and to this day I watch his nature films—especially if they have the pretention to say something—with great incredulity. And nevertheless—and despite Raimond Madar's own opposition—working with him and my name making it into the credits of his films opened up the path to independent filmmaking for me. Even regardless of the fact that I didn't have the respective education—I had only somehow, through trials and tribulations, managed to finish my genetics studies and allow myself to be directed to Obinitsa Grade School, at which I never appeared, however. I was to become an author.

To this day, I'm amazed at how I managed to get independent work so quickly; and secondly, by how I managed to convince the film studio management that the completely unknown Herbert Treumann was a suitable cameraman. I was already in love with him by then; it had happened practically at first sight. It might also be that Herbert was somehow able to win over even the unfeeling geezers at the film studio (a few of whom were indeed younger than I am now, but they were still geezers all the same—blasé and bulging with importance) with his personal charm. He had then, and to this very day still has the kind of charm that worked and still works on people, regardless of their gender or sexual orientation. All in all, however, it turned out that Herbert Treumann was also a cameraman with a very steady hand and a sharp eye. He could have become a great cameraman, but oddly, he didn't especially value his abilities in that field; although maybe as the new times rolled around, he found that it was easier for him to earn money in his studied field, in law—and good money at that.

Actually, the entire success of *The Railway Watchman's House* is owed to Herbert Treumann, without exception. I don't know whether he knows this himself, because I've never spoken to him about it explicitly. That summer, all of my thoughts and feelings were fixated on him alone, and it's plausible that I rose higher than my own level only thanks to the fact that my desire to shine before him was so powerful.

Back then, as always, Herbert had a girlfriend—Kati, a first class blond who came to the set from time to time, tanned in the grass next to the railroad tracks, and soon went away again because of boredom and the mosquitoes. Herbert could be very delicate with her, but he could forget about her as well. He never spoke about Kati. Beside all of his convincing, manly beauty, he was somehow bizarrely monkish. He could lie in the grass for hours and stare at the sky, his eyes glinting. It seems to me that he never dreamed about love, or about anything of the sort. I don't know what he dreamed about. I lay beside him, at a slight distance. Crickets chirped on the railroad, we didn't speak.

Back then, I burned with frustrated lust, and from time to time even with rage over Herbert's brilliant indifference. Now, those summer evenings seem to have been something akin to happiness. Maybe the only "real" happiness that I have ever experienced. Sometimes, I ask myself whether Herbert would have reacted to me making an actual pass at him. Maybe he wouldn't have had anything against it. Maybe. But that, I will never find out. I no longer feel anything for him in that sense—perhaps only a little nostalgia for my former feelings.

Herbert is himself, however, blasé, to a certain extent. As we all are. I can't imagine him still lounging next to a railroad and watching the clouds for hours on end. His clientele is very broad, and gives him no respite; but still, it seems to me that he even treats his legal work with a certain smiling indifference. Perhaps that's the reason he is so successful. He was even surrounded by brownnosing businessmen at the Eurovision evening, the majority of whom have a criminal background, and none of whom I recognized, although a few of them are probably big "doers" in Estonia, as people say here now. In addition to those temporary satellites, he had, as always, a stable female "Sputnik" this time. I don't remember what her name was—I let it slip past me, because there's no point in remembering Herbert's women's names anyhow. Next time, he'll already have one that is new, although identical to the last. I don't know what their use is. His disinterest in them only appears to increase with the years. But it's also true that for a person of his position, a blond is, of course, part of the collection of compulsory accessories; just as a suit and a good car. Herbert has a silver Mercedes coupé, and probably a few more cars on top of that.

When we made a film together, he generally limited himself solely to his work, and took my frequently vague ideas and instructions into account with great precision, almost devotedly— which made me quite amazed. Only once did he give me advice on the content, and even now I don't know whether it was more beneficial or detrimental.

Specifically, I had planned to use Liz Franz's songs in my film. I had no other idea for sound design. When I told Herbert about this (right at the beginning, because it was very important to me), he was both quite amazed and critical at once. I realized that for him, Liz Franz was a singer far behind the times (and that she probably is for the majority of my generation), and that my desire to use her old songs in my new film was even a little ridiculous. Herbert, who otherwise never spoke badly about anyone (he was too indifferent about people for that), seemed to regard Liz Franz so much as poisonously, scornfully. I didn't speak to him about Liz Franz anymore, because I saw that it could lower me in his eyes.

I betrayed my "poor girlfriend"—*бедная подруга*, which I started to call her in my mind only much later, of course: during the second phase of our acquaintanceship, and I myself was Liz Franz's *pauvre ami*, poor friend, in my own mind—yes, I betrayed Liz Franz, who at that time wasn't yet my friend or my girlfriend in reality, at the first chance I had. Ultimately, the music for the film was written by Asko Lepp, who back then was a young, promising composer, and still is to this day. In those days, I only liked that exceptionally intellectual music, which also had some sort of eastern pretention, because Herbert Treumann liked it. Now, it feels somewhat fake and hollow to me; just as my entire film does, incidentally. Yet, it could also still be true that Herbert Treumann's advice was useful, and that Liz Franz's songs would have had a ridiculous, anachronistic effect on the film. I'm unable to judge them adequately to this day. They're simply a part of me, a much greater part than Liz Franz herself.

However, Herbert Treumann is worthy of his name, because although it's a long time since I've been of any use to him, he has remained loyal to me in his own way. That loyalty is just as baffling to me as his indifference for people. He is never intrusive, but calls me regularly and always invites me out somewhere when he knows that I'm in Estonia. On the other hand, he has never looked me up in Paris, although he has been there. It may be that he has avoided it out of discreteness, maybe out of some odd fear that something undesired could possibly happen between us in that new environment, which is furthermore "my" environment. Or, he is simply jealous of my new life. I don't know. But his invitations are always benevolent and grand. This time, it was that Eurovision dinner, the one thousand kroon ticket for which he treated me to. When he called and invited me, I wanted to know only one thing: no cultural figures are coming, are they? He confirmed that none were, because he had organized the evening to some extent, and he also generally avoided associating with cultural circles. He apparently doesn't understand them—there's always someone there who gets loaded, and then attacks him or starts to pick a fight with him, while incidentally, they fawned over him inexplicably beforehand.

I avoid Estonian cultural figures because some of them remember me or have heard something about me, and they always have some particular opinion on what kind of a person I am; likewise, I can tell that I'm firmly fixed in the local cultural hierarchy that they've arranged with microscopic precision, the ranking-criteria for which is difficult for me to understand. I've become a layperson in those fine points; "I just don't get it," as I heard my high-school-senior nephew say. That means: I'm unable to analyze. They—Estonian cultural figures—are in turn unable to hide their satisfaction over the fact that although I am abroad, I haven't actually gotten anywhere. They insinuate that there are already new, famous figures in Estonia, and I'm just as good as forgotten. As for me—I haven't heard anything about those new people, although they've sometimes apparently achieved international success. I don't know what people mean by that. Maybe they've gone to some festival. And so, we have *nothing* to talk about. Furthermore, I'm sometimes left with a sort of bad taste in my mouth from speaking with cultural figures; it's as if I'd like to rinse my mouth, but I don't even know of what.

And so, luckily only businessmen, lawyers, some top criminals, a number of foreigners of unspecified status, and for some reason, also a couple of diplomats were on the twenty-fourth floor of the Radisson SAS. Apparently, people in Estonia have also learned to decorate their evenings with diplomats. Such a practice is mandatory in France. Even an Estonian ambassador not only fits the bill, but is the jewel of every Parisian dinner, as stupid as he may be. No one among those present at the Radisson seemed to recognize me, nor did anyone evince any hostile prejudice, although my velvet jacket didn't exactly correspond to the evening's dress code—which was more or less free-choice. Although one of the criminals was even in a tuxedo.

Herbert acquainted me with the guests' backgrounds when he freed himself from his satellites for a moment. He did so in unrestrained words that he probably never uses in his legal career. He still speaks to me in the same way that we spoke back when we lay side-by-side in our tent (it was stuffy in Arnold's cabin) on the nights of film shoots, endlessly discussing very important and abstract matters. I was sleepless and elated because I was in love with Herbert, and he lay right there in my reach (although I never reached my hand out). Why he was sleepless, I don't know.

Still, that company at the Radisson was generally quite depressing, and I had already gotten to the point of regretting coming at all. Everyone was actually *watching* Eurovision. To pass the time, I attempted to converse with Herbert's girl, who was growing bored next to me, but she turned out to be practically aphasic—or else, I was unable to pronounce a single sentence to which she would have responded.

The pair sitting across from me—some colleague of Herbert with his wife, who appeared to be slightly more intelligent than Herbert's blond—tried, in turn, to converse with me. They praised the Eurovision show's good production, and expertly mentioned the names of the figures responsible, which meant nothing to me. One of them had apparently also directed some television series, of which the woman was critically minded:

"I don't understand at **all** how he could stoop so low!"

I thought she meant Eurovision, and chimed in that truly—it's hard to come up with anything more vapid and pointless than Eurovision. The married couple ignored me after that, and I was fine with it, because I would only have said something wrong again anyway.

The food was luckily very good and I drank quite a lot of wine, became drunk, and Eurovision seemed really fun to me. For variety, I also fantasized about whether the diplomats' sitting in front of me, at another table, with their backs' facing me, were a couple or not. The pair was the Swiss ambassador—an older gentleman—and some young embassy advisor. Both had come without women. Some sense of cohesion seemed to dominate between them, which, of course, could also have stemmed from their common origin. In addition, the young man seemed to have power over the older one. He, by the way, perceived that I was watching them, and looked in my direction several times. That glance was strangely swift each time. The young man was generally handsome, but with a face that was somewhat too brutal. That is, he had a sufficiently delicate and cultivated face, of course—the brutality was hidden. Yet, I believe he is erecting his career step-by-step upon the very types of old men (or older women), who are taken in by him and to whom he always makes promises at the given moment; whom he is always able to keep on a leash of just the right length. It also appeared to me that he saw that I saw through his game (one dog sure recognizes another!) and hated me because of it.

There was a bet going on for common entertainment during the evening. Everyone could make a one hundred kroon bet on a single song. The jackpot was to be split among those who guessed the winning song. Oddly, the MC, who was probably paid extra, didn't come to me asking for money. It was as if I was invisible. Still, I was already so drunk that I would have wanted to make a bet. I would have bet on Cyprus's boy band, although I didn't really like them that much either. However, neither was I unable to see any kinds of other criteria there for telling the songs apart, aside from an erotic attraction to the singers. At the end, it turned out that those same Swiss diplomats had made the right prediction: both—the young as well as the old—had bet on Latvia, as did Inga —the wife of one of Estonia's richest individuals, investment banker Rain Lõhmus. They all then split the winnings evenly between them, and thus earned back the costs spent on the evening. I've come to understand that many things are free for the rich. It's a fact of life.

Having heard from Herbert that I live in Paris, Rain Lõhmus complimented the city, where he enjoyed going from time to time. He also agreed with me that onc needs to spend a great deal of money there to feel well. He apparently couldn't imagine my relative poorness, just as I couldn't imagine what his assets, which stretch into hundreds of millions of kroons (tens of millions of euros), really mean. Another person's life is so abstract, and in my opinion, the great peculiarities of his, that people speak of (such as wealth or talent), have nothing to do with the physical/psychiatric individual, with whom one must speak. All things considered, all people are more or less ordinary.

Rain Lõhmus said he had recently flown from Paris to New York, and that flight route seemed to him to be the most suitable for visiting New York. I asked whether he flew on a Concorde. He acknowledged somewhat too quickly that yes, he had flown on a Concorde, and it wasn't so expensive at all. I inquired as to how it was flying on a Concorde, because I've only seen documentaries about it. He said it had been a little like a Russian airplane: cramped and stinking of jet fuel.

After that, he introduced me (having heard that I was involved in the film industry) to a burly guy with tattooed arms (he had taken his jacket off from over his white T-shirt) and a shaved head, who had arrived later, and whom I had heard speaking in Russian with his female companion (who is most likely regarded as beautiful). I had thought him one of the top criminals, but it turned out that he was actually the renowned young writer Kaur Kender. I was initially bothered upon hearing that there was in fact one other cultural figure there, and that I would furthermore have to speak with him. Luckily, however, it turned out that my name meant absolutely nothing to him—that barely noticeable transition of flattery into contempt or vice versa didn't show in his expression, which is a rule when you are introduced to a cultural figure as being a cultural figure.

We got to talking, and spoke for quite long about the film *Star Wars: Episode II—Attack of the Clones*, which I had just gone to see in Tartu during the day. Asko invited me, and (of course)

I didn't decline. That time, in the dark cinema and looking at
him from the side, his eyes, showing between his long eyelashes,
appeared dark and shining; somewhat like Herbert Treumann's
eyes when he sat next to me during the test showing of *The
Railway Watchman's House* fifteen years ago. I found that *Star
Wars* was a perfect work in its own manner, and the relatively
well-contemplated psychoanalytic symbolism as well as the
complex of mythological archetypes even surprised me. What
was astounding, of course, is what simple means can be used to
captivate people; how primitive the "modern fairytale" still is. Or,
well, just as primitive as always, apparently. It was easy for me
to pose my reasonably polished positions to Kaur Kender now,
because I had already voiced those thoughts in front of Asko,
also having had to change my opinion about his stupidity on the
basis of his clever responses. No, Asko isn't stupid in the least,
and at that moment, I felt a strong longing for him. I realized
that everyone at that dinner (except the women) was thirty or
well over it, while at the same time seeming to be perfectly of the
same age—early-middle-aged, just as I am. And also that there
really wasn't anyone there to look at. In the meantime, it seemed
that Kaur Kender was giving me the eye; I was also charmed by
his flexible and quick intelligence. Picking up steam, I told him
about my trip to Riga. He asked me a couple of questions about
it, and promised to use my views right away in an article that he
was to be writing about Eurovision for the German weekly *Die
Zeit*. Back in my day, I certainly wouldn't have dared to admit so
openly that I didn't have my own ideas, and that I was copying
them from others. Nor would I have dared to speak about my
successes (that *Die Zeit* order), although I would have feverishly
yearned for someone to bring them up in conversation, thus
giving me the opportunity to speak about them modestly. The
new generation is nevertheless more honest and open-minded, in
a certain sense. Past midnight, I realized, by the way, that he was

very drunk, and *that* was likely what I had interpreted as flirting.

Past midnight, everyone was quite drunk and in a generous euphoria from Latvia's victory; I was the only one that started sobering up. The thing is that I usually don't want to drink much. I very much like the first, fresh buzz. This buzz comes around after around a couple of schnapps (German *Schnaps*), or after the third or fourth glass of wine. Then, for some time I am possessed by a certain warm, lonely feeling of happiness. But I don't want to drink more: the wine becomes disagreeable, the unpleasant physiological perceptions that go along with light alcohol poisoning start to poke their noses out from the enjoyable intoxication, and I start drinking water or juice; sobering up.

It could also be that this is simply a cautiousness, which I've grown into. It's dangerous for a homosexual to let him- or herself go (*se laisser aller*): who knows what will happen when the person is drunk. Perhaps the person will get too bold. Control has to be maintained in every situation. Actually, that control is also maintained when very drunk (I've tried it), and I don't really believe in memory gaps. They are relatively relative, and primarily serve the aim of excusing oneself: not remembering means it never happened, or if it has happened, then it didn't mean anything. Therefore, I generally avoid and despise passes made by drunk men who identify themselves as heterosexuals, although I believe that these are completely genuine. However, they are also completely cowardly. They'd like to give it a try, but in such a way that it's as if it had never happened. A man who doesn't remember anything afterwards. We've checked it out, thanks, no more for me. Maybe I'm generally too cautious.

It started growing light outside again after three o'clock. That is, it hadn't actually quite gone dark: the northern sky behind Toompea had kept glowing above the sea. A beautiful view opens up from the twenty-fourth floor of the Radisson; it's as if Tallinn's tiny downtown is in the palm of a hand. Looking to the south, towards Lake Ülemiste, it appears as if you are somewhere in a village, in the center of which that sort of lookout tower has been built, for some reason. Below are tiny wooden houses, squat garages, a few ugly panel apartment buildings (HLMs) in the area of the Central Market, and a forest right behind them, then the large Lake Ülemiste. The city is pressed between a lake and marshes and the sea—it was never meant to grow to such proportions, and is now stretched out from the east to the west like bowels. At the same time, the downtown is still full of open plots and run-down shacks, so the city lacks any kind of practical purpose for building skyscrapers, just like in Tartu. Especially given the fact that the view from them is treacherous (giving away the city's smallness). But it is also beautiful. The view towards Toompea and the sea, with its many church towers, is truly beautiful on a summer night.

In all honesty, Tallinn has never grown out of being that small German trader's town, which was called Reval, and is now called Old Town (*vieille ville*). The New Town is merely chaotic slums, villages, and hamlets beyond its old walls. The Old Town, a.k.a. Reval, is called medieval, although its silhouette—no matter whether seen from the sea or the Radisson—is rather baroque: apparently, Reval's final blossoming arrived at that very time, before its ultimate decline into becoming a provincial governorate center, and it was right then that new tower spires with modern forms were erected upon the churches and Town Hall. As I had never seen Tallinn from such an angle, I eyed it like a completely strange city for the first time in my life. I realized that I will never come back here again for good, and that I will soon no longer have any reason to call it my hometown. It did appear very beautiful to me at that moment. The sky had just erupted into a reddish glow from the northeast. The sun now sets in the northwest and rises from the northeast; the sea, however, reflects its glow from beyond the horizon back into the sky throughout the night.

Two cathedrals located upon the towering mound of Toompea hold the most prominent place in Tallinn's silhouette: the old Catholic/Lutheran Dome Church (Sainte Marie), and the Aleksander Nevski Orthodox Cathedral, erected at the beginning of the nineteenth century. Incidentally, the one tower's baroque volumes harmonize fantastically with the other's numerous cake-top onion domes. Sainte Marie is, however, higher than Aleksander Nevski at the top of the hill, and dominates over the entire town. The most imposing tower in Lower Town is that of St. Nicolas's (Saint Nicolas) Church—a former German congregational church, now a museum and concert hall. Its tower was destroyed during the Soviet bomb attack in World War II, and the restored tower was destroyed once more in a fire, so what can be seen now is the second copy of Saint Nicolas's baroque tower.

Another medieval congregational church was St. Olaf's (Saint Olaf) Church, the tower of which is the only one that has remained un-modernized (although it has likewise been rebuilt, following a fire that happened centuries ago), and to this very day consists of a sharp needle that is said to have been the highest construction in Europe and the entire world during the fifteenth century. It served as a landmark at sea, because Tallinn's (etymologically *Talilinn*, *Talvelinn*, Winter Town, *Ville d'Hiver*) primary function was as a trade port, as well as a wintering harbor for Hanseatic ships. Still, Winter Town is its most beautiful on summer nights. Maybe because the summer is so short here. It might also be true that everything identifies itself in relation to its opposite.

I left before the last partygoers. Two blonds, most likely prostitutes, but the kinds that don't define themselves as prostitutes, had popped up next to two unidentified foreign men that I had deemed a gay couple (I don't mean the Swiss diplomats—they had long since left) over the course of the night. Simply beautiful girls. The male foreigners, who were dressed exactly alike (a tight white T-shirt, black jeans), indeed continued conversing only amongst themselves; the blonds crept after them while at the same time keeping as great a distance as possible, and signaling that they belonged to one specific foreigner of the pair, although they were unusually similar to one another—the foreigners among themselves, just ~~the~~ as the blonds among themselves. Perhaps the blonds kept an eye on their respective partners precisely in order to avoid mixing them up. Women are often pedants at these things.

I decided that I was already sufficiently sober to drive (I had drunk water and cranberry juice in large quantities), and that I now needed to leave that city. The hotels were probably chock full in connection with Eurovision, and I didn't want to show any sign of myself (*signaler*) to my parents; and so, I decided to drive to Anton's place on the island of Hiiumaa, as he has always invited me to come and visit. By calling directory assistance about the ferry times, however, I found out that the first ferry to Hiiumaa on Sunday morning only left at ten-thirty; and so, I set course for Virtsu, from where ferries depart for Estonia's—more specifically, Livonia's—largest island, Saaremaa. I had no definite plans for what I would do there, but for some reason I didn't want to drive back to Tartu either. I suddenly had the feeling that it would be useful to cover my trail a little—to make an unexpected maneuver, preferably across the sea. Nothing loses a trail better than water. I was apparently in *quite* an inadequate status from sleeplessness and the repercussions of alcohol. The night was very, very cold; the surface air temperature in many places certainly fell below water's freezing point again. The streets of the suburbs that I drove through (passing quite close to my father's house, too) were empty: along the street were only a couple of groups of drunken partiers and a couple lone partiers staggering home. One group was waving an Estonian flag, for some reason; perhaps it was simply the first flag handy for lack of a Latvian one. The whole of Livonia has probably never had any common flag; the developing statehood was still too weak for that. I wonder what it could or might have been.

After the hamlet of Risti, I turned off onto a small side road to sleep a little and while away the time. The wooing of nightingales in the bushes was so loud that I couldn't get any sleep. It also immediately got cold in the car, although the sun had already risen. Then, the sun started shining into the car, warmed it up to a pleasant temperature, and I fell asleep. When I awoke, it was quite stuffy, and my head was drowsy. I splashed water onto my face from the ditch; the thicket had a very strong and fresh aroma, even sweet.

There was also an abundance of groups on the ferry that had been at Eurovision in Tallinn. Some were tired and quiet; some continued drinking, waving their beer bottles around and making a racket that was plenty unpleasant. Eurovision songs played on loudspeakers on all decks of the ship, and in all of its lounges. I suddenly felt very marginalized and excluded (*exclu*); I would have liked to be at home in Paris, where it would have been a piece of cake to ignore Eurovision, and there wouldn't have been a trace of it left by morning. In that moment of weakness, I was furthermore hit by a strong desire to be with Liz Franz. I wondered if she would have entered Eurovision if it had been possible (when she was still performing, the Soviet Union didn't participate in that song competition), and I decided that she wouldn't. Never. At the same time, I fantasized about what her Eurovision song, her performance costume, her accompanying band would have been like. She would undoubtedly have won if she had entered. Her costume would have been black, of course. Maybe a black suit. It seems to me that in Moscow, Liz Franz dressed in a black suit from time to time; was like a man. Sofya—that girl, who laid tarot, and with whom she lived, and whose name actually wasn't

Sofya (it was her artist's name, in the event that chiromancy is an art), but simply Natasha—was a woman. Holger said to me one time, when I cautiously and conspiratorially asked him about Liz Franz: "Well, yeah—she *is* a lesbian, too."

That bit of information surprised me greatly. I'd never seen those things in that way. But Holger's statements aren't one-hundred-percent believable, of course. Lesbianism could simply have been a part of a slandering campaign that nationalist-minded intellectuals promulgated about the traitor (gone to Moscow!) Liz Franz back in those days. At the same time, Holger—who works as the cultural editor for the tabloid *Õhtuleht*—is generally very well informed; especially in what concerns cultural figures' sexual orientations. Holger himself is one-hundred-percent gay, but he has a wife and two children, and believes that no one knows anything about him, and takes very malicious revenge on anyone who breaths a word about his sexual preferences. However, he considers himself to be very open-minded. He has one long-term relationship abroad, in Belgium, with a quite lovely, naive young Belgian man, who is not so young anymore now, of course. They stayed at my apartment in Paris, because Holger is very frugal and never spends money on a hotel if it is possible to do things otherwise. He also brags that he practically never pays to go out to eat, because he can fill his stomach as well as drink himself silly by the end of the day, at all sorts of presentations and vernissages.

And so, I don't know about that lesbianism. And actually I'm unable to imagine Liz Franz on stage in anything other than that very severe, but at the same time inexplicably sensual black dress and a silver neckpiece, which was practically invisible in the black stage box, so when she turned her face downstage for even a single second, leaving her black bob facing the audience, it was as if she disappeared from sight. This was an exceptionally effective trick, because her voice, which indeed faded away into almost a whisper for an instant, nevertheless projected perfectly forth into every corner of the auditorium thanks to her amplification. It was a small private theater attempting to be alternative, which was nevertheless located in the chic Sixth District near Saint Sulpice Church. As Paris was unfamiliar to me at that time, I don't remember its exact address: I've gone walking in that area a couple of times, and think that I recognize the building, but there is no longer a theater there; presumably, it has been liquidated or moved to some cheaper space.

On that cold January evening in 1991, however, an unexpectedly long line wound around in front of its modest door. Plastered onto the wall beside the door were a number of small posters only in A3-format (it had all come somewhat too suddenly, especially in the French conception), which depicted a black Liz Franz on a red background, her head lowered, holding a microphone in two hands, but combined in place of which was actually a white rose.

The concert was initially meant to be a small, closed event, and was only supposed to happen in March, in connection with the release of Liz Franz's album *Hääl / Голос / La voix / De Stimme* by the small record-label Paon (Sony later purchased the trademark, and it is probably no longer used at all anymore). However, the bloody events of January 10th in Vilnius and Riga had suddenly brought the Baltic States to the center of attention, and Liz Franz's publisher made an enormous effort to move the whole thing forward.

And so, it was late January, 1991, it was quite frigidly cold for Paris (probably even below freezing), and people were standing in line because the theater was small, seats were few, and the ticket seller couldn't manage to let them through so quickly. On top of that, the majority of people had invitations, and entered from the side. There were probably only enough tickets for very few overall: the auditorium was crammed full to the brim, and all of this together induced a sort of special, dramatic atmosphere of anticipation. As it later turned out, that was Liz Franz's last concert. She did have offers afterwards, but she declined. She knew that her success in the West was limited and short-term; was associated with political events. She preferred to leave the stage accompanied by genuine ovations, not to panhandle for pitiful *succès d'estime*—polite applause—from further auditoriums somewhere in her homeland. She "died" (as a singer) in the radiance of projectors and a storm of applause, just like the unhappy French-Egyptian songstress Dalida dreamed of in her song "*Mourir sur scène*." Dalida, of course, took her own life with an overdose of barbiturates, if I'm not mistaken. Yet, in that small "black box" on that January evening, it felt as if Liz Franz's career was just beginning. I was there as her official interpreter. It all happened like this.

32

I planned to write about how it all happened after a short break—the next morning, at the latest. But the pause became extended, and now it's already the fifth, no—the sixth morning. I fell ill and wasn't even capable of thinking about what I still wanted to say in the meantime. Furthermore, it all seemed perfectly pointless—both what I've already written down and what I still plan on writing. It was suddenly clear to me that Liz Franz would only laugh scornfully at it. Scornfully and ruefully. And would forgive me for everything. You poor friend! (Meaning me.) Oh, how he's fallen into the clutches of such fallacies! He's listening to others. He certainly knows for himself that it's not all like that. I heard Liz Franz's gentle and commanding voice:

"It's not like that!"

She always triumphed over me with those words. "It" was never like that, as I claimed, in the event that I dared to express my differing opinion to her's, and especially when that opinion somehow concerned her personally.

I had started feeling poorly on the Eurovision night. However, I ascribed it to Eurovision, the company, wine, overeating, and sleeplessness. But it didn't pass. On Saaremaa, I planned to visit Tõnu—a botanist, who I was in love with during college. He was very handsome, and when I last saw him four years ago, he was still quite handsome and had hardly aged. He had only become worried. He has a wife and two children; they live in the country. Tõnu does translations, writes for the nature magazine *Eesti Loodus*, and composes articles about plants for the national dailies, but it is hard to feed a family with all of that. His wife works as a teacher at the local primary school. They live in an old farmhouse together with the farm's old farmwife, who took them in as caretakers, promising to bequeath to them. Her health was in poor shape: she was already well over the age of seventy, and wasn't supposed to live for very much longer. Now, Tõnu and Maire's older child—their daughter (I don't remember her name)—will soon be graduating from high school, but the "old farmwife" is apparently still as fit as a fiddle and has only turned more ornery, constantly suspecting them of stealing household implements (pots, spoons) or her personal effects (pantyhose). However, the family has nowhere else to go, and they have probably already gotten used to the old woman's terrorizing. The location is very beautiful, otherwise—in Jämaja, on the Sõrve Peninsula. When the old farmwife one day "buys the farm" all the same, the property will be theirs, and they will at least have something to bequeath to their two children.

I wonder what will become of those children? They seem to be very talented. The boy already seemed suspicious to me. Too sensitive. I fear that he will turn into an open gay, will live out what Tõnu has buried in his marriage. Specifically, the thing is that Tõnu—unlike Herbert—was an obvious homosexual; everyone in our class knew it. He constantly fell in love with handsome, masculine college students, and didn't go without displaying it, either. But then, a few years after university, he married Maire, although he definitely didn't love her. I was at the wedding, and watched it closely. Tõnu was as white as a sheet; only Maire appeared satisfied. A homosexual man's marriage is self-castration in a certain sense—a sacrifice, but I don't know to what goddess's altar. As revenge for this sacrifice, he will torture his wife with unfeeling loyalty for the rest of his life (other women don't interest him anyway, and he has crossed out his homosexuality). Maire has completely lost her former sheen, and yells at the children irritatedly; they only speak to each other in a kind of demeaning, jeering tone. It is also true that they have many financial worries.

Tõnu was nevertheless happy to see me: he almost hugged

me with his wife watching, but then withdrew into himself again. His son Rainer watched that scene attentively. I had even had some of fantasies in connection with Tõnu while driving to Saaremaa, but they crumbled to pieces when I was actually there. On top of that, I was sick too: my head was splitting, I was quite weak, and probably left an impolite impression, driving off that same evening without staying there overnight, which Tõnu very much seemed to desire. At any rate, Tõnu envies me because of my life. It was actually he that [who] dreamed of Paris while in Tartu, not I. He took French-language classes, which I had received in high school all the same. He now translates French literature, but outright jaw-droppingly small sums are paid for it. I, on the other hand, dreamed during my college years of a life in the country, on an island, in an old farmhouse. Along with someone else, of course. With Tõnu, with Herbert Treumann. I know it wouldn't have been feasible. Men depend too much on their social position, on public opinion. Only women are capable of following through in the name of their love, of casting everything aside. Actually, I despise men.

I didn't drive from Tõnu and Maire's place directly back to the harbor, however: I wanted to sit and rest a little, so I turned into the Jämaja Cemetery, which I especially enjoy. It is one of Estonia's most beautiful country graveyards. Saaremaa, where the topsoil is generally very thin upon the limestone bedrock, was already scorched brown from the drought from place to place. The grass had only grown to quite a stunted height, and had already blossomed in late May, as it normally does in July. Sulfur-yellow birdsfoot trefoil (*Lotus corniculatus*) was also visible between the brown stalks. Only small patches of potatoes had risen and already withered on Tõnu's strip of field. The plot (*lopin*) of land that belongs to them, actually to the old farmwife, is an important source of food for the family. By the way, Tõnu has become religious over the last few years, which makes conversing with him practically impossible. He has a quote from the Bible for everything, no matter whether it is from the gospels or the epistles. He deemed the drought to be a sign of "the end of this world's era," and I was amazed by how easily he has sold out his once extremely skeptical worldviews for those cheap consolations. No doubt he needs religion for fighting against his own "vice" as well.

Thanks specifically to its thin soils lying upon limestone, Saaremaa was one of the most developed regions of Old Livonia during the Middle Ages. Its lands were easy to cultivate with rudimentary wooden plows, and the thin layer of soil is actually fertile, although susceptible to drought. However, the medieval climate was relatively moist. Saaremaa's population is said to have also developed maritime trading and gone on raids along the western shore of the Baltic Sea. The land's new masters—bishops and knights of the German Order—had to enter an initial contractual relationship with them, in any case. Saaremaa also has some of Livonia's oldest churches—odd, single-chambered "tents" without towers or decorations, on the walls of which magical semi-pagan symbols can still be found.

I like Jämaja Cemetery more than anything else on Saaremaa, however. It is located right on the seashore—and on the shore of open sea, at that—facing the West, where the dead of all ancient religions headed, of course: in the direction of where the sun disappeared as well. The sun was indeed disappearing on that evening of May 26th. The air chilled quickly, signaling the fact that it is still only spring—the sea hasn't warmed up yet. Jämaja Cemetery's boxwood hedges started giving off a strong aroma. There are very many evergreen boxwoods (*Buxus sempervirens*) there—the portion of them that hasn't been trimmed has grown into large bushes. The box normally doesn't tolerate the local winters: for example, the orderly box hedge surrounding the small fountain on Viru

Square in Tallinn is covered up with pine branches every winter. For some reason, I am always reminded of those snowy pine branches there around the silent fountain when I think of Tallinn and winter. Yet, thanks to the open sea, which ices over on extremely rare occasion, the climate on the western coast of the Sõrve Peninsula is apparently mild enough that the box grows there as freely as it does in France. And the somewhat sickly-sweet, somewhat tart smell of box dominates the entire Jämaja Cemetery. For me, it is the smell of Parisian parks, and especially of provincial parks in France, the smell of French soil itself—rich and brownish, evergreen.

To me, Jämaja Cemetery feels like an island, which has drifted there from elsewhere—from far in the south—and could go back to sea again any day, along with all of its corpses. There are also strange crosses there. For example—one row of small, mossy crosses made of juniper, with the words "Bird's children" etched into the first. Apparently, they are markers for the Bird family or for Bird Farm. Yet, it appears almost as if they really were small graves made for birds; perhaps for sea birds.

In Estonia and Livonia, only nobles used stone burial vaults that were closed by stone covers on the surface. There is also a section of them in Jämaja, but all of the graves have been pried open and robbed at some point. The soil in these parts appears to be more definite if one considers Christians' belief in the "resurrection of the flesh."

Jämaja Cemetery has always put me into a better mood with its smells of box and the sea, but this time, it made me sad. I sat on an old, mossy bench, the lilac bush above my head was in blossom and emitting its aroma (spring is later by the sea), and I had the feeling that I was losing someone or something with the disappearance of the sun, behind the sea. Tears even came to my eyes, at which I was highly amazed. I hoped that I would perhaps start to cry for real, but I didn't. I didn't even understand what I was upset about. I got up and drove to the harbor, where I managed to make the last ferry.

I was already thoroughly sick in Tartu. It was in the early hours of Monday morning that I arrived. Strangely, I stayed alert the entire way—in some other, somnambulant state (*état second*). Driving into the city, I turned onto the wrong street, which was a one-way in the other direction, but luckily, no one came in the oncoming direction at night. Luckily, I also remembered that there is a pharmacy with extended hours below the Town Hall. I acquired a thermometer there. For some reason, I didn't buy any medicine—in my mode of thought, which had slowed abruptly, I namely decided that I should first ascertain whether I had any kind of an issue at all, or whether it was **purely** psychosomatic (conditioned by my aversion to approach my most embarrassing and painful confessions, which threaten to reveal too much—I'm not sure whether about me or Liz Franz); in short, I should firstly take my temperature, keeping in mind that the thermometer should be "down" for ten minutes, as my grandmother always required, and *then* I should act according to the thermometer's decision. It was, of course, the new type of thermometer that no longer needed to be held underneath your tongue for ten minutes, pressing it in so hard that it became painful (it was of the utmost importance to convince my grandmother of the authenticity of my sickness); however, I nevertheless went home with it and took my temperature only then. I didn't know whether I should believe that number, which was shown almost instantaneously (mercury, with its slow and material expansion, still seemed more trustworthy), and which furthermore was unusually high: 101.7.

It appears to me that I haven't had such a fever since childhood. There have been prolonged sicknesses practically without a fever or with a couple of bars on the thermometer, lacking any apparent reason and other symptoms, apart from a subjectively very bad feeling, which could, however, also be called depression. I was struck by such bouts of sickness on average after every other time that I was with Liz Franz, so the first few times I so much as suspected that I had gotten some infection from her. Yet, my sense of well-being normalized in a week or two, and the sickness that I started to call the "Liz-Franz syndrome" didn't leave any apparent consequences. During those pseudo-flus, I mainly submitted to feeble accusation of Liz Franz (I was sick **because** of her too!) and even feebler self-contempt, because I called Liz Franz two or three times a day in addition to her already regular phone calls. I called in order to inform her that we would never meet again, and what I thought of the whole thing in general, and that I'd had enough of playing the role of that old maid's call boy, etc.; but actually, I merely stayed condemningly silent and listened to Liz Franz's worrying and caring statements. She recommended not eating, drinking a lot of water, and sleeping with wool socks on to get over the sickness. I have to say that such a caring display was somehow pleasing, although I never followed her advice out of defiance. Only now did I act according to them for the first time, in Tartu. I didn't even want to eat; on top of that, I didn't really have anything at home, and I couldn't make the effort to go to the store. Luckily however, I did, have four large bottles (eight liters) full of Rõuge water.

Rõuge is a small village about fifty miles to the south of Tartu, on the edge of Livonia's tallest "mountains" (up to 1,050 ft above sea level), on the rim of a very steep and deep valley, at the bottom of which is one of the deepest lakes around here. On the shore of that lake is a romantic-style pre-war pharmacy building, where a nice, clean old couple—former pharmacists—now run a home restaurant. The windows in the dining hall, previously the pharmacy room, look out over the lake, and that strangely bright state of mind that characterizes all of Rõuge prevails there. With its mighty overlooks (from the church, for example), it's as if Rõuge was transported to Livonia from somewhere else, from

Southern Bavaria (Liz Franz and I once stopped in Feldafing on the shore of Lake Starnberg, where Thomas Mann wrote *The Magic Mountain*). I recently visited the Rõuge pharmacy-restaurant for the second time, and namely for the water. I had empty bottles with me. Upon ending up there for the first time by chance, I had asked for regular water with my meal (ordinary Livonian food: pork and potatoes) and in addition to their homemade currant wine (currant juice fermented with sugar), which turned out to be surprisingly potable. With its especially good flavor, that water surprised me even more than the wine (which, as it became clear, likewise owed its good qualities to the water). I wouldn't say that I'm especially picky in terms of water. In Paris, I drink mainly tap water, which—true—is also sufficiently high in quality. It is a part of my money-saving policy, the results of which are, however, annulled by the compulsive wastefulness that takes place about twice per year in the form of buying new clothes, always outside of sale periods, when not one normal person—especially a poor one like me—purchases clothing in Paris.

But I immediately realized that Rõuge's water is very pure. I believe that anyone can tell when water is truly pure. It then has something like a slightly sweet taste, although its sugar content is naturally zero. This is probably a special signal by our taste receptors, and perhaps derives from broken-down carbohydrate residue found in spit. Rõuge's water reminded me of Evian by flavor, but was fresher. I asked the old man—who was serving as a waiter while his wife was in the kitchen, and who in the meantime, between filling orders, continued playing his chess match with a villager who was knocking back homemade wine; thus playing on two boards, in a way (I was the only patron)—if they'd been told that they have good water. It turned out that they were completely aware of the fact. As they are located at the bottom of a deep valley, their water well is set upon an aquifer, and chemical-microbiological analyses show that their water can be bottled straight from the source according to the European Union standard. I had forgotten that they were former pharmacists. Thus, I took empty water bottles along the next time, and filled them directly from their tap with the pharmacists' kind permission.

And so, I now drank that water. I slept for a while wearing wool socks, because it felt cold in the room the whole time. I sweated and drank the water again. At first, my dreams were tormenting. I fought Liz Franz, ripping long sentences that were similarly long wooden peasant carts from her hands. I realized that everything I've written is completely pointless. Yet, I still decided to get one sentence: it came free surprisingly easily, and Liz Franz was gone. I trudged along the path, uphill, the cart behind me. When I looked back, Liz Franz was on the cart and pitying me. I started feeling very sorry for myself as well—I collapsed into her embrace, cried, everything around us turned white, and I promised to destroy what I've written.

I awoke with the feeling that my health had mended, but I didn't rush over to the computer to delete files, finding that I'll always have the chance to do so. I actually haven't turned my computer on a single time over the course of all these days, and Asko, who was able to see whether I was at home or not through the house's internal network display, most likely believes that I'm still away. In any case, he showed no sign of himself. It did sound as if someone was knocking on the door once—I woke up to the knocking, but didn't go to open it. My fever was up again by evening, but as I hadn't eaten anything for two days, the night was easier, my sleep sounder, and my dream less tormenting. Specifically, I arrived at a large hospital/boarding house in Japan, where I was supposed to have a cancer operation, and where I was simultaneously supposed to finish my notes. It was a large, white ward with several beds: other Estonian cultural figures had also arrived there, although none of them recognized me, and

I only spoke with the personnel in French. The new-patient/ guest reception took place with a "large appointment," during which a number of doctors and members of the Cultural Affairs Committee dressed in white doctor's coats entered the ward; neither could be told apart from the other. They heard out the fresh arrival's wishes, and scheduled an operation time. My only desire was a laptop, because I had left my own behind with the knowledge that they would be provided by the hospital. The head doctor said that, yes, they had one for the entire building: it's sometimes in one person's hands, other times in another's, and I could certainly use it someday. I protested loudly that I must write absolutely every day, but the committee had already left. After that, I attempted to exchange Russian rubles for Japanese yen, cursing myself for not having taken yen out immediately—I would definitely lose a lot now because of the exchange rates. I looked for a bank—I was along the Seine, but the streets were devoid of people and unfamiliar; I was in Paris for the first time in my life. It was dark, and a fine drizzle fell. The streets led steeply down to the river, but I needed to find the Louvre Métro station. Then, I saw that I was by the back gates of the Louvre—there was a large sign reading "Louvre," but the gates were closed and the Métro station should have been somewhere on the other side. I wasn't sure whether I could even get all the way there in that rain, or whether I would get drenched first. It was cold, too. Corresponding to this in reality, of course, was my sweating and the fact that the back of my shirt was soaked.

Today is Saturday, and I plan to start eating, although I don't know what yet. I don't seem to be hungry, although I'm weak. Nevertheless, my mind is rather clear. I fetched a bottle of Evian from the store downstairs to replace the Rōuge water, which had run out. I suppose I'll have a look at what to eat during the day. Maybe semolina porridge? My grandmother always made that porridge when I was sick and didn't want to eat. I *had* to eat. I've

Tõnu Õnnepalu

never gone so long without eating before now. I see that there's nothing special about it, only a bad taste in your mouth the whole time that doesn't even want to go away with water. Liz Franz's systematic state of not eating seems significantly less mysterious to me. Yet, a voluntary fast or one forced by sickness is still something different than that almost constant spit swallowing and the pinch of hunger, which I went around Paris with in January of 1991.

I had arrived in France in the first days of October and worked for a month picking grapes at a Vaucluse vineyard. I was supplied with both the invitation necessary for a visa and the address of farmer acquaintances (his aunt's) by Denis S.—a young Estophile, whom I had met in Estonia and in turn introduced to our young filmmakers, all of whom I still knew at the time.

Back then, Denis S. held Estonia—that completely unknown land—in very high regard, and believed that all kinds of never-before-seen artistic pearls could be discovered there and introduced to the French audience (and namely by him personally). He did indeed encounter disappointments and semi-disappointments upon coming into contact with the actual art phenomena; however, these did not convince him to give up in the very least, because he was certain that the true treasures were hidden by the censorship and official art policy, and that he would need to win over the locals' trust in order to gain access to them. Until then, he translated a couple of second-rate authors' short stories, in which he found something unique, and tried to find a publisher for them in France. He was in fact successful at this, but only in connection with the events of 1991, when people abruptly began searching for any material at all about those countries that had suddenly appeared on the map. Denis S. turned out to be practically the only native French-speaking expert on Estonian language and culture in France, in addition to Jean-Luc Moreau, who translated the Estonian poet Jaan Kross, and his advantage over Mr. Moreau was that thanks to his practice, he even understood Estonian speech.

That time, in the spring of 1990, I attempted to comprehend what really forced Denis S. (both he and the vineyard will remain anonymous here, because they broke immigration and labor laws by inviting and employing me, and I don't know how quickly those violations, or so much as crimes, expire in France), who was in fact a student of Paris's Grande École (which promises one of the most reliable careers), to become involved in something so marginal and having so little perspective as Estonian language and culture. Yet, I wasn't yet familiar with French society and its logic. On the basis of analogy, I believed that it was just as simple to become someone there as in Estonia. I, for example, was with my film *The Railway Watchman's House*, and with my second film, *The Boat* (I didn't know why, and most importantly **for whom** I made it; I filmed it alone—Herbert Treumann's period in my life had passed along with the completion of *The Railway Watchman's House*), despite its obvious shoddiness, its trivial philosophic-pretentiousness, and the fact that I hadn't the slightest idea for whom, how, and for what purpose I should keep making films at all—despite all of that and my inner conviction that I was no one, and that the only sensible act would be suicide, I was not only a promising, but also an already-acclaimed young documentary filmmaker in the eyes of the small but influential social faction that was composed of cultural circles and the satellites orbiting them. I came from a nation of one million, which despite belonging to the Soviet conglomerate, still (and even more so) formed quite a closed universe in the cultural sense. It was relatively easy to rise to stardom even *there*, even though that star was not visible outside of the bounds of that universe.

Yet, at that time we had very distorted conceptions of what was "outside," although we regarded ourselves as citizens of the world and fully entitled members of the Western cultural sphere. The illusion was further amplified by the fact that the larger universe, the Soviet Union, was quite closed-off in turn, and in addition to national attention, one could even enjoy a certain "Soviet-wide" recognition; especially if your work was accompanied by buzz that the authorities had somehow banned it—which, even right at the final moment before the ultimate breakup of that system, happened with my *The Railway Watchman's House*, the debut television screening of which (which was already advertised in television programs) was cancelled for "technical reasons." I personally was certainly never summoned for a "conversation" with the KGB, or with any other state organs. Those organs no doubt understood that I didn't pose any danger in the least to the crumbling regime. Yet, there had apparently still been some kind of trouble with the film studio management. The main thing was that the buzz (*bruit*) was set in motion, and it was a considerable benefit for me later on.

And so, I was amazed at Denis S.'s extravagant interest in Estonia, because I didn't grasp the fact that coming from a nation of sixty million, it is much more difficult for him—even despite his good schooling and obvious abilities—to erect any personal position for himself among those millions. Especially because as the son of provincial pharmacists, he couldn't hope for family ties and acquaintances among the elite. He made a rational, although risky choice by building his future career upon a rare area of knowledge, in which he had, in any case, hopes of becoming a leading specialist in France. The risk in this was, of course, that the position of leading specialist could turn out not to be especially esteemed. (For example, Vahur Linnuste, who was active for decades as an Estonian-language lecturer at the National Institute of Oriental Languages and Civilizations (INALCO) in Paris, was a completely marginal figure in Paris's academic circles, indeed being that much more colorful for it; but I must rest on the topic of him further, and with special thanks at that.) And so, Denis S. went out on a limb, and as it has become clear by now, that risk paid off. Not highly, but well. Denis S. was selected last year as a professor of Estonian and Finnish languages and literature at the University of Caen, which from what I know is a practically lifelong job in France. Denis S.'s climb was thus even quite rapid, because he executed his career plans in only twelve years.

Yet in the spring of 1990, I wasn't able to see the first rungs of his conscious and rational career ladder in his very thorough, intelligent and lively Estophilia. As an outstanding young Soviet Estonian cineast, I had low regard for such career building. In France, I've realized that if you don't want to blend into the mass of faceless and impersonal salaried workers (*salariés*), it is (if you don't happen to be of very good origin or have very special talents; preferably both at once) common and practically inevitable to become an administratively identified, but easily replaceable bolt in a large machine, which reproduces the wealth of that powerful land day after day.

I, on the contrary, didn't have any kind of clear plans for the future or my career when I landed in an Aeroflot plane at Charles de Gaulle Airport in October, 1990. There were primarily doubts, fears, and vague hopes. The doubts were in connection with my film career to date. It seemed to me that something sounded wrong there (*sonner faux*); that it had somehow come too easily and thanks to preconditions and chances, with which I had nothing to do. That I was simply the product of a system, and a crumbling system that would soon come to an end, at that. And so, maybe even merely a product of decay. That neither my works nor my abilities had any value in any scale, even a touch outside of that system.

My fears were in connection with money. In 1990, there was already a clear sense that money would start playing an altogether different and more important role from then on. It hadn't been that important up until that point. One could always get money somehow. I'm not even able to say what I lived off of during those last years in Estonia, but there was always some kind of money for the most part, and when there wasn't, then someone lent it. You couldn't really get anything for rubles anyway. But I was able to get by, and quite lavishly in my own way from time to time.

The scary thing was not that old money, but valuta. That's what it was called, using the old Italian banking term. Currency. Everything could be attained for valuta, and valuta was just as good as unattainable. The market rates were already such, that with my ruble-based income, which I could live on for a month, I would have been able to get perhaps a couple of cups of coffee at a café in Paris. It was clear that from then on, I would need to earn valuta. And that positions (like my cultural position) and abilities that were acquired in the old system might not be worth a single penny in valuta. Amazingly, however, I earned my first valuta from a film—that very same *The Railway Watchman's House*. It was shown on Finnish television in the winter of 1990; by then, it had also been shown on Estonian television several times already—perestroika, a.k.a. the breakup, was reaching a terminal phase. Although distribution rights belonged to the Soviet-wide organization, I was still paid one thousand Finnish marks (a currency that was about equal to the franc) in cash by the understanding Finns, and in secret from the Soviet authorities. I was greatly tempted to buy myself sneakers (*baskets*) and jeans with the money, but I suppressed that desire. Nevertheless, I was unable to resist the shoes. Specifically, while walking on a street in Helsinki (I was invited to give a television interview for the screening, and the payment was arranged for that same reason), I saw how outrageously ugly my shoes were compared with those of everyone around me. So, I purchased a pair of shoes (sweating profusely while trying them on and making my choice, because the selection was sickeningly large), and ultimately, I still just bought very expensive brown shoes costing five hundred marks, because I had liked them right away.

I was wearing those same shoes when I stepped onto French soil in October. I had left myself the remaining five hundred marks for travel money, but it was confiscated by customs at Leningrad's Pulkovo Airport. At that time, tensions between the separatist Baltic States and Russia were already quite great, and were also expressed in the behavior of Soviet customs officials. Understanding from my accent that I had come from Estonia, the customs official pulled me aside. I was searched in a separate room, and they easily found the five-hundred-mark note that I had simply stuck into my breast pocket. I hadn't even taken any effort to hide it, having fatalistically banked on my luck. But I had no luck, and the illegal currency was subject to confiscation. Luckily, however, I was still allowed to board the plane to Paris. I thought about the confiscated five hundred marks and my completely empty pockets throughout the entire flight. The first skill that I had to acquire in Paris was jumping over the turnstile in the Métro. However, many people did so, and I started to feel that it wasn't really that bad. I also located Vahur Linnuste's apartment, was given something to eat, and finally reached my vineyard in the south of France.

Picking grapes was something like harvesting potatoes: extremely tiring bending-over, as the bunches were low down— they had to be cut using small, bent branch-clippers, with which I bloodied my hand all the time in the beginning. The bucket filled up quite quickly, and had to be poured out into a high tractor box. I wasn't used to physical labor, especially in such amounts. The other seasonal laborers there were acquaintances of the family who owned the farm: a couple of pensioners (including Monique, who took me under her wing; a certain flirtation developed between us, and I was very thankful for that motherly attitude); six or seven young friends of the family son, with whom I shared a room and made meals; and two old Moroccans, who had been there every year. My relations with them were poor. They pointed out my mistakes all the time: uncut bunches or over-cut vines (as I saw it, everyone cut those vines away). They apparently sensed—and apparently instinctively—a new structural competitor in me, as a representative of the opening Eastern Bloc. But I have learned well that immigrants and foreign laborers are hated the very most by slightly older, earlier (*plus anciens*) immigrants and foreign laborers. And they also know those "newbies'" weak points well.

In addition to the Moroccan geezers' systematic harassment, I was depressed by the tempo and duration of the work. I had never had to work like that before. Harvesting potatoes in a kolkhoz was child's play next to that. Work lasted for nine hours with a one-hour lunch break and a couple of five-minute drink breaks, during which we were, by the way, given the previous year's wine, which made it even more difficult for me to bend over, but only stimulated the French workers. The most depressing thing *was*, however, that no one else apart from me appeared to tire. However, those friends of the family son were no farm boys either, but were all from the local small town, where they had gone to school together. Although I didn't really joke around with the others, much less break out singing (my Tallinn-High-School-No.-1 French proficiency turned out to be the kind that exists in books, but which is not spoken or understood at all, at least in Vaucluse—they had many laughs over my literary expressions), I wasn't able to keep up with them very well, and someone had to duck into my row to help me catch up from time to time.

All the same, I must say that no one aside from the Moroccans reproached me even once. Still, I was an item of interest in a certain way as well. They were able to ask me whether we supported Stalin, whether we had reindeer, whether I knew what happened at Chernobyl (I didn't understand what that "Chernobyl" was at first, and gave the impression that I was indeed a victim of Soviet disinformation, which they enjoyed greatly), whether I knew what U2 was, whether Estonia had a strong soccer team and who its goalie was. The fact that I didn't know a single French, German, or English soccer player seemed especially exotic and wild to them. I asked falsely whether they knew Dmitri Gvozdikov, a famous Soviet player, but even that trickery didn't really work out, because they actually did know the names of a couple of Russian soccer players, but they'd heard nothing about Gvozdikov, whom I had invented right there in the field (*sur-le-champ*).

I have indeed gone through quite proper integration, if you look at it that way. Specifically, on the second day that I had the fever here in Tartu, I called the landlord and asked him to bring around the television that he had offered, but which I had said there was no rush in bringing. He did. And yesterday I watched the broadcast of the opening World Cup game from Seoul. Despite all of my integration, I certainly do not usually watch soccer, but having a fever, it was completely fitting. Lebœuf, Djorkaeff, and Trezeguet are familiar names and faces for me. I find, by the way, that Lebœuf is very likeable, although the British player David Beckham is my favorite. Apparently, there is something exotic about an Englishman when viewed from France (from across the sea, *Outre-Manche*), and exotic is often erotic. I fully rooted for the French team, and felt regret for Zidane's being left out. The TV camera repeatedly zoomed in on Zidane's watching the game, and it's true (I found) that there is something majestic about him; special, in any case. I don't know—maybe very great fame makes a person special, gives him or her that kind of an attitude. I rather think, regardless, that one needs to have something special in order to achieve very great fame—even in soccer. And, by the way—why "even" in soccer? I haven't known for quite some time, whether soccer is a lower art form than film, for example, in the peripheries of which I'm vegetating. The ability of Zidane, Lebœuf, and others to bring a large group of spectators to the point of catharsis at the price of almost superhuman exertion is, in any case, something to which I don't measure up. And so, I can't make a decision either. Nor do I want to. I was crushed by France's loss (0:1) to Senegal. Apparently, one-to-one, kingly brilliance is decisive even in such a collective activity as soccer. Without Zidane, the "blues" (*les Bleus*) didn't have the right momentum. All the same, I must admit that the feeling of being crushed and those fixations disappeared from my mind about ten minutes after the end of the broadcast. All the same, I'm not *so* integrated to have lost sleep over France's loss.

But, yes, I was speaking about my doubts in 1990, which were in connection with my creative work, fears associated with money, and I also mentioned hopes. Officially, my hopes in traveling to France were in connection with plans to study the film business somewhere in Paris. At least that's what I told Denis and my acquaintances in Estonia. That's what I even told myself, still not really being able to convince myself in spite of it. I knew that I would never go to school anywhere anymore. I abhor those institutions of internment, where some determined pinheads, who have managed to climb up to a teacher's or faculty-member's position have the right to judge you: you're smart/ stupid, right/wrong, a success/failure. I completed my official, mandatory studies, and stuck into my pocket a diploma that I've never used. Good enough. My actual hopes in connection with that first true trip abroad—Finland had not been the real abroad just yet, although the differences in the system, the cleanliness of the streets, and the wealth just fifty miles away from my home city had seriously astounded me—those hopes were invariably connected to love and sexuality, or sexuality and love.

I understood, of course, that they were absurd in a certain sense; that there is no such direct path. That people's hopes may be associated with them for the most part, but that one must choose the suitable means for reaching that goal. If you don't have blinding beauty, then you must earn money, achieve power, fame, a high position. And as that previously mentioned Estonian novelist Anton Hansen said: then love, too, will come. It is one of his most quoted sentences, which our nationalist peda- and demagogues never tire of exploiting. In Hansen's novel, a peasant farmer chides his impatient son with those words ("Work hard and persevere, and then love, too, will come"). For some reason, however, the boy's response to his father is never quoted, sounding something like: you and mother have indeed worked hard and persevered, but there is no love on Vargamäe (*Mont-du-Voleur*, their farm's toponym) to this day. Yet, unlike the average Estonian schoolteacher, I truly have read Hansen's *magnum opus* from cover to cover; indeed not when it was in the school curriculum, but earlier. There were periods around the time of my puberty, during which I devoured books quite indiscriminately, also (and maybe especially) including the kinds that for my peers were considered literature that was already old-fashioned, no longer interesting—just as that same Hansen was. And so, I did not rely on literature teachers' distorted information even in that paradox of nationalist love, but rather proceeded from the original text. What is the point of love's coming when you've already worked hard and persevered, and you yourself are old and ugly? I decided to go straight to looking for love, immediately. And to this very day, I don't believe that if those searches have not been fruitful, the reason for this might be scant work and exertion. I don't know it what is.

I had made my start already in my homeland. I suddenly realized that I was twenty-seven years old and *still* practically a virgin. I didn't even dare to put it so brutally to myself. But the times had changed, and freer winds blew in traditions. People started to talk about everything—in the newspapers, even about homosexuality. It so much as felt that people were treating it quite liberally. This was, of course, an optical illusion caused by the perestroika era euphoria. "People" on average still regard it as disgusting, perverse, and scandalous. The thing is specifically—and one must understand people—that for every person, his or her sexuality is, to some extent, a mystery and a burden. It always has elements, fantasies, lusts that somehow don't fit with what is written about in books; with what is shown in sex scenes in films, and even in the most raunchy pornography; with what men talk about amongst themselves when drinking, and what women confess to their treacherous girlfriend in a burst of trust.

Naturally, a normal person denies the existence of that dark area within themselves. If he or she is in a position of power in terms of a sexual partner, then the person forces that partner to follow their personal fantasies, calling them normal. If that opportunity is lacking, then there are still prostitutes, pornography, masturbation, or discontent. Some kind of discontent probably always remains, because not a single existing world corresponds to all of our fantasies. In any case, one never manages to domesticate everything frightening that sexuality holds by using the measures mentioned here. Something is left to haunt somewhere. During a moment of depression and loneliness, the thought might even flash through one's mind: maybe I'm not actually normal. (Heaven forbid!) So-called "official perverts" do exist in order to eliminate and dampen those haunting thoughts and doubts; the most prominent group of which is, in turn, made up of all kinds of gays. All of a person's personal gruesomeness, all of their deviance, inhumanity, non-understanding, all of their forbidden desires can be projected upon them. They are very necessary. But they must never feel too good about themselves. To the reassurance of decent individuals, I can acknowledge and confirm here that for the prevailing part of my sexually active (or passive?) life, I have felt either quite poor, poor, or very poor ("a bullet to the head," as they say) in this area. The punishment for existence is practically permanent, although one becomes used to it, as with everything.

In the fall of 1989, however, I thus decided to rid myself of my virginity, and took a leap into the unknown. To accomplish this, I used the personals section of the independent private-weekly *Eesti Ekspress*, which had just started to be published. The newspaper's readership at the time was relatively young, progressively minded, and alternative. Now, probably the entire Estonian population reads it; at least that's the impression I've been left with. I don't read it, nor do I know what the personals section of the paper is like now; presumably, it is too expensive to publish private ads there. Many such ads were placed back then. And according to the logic of an inflation economy, the majority of ads were in the "wanted" section. No one wanted money (or if they did, then valuta); everyone wanted to exchange their rubles for something (in their minds) more reliable. People bought up all kinds of building materials, for example, the decomposing heaps of which can still be seen now when traveling around the countryside.

I don't know which transaction—buying or selling—my offer should be classified as, because it is clear that human, and especially sexual relations are buy and sell transactions as well, although their nature is concealed by several romantic preconceptions, with which I myself was stuffed to the brim. In any case, my *annonce* appeared in the "Acquaintance" column, under the subsection curiously entitled "Looking for Gentleman."

The ads in that column truly were looking for "masters" in a certain sense: preferably foreign and solvent ones, who would put the seeker on a leash and lead them to a more pleasant place somewhere. The seekers were *evidemment* "ladies," who where possible identified themselves as "sparky blonds." I believe that my ad, which I took to the *Eesti Ekspress* drop-off for personal ads at the Tallinn Central Post Office, shaking from fear and excitement, was the first **such** ad in that paper (it was followed by an entire wave of them, which receded over time, because it became clear that it was a relatively closed circle, and other places and conduits for acquainting also appeared). I don't remember the wording of my ad. It was most likely too embarrassing for my memory to retain. There are luckily files that can be deleted, and without a trace. It definitely mentioned my age, as well as probably the age of the sought-after partner in order to keep old men away; something literary/poetic in addition, in order to signal my high expectations for the partner's physical/mental parameters. Those ads are, of course, a unique concise form, in which one hopes to express a great deal, but forgets to add anything the slightest bit revealing about themselves ("I'm not exactly the most handsome, bold, or rich; actually, I'm rather ugly, cowardly, and poor." etc.). I certainly didn't use such open words as "gay" or "homo." Yet, the message got through, and reached its addressees. Namely, a lifetime obligation to conceal and lie is brilliant schooling that makes gays good spies and code breakers. It's unfortunate that state espionage services can't use us for these purposes: an opposing spy would have certain overly simple measures for coaxing the agent over to his own side, and even if that were avoided, the gay agent could develop a double game simply out of boredom, habit, a double-crossing instinct.

When I went to the same window a week later to ask for the letters under my number (I feared there wouldn't be a single one, or that there would be one or two pink envelopes in an old person's handwriting), I received an entire pack. About twenty-five. A few more trickled in after that. All of them had "gotten it"; so what that some of the responses eked out with great effort onto half-sheets of graph paper reeked of a more-than-lacking sense of literacy. Yet, there were also true letter-novellas, letter-poems. I realized that my "vice" is democratic in the utmost sense—meaning, permeated throughout all layers of origin and intelligence; and that suppression and frustration, the full extent of which I only saw through others, is just as democratic. You get the feeling that you're still somehow getting by.

Then followed the phase of replying and calling, of meeting. My all-excusing imagination started up immediately, and I replied even to handwriting with the most unpleasant, rounded, rolling tails. I didn't allow myself to be bothered by an alarmingly unerotic voice on the phone, either. My virginity was won, if it really was won, by one such guy with that same sort of rolling handwriting, and a lightly sleazy voice. I'd made my decision; now I had to act. I couldn't let myself be led by my feelings any longer. For where had my feelings led me so far? Only into platonic affairs.

The guy was also unpleasant in appearance. That is, he was actually a completely ordinary, somewhat chubbier twenty-nine-year-old father. He was, by the way, really a father. It was midday—we went from downtown to his HLM district (probably Mustamäe) on a packed trolley. His wife and daughter, pictures of whom were hanging on the wall, whose clothes and toys were scattered around everywhere, weren't at home. His face was burning more and more the entire way there in the packed trolley, where our conversation only stagnated more and more; he watched me with lust, which seemed absolutely baffling to me. To me, he was more or less repulsive. But as I said, I had to give that thing a try. At the apartment, he probably offered me some kind of a liqueur or wine. I was nervous, he aroused; no doubt it was possible that his wife could come home soon—we needed to head to their wedding bed.

When Linda told me about her impressions of sex years later, I was able to picture them wonderfully on the basis of that same first experience. That's just how it was. He got on top of me, dreadfully turned on (I was as cold as a fish, covered only in a nervous sweat), performed something there, panted; it was annoying and I waited for him to finish already. Luckily, he came quite quickly, and I didn't allow any true penetration to happen, of course; but that didn't seem to be very important, either. I generally couldn't figure out what he needed me for, and whether it really wouldn't have been more interesting for him to be alone with his own fantasies. Then he wanted—probably out of politeness—for *me* to have my own turn at it. Somehow, with difficulty, that came through as well (I didn't dare tell him that I wasn't interested—I was afraid of looking impotent), and was finally able to get out of there, out into the fresh air. He naturally didn't keep me there; on the contrary, he so much as helped me dress and look around the bed for my necklace, which had broken in the throes of passion. My glasses remained unbroken, luckily. Taking the trolley back into the city, I felt adequately disgusted with myself: at home, I washed myself carefully and at length. The next day, that episode already felt like an unpleasant hallucination. I wouldn't say that the loss of my virginity changed me. Or if it did, then it made me slightly more cautious. With the other correspondents, I went to a café for starters.

Long and interesting correspondence developed with a couple of them. They told me their own story, and I told them mine. They were all very similar for the most part. Each had had a more-or-less unrequited love for a classmate or an older student in their youth. Very high and practically unrealized ideals. Our meeting was always a great mutual disappointment, because both had already managed to construct an entire fantasy that crumbled when faced with unjust reality. I traveled with one of them to Riga, on the night train, where nothing happened between us, of course. I even lived with another—a Tōnu—for a month, out of a sense of obligation, and a certain routine sexual intercourse took place, during the course of which both of us tried to find some elements of our fantasy in the adjacent body. He who seeks, finds. Sex is undoubtedly also a question of compromises, conformism, coming to terms. Ideals must be blunted, ideals must be destroyed.

Even so, it seems that even a year later, there in the Vaucluse cru, they (my ideals) were just as intact as they were in high school, when I filmed Martin in close-up, when I was impressed by Veiko. Just as intact as they were later, when I lay in the grass at Herbert Treumann's side (that aroma of a summery pine forest mixed with the diesel stench of a passing train is, for me, still the smell of ideal love, of absolute harmony, of eternal loyalty; happiness, although the smell of non-existent happiness). Perhaps my ideals have remained so untouched for the very reason that I have systematically left practical opportunities untaken. Even though they exist, it seems, always and everywhere. They weren't lacking in the Vaucluse cru, either.

The family son, Gilles—a large, strong farm boy; a cheerful fellow with brown eyes and bleached-blond hair—behaved quite openly as a bisexual. I must say straight away that in the Mediterranean cultural sphere, there is nothing scandalous about this in principle (the main thing is to preserve a "macho" stance); yet, he nevertheless balanced on the verge of scandal. He had an official *amie*, Catherine, but on top of that had an entire harem of friends, who all worked there in the cru, and whose relationships with one another and relationships with Gilles were very much ambivalent. One of them, Roger—a slightly effeminate young man with long, curly hair—was apparently Gilles's actual and preferred sexual partner. One Saturday evening, we all drove to a disco at the edge of a tiny nearby town (Gilles had a Porsche, and I was able to sit in its backseat—he had great fun demonstrating to me, a Soviet, that thing of wonder; the backseat of a Porsche is, of course, extremely uncomfortable), and after midnight, when we started coming back, I was witness to a true triangle of passion.

Roger sat in Gilles's Porsche, where they kissing. Catherine was crying in Laurent's Renault, then came out, banged on the window of the Porsche, threatened to drive off immediately, and warned Gilles to watch out to not get AIDS from "that slut." Then she cried a little more, and indeed drove away with Laurent, who took me home as well. Catherine lived right in the same area, and after a short time, Laurent was back there at the vineyard.

We overnighted in a wing of the main building—I was still sitting outside on a bench in front, and hadn't gone inside to sleep. The night was quite warm, the cypresses emitted their aroma, and some nocturnal birds hooted in the hillocks. The landlord's small hound dog, which was kept for looking for truffles, came and licked my hand, then lay down in front of my feet. Laurent asked whether I might want to come to his place, saying he had wanted to invite me over for a long time, and that tomorrow was Sunday. I would sleep at his place, and he'd show me around the area the next day. I turned it down. Said I was tired. I actually quite liked that stocky Laurent, but even more to my liking was André—a tall boy with a dreamy face, next to whom I slept every night (we were four to a room). Nothing ever happened between us, of course; I probably don't need to emphasize that anymore.

I don't know what's become of all of them. I've never gotten into contact with any of them again, although a couple of times, I've considered driving there to Vaucluse to see them. Hopefully neither Gilles nor Roger got AIDS. Gilles is most likely married to Catherine, and they have a couple of children; Gilles has taken over the grapes and truffles from his father. It's still difficult for me to imagine that they're all already middle-aged. It's good that I haven't gone to see them—nostalgic journeys to the shadows of your past are perfectly pointless: there's nothing there any longer.

33

I already spoke briefly about my ridiculous attempts to invest the money earned from stooping in a cru into the Paris gay scene. There *isn't* anything there to talk about at length. The most significant circumstance in that fall of 1990 was actually meeting Sven—a gay who had moved there from Estonia one year earlier and who, by the way, lived a highly active and multifaceted life on that scene.

Sven was a couple of years younger than me and graduated from the same High School No. 1, where his French also came from. In barely a year, his proficiency had become so flexible and rich in terms of modern, idiomatic expressions that he could no longer be told apart from any of the locals. He had no accent at all: a result, which I haven't even reached in eleven years. Sven's language was simple, while I, on the other hand, always try to express myself complicatedly and end up crashing and burning, sounding ridiculous or, in any case, not one-hundred-percent myself. Sven acted as a small-time prostitute, for which his job as a hotel night porter offered him good opportunities. He had also submitted an application for asylum, and recommended that I do it as well. He was very accommodating in his own way, and truly helped me without any benefit to himself; I personally certainly would not have been brave enough to take on the French administration. It became clear, by the way, that it wasn't so bad for a person tempered in the Soviet administration—not even immigration officials.

Nevertheless, I would rather not rest on that stage at greater length, because it was one of the most difficult and unpleasant ones, and it is *still* a little too distressing to recall. I'm quite a poor liar if it must be done consciously and purposefully. But luckily, no one really expects an asylum applicant to leave a very truthful impression. No doubt all kinds of drama has been seen there, one more veridical than the next. I, of course, slapped together my personal KGB legend. Luckily, Leningrad customs hadn't confiscated the videocassettes with my two films, and they were very lucrative for me from that point onward.

One way or another, I stayed and waited, although there wasn't really any hope for my application's finding a positive resolution. However, in 1990, things weren't in the least as strict as they are now. Nowadays, a person the likes of me wouldn't have any hope at *all* of getting asylum. The demand is too great, and competition for the lone "free spaces" in rich France has become too sharp.

I lived at the home of Vahur Linnuste, that Estonian-language lecturer. In those years, his apartment, which he had halfway built into the rooms of a former horse stable in the courtyard *rez-de-chaussé* (ground floor) of an old Marais house, was a true gypsy, or to be more precise, Estonian camp. Often, ten or more penniless compatriots slept on mattresses on the floor and in beds: Estonians, who in the spirit of the 1930s had come to discover Paris, and had found before them quite a different kind of city that was frequently disappointing, unfriendly (they weren't welcome!), and dreadfully pricy. Vahur Linnuste not only housed them, but also fed them, acquiring food donations through Lithuanian immigrant organizations. Even I went with him to haul those large packages of canned and dried goods home from a suburb somewhere, which involved several Métro transfers.

Among the Estonians that Vahur Linnuste housed were both young university students and renowned cultural figures. There were also thieves and adventurers, who took this or that from his dwelling along with them, from time to time; but Vahur Linnuste made nothing of it. Estonians generally regarded him as a hippie and a weirdo. People loved to talk, wrinkling their noses slightly, about the hygiene conditions of Vahur Linnuste's apartment. It's also true that he later turned off the hot water heater, because his electricity bills became too large. It's also true that, at least when I lived there, not one of the overnighters attempted to clean or wash anything there. Every once in a while, Vahur Linnuste organized a dishwashing bee; however, participation in them was not always enthusiastic.

Beneath Vahur Linnuste's apartment was a vaulted cellar, where he kept the wine bottles that he went to bring from Spain every year in his small car. The wine certainly wasn't much to brag about, but his guests never turned it down. Afterwards, safely back in our homeland, it was good to talk again about the awful headaches from Linnuste's awful wines. I don't know many Estonians who would have stayed at a hotel when visiting Paris at that time. I lived at Vahur Linnuste's place for two months. Mr. Linnuste himself and his very young French wife, who had slightly anarchistic views, and who had run away from her own bourgeois home, resided on a *mezzanina* built in the high-ceilinged space. The *mezzanina*'s plank floors creaked rhythmically several times per day. People spoke of Mr. Linnuste as a sexual genius. That young woman, Jeanne, loved to talk at a whisper in the kitchen about one artist or another, who was actually an *anarchiste*, and who was secretly repressed by the authorities for that reason. She further pronounced *anarchiste* in a specific whisper, which is favored by the swishing *ch* and *st* found in that French word. Since that time, anarchy has for me always been associated with Vahur Linnuste's uniquely-smelling kitchen and Jeanne's urgent whispering.

I myself don't even know how those months passed, but pass they did. The weather turned gradually colder, and the integration outfits I'd bought from department stores weren't especially suitable for winter. I had somehow thought, like all Estonians, that Paris *has* no winter; that the chestnuts blossom year-round; and had stuck to that belief even despite the harsh onslaught of reality.

My money finally ran out in about mid-December—I couldn't go to the Marais gay bars in the evenings anymore then, either (Mr. Linnuste's apartment was located in a fantastic place for that). I wandered around the city for days on end, down streets and across parks, and sat in Notre Dame or some other church to pass the time—those places are free. I strove to figure out the secret of Parisians' identifying good looks and self-confidence. For some reason, I refused to consider the fact that they all possess and circulate sums of money that exceed the quite finite emptiness that governed my pockets, by an unending number of times. When the sun was shining, I attempted to doze off on a park bench. It was still very warm in November, but the temperature started to gradually grow colder in December: the sun no longer really reached far enough to shine upon the benches. I sat and thought in amazement about how I hadn't met anyone in that large city yet; that no one had come up to me and invited me to go along with them. A couple of times, someone asked for the time or for money. I longed for Tallinn and my acquaintances, for my secure life, where my belly was full. I came up with stories that I would tell when I went back there some day. At the same time, I didn't want to go. I knew that something had to happen to me in Paris; that I had to meet someone who would change my life (in my imagination, it was, of course, a French Prince Charming— simultaneously harsh and sensitive, athletic and poetic; in short, a true chimera), and that I was not allowed to leave the city before that. I mustn't give up. I figured that I *could* always go and jump off of a bridge into the river if it didn't amount to anything. Watching the brownish water from the bridge, a leap nevertheless didn't seem all that realistic. I lied to Denis S., saying that I went to the National Institute of Cinematography to check it out, that I was preparing for enrollment the next summer, getting the corresponding paperwork in order, working at a library. The last part wasn't quite a lie, because as the weather grew chillier, I truly discovered the opportunity and warm refuge for many *clochards* (drifters) that is the Beauborg (Pompidou Cultural Center) Public Library. If I read anything there at all, then it was the books that I had already read in Estonia: Mauriac's *The Desert of Love*, *Thérèse Desqueyroux*, *The End of the Night*. The library was located on the upper floor—going up the escalators installed in glass tubes, a wide view of the city unfolded. Interestingly, it all didn't seem romantic or inspiring at all. I had practically forgotten that I'd once made some kinds of films, had come up with some creative works. Naturally, no one in that city had heard anything about my films either; no one reminded me of them. I thought mainly about what we would have for dinner at Linnuste's place in the evening, what sauce would be on the macaroni that day. Or if it'd be without sauce, just oil.

In early January, I'd suddenly had enough of it. New Year's was over, 1991 had begun, and nothing seemed to be changing. On New Year's Eve, I had ambled along the Champs-Elysées, where an estimated one million people were celebrating. Everyone was with someone else; one had to look out to not be hit on the head by the cork from a champagne bottle, or by the bottle itself. I left there in a deep depression. Wandering around empty and quiet, incredibly light Paris on the morning of January 1st, I came to a decision. I decided to go back home, to say "to hell" with the asylum application, to bury my hopes. To tell the truth, I once again deftly placed my hopes in the other side, which had inconspicuously become Tallinn, even Tartu. I intended to publish a new personal ad in the newspaper; I was confident that everything would go differently this time. In addition, I intended to start doing business and earning money. I certainly didn't know what business for certain; perhaps some kind of an import, such as Rhône wines—I would use my ties. I knew that several of my male classmates had already become importers (*importeurs*) for something; that they had made money, and that it all wasn't so impossible.

First of all was the main problem of where to get money for the trip back. A bus ticket to Warsaw cost five hundred francs; it was supposed to be quite cheap to go on from there to Tallinn—maybe only fifty francs because of the exchange rate. However, my pocket only held Latvian santīms, which couldn't be used for anything; otherwise, I would have spent those away as well. Sven had promised to get me a job as a night porter too, but he hadn't gotten any bites so far. It was then that I met Hannes Liiva.

Today is June 3rd. Poplar fluff hovers above the Emajõgi, the air is heavy, the trees dark and dusty; the poplar fluff and elm seeds form gray dust devils on the park paths, stirred by a lazy breeze. For some reason, I was reminded of winter yesterday. As if summer was already coming to an end. Hawthorns (*aubepines*) are blossoming, and even starting to finish the process. I'd like rain to come, but it won't. Proper rain. It sprinkled a little in the evening, only making the air moist; today is even more suffocating. The days are very long. The most agonizing thing when I was sick was the very fact that the day never seemed to end. Still that dry, unforgiving sunshine; the boring blue sky outside the window. I longed for Paris's normal, dark nights. They're already talking about damages from the drought on the radio. On the western coast, it practically hasn't rained at all for two months already—the new crops have been ruined from place to place, hayfields and pastures are scorched. This drought-spring will probably be a mercy kill (*coup de grâce*) for many an agricultural company already breathing its last breaths in financial debt. But these days, that doesn't yet mean starvation, or even economic recession. I don't even know why I'm reporting this—what do those scorched Livonian fields have to do with me? The overproduction of food is still dominant in the European Union; dearth in Livonia would only mean relief for the exporters there.

Of course, I'm not familiar with the global mechanisms of causes and consequences: those patterns are undoubtedly too complicated for such a primitive machine as the human brain. And so, I don't know specifically what could significantly sway that which we call balance, but which perhaps is more precisely a certain state of extremity very close to the breaking point, to the system's self destruction, to a shift of state. Universal balance, if such a thing exists, isn't swayed by anything, anyway. All in all, even "nature's balance" is probably much more powerful than people believed in my youth, when the fear arose that man could destroy it. Man can only destroy his own civilization, but that destruction matures in a civilization one way or another—civilizations are attempts to go as far as possible in one direction, to remember as much as possible, but time and again, the rubber band tied to the boot of humankind yanks us back, into oblivion.

I dealt with such thoughts when I was sick. I somehow identified with that parched land talked about on the radio news, and to me it seemed that as soon as it started raining, I would recover. I reached for my bottle of Rõuge water. Luckily, I still had that—water!

Hannes Liiva, however, I met (naturally) at Vahur Linnuste's place in January1991. He came to one of those "Estonian music nights" that Mr. Linnuste organized from time to time. He had, by the way, a true old-fashioned radiola (unfortunately, I don't remember what brand)—almost the same kind as the one on which I endlessly spun the Liz Franz record with the pink and white sleeve during my puberty. The other sound-maker was slightly newer: an old portable radio/cassette player that occasionally jammed the tape, and which otherwise emitted quite a tinny sound. The Estonian adventurers had apparently spurned them for being too shoddy, and had left them there.

On the other hand, Mr. Linnuste's collection truly held an abundance of Estonian music, peppered with the terrible academic screeching that was produced by the numerous members of the ESSR Association of Composers's family on the eve of every new congress, Soviet variety, the humorously naive performances of expatriate Estonians, and the newest local Estonian alternative rock. I didn't know where he had gotten all of it.

That evening, Vahur Linnuste had so much as put on that same Liz Franz record. Specifically, he found out that Liz Franz's solo record would be issued on Paon Records in spring: they had addressed him in the matter of translating the lyrics. *Too bad*, I thought, *that I'll already be back in Estonia by then.* At the same time, listening to that record after a rather unrestrained consumption of red wine deepened the most sentimental homesickness within me. In those years, Liz Franz hadn't been so important to me for a long while, but I hadn't forgotten her either. On a number of especially damp and dreary days before Christmas, when all of the store display windows were decorated with shimmering dark-blue, red, and gold; with actual pine branches; and on the streets in front of flower shops, there stood clumps of bound pines, which, when sniffed from quite close up (I often touched them semi-secretly—I didn't know if I was allowed to or not), dispersed their own familiar scent among the powerful smells of the street—on some such December evenings (and those display windows were a million times more brilliant than in my childhood, casting me back into my childhood with a force that much greater), I hummed a Liz Franz song to myself for encouragement or the enjoyment of self-pity; actually, for the most part, that very same "I Long for the Bosom of the Rowan Tree." She didn't have any songs about pine trees.

When I was there in Mr. Linnuste's apartment, standing amid the visitors and quite drunk, engrossing in my dearest melancholy, accompanied by Liz Franz's old songs, Hannes Liiva struck up a conversation with me. He had already caught my attention beforehand with his appearance. It was absolutely gray. It wasn't that his hair was gray. It *was* gray, that is, but not from age. His hair's natural color was gray—that kind of gray-sand whisker gray. His face also had a gray tone, and all of the lines on his face somehow pointed downwards, as if hanging from the corners of his mouth, eyes, and cheekbones were normally tin weights that he left at home when joining a crowd. I can't confirm that his clothes truly were a gray tone, but he certainly didn't wear anything colorful. He seemed uncommonly antipathetic to me. Not hostile or ugly, but somehow warding everyone off. I don't remember the pretext under which he spoke to me, but in any case, it soon turned out that he had a car and was planning to drive it to Estonia. I immediately pricked my ears up. In short, the outcome of our conversation was that I went to go and live at Hannes Liiva's place on the following day.

The thing was that there was something wrong with his car, and it had to be fixed before heading out: Hannes Liiva spoke practically no French at all, however, and hoped to use me as an interpreter at garages. He agreed to take me along with him to Estonia for free in exchange, especially because of the fact that I could also take turns driving the car. The vehicle itself was a large old Citroën—the kind of luxury model that settles close to the ground when stopped, but heaves its belly up from the ground again when started, and is probably capable of boosting itself even higher in poor road conditions.

But right then, that grand Citroën, which probably a couple of decades old, was squatting on the driveway to a tiny *pavillon* in a garden suburb close to Paris, its belly close to the ground. Hannes Liiva resided in that *pavillon* and was supposed to be renovating it as rent. He was living in France for his second or third year already—he possessed some kind of a residency permit, and even received unemployment assistance. He worked for a short time in construction, but had gotten into an argument with the other builders: they had started to taunt him. Maybe he simply hadn't understood what they were saying. He had arrived in France with his Jewish girlfriend—they were supposed to travel to Israel, but got stuck in Paris. The girl had arranged all of their affairs, had mastered the language. But then, the girl dumped Hannes Liiva and hightailed it to Israel herself. He still hoped to fly there after the girl. He hated France, the French language, and the French people with all his heart: in his mind, everyone there and everything about them was bad, poor-quality, deceitful, etc. Yet, he wasn't planning on turning back to Estonia permanently, either. He was able to live off his tiny unemployment sum, and had so much as bought a car. The one-room *pavillon* was extremely cold in winter, of course—a draft blew through the glass door and sagging windows, but that was no rarity in France. A warm room in winter was a higher, bourgeois luxury. The winter *would* pass soon, of course, and then it would be warm again. Hannes Liiva didn't even allow the electric radiator to be kept on too much, because he had to pay for electricity himself. Interestingly, he wasn't cold. He was oddly indifferent about everything—he slept a great deal and ate relatively little, but was still rather more chubby than thin. I couldn't stand sleeping so much: I became hungry and cold. I didn't have money for buying Métro tickets and traveling to the city, either. I realized that by leaving Mr. Linnuste's place, I had gone out of the frying pan and into the fire.

This all the more so because the car repair wasn't going anywhere. As towing it was too expensive, we went from garage to garage and attempted to find out what the car's problem might be by way of verbal questioning. From outer inspection, the problem was based in the fact that the car wouldn't start, wouldn't even "turn over." They recommended buying a new battery (the old one was dead, too). We bought a new battery. Hannes Liiva sat in the car and cranked the starter relentlessly, until the new battery ran out as well. Then, we took it to a garage to be charged. The mechanics in those parts were all Italians—talkative and full of laughter. They recommended bringing the car to them, saying they would certainly fix it. Charging the battery cost a pretty penny. One time, Hannes Liiva bought a broiler chicken from the Auchan supermarket, and baked it in the oven. It was a party—life seemed possible again. The wintry garden suburb was extremely depressing otherwise. Its emptiness, stagnation, the sounds (a chainsaw, a barking dog) all reminded me precisely of childhood. I wouldn't have even dreamed of such a regression. In Paris.

The bloody events of January 10th in Vilnius that were shown on the news were a small, stirring *entr'acte*. But even thinking about them didn't entertain me for very long; and on top of that, nothing further appeared to be happening. At least Hannes Liiva and I had something to talk about for a while. I didn't want to go back to Vahur Linnuste's apartment, because I believed he was already tired enough of me; on top of that, I had announced prematurely when I left that I wouldn't bother him anymore. And hope of driving away, some kind of hope, existed nonetheless.

Then I decided to ask Denis S. for a loan. It was a very unpleasant decision, because I had already borrowed from him for the train ticket when I traveled to Vaucluse, planning on paying it off from my salary; however, my salary ran out in Paris before I could manage to pay him. He hadn't asked, either. Finally, I got my nerves together and called him. Denis S. had just gone looking for me at Mr. Linnuste's place, and was very happy that I called. He apparently had need for me. Specifically, the thing was that in connection with the abrupt increased interest in the Baltic States (I had known nothing about it while messing around with Hannes Liiva's batteries in my garden suburb), the record company Paon was planning to move up the release of

Liz Franz's record. And as he was busy, he thought that maybe I would like to be Liz Franz's interpreter—the record company was looking for someone. They would most likely pay for it, too, Denis S. added perceptively.

Of course I wanted to. I would have wanted to even without pay. It suddenly seemed like the Great Opportunity for me. All of my former adoration for Liz Franz re-awoke, as if it had only been in an enchanted sleep. Liz Franz in Paris! And I her official interpreter, at her side, in her brilliance, a part of her brilliance! I was thrilled to the utmost extent. I informed Hannes Liiva that I needed to move back in with Vahur Linnuste for a while, to which I no longer had any psychological objections, either: I now had a *function* in local refugee life! It turned out that Mr. Linnuste didn't have a single other Estonian there at that time: it was the dead of winter and the ebb of tourism. I stayed and waited for Liz Franz's arrival; I counted the days until then. In the meantime, I also ended up on television.

Specifically, one television channel (probably France 2—back then, they were all the same to me) organized a panel discussion on the Baltic States' fight for freedom in light of the recent events. They sought, via Vahur Linnuste, a "testifier" (*témoigne*) for the show, who would add truth, value, and immediacy with his testimony (*témoignage*). Of course, I didn't have any testimony to offer about the fresh events in Vilnius, or even in Tallinn, but that really wasn't a problem—the given station had a Moscow correspondent for that. I was required simply as a zoological sample specimen—more as evidence (*preuve*) of the existence of the nations being discussed, of the Balts (*les baltes*), than as a testifier. I was allowed to open my mouth only once over the course of the show. It was a live broadcast, by the way; I was very nervous about my French. Yet, I was only able to utter a single word, which I pronounced intelligibly:

"*Non.*"

The question was whether I believed in the Baltic States' independence. However, that "*non*" didn't stem from a fear of the Soviet authorities, as some probably believed afterward, nor from conformism; but on the contrary, from willful and demonstrative non-conformism. In my opinion, it was already banal to talk about one's belief in independence—everyone was sick of it; I also never participated in the events of the "Singing Revolution," which to me felt like totalitarian mass hysteria. I had thought better of my people, had somehow subconsciously—which was probably a widespread understanding among Estonians during Soviet times—regarded us, Estonians, as being different, more sensitive, more individualistic. That mindless collective singing of the masses, all standing together on the Song Festival Grounds, swaying and holding hands, displayed to me clearly that Estonians surrender to mass psychosis just as easily as Russians, Germans, Chinese—whatever nations.

Thus, "*non*" was my answer to the new mainstream, but I hadn't realized that it wasn't yet in the least bit mainstream there in France, and that on the television show, I was expected to have a brave, idealistic, and naive belief in my country's future—that was supposed to be a part of my species's zoological attributes. I had indeed planned on giving my "no" a nuance, explaining that I naturally hoped and highly desired Estonian independence; however, in a strict sense, I didn't have the basis for believing in it, as I had no idea what the belief was and for what purpose it was, and adding that the Soviet authorities in particular demanded that we believed in them, but that new freedom must also come with a freedom of belief, in which the political regime would persevere on something more natural, broader than blind *fide*, etc., etc.

But the show's anchor immediately cut me off. At the time, I didn't yet know that one must speak over the others on French talk shows, fight aggressively for his or her own space in the national medium, compete mercilessly with the anchor and the co-guests, shout, wave one's hands. To tell the truth, I saw that it was going on around me, but was unable to copy it. And so, the sole word that I have ever appeared with on France 2 (later, in connection with my film, I was also on Arte once), was that "*non*." It brought me hatred and disdain from the old Paris-Estonians, and from that point onward, I became a *persona non grata* at their regular Wednesday tea evenings; which, however, was no big issue, because as life showed, I no longer needed their tea, madeleines, and sandwiches, and I actually felt great relief that I no longer had to participate in their inter-factionary battle (there were five older ladies to each faction, whom I moreover chronically confused). On the other hand, my television appearance had a favorable effect on the immigration officials, because very soon after, an official letter was delivered to Vahur Linnuste's address, informing me that a positive decision was made on my asylum application. I was only shown mercy among the local Estonian refugee community when my documentary *Borders*, which I had filmed in France, became a little well known. They then invited me to appear at their tea evening, but I didn't go. The only person who didn't forgive me for my "*non*" for a full ten years was Madame Monclin.

Hilja Monclin was namely an Estonian, who immigrated as a child, before World War II. She had practically forgotten her Estonian, so it was easier to understand her when she consciously spoke French—not French mixed with some kinds of odd vocables that were apparently supposed to be Estonian. She was married to a wealthy man, and probably felt bored. In those years, she finally found a suitable form of entertainment for herself. She became a heated freedom fighter, and one time, she so much as haggled off of Arnold Rüütel, who at the time was the Chairman of the Republic of Estonia Presidium of the Soviet Supreme and was on an unofficial visit to Paris, some kind of paper confirming that she somehow represented the Republic of Estonia (which at that time did not yet exist diplomatically) in France. Even now, she regards herself as Estonia's sole fully authorized representative in Paris, and believes that her being driven off was merely a machination of Prime Minister and later President Lennart Meri. She only referred to Lennart Meri as "*sale petit bonhomme*" (wretched little man), and hoped her time to shine would come when Rüütel came back into power. Yet, she hadn't noticed that the fight for freedom had long since ended. It truly is difficult to pay notice to the passing of ten years in Paris: really, nothing has changed.

Only then, at last year's New Year's Eve embassy reception, did I discern that I had apparently finally escaped Madame Monclin's *disgrâce* (disfavor). Madame Monclin appeared to be somehow less combative, resigned, at that reception. She said that maybe I was right, and Estonia *hadn't* become free (her Estonian had made great progress in the meantime, that must be acknowledged), because what freedom was that, when even Arnold Rüütel had to dance to the beat of Moscow's drum and wasn't able to call her, Hilja Monclin, a fully-authorized and extraordinary ambassador, as he himself (Mr. President) deemed right in his heart.

I don't know if I was right or not: is Estonia independent, or isn't it? I've probably become too distanced to be able to decide. And undoubtedly, I'm only talking about all of this in order to not talk about me meeting Liz Franz—to delay it, although it already happened long ago: eleven, soon eleven-and-a-half years ago.

And now, one more event has disrupted my documentation of those former events, which nevertheless extend right up to today, and probably into the future as well. I don't know what to think at all anymore.

Over the entire course of the week that I was sick, and right up until now, I hadn't thought of checking my mailbox. No letters aside from my rent bill come to me here, and the latter had already arrived. As far as I know, no one who might write to me has my address. Today, when I went down the stairs (the large stairwell is pleasantly cool and dim in this suffocating weather), I remembered that mailbox. It contained a pile of variegated junk mail, of course—I was just about to throw it into the trashcan, when I felt that among the colorful garbage was something thicker in the shape of a long envelope. It was indeed an envelope—quite thick, with my name on it, the correct address even up to the zip code, and two US stamps. The address was written in upper-case letters: exactly those upper-case letters, in which Liz Franz wrote the addresses of all of the postcards she's sent to me. I didn't dare to open it immediately—my legs went weak upon seeing the handwriting, and for a moment I was overcome by the desire to toss the envelope into the trashcan along with the junk mail. But curiosity won out over fear. I sat on a park bench in front of the monument to Russian Imperial Army General Barclay de Tolly, and ripped open the envelope.

There was a rehearsal for *Evita* underway on Town Hall Square. Open-air performances of that famous, although perhaps slightly outdated musical are the highlight of the 2002 summer season in Tartu. *Evita* tells the story of the rise of Argentinean dictator Perón's young wife: of her happiness, popularity, battle with illness, and early death. Madonna played Evita Perón in a film made a few years ago, and the massive portrait floating in the air next to Tartu's Town Hall also suspiciously resembles that pop star. Still, some local actress should be playing Evita in Tartu. The sound system on Town Hall Square is decent, in any case, and I've been able to hear the rehearsals from my room without going outside or opening the windows. I found out that there will be a full ten performances during the run—evenings at nine o'clock from June 7th through the 20th—and thought about where I should head that is away from Tartu for that time. I so much as considered returning to Paris, but some stubbornness held me back from making that decision. If I've decided to solve the mystery of Liz Franz's disappearance in Tartu, I thought, then I should solve it in Tartu; or I at least have to more or less finish off my notes here, because I'm not sure whether I'd continue writing them in Paris. But everyone has their limits, and to hear "Don't Cry for Me, Argentina" for ten nights—that, I'm not even prepared to do in the name of Liz Franz, or becoming free of her.

I met with Signe the previous day, and she complained that she is worried about her great-aunt, whom she goes and cares for. Her great-aunt lives on Rüütli Street right near Town Hall Square, has lived there for her entire life, and has nowhere else to go; especially seeing as how she has terminal cancer and can't really move. Signe apparently doesn't know now how her poor Great-Aunt Elli (actually Eulalia) will survive all of those *Evita*s, because she has already complained about the "holler and racket" coming from the street, which she has never normally complained about otherwise.

I comforted Signe, saying that her great-aunt will certainly get used to it, that the musical has pretty sing-along melodies, and that sure enough, you'll see: soon, she'll even be humming "Don't Cry for Me, Argentina," and in the end, will die a gentle death with Evita's name on her lips.

That last part was, of course, a harsh joke, but I know Signe's ambivalent attitude towards her Great-Aunt Eulalia, caring for her is a heavy burden that she masochistically enjoys at the same time. Signe then complained that she's more worried about herself, because *Evita* apparently also drifts wonderfully through the windows of her apartment across the river, and for some reason, as silly as it might be, "Don't Cry" always makes *her* cry; especially seeing as how she's now weaning herself off anti-depressants, because even the cheaper Prozac variety is too expensive for her at the moment.

*

My poor girlfriend, my бедная подруга, I thought when I had managed to acquaint myself with the contents of the envelope over the course of a few seconds. You certainly know your *pauvre ami's* heart very well. But still, not quite to the core. Or you *do* know it to the core, but your poor friend himself always remains on the surface, regarding that changing and volatile surface *as* his heart?

The envelope contained two pairs of plane tickets, and I inspected those first off. The first were in my name with an itinerary of Helsinki–Paris–New York. Air France. The second pair was for the same itinerary—and as I confirmed, also for the same dates: departure to Paris on June 9th, from there onward on June 11th; yes, there would be time left for getting my affairs in order at home: the 10th is a Monday, and there's the morning of the 11th on top of that—but in Asko Lens' name.

No, Liz Franz, you don't know your friend's heart. Why do you think I want to fly with Asko? I *would* have wanted to, but now . . . I don't know. Everything is happening too fast, coming and going, I haven't, to admit the truth, actually and deeply fallen in love with anyone for eleven years—the entire Liz Franz period. My heart has probably numbed; maybe it is, in fact, age that is coming without me noticing, I've thought. Maybe I've been scared by Liz Franz's affection for me—that dogged and relentless passion, the frightening reflection of which I've seen in each one of my fledgling affections; and that reflection has made me disgusted by my own feelings.

Yesterday, I saw Asko on the stairs again (it is still somewhat tiring to live in the same stairwell as your romantic interest when that interest is so ephemeral): he was going the other way in the company of a girl, I wasn't sure whether it was Mailis or someone else. Her face seemed thinner. I said hello to him with genuine indifference, although something stirred within me all the same—some feeling of offense, maybe, or grazed self-love. Apparently bothered by my indifference (I actually know absolutely nothing about his feelings or thoughts towards me), he sent me an e-mail afterwards, in which he invited me onto the "roof" later that evening—yes, like the first time. Everything seemed so promising and romantic then. That was a month ago. What would we do there on the roof now? I hoped that maybe it would be a bigger party, to which other university students would also come. But in the evening, he e-mailed again and informed that something had come up, and perhaps we'd see each other tomorrow—so, today. Will I tell him about those tickets there on the roof? He'd certainly like to come to New York. Exams are probably supposed to finish this week as well, if I've understood correctly. And if I had been given such an offer in my youth, I wouldn't have hesitated, in any sense—exams or not. Such offers aren't made several times in your life. But how will I explain it all to him, when everything between us is so undefined? And can I even be *bothered* to explain, and can I even be bothered to travel with Asko? Maybe when I'm in New York I'll actually meet . . .

Already! That machine is already starting up—the machine of useless dreams. And will I go there myself in the first place? Is it a trap? Because it's undoubtedly a trap, what else could it be? But just as undoubtedly, I'm trapped anyway. Liz Franz knows about everything, regardless. My "conspiracy apartment," my relationships, my dreams, everything. It's probably worth knowing just one person's desires and dreams quite well enough if you *do* know everything about him, his primary mechanism.

In addition to the flight tickets, the envelope also contained a voucher for high-speed Tallinn–Helsinki ferry tickets. The flight times apparently didn't match up well, and actually, I like to depart Tallinn by boat—seeing the city's silhouette, in summer, when it's light. Liz Franz knew that because it is her own preference as well, which she can never bring to fruition, however, because there are more Estonians who would potentially recognize her on ferries than on planes. By the way, the tickets were round-trip—naturally, because they aren't business class tickets. So, complete freedom: stay in Paris, come to Estonia. The return flight is on June 25th, but it can be changed.

No, you know that side of me brilliantly, Liz Franz. That maniacal fear of oppression. Not one ticket may have locked-down return dates, because your duckling might become fed up and start itching to return right away, on the first day. However, if he *has* the opportunity to turn back, then perhaps he won't do so and will take things more calmly, because he supposes he can do so another day, too. If there isn't that option, then you can be certain that for the entire time he's forced to be there, he won't think of anything other than how to "escape," and won't see or hear a thing. Like in a cage. Or a box. But the box in which you've transported your duckling for eleven years has large, pretty ventilation holes in it. He is completely calm in there, he doesn't struggle. Quite relatively calm.

Additionally, the envelope contained a postcard with a picture of the Statue of Liberty, upon which Liz Franz had written in her usual style, but in what was a little like strange handwriting (no doubt it felt that way because I haven't seen her handwriting in a long time): *Go alone or together. Don't hesitate, everything's arranged. You'll be met at the airport, you'll be recognized. Don't worry about straw. Your That.*

And next to the signature was further taped a large, blue iris petal, which crumbled into dry shards beneath my fingertips and fell to the sidewalk. That reminded me that the whole iris section is now in full bloom at the botanical garden—the most spectacular strains: multicolored, velvety, violet. I wonder whether they're blooming so late in New York as well?

There was no date on the postcard, as always. I inspected the postmark: it was indeed from New York, but the date had smeared on the stamp. On the other hand, the Tartu arrival stamp was clearly legible on the backside of the envelope: 05.30.02. So, it's already been lying around in the mailbox for several days. There was no sender's address, of course. But so basically, she still left me just about ten days of spare time. That's even short: Liz Franz usually organized all trips and meetings two months, half a year in advance. That habit was no doubt left over from her days as a singer, when concert tours were in place for an entire year and even longer. She also knew that I have a US visa. I had it put in my Estonian passport a couple of years ago when I planned on flying to New York for the summer, to prove my independence to Liz Franz. But that travel plan somehow fell through: in the end, I still came to Estonia in July, just as Liz Franz did. She certainly didn't scoff at my travel plans *directly* that time.

Asko doesn't have a visa, of course, but there should still be time to arrange that, in any case. Today is only Monday. Should I give up this apartment then? But if I come back to Estonia from New York anyhow? There's nothing for me to do in Paris during July and August anyway. That Forest Brothers' film project is unfinished here. That Liz Franz project. Now that she isn't so disappeared anymore, I'm actually even more in a rush with it. I know that as soon as I see her, it could all collapse in a single blow. She'll say: "It's not like that!" And I'm already breaking down into doubt—over everything that I've written here, and over what I still plan on writing.

But no, it won't go so easily for her this time. I'll complete my testimony. In spite of her, and in spite of myself. I know—it's not so simple to stop me anymore, not even with transatlantic flights or anything else of the sort.

Actually, I'm awfully interested in what awaits me ahead. Has Liz Franz really left Umberto, is she living with her Juri? And do Father Vincenzo, Father Salvatore, and Father Serafimo walk in and out, play the flute while sitting on the floor in the evenings? And Liz Franz, free Liz Franz watches them all with a motherly, gentle smile; at the same time, proudly; at the same time, melancholically, resignedly, mourning within, like Maria Callas withdrawn from life.

She's sitting in the corner in her high-backed, red plush upholstery diva's armchair. It is from that chair that she rises when I walk in. She walks toward me wearing that very same brilliant, although also somewhat questioning, even childishly shy smile—just as she did then, the first time, in that Paris hotel foyer.

34

She rose from her armchair, where she had been waiting for me. I was running slightly late because I had misjudged the distance, thinking it shorter than it was, as always happens in Paris (I somehow reduced that city's dimensions to the scale of Tallinn and Tartu); I was out of breath from my quick pace, and even somewhat emphasizing it so that she would see I had hurried. With her first words, she was able to immediately erase the embarrassment of my excuses; to create some kind of natural, almost comradely atmosphere. I was in seventh heaven. I was certain she knew who I was, because in any case, Denis S. had told her about me. I quietly hoped that perhaps she had even seen my films, and perhaps they had left an impression on her. She would then be the first person I had met in Paris who had seen my films. I'd generally gotten used to the idea there that all of the people shuffling around me have never seen *The Railway Watchman's House*, nor do they wish to see it, and if it were to be shown to them by force, then they would give it a shrug in the best case. I'd once again become accustomed to being a nobody. Liz Franz was able to rise from her armchair and walk up to me, was the first to reach out her small hand to me with such a movement, such an expression that all at once I became *someone* again—all of my suppressed vanity and self-awareness came back in a rush.

I don't remember what we talked about. We waited there for a *Le Monde* journalist, Nicole Zand (that was her pseudonym), who was supposed to do an interview with Liz Franz that I was meant to interpret. She ran late, and quite a heart-to-heart took shape between us right there in the hotel foyer. Liz Franz seemed so simple and natural to me. I gazed upon that short woman with bobbed hair, who had risen from her low armchair so gracefully and nimbly, and had walked towards me—I knew her already, long ago. Which, in a certain sense, was indeed so. I naturally didn't tell her right away about how I would cry and masturbate while listening to her record at the age of fourteen. I haven't told her about that to this day, to tell the truth. But I believe that she had an idea about it all. Somehow. And straight away.

My interpreting (*interprète*) turned out to be very easy. After exchanging the first polite formalities, it became clear that Nicole Zand spoke quite decent Russian, and they continued speaking without my assistance; I was only able to help Madame Zand on a couple of occasions, when she couldn't remember some Russian expression and searched for it in French. Liz Franz spoke Russian with a very heavy accent; I was amazed at how she pronounced it so purely when singing. Apparently, it was a question of will, of style.

Madame Zand was an older Jewish lady with dyed red hair, quite lively and nervous. Her husband had worked for years as the *Le Monde* Moscow correspondent. They had been to Tallinn, also. It was during the sixties or seventies. She had been astonished by the old, pre-war European/German aura there. All of those little ladies wearing hats and sitting in cafés, eating cream pies. She wanted to know whether Estonia still is like that, now that it was becoming free again.

I noticed that Liz Franz replied quite tersely and stalely, but Nicole Zand liked her answers and burst out laughing several times. Liz Franz was apparently used to giving interviews and knew what would have an effect, what would go in, and what there was no point talking about. She never went into details or nuances, and replied directly and without mincing words, although perhaps not always quite honestly (when I think back to it now). I was enthralled by her "performance." At the end, she suggested to Nicole Zand that she also speak with "the young, renowned cineaste," by which she meant me. Nicole Zand cast me a quick glance, sizing me up, and gave me her business card, even writing her direct number on it, requesting that I get in touch. (Once, that business card even truly was helpful.)

When Madame Zand had left, Liz Franz made an effortless proposal to go to a café somewhere and have a bite to eat—she was apparently dreadfully hungry. No-no, don't worry, she made a disallowing gesture—her publisher would pay for all of the café receipts, even for mine; that's what they'd agreed. Truly—from the very beginning, Liz Franz showed exceptional discretion and skill at disguising her offers in monetary affairs. She asked me to be her guide: apparently, she had indeed been to Paris once (I now know that it was with Umberto; back then, I didn't know about Umberto yet, or really anything about Liz Franz's life at all—all I knew was that she lived in Rome), but knew the city poorly. So, I played the expert and took her to Contrescarpe Square, in order to show Liz Franz the picturesque Mouffetard Street Market. Contrescarpe's cafés were so chic, in my opinion—on cold, gray days, I had dreamed of sitting there in the warmth behind the glass and eating that, which the entire square smells of, while drinking a hot, fatty *café crème*.

Now, I nevertheless didn't dare to order anything other than a chicken salad; the names of many foods on the menu were also completely unfamiliar to me. Liz Franz luckily didn't demand that I translate the menu, but rather chose a Nizza salad right after me—a salad which, by the way, she only picked at, so I was amazed at where her ravenous appetite had gone. I, in any case, cleared my plate entirely. We also drank red wine at Liz Franz's proposal, as cheers to our acquaintance. I don't remember what we talked about in the slightest, but we talked the entire time; it had already long been dark outside, we had ordered more wine, and I was quite drunk—Liz Franz didn't pick up on it. All of a sudden, she looked at her watch and shouted, horrified, that she definitely needed to go—her publisher was apparently already waiting at the hotel. Which doesn't mean that we picked up the pace on the way back. Liz Franz never ran anywhere.

And I'm disappointed to be leaving Tartu. Even though a couple of days is still time, but I'm already disappointed. I've gotten used to it here—still, more than a month, that's a long time. Spring has turned to summer in the meantime, and because of the drought, even *that* season has the appearance as though it were coming to an end. Suddenly, it's difficult for me to imagine Paris; even more difficult than New York, of which I have two fixed conceptions: one in a general-, the other in a mid-scale. In the general scale, it is a dark abyss between buildings, where human insects swarm. Closer up, it is a mass of nondescript faces flowing past; by the way, the point of view—meaning I—in place, is being constantly nudged: the camera jiggles. Then there is also some imagery of the ocean—of the fact that the sun rises from the ocean, because it lies to the *east*. I've been to the ocean in France and Portugal— the sun sets in that direction; very magnificently, I must say.

Yet, I've already developed my own customs in Tartu. Such as going to the market—although I've now switched over to the open-air market behind the bus station, where there is more fresh stuff, Livonia's true bounty and copiousness. As if there *wasn't* a drought. I haven't wanted meat anymore since my sickness—my stews have changed in character. Yesterday, June 4th, I acquired my first bunch of fresh carrots: thin, crooked, and very sweet. The local fresh cabbage is also ready—tiny, tough heads. My stew was indeed composed of that bunch of carrots (twelve kroons), one head of cabbage (seven kroons), and a little bit of water and salt. Those young plants boil to softness in a few minutes. Sour cream is to be added when eating. For dessert, I had sweet cottage cheese with fresh honey (first harvest: willow, maple, dandelion .. .) and fresh strawberries, a pound of which for now still costs fifty kroons (three euros), but which I cannot refuse myself because of their smell, with which the entire aisle between market counters is filled. These kinds of strawberries are never available in Paris, anyway, and on top of that, the season for them will already be over when I get there.

My second Tartu custom is taking a walk at ten o'clock every evening along the left bank of the river to the pool; meaning to the swimming area upstream of the city, where the water should thus be tolerably clean, because aside from Tartu, there are no significant sources of pollution on the Emajõgi. Nevertheless, I still haven't taken a dip in the river. I sit there on a bench on the sand, and listen to the hooting of nightingales; I watch the behavior of human couples in love, which is indeed quite unvaried; I observe how the red sun slips downward in relation to the river, turning everything sweetly pink.

The third custom is walking on Toome Hill and on the streets lined by wooden houses behind the hill. Yesterday, there were even a few good downpours. It seemed as if it rained quite heavily, but the ground didn't even become moist—the stone pavement did darken for a moment, but dried straight away. The park paths remained dusty. There were two rainbows over the Emajõgi, stacked one above the other. I stood in the ruins of the cathedral and watched the sparse rain falling into the church, as it has fallen for several hundred summers already. Asko hasn't shown his face, and I haven't chased him, either. I suppose he knows best; that is—he doesn't know anything, of course. He doesn't know that someone, a once-renowned songstress, whose name he has perhaps heard mentioned, but whose songs he would hardly know, has, for some reason, bought transoceanic plane tickets in his name. And in all likelihood, he will never find that out. Things are starting to be too much of a hurry in technical terms (a visa), also. I'd always imagined—dreamed, rather—that when I went to New York some day, it would be with someone; that I wouldn't go there alone. To tell the truth, that *is* the reason why I haven't gone. Amid and I were supposed to go, but everything ended before that. Everything has always ended beforehand, and for the most part, everything has ended even before it has managed to start at all. So, I must travel there alone, and that is logical as well, of course. *Liz Franz* is waiting for me there.

There was a period, when I read all kinds of Buddhist literature. To me, it seemed like that radical un-religion offered some kind of a solution. I still remember the teaching of one Tibetan Rinpoche, who said that everyone dies just as he has lived. Everyone flies to America just as he has lived in Europe. It truly does seem logical in every respect, even if I no longer believe that following the teachings of Rinpoches might somehow decisively save me from myself. Everyone lives to the end with that person, as whom he was born.

My obligations as Liz Franz's interpreter in late January 1991 were, however, really quite simple to fulfill. As I had hoped, I *was* able to sit next to her at lunch tables and gorge myself. A true interpreter doesn't eat, but interprets. But Liz Franz spoke with her publisher in Italian (true, in quite stiff Italian), in even stiffer German with her tablemate (but Liz Franz was never ashamed of her linguistic deficiency—she spoke as she spoke), and, naturally, in Russian with some Russian *comtesse*, who was as shriveled as a dried plum and decked out in gold, but had shining eyes. For some reason, there was always a Russian *comtesse* or *princesse*, a countess or a duchess, at the table. The publisher apparently had some particular weakness for them.

He was, all in all, a unique old gentleman, that Monsieur Mieroslawski. More than anything, he loved antique items and odd objects brought from distant lands. On the street, he routinely dragged us in front of the display window of some antique store, if not *into* the store, for us to gape with him at a lamp stand made of large seashells; probably decadent work of the late nineteenth century. Or at a little Chinese chest guarded by a golden dragon: when the chest is opened, the dragon starts to spurt fire and smoke, as *Monsieur* Mieroslawski explained to us in French (because I didn't understand Italian), and as I had to translate to Liz Franz, who was bored but feigning great interest. The ignition mechanism wasn't working at the moment, but it was apparently possible to fix.

Mr. Mieroslawski's apartment on a quiet cul-de-sac near the dome of *Les Invalides* (with a view, if you parted the heavy velvet curtains, towards the golden cupola of *Les Invalides*, onto the square) was a genuine exhibition of old stuff. The curtains kept away the daylight, so that Mr. Mieroslawski's self-made mise-en-scène could have a better effect on the viewer. An African mask grinned beneath a spotlight, while in another corner a Japanese aquarium sparkled with its green plants and red and white fish. All of the furniture was heavy and antique; the ashtrays, dishes—nothing originated from either this century, or from this part of the world called Europe at all. We visited Mr. Mieroslawski at his home for a goodbye dinner before Liz Franz's known departure (she didn't actually fly out, although she even had herself transported to the airport). That home-dinner dinner, which was served by a butler, was extremely excruciating. I felt poor in my shabby clothes. Everyone there was indeed dressed in a bohemian manner—a well-known TV journalist and cultural commentator, a music critic, a professional musician, and a presently fashionable columnist for *Le Nouvel Observateur*—but I immediately saw that those bohemian, open-minded pants, jackets, and shirts were very, very expensive.

I also felt slightly demeaned because I was the only interpreter there. The publisher's wife did ask me out of politeness what I did in my home country, but she took no notice of my reply, because while I had been formulating it, the entire table had managed to burst into laughter over a TV anchor's joke, which went over my head (just as most of their jokes), because it had to do with some inner ring's references that targeted, as far as I could understand, considerably high spheres—all the way up to President Mitterrand. I had to translate those jokes for Liz Franz.

To my satisfaction, she did not have all that great of an interest in the dinner party's guest of honor, either, because no one could be bothered to converse via an interpreter, and furthermore, they had quite enough of their own Paris affairs to discuss, and each one wanted to be in the spotlight of attention at least once during the course of the evening. I also noted that after each guest's departure, everyone there started talking mercilessly behind his or her back, although it all left a friendly, private impression. Now, having encountered Paris's cultural circles somewhat, I know that it is an ordinary, even normative scenario for an evening. I've also learned to take part in the conversation and understand their jokes. The only thing I haven't acquired is how to produce their jokes. I'm too slow and am never able to seize upon that infinitesimal slit in the conversation, into which I could jab my own poisonous allusion.

Naturally, at that dinner, no one spoke a word about the previous day's concert (aside from a couple of polite statements dropped during the appetizer), at which a couple of the guests *had*, however, been present; nor of Liz Franz's record. In my naivety, I had envisioned that Liz Franz would be asked to perform one or two of her prettier songs (I now know that she wouldn't have done so anyway). She was dressed from head to toe in black again, just as on stage, but this time, it was a pantsuit that more resembled a regular suit. I had liked the previous evening's black velvet dress more, of course, but I also saw that it would have been out of place at that "bohemian" dinner. All the same, I would have liked to see that extremely effective image again and again: Liz

Franz during her last song, which was her hit song "Prayer" from the freedom movement, on a dark, black stage, kneeling right at the edge of the stage in the projectors' spotlight, her head slightly lowered, the microphone held between her hands, as if pressed against her chest; just like that white rose on the concert poster. The silver microphone *looked* like a white rose in her hands at that moment. Then, the fading of the last sounds, and then several more seconds of tense silence, Liz Franz frozen in the same pose, rarely unmoving; then, the storm of applause breaks out, people rise to their feet, shout "bravo," whistle; everyone had the feeling that they were present (*assister*) at something very special—as Nicole Zand wrote the next day in *Le Monde*, probably summarizing the feelings of many: *the few chosen ones, who had the fortune to make it in to that concert, partook in a powerful and, at the same time, inexplicable common experience, which can be summarized in two words: freedom's birth.*

Truly—upon reading those words in the newspaper, even I felt that Nicole Zand was absolutely right. I was very proud that I had been able to share in that event. And overall, I was in a euphoric state of mind. Even *I* was free once more—I had money again.

The next morning after the concert, I had to do quite a heavy amount of work. Liz Franz was attacked by an entire horde of radio and newspaper journalists (she had gone on television without me), and this time, I truly did have to translate. A small meeting was held at the record company following that tense session, during which a rundown of the record launch was made; a contract was likewise signed for the release of a new record, for which Liz Franz was supposed to receive quite a nice little (for me, back then) advance. I must say that the record has never been released, nor will it probably ever be, given the fact that the Paon record studio doesn't exist, and Monsieur Mieroslawski can now dedicate himself entirely to his true passion, which is the collection of old and odd items. He was apparently still able to get quite a pretty sum from the sale of Paon.

Translating Liz Franz's contract in the small Paon office that afternoon (luckily Mr. Mieroslawski didn't realize that I didn't understand the contract's legal wording in the very slightest), my mouth became dry and my head was buzzing. When the meeting ended Mr. Mieroslawski invited the two of us to come to his office (I grasped that Mr. Mieroslawski had strangely started to like me), where he firstly took us to his window, making a sweeping gesture and asking us to marvel at the view from it.

Presumably, that view was one of the pearls of Mr. Mieroslawski's collection. Namely, outside the window was a small monastery courtyard—a garden, the existence of which could not be discerned from the street in any way. It had a couple of ancient, pruned trees, a few oddly-shaped hedges, a grassy square, a small pond with greenish water, and a moss-covered fish on its stone bank, from the mouth of which water gurgled out into the pond. It truly gurgled. Mr. Mieroslawski opened the window, and through it came genuine quiet, unbelievable for Paris's 7th District. A black thrush sang quietly, but somehow passionately, reminding us that winter would soon turn into spring. Then, Mr. Mieroslawski closed the window again, went over to his large, empty desk, took an envelope out of its drawer, and handed it to Liz Franz. The envelope apparently held cash. Then, he said a couple of words more about the upcoming dinner (something to the effect that we were both expected), after which—as if he had recalled something else at the last second—he turned not directly towards me, nor towards Liz Franz, but somewhere between us with the question, or more like the statement of his opinion, that the interpreter also deserved his fee. I had counted on perhaps a couple of hundred francs, although I had also already come to terms with being forgotten about completely.

Mr. Mieroslawski left a pause for excitement after his words, as if expecting me to name my price. After that, he stuck his hand into the breast pocket of his moss-green cashmere jacket, pulled out two banknotes (it suddenly seemed to me that all of his drawers and pockets were full of cash), and handed me two five-hundred-franc notes.

"Will this be sufficient?" he asked politely.

I was only capable of nodding dumbly. "This" exceeded all of my expectations. "This" was a moment of enlightenment, during the course of which I realized what money was. Money wasn't, of course, those rubles, with which I had run the majority of my life. Nor was money the one thousand Finnish marks that I received from Helsinki for screening my film, because in my opinion, it was still very little money for that one film. Nor was money the nearly four thousand francs earned for stooping on a cru, one thousand of which were spent there on food. It was sooner a little than a lot for an entire month's worth of very hard work. Money, I realized at that moment while standing in that quiet office with a view of a monastery garden, is when Mr. Mieroslawski takes, with an absent-minded and almost indifferent motion, two five-hundred-franc notes out of the breast pocket of his green cashmere coat, and hands them to you, asking if it is enough. Is it enough for walking around through the city with Liz Franz, and for the numerous café sessions, which Liz Franz proposed again and again, and which she treated me to, and to which I quickly became accustomed? Is it enough for the several luxury (Thai and Japanese style, in the private rooms of the most expensive restaurants) lunches, where immigrant Russian *comtesses* and *princesses* jingled their gold?

Truly—is that enough? It's never enough, but it's bearable if you receive it just the same, for nothing, on top of it all. *Then* it is money. Otherwise, it's a salary, earnings, or I-don't-know-what. According to the common laws of economics, added value is created during the course of work. You receive a part, often only a trifling part, of that added value as a salary. As such, you basically give money—you don't receive it. You make money for others, and money is exactly that, which is in those other hands. "Straw," "sticks," "dust," to use Liz Franz's agricultural (always a country girl!) euphemisms. Money is rain that falls upon a rich field, but it doesn't rain on a poor one. Money is freedom.

I, for example, felt exceptionally free thanks to the two five-hundred-franc notes that appeared out of Monsieur Mieroslawski's coat pocket. I was no longer dependent upon Hannes Liiva, or on his Citroën lying on its belly in his driveway. I could purchase a bus ticket and travel back to my homeland on my own. But I didn't rush with that, initially. There appeared to still be much more interesting things ahead of me in Paris than in poor and wintry Tallinn, where there was nothing available at *all* anymore, as the rare tourists that arrived from there had said at Mr. Linnuste's—everything was apparently based on ration coupons. Moreover, I was in no hurry because Liz Franz initially remained in Paris. Specifically, she used the freedom contained in that rather fat little envelope handed to her by Monsieur Mieroslawski thusly, that she left unused the return ticket to Rome, which Mr. Mieroslawski had purchased. She indeed had herself driven to the airport, but upon arriving, before checking her baggage, she shook off her escorts, waited a little while, and then took a taxi and headed back to the city. She had informed me of her plans beforehand, saying that she wanted to "stroll around" in Paris for a few more days without having bothersome obligations and escorts (but I wasn't a **bothersome** escort—that, I realized immediately), because new obligations would once again await her in Rome, anyway.

She took a new hotel room as far away from the old one (and likewise from Monsieur Mieroslawski's pathways) as possible, on Courcelles Street on the right-hand riverbank in the 17th District. Interestingly, it is quite close to my current apartment and I pass it often; however, it is a long time since I've felt anything when looking at that hotel's facade, although I can think—again and again—back to that decisive (if it *was* decisive) evening with Liz Franz, which happened there in that very hotel room. Sometimes, I've thought of stepping in to see whether that same receptionist is still at the table—a boy with a dreamy face, who watched us somehow too sharply that time, and who I ineptly tried to make eyes at. Even if it is the same, he is by now already a rather middle-aged man—no longer a boy. Just as I am. Although, I don't reconcile to that. Looking at shorts yesterday in the Tartu Department Store, taking into account the fact that according to Martin, people in New York walk around in shorts, unlike in Paris, where only American tourists wear them—rummaging through those overly athletic and boyish shorts there at the department store, not finding anything that might be simultaneously youthful, sufficiently chic and solid, I suddenly realized that I *am* already an old man, or will be becoming one very soon, in any case. That I'm no longer a boy. That realization struck me very painfully. Life, which has always seemed dreadfully long, suddenly appeared incredibly short. Youth has passed, and there's been nothing. Nothing of that, which I dreamed about throughout my entire youth, and which I'll probably remain dreaming about—an old, pathetic "youngster," ridiculous in his pubertal implacability. (Three pimples appeared on my nose after my fever: I looked at them, like—see, puberty **again**! Another one!) Actually, there's nothing more for me to expect. What's been has been, and I even thought with a certain sense of satisfaction that the plane *might* actually crash into the ocean or something like that, and although I don't want to die, there wouldn't be anything especially sad about it if taken rationally: it would simply be cutting agony back to a normal length. For agony already began long ago, and maybe eleven years ago, when I knocked on the door of Liz Franz's hotel room on Courcelles Street at the pre-arranged time—four knocks, likewise an agreed signal (so she wouldn't have to open it for the maids, etc.). I was twenty-eight years old then—it already felt as if life was well over, but I was actually very young; furthermore, I looked younger than my age. Actually, the other day at the aquatic center I was asked pressingly whether I really wasn't a student. Yes, I am a student—Liz Franz's eternal, blockheaded student; but I don't get any kinds of discounts for it when using public transport and athletics institutions.

35

Liz Franz, who opened the door for me at eight o'clock in the evening, was wearing her black velvet performance dress, on the shoulder of which was still pinned a live, white rose blossom. The room was dim—there was only one floor lamp lit, which was behind the back of Liz Franz's armchair, so that (as it later turned out) she remained in the shadows the entire time and could observe me quite well. Now, I also know that she was very heavily creamed, powdered, makeupped, etc.; but that time, it all seemed like her natural brilliance. She appeared small, fragile, and very young. She spoke in her quiet, low voice, into which some kind of street-boyish audaciousness, or rather vulgarity broke from time to time. There was a bottle of wine on the table that she immediately asked me to open, because she apparently could never manage to work those corkscrews (I was proud to be of manly service), a large tray of several kinds of fruits that immediately made my mouth water, and another plate with a selection of cheeses—expensive ones, at that; that much I could already tell.

Liz Franz had asked me to bring my films along. I hesitated for some time over whether to take both of them, or only *The Railway Watchman's House*; in the end, however, I stayed only with *The Railway Watchman's*, deciding that it is more impressive alone. I very much wanted to make an impression on Liz Franz, not realizing that I had already *overly* done so. Liz Franz had gotten a VCR for her room, and proposed that we start watching the film right away, leisurely sipping wine at the same time. She had discretely placed my chair next to the small table so it would be as simple as possible for me to reach my hand out towards the trays.

And so, the first ever projection of *The Railway Watchman's House* took place on French soil. I was very excited and even forgot about the food, only sipping my wine nervously, pouring more for myself, also forgetting Liz Franz, who had to ask me for some, but who, by the way, was able to do so well, without causing embarrassment. She reacted in a lively and unrestrained manner, laughing several times—incidentally in the places, which were also funny in my opinion, but at which I hadn't heard anyone laugh else yet. In Estonia, *The Railway Watchman's House* was regarded as a serious, almost pathetically patriotic film. As I saw it, Arnold Ratas was nevertheless quite a funny fellow. Liz Franz applauded spontaneously and shouted "bravo!" when the credits rolled. I blushed deeply from gladness, but luckily, it probably wasn't noticeable in the dim room. Then, she asked in a businesslike manner whether I could lend her a copy—she could make more copies and give a few to her acquaintances who were involved in making and distributing films. She said that in her mind, the film should be shown in France as well as Italy and elsewhere, and by all means, I should make more films. I wasn't really planning to travel back to Estonia now, was I? I replied that I probably was, because I had no work or money in France, and it was hardly likely that anyone there would be interested in my films, either.

"You know," Liz Franz replied somehow especially confidingly, conspiratorially (*complice*), "those are all the sorts of things that can be dealt with. They're not important things. Don't worry about them. What's important is that you know what you want to do, that you have your own path beneath your feet. There are always helpers to be found, you'll see! [And truly—I had already seen that.] Do you think that I had money, that someone had an interest me when I left home, when I went to Riga, when I went to Moscow? I didn't have a single penny, but whenever I was starting to get disheartened, someone came along. Believe that:

someone always comes. Otherwise, I would have been dead long ago—seriously! You might think that I'm just saying that, as they say. But I watched your film, and I've seen many films over the course of my life, and many of them are so identical that—get out of here. I hadn't ever seen *such* a film before. It had love."

I wonder how she could have spotted that, I thought. Herbert Treumann actually only featured in the credits, I mused, and continued listening even more intently; Liz Franz seemed to know me better than I knew myself—there was something intoxicating about that.

"That really is the only important thing in art," Liz Franz continued. "That it has love. And hate, too. But there's no hate if there's no love. I'll tell you the kind of thing that maybe no one has ever told you: you've loved a lot. You probably aren't able to appreciate it, nor should you be; but actually, that's the most important thing."

I thought about Herbert Treumann, about how he lay next to me in the grass and chewed on a stick of straw, his shining eyes gazing into the summer sky; about how the shadows of pines on the grass crept ever closer to us; about how the rumble of passing trains started echoing back from the edge of the woods ever more clearly towards evening (and how one could hear when a few stopped at Mustjõe Station in order to let trains going in the opposite direction pass); about how the door to Arnold's cabin had swung open several times, and Arnold had no doubt peeked over at us, but we weren't in a hurry to go anywhere, although apparently for different reasons. Herbert Treumann wasn't in a hurry because he wasn't in a hurry to go anywhere at all, and I because I was at Herbert Treumann's side, and wanted that moment to last forever. But ultimately, the shadows of the pines still reached us, and the mosquitoes had become quite bloodthirsty. At first, we sat up, and Herbert said something ordinary and daring—proposing, for example, that we go for a swim or head to town on the last train (not that! Then we wouldn't get to sleep in the same tent together that night!). And life, to use the proper railway imagery, reverted to its normal rails . . .

That picture flashed through my head abruptly, and I suddenly started feeling sorry for myself because of my unrequited love. No one had ever told me that I had truly loved. I asked Liz Franz stubbornly, like a child:

"What good is that loving? It's always just a mirage, it never actually leads anywhere."

"That's not how it is," she replied gently. "You'll see—actually, it's not like that at all. The main thing is: don't doubt yourself. Some day, you'll get it all back in spades—honestly!"

She said that "honestly" like children say it to one another, and there was something very convincing and moving about it, although rationally, I didn't believe her words. I didn't believe that life is somehow fair, or if it is, then in such a great scheme of things an individual's chronic and ultimate bad luck hasn't yet ruin anything of that fairness.

"I'd like to sing to you as thanks," Liz Franz said all of a sudden. "I simply can't do anything other than singing, and your film truly moved me, so please don't be peeved. Maybe you know one of my songs, maybe you like one of them more than the others?" she asked in the strangely timid tone that, by the way, enters all artists' voices—no matter how famous and experienced they may be—when they speak about their own works.

I couldn't have expected that. Liz Franz singing to me! Or, to tell the truth, that dream was so old, already buried too long ago for mr to still think about its realization . . . Maybe Liz Franz really was right—you truly do get everything, but you get it when you don't especially want it anymore.

"I know all of your songs, I believe," I replied with faked thoughtfulness. I had already learned to speak with her in the familiar tone, and it offered me a vain sense of gratification. Liz

Franz had proposed that we switch to speaking in the informal on the second day, but I initially still naturally spoke to her in the formal, so she had managed to make several mild remarks to me.

"I don't know—maybe you've had enough of the song," I said with false wisdom; from colleague to colleague, so to speak. "Because it's such an old and simple one, but I still like it the very most, I have since the very beginning. That 'I Long for the Bosom of the Rowan Tree'."

"I knew you would want that," she replied, satisfied. "That's my very best song. Only stupid people regard simple songs as too simple. All good songs are simple."

And so, Liz Franz sang to me. She rose, said commandingly: "Sit here!" while pointing to her armchair. I sat there obediently. She went behind the chair. I turned my face towards her, but her own face now remained almost completely shadowed in the light coming from behind her. I realized that she didn't want me to watch her; I turned my head the right way again, closed my eyes, and attempted to imagine myself sitting next to the radiola once again—I tried to bring myself into that magical state of years ago.

She sang quite differently than from on the record. It was hard for me to get used to it during the first verse; I was even disappointed—those two songs didn't seem to match up in my head. That version recorded twenty or more years ago, the young Liz Franz version that was in my head; and the song, which now sounded from behind my back there in a dim hotel room—quietly and pensively, in a rather low, husky voice.

By the second verse, I realized that it was actually better. And during the third, I was already completely enchanted. I felt that she sang not only *to* me, but *about* me as well. Almost as if I had sung it myself. Then, I don't know whether during the last notes, maybe over the entire last verse—but it was as if I didn't grasp what was happening at first, it was like I was in a trance—I felt a hand sliding over my eyes, another over the back of my head. My head was suddenly in her hands, literally. I was so surprised that I was unable to react in any way—I froze, as still as a mouse. I hadn't expected anything of the sort, nor had I desired it. But at the same time, that stroking was good. I was quite drunk. And no one had touched me in so long. I even felt slight arousal. Liz Franz leaned down—I sensed her perfume a little too suffocatingly. She brushed her lips across my eyes, which were still squeezed shut, my face, my mouth. Sensing that I didn't want to kiss, she kneeled in front of my chair and unbuttoned my shirt, stroked my stomach, my chest. I remained unmoving. I didn't know what to do. I would have liked to run away. But at the same time, I didn't want to lose Liz Franz. I figured that I would still have great need for her. I didn't dare push her away. To increase my arousal, I imagined that, kneeling in front of me in place of Liz Franz, was the young hotel night porter, who had looked straight at me when I came up. Liz Franz was already undoing my belt and pant buttons; I thought with embarrassment about how I was only half erect, and that thought reduced my arousal even more. But Liz Franz was very skillful. She finished her performance. She said—come, let's go, it's more comfortable here for you, taking me by the hand and pulling me onto the bed. I was forced to open my eyes for a moment during that movement, but I closed them again immediately, in the bed. It really was more comfortable there. My orgasm was certainly quite soft, but I nevertheless felt great pride afterward; although shame, too. I quickly buttoned up my pants.

"Don't worry, it's nothing," Liz Franz said in an ordinary voice. But I was certain that there *was* something, that things had taken an unexpected turn for me, and I wasn't sure whether it was good or bad. We sat back in our places. She was exactly the same as she was before, only blushing, and the white rose had disappeared from her shoulder; she had apparently taken it off. (The next day, I saw that rose in a glass of water on the little table; it still hadn't withered.) We drank more wine. She said I could stay there, that I needn't go across town at night. I actually would have liked precisely that: to walk out in the fresh, cold night air a bit, to collect myself; but I didn't want to be an ungrateful lover and run off right away. It ended with me sleeping next to her in the wide hotel bed. She didn't touch me anymore that night, but I woke up in the morning to her stroking me. As my morning erection is always stronger, it was quite pleasant; this time, with the help of the hotel boy (I imagined him walking in, holding a tray; that Liz Franz would invite him into bed as a third), gratification came more deeply and more powerfully. The morning outside the curtains was unexpectedly sunny. I noticed that spring flowers (tulips and daffodils), which definitely hadn't been there in the evening, were in vases in the room. That is—Liz Franz had gone out and brought flowers without me hearing her. A breakfast tray was actually already set upon the table. I was indeed hungry. We ate—that is, I ate; Liz Franz only sipped orange juice. She had apparently also managed to take a shower, to carry out all of her cosmetic procedures. The thought that I had become Liz Franz's lover certainly seemed completely absurd to me, but I didn't start drawing conclusions over it at any great length. Instead, some new cockiness raised its head within me that morning. I sensed that I would have new rights from now on, and that I truly might not have to really worry about money, or about my own life; everything would work out. Later, we went for a walk in Monceau Park, and it was the first day that there was truly spring in the air following a gray and cold month of January. The starlings whistled quite loudly, and the yellow and white noses of crocuses could be seen in the grass.

My departure is at hand. Before leaving Tartu (I didn't give the apartment away, but I'm unsure of whether I'll go back there or not), I called Asko and said I was going away for some time, and that I wanted to see him before I left—to give him the Leonhard Cohen record that he had asked for to copy. Interestingly, he was there lickety-split. His handsome gray eyes expressed true sadness over me going away—he asserted that if I come back at the end of June, he'll definitely have more time, and then we can do something together. I would have wanted to stroke his young face and young hair in goodbye, but I didn't, of course. I just don't *know*.

Now I'm in Nõmme, in Tallinn. Contrary to all of my promises and "principles" (which I certainly truly do not have, not even in quotation marks), I slept in my old room at my parent's place, which is full of all kinds of old things: it's being used as a storage room. As the room is still called "my" room, but as I haven't slept there in years because I was always "at Susanna's," a number of things have collected there over the years: boxes, baskets of yarn and fabric scraps, my father's stacks of old magazines that he can't really bring himself to throw out, and old clothes that my mother has packed up to someday take them to a church "for the poor," although I don't believe the poor want them. They're brought more fashionable and better-quality clothes from abroad than those ugly Soviet-era suits and dresses made of bad material. Apple trees and the greenhouse are visible through the window, but it's as if I don't recognize them anymore. At least not this morning. My departure protects me from remembering. Today, I've never been a child or a young man, I've never looked at pictures of Liz Franz that were cut out from an issue of *Youth*, I haven't listened to the radio in that house or dreamed of the freedom that Liz Franz's songs vowed to give me.

Everything is arranged, all I have to do is wait it through and call a taxi. I don't want my father to bring me to the harbor in my

Opel. I want to leave alone, without seeing anyone. I think again to make sure I haven't forgotten anything. The parking tickets have been paid off—that's essential. Otherwise, reminders will start coming to my father's name (as the car is registered to him), his bank account will be frozen, a debt collector will come to the house to list his assets. No, I'm not exaggerating. Estonia is a very harsh country in regard to exacting the payment of parking tickets. And those are very high.

I managed to get by this time with only two tickets: one amid the HLMs near Tallinn's Central Market, where in my opinion there's no need for paid parking. The other was in front of my building in Tartu yesterday, when I parked the car to bring down my suitcase. The Tartu ticket was only three hundred kroons (twenty-five dollars), and I was almost thankful to Parking Officer Astrid Hansen for writing such a small amount. In Tallinn, it was immediately put at six hundred (fifty-one dollars). For my father, nine hundred kroons would be over half of his monthly pension. However, one fine (six hundred kroons) is more than 10 percent of an average Estonian salary. Estonia advertizes itself in the international finance media as being a country with very low taxes. This information is generally true in what concerns foreign investors, businesspeople, and the fraction of the population that belongs to the highest income percentile. The taxes might truly be quite low for them. Yet for the lower classes, there exist mechanisms by which they can basically be robbed blind. One part of this system is all kinds of penalties (German *Strafe*, punishments, which my grandmother still called "penalty strikes"), the size of which does not depend upon the individual's income, and which are extremely high in comparison with incomes and the punishable misdemeanor. I believe that every ordinary family that owns a vehicle pays at least one parking ticket per month on average.

Near the market, when I removed my yellow ticket notice from beneath the windshield wiper, I saw a depressing scene next to me. I was angry, but that poor family man who had gone to the market in his at least twenty-year-old Renault to make his purchases (thanks to the market sellers and bulk retailers and importers dodging taxes, the market in Estonia is cheaper than shopping centers), hoping to save ten to twenty-five kroons—that poorly-dressed young head of a family in the company of his four-year-old daughter, was obviously depressed. Six hundred kroons is, for example, more than an unemployed person's monthly state welfare. And although that father was probably not unemployed, the fine apparently punched a big hole in his family budget. He most likely doesn't have that much extra money, and he and his wife will have to wait until the next payday. Awaiting him at home is, by the way, either an ugly scene—"again, you . . .!" and "Can't you just one measly time . . ." etc.—or, which is even worse, his wife's resigned, hopeless gaze: never, never will we work our way out of this swamp that is poverty.

And just go ahead and miss the deadline or try to not pay the fine! On the basis of a concession, parking organization, exacting fines, and towing vehicles have been given to private structures (from what I'm aware, it is some security company; i.e. private police), in whose economic interests it is to exact penalty amounts that are as large as possible. The debt collectors that demand the payment of overdue fines are, in turn, private companies, which likewise depend on receiving the money to survive. According to the law, not only can your bank account be frozen instantly, but the names of "debtors" are also published on public web pages. You can end up on these as well if you are, for example, in debt to some private cell- or landline-phone operator for a monthly phone bill. And your name is not erased from the database even when you have erased your debt. You remain on a black list. Interestingly, no one protests against these sorts of totalitarian measures. Apparently, it's some kind of national peculiarity. "Blame" (German *Schuld*, French lacks an exact equivalent:

faute, *tort*, *péché* (sin) aren't quite the same) is an argument that convinces everyone.

"But *he's* the one to blame! Why does he park his car incorrectly then? what does he leave the bill unpaid for!"

In the event that "blame" befalls someone personally, the individual attempts to hide it from others (but the mechanisms for uncovering "those to blame," as I've said, are becoming ever more efficient), snorts angrily, curses (*jurer*) softly, justifies the action, saying that others do it too. And tries to go without paying the fine or the debt. Because he or she knows that parking fines don't expire. Their payment can even still be exacted from the person's grandchildren. Not a single amnesty will extend to them. The person pays it. His or her six hundred, 1,200 kroons. Tõnu told me in Saaremaa that he got two parking tickets while visiting Tallinn, and the trip to Southern Estonia they had planned (with their children and tents) will likely be cancelled now, because the family budget is in the red. The children were apparently very disappointed. But he wasn't even outraged. He was resigned, and those tickets somehow suited his new religious worldview. One *must* be lower than grass, pay their fines. You'll get what's yours later. Ten-fold and one-hundred-fold. He even criticized me for "talking badly about others" when I reminded him of the scandal that for a long time surrounded the current prime minister, who as president of the central bank had somehow been mixed up with the disappearance of ten million dollars of state money in some failed money laundering scheme. It's very possible that he truly isn't to blame. But the case never found any final elucidation (*élucidation*)—it was basically covered up.

In all probability, democracy will never succeed in old Livonia. In all probability, the self-government of a people ruled by others for centuries will only develop into some special form of totalitarianism. Freed slaves start ruling other slaves especially uncaringly. While the masters have something of a conception of their subjugated people's humanity (*humanité*), born from distance, the subjugated people themselves know very well that humanity is a needless attribute; that one can rule (they say "run" instead, because the largest political structure that they imagine is a manor, a kolkhoz—in short, a farm) much more effectively without it. Sometimes, especially when going away from here, I feel very sorry for the country and those people. Maybe that pity is really only my outwardly projected self-pity. It's very possible.

I assumed naively that Tallinn, where the opening night of the musical *Evita* wasn't, would somehow be quieter than Tartu. Yet, thanks to some kind of a festival called "Old Town Days," the entertainment hysteria here has actually risen to an even incomparably higher degree. On every street corner in the city center is a stage, where some kind of a racket is being made. A dance ensemble costumed in some kind of a national dress (*costume national*) is performing on every green area, making identical rhythmic movements called "folk dance." For some reason, it reminds me of film clips from Germany in the 1930s. When I spoke to Martin about totalitarianism, he chimed in excessively. He apparently has those exact same feelings. That scared me. Hopefully I'm wrong. The majority of my compatriots really don't think it so. But, at the same time, people have never believed that they really do live in a totalitarian country, that they *are* the tools of a dictatorship. And the victims. They pay their fines and tithes without objection, and forget them in the whirlwind of cacophonous mass-media entertainment. They ready themselves for a new working week; hope that life will get better. It is certainly some personal hysteria of mine that in this drought-scorched spring, amid the withering fields (but who thinks of them any longer in cities, where the only worry is drying grass?), allows me to see raging mass public events in such a grim, almost eschatological light; almost like Tõnu there on his Saaremaa.

Religious people are sometimes very convincing, regardless. They possess old, tried-and-true formulas. I have no formulas at all, and actually am more troubled by the question of what will happen in New York. Will Liz Franz herself come to meet me at the airport? We'll embrace. I'll feel annoyance. She'll have put on too much perfume again. The wrinkles on her neck will have become even more visible. The whole circle will start from the very beginning, or will simply continue. Everything will be just how it used to be. Just as it was in the beginning, so it will remain. Or will a decisive battle happen between us? Who will vanquish whom? I'll finally tell her everything, there will be catharsis and release. Or are there no such things in life? Have I already long since and hopelessly mixed up my life with Liz Franz's songs?

36

Paris in the evening was gray and white. As always. The sky was gray—a large gray sky with large gray clouds. A sea of clouds, as they say, and in Paris's case that expression is true. An ocean of clouds. Powerful rolling waves of clouds. White buildings. Gray shutters with peeling paint. It was very calming to see them. I slept almost the entire way on the plane. Getting close to home always makes me sleepy. I became drowsy again on the bus and in the taxi (I took a taxi from the bus's last stop at the Arc de Triomphe, because I couldn't be bothered to wait for the 92 bus—I was suddenly in a hurry to get home to my apartment). I almost didn't even look out the window. I know what's there. That, I truly do know. And luckily, it's always the same. It was raining; the bus's windshield wipers were going (they were what made me drowsy), then the taxi's windshield wipers. There were Sunday evening traffic jams on the drive into the city; however, the bus didn't take the A1, but rather something else along Nationale, through Bourget. Only then did it plunge into the ring-boulevard tunnel, into a traffic jam. Vehicles' taillights edging forward slowly and choppily in multiple rows. Some kind of a sluggish, red braid; a current. Then gray and white air again, buildings, dark sycamores, unfamiliar duskiness, rain.

In Tartu, it felt as if it didn't rain anywhere anymore—not yet. And that if one were to go even farther to the south in that desert climate (a good 995 miles, which separate Tartu from Paris), then the drought would only deepen, the sand would become ever hotter, the oases more infrequent, the grass more burnt, the camels thirstier. I purchased a light-colored suit when I was still in Tartu, because it seemed like that is inescapable there in the desert. Only in light-colored clothes can one stride along beneath the unforgiving sun.

Waiting for the bus in front of the Charles De Gaulle Airport's D-Terminal (a good half hour or more, probably because of the traffic jams) and trembling in the chilly, dank wind, I realized that at least here in this city there is nothing to be done with a light-colored linen suit right now. Our fashion-makers recommend something darker for the fall/winter period: gray, black, blue.

On top of that, on the plane, I had dropped a little piece of chocolate from some kind of a cake with an egg-cream filling—the taste of which I didn't like at all—between the legs of my new, light-colored pants. But I ate it dutifully. Airplane food is becoming ever more ridiculous with each passing year. Only the boxes and packaging are becoming more complex and perfect. Soon, you will probably just be brought a pile of boxes and cups, which you can crackle during the flight, searching for the tiny scraps of dried food that have to be disentangled from the several layers of paper and plastic wrap. Then, the stewardesses will gather up the boxes, cups, and fragments of paper and plastic anew, and a profusion of smiles and multilingual niceties will be mutually exchanged, having once more produced a nice little amount of garbage all together. The flight time won't just go to waste, but rather the used material will be used for recycling (*recyclage*) and to produce new boxes and cups, plastic packaging, paper napkins. People will get work.

Still, the chocolate stains on my pants, right between the legs, really did depress me. When my seat neighbor asked me whether the foil-wrapped confection (the old racist name of which was something like a "nigger kiss" or a "nigger head") was good, I said: *médiocre*. This was now the confection's punishment for me calling it mediocre, while still continuing to eat it.

My plane neighbors were an international family: the husband was a Brit or an American, his wife French. The woman had large, moist, bulging eyes, with which she watched me questioningly from time to time. Apparently, no matter where she turned her bulging eyes, it felt as if she was watching you questioningly, in amazement. She had a pretty, thin face—just like the man, whose hairline was already receding quite far— and I would have gladly been either member of that couple. Or their child. Whenever I see a pleasant, intelligent, friendly, harmonious married couple, between whom there dominates some kind of a mental connection (this appears to be extremely rare among the millions of marriages), I automatically want to be their child. That's how it has been since childhood. Back then, I was convinced that I actually had parents other than the ones that claimed they were mine. That I was a foundling who came from a much better, finer family. For some reason, I didn't doubt the identity of Grandma Martha. She was the victim of a conspiracy (*complot*) as well.

The woman was reading Jung's autobiography and occasionally showed a spot to her husband, who nodded. On occasion, she closed the book and stared with her bulging, inquisitive gaze directly at the old, wise, laughing Carl Gustav Jung on the book cover. It appeared as if some kind of dialogue was on the verge of springing up between them. I don't know if the woman saw that I stained my pants. I hid the stained part with an issue of *The Economist* that I had bought at Helsinki Airport. I was embarrassed in front of the woman.

At night, I dreamed of my mother justifying herself to me for having belted me in the basement during my childhood as punishment for having gotten my new dress pants dirty. It had apparently been a difficult time in her life. I, however, accused her in turn of having taken it out on the very weakest. Upon waking up, I realized that staining my pants with chocolate had been an unconscious, deliberate step. Only that I don't know to what ends. Whether: a) to get the attention of "grown-ups," b) to put things right—look, I *am* rubbing chocolate on the front of my pants (especially given that the brown stains are like *caca*) and you **may not punish me** for it!; or c) precisely in order to plead for punishment: go ahead and whip me!

That woman with bulging eyes perhaps reminded me of my mother, maybe of Liz Franz. And indeed: why wasn't I being punished? Why is the world so indifferent towards me?

The apartment was filled with chilly, dusty air, as it always is when you've been away for a long time and the sun hasn't heated the roof. An entire mound of letters was lying beneath the door—I checked through them quickly, not one was from Liz Franz. Nor from Amid. I'm still waiting for a letter from him, although he's never sent me a single letter; nor will he ever send me one, either. I'm waiting for him to call out to me for help when he's in trouble (because he *is* in trouble—that, I don't doubt). But he knows that I can't help him. And so he stays silent. I was, however, surprised by the fact that Liz Franz hadn't sent a single card to Paris. That is, she knew where I was the whole time; she didn't have to look for me? Yet, I didn't brood over those questions, nor did I care to open the bank statements, phone bills, and other such envelopes. No doubt tomorrow will come. I know that I have quite enough money in my account, and that those bills are paid automatically. Although I have compulsively wasted the money received from Liz Franz (I've felt that I'm not allowed to save it—it must be destroyed, just as myself), the conservative side of me has nevertheless acted on its own whim and gradually collected small savings in my account, below which not even the wasteful, self-disciplining side is permitted to deplete the account balance. There must be at least twelve months' worth of rent and living money there. A year is a long time—one can always manage to kill himself or undertake something else over the course of it.

I opened the window, pushed wide the shutters, looked down into the courtyard. It was gray and white there too; the rain fell to the bottom of the courtyard, in the dusk. The pelargoniums on people's balconies had grown large and were blossoming red.

Some kind of deciduous tree that resembled a maple was growing in a pot on one balcony. Even that tree had flourished nicely this spring, already offering quite lush shade. Judging by that tree, you could see whether the weather is windy or still, because neither the street nor large trees are visible from my windows.

In the morning, I saw that the small tree was moving quite intensely, which meant that it was windy. Windy and gray. I could no longer quite imagine that the sun could be scorching somewhere, that the grass could be brown. The wheat on the fields along the road to the airport was very strong and robust, the thick heads erect atop the blades. Tartu, Livonia already seemed like an unlikely, exotic mirage to me. Was it true that I had an apartment there, things in the cupboard? I don't believe it. Night and deep sleep had erased all traces of it. I hadn't come from anywhere, I'd been here the whole time. Nor did I quite understand why I should go back to the airport tomorrow and fly on to somewhere else, either. Paris is so quiet and drowsy. Better to nod off there in my accustomed life, which is gray and white; gray and white.

It was dark outside the window already at ten o'clock in the evening—I went under the covers immediately; obediently, like a child. The sounds of the building lulled me to sleep. I attempted to listen to them, just as I once attempted to listen when my mother sang me a lullaby ("The wind sang the sparrow to sleep, the sun sets behind the woods . . ."); I wanted to listen all the way to the end, but at the same time, I wanted to fall asleep during the song so that I wouldn't have to wait for sleep alone afterwards. You can always become afraid again when you're alone. My mother sang that song very rarely. Maybe only a few times altogether. I didn't want my grandmother to sing to me—she had a nasty, jarring voice.

Now, I listened to the sounds of the building, which lulled me; trying to lengthen that pleasant, almost erotic state of drifting to sleep. The banging of the elevator doors; someone's footsteps in the stairway; someone's television somewhere on a lower floor; the rattle of metal shutters being pulled shut, which echoed in the courtyard; the steady noise of the city and the ring boulevard; the melancholic honking of a rescue vehicle from time to time . . . I probably didn't hold out for very long, and slipped into unconsciousness.

It is oddly quiet here in comparison with Tartu. As if the large city were an immense absorbent, gray-and-white sponge that ever gulps down noise into itself. The voices of all those millions of people and the sounds of their cars get caught up in a mutual resonance that extinguishes them, so everyone is left alone, is left to him- or herself, like in Ernst Enno's poem *The Shadow*:

> *The train rushed, the sun shone*
> *and silenced every speech,*
> *left alone were the rumbling rails*
> *and the wheel's shearing haste.*

I have the collected poems of Ernst Enno (Estonia's only mystical poet, whom I have already mentioned) on my shelf here. Here, I have everything to which I'm accustomed. Where indeed did that senseless fantasy of hiding myself in Tartu come from? Here and only here can I turn invisible; can I melt perfectly into that which surrounds me. Even Liz Franz wouldn't find me anymore. She would search for me, but she wouldn't see me, because her eyes would be struck with darkness. No matter where she looked, it would be the same everywhere: gray, white. It would start raining again. That erases even the last traces.

During the day, I managed to do a ring around my main paths. Gardens are the mandatory elements of my accustomed route. Monceau Park as the closest; the gardens of Tuileries and Luxembourg. Luxembourg has the most magnificent flowerbeds.

Right now, they are only in their early phase: the summer flowers have just been planted, and haven't had time to grow up yet. Full blossoming will arrive in August. There was a photo exhibit on the iron fence of Luxembourg Gardens, as there always is in summer. This year, it is someone's pictures of the daily lives of simple Nepalese mountain dwellers. A smiling shepherd carrying a black lamb with a broken leg over his back. A woman and a small child shielding themselves from the starting snowfall beneath canvases. A napping infant in a basket on its mother's back. Dancing lamas driving out evil spirits. Honey hunters—the Himalayan honey bee (*Apis laboriosa*) is the world's largest bee that builds its hives on high cliffs, and honey hunters risk their lives scaling them in order to bring back honey, using rudimentary rope-ladders and poles. I suppose they get stung as well. But I guess that honey still costs something, too. Just as salt, which is collected from salt lakes and carried over gorges on the shoulders of animals and people.

The Nepal exhibition appeared to be very popular—many people stopped before the pictures at that coming-home-from-work hour; only the sun, which shone over the park's treetops into viewers' eyes was slightly bothersome: you had to squint, shield your eyes with your hand, just as those mountain dwellers in the pictures on their way across a glacier, into the sun. In the city, where there is so much of everything—in excessiveness, a life in which there is so little of everything (sheepskins and a smoking fire of yak pies against the cold, barley bread and yak milk against hunger, prayer wheels and bows against all else bad) seems alluring. And that sort of a conception for the exhibition—hanging the pictures outside on the fence—is charming in itself. Why should pictures be hung in dim museums with dead air, where no one lives and nothing goes on? Museums are extremely perverse institutions. Museums' pictures could also be brought out onto the street. Over time, they would blotch and disintegrate in the rain, would be stolen (but would they go for so much anymore, if they were brought outside en masse?). Yet, there are millions of pictures in this city's museum repositories—they would last for years. And if everything were to run out, then artists could start making new pictures. What point is there in making new pictures now, when there is nowhere to even put the old ones other than in museums, for torturing tourists?

Walking past a newspaper booth and reading the *Le Monde* headline, I remembered that the first round of parliamentary elections was held on Sunday. And so, I belonged to that group of fifteen million French people (36 percent of the electorate) that "shunned the urns" (*bouder les urnes*), as they say. Most likely, I'll never go voting in my life. Chirac's people will get a majority in parliament, also; it promises to be a stable single-party government.

In order to feel that I had really gotten there, I went to the movies. Watching a film in the darkness of a cinema, you are borne somewhere far away, so when you step out into the light on the street, there is a feeling as if you've come home from somewhere distant—as if you're finally there in reality. I also use the cinema trick in foreign cities in order to achieve the feeling of reality, of regularity.

Because one's surroundings *should* be regular. Like a regular pencil. In school, when someone left their regular pencil at home, we asked one another: where's your other "regular"? A "regular" was essential. You can have colored pencils, but you need a regular one. You're not going to write in red, blue, green, yellow. You need a "regular" for writing life—you never grow tired of a "regular." Paris is very regular. By emerging from the cinema, I had once again found the regular from the bottom of my bag.

By the way, I watched Pasolini's *Teorema* at the Accattone. It runs there all the time, once or twice a week, but I haven't seen it in several years. It's good to occasionally re-read your dear old fairytales. From them, from their influence, you see that you actually haven't changed. Nor will you, probably. Yet, to my surprise, the part in which the guest consolingly strokes the back or the neck of the broken family son, who has come to the edge of his bed in the night, wasn't in the film. I don't know whether I had thought it up, or if it had been lost from the copy, because it was a very defective copy: smaller clips were constantly missing from it.

Ultimately, what happens is that old experts have to re-tell *Teorema* to the new ones, to the neophytes, because all that is left of the film are fragments overflowing from a black rain of defect. Separate competing versions, and schools of it, develop, because different experts remember the film differently. Then, someone reconstructs it according to his or her own taste and the fashion of the moment, to the ideological zeitgeist, and attempts to canonize the new version as the only true one. The person can be successful at this, too. People *do* start to believe in it. A new religion is born.

Already then, in the spring of 1991, I realized that Liz Franz's life—the life that she still had when she no longer sang—was founded on lies. There are perhaps two or three main lies—they are simple, even primitive, but nevertheless, she believes in them unyieldingly. Nothing can shake them. Not any truth. And did I then have truths, with which to resist them? I had none. But from then on, I had money. Not that Liz Franz started giving me money right at the beginning. She did, that is, but not directly, not in the form of money. Thus, it was possible for me to lie to myself in turn, claiming that I didn't receive money from her, that I wasn't doing it in exchange for money, that I wasn't Liz Franz's bought toy, her doll. She did, however, dress me up like a doll straight away.

"Clothes are a masquerade. But you very much need a mask right now. You mustn't give yourself away too easily. You mustn't be too easily definable. You can't imagine how people fear clothing. Like birds and scarecrows. It's very easy to scare them with clothing. Have you noticed that you're feared?"

And when I replied that I hadn't, she said:

"Exactly! You need clothes. Let's go see."

I weakly protested that I had no money, although I certainly did understand what she was thinking.

"Don't worry, I'm sure you'll pay another time when you get money," was her reply.

And she bought me everything new. Not only from the tip of my head to the heels of my toes (indeed, shoes as well), but underwear, also. She bought me underwear regularly from then on (primarily Calvin Klein, but also Dim, Homme and others); actually, she brought me a small gift every time that she came to Paris—meaning quite a large bag full of all kinds of clothes, among which was doubtless a pair or two of underwear, also. I've lived off of the stockpile from those beginning years practically up until now. Just yesterday, I saw that—huh, the last of them are starting to wear thin, to unravel. I believe that the underwear was a double game: knowing homosexuals' weakness for underwear, Liz Franz apparently also got a certain enjoyment out of dressing my most intimate part. That way, it was as if it belonged more to *her*. And to her it belonged. In those first years, I had practically not a single sexual partner in Paris, in spite of my tenacious efforts (not counting some one-night stands that were forced and reluctant, just to defy Liz Franz), so in my eyes, all of those pretty new pairs of underwear were all for naught. Only Liz Franz's hands, which I began to hate ever more, slipped between their wide, comfortable elastic bands. Before that, I truly had owned only quite awful Soviet "tighty whities." But I hadn't been able to consider it a very significant handicap, either.

And so, Liz Franz dressed me in new clothes. They weren't very expensive at first, because formally, it *was* for my future money. I intitially even kept some kind of a tally. True, it hadn't been at all precise or exhaustive from the very beginning. And when that tally reached over three thousand francs, I gave up keeping count entirely. It was easier to not think about it. It was easier to think that when I became rich, when I made a film and became rich and famous, then I could pay back Liz Franz not only all of that money, but a heap more on top of it. Throw it in her face and leave.

However, there wasn't even a question of me being able to leave at the drop of a hat back then, to somehow end the relationship. I was up to my ears in debt. I understood quite well that Liz Franz's "sexual servicing" was the interest payment. Love. That there was not. But Liz Franz never acknowledged that. That was her lie number one. She was certain that we were meant for each other. And if I really was mostly gloomy and bad-tempered, if I made nasty scenes and was never the one to kiss her first, then it came from the fact that I still don't understand how I love her. That I actually love her so much that I don't dare let it come out. I'm afraid to suffocate myself under great passion. Actually, I suffocated under Liz Franz's dogged and truth-denying passion. I would have liked her to understand, her to admit it. But what resources did I *have* to make her admit it? And what right? To admit that she is an aging woman, who has decided to redeem happiness—in exchange for what she still has, for money.

That was actually lie number two. To claim (to herself) that it was happiness. I couldn't fathom how she could be so blind. So, is it love when you tie yourself to someone, make the person dependent upon you, feed the person's hatred with your money? Yet, it is true that under the name "happiness," people yearn above all for someone being tied to them, dependent upon them, needing them. I needed Liz Franz more and more. Although it was just then that I became quite financially autonomous. Firstly, I was invited to appear on a serpentine string of several radio stations, because the Baltic fight for freedom was still a fashionable topic. And they even paid for it. As I had money, as I was quite indifferent regarding the reply, I dared to ask for it. And they paid, too. Secondly, thanks initially to acquaintances of Liz Franz that she had activated, one television producer expressed an interest in my films, and it ended with Arte acquiring the rights to show *The Railway Watchman's House*—paying both Moscow, to which the rights formally belonged, and me. And it wasn't a small amount. Back then, the sum felt like an entire fortune to me. True, when I had rented myself an apartment (that same one that I still have to this day), had paid for all of the security deposits and commission fees, then half of the money was gone. But Liz Franz encouraged me to take that apartment. It was relatively cheap. And it was beneath the roof, on the top floor—just as I liked it. I can't stand having someone above me. Stomping and walking around up there.

Liz Franz's acquaintances were actually needed once again for renting the apartment, because people will hardly rent an apartment to a foreigner who lacks regular income. But that real estate agent, as I found out later, was Umberto Riviera's agent in Paris. And back then, such a recommendation was worth even more than good personal papers. I've heard that getting an apartment in Paris has become much more complicated now— potential renters compete for some miserable servant's room with their *dossiers*, one better than the last. For you to be let through the first round at all, you must be at least third-generation French (even better if you're ethnically French),, have had a steady job for some time, and have a solid amount in your bank account. Only after that will they start seeing whether you also leave an otherwise polite and pleasant impression, whether there is no danger that you'll get a cat or a dog, are thinking of having children, will invite guests over too frequently, will start pounding nails into the walls to hang pictures. I've repeatedly thought about changing apartments, have dreamed about a new life that would begin in a new apartment, have read apartment notices like poems or litanies; but I've rarely even reached the point of going to look at one. And when I *have* gone and looked, the places have been depressing. Dark, filthy dens, most likely cold and damp in winter. With a view facing a wall or, oppositely, directly onto a heavily trafficked street, so you practically can't open your windows at all. In short—I've remained in the apartment that Liz Franz and I went to see together in April of 1991. At that time, I believed that by acquiring a personal apartment, I would become independent of Liz Franz and her hotel rooms (which was still a change from being at Vahur Linnuste's place, who on top of that had probably started to tire of me), not realizing that the apartment would become "our" apartment—a part of that false construction, which Liz Franz stubbornly called "us."

It had no furniture, but Liz Franz bought all of the necessities. And all in all, I truly must acknowledge her exceptional intuition in real estate. Because nothing similar can be acquired in Paris for a price anywhere close to it (they're not allowed to raise the rent arbitrarily, so it has remained relatively low). It is warm and dry in winter, because the building's central heating goes down via the upper floor, and I have to turn off one radiator most of the time. French people generally freeze in winter like rats in a den, wearing a pile of sweaters one over the other, not having the nerve to turn on their electric or gas heating. Yet, heating is also mysteriously cheap in this building. It is probably also notably chillier in the lower apartments. The place was built during the thirties, likely for the middle-class of the time. Even now, only "whites" live there. Still, I've almost unceasingly plotted escape-plans there. "Escape" primarily meant going back to my homeland. Because there, I imagined, I would manage even without Liz Franz—it probably wouldn't be as easy for her to come after me there. I imagined myself living in a solitary forest ranger's cabin, almost like Arnold Ratas in his railway watchman's house. Poor, but independent. I knew that Liz Franz hates the country; that she hardly ever goes there. Specifically, she claims that she got more than her fair share of the country during childhood.

"I've lived in the country once before already," she said. "I know what it is. And I don't believe I could manage to live in the country anymore if that *was* the country."

An enormous number of flowers had apparently grown on the meadows there—before hay-season, they were apparently like a multicolored sea with a changing appearance. She had often hid herself in the meadow grass and listened to how at first her mother, then also her grandmother called out for her worriedly. She had apparently watched the bellflowers, the quaking grass, the chamomiles, the angelicas swaying above her head (she hadn't seen such large, tall bellflowers, chamomiles, or angelicas anywhere since), and imagined that she would never be found again. Then, she imagined that the flowers and grasses were people; that she was in a city, a large city. She sometimes went home only in the dusk of evening, and had been in big trouble.

"But I knew that they couldn't actually do anything to me."

Truly, I've always been amazed by how adults can successfully instill fear and obedience in children with empty means. What can they really do, actually? The children will generally live longer than they do, and will take revenge, anyway. It's possible that the system has indeed begun to fall apart. Children no longer listen.

Another place where she loved to disappear was into the woods beyond the meadow. It was a pine forest and she feared it, but she hardened her heart, loudly sang Soviet songs that she had heard on the radio, and pressed ever onward. Then, she imagined that the pines were the tall buildings and towers that she had only seen in pictures—Moscow. And she was no longer afraid of them. She could sit atop a stack of logs in a clearing and count a nightingale's coo-cooing until she got a suitable number:

fifty-five. She was certain that she wouldn't live any more years than that, anyway. She was five at the time, and fifty-five seemed like a magical age; a witch's age. She told me this when she was just forty-four. Fifty-five probably still seemed far-off to her even then—an unimaginable age. As it is to me right now, also: I actually don't imagine that I'll still be alive at the age of fifty-five.

She would sometimes exit the woods only at dusk as well.

"Those pine forests are so forbidding in the dusk, all the same. I never want to see that again," I remember Liz Franz saying.

For unlike her forest fantasy of Moscow's towers and buildings, the pines didn't light up as the dusk approached. They only began to rustle suddenly, to blacken. Occasionally, she became truly afraid then, and had started running, imagining that wolves were already at her heels.

"There's actually nowhere to hide yourself in the country and the forest," she asserted, as if guessing my escape plans.

But here, in New York, she is undoubtedly perfectly in hiding—from me and for as long as she deems proper. She doesn't need to come out at night as she did then, from the meadow hay or the pines. And all I can do is wait. And wonder. What's it all for? It's seven o'clock. I woke up at already four o'clock because of the time difference. It was still dark then. I saw how the cloudy sky started to dawn. That time was incredibly quiet. Only large semis and garbage trucks drove on the street below. Three yellow taxis were parked at the taxi stop, and it appears that they're still parked there now, although they've probably actually switched out. The Chinese are already moving about, but the street is still relatively empty all the same. The large ventilation fans on the roof below the window here aren't rumbling yet. It seems that work hasn't started in the workshops below yet. Yesterday at nine o'clock, when I came "home" (well, still home) dead tired and climbed the red steel staircase, they were still sitting at sewing machines amid piles of cloth scraps. The scraps are vividly colored; at least that's what it seems like when you walk past—red and blue in the bright light of neon lamps. What are they sewing out of them? And why did Liz Franz (if it was her at all) rent such an odd apartment for me? It is on the corner of Grand Street and Forsyth Street in Chinatown, although it is formally already more towards Little Italy, but actually completely China Town.

True, the room is very large. Large and empty—it is the first room of a Norwegian artist's atelier. He works in the other room during the day. There's an incredible amount of noise here during the day—not only street-noise, but those previously-mentioned ventilation fans right under the windows as well. Only hot air came in through the windows yesterday. And very thick air. Chinese food, rotting fish-water, melting ice-water that trickles into the gutter from beneath the large fish counters down there in the heat. More of I-don't-know-what. The prospect of having to spend two weeks in this racket and stench, in a completely desolate room, seemed extremely scary to me yesterday.

The room is truly desolate—there is only an inflatable mattress on the floor and a wicker chair with a broken seat. I currently have my laptop on some drawing board that I found in the Norwegian artist's atelier (he doesn't sleep here), one end of which is supported on the windowsill and the other upon my lap. True, there is also a kitchenette with a refrigerator and a gas stove. The Norwegian artist has apparently, he claims, been paid the rent. For two weeks. I don't know how much. No one is actually allowed to live here—it's an atelier. He said that if someone should ask, then I should answer that I work here with him. But by and large, no one here apparently asks anything. The Chinese sweatshops below are most likely half-illegal. But I must admit (as a plus to the apartment) that one can see trees, the sycamores of Forsyth Street, from the window. There are tennis courts between them. The wind stirs the sycamores, the sky is gray. The mugginess was replaced by cool air after a thunderstorm yesterday. But it was truly stifling before the thunder. I felt like I didn't have the energy to go anywhere. Two weeks here, in this awful hole! Liz Franz, you are still able to surprise me.

I flung myself down upon the inflatable mattress quite hopelessly; the ventilator made some kind of a breeze out of the hot, stinking air, which nevertheless cooled the room down somewhat. The noise was almost deafening. But amazingly, I fell asleep. When I woke up, I took a shower, shaved, and made myself a green Chinese tea that I bought and brought with me from Le Palais des Theés in Paris. I sat right here at the window. The window was open—only a fine, black metal screen separated me from the outside. That same stinking mugginess blew into the room through the screen, but the hot tea cooled me down. I watched the yellow taxis parked at the stop in the heavy metallic sunlight shining straight down; I watched the bustling Chinese. Some women carried black umbrellas; some opened them when stepping out of the shade of a side street into the sunlight. A mottled fruit stand was visible farther away. I had come past it and knew that it held an abundance of unfamiliar weed-like clumps of grasses, roots, some kinds of dried mushrooms, and creatures that the Chinese sort through expertly. I sipped more tea. Suddenly, I felt that I had arrived. That there *is* nowhere else to go from here any longer. And I furthermore had the strange thought that Rome must have been just the same. Once, two thousand years ago, when it ruled over the entire known world. It had to be just like that: the stench, the unfamiliar goods, all possible races of people, haulers, market counters, foods, eating, trash, carts, a multilingual din, the unbearable sun, panting dogs. And a strange peace. *Pax Romanum.*

It probably really is true that everything turns into its opposite upon reaching an extreme. I realized that I haven't experienced such peace in a very long time already. (Im)patience had suddenly disappeared. I knew that I now may patiently wait. See. What happens. That there will be some resolution in the end, anyway.

37

Today, the Chinese have umbrellas because of the rain, not the sun. It's raining, the wind is blowing. Steps boom on the steel stairway, the steel doors clang below. I still don't quite have a very good idea of what Liz Franz was thinking by putting me here, above a Chinese sweatshop. And what she's displaying by not showing her face. No one came to meet me at the airport, but I knew that already beforehand.

Artur Kallas, who I've known for a long time somehow, originally probably by way of expat-Estonian circles, sent me an e-mail saying that he has been "requested"—even now, he hasn't said who requested it, and neither have I asked, making as if I know who it was, anyway—to come and meet me at the airport, but it isn't that easy for him to do so, and perhaps I could take the bus from Newark to the city on my own. Which I did.

Stepping out of the air-conditioned airport air was a true heat-shock. It was six o'clock, it was over eighty-five degrees Fahrenheit, and a white humidity veiled the air. It seemed as if the sun was shining, but I couldn't tell from which direction. Everything was uniformly, tremendously, blindingly milk-white. I saw the sun only when the strange old-fashioned bus—which reminded me of my very first memories of a bus from childhood: the red-and-white snub-nosed bus no. 18 pulling up to the Vikerkaare bus stop—turned onto a viaduct. The sun hung there—a red disc with beautiful, sharp edges, at which it wasn't the slightest bit painful to stare. Earlier, it had been the darkest spot in the sky.

I spent that night at Arthur's place on 56th Street (East). He took me to the river in the evening. Already, while waiting for the bus at the airport, I grasped that everything here is a couple of times greater than life-size, as if it wasn't a land of people, but of some kinds of gods; and that the people have, to some extent, also attempted to grow up to those dimensions, although they nevertheless haven't achieved very great success in this endeavor. Many are normal-sized, even small. I'm not even talking about the Chinese here, but there isn't much to brag about in Chinatown, either.

And so, the river and the bridge visible from there no longer expressly surprised me with their size. As I hadn't, in fact, imagined anything from here before, nothing has expressly surprised me, either. I've automatically adopted all of it immediately, because nothing at all here contradicts it in any way. That's the way the world *is*. Now, here. I'm in complete agreement with it.

Yesterday, I reached the old harbor on my walk: I enjoyed the strong smell of sea, and even of the tar there. I don't know what emits the latter. It was strangely devoid of people up there on the riverbank beneath the viaducts and Brooklyn Bridge, on the side of Chinatown. One could sit there in absolute solitude and watch the rippling, oil-blotched water. I've already even learned the fact that here, there are many places practically devoid of people. That if you don't want to, there's not the slightest need to plunge into the flow of people.

Sitting there amid the fish-scented breeze and noise of the bridges on a wooden bench on the riverbank, I did suddenly feel a sharp longing for Liz Franz. I would have liked her to be there as well, for her to sit next to me. All of a sudden, I realized that I have nothing serious to say to her—that all of my preconceived truths and accusations would have slipped my mind. That we'd speak of this and that like always, never once touching upon what's primary. If she were there next to me, I wouldn't be thankful for her being there, but sitting alone, I thought that I would be thankful even for that. It's someone, notwithstanding.

Every Chinese person who bustles about there between the stinking counters of goods, who loiters on stairs and in doorways, who plays squash in Forsyth Street Park (I've already grown used to the arrhythmic afternoon thwacking beneath my window) or does his or her slow Chinese aerobics on the athletic court in the morning—every one of them has someone. And not just someone, but likely a whole lot of someones.

That old woman who came from the market wearing soft slippers, her body bent to one side from the weight of her bag with a fish tail sticking out of it, and a look as if that trip to the market might be her final (*ultime*) effort in life, after which she would quietly depart this world. But actually, an entire big Chinese family certainly awaited her fish, and she will go to the market many, many times more, and will make her way home every evening, wearing that same death mask (it was probably just an ordinary old Chinese face that I wrongly interpreted).

In that sense, I am even poorer than all of them, even that undoubtedly poor woman. I don't even have Liz Franz. Not in this city, or in any other around the world do I have someone, who I can say without a shred of doubt is there for me. No one aside from Liz Franz, who has disappeared. Who has taken it upon herself to play cat and mouse with me.

It's possible that I'm being overdramatic by saying that I have no one. I did actually go out to eat (as they say) with friends last night. Those friends were Artur, Carl Frederick, that Norwegian artist in the first room of whose atelier I live, and his friend, or more like lover, as he emphasized to me when I asked about "his friend" on the first morning while eating bacon and eggs together in a coffee shop. This "lover" bears the handsome name Laurent, reminding me of someone from my early French past, but I don't remember whom. Laurent is indeed a Frenchman. When they arrived with Carl Frederick in front of that John's Street restaurant, where Artur and I were waiting for them, I saw with my own eyes that Artur's comment—they look like brothers—was absolutely right. The same height (quite short), the same slender, boyish bodies (Carl is about my age, Laurent something over thirty), wearing identical black jeans, and all of that probably reflected somehow in their faces, making their facial features similar as well. Maybe they *are* similar, because both have a small, thin nose somehow slightly squinted eyes with bags under them, into which it's like they've secretly collected all of their old age—so that, for brief instants, their smooth faces appear to belong to an ancient old Chinese man.

At first, I ascribed that Chinese-like expression in Carl Frederick's case to him spending a long time in a Chinese sweatshop in Chinatown: we undoubtedly become similar to our surroundings to some extent, and homosexuals are famous for their chameleon-like ability to adapt; for their mimicry. In my opinion, there is also a certain amount of Chineseness to Carl Frederick's paintings, which hang on the walls of my side of the atelier. When I said that to him, however, he appeared surprised. No doubt he personally regards them as foremost New-York-like. Viewed from a distance, they are almost or fully uniformly dark (primarily brownish, blackish) surfaces only vivified by a color-coat relief, a spatula—or I don't know what it's called—smoothly drawn, knotting lines. At first, those large greenish-brown rectangles glistening oily even seemed a little repugnant to me; then, however, I looked at one more closely, and saw that yet a second color glows from beneath the brown, knotted surface—blue, with which the lower coats are painted. In my opinion, there *is* something Chinese about it. Even the paintings' paint-smell, which they don't stop secreting, although they are said to have been completed a year ago and longer—apparently, the coat is so thick that it will stink to infinity, for me becoming mixed up with the stench of Chinese food and rotting fish from below; I no longer know which is which.

The weather is, by the way, still cold and rainy: Chinatown was drenched by rainfall all day yesterday—sometimes a strong downpour, sometimes large, gray wisps of fog that floated across the street, thoroughly soaking up that soupy bouquet of smells and adding its own particular moist, doggish, oceanic smack. The humidity even penetrated through the large windows into the atelier, and probably even into my dreams, because upon waking in the dusk of morning, it seemed as if the trucks giving their long, low honks while speeding across the intersection, were ships signaling to one another on a foggy sea.

I have two types of information about Carl Frederick's success as an artist. According to him (I asked), he lives off of his art—which wouldn't be that bad at all, given the fact that in addition to the extremely spacious atelier here in a Chinese sweatshop (which he indeed recently partitioned into two in order to start renting out the other half), he apparently rents a quite expensive apartment in West Village. And I'm unsure of how regular Laurent's income is.

Still, what seems closer to the truth is the version that Artur presented to me, according to which Carl Frederick has not sold practically a single painting in his life, nor has he made it into any gallery, and he lives off of his art in the sense that it is a thing that he does every day and it gives his life content, gives him moral support. His *financial* support comes from Norway, however, where Carl's mother has collected a large fortune in the slimming business (diet products and the magazines promoting them). And it's true that although Carl's paintings do not lack a certain finesse, I still have the feeling that I've already seen such paintings repeatedly—even despite the fact that I never go to museums, or to art exhibitions. At the same time, they could decorate any bohemianly high-bourgeoisie Newyorker's home, or even a rather chic bureau quite nicely. But unfortunately, potential customers are not familiar with the name "Carl Frederick Schultz." I suspect that those able to cover a canvas with a rather fine and unique coating of paint do not number so few in a city the likes of

New York. And many of them do not have a diet-queen mother in Norway—so, by way of pure biology, they're forced to develop a more aggressive sales strategy. It's no secret that art no longer says anything to anyone in and of itself; however, some artists' signatures are indeed impressive—just as impressive as those signatures of bank presidents printed onto dollars and other bank tickets. People value stability, a stable currency.

In the morning, I looked through Carl Frederick's record collection for something to put on, but I didn't find anything. There were several large collections (a good ten records in a box) of "Meditation" music that comprised classical music and romantic pop hits. It was surprising to me that there are still so many of those hits—it seems as if there are only around a dozen (Saint Saën's "The Swan," the chorus from the opera *Aida*, a Bach toccata in I-don't-remember-which key, the old English song "The Green Sleaves," and a few others). But they nevertheless number in the dozens, if not the hundreds. Consequently, it isn't true that a modern person's cultural layer is thin. It's possible that the layer is actually exceedingly thick, and as a result, it's difficult to add anything to it. The volume of human memory is not infinite.

At the restaurant, I further heard that Carl Frederick is involved in Chinese *tai-chi* exercise. In terms of books, I found two volumes in his atelier: the thick, illustrated (Taschen edition of) *Alchemy & Mysticism* from the series "The Hermetic Museum," and the thin *The Secret of the Golden Flower. The Classic Chinese Book of Life*, the first (numbered) sentence of which sounds like this:

Naturalness is called the Way. The Way has no name or form; it is just the essence, just the primal spirit.

I indeed must say that Carl Frederick has apparently not really read either book. He was given *The Golden Flower* with a dedication as a gift in 1996, but it looks exactly like a book that has been opened and leafed through two or three times at the very best. But from their presence, one can conclude that in all likelihood, Carl's paintings have some kind of an alchemic, mystical intention that I did initially incompetently call "Chinese." Maybe they really are deep paintings, by the way. I'm unable to say anything to it.

Here in the atelier, I watch the park-corner and the street-corner that can be seen from the window more readily and at greater length than I do Carl's paintings (which aren't disagreeable to me, either; at least nothing pretentious is **depicted** there, like surrealist-psychoanalytical figures, for example). As there is a fine black metal screen in front of the window, I can't tell very well whether it's raining or not.

Right now, it's evening, and as it turns out, Friday evening (already Friday! I caught myself thinking: one Friday, one Friday evening more, and I'll be flying out—yes, only to where: Paris, Tartu? And will I *see* Liz Franz at all, will I *see* her again at all, ever?)—it's raining, which is visible from the cars' moving windshield wipers, the Chinese people's black umbrellas, which make up a quite dense current. For a couple of hours, I've sat here at the window and watched, as if hypnotized, that current of cars edging forward in the rain—that orderly current of yellow, white, and red car taillights; that chaotic current of black umbrellas. The yellow taxis standing. People disappearing underground through the subway entrance, and resurfacing in bursts when a train has arrived underground (it's the last stop of the small Shuttle line (S)). The current of both vehicles and pedestrians is significantly denser than it has been on previous evenings. The dark tops of the sycamores stir above it all, however. I don't know whether it's almost dark already, or if it's only duskiness due to the rain. It doesn't turn all that dark outside at night, either; the tops of the sycamores remain green in the glow of the city sky, as if white nights had arrived in New York as well. I don't especially want to go out and personally plunge into that somewhat feverish, Friday-night current. I have the feeling as if I *were* already within it, amid it—as if I were sitting on a dock, which it surges past; testing the water with my toe, but not jumping in. But I can watch it like a picture, and much more eagerly than any one picture. It moves.

Still, I could have gone out tonight, too. That is, Laurent called in the meanwhile. There's an answering machine here, and I normally don't pick up, because no one calls me here; however, I hear those rare messages left for Carl Frederick (he doesn't appear to be especially sought after). Just now, I heard a voice that announced it was Laurent, and that the message was meant for me, and that they were going out soon, and if I wanted to come as well, then I should call within half an hour. I replayed the message once and memorized the number. But half an hour passed, and I didn't call.

I nevertheless hadn't been mistaken in sensing that Laurent felt a certain interest in me. I believe that he feels a certain interest in all new acquaintances, in all new opportunities. And on top of that, we spoke to each other in French last time, although his English is also very good and he likes speaking it. Laurent is from Grenoble, lived for eight years in London, one year in Paris, and has lived for two in New York, where he apparently wants to stay. He seemed sharper to me than his lover Carl, in a certain sense—but more vulgar at the same time. Quite a considerate guy, I believe. That French mathematic-bookkeeping consideration that I know quite well.

When Carl Frederick was in the bathroom, Artur said the same thing that he had told me earlier: it's like they (Carl and Laurent) were made for each other, are like brothers. Laurent laughed and said that that's definitely not how it is:

"You always say the wrong things."

Carl Frederick believes that Laurent is the love of his life, is his fate. Someone apparently predicted it to him before he met Laurent, and they also otherwise match up perfectly (in astrological and I-don't-know-what-other terms—alchemic?). From Laurent's reply, however, I realized that he sees things through a slightly different prism. I believe that such a thing as "the love of (my/your/his) life" has no meaning for him. As a rational Frenchman who analyzes his feelings, he understands that there's no point in betting on such a card if you want to save yourself from having unnecessary miseries. Yet for variation, he gladly put up with Carl's affection, allowed him to hold him around the waist, to go around arm-in-arm. At the same time, he flirted with both Artur (mainly), and even me. And now, he was inviting me out in the evening, because that perspective apparently seemed more entertaining than being with the one, for whom he is the "love of his life."

I weighed up going or not. It would, of course, save me from a lonely Friday night that always puts me in a somewhat exiled, melancholic state of mind. But then, I decided to give in to that very mood precisely. It is so familiar, predictable, and safe for me. Ultimately, when I become tired, I'm always glad that I'm not in a pointless bar somewhere, but am in my room, in my bed. Such an attitude towards life is no wonder when you're single, of course. Laurent namely inquired whether I was single straight off at the beginning of last night. Am I, by the way? There hasn't been an official divorce, of course. Consequently, I am still married to Liz Franz (indeed, without ever officially *being* married), which, by the way, is also proven by me being here. Maybe that kind of marriage-form is actually ideal for me. I can't imagine myself really living with anyone for longer than a few months.

And so, I didn't call, I even forgot the number, and instead went down to the street and did a ring around East Village. Music was playing from the Latinos' stores and bars. Couples and singles had dressed up for going out (while leaving the impression that it's all chance, casual). A couple walking in front of me—a handsome Spanish-type boy and a blond American girl—were already arguing. In spite of that, the night was still young.

Still, people rarely go out as "single": for the most part, singles join up into pairs or groups on Friday evening, and go out as such temporary constellations. Take for example, that fat girl and the tall, pretty girl who got into her car. The fat girl is the tall, pretty girl's escort just in case there are no bites. And for passing the time. Your mood can nevertheless turn sad easily when alone. Mine did.

A light was on in the lower-story window of a redbrick house with a romantic outside staircase; the curtains weren't drawn, and bookshelves could be seen in the yellow light of the room. The thought suddenly came to me that I would live here in this city if I had such an apartment, warm and yellow light, bookshelves from which I happily wouldn't pull myself away, even on Friday night. Then, I remembered that I don't have all that many books: everything has been left behind somewhere. Then, it seemed to me that there should actually be a person there in place of the books. Yes—a loyal soul, just as loyal as the bookshelves, as the floor lamp casting its yellow light, as a dog. Like Liz Franz.

An absurd hope suddenly filled my soul: in one such apartment—maybe in some bourgeoisie/bohemian East Village house, maybe actually somewhere high up above the city and Central Park, because it can't be second-best; because it can be not only the very best, but completely unexpected—somewhere there, Liz Franz is waiting for me; yes—a young, genuine, jeering Liz Franz; a mature, loyal, motherly Liz Franz. A loving Liz Franz. And that life, of which I once dreamed *would begin*. My sole and unrepeatable life. That still hasn't arrived yet.

But that mirage quickly passed. I felt that the misty rain was already becoming unpleasant, that my feet were getting wet. I turned back. I further stopped in front of a few Chinese and Vietnamese diners here on Grand Street, considering whether

I should buy something or not, but the thought of choosing, of deciding what I wanted out of obligation held me back. I didn't step in anywhere.

Now, it's morning. The city has unnoticedly started up, the Chinese are in a hurry, the cars are driving. At six o'clock, when I woke up, it was still quite empty and quiet. Just those trucks speeding across the intersection while blasting their fog horns. I managed to somewhat regret not going out last night. It would have been interesting to see how far Laurent's interest in me extends, all the same. And to enjoy Carl Frederick's miseries, to pass the time. Although, *I* have no significant interest in Laurent. But another's interest always boosts the tone a little.

I ask myself: am I still capable at all anymore of having a lasting interest in anyone? Proper, deep falling in love is probably still somehow connected with youth and foolishness. There isn't actually such a big difference between people for there to be a point in fixating one's feelings on any one of them. More than on anyone else.

The day before yesterday, I watched those model-boys' walking on Chelsea Street. Bodybuilding has been brought to the level of art—it feels like there's nowhere else to go onward from there. And those biceps, chest muscles, and butts are identically alike. All are approaching the ideal, the standard. And actually, none of them need anyone for anything other than being a living mirror. Homosexuality, it seems to me, is some men's deeper-than-usual doubt about their being, their identity. We need more affirmation of it than others do. We feel that something is lacking. We look for what is missing from others like us. To get ourselves that perfect body; to exchange it for our own imperfect, doubting existence. To become him. But that will never happen. Yet, what then is the purpose of gyms, of bodybuilding equipment, of special food compounds, of cosmetics products? Every person who shows even the slightest bit of effort (and that effort is not the least bit greater, not even the monetary expense is greater than when infinitely searching for that unattainable, ideal partner) can make himself that body he lacks **on his own**. From then on, he only needs others for comparison, for affirmation: he has truly become his own ideal.

There are, of course, a further number of old-fashioned people who obstinately do not go along with the times—such as Carl Frederick, who believes that his life's perfect alchemic formula is in someone else's possession (in the given case, apparently the unfaithful Laurent). Or like me.

Watching the swelling bustle of Chinatown below on this successive gray and chilly morning, I'm pondering the fact that if Liz Franz hasn't yet surfaced up until now, then there must be some point to it. She is giving me time. But for what? For finishing these notes, my protocol? In order to then come and annul all of it. Or for me myself to see that it cannot be told. That there *isn't* anything to talk about.

Yes, I suppose I don't really have much of anything to talk about anymore. A relationship between two people that lasts eleven years can actually be summarized in a couple of sentences. This relationship hasn't changed significantly over that time. I believe that even life-long marriages can be described exhaustively in a few sentences. What is long and interesting is perhaps only what happens before the two people meet—that, which leads them together. Each of their own stories. The crossing of the two stories is still just one point.

Yes, that geometric conception of life seems realistic to me. Straight lines either cross or never meet, in the event that they are parallel (a friendship?). And the crossing is only one point. What's there really to say about it? Because following the meeting, up to which the gravitation between the two individuals has led (if we jump from a mathematical to a physics metaphor), repulsion inevitably takes place. Detachment begins. Sometimes, it is formed into a marriage. True, even this can last for years—occasionally, even the entire remainder of a person's life.

38

And so, my "marriage" to Liz Franz lasted from late January 1991 until early April 2001. (Or has lasted. Then, a hiatus began. An entr'acte. The diva went backstage.) Ten years. And it's not as if I really have anything to say about it especially—what haven't I already said. Every marriage has its ups and downs. By the way, those ups and downs are different for the partners, for the most part; often on opposite poles. To tell the truth, I never really understood what Liz Franz saw in me. She indeed spoke about how talented I am and that a great future awaited me, but those talks led me to desperation, because at least initially, that future wasn't to be seen anywhere, and neither did I see any reason in regarding myself as being more talented than thousands of other documentarians. True, thanks to the fact that Arte bought *The Railway Watchman's House*, and that it ended up right in the middle of that small wave of Eastern-European fashion, which swelled during those years (and subsided quite fast), I received a contract from that same Arte for the making of a new film.

In the spring of 1993, *The Limits* (*Les Frontières*) was indeed shot according to my script: a personified (basically my own) story about borders and their crossing in Europe. But there's no point in stopping on this for very long. It is undoubtedly the most renowned of my works, if "renown" can even be spoken of in their case at all. Looking out of this window at those mouths of the subway and the Chinese flowing out from them, as well as just those bustling along the street, I can be certain that not a single one of them has ever heard my name or seen the experimental documentary *The Limits*, which even the BBC showed on a couple of occasions. Unfortunately, the same applies to those actually rather numerous whites that cross my field of vision on the street. It applies to practically this entire city, and practically all of the cities and villages in the world. True, perhaps even around one hundred people who know I'm the author of *The Limits* could be found in this city. Maybe even two hundred, given those Estonians, who have heard of it and haven't yet managed to forget. Maybe their friends. Now, Richard, Heinrich, and Marco (who certainly forgot about it immediately), too. But more about them later.

For me, the strong side of our "marriage" was undoubtedly the material insurance. Although I developed certain incomes in Paris that from time to time, during the period of *The Limits*, were even quite large, my expenses grew even more quickly. Going to gay bars alone takes an unbelievably large amount of money. But right at the beginning, I worked for almost an entire year as a night porter at a shoddy hotel in the 11th District. I received minimum wage, which back then was below five thousand francs. That was a hard year. But at least I now know what "going to work" means; what it is that people generally do. Or what they allegedly generally do.

Because in my opinion, the picture that our hard-working society creates of itself does not really conform to reality. There is almost not a single person among my group of acquaintances whose life might correspond to that devout portrayal. None of them goes to work for eight hours a day (ten, twelve, as it's fashionable to say about oneself now). This also applies to my very newest acquaintances here. Carl Frederick has apparently not gone to work for a single day ever in his life, if one means by that a salaried job in a company or an institution somewhere. However, he does indeed visit the atelier here to paint more or less every day. Thus, he does in fact go to work, and apparently, he has a great need for it. Going to work is an immense psychological support, a feeling of security, a source of the meaning of life, *réconfort*. Carl Frederick comes at around twelve o'clock, dons a paint-spotted smock, takes his tubes and spatulas, his unfinished canvas. He then scrapes and keeps busy there. True, his going to work is very costly, given the rent for the atelier and expenses made on materials. Yet, in both the state and private sectors, there are undoubtedly millions of jobs that are even more costly in an economic sense, but the importance of which as a guarantor of social stability and well-being is difficult to overestimate.

Seeing as how work as a night porter was excruciatingly tiring (I was almost used to it by the end of the year, but then the first film monies came in, and I left my working-class career right then and there) and the salary for it was so small, the small presents and occasional little sums of money (just around a thousand francs) given to me by Liz Franz for making ends meet at the end of the month felt completely justified to me. All in all, I had remained in France at her persuading. Homesickness became unbearable from time to time. Suddenly, it seemed to me that only *there* is true freedom, true peace of mind, true sleep. That I am needed there, my works are needed there. That I'm understood there. And I understand everything. How simple life is in your homeland! Everything is familiar, everything is clear. One episodic friend and lover of mine in the meantime, Jüri, who was likewise an immigrant (although I met him in the summer of 1997 in Estonia), tended to say pathetically that life abroad, among a foreign people, is perhaps one of the most difficult trials that can ever arise in human life. That certainly felt like an exaggeration to me, because every life undoubtedly has its own great trial, and what is easy for one person is overwhelming for another, etc.

I've noticed that for some, immigration is not the main trial in the least. It appears to also heavily depend on the immigrant's age. Those who have left their homeland before the age of twenty, before twenty-five at the latest, adapt incredibly well. For them, their home country primarily signifies childhood, their parents.

But no matter how strong the sentimental connection is with them, there is an at least equally strong (unconscious) wish to separate from them, to flee as far as possible from childhood and its dependency. Becoming grounded in adult habits appears to be more fatal.

I don't know what has happened to me here in New York (but it *is* true that I've been here for just barely a week) that I haven't yearned to go back even once yet. Not to Paris, to my accustomed apartment (how immensely quieter it is there! how immensely simpler, more accustomed, and cheaper practical life is there! I'm unable to buy anything other than milk and stuffed Taiwanese cookies, dried plums from the Chinese shops here below), or to Tartu. It's as if both are too small, too unimportant for me to miss them. No, I truly don't know what has happened to me here. Maybe anticipation is propping me up, also. It *is* clear that I can't fly away from here until I've seen Liz Franz. I'll so much as overstay my time here, regardless of money. And I'll wait.

Actually, I believe that it's not impossible to meet people here by chance, either. All in all, the city isn't so big. And our first meeting was a coincidence, if you take it like that. And eventually, I'm certain she'll turn up on her own sooner or later. She's letting me wait on purpose. She'll call one of these days. Yes—apparently, that is one reason why I sit here at the window in the atelier so much.

The movement of the sycamore leaves, the movement of people on the streets, the thwacking of the young Chinese players' squash game on the court below, the sun's apparent movement on the arching sky above (it is so high the entire day that not much of it can really be seen from this room)—it's all a riveting sight, yes; I can allow myself to lull, to drift off, to slip into some other state from that, and the noise, the smells accompanying it, to which I've already begun to grow accustomed; and all without really thinking about anything. Yet, beneath that state and the amazingly calm act of sitting, is actually the anticipation for the phone to ring and Liz Franz's voice to sound on the answering machine.

Would I pick up immediately? Or would I let her call one more time? Or would I call her back at the number that she leaves, but not right away, the next day? And how would Liz Franz be dressed when we'd meet? And where would we meet? In Central Park. Yes, I think so—in Central Park, next to the angel. That would be simple. And dramatic, Liz-Franz style. I *have* been her angel.

Specifically, she once developed a theory that we actually aren't regular people, but rather angels; that there is something about our meeting that is a great deal more than the meeting of two people. Appertaining to this was also the teaching that sexual relations are of no importance. This means that which has been between us lacks importance, because during the period of her angel theory, our relations had once again become bodiless— aside from obligatory kisses upon meeting and saying goodbye, which in my opinion were not at all so immaterial, so passionless, so angelic on Liz Franz's part: they were a wife's kisses.

For some reason, however, she needed to wash us clean even of that; although in my opinion, it hadn't held any particular importance. I don't know why such decisive importance is ascribed to the touches shared by two people, be they internal (if a certain contact between mucus can be counted as internal) or external. Just as though some hugs or caresses, some orgasm might change the course of the world. I still understand this if they have a true, material consequence. When one has a child. Or some disease. Then, I understand..

Perhaps *that* is just what Liz Franz wanted to tell me, because actually, I was the one who ascribed such great importance to our sexual relations. I imagined that she paid me for it. But maybe she really didn't? That idea is new to me.

And how will Liz Franz look when we meet? Has she let her hair grow out in its natural color, will I finally see how much or how little gray hair she has? Will she perhaps wear glasses, smile at me from behind them with the mild smile of a grandmother? No. I don't believe so. That would be a different woman, not Liz Franz.

Or has she had yet another plastic surgery done, been "rejuvenated," and now hopes to see the effect her alterations have on me? Poor girlfriend! That effect can only be negative. And I hope that you at least won't come to our meeting wearing tight black jeans!

I despised those jeans from the bottom of my heart, and she wore them—I know—just because of me. She apparently believed that they, along with a bob, would give back to her that unisex look, which was once her trump. But many people look a little unisex when young. The genderless beauty of young Renaissance angels, the code of honor at that time, which allowed the role of passive sexual partner only to a boy under the age of eighteen—all of that speaks of gender universality at that delicate and flushed age, when moreover, lust is also the strongest—the blood is pounding, so to speak. Later, alas, gender traits develop to become ever more obvious. Drag queens (transvestites) wage their own pathetic, heroic battle against this law of nature, which boringly divides humankind into men and women. Just as with Liz Franz. I believe—and Juri Katz's photos serve as vivid proof of this—that during her youth, she could truly even deceive people; that she could often be thought a boy if she walked around in pants and a baggy sweater. But her features unfortunately became much more high relief with age, especially concerning her lower body. And skin-tight Armani jeans unfortunately emphasize those features, not hide them. A rear is a rear, and Liz Franz's rear had bulged to quite decent proportions despite all of her fasting and general slimness—as if all of her despised womanliness had collected there. Yet I have also noticed, by the way, that women who are ashamed of their bottoms bulging around middle-age start wearing skin-tight pants, naively believing that they'll somehow make it smaller; as if with a corset or something. And so, they emphasize to the point of ridiculousness their figure's weak (or precisely strong, the very strongest) spot, which would remain unnoticed in other clothing. When worked into jeans, the body jiggles when the person walks, and in spite of everything, creates folds and bulges. I've asked around to see whether homosexual men perhaps actually like this. But I've come to understand that generally, they don't. That upon crossing a certain line, an erotic butt becomes unerotic. However, I never told Liz Franz that she could forego those "boyish" jeans on the eve of her fifty-fifth year.

On the other hand, Liz Franz's skin-tight pants were also a good lesson to me. I realized from them how miserable our attempts are at inciting belovedness out of love with all kinds of tricks, clothing, and measures. All of those techniques are absolutely counterproductive. We want the person to love us and no one else, yet in order to achieve this, we strive to disguise ourselves precisely as someone *else*, who we believe could incite desire in the person. These small measures perhaps have an effect at first sight, on the street, at first meeting. But all in all, the truth is that love is blind. It does not see the shortcomings in the person who is loved, nor does it see the beauty and virtues—be they true or false—in those, who are unloved. You can't help it. Love, as strange and contradictory as it may be, retracts into its shell. Thus, I was able to be as nasty and cruel with Liz Franz as I pleased—her love didn't change the tiniest bit because of it. And she could disguise herself however she wanted, be whatever way she wanted, as far as I was concerned—those attempts only annoyed me.

I believe that if she had suddenly turned around, begun to fend me off, jeered at me, berated me—in short, if she had changed to be like she was with others with me—then I would have immediately changed my attitude. Then, I would have had to start fighting for her approval, her attention. Now, I knew that no matter whatever I might do, it wouldn't change anything. I didn't know this right away, of course, and I initially attempted to free myself by way of stubborn periods of silence, treacherous rejections, failed appearances—which, true, were never all that consistent. Sooner or later, I needed money. Or comfort. Or affirmation. And I picked up the telephone receiver to call her.

39

The rain subsided yesterday; true—yet another thunderstorm swept through in the afternoon and wet the pavements. But today, the sun shines from a sky in which there are only a few small, scattered white puffs of cloud. A pleasant, chilly breeze is blowing from the direction of the ocean (I suppose). You couldn't want any better weather. What makes me surmise that Liz Franz will call soon? Because the *sun* came out! Specifically, whenever there was beautiful weather at the time of our meeting, she always claimed it wasn't just by chance. She hinted that one can even exercise control over the weather by will.

"Oh, you'll see—the sun will come out," she assured confidently when the weather was grayer than gray.

And truly, it did. Practically always. Was she able to always instinctively set our meetings for a meteorologically favorable period? Because I can't explain that phenomenon in any other way. Otherwise, right should be given to the Buddhist conception of the world, according to which everything is an illusion. And that the illusion can be dispelled with one's will. Or else summoned. Thus, replacing illusory bad weather with illusory sunshine is no problem. In that case, however, Liz Franz should have been a high-level yogini. And in that case, love (another's love for you)—that *greatest* illusion—is apparently not in the realm of those summonable and dispersable illusions, because she had no success at summoning it. Or however you take it. Because in my youth, during my radiola period, I was undoubtedly in love with her in my own way; in love with her songs, her voice, my conception of her, the freedom that she seemed to sow around her. That love was platonic, of course, but have I—actually—had other kinds, "real" ones?

But how low the real Liz Franz dipped in comparison with that object of platonic love! Did those two have any connection at all? It often appeared to me that they didn't. Because she truly even stooped to the point of using the most ridiculous means. To some kinds of completely brainless, feminine "spells."

For me, the limit or bottom of these was her habit of leaving her things at my apartment. They allegedly took up too much space in her suitcase, and she would need them again another time. These were actually extremely small objects—primarily lingerie that she slipped into my wardrobe. It could also be, of course, that she bought those small, black silk pieces of underwear for me extra, and didn't want to show them to Umberto. But I don't believe that Umberto rummaged through Liz Franz's dresser drawers. Amid, however, did discover those black lace panties in my laundry one time (he was taking a towel out of my closet), and from that point onward, he believed unrelentingly that I surrender myself to a secret fetish—that I myself wear women's underwear beneath my clothes from time to time; that I get off on it. I certainly told him exactly how things actually were, but the truth is rarely believable. Or did he believe it, and drew his own conclusions in his mind on that very basis?

There was a powerful thunderstorm over Chinatown last night. I was just falling asleep (I still haven't quite gotten used to the time difference, and gladly snuggle into bed as soon as it gets dark). I was awoken from a half-asleep state by the first flash of lightning beyond my eyelids, which was so bright that I thought something had exploded in the room. Only that the thunder rumbled a few seconds later. Squeals and excited shouts sounded from the street below. I've never heard such a spontaneous and lively reaction to lightning. Like the twittering of a flock of birds rising into flight. When I rose and looked out the window, the street was indeed already almost devoid of people—the flock had hidden itself away. Another couple of bright lightning bolts made the tops of the sycamores glow neon; after every flash, the street seemed dark and empty, like in late fall. The wind turned the treetops upside down, made white whirlwinds of trash on the pavement. I had the windows wide open, and a red plastic bag suddenly swept across the floor with a rustle.

The lightning and thunder quickly faded into the distance; they were probably already somewhere over the bay, towards the Statue of Liberty. In this city, one surely probably doesn't have to fear it striking inside. But I can't imagine how powerful the skyscrapers' lightning rods have to be. Most likely some very thick, wrist-thick or thicker copper wire that runs from the tip above deep down into the earth. The amount of current caused by a single strike is enormous.

A downpour erupted outside, rain started pounding in through the screen—I had to go and shut the window regardless of the fact that there was no danger of lightning. (But ball lightning? That red steel stairway to the Chinese sweatshop, which I'm already used to clanging up and down, would be a favorable spot for ball lightning to do its thing . . .) Right at the moment that I was pondering ball lightning while shutting the window (thinking about how it would run along the cast iron handrail, sparkling cheerfully on the newel posts, setting alight the Chinese workers' bags of cloth scraps that are piled on the landings for the evening), the phone rang.

I was a little surprised that someone was still calling here so late, because as far as I knew, Carl Frederick is never in the atelier in the evenings. I listened, uninterested, to what was being spoken on the answering machine in an odd accent in English, before I realized that it was intended for me, and I still didn't understand who was calling yet. I picked up the phone and turned off the answering machine. It was Umberto Riviera. At first, he asked politely how I'm doing here in New York, apologizing that they haven't had time to deal with me until now, because they've been busy. I mumbled something unclear in reply, because I was truly confused. Umberto Riviera has never called me before. Now, he spoke in a voice as if we had last been together a week ago. Actually, it's been over a year since we last met. And Liz Franz has always been with us, too. After that, Umberto Riviera got down to the matter at hand immediately, and asked what I'm doing on Wednesday evening—meaning the day after tomorrow. I replied that I don't especially have any plans. He said:

"We would like to show you some interesting places."

I actually realized only then that he was speaking in English, as we've usually spoken in French. I didn't start switching over to French either. To tell the truth, French didn't even come to mind at all at that moment. I wouldn't have been able to utter a single sentence in French. I tend to have these sorts of memory gaps. I replied politely, "Oh, great!" and "Of course!" And he scheduled to meet at nine o'clock in the evening (he said he unfortunately couldn't make it any earlier) at Townhouse Bar on 58th Street, on the corner of 2nd Avenue. He gave me the building number as well (236), and expressed worry over whether I would be able to find it. I stammered that I would, definitely.

"Good," he concluded tersely. "Then see you after tomorrow. Have a nice time."

"Yes," was the only thing I was able to reply. Then he hung up. The downpour outside was already starting to subside. I pulled the window up again—through it came fresh-smelling coolness; I felt that my face was flushed. I dressed and left the building, because I knew that I wouldn't fall asleep right now anyway, and that cleansed post-thunder air drew me to it. I hoped to calm down while walking around.

Still-frothing streams of water flowed in the gutters, sweeping along scraps of paper and plastic cups. The Chinese were already pouring out onto the street again, although more sparsely than before. Above the buildings could be seen a clearing, darkening sky; the crescent of a new moon flashed in the view from one street. Umberto said "we": does that mean he'll come with Liz Franz? But then why did he call, and not Liz Franz? We've never spoken without Liz Franz's mediation. What's more—Liz Franz had strictly forbidden me from doing so right at the start. One time, namely (it was in our very first spring), I called Rome, and Umberto Riviera picked up. I already knew then of his existence. Liz Franz never called him her husband. She had only said curtly:

"I live alone, although I live at someone's place. His name is Umberto Riviera. I'll tell you about it at greater length sometime."

That "sometime" indeed never came, but I gradually found a thing or two out about Umberto Riviera: piecemeal from Liz Franz, and in greater and juicier pieces from the previously mentioned cultural journalist Holger. That time, however, as Liz Franz had left me with the impression that their relations were open, more or less like friends, I not only started talking to Umberto Riviera after he picked up the receiver (which I didn't do for years after that, so Umberto Riviera might have developed a phobia for silent phone calls; although Liz Franz asserted that in Italy, there are frequently wrong numbers and malfunctions, so you can't hear the caller's voice), but in addition, I also announced to Umberto that Liz Franz was supposed to come to Paris soon, and I would like to ask her something about the trip. The thing is that I hate any kind of cover-up and intrigue. Because I'm not good at it. That time, my principle was to state everything just as it was. Now, I've realized that there is truly no point in that—it creates more misunderstandings than perpetual white lies and concealment, to which everyone is accustomed, and which is even *expected* of you. It's polite, decent (*décent*).

Incidentally, I immediately understood from Umberto's momentary silence that time that I had done something improper: he was apparently aware of either nothing or, in any case, not everything concerning Liz Franz's upcoming trip. He certainly knew nothing about me. After about an hour (Umberto claimed that Liz Franz wasn't home), that call was followed by Liz Franz's call to me. From the icy tone that she was unsuccessful at hiding (she had to be truly enraged), I realized that I had made a big mess (*grosse bétise*), and on top of that, had left a half-witted impression of myself. I was very ashamed. Liz Franz said:

"What is between us concerns only us. No one else has anything to do with it. No one else, no matter what relationships either of us might have with them. Everyone is his or her own person; everyone has his or her own life. I believe that you don't have to mix everything up, that no one has any **right** to know about the other. No one, whoever he or she might be. A mother or a father or a husband or a wife. No one."

I understood. She was undoubtedly right in a certain sense, and actually, I also believe personally that no one gets any right over me, regardless of the character of our relationship. I "got the message," as they say, and over the years, I didn't breathe a single word about Liz Franz to anyone. I noted that Liz Franz was also right then, when she said:

"If you yourself don't tell, then no one will find out. People always tell things themselves, that's why everything comes out in the first place. Others only know about you what you show yourself."

Yes, because it's awfully hard not to tell about things. At least to someone. And if you say it to someone, you've said it to everyone.

The more jealously I hid our relationship, the more shameful it felt to me. "My secret" (now that I talk about it here, it seems quite innocent to me, all in all) acquired monstrous dimensions within me. I began feeling like a monster myself. Observing people on the street, it seemed to me that they were all normal; that all of them have some kinds of humanly acceptable relationships, and if they were to hear my story, they'd blush from embarrassment. They wouldn't believe their ears; they would look at me with an expression that expressed sympathy, disgust, and contempt all at once. And so, I kept quiet. That's probably what is called a dual life. I know that it's not easy, and that exiting it is a long process. Speaking about it out loud indeed brings relief, but always brings new complications as well. Amid was the first person who I told about Liz Franz; that is, about Liz Franz and me, about Liz Franz as a constitutional component, an organ of myself. I felt that Amid would understand me. He himself namely liked to confess to me. (But confessing and hearing a confession are two separate things, just as understanding and searching for understanding.)

40

I already spoke about my meeting with Amid. I was narcissistically blinded by him: how could **I** have such a handsome "lover" (it appeared to me that he would become my lover)? Classic. *Mon amant arabe.* My Arab lover. It had always been a fantasy of mine. Nevertheless, many fantasies are complete clichés, just plain.

Yes, an "Arab" (I already said that Amid was actually Kabyle, Berber) is something different. Something radically different—someone, into whom you can project all of your dreams. A blank page, in a certain sense. An Arab is almost like a True Man.

Homosexuals' main tragedy is namely based in the fact that they don't **actually** love each other. At least that's what Proust's theory claims, and I generally agree with it. The sexual relationships between homosexuals, within the entire gay scene that "simmers" in Paris's Marais or here in Chelsea, has always reminded me of life in a harem, where women establish relationships with each other out of boredom and the lack of anything better; even fall in love with one another (and seriously, hotly, tragically, at that)—but all of that functions only thanks to the enclosed nature; the latticed windows of the harem rooms; the special, sleepily lustful atmosphere that governs around the splashing fountains and the fruit trays, amid the beautiful golden mosaics. The appearance of their master shatters every time, that spider's web of relationships woven from those fine, gentle bonds; from those soft hugs. Who is the master's new favorite? The question burns in all of their hearts at once; even secretly in those older women, who know they will never rise to that standing again, and that their part from now on *is* those cloying embraces with one another, the common hopeless indulgence at bowls of sweetmeats, boredom.

Another tragedy is based in the fact that the True Man doesn't actually exist, not even among heterosexual men. Some of them merely play that role more masterfully than others. A master is a master only when he spurns you. The favorite knows that the master has weaknesses. That he is actually weak. That the flesh *is* frail. Only our fantasy creates that legend of the mightiness of the flesh again every time that we're alone. Our fantasy, or a year or two of gyms, of diet products. And how *much* might! But when viewed from very close up, it's never so. Even the most imposing biceps and triceps feel pain and fear. Inside of every man resides a simple-minded child yearning for love and fearing punishment. And although Amid wasn't any bodybuilder (to tell the truth, they seem unerotic to me—their body is like clothing that they can never take off again), he was an Arab. He rode up, so to speak, on his fiery stallion, symbolically abducted me from the stifling, dusty Luxembourg Gardens with its leaves drooping from drought and wilting flower beds on that August evening in 1998. Our first night together, however, didn't take place somewhere out on the steppe; in a desert beneath large, blazing stars; beside a fire; not even on the bank of the Seine or in the undergrowth of the Boulogne Forest; but instead in a nicely bourgeois manner in my 17th-District apartment, in bed. Sitting on the bed. We talked; or rather, Amid talked. Moreover, he was able to leave the impression that he was good, in the sense that he was caring and attentive towards me. That—I have grasped—is an extremely valuable and rare quality. For the most part, people only care about their own desire, their own fantasy that they try to carry out on another's body. It is, for the most part, the hopeless clash of two different fantasies. Actually, that was also the case now. Amid spoke, I listened, waiting for him to finish, absentmindedly stroking his back, gradually even forgetting lust.

He spoke. The night was especially stifling; it could have been a good one hundred degrees in my attic apartment, which the sun had heated up all day long. We didn't sleep that night, because Amid wanted to talk. His dark eyes glistened in the half-darkness of the room, which was illuminated by the glow of the city sky shining in through the window. Even a couple of pale, hazy stars might have been there in the sky; I don't remember anything about that. I only remember that he spoke until morning, until full daylight, and then left—I collapsed into sleep, absolutely exhausted.

And so it started to be every time. In every relationship there is some kind of a base pattern, upon which the entire relationship is also founded, and which is put in place right at the beginning. From then onward, the pattern will never change again. A change would be the end of the relationship. Quite soon, I realized that *that* was what he was looking for from me: two listening ears. And a difference. I was likewise different to him, exotic. He probably wouldn't have been able to confess to any actual Frenchman, much less to a French Arab. He grasped that if I *did* have prejudices about him, then they were so mythological and generalized that they practically wouldn't disturb us. It was no doubt also important that in that country, I was even much more foreign than he was. Amid had actually been born in Paris, had naturally attended a French school, had studied well and enrolled in university. His department was *Lettres*—literature and philosophy; his major was French literature. He wished to become fully French, to assimilate, to forget his entire Arabness (which was, as I said, in fact Berberness).

His father had been a *harki*, i.e. an "Arab" who fought in the French army during the Algerian War. Moreover, Amid's father was among those few *harkis* lucky enough to evacuate along with the French, and thus escape the Algerians' revenge, the bloodshed, to which tens of thousands of *harkis* betrayed by the French, abandoned, fell victim.

Of course, no luck awaited him in France in 1962. There was even nowhere to put those tens of thousands of white French people (those famous *pieds noirs*, "black-feet") that suddenly appeared in their motherland: *they* were also despised and mocked, not to mention the Arabs, against whom people likely held enmity, despite the fact that many of them—just as Amid's father—had fought namely for Algeria to continue being a *départemant* of France, in the schools of which children learn about how "our ancestors the Galls" were blond-haired and blue-eyed.

Amid's father struggled to make ends meet in the suburbs of Paris—in true *bidonvilles*, shantytowns; in places, the existence of which, on the outskirts of Paris in the 1960s, couldn't even be imagined now. He worked on building projects, performing difficult physical labor for which he was paid poorly; but the situation nevertheless improved gradually. He married Leïla, Amid's mother, and they received an apartment in a new HLM in Argenteuil (when I visited, that "tower" of course already had quite a worn-down appearance, the stairwell was full of graffiti, and I had to edge past the young Arabs hanging out on the steps with quite a dangerous aura about them).

Amid was born on May 21st, 1971; his sister Aïcha had been born a couple of years earlier, and Leïla and Amid (Amid's father) had no more children. Amid remembered his father as an old man, although he was only around thirty-five to forty years old then. But he had apparently been gray-haired. He had apparently started drinking in France, which certainly wasn't a religious problem—because he wasn't religious, but had rather already received a modernly secular national upbringing in Algeria (specifically, he was an orphan and grew up in a state orphanage); however, it did indeed turn into a health and family problem. His father often came home drunk, dreadfully angry, and beat Amid's mother and sometimes Amid himself, who had indeed defended his mother (and gotten it twice as badly for doing so)— they all feared his father awfully. He had hoped his father would die, but when he did fall from scaffolding at a construction site and perished (Amid was then seven years old), he felt guilty and sorry for his father. His father had been a quiet, mild-mannered, miserable man when sober.

His mother Leïla, who hadn't worked at all before, got some kind of a cleaning job with great difficulty—they lived very poorly and only thanks to welfare. In school, Amid was teased over his clothing. Maybe that's the reason why he dressed so well. Where he got the money for it, I don't know. Now, I tend to believe it was from prostitution. He did tell me about a couple of older men that he had had (I now believe that there were even more—oftentimes, his evenings were "very busy"), but never about the money that he received from them. He didn't get money from me. Every once in a while, I would only treat him to dinner or invite him to the cinema. My money was to listen to his confessions, which always revolved around the same exact things over and over—they began to repeat quickly: his father, mother, and sister (he appeared to outright adore both of them); him being outcast as an "Arab"; the arrogance of the French; his geezers, about whom he told quite funny stories.

For example—one of them, Claude, always awaited him in a flowing ballroom gown, a crown upon his head, chandeliers that held real candles were lit everywhere in his large, magnificent apartment, music played, Claude's butler/lover (*"qu'il me déteste!"*—"how he hates me!" Amid said, laughing) stiffly poured champagne (which Amid said he abhorred) into their glasses, an icy expression on his face. After that, Amid had to ask Claude to dance. *Rien que ça.* Nothing more. I nevertheless doubt whether there was *rien que ça.* But that's what Amid claimed. I fear that the fact that he still didn't dare to admit the entire truth to me in his confessions (it wouldn't have done anything to me, anyway—I didn't feel threatened by geezers) indeed became fateful for him. He still remained guilty. He once asked me whether I believe in God, and when I responded 'no,' then he didn't speak about it anymore.

In September, Amid invited me to come to his home one time. Along with Leïla and Aïcha, we ate couscous, which was truly good, and drank sweet peppermint tea. Their apartment only had two rooms and a miniscule kitchen. It was decorated in quite a French fashion, the rugs were cheap and worn. But everything left a very warm, safe impression. Amid's sister Aïcha turned out to be an all-around modern French girl, and was already close to finishing her studies in literature. Unlike Amid, she knew Mauriac very well, and we spoke about *Thérèse Desqueyroux*—we got into a fervent conversation. Thérèse was also Aïcha's literary alter ego.

It was then that I saw Amid can be very jealous. On the one hand, he was proud that I impressed Aïcha (his mother Leïla almost didn't talk at all, only smiled her mild, warm smile; she appeared to already be quite an old woman), but on the other hand, he appeared to be suspicious that something was sprouting between the two of us, which he and I didn't have. That some part of me didn't actually belong to him, that his older sister could take possession of it. Amid became gloomy and soon announced that we were leaving—that Rachid, his friend, was waiting for him, and that I apparently had things to do as well. I had nothing to get done at all, and I was just hearing of Rachid for the first time ever.

After that "presentation to the family"—I was naturally just a friend, which I actually *was*, too; and, by the way, neither his mother nor his sister appeared to have the slightest clue about his hidden life—after that presentation, which overall went well even beyond expectations (I had feared that visit quite intensely, had imagined god-knows-what—some kind of a dark "Arab family"), our relationship remained as it had been on the surface, only that Amid's visits and confessions became ever more infrequent. He no longer said a word about the old men. The closer that fall came, the more closed-off he became. I felt that he was hiding something from me, and that geezers weren't the issue, but something more serious. Ever more often, we only went out to eat or to the cinema, and he no longer came to my apartment. Amid naturally didn't allow anything to show when we were out. And then Liz Franz came. To Paris.

I had certainly spoken to him about Liz Franz (in connection with the appearance of black silk sex-lingerie in my wardrobe), but like I said, he hadn't believed me. Or taken me seriously. Now, I said that she was simply an older lady, my long-time acquaintance, a former songstress, and I proposed that we could go out to eat together.

The dinner at that Moroccan restaurant was very tense. Although Liz Franz did everything to be sociable and I hoped they would have a mutual liking for one another, our conversation petered the entire time. I, by the way, also had to play the role of translator, and conversations with a translator are already very arduous. By the end, Amid was practically silent—Liz Franz and I were forced to speak among ourselves. We even exchanged a couple of sentences in Estonian. When that happened, Amid said with suppressed rage that it was now time for him to go, rose from the table, and walked off. I didn't see him anymore until that time on the street, several months later, when he had grown out his beard (it was only the sparse whiskers of a young boy—somehow very sad and pitiful), so I barely recognized him.

I realized that same evening, in that same restaurant, that something had gone very wrong, and I took revenge for it upon Liz Franz, whom I also, by the way, deemed as the guilty party. Had she really needed to come to Paris again? I practically threw her out of my apartment the next day, and thought with a certain dark satisfaction that there it was—I'd gotten rid of both of them, I was completely alone now. That wasn't true in Liz Franz's case, of course. She showed understanding, as always. And after a couple of months, I confessed to her my entire story about Amid, and she comforted me.

But that time before Christmas (I remember that I was walking down along decorated evening window displays, feeling very alone, missing Estonia, where there should be snow on the ground), when Amid came past me on the street by chance (this was also the reason why I didn't deem meeting Liz Franz in New York by chance as impossible), he had truly changed. Or wanted to be changed. Strict, masculine. He didn't extend his hand to shake, and mine was left hanging in the air awkwardly like the ones on those mechanical dolls, which move this way and that beneath the gazes of children staring at them in wonder in the window of Printemps Department Store—dolls making preparations for Christmas, packing presents (presents that are actually empty boxes and don't have to hold a surprise for anyone, because dolls don't give each other presents, don't feel joy or sadness). My hand hung in the air, and I was suddenly unable to do anything with it—I let it slowly, "unnoticeably" sink down. Like a broken doll. Amid didn't look directly at me, either—although for a moment, I caught a happy little flicker of recognition in his gaze, which he quickly extinguished. Some kind of new, unfamiliar gleam burned there instead.

"My life has changed," he declared to me immediately. "*J'ai tourné le dos à tout ça.* ['I've turned my back on that whole thing.'] Allah is great."

I was unable to respond with anything. I lack absolutely any kind of information on the relative, and even less on the absolute greatness or smallness of Allah, Christ, Jehova, Buddha, and other religious heroes. All I saw was that Amid was just about to turn to leave. He nevertheless took pity on me, asked indifferently:

"*Et toi? Ça va?*" ['And you? Is everything alright?']

I mumbled pointlessly:

"*Oui, ça va, ça va.*"

And then, as if he had remembered something else before heading off, he said rapidly, in a half-whisper, as if passersby might overhear us:

"Forget all of what I told you. There's never been anything like that."

He said this while wrinkling his brow and in a voice that would not tolerate objection, the likes of which I had not heard from his mouth before. And then, he disappeared. Very quickly. It was the last weekend before Christmas and the street was filled with feverish shoppers—Amid was absorbed into the crowd before I could even react in any way. It was like I was nailed to the ground; I was suddenly afraid, my legs were weak. I didn't even make an attempt to run after him.

So, he disappeared from my life just as spontaneously and abruptly as he had appeared. Maybe he was done telling me all of his tales. It took more than a single night, but well under one thousand. Religious types probably say: God gave, Good took away. The second half of that sentence is especially correct in the given case. I didn't make an attempt to win Amid back (I truly know that that will never work), but in spring, in April, when the weather became warm—I walked big circles around the Saint Germain Forest, where the trees were gradually leafing, the birds were singing, and there was no one in the evenings—I was struck by such a feeling of missing him one day that upon arriving home, I picked up the phone and called Amid at his home number. He had given me the number the time, when I went and ate couscous at their place, but I had never called it even once. The number was correct—Amid's sister Aïcha picked up. I asked cautiously whether Amid might be home. Aïcha was silent for a while; I had the feeling that she would hang up, but she didn't.

"No. He doesn't live here anymore," she finally replied. "If you want to talk, we can meet up. I don't have anything to do tonight; I can come to the city. If that suits you."

Yes, it suited me, although I already felt regret over having made that call in the first place. What did I have to talk about with Aïcha? Why did I need to reheat that finished story? To hear more of Amid's tales? Actually, back when he was telling those stories, on those unending, scorching, sleepless nights, and I (idiot!) waited for when we would finally get down to business— then, I occasionally hated him and his tales.

What the hell is it, I thought, annoyed, *that people only want to tell me their own tales?* As if I were some kind of a silent vessel, an eternal listener. Why can't I tell my *own* tales to someone? And why did the person, whom I'd actually wanted to know more about (in the hopes of gaining greater power over her, in the hopes of solving the secret of the power she held over me), why did Liz Franz never, ever properly tell me her own story, why did I have to pry single details out of her?

But here, on these pages, I'm settling that injustice. This is my little revenge. I'm not only telling my own tale, but I'm telling the tale that Liz Franz left untold to me as well.

I waited for Aïcha in front of the Péreire Square RER station; Argenteuil trains come there, and it's close to my home. Afterward, we sat in the café right there on the edge of the square, which I walk past every day, but the name of which I don't know even now. It seemed that Aïcha had aged. Maybe she had changed her haircut, but I didn't remember what it was like the first time. I ordered a glass of wine, Aïcha a Coca-Cola. I remember that glass of dark liquid in her hand; for some reason, I had the feeling that it contained blood—old, congealed blood, although wine should really be more like blood. She cut to the chase, informing me immediately that she knew about us, or, well (*enfin*), could tell. (And actually, she *didn't* know, I thought sadly—she didn't know that innocent, pitiful truth regardless.) Amid had apparently never spoken about it (his homosexuality). Nor did *she* tell her brother that she loves women. Or, mostly women. (She said that in an almost indifferent tone—it wasn't any "admission.") Behind "that" which happened to Amid, however, was namely the same

Rachid, who she had initially thought was Amid's lover—which, in a certain sense, wasn't actually false, because Amid was infatuated with him; Rachid had absolute power over Amid.

"At home, when we were little, no one ever spoke about religion or the Prophet. For us, '*Inch Allah*' was just a saying. As far as we knew, only old, uneducated people went to the mosque—'religious types.' There was something vaguely disgraceful about it, almost like a spiritual restraint or something. Obscurantism. The thought never even crossed our minds that we should go to the mosque sometime because we're of Algerian descent. Our father was an atheist, and in the elections, when he received citizenship, he voted for the communists. Our mother didn't say anything about those things. She did always wear a headscarf outside, but to this day I don't know whether there is some kind of a religious background to it. She cries a lot now, in any case. We don't know where Amid is, you know. At first, he started going to the mosque after Rachid, in some group or circle of theirs. Then, he grew a beard. It was ridiculous—he doesn't have a proper beard yet. Then, he started telling me that he's ashamed of me. That I live indecently, that I go around naked. I laughed in his face. Not that he dared to say too much to me, either; I'd always been his older sister. We were very close."

It seemed to me that Aïcha's eyes were moist, but I wasn't certain, either—it was already evening, and was dim beneath the patio's awning. It might have been around perhaps nine o'clock; a lot of people were still bustling around the Métro entrance. There is quite a narrow passage between the café tables and the street there, so people have to jostle past, brush the tables. I thought about my sisters, or to tell the truth, about Külli. All in all, blood ties don't count for anything. We will become strangers, and it'd be better if we don't even meet again. And so-called bonds of love count for even less. I didn't even have the feeling that Aïcha was talking to me about someone I knew. But then, right at the moment when her eyes became moist, or when it seemed to me that they did, it suddenly appeared as if Amid was sitting across from me. And as if all of that had already happened. Amid's eyes also moistened easily at his own stories. He actually had a very gentle soul, was still partly a child. *That* is the reason why his sparse beard had such a horrible effect on his face. Like some kind of a fungus, a cancer, eczema. And once again, I was listening to someone. That time it was the brother, now the sister. I realized that Aïcha had just as good as forgotten about me—she stared at the street, somewhere into the dark-blue spring evening sky above the square in the middle of the ring road; into a sky, where—as if in irony—a beautiful sliver of a young crescent moon hung. No, she didn't see me, or probably anything else around her, either. But at the same time, my presence was important. I was listening to her. Now, *my* eyes moistened. Not over Amid, who had disappeared (I digested that tale only later, in retrospect), but over myself, whose mission in that large city was to be the listener of a Berber family's stories. A confessor. Although I've always felt more like I'm a boy, an outcast altar boy, not a confessor. Muslims, by the way, probably don't have a confession. But Aïcha, as she confessed to me during the course of her story, had once, apparently influenced by reading Mauriac, out of some kind of romanticism (there was something very French about that rational analysis—Aïcha had still assimilated very well, better than Amid, who actually never truly got his head around the French literature that he studied), had once considered having herself baptized—becoming a Catholic.

"Oh, you know—the Virgin Mary and all that," she said bitterly, smirking self-ironically.

She had apparently even fallen in love with a girl during that time, whose name was, specifically, Marie. Now, she was glad that she hadn't gone through with it; that she always turned back at the door to the church. Something had nonetheless held her back. Because later, from Amid, she saw clearly how idiotic it is—religions, turning to faith. How blind, how cowardly, how pathetic!

What happened with Amid was that he began to show up less and less often at home. He had been out on nights before as well, but apparently for other reasons at the time. And back then, he had always been quiet, sweet (*doux*) when coming home; had wanted to chat with her and their mother, as if wishing to make atonement for some invisible guilt, although they didn't reproach him for anything—not even in their thoughts. Now, however, he was moody and severe when he came home—he watched everyone with a scornful glare, offended his mother, made her cry, apparently was also hurt by it himself; but became only more self-righteous from it, and soon ran out again. Until he didn't come back anymore. He called one day from somewhere in England; from where, he didn't say. He spoke with his mother; he refused to speak with her, Aïcha. He asserted that everything was fine with him; that they shouldn't worry or expect him to call too frequently. He now served only Allah, and was apparently happy. They came to understand that he was studying at some Koran school in England. It was as if their mother collapsed during that time, went gray very quickly. Amid never sent them his address, nor said what his phone number was. Now, two weeks ago, he had called again and informed them he was on his way to the Holy Land, to Mecca, and that Allah is great.

"He hasn't called you, has he?" Aïcha asked abruptly in a strange, cautious voice.

I realized that question *had* been the whole point of our meeting. That she had had a tiny hope of finding something out through me. She indeed admitted that when I called them, hope had suddenly sprouted within her—perhaps Amid was actually back in Paris, perhaps I had seen him or he had called me, and that was why I was looking for him at home. Yet, I naturally had nothing of which to inform Aïcha. I believe that she believed me. I gave her my number to call if she heard anything.

About a year later, she called me. But it was only a hopeless attempt, trying her last resort, so to speak—that perhaps I did in fact know something that they didn't. They haven't received a single sign of life from Amid since the time that he went to Mecca. They didn't dare to search for him officially, either, because . . .

Back then, there was already quite a lot of talk about Islamic extremists: about "integrists," who grew out of just the same kinds of suburban mosques that Amid attended with his Rachid (Rachid disappeared, also; it's possible that they are together to this day, and that the asexual—but that much more erotic—form of marriage, a brotherhood of belief or arms, is still the most lasting of any of them), and who caused an ever greater headache for France's government. Rationally, I certainly associated those stories with Amid when listening to the radio or reading the paper, but emotionally, I still didn't believe that he could have anything to do with all of that. As much as those "integrists" were shown, they appeared to be truly brainwashed guys. And "brainwashed" is still saying it lightly. The name for it is rather a lobotomy, surgery. Something has been cut out of those people; some spot has been numbed. And not only them, of course. When I heard about Le Pen's success in the elections, now a month and a half ago in Tartu (how distant that all is!), I mused that everything is so symmetrical and that the movement of human societies in some direction is just as rational; just as much led by some kind of intelligence as the dynamics of schools of fish, of clouds of plankton in the ocean. From time to time, the human population undertakes self-destructive onrushes. People—most of them—are probably the happiest during that time.

However, some kind of a short circuit between the talk of Islamic integrism and Amid's story happened in my consciousness only last fall. After September 11th, people in France spoke a great deal about how there were also Muslims of French origin among members of Al Qaeda, about how a certain Zaccarias Moussaoui was seized in the US, etc. All of that didn't yet have an effect on me, however. Then one day, I read a report in *Libération* about that prison camp for "terrorists," which the US authorities set up at their Cuban Guantánamo base. It was shown to journalists in order to apparently convince them that the prisoners were kept in decent conditions. But maybe it was for just the opposite reason—to send a frightening message. Because the description was truly awful. Small iron cages, where there was nowhere to duck away from the scorching sun, from the one-hundred-degree heat. Young boys nabbed in Afghanistan, some just sixteen years old, who are held in chains, who are almost turned into animals, stultified, no longer understand what is happening to them. I guzzled down that description greedily, because suddenly, it dawned on me that Amid could be among them as well. Although he isn't, of course. But in any case, he has probably, and irreversibly, been launched into a world, the laws of which were certainly not made for him. Amid—gentle, mythomaniac Amid, who was inclined to fantasize, among those scarecrows costumed in rags that wave in the desert wind, in turbans, beards, Kalashnikovs! In some camp, next to a campfire (but if he *is* happy?—that very idea suddenly seemed the most gruesome to me), somewhere on a mountain pass, in a cave, from which the Americans' extremely sophisticated bombs burn people out like fleas.

Actually, it was only at that moment that I realized I'd lost him. That I'd had someone at all—someone who talked with me, or if not with me, then to me, in any sense—and that I've lost him. All of a sudden, I felt immense rage. Never before or since then have I felt such a nameless rage—it was almost some kind of a strange force, it horrified me. But somewhere, secretly, I enjoyed it, and enjoyed it tremendously—much more than a single orgasm.

I cursed all religions, all gods—as many as came to mind. They suddenly seemed so ridiculous in their imagined nature: those worthless pope-figures, those monstrosities of words, the ultimate achievement of human idiocy! May they be damned! And if they truly should have even *some* kind of power over their whole gang (although in the monotheistic picture of the world, those mafia bosses are depicted more as lone endeavorers; almost as romantic Don Quixotes), then they could be so nice as to do for sucky humankind, which of course doesn't deserve any good deed, the only deed that they owe it all the same, no matter whether separately or by group, given the centuries of bowing down and mutual hatred, which that gang of apes, who thought them up, has poured onto their alters—yes, they could then go ahead and do that ultimate (*ultime*) good deed for mankind: free us of all religions. Please! So it would be over, now and forever. And please, also free (the one or all of you, in the event that you really have divided the world up into areas of influence among yourselves, like the Chinese mafia) us from all future and existing upside-down religions, anti-religions that don't dare to say their own names. And then, off from whence you came. Be on your own.

After that burst of rage (which I reproduced here only approximately: it wasn't so verbal or rational at all), I momentarily felt an almost enlightened enjoyment—my entire body warmed, and it was as if a beatific light surrounded me. Then, it faded and I was gripped by fear. I started feeling sorry for myself. I sat down right there on the floor of my apartment, and cried like a child. Like when I had disobeyed my grandmother and awaited a nameless punishment that was supposed to arrive when my father came home. I was completely alone in the world. I probably haven't cried like that since childhood. Everything vanished into it: my life abroad, homesickness, fear of the future, the slow wearing down of hopes, Liz Franz. That cry was an enjoyment in turn: an even deeper enjoyment than rage and cursing. I fell asleep right there on the floor.

The next day, I called Liz Franz to invite her to Paris. I had decided that I needed to put an end to it; that I would tell her everything the way it was. No talk about a duckling that she should set free—as I had said to her last spring on the Bridge of Artists, where we sat on a wooden bench in the sunlight, without any visible consequences. The river glinted in its springtime way, the high water carried clods of turf and logs out from under the bridge. It was then that I told her: set your duckling free. She said she already *had*. I didn't believe her. I realized that she answered me just as figuratively as I had asked. That in a certain sense, I *was* free, of course—our relationship had changed greatly, because time had simply worn it down; we were accustomed—I to her bulldogish love; she to my feeble, yet tenacious hatred. Yes—apparently old spouses are truly quite free of each other by the end, because they simply no longer notice the phenomenon next to them. It's no longer next to them: it is they themselves.

But now, on that morning after the cursing and crying, I wanted to say straight to her: let's end it, enough. Don't call, don't send me money, don't write. I won't reply, anyway. And I'll return the money. I can't return what you've already given, but actually, I believe that we're even.

I felt that I would make it happen that time; I was calm and decisive. But no one picked up the phone. Nor has anyone picked up since then. And apparently, I'll see Liz Franz tonight. And I no longer even know what I'll say to her. It's like I've already said it all. But as always, she has outplayed me. By being the first to say it herself, and not with words, but with actions. It turned out all the same, that I needed her more than she needed me.

To tell the truth, I can't even quite imagine the woman, who should be waiting for me there at Townhouse Bar tonight. Or will Umberto come alone after all? One way or another, something should become clear tonight. I just don't know what I'll do with the time in-between. Probably go for a walk. One can walk endlessly here in this city, even more endlessly than in Paris—that, I've learned quickly. You are faced with something new all the time, you forget about yourself. Life lightens. Only your legs become heavy by the end. By the end, you're so tired that upon reaching home (I naturally already say "home" in regard to the sewing factory place, because what other home do I have currently; I can even tell one Chinese apart from the others—that old man with a gray, nicely-trimmed beard and gold-rimmed glasses is probably some kind of an owner or a boss here; he greets me kindly, and I like him—I'd like him to be my father), you collapse into bed and sleep. The city has swept through you like a river; you don't remember a thing.

41

Although I'm no longer capable of the rage of my curses from that time, I wouldn't take anything back, either. I know what I'm talking about when speaking of religions, beliefs. I know that belief is not only an opium, not only brainwashing—that it is something much worse. Destruction, a loss of self. The living you is exchanged for the seemingly living you. Like in those old Estonian fairytales, where the Devil switches a real child for one made of birch bark, rags, and a drop of human blood, which the mother then cradles and raises like a real child. Until something dreadful happens. Such as the birch-bark child catching fire in front of the oven, and burning the entire house down. Or the Devil coming to reclaim his "own," or the false child starting to terrorize the entire family, to submit everyone to its undefeatable will.

A "clash with reality" generally doesn't destroy belief. Reality always has some flaw about it for a believer; it isn't quite right. For example: God never does wrong, although it should even be clear to a child that if a god truly exists (a hypothesis that indeed cannot be conclusively refuted, just as it can't be proven) and if it is all-powerful, then it primarily does wrong, and sometimes also a little bit of good just to pass the time. But go ahead and tell that to a believer. One possible response is that the Lord's ways are impenetrable for our minds and dark to our understanding. In short, that everything evil is somehow good. Another option is that someone else is doing the wrong. Whether the Devil. Or a person. Or the Devil through a person. That's it. The religious world is hermetic.

I know this first-hand. Actually, my belief in Liz Franz has lost nothing of its exclusive force upon coming into contact with the true Liz Franz. So what that the true Liz Franz was a pathetic old woman who paid to keep me as her last great whim; who incessantly deceived herself by imagining that I loved her . . . And *didn't* deceive herself. Because I did love her. Or, rather—I believed.

Not just that one, who dyed her hair; who spent an hour or even two in the bathroom each morning; who put on those ridiculous, tight Armani jeans; who left her lingerie in my closet; who tried to cook for me, which she wasn't capable of doing, at which she was inept and clumsy, and as a result of which, as the result of hours of toil, were readied only over- or undercooked spaghetti with bitterly burned garlic, which she called *allio et olio*, and which truly wasn't fit for eating (I'm not a snob in terms of food), so we still had to go out or order in afterwards; or else I myself had to whip something up.

Not that older woman, who showed signs of several health problems, because lately, she often looked especially poorly and probably only propped herself up with medicines (I saw them when rummaging through her large cosmetics bag in the bathroom; their names didn't mean anything to me, but there were at least six different kinds of capsules) and, of course, with willpower. I suppose she had been afflicted at Umberto's in Rome, then. And I didn't care. I had become completely immune to her sufferings. So it goes with everyone who loves us. They'll love us anyway. No cause for worry.

But she was unwell. It seemed as if she didn't go out anymore in Rome, because whenever I called, she was at home. In Paris, when we walked along the river, she could never keep up pace with me. I certainly slowed down, but not so much that she didn't start running out of breath, either. I simply showed mercy by taking a seat on the Bridge of Artists, because I felt that she was just about to collapse. And at the same time, she appeared weak enough for me to dare to come out with my duckling talk.

But she still had sufficient strength within her to give me that unexpected reply.

Or take her habit of giving me little memorabilia as gifts. What a pathetic way to tie another person to yourself, to remind them of you. For she always brought me some little, useless, pretty thing. A porcelain figurine of a saint; a blue, glass pyramid; a crystal ball; a silver letter opener in the shape of a dagger (I had to give her a franc for it, because otherwise, gifting a knife is supposed lead to a fight); a chalice encrusted with gold on the inside, bought from an antique store in Rome somewhere.

I was already used to it; I even waited with a certain excitement to see what kind of "little thing" she would bring me on this occasion. There grew to be so many of them over time that I was forced to throw other things away, to give them away. And still, they lay around occupying all of the shelf-space in my small apartment, because I couldn't bring myself to throw them away or give away the most valuable of them, either. And who needs them? I personally am not reminded of anything by memorabilia. No more than what I already remember. Yet, I grasp that bringing them, that decorating my apartment with them was a feminine "*woodoo*" similar to giving me underwear as presents, to leaving her underclothes in my closet. I started calling Liz Franz the Goddess of Small Things, in my head, after Arundhati Roy's famous book (which in my mind was only half-good in terms of the story; her literary pretention was annoying, however). That was funny to me. I sometimes laughed alone. Occasionally, completely lowbrow things are endlessly funny to me—I can break out snickering to myself about them when they come to mind, even after one hundred times. And Liz Franz's little things collecting dust everywhere reminded me of that goddess nickname quite often. Quite often, I had a bit of a laugh.

That was the true Liz Franz. But there was also the ideal Liz Franz, who came from a completely different time, from the radio, from youth. And when the true Liz Franz went and changed that ideal, then it was paradoxically only raising her higher; only swooping up to an even more unattainable height, which I had erected for myself while masturbating, crying, praying in front of the radiola during puberty. Yes—praying with the words and tunes of Liz Franz's songs; praying to her with her voice; and always receiving a response, also. My goddess always answered me: all I needed to do was take the black disc out of the multicolored pink and white sleeve, push the arm of the gramophone to the right place, and let the needle down.

Still, at the time that we became acquainted, I almost didn't listen to her songs at all anymore. Although, a couple of moments of weakness arose, I must admit. However, I put an end to them by destroying all of Liz Franz's phonograms. I think that she knew that—she did have time to rifle through my records when she was at my place, just as how I rifled through her cosmetics bag (just as mysterious as her medicaments were a number of tubes and jars: beauty chemistry is a true higher science, in which it is practically impossible for one not dedicated to the subject to orient him- or herself). But that doesn't mean I didn't progress my fantasy of Liz Franz further.

Specifically, at that time (during the first years of our "marriage"), I started to pick up an interest in opera. True, opera had somehow already fascinated me during childhood: its costumes; divas descending stairs and effectively "entering," whom I mimicked at home alone, dressing in my mother's dresses, adorning myself in her cheap pearls and silver brooches (one of them was more valuable: my mother called it a "filigree"). Yet, I couldn't put up with opera pieces—in my opinion, it was outright unbearable, that screeching in high notes. By dressing myself up as a diva and squealing in a terrible voice, I simultaneously parodied, mocked the opera. At the time, I probably already instinctively perceived that it is an anachronistic, defenseless, dying-out genre;

incessantly prolonged agony; a genre on its deathbed, where it can no longer manage to protect itself against scorns and jeers, but can nevertheless proudly turn its feeble head towards the wall, remaining forever—and against all reason—idolized.

I believe that when Liz Franz did not become an opera singer, when she wasn't accepted to the Tartu School of Music that time, thanks to the "dual-bony" conspiracy, it was due to her luck; it was a part of her fateful, unhampered climb. Because by the time that she would have become a singer (and due to the mediocrity of her natural requirements and lack of cultural/birth prerequisites— the country girl that she was—she would have, in the best case, become an average singer, the *prima donna* of a provincial theater), the era of great opera divas was already over, anyway. Maria Callas was and will forever remain the last. Together with her decadent directors (foremost that Visconti, with whom she was able to fall hopelessly in love), she made that dying, already half-dead opera blaze brightly once again. The ultimate blossoming of many human and cultural phenomena arrives right before their end— to tell the truth, just after their end, as some kind of post-gust that can romantically (but in opera's case, this is entirely proper) be compared to the red splendor that an already-set sun creates upon the clouds.

By the time that Maria Callas appeared, opera had already ground to a complete halt. A singer—for the most part fat and ugly, which costumes and makeup grotesquely attempted to hide—entered the stage, spread her arms wide, and performed her aria. The audience expertly evaluated the quality, the length of her high notes. It was a certain type of *cuisine des connaisseurs, haute couture*, designated for the same strata of society as they were. A plus for lone eccentrics, for decadent (mostly old homosexual) fans.

Maria was also fat and ugly at the beginning—she outright re-garded herself as a frog beside her stunningly beautiful sister—and likewise spread her arms wide, as she had been taught. Yet, within her burned some godly, devilish flame. She realized that it wasn't right. She felt that opera shouldn't be sung, but rather lived. And instinctively, she also sensed that, with which she never consciously reconciled: that the same "living," that "giving life" is like giving an *actual* life, like giving birth; that it means she isn't actually *giving* herself away, that she herself is left with no other life than that, which feeds her art—opera. Her artistic instinct was perfect. Although she hadn't received any modern stage training, she possessed all the necessary body techniques; invented them herself. That's what they said about her famous "falling from the bridge" in Visconti's staging of *The Sleepwalker*. She actually didn't fall anywhere, but it seemed to everyone that she did—that she descended, her eyes closed, like a true sleepwalker. Everyone gasped. The secret of that illusion of falling apparently merely lay in a complete exhalation: she let the air out of her lungs, and it was as if she suddenly collapsed.

Or Visconti's story about how when Maria entered as Norma, she always reached her high note precisely at the moment when her left leg hit the eighth step. Everything was subjected to precision; the entire opera lived and breathed in Maria with that fateful, undeniable passion, with which (probably only) women love. And when she had fallen unhappily in love with the homosexual Visconti, then even *that* was actually only a necessary sacrifice to her altar of art.

There had apparently been a scene in that very same *The Sleepwalker*, where she walks up to a couch with her eyes closed, and truly closed. At that time, Visconti used a cologne that was quite rare: always only that cologne. Maria asked him to spray it onto a handkerchief and always place it there on the couch before the beginning of the performance. That was indeed the smell, to which she led herself. Luckily, no one in the orchestra came up with the idea of using that perfume, because the diva may then have marched straight into the orchestra pit.

It goes without saying that Maria's vocal material was never flawless in the least, and there were better singers than her technically during her time. Many believe that her performance technique, her never-before-seen naturalness, her organic nature, her vividness were "merely" compensations for her average voice— in a certain sense, the utmost resolution to become an opera diva in spite of her voice. Yet, even when listened to on records, Maria is by far more powerful than every singer who has ever been and been recorded. So what that it isn't always so shining, so pure, so carrying. But along with the notes, feelings emanate from her, which come from so deep down that I am always reminded of I-don't-know-what that is bloody, carnal: birth, an orgasm, a scalpel that slices into a body.

Naturally, Maria paid the highest price for it: she paid with her life. Not in the sense of someone "sacrificing" their life, dying for someone or something. Who needs our death, a corpse? She paid with her life in the sense of how I've said: she gave away her entire life, until she was truly so exhausted that she no longer had anything to give. But *that* wasn't the victim any longer—that death, which came at fifty-five years of age, when she already hadn't sung in years, but rather lived as a recluse in her Paris apartment, completely crushed from the failure of her "personal life." She had already brought her sacrifice; those last, silent years were still only a post-life, the dismal agony of an empty shell.

And she never acquired that personal life, which she craved. Not from Visconti, naturally, or from her boring old husband, who was foremost her impresario, and with whom she read a fresh critique about her last performance side-by-side in bed every evening; nor from that "love of her life"—that monstrous billionaire, the ugly-as-a-frog Aristoteles Onassis, who finally, simply out of a delirious passion to obliterate the goddess (diva!), to thereby acquire for himself even more power and greatness, switched Maria out for Jackie Kennedy.

All of that yielded, if viewed in retrospect, to only one thing: Maria Callas's infallible artist's instinct. She had to become unhappy, and she always found—even with her eyes closed—her murderers, her torturers (and her inspirations); just as she had led herself to Visconti's perfumed handkerchief. She also killed her own child—meaning the fetus that Aristoteles Onassis had conceived within her, but to whom he did not allow Maria to give birth.

And even regardless of that abortion and the undoubtedly numerous sexual encounters, Maria remained a virgin in a certain sense, just as every female artist probably does, and maybe even every male artist. She never had to truly "belong" to someone, to a single man, to a single person; although that was what she longed for most fervently—the only goal, in the name of which she believed she was improving her art.

Even her ashes, which according to her last wishes should have been sprinkled into the water off the shores of Onassis's Scorpios Island, where Maria believed herself to have once been happy, were simply cast "somewhere into the Aegean Sea" from a Greek naval ship during an official ceremony. Maria Callas belonged to the Greek people, the government claimed. And the millions she had earned with her art were divided between her hated mother, her envied sister, and her detested husband.

*

At that time, I started to gain an interest in opera simply out of boredom, as far as I know; likewise, listening to opera records (which, for the most part, were also still boring) was a certain expression of defiance against Liz Franz. She, namely, was not interested in opera. I liked to torture her by listening to Maria Callas the entire evening. Yet now, I see clearly that my enthusiasm for opera, my idolatry of Maria Callas (which indeed never went to such extremes as buying all sorts of bric-a-brac, looking into the fine details of Callas's life, the pilgrimages undertaken by many Maria fans) was nothing other than giving a certain new shine to Liz Franz, who threatened to dull in her actuality and aggravating closeness. For me, Maria Callas was actually Liz Franz. The true, actual Liz Franz; Liz Franz in her ideal and, at the same time, in her real form, in a higher sense.

I certainly must admit that there was a *great* deal parallel about them. Liz Franz's art also belonged to a genre that was dying out. She was one of the last links in that line of great lyrical variety songstresses, among whom were such greats as Marlene Dietrich, Edith Piaf, and others. There was always something deeply personal in their art; they themselves *were* their art—they were absolutely non-standard, so in that sense, it is nonsense to talk about some kind of a "line." In my opinion, modern pop stars (such as Madonna, for example) no longer belong to that category. They are already products; they're not really people any longer. Yet that—people turning into products—is probably a universal tendency and doesn't only affect pop artists. They merely express it in a pure form that is visible to all. They are role models, idols, as always. Their followers include, for example, those countless "superbodies," whom (I'd like to say **which**) one encounters in this city at every single step. Those large, perfectly proportioned, absolutely ripped beings with absolutely smooth, flawless skin, hair that shines metallically, a strangely empty gaze, and expressions that are interchangeably identical are no longer people in the old sense. Such beings have never before lived on planet Earth. The classical Greek beauties are runts next to them. I believe that it all started with female pop stars and then quickly spread to supermodels, until it took over homosexuals—those ever-brilliant imitators, who always carry the imitated phenomenon to unheard-of heights. And from there, from those pioneers, it spreads on across the entire society. Every "office girl" wants to be at least like Madonna, or whoever all of those supermodels might be—Linda Evangelista? That one's probably old already? Every little investment banker wants to resemble that nameless, machine-like ideal that is consciously cultivated at gyms; for feeding which the pharmaceutical labs develop ever-newer series of extremely expensive food substitutes and pseudo-hormones. Of course, following those ideals is accompanied by dark and painful repercussions, just as in the case of any ideals (which, by nature, are all inhuman). Nutritional and mental disorders, suicides. No one knows yet what becomes of those half-artificial, futuristic beings upon aging.

And so, Liz Franz's art belonged to an old, by now practically abandoned current, in which personality still counted. Now, people want to be unique (meaning they want to stick out), but personality is despised. Personality is now actually something almost as horrible, as embarrassing as "soul," "heart." The latter is an organ, the well-being of which must be cared for with diet and exercise. And that's it. No kinds of metaphors.

Actually, Liz Franz withdrew at precisely the right time. She knew what others didn't know yet: that her art is at its end; that its time will no longer come. That it's time for it to die. Or is that merely my fantasy?

I definitely no longer remember whether I ever thought specifically about killing Liz Franz. It's true that I often would have liked to exterminate her from my presence, to turn her off like a radio. But all the same, I probably never made it up to imagining the act of murder, a knife, a pistol, even poisoning. We cannot kill our own gods, not even in thought. If they die, then it is only by their own free will.

42

When I reached Townhouse Bar last night, Umberto Riviera was already there. The bar itself didn't exceptionally surprise me, because I had informed myself about it in advance and was aware of the character of the establishment. The local gay magazine *HX*, which, as always, is tantamount to an advertising catalogue for goods and services aimed at a group of consumers with relatively high purchase power, characterizes Townhouse with the following words: "Upscale professionals and their fans gather around the piano or cruise the downstairs club. [. . .] Take your pick of three bars; lots of suits and blazers."

In short, I thought while crossing the first bar room and gazing at the figures sitting nicely on couches: *vieux Monsieur meets his escort*. I also debated with myself which category I should belong to, and didn't actually have the time to decide (I had neither a blazer nor a suit, and I am probably already too old to be an escort), because before I could, I saw Umberto Riviera, who was standing next to a grand piano in the very back corner. Liz Franz wasn't there. Umberto introduced me to his companions. Firstly, Marco.

Marco was a tall, young, handsome Italian. He winked at me, but I know that doesn't mean too much in this city; it is more like a mutual expression of politeness. It isn't nice to simply breeze past another person if you notice even the slightest something likeable about him or her, of course. I immediately realized that Marco is one of Umberto Riviera's latest *placements*, brilliantly chosen as always. I wonder whether Liz Franz, who so successfully advised him *immobilier* (in the field of real estate), also gave him advice in choosing that slim *mobilier*, who probably visits the gym regularly (but not too often)? In any case, it was truly a first-rate capital placement.

After that, Umberto introduced me to the pianist, who was a thin man with glasses, his eyes oddly bulging behind the lenses, as if they were amazed all the time. He nodded to me without a break in his playing, the smile on his face didn't change form. It was the kind, as though he were incessantly in wonder at the whole world, but could somehow never manage to decide which way he should start expressing his wonder. He was playing tunes from some musical.

On from there, towards the wall (Umberto stood directly next to the pianist—stepping away from that position, he whispered into my ear that the pianist, whose name I don't remember, had AIDS, that he was dying, but was now on his feet once again, incredible!), two bona fide older m'ssieurs leaned against the lid of the piano. I must say, however, that out of the entire group, only the pianist was wearing a suit, as promised in *HX*. Umberto wore sheer black "sailor pants" and a black polo shirt, from the material of which it was obvious that it was a very pricy designer shirt; maybe even of Yoshi Yamamoto's own making (Artur Kallas had dragged me to the Yamamoto shop—he buys everything from there). In any case, something very upscale. The same and even more was true for Marco, who was likewise wearing black (probably a silk T-shirt, jeans, and black athletic shoes with white laces), only that the black was tighter against his body, emphasizing its sculptured forms. The two older m'ssieurs were, however, dressed rather summery and sportily, both wearing white shorts, white socks, and white running shoes.

The younger of the two, who still had quite a rosy face and good posture, and who (as it immediately became clear) was already quite drunk, was Heinrich. Heinrich informed me, while already making eyes at me quite intensely, that he is my neighbor, a Latvian. "By the way." He truly did have a very familiar face—that strong Baltic German type with a nose that tends to redden, and copious numbers of which can be encountered from Munich all the way to Tallinn.

"My mother was namely Latvian," Heinrich specified. "But unfortunately, I can't speak our mutual language." (Estonian/Latvian, he was thinking.)

I told him that I visited Riga just recently, and that the city is "wonderful." Heinrich said that I'm lucky: he has only been to Riga once in his life, several years ago.

The oldest of the m'ssieurs, whom I estimate to be around eighty years old (it's possible that he's already well over it), waited his turn in line to be acquainted while maintaining an imposing pose, erectly leaning on the piano lid, as if he were supporting the piano and not vice versa. Adorning his summery outfit was a shirt with palm trees and little red fish, which reminded me of the summery short-sleeved shirts of my childhood, which I wore at the seashore in Kloogaranna. Back then, people traveled en masse from Tallinn to Kloogaranna on a electric train; now, the place is said to be practically abandoned, *desaffecté*, as traveling by electric train is regarded as a sign of the lower class in Estonia.

The thing was that once, I asked my mother among the sand dunes at Kloogaranna, where she had lain out—having first rubbed her body in sunscreen, which was a white semi-liquid substance squeezed out of a round, flat, about palm-sized flask (I terribly enjoyed when my mother rubbed me with it, but unfortunately, sunscreen wasn't to be wasted just the same)—specifically, I asked her what "those" were, pointing to her breasts. I was truly interested in what sort of things they were—those large, rounded objects. My mother replied:

"Palms."

It sounded cryptic, but truthful. We also had a palm at home, a large cabbage palm with a hairy trunk, which finally grew so tall that we had to give it away, and from then on, those forked leaves were for me somehow embarrassingly associated with my mother, and the word "palm" turned into a word with dual meaning *par excellence*. Yet, I was already used to words often meaning several things, and to the fact that people don't make anything of it—as if they were always aware of what was meant exactly at the given moment. Occasionally, it appeared to me that just a single word would actually suffice. Everything could be a "palm," for example. Now, in retrospect, I've realized that no doubt (and I recall that it was so) my mother's sunbathing bikini-top had a palm pattern on it, and she thought I was asking about those figures; it didn't even cross her mind that I don't know what **those** were.

In any case, there were palms on Richard's (because that is how the old gentleman introduced himself) extremely youthful shirt, and it was funny to me on the inside. When Richard later excused himself and went to the restroom, Heinrich—with whom I had already managed to fraternize to a certain extent by that time—explained that Richard was sixty-four years old. He had been fifty-nine for years. Then, he organized a party, where discretely, without naming numbers, his sixtieth jubilee was celebrated. About five years ago, Richard increased his age to sixty-two, and lately, he fixed it at sixty-four. No one knows how old Richard actually is, or what his life has been like in reality; where he is from. He personally claims to have worked in Hollywood, and he seems to truly know some stars of his time, of whom few are indeed still around. When he and Heinrich became closer acquainted several years ago, Richard—who generally introduces himself by the name Richard April—informed him that his actual name is Richard Goldberger, and that he isn't a Jew.

"I've got nothing against him being a Jew," Heinrich said. "My boyfriend, Juri, with whom I lived for eighteen years, was also a Jew."

At that moment, Umberto walked up from the bar, having asked beforehand whether he could offer me a drink, and having recommended a martini, which is apparently a New York specialty and something completely different from what is consumed under the name "martini" in Europe. Behind him came a waiter with a silver shaker (I think that's the name of the cocktail-mixing utensil) and misty glasses, which he had apparently chilled in ice. He poured the martini into the glasses so they were full to the brim, and placed three olives skewered by a small plastic sword into each. Umberto explained that it was practically pure Beefeater gin, to which a couple of drops of vermouth were added. He proposed a toast to my arrival in New York (I had already managed to tell him that I like it here, and that I am very pleased with my Chinatown studio).

The beverage was probably strong indeed, although it didn't taste that way. However, it went straight to my head. This was especially due to the fact that when the first burst of alcohol reached my brain, yet another short-circuit happened there. Umberto had apparently signaled to the pianist, because he had begun to play a new song. At first, it was an improvised introduction, which indeed seemed familiar to me, although I didn't understand what it was. However, I noticed that Heinrich started to cry. I hadn't realized that he was so drunk, but the music apparently reminded him of something. The large German nose on his rosy face bursting with health turned even redder. Then, it hit me that the tune was Liz Franz's Moscow-era song, "The Farewell" ("*Прощание*"). And then, it further hit me that what I was drinking was a martini. And that the drink, which I loved to drink at the Gunpowder Cellar in Tartu when I had the money, was called by the same name, and that at the best of times, it was also accompanied by a Liz Franz song spun on the bar's turntable. The picture suddenly became very clear to me, although I didn't understand what that clarity meant, what it was that I was seeing.

Heinrich, who dried his eyes, explained that his boyfriend had died five years earlier of AIDS, and that almost all of his friends were dead—only he alone has escaped the disease. He's lucked out in life.

"He was a Latvian too, by the way, he was from Riga. He was so sweet."

Heinrich started to cry again, because the well-known melody of "The Farewell"'s refrain is truly powerful. I asked, because it was clear to me:

"Juri Katz?"

"Yes, his real name was Juri Katz, but he changed his name, too. Here, he was Yuri Antonoff. How do you know?"

He asked that without any great amazement, and I mumbled that I knew someone, who knew Juri Katz.

"Liz Franz?" he asked with some sort of particular expression. And he sighed. But at the same time, I was attacked on my other flank by Richard, who had apparently been striving to win my attention for some time. Now, he tapped me on the wrist and asked something. I was in such a great state of confusion from everything I had heard (and a new martini had already appeared in front of me) that I didn't understand what he wanted at first. But he asked—in a certain shy tone, yet still commandingly and while making eyes at me at the same time—whether his hairdo was all right. The sparse clump of hair, which was dyed reddish-blond and was in a comb-over, had truly probably been an object of special care, and even now, it stood flawlessly in line. I assured him that it was OK. Then, he clasped me by the wrist and told me a story that he probably thought up right there on the spot about how had been propositioned in the bathroom. In his opinion, that was scandalous. He doesn't tolerate someone touching him while he urinates ("while I am p i s s i n g !"). Richard was suddenly terribly funny to me, and seemed absolutely cute. His face was oddly smooth, but Heinrich had already briefed me about how he had had several plastic surgeries.

Yet, at that moment, I nevertheless wanted to hear more about Juri Katz than about Richard's Westie (some kind of a smaller breed of dog, as I understood it), which he said I must meet by all means. "Why don't you move to New York?" Richard asked. I thought, chuckling to myself, that indeed—there is someone for everyone everywhere, and over the course of a second, I imagined my life with Richard, with his Westie and his manias (he was definitely a mythomaniac and I would definitely have to listen to his stories from morning to night, which would quickly begin to repeat themselves, but so what—I'm used to old people; furthermore, my secret calling has always been to become a housewife—foremost Liz Franz's housewife, yes, Liz Franz's wife, who would wash and iron and cook and clean and go to the store and to cafés with girlfriends; and who would wait—that thought put me in a good mood). I turned towards Heinrich and asked whether Yuri became a Catholic. He was very incredulous. No, he hadn't had anything to do with any religion, as far as he knew.

"And you don't know anything about Father Vincenzo, Father Serafimo?" I asked.

Heinrich replied that he had indeed known a Vincenzo, years ago, but that he hadn't been any kind of **father**! He laughed, he was no longer crying. He appeared to be surprised, but not excessively. "Why?" he asked. I replied that it was nothing; I was simply asking because if he already knew Juri, then perhaps he knew someone else. But Heinrich, who was already seriously drunk, put his old record on again and began talking about how he has known many, many people (men), but how they're all dead. All of them! How he has a picture, where he is with his friends at the seaside in Key West, and how everyone in the picture is dead, except for him.

I saw that I wouldn't find anything out from Heinrich, and I didn't want to touch him more with Juri, either. Umberto and Marco had meanwhile sat down on the couch, and were having a lively conversation there in Italian. All in all, that didn't amaze me in the least—Marco and that whole thing. I'd known that about Umberto, right? Only that the rest of the company was a bit odd for Umberto. I asked Heinrich how he knew Umberto, and he replied that it was through Juri, from which I deduced that they must socialize with Liz Franz—Juri and Liz Franz. And that the whole story about the monks was Liz Franz's next subsequent brilliant mystification. And that at any rate, Juri was dying at that very time, and Liz Franz's great crying sessions back then . . . But I was already too drunk to think about it, and I'm not sure whether I thought about it then at all, or I'm only putting two and two together now. And none of that amazes me. Everything suddenly (at last!) seems so logical.

Umberto and Marco stood and proposed that we move on to show me more places. The next was supposed to be something different. It was located quite near by—the bar's name was Red, and as I can read from *HX*, as it's already open next to me here, the bar is described as: *Strippers, porn stars and dancers mix with well-to-do gentlemen.*

I don't know for sure whether I drank four or five martinis over the course of the evening; in any case, it was significantly more than I am used to. As I deny memory gaps caused by alcohol, I also cannot claim that I don't remember what happened there exactly. And I *do* remember. The only thing that alcohol truly does warp strongly is a sense of time. I got home at two-thirty, although it felt as if it had only been a couple of hours. The taxi drove down Second Avenue, where the traffic was still surprisingly lively: looking ahead, it was one long river of lights stretching forth. I didn't really think about anything in particular there in the taxi. To some extent, I thought about that dancer with an empty expression grinding on the podium, into whose waistband Heinrich stuffed dollars (every now and then, the boy removed them and stuffed them into his sock in turn). The dancer came to our table and touched me; it was pleasing. But all the same, I didn't have the desire to go into the backroom with him, as Heinrich recommended. I was appalled by his seemingly frozen gaze, and it's not as if he was the most handsome, either—his reasonably white body, I mean. Creating that New York "super body" is apparently such an expensive project that you can't allow yourself one with stripping. Or else by having such a body, the person already moves around in other commodity circulations with a higher price level.

Heinrich, however, did indeed go into the backroom with the boy, and came out about five minutes later, by my calculation. "Twenty dollars," he said. His face was unchangingly pink. He put his arm around my shoulder, stroked the back of my neck; I noted with amazement that it wasn't unpleasant. I mused that I sure have been very picky and selective. Richard hadn't come to Red—he withdrew at a dignified pace, supporting himself on his umbrella (his calves, which showed beneath his shorts, were just about as thin as the umbrella, only white; seeing as how the umbrella was black). I had managed to avoid kissing Richard on the mouth, having turned my cheek. The others didn't seem to make a big deal out of the mouth-kiss, not even Marco. Yet, drifting down the river of lights on Second Avenue in a taxi (for a split second, I really did have the feeling that it was a boat), I actually thought more about the words that Umberto had said to me upon leaving. Specifically, he scheduled a new meeting. It had all happened when we were already on the street, probably so I wouldn't be able to ask too much. By that time, I was already so drunk that I was giving Marco the eye the whole time. Marco put his arm around my waist, and we walked side-by-side the entire time that Umberto, who didn't appear to be bothered by that one bit, conversed with me in a businesslike manner, asking whether I was an early riser. I said that I certainly am otherwise, and especially here in New York, but probably not tomorrow. No, not tomorrow, but on Sunday, Umberto Riviera reassured me. To put it briefly, he invited me to take the ferry to Staten Island on Sunday morning by five-thirty—sunrise. That a kind of little outing was planned. It was apparently Liz's idea for me to visit Staten Island. Now, it was finally possible for me to ask whether Liz herself would come, too. I feel as if Umberto Riviera answered that she would indeed. ("Yes, she will also be there.")

But at that moment, I was more involved with Marco, whose embrace aroused me. Then, however, Marco released me in order to hail a taxi. As they put me into the taxi, Umberto confirmed again that we would meet then at six o'clock on Sunday morning at the Staten Island ferry terminal on South Street.

I had walked past there and even considered going for a trip, but hadn't. I was thus familiar with the place, and all I had to do was remember the time: six o'clock on Sunday morning. That didn't surprise me one bit. Nothing on that evening surprised me, nor does it to this very moment.

Even today, I woke up at six o'clock and went out. The sun already illuminated the top floors of the buildings. Chinatown was still quiet, but people were moving about. The viaduct and bridge along the river already rumbled from cars and trains. Runners ran past me on the shore; an old Chinese woman exercised, looking out across the river, turning her head back and forth downstream and upstream, so it felt as if she was watching me inquisitively with her dark brown eyes, furrowing her brow. But actually, she was focused on her breathing. Or on I-don't-know-what.

It was already quite difficult to get past the fish market—there was *such* a mob there. Fish-smelling mud made by the melting ice squelched underfoot; speedy forklifts crisscrossed around the stacks of crates—watch out not to be run over. Stores' and restaurants' muscular Latino boys, the Chinese fish market's Chinese boys (that's how I designated them to myself) pushed handcarts holding a couple of crates of large, unfamiliar fish, all packed into ice, or a netful of oysters. Fish, fish, fish in crates on the ground everywhere. I didn't recognize a single one of those fish apart from salmon. A few also resembled rockfish. The fish merchants who had their transactions made were already having breakfast at the coffee and pastry cart, and again and again, I have the feeling that there is something very old-fashioned about this city—a lot of what we in "Old" Livonia, for example, have long since lost. Like the fish market. In the old days, that kind of a fish market (smaller, of course) could also have been held on the bank of the Emajõgi every morning.

In any case, I realized that six o'clock isn't an especially early hour here. Even *that* is somehow old-fashioned: that early waking. Even large, black, shining Lincolns were already pulling out of the garages beneath the skyscrapers. Maybe they had to take their masters to catch a flight, who knows. Even the rich start off early. So, five-thirty on a Sunday morning is nothing special. And what is special about the fact that I'll finally, on the last day, meet with Liz Franz after all? We'll take a ferry to the island, we'll talk, I'll be able to get everything off of my chest, everything that has so far been left unsaid. All of my hatred, all of my indifference, all of my foulness, all of my love. I won't let her interrupt me. I'm no longer that weak child, whom she once met without knowing it. Whom she—that time in the beginning, appearing merely as a voice on the radio, on a record—took over from my grandmother, from that *reine-mère*. Of course, a true queen must come after the mother-queen. But in the end, the little king must grow up as well. Has grown up. Has realized he *isn't* really a king. And with that, the queens' power is broken.

Liz Franz, you know that this meeting will be completely different from all of our former ones. Something completely new. *That* is why you've delayed it further and further. You're afraid, Liz Franz—in the end, *you* are afraid. But I'm waiting. And time no longer frightens me, either. I know it will go quickly.

43

Trrrrrr-trrt. Trrrrrr-trrt. I hear the sound of the Chinese sewing machines downstairs coming up through the floor like the songs of chickadees. Today is Saturday. According to the *New York Times*, the air temperature in Manhattan will rise today to ninety-two degrees Fahrenheit, which is well above the average indicator for June 22nd. Yesterday was the summer solstice. Light has achieved its climax, the heat—not yet. That is, an unnoticeable withdrawal has begun. I had barely managed to write that anticipation no longer appalls me; that time goes by quickly, when all of a sudden, it stopped. The resounding thwacks of the squash balls through the dull roar of the ventilation fans on the floor below, which almost drowns out the street noise. Yet the "*kuks-kuks*" of the balls is of such an audio frequency that it sounds through it. The same goes for the sirens of police cars. The sewing machines below have silenced; apparently, the Chinese women reached their weekly quota and went home. I've already managed to do everything today to pass the time, but it's still just three o'clock and I don't dare go out yet: I'm waiting for evening, when the heat subsides.

In the morning, I took the subway to Brooklyn and visited the botanical garden. The heat was already quite powerful then. The roses in the rosarium shed their petals visibly, and audibly. The petals outright pounded down, although there was no breeze. The smell of wilting roses was a bit sickly sweet; it seemed that it could make your stomach turn.

Reigning above the pond and the fiery paths in the Japanese garden, however, (I eyed the blue Japanese irises flowering on the surface of the water, their cross-like blossoms, and wondered whether the dry petal that dropped from Liz Franz's delivery onto

Barclay Square in Tartu might have come from them; but hardly) was the sappy aroma of conifers, the smell of midsummer, which is identical everywhere that pines and their relatives can be found. Along the Koiva River in Livonia. In the Brooklyn Botanical Garden in New York; along the Mediterranean in Antibes, where Liz Franz and I spent a couple of days around midsummer, the sun's standstill, the solstice (*solstice d'été*) of probably 1993—yes, 1993. One night. Even there, I was surprised most by the aroma of conifers streaming from the hillsides, from the graveyard, down to the beach. Cypresses, Stone pines. Our hotel was somewhere on the upper side—at night, that smell gushed into the room through the open window. It was like incense. It was hot, as it is today. Neither of us slept. I lay on my back, my eyes open; the white curtain in front of the balcony door moved in the warm breeze. I would have liked to be alone, to masturbate. Liz Franz placed her hand on my chest. I waited for a few moments for her to stop stroking me, to pull her hand away. But her hand remained in place—a fiery, heavy hand. I felt that it was suffocating me; that I was unable to breathe. I pushed it away. I pushed that hand off of my chest. A few seconds of silence followed, as if time stood still, and then Liz Franz turned over onto her side, curled up into a ball, and emitted a long, animal-like howl. It was a sob. She was crying. She was crying over me like a woman, and then she cried like a little child. I didn't do anything: I lay there, on my back, with my eyes open, waiting for her to shut up. I didn't do anything—I didn't stretch out my hand to comfort her. I didn't *want* to comfort her. I certainly didn't feel good about it, but I also enjoyed her suffering. I was surprised the most by that power. By how I can cause such an outburst of feelings. I'd never known that I was capable of that. I myself had always been the person whose hand was pushed away—no matter whether it was directly or symbolically. The person who already knows in advance that his hand will be pushed away, so he doesn't even dare to extend it. Interestingly, one can nevertheless do to others in life what has been done to you.

The next day, we drove a rental car down the road along the sea in Côte d'Azure, that very same scent of conifers blowing in through the window. We were silent. I felt guilty, and blamed Liz Franz for causing that feeling of guilt. Every now and then, I thought that it would be good to speed off of a high cliff somewhere. To put the pedal to the metal, and when we had achieved the maximum speed, to turn the wheel sharply. Yet, the thought of what people in Estonia might say about that twin death held me back. And naturally, I wanted to live as well.

I don't know why that scene, that pushing her hand away, came to mind there amid the scent of pines in the Japanese garden. It comes to mind often. It haunts me. I don't know whether Liz Franz remembers it. It's possible that she doesn't. People see things completely differently when they are together, too: one remembers things that the other claims never to have never happened at all. Because luckily, forgetfulness exists; and luckily, it is man's primary state. Luckily, almost everything is forgotten. Otherwise, we would suffocate.

Afterward, I further sat on a bench beneath the lindens along the botanical garden's allée. The sweet smell of linden blossoms dominated there, but even it already held the sickly sweetness of wilting. One night on the bank of the Hudson, down there around Battery Park, the smell had been fresher. The sun had been setting; there were roller-bladers, walkers, bikers along the shore. That evening, probably two days ago, I sat there on the bench for a long time, watching how the yellow sun descended almost straight down between the Jersey skyscrapers on the other bank. That time, I didn't wait; time went so quickly. The sun descended, disappeared; I rose, and moved onward—an entire hour or even more had passed in the meantime without me having noticed. One small bird sang in the low bushes on the bank at the river bend. It was incredibly quiet there (until a riverboat sailed past), so the little bird's song could be heard clearly. The clamor of the city faded into the distance, the voices and shouts of people echoing from the grass—I don't remember them. I don't remember the tune of the bird's song, either. It was foreign to me. Yet, there is something universal in birdsong. No matter how foreign it might be, it is always just as comprehensible, or incomprehensible. Its effect is the same. Whenever you stop and listen, the story it tells is one and the same: nothing. That "nothing" is calming. Distancing. Distancing you from your greater life, from yourself. I don't know if there exists some similar universal element in people's song, in their music—something in common with birds. I believe that there is. Our phylogenetic distance from birds isn't so great, all in all. Those few (hundred-) millions of years.

One green linden leaf tumbled through the air in front of me, and fell onto the path. It still had a fresh, lively appearance, but would wilt immediately in the heat. Soon, many such leaves that have fallen and dried before their time will already be everywhere. I know—that's just how fall comes in Paris: in the form of those rustling leaves, which already start to rustle in June. And the rustling of which ends only in December. I believe that it is the same way here: New York is farther to the south than Paris, but still falls into the same natural zone, temperate zone. Just as Livonia. Yes—just as Livonia.

I rose from the bench underneath the lindens and exited the botanical garden, back into the subway. I didn't even manage to spend more than a couple of hours there in Brooklyn; it wasn't even midday yet. That arctic temperature held sway in the subway car, just as always. Some stores are even colder. That is apparently Americans' conception of the temperate zone: the average indoor and outdoor temperature must always be just right. I'm amazed that they don't all cough or sniffle. Man is a very adaptable animal. In any case, it was very cold in the subway car. But I forgot about that the next moment. I hadn't looked at whom I sat across from. But on the other side of the aisle, directly across from me, sat a black man, the likes of which I hadn't seen before. Across his massive, but still proportional, even sensitive wrists ran fine, tumescent blood vessels, like some forked African river. I am already used to all kinds of pumped-up bodies here, but the black man was something else. He was already on the other end of the standard, or corresponded instead to some kind of ancient standard that once held sway in our—man's—hot, common home, and which fascinated me there in the ice-cold subway car above any sort of ordinary degree.

I wasn't able to *not* watch him. He touched his powerful lips, cheekbones, with his hand. Everything about him was perfect, large, massive. I didn't see his eyes—they were behind light-blue reflective sunglasses; the kind of mask-like sunglasses that cover half of the face. I felt as if that reflective glass surface *was* his eye. He turned it towards me from time to time. I don't know what he thought or felt. I can't even guess. He wore a white, skintight shirt that didn't leave any part of his body's form unemphasized; but on his legs, he wore light-blue trousers seemingly made out of silk, on the sides of which were large white snaps closing the slit that ran down his pant leg, as well as one white stripe. He leaned over and snapped one opened snap shut; while doing so, a piece of brown knee, his calf, showed between the shining, light-blue cloth. Then, he rose and got off at some Brooklyn stop. I probably should have followed him, but I didn't. I would have been prepared to be that black man's slave. For at least five minutes. Even in exchange for money. But I only had my last one-hundred-dollar bill in my pocket, and I considered it to be too much. And so, I didn't follow him. I didn't find out what happens when you follow your momentary, but that-much-stronger passion, which arose as if from somewhere out of a very distant past—long ago, hundreds of thousands of years before your birth. That even scared me—that chasm of time, that passion's determination to cross it.

When I exited the subway station on Canal Street, the black man was already out of my mind. The heat had begun to rise decisively—I searched for shade along the walls of buildings, but Grand Street, along which I mainly had to go, was just in line with the sun: there was almost no shade there. On top of that, midday started to approach. I was hungry; I purchased a large cupful—I suppose it was nearly a liter or a gallon, which is almost a liter—of chicken-noodle soup (three and a half dollars). A pound of dark-red cherries from a street vendor (two dollars). When I got up into the room and opened the cup of soup, it was still so hot that it burned my mouth. It was then that I remembered the black man. And not just remembered. I left the soup to cool on the kitchen counter. I undressed myself. **Black bull**, yes—I found the right word for him. Black bull. *Taureau de nègre*. But I didn't submit to him. I *was* him. Yes, I was him myself. That was even better, I believe, than if I had followed him. Although he so lustfully touched his lips, cheeks, neck, on which the blood vessels bulged. We are nevertheless the freest in our lust when we are alone. No one bothers us. When I finished up, the chicken soup still hadn't cooled yet; I burned my mouth regardless, but otherwise, hot soup on a steamy day was just the right food—it made me sweat.

Afterward, I read through *The New York Times*'s top story, which began on the front page and continued further at great length on the sixth page, with photos, and told about how a nineteen-year-old Arab had intruded a house in a Jewish colony on the West Bank, and had killed the mother of the family and three children. It's also possible that a number of the victims (the two remaining children that were at home out of the seven total were wounded) were a result of gunfire from Israeli soldiers, who managed to shoot the intruder after a long battle and throwing

grenades into the house. On another day, Jewish colonists drove
to a nearby Arab village and threw a twenty-three-year-old Arab,
a stonecutter, off of a roof after an exchange of words and stone-
throwing there. I fell asleep before reaching the article's final
conclusions, and slept like the dead, not grasping where I was or
what time it was when I awoke. But it was only one-thirty. I made
tea. I photographed myself (on time exposure) nude against the
studio's white walls, windows, monochromatic paintings. I felt
that a documentation of that day should remain, and it should
be that very kind. I don't know for whom, but it must. For a
moment, I thought about sending those nude pictures to Liz
Franz. Let her look. My body is already starting to age. I want to
see it myself. To document the process, upon reaching the peak of
which comes the descent; a process, which has probably already
crossed that point unnoticed, just as summer did today. Although
on the surface, nothing has changed.

Then, I took a shower, and noticed while drying myself that a
large amount of hair is coming off on my towel again. I wonder
whether I'm balding? I wandered around on the atelier side.
Yesterday, when I came home during the day, the little turtledoves
(that's what I call them, Carl Frederick and Laurent, to myself)
were painting together. Yes, Laurent stood in front of the easel
(Carl himself never uses that easel) with a serious look on his face,
and painted the white-primed canvas black. I said that he had the
same style, having Carl's relative monochromatism in mind. He
replied that be that as it may, he wants to be original. Today, I
saw that truly—they have nothing in common in what concerns
painting style. Laurent's technique consisted of him drawing the
contours of skyscrapers with disproportionally large windows,
like children do, into the fresh coat of black paint with some kind
of a stiletto (which revealed the white base layer, making fine
white scores), and in the black "sky" above them, had written in
block letters: I LOVE NEW YORK.

Viewed separately, Carl doesn't seem to be a great artist per say, yet from viewing that funny drawing, I nonetheless realized that not only his painting skill, which is ultimately merely handicraft-skill, but also his spiritual finesse is still from a completely different class than that of the "love of his life." Which, at the same time, means that that love of his life is purely the fruit of his overly refined fantasy. It happens. Frequently. That's probably almost always what happens when one strays into such categories. The dream of love is the fruit of a life devoid of activity, and still, art can be born of only such a life. Love always deceives us. It never leads us towards the being, whom we crave; whom we believe to be the object of our love; on whom we are fixated. It's always an error of perspective. Because love has always fixed its target farther than the one we love. Our beloved must be destroyed just as *we* must, because love's goal is new. If not a child, then something else. Maybe. Maybe that's just the wrong path, but what does "the wrong path" mean? In nature, where we are, wrong paths do not exist: all paths inevitably lead somewhere, all paths are right, no one goes without dying, no one escapes that mill, everyone is reduced to a proper powder.

But still—what incredible power, that love; with what blindness it strikes us (for would we otherwise dare to step into that arena?), with what massive ability to deceive ourselves it equips us. Carl sees in Laurent everything that is not there, and doesn't see the sole thing that is: an ordinary boy who is looking for adventures. Simply a kid. Yes, when he bought ice cream on the street one night that we went out together, and he fell behind us while licking it from the cup, when I looked back then and saw him coming, so seriously involved with his dessert, then at that same moment, I saw within him what he is maybe most of all: a child. Maybe all homosexuals are children who haven't grown up; I don't know. But if Carl *does* see a child in him, then that only makes him greater in his eyes, paradoxically. For he has erected his entire fantasy upon that—upon that simple boy, who has nothing to do with his conceptions at all. How simple it is to see this in others, and how impossible to see through it in yourself!

That time on the street, Laurent picked up his pace and whispered to me upon catching up (I had fallen behind Carl Frederick in turn): "Don't you find that you and I are like brothers?" He winked at me. I realized that he wouldn't have anything against a little adventure. But brothers! *Tu parles!* More like sisters. Yes: a big sister and a little sister, and only incest could take place between us. Or boredom. But I patted Laurent on the shoulder and confirmed: yes, of course, like brothers. I don't know what mania it is that people have. Liz Franz also claimed once that she and I are brothers. But I know very well that I haven't a single brother.

I recalled what Linda said one time about her grandparents, who lived in some nursing home where Estonian refugees in Sweden—not exactly an actual nursing home, but the sort of half-service home for the elderly. Her grandfather, who came from the island of Saaremaa, had been the captain of a ship, and was eighty-four years old, said one day:

"Salme, I don't love you anymore. You've tired me out."

And he moved in with his "girlfriend," as Linda put it. That "girlfriend," whom he refused to introduce to his children and grandchildren, had (according to witnesses) been just as old as Salme—something over seventy; however, the turtledoves' life together had recently ended with interference from the nursing home administration and hospital authorities. Specifically, Linda's grandfather had been making love to his girlfriend so passionately that she broke a rib while falling out of the bed. I don't know how that love affair continued or ended, because I haven't remembered to ask Linda, and I don't know why it came to mind just now, either. In any case, it appears that age counts for nothing. People don't become wiser.

In order to drive away such fruitless musings and while waiting for the sun's descent, I turned back towards the *New York Times* again. I'm incapable of reading a single book when in a state of anticipation. Not to mention a newspaper. I did read through several articles. An article about how cell phones are bothering subway passengers. That is, everyone certainly uses their phones "when necessary," or at least "in case of emergency," but others' calls seem too loud and too long to them. The idea of making separate subway cars for people talking on cell phones has been put out there; but firstly, people don't like that sort of segregation, and secondly, it's not at all practical, because people often storm into a subway car at the last second before the doors close.

It's very difficult to find a way for how people might live according to their ideals: among other members of their species, but privately. Indeed being objects of wonder, but not allowing others to take advantage of them. The ideal of love quickly becomes anachronistic. Everyone actually wants to live for themselves, and for others to live for them, too; but as everyone wants to live for themselves, to follow their own personal fantasy, there is no one who would live for others. Then, politeness games are invented, in which reciprocal interest and admiration are shown—tit for tat. Afterward, each can withdraw to his or her own life-capsule again. In the end, it's the safest there. Life is ever more similar to what is said to be our greatest secret longing: embryo, placenta.

After that, I read through two articles about forest fires that are wreaking destruction on several states—on Colorado the most. Already thousands of square miles have burned down, eighty houses. The forest fires this year are apparently earlier and more extensive than ever before. One large fire was set by a lost camper, who wanted to signal his location with the flames. Blame for sparking a second fire has been placed on a young woman (the mother of two children and a forest ranger on top of that), whose task was also to discover illegal campfires.

Specifically, she went into the forest to burn a letter received from her cheating husband. Her neighbors believe she had to be extremely shaken up by the letter for her to have undertaken such steps. She apparently actually *loved* the forest, like everyone does in that vicinity, which is said to stand out for its lack of malls and recreational institutions. The woman has been arrested and is being accused of willful arson.

44

In the end, every wait ends somehow abruptly, even rushing. I set my alarm for Sunday morning, but I woke up a little bit before it sounded. As if I had a long trip before me, a departure. Then, I always wake up a little before my alarm.

It was already almost light outside. I made tea in order to rehydrate my body, because I had sweated profusely during the night; my sheets were soaked. The night had been hot. Even the empty streets were still warm; the walls of buildings and the asphalt still radiated the warmth of the previous day, like good old ceramic stoves. In some places (there, where the fish market is held during the day), the pavement stank of fish. In other places, however, the smell of hay invaded my nostrils. I deemed it a smell-hallucination. Yet, on the balcony of the Staten Island ferry harbor, which looks out towards Battery Park, that smell of hay was absolutely clear and undeniable, and I realized that it simply came from cut grass—from the grass that had wilted in the previous day's heat.

Although I woke up early, I still ran late. My skin was lightly sweaty from the quick walk across the embankment. I was overcome by the thrill accompanying that early-morning, dawn exit—some kind of exaltation. I hummed the dramatic melody of the *Norma* finale to myself. More or less. Where Norma (Maria Callas) declares in a commanding voice to her lover, Roman officer Pollione:

"*In mia man alfin tu sei.* ['Finally, I have you!'] No one can shred your ties. I can!"

Pollione wails: "You mustn't!"

Norma: "I want to!"

Then, she orders Pollione to swear in the name of his children, his fatherland, and his faith that he will abandon Adalgisa, whom

Norma has decided to destroy. At the stake. Pollione begs for mercy. Norma: "You still beg? Too late!"

Norma relishes his sufferings and her triumph in advance in an aria as brisk as a merry-go-round: "At last, I can make you as unhappy as I am myself!"

Then, however, she changes her mind and herself declares to the priests that she has sinned—she, the priestess, has desecrated the altar (she is a mother!), and according to the druid laws, she must be burned. May the pyre be erected for *her*! Everyone is horrified to death. However, Norma orders the priests and the crowd in a low, booming voice:

"Si, preparate il rogo!" ["Yes, stack the pyre!"]

That *rogo* emanates from Callas's chest in such a voice that it is clear: the insane woman really has decided to mount the pyre. Her flesh is already burning, from within.

An extraordinarily beautiful, sorrowful aria follows (*Qual cor tradisti, qual cor perdesti*—That heart, which you betrayed, the heart, which you forfeit, now manifests itself before you at an awful moment: you strove to escape from me in naught . . . Cruel Roman, now you are one with me . . .). The aria turns into a duet, Pollione declares that he will burn with Norma, that his love has been reborn . . .

Thinking of that nineteenth-century industrial tragedy and its final scene bursting with a rush of feeling (Callas is truly sublime there, as Pollione says about Norma) made my mood especially vigorous—I picked up my pace, the air along the river was so fresh, a breeze blew in from the sea, it was almost cool.

The fish market was closed on Sunday and didn't pose an obstacle. Regardless, I was running late. Yet, I didn't worry about that, because I knew that Liz Franz was used to me running late, and that she would certainly somehow excuse my lateness to Umberto, too. I didn't care how. Nevertheless, when I saw the time illuminated in neon on a high-rise across the river (and it was 5:59), I was amazed that I had run late anyhow.

In all likelihood, I've never made it to a single meeting with Liz Franz by the right time, and she has never once reproached me for it; not even when I've failed to show up entirely. I was even more amazed, however, when I saw neither Liz Franz nor Umberto at the ferry terminal. Lone people, waiting, were dozing on the benches—probably nighttime partiers waiting for their ride home, for the most part. I looked at the schedule and found out that the ferry didn't depart until 6:30. So, there was time. Regardless, it was strange that Liz Franz wasn't there yet. Because she, on the contrary, had never run late for our meetings. I had never had to wait for her. Never.

It was then that I exited the stuffy waiting hall onto the balcony, and breathed in that smell of hay there. I remembered that it was St. John's Day Eve in Estonia. There were other people on the balcony as well. Two very fat girls, who had somewhere picked up a tall Latino university student with an intelligent air about him, and who looked very good for being with them. The girls had decided upon acting brutally: that was apparently their style. They talked about someone's penis, roared with laughter (they were probably quite drunk), attempted to touch the tall Latino boy, who somehow unnoticeably squirmed away from their touches, and patted them on the butt in consolation. The fat girls became ever more brutal, their speech ever more obscene, and I wondered: how many options do they really have for finding what and whom they dream of in life? Brutality is perhaps their only consolation.

Three white cruise ships approached from the ocean, one after another. The harbor janitor—an old man who was sweeping aluminum cans and cigarette butts into a dustpan with his little broom—had bought a cup of coffee from somewhere, came up next to me and leaned on the railing to drink it, and pointing at the white ships, said: "I call them . . ."

But I didn't understand what he called them. It had to be something derogatory, because he added: "Not like in the old days." Presumably, the oceangoing vessels didn't resemble those floating cargo shelves of old, those in his childhood. One ship that appeared from beyond the point, passed the Statue of Liberty, and disappeared around the corner, was nevertheless slimmer than the others; I wondered whether it might be the *Queen Elizabeth II*, the last ship that crosses the Atlantic regularly; although the likelihood that the *Queen Elizabeth* reached New York on that exact early morning had to be extremely low.

Two tall girls had landed at the railing on the other side of me. That is, I regarded them to be girls at first, but then realized that they were "girls"—two drag queens. They chatted with each other in a low, manly voice; at the same time, the legs showing from under the hems of their dresses appeared quite feminine. Not to mention their breasts. But getting silicon breasts is no problem for professional she-male prostitutes. Only that they are said to sag later, and are then extremely ugly. A drag queen who has lost his commercial appearance hardly has sufficient savings for a new operation. Yet, these two were just at blossoming age— the worries of old age were far from them. One wore a jumper made of shining red, stiff material, and red shoes. The other, his sister (*sista*), was black, however; hovering over his black jumper was also a black veil, which extended down over his knees, and he likewise wore a black-veiled hat.

When I was studying them, Umberto greeted me. They had come up behind me unnoticed. Umberto and Marco. Umberto was in a white suit (I had also put on my light-colored suit and a white shirt), Marco in a black one. Marco wore black sunglasses as well, despite the early hour and the fact that the sun was still behind the smog on the horizon, and wasn't blinding in the very least. Umberto held a small, red cardboard box about the size of a smaller shoebox. Out of impatience, I forgot the usual, required discreteness and asked where Liz was. Did she not actually come?

"Elle ne viendra plus," Umberto replied. *"Elle est ici, dans cette boîte. Ce sont ses cendres. Nous allons les disperser dans la mer. C'était sa dernière volonté."*

I was thankful to him for saying that in French, because I probably wouldn't have made head or tail of it otherwise. Even then, it even took me some time before the words' meaning sank in (still, those words along with the neutral resonance of Umberto's voice did stick in my mind: if I were a recording device, I would be capable of playing them back in identical form). And so, that small shoebox was Liz Franz's ashes. She wasn't coming anymore. This was her last wish. OK. I knew that.

I believe it was a particular defensive reaction against the unexpected: that definite conviction that I had known. The entire time, the entire way here from Tartu, and the entire time here. That she wasn't coming anymore. The red shoebox as the location of Liz Franz's earthly remains certainly didn't seem especially real to me. But apparently, I had to take it as being real. I've always preferred to believe the world in the way that it presents itself to me. As I'm told.

The ferry had arrived from the island, and they started letting people on board. The few tired passengers who there were spread out and plopped down onto benches. At Umberto's direction, we went to the stern of the ferry. No one was there. The ship tooted—it was lower, more booming than the horns of trucks speeding across Grand Street at night. It was indeed already moving, having pushed off from shore unnoticed, and for a moment, I was gripped by panic: I can't get back again! I had apparently subconsciously planned an escape, jumping onto land at the last second. Now, that second had passed. The ship sailed out from behind the high pile wall, and I saw that the sun was already quite high above Brooklyn Bridge. I recalled how I took a walk on that bridge one day. There is a plank pedestrian walkway on the bridge's upper story; quite a crowd passes through there. For a while, there is a road for vehicles beneath that plank walkway, but the river can be seen through it in the middle of the bridge (there are gaps between the boards measuring about a couple of centimeters), very deep down, and while looking at this, I suddenly became afraid. I took my camera out of my pocket to take photographs and dispel the fear, but the camera strap pulled my keychain along with it (the three keys to my Chinatown studio, two of them for the front doors below), and it fell. Luckily, I thought I heard some kind of jingle (the traffic passing below makes quite a din), and I looked back and saw my keys, which had luckily become caught in the gap between two boards. I lifted them carefully out of the gap. They were small keys, and could easily have dropped through the crack. When I leaned over and looked into the depths visible through those boards, I suddenly remembered that I had seen that bridge in a dream. That *kind* of a bridge, I mean. In the dream, the bridge started in the Tondi district of Tallinn. First of all, I had met an older lady on the tram, who wanted to strike up a conversation with me, claiming that she'd known me for a long time; I, however, said that I had lived abroad for many years and didn't know anyone there. I got off the tram to get away from her, and decided to go by foot. There was an industrial neighborhood there, just as there truly is in Tondi, but more massive in scale, more awful—something akin to nineteenth-century London (or New York). I passed between the large, cast-iron industrial buildings, then came upon narrow medieval streets and a small gate. It had to be a monastery, a nunnery. I stepped through into a tiny, mossy courtyard. I knew that I wasn't allowed to enter; that the gate had been left open accidentally. I exited, and sure enough, a nun wearing a tiny shawl, a Lilliput, who carried a large collection basket walked past me. I didn't give her money, although I regretted it a moment later, because doing so probably would have washed me clean of guilt. New alms-collectors arrived right away, however: an old monk with a small choirboy, who carried the basket. I took two metal five-kroon coins, which are quite scarce in Estonia (mainly one-kroon coins are in circulation), out of my pocket, and I was proud that I had such large monies to give. But then, I saw that the little boy's basket, where I put my coins, was already filled to the brim, and it contained precisely a large number of five-kroon gold coins. I was disappointed that my donation incited so little attention. It was then that I reached the bridge. It started from the railway station and led across a very wide river, which I had never seen specifically. On the other side of the river was seemingly some kind of a wasteland, which I identified as Russia, maybe Siberia. Winter appeared to hold sway there. Still, I now needed to cross the river in order to make it home. The bridge was built out of exactly the same kind of crossways boards as the Brooklyn Bridge's pedestrian way. I believe that I've never seen such a bridge before in my life. The boards were orderly at first, but then became sparser—some of them were broken, rotten, delinquents had broken them, the bridge swung. The river swirled blackly below; the water appeared to be very cold. I got down onto my hands and knees in order to somehow crawl across the sparse boards, but I woke up before I crossed it.

I also failed to cross the Brooklyn Bridge in real life: I turned back halfway across, because I had nothing to do in Brooklyn. I was also satisfied that the dream, which had astounded me that time, and over which I had wracked my mind, had been resolved in a kind of way. At the same time, I felt that something else was resolved; that I now knew something, but I didn't know what it was.

Now, on the morning of June 23rd, as the Staten Island ferry sailed out of the harbor, the golden disc of the sun hung above Brooklyn Bridge in a golden fog, already warming the air quite well. The water behind the stern of the ferry, the wake-water, likewise glinted gold. It suddenly looked very beautiful to me. The drag queens, red and black, had followed us to the stern, apparently out of a professional interest (we were still three potential customers, and furthermore, I had been watching them), but situated themselves discretely at the other corner of the stern platform. The platform wasn't all that wide, of course. They no longer chatted, but yawned widely. I suddenly grasped that this was a funeral, and I had the bizarre thought that those two drag queens were likewise funeral guests, that they belonged to the cortège, and so, there were five of us. Three men and two women. Or however you take it.

I don't know what's done at funerals—I mean at these sorts of ashes funerals, because I've never participated in such a ceremony; although there wasn't any ceremony at all. As if it had been ordered, standing there on the stern platform, which was separated from the wake-water by only a small folding gate (passengers disembark and board there when the ship docks), was a small, gray stepladder, probably designated for some crew needs or maintenance work. The ferry sailed very quickly—much more quickly than the ferries to the islands of Saaremaa and Hiiumaa; Manhattan grew distant very fast, its skyline was already wrapped in yellow haze. The golden glint suddenly seemed so beautiful to me that my eyes moistened. For some reason, Umberto climbed up onto the small stepladder, although he also could have gone to the railing just the same. This way, he was higher up than us. He opened the box, and scattered the whitish-gray ashes from it, further tapping the box against the railing post. His lips moved, but I didn't hear what he said because of the engine noise. Was it that you are taken from ash, and it is ash that you must become? And if it was, in what language? In French, it is *poussière*, dust. In Estonian, *põrm*—dust, ashes. I don't know what it is in Italian. The ashes themselves drifted up and down in the wind a bit; some of them dropped immediately into the golden, glinting wake-water, disappearing there in an instant, not leaving a trace for a mere moment. The whirling wind carried a small cloud of ash back to the deck on the ship's stern and blew it into my face, so I had to rub my eyes. Although I'm not sure whether it was really Liz Franz's ashes that got in my eyes. It also might just have seemed that way. I was satisfied that Umberto and Marco (who stood at a slight distance, his expression unreadable behind his sunglasses; apparently indifferent) didn't say anything. Umberto went and threw the empty box into the trashcan, and then they stood along the railing and remained silent. The two drag queens didn't move from their place, either. In my mind, it was very important that no one say anything, that everyone remain in place as still as possible, because I needed to think about the chemical composition of ashes.

Needless to say, ash is a mineral component of the human body, which collects after the body's cremation, i.e. incineration in the oven of a crematorium. I have seen several documentaries about crematoriums, and therefore generally know what one looks like. In the end, ash is further ground down to a finer state in a ball mill, because there are always smaller bits of bone that didn't crumble. I don't know why that mineral component in particular is regarded as being so important while the oxygen, carbon, hydrogen, and nitrogen (which actually make up the overwhelming majority of the body's mass) are allowed to fly out of the chimney without any feeling of remorse.

And so, the organic part of Liz Franz's body had mixed with Earth's atmosphere already some time earlier, a part of the water had probably rained down among precipitation, and a part of the carbon dioxide had joined the gaseous dome causing the so-called greenhouse effect, while a part had most likely been assimilated by the flora, as it was currently spring-summer—a period of intense vegetation in the northern hemisphere.

But of what elements is ash composed? Calcium, phosphorus, magnesium, potassium, sodium, iron, plus all kinds of microelements and virtually the entire periodic table. It is probably true that a number of those mineral substances' particles spend a much longer time in the human body than actively replacing carbon, hydrogen, and oxygen atoms do. The mineral content is highest in bones, and the bones' metabolism is not as fast as that of soft tissues. Yet, is it possible that some particles (atoms) stay in a single human body from the moment of birth until death? This could be studied by branding particles, but it would be a very long-term project, and a negative result would still not be proof that it isn't so.

The orange Staten Island ferry was already docking. I looked at the clock: the crossing had lasted twenty-five minutes, but had gone by so fast. Umberto took me by the elbow and said that they were going back right away, but that I could walk around a bit on Staten Island—Liz apparently wanted that. And no doubt I wanted to be alone. But they invited me out to dinner. In Liz's memory. There, he'd tell me how it all was, and he apparently had something to give to me from Liz as well. (*I wonder whether that "something" is money?* I thought automatically.) He had reserved places at the Indian restaurant Nirvana (he stuck the restaurant's card into my hand), and they expected me there at eight o'clock.

I disembarked the ferry and walked straight forward through the immense terminal waiting-hall, along the long concrete galleries, from which one can board a bus, but I didn't want to board a bus—I only wanted to go forward. Staten Island is one borough of New York. Visible there was some building with a tower, probably city hall; a stairway led up the hill next to it. It seemed to be the most direct path, and that was the way I went. At seven o'clock on Sunday morning, the streets were completely quiet and empty of people. It smelled of the flora; quite a strong breeze blew from the sea, the trees rustled. Soon, a series small, idyllic wooden houses amid large trees began—clover blossomed in the grass in front of them, flowers could be seen in the gardens. A fat man walking his small black dog went past me. Otherwise, the houses still slept. It was somehow odd in that great sunlight: that void of people, silence, the smell of plants, hay—yes, the smell of hay again.

The houses along the street that led down the hill were set more closely together; some of them were crooked with run-down porches, the street was deteriorated. In front of every house was a teeny yard—in some of them grew weeds, corncockles with blue blossoms, orange lilies in others. I heard one door open, and I looked back. A large black mamma came out onto the porch holding a small, sleepy tot. She stepped off of the porch and onto the street, yawned and stretched, looked around. The little boy squatted down and started digging around in the dust there in the street. Another street led back up the hill—at the tip of the knoll was a square with benches, a little bit of sea was visible from both sides along the street. I sat down on a bench. That smell and silence around me—suddenly, I realized what they reminded me of. Summers in the country, at my aunt's house, where my grandmother took me for a couple of weeks every year. It always smelled of cut hay there. Because our visit to the countryside—the *reine-mère* summering with her little prince—always happened right around the summer solstice. You almost didn't see people in the country, there among the hummocks and the fields. There, there in particular, on the kind of warm night where the smell of hay—that smell of spring turning into fall (because around the summer solstice, when strawberries are ripe and everything seems to still be in blossom, the process of ripening, stiffening, in short—fall has begun in the vegetation) entered the room through the mosquito screen in the window, filling the entire house—there, I discovered lust within myself.

It was intoxicating and very awful. Intoxicating at the beginning, awful when something suddenly discharged from there, when a stain came onto the sheet. How to explain it? What is it? Why is it so enjoyable when you do that? And why do I imagine such things while doing it? It must be something very bad. Some kind of sickness. It must be hidden, no matter what the cost. Only the stains will remain—what can you do ...

Sitting there on the hilltop, I mused that basically, my life has changed very little from that point forward. All changes have been so superficial. Simply, yes—you learn to hide things better, even from yourself. It's called getting by, the skill of living. It causes less embarrassment, pain, and trouble, until it no longer does anything. You get completely used to who you are. Is now the time?

Walking down the other street, back towards the harbor (it was already starting to get hot, the smell of hay receded), I thought that now, there *is* no one, who might sing about that land. Liz Franz was the last, yes—suddenly, I was hit by such an inspiration; I even came to a stop, watched a bee climbing through the clover with interest, and said aloud:

"She was the last."

Not even that land exists any longer—those meadows, which suddenly sprung up before my eyes; those wide Tänassilma meadows, where the "flowers," as Liz Franz asserted, had grown above her head every summer. They no longer exist, no one goes "round" there anymore, nor disappears into the blossoming hay in midsummer. In its place are thickets of willow, of alder—forest. A different kind of place, a different kind of smell. I tried to imagine what it might be like right now. The time there must be—yes, around three in the afternoon. On St. John's Day Eve. The bonfires are already piled up and ready for evening, although it is a long time since anyone has remembered for whom or what they are lit. And there's really no one to be seen. I saw only an alder thicket glinting in the boring light of a summer afternoon, a dusty gray road that disappeared into it, white cumulus clouds above everything. It was still so long until evening! It dragged and dragged, and no one came down the road. I was unable to imagine anything from Livonia aside from that white, dusty road between the clumps of alder. For some reason.

The ferry going back was larger, a lot of people boarded; I was amazed at where they all came from—from that island, which on the surface seemed still to be in such deep slumber. In spite of that, on the way back, I saw an entire group of black boys standing in front of a small diner; a group of women busied themselves in a self-service laundromat—likewise blacks, Latinos.

On the ferry, I sat on the stern again, outside—there were benches there on that larger ship. An ugly Latino woman, her face blotched from some sickness or an unbalanced diet (poverty), sat next to me with two children in tow: a girl of about four or five, and a boy of two or three. The little boy had immensely large, dark eyes, which took up (it seemed) about one third of his face. He studied me with those eyes: timidly at first, then with a particular interest. He demanded the cup of coffee from his mother, acted as if he took a drink, and handed the cup back to his mother, still staring straight at me the entire time, as if questioningly ("with big eyes," but they were constantly big). He was wearing nice, new clothes and little boots with gold shoelace clasps; everything quite cheap, of course. The girl sat on the other side of her mother, was silent and stayed in place the entire time; I didn't really get a look at her face. The mother hugged the boy; the little boy pressed himself against his mother, still staring solely at me. Children watch people that way. Something simply captivates their attention, causes some kind of a puzzle that they are unable to express. Which they strive to solve all by themselves. No one knows what puzzles they are; we ourselves have forgotten them. But maybe we are still striving to solve them. I suddenly felt a great, undefeatable exhaustion. The cool sea breeze was so pleasant. I thought vaguely, having that ugly Spanish mother and her two beautiful children in mind: *That* is *life*. *That* is *life—yes, that* . . .

I awoke when the ferry bumped against the jetty. I indeed hadn't been able to watch Manhattan's approach. The past morning felt like a dream to me. But disembarking the ship in the line of people, I noticed that that very same little brood was walking in front of me: the daughter at her mother's left-hand side, the boy at her right, their dark bobbing heads, their light-blue backs (each was wearing something light-blue). Now, the little boy no longer looked towards me, looked back; he was already more interested in what awaited him ahead.

45

When I reached Nirvana (30 Central Park South; the top, fifteenth floor) and the doorman, who looked South Asian and wore Indian dress, invited me into the elevator, making small talk about a beggar whom he had watched for several hours on the other side of the street, sitting next to a park (the beggar hadn't done anything, just lain around there, but people still gave him money: tourists!), I mused as I rode up the golden Indian-style elevator alone and checked the time that St. John's Day Eve was already ending in Livonia: it had to be three o'clock in the morning, the bonfires had burned down, people were, for the most part, completely drunk, sleeping a heavy, vodka-infused dream or already sobering up again, meeting the dawn with pale faces; a dawn that is probably already erupting from the northeast—yes, it must be starting to grow light there already, and the damp summer morning that makes one quiver is unusually quiet, only music still echoes across the lake from somewhere—maybe it is Madonna, maybe the Pet Shop Boys, or else something ethnic, Estonia's version of country music, because nobody cares at that hour, and most likely, someone has simply forgotten to turn off the speakers next to a campfire or those sounding from an open car door, and in that racket, a lone old man raising a bottle to his lips is talking to himself while sitting by the fire, until even he falls to his side in the trampled grass. St. John's Day has begun, and when the elevator reached the top, I was stuck by the recognition that it hadn't been for naught, regardless: that this year, all of those bonfires, without anyone having known, were lit in honor of Liz Franz, who hated St. John's Day from the bottom of her heart.

Umberto and Marco were already there, and the "Latvian" Heinrich had additionally been invited for some reason. They sat at a table by the window, where there was one more open seat, for me. Umberto and Marco sat with their backs towards the window, yet still saw the view from it thanks to special mirrors placed on the opposite wall, which was apparently (as Umberto immediately explained apologetically) the restaurant's main trump. The food was allegedly mediocre, but that had again been Liz Franz's wish—for me to see that view. She had **wanted** it.

"She was like a little child, you know," Umberto said in English. *"Come una bambina,"* he added in Italian, smiling without me having grasped the point behind the smile.

I did, however, immediately agree with his assessment. Yes, Liz Franz was like a little child. How had I not realized that earlier? A little child, who **wanted**. When she didn't get it, she started to cry. This time, she had wanted me to admire the view that opened up from the window of her last residence. Specifically, they had lived right near there, and the view looking out from their apartment was similar, although they were lower. Umberto didn't name the address, however; only gesturing vaguely towards somewhere to the west, where the red disc of the sun was vanishing into the haze above the buildings. I realized that they didn't wish to disclose their address, and that most likely, I will never see Umberto or Marco again in my life.

And so it is, in all likelihood. Namely, I'm writing these lines already two weeks later, in retrospect, simply endeavoring to summarize, because I no longer have the desire or the care to rest on all of it at greater length—new things, as surprising as that may be, have come up, and they don't number few.

Specifically, I'm sitting . . . But it's better, I realize now, to leave *where* unsaid. It no longer has any importance. And truly, better to follow Liz Franz's teachings, to not leave excessive traces, to speak about yourself just as much as necessary and as little as possible. I'll only add as much as that I am truly busy with the realization of what had come to mind on Brooklyn Bridge, but which I hadn't understood immediately. What else? Oh, right. At the beginning, I spoke a great deal about that Asko. That was simply a fantasy. Not that Asko might have been a fantasy: he existed then, and continues to now, but I don't think about him anymore. I decided to put an end to such things—to such fruitless, demeaning fantasies. I suddenly saw him clearly for who he is, and it truly isn't worth the effort. I have other cats to whip (*d'autres chats à fouetter*), as the French say. Most likely, I will never see Asko again in my life, either.

But the view from Nirvana was truly odd. Treetops, yes—a dark-green, churning mass stretching out to the red fog on the horizon, the likes of a tropical rainforest in documentaries when it is shot from the air. This was naturally Central Park in the given case, and it was encircled by buildings from the east and the west. In the west, they formed a dark, zigzagging mountainscape at the moment; in the east, however, the windows of the buildings— living there are the richest of the rich, film stars, old money— reflected the purplish glow of the sunset, which was just about to die out. During the time that we ate, lights flickered on in the streets and windows (although sparsely: the rich, for the most part, are already out of the city during this season), the treetops darkened until they began to blacken uniformly—green leafage was only visible in the vicinity of the park lanterns, as if an abundance of bonfires had been lit in *that* forest as well, or as if the churning mass of trees was merely grass on a hayfield guarded by tiny fireflies all in a row.

For the main course, I picked spinach with cheese from the menu, because I didn't want meat on the evening of that hot day (it was indeed almost the temperature of a frosty night in the restaurant), and I wasn't hungry in general, although I hadn't eaten the whole day; I had lain in my studio, stared at the ceiling, sweated, sometimes slipped into a sort of dreamlike state, of which I was brought out by a siren or the shouts of the

Chinese, a sharp note in music sounding from the shops on the street.

I did, however, immediately become quite drunk from the mango-champagne cocktail that Umberto refilled again and again for me (the bill that was brought to him at the end of the night came out to three hundred and twenty dollars divided between the four of us, to which he added a forty-dollar tip). I didn't ask anything, because all of a sudden, it didn't really interest me. The food seemed very good in its moderate spiciness, although now in hindsight, I feel that I have also eaten better Indian food. The story that Umberto presented to me was generally this.

Liz Franz was found to have throat cancer a year and a half ago. She had refused to undergo any kind of chemo- or radiotherapy, and when she had refused something, then it was refused—she couldn't have even been physically forced to do it. And so, those incessant coughing fits, that unwell expression, the tiredness while walking, which I had regarded to be partially a circumstance of age and an overly-forced diet, partially a symptom of psychosomatics, had actually been symptoms of a developing sickness.

When things took a turn for the worse and she was suddenly unable to really talk—it had been in winter, when she "disappeared"—Liz Franz decided that they would travel to New York. Umberto had that apartment in New York, and he had also made proposals earlier for them to be there for longer periods, but back then, Liz Franz had always turned it down. On top of that, Umberto's New York trips had been a vacation for both of them. Liz Franz traveled to Paris or Tallinn in turn, while Umberto was with Marco, who indeed lived primarily in that New York apartment. Marco apparently does some kind of work in "showbiz," but I'm not confident of that version's correctness. Marco himself remained silent for practically the course of the entire dinner, just as (oddly) Heinrich, who had otherwise left a talkative impression. We all only listened to Umberto's storytelling. Or ate and drank in silence.

Liz Franz had, by the way, apparently been fully aware of Marco, just as Umberto had known about "us": meaning Liz Franz and me. He was now genuinely interested in whether we had truly been lovers. ("I mean, you are mostly gay, as I understand.") I said hesitantly:

"In a certain sense, yes—we were. For a while."

And suddenly, that seemed like a lie to me; a boast. I had never been Liz Franz's lover.

Those last months in New York, the three of them had lived together by Liz Franz's request, and Marco and Liz Franz had apparently become great friends ("Didn't you?" Umberto Riviera asked Marco, who nodded indistinctly; he was still wearing sunglasses, although it was already night outside), and at first, when Liz Franz was still well, they spent a great deal of time together, because he, Umberto, had a lot to do, but Marco was often at home during the day. It is from that remark that I assume Marco's work in "showbiz" was indeed something of this sort: making the bitter time of older gentlemen and ladies sweeter. Entertaining those, whose minds are no longer entertained by "show"; who no longer find a footing in art. So, yes: "showbiz" indeed, in a certain sense; even in a higher sense.

Liz Franz luckily didn't refuse painkillers: in the end, she had a morphine pump, the kind of device that is hooked up directly to the vein, and the button for which the patient pushes independently when necessary, giving him- or herself a new dose of painkiller. Studies have apparently shown that in this way, a patient even uses less morphine than prescribed by a doctor in the case of shots. Luckily, the attitude towards pain has progressed, Umberto confirmed: people no longer believe that suffering is medically indicated, or that morphine causes addiction as a painkiller. Even just recently, it had apparently been absolutely crazy: specifically, it was a generally accepted theory in medicine that infants under the age of one year do not feel pain, in the sense that it doesn't do anything to them. They can't *talk*, of course. And older people were also allowed rather to suffer as long as they didn't scream too much.

In the end, Liz Franz had no longer been able to speak, although she made all the necessary arrangements in writing, which—true enough—weren't all that many. She had written that postcard for me in advance, and asked Umberto to send the airplane tickets to me after her death. How Liz Franz knew about Asko, Umberto didn't say; nor did I ask. Liz Franz actually had those tickets booked already right at the beginning of May, because she was convinced that she would die in late May. All the same, she hadn't left anything to chance, worrying that maybe there wouldn't be any flight tickets available afterward, which, by the way, would have been true as well, because flights were reduced after last fall, but everyone wanted to come to New York again now. Liz Franz had actually also booked those tickets in mid-May, and had Marco put them in the mail. She had apparently had Marco confirm repeatedly that he really had done so; luckily, Marco had put the post-office receipt in his pocket—that calmed Liz Franz down, more or less. With Marco's help, Liz Franz also made an arrangement for that Chinatown studio, and had asked Artur to meet me at the airport. She hadn't wanted to overburden Umberto. She had apparently still wanted to be independent, even after death.

They had been to Staten Island once in early spring—Liz Franz had liked the trip, and that was probably where she had come up with the idea that we carried out in the morning. She actually died on May 26th, under morphine, in the early morning, at home, alone, likely without any suffering. When her condition was still stable, she had sat on the balcony for days on end. Umberto had thought she was watching the park, the trees:

"You know, she was from the country just the same, and those who are dying always turn back to their childhood."

Yet, Marco had said (and it was more or less the only time aside from ordering food that Marco opened his mouth, confirming that it really had been so) that actually, she was only watching the street, traffic, the people who could be seen very well from their fifth-floor apartment. She could apparently sit there for hours and hours, as if to drink up that river of people and cars with her gaze. It seems that it doesn't dry up there on nights, either. She had never gotten enough of it (only in the end did she sit in the room, watching—when she was conscious—the sky, probably, because nothing else was visible from her armchair).

She and Marco had apparently liked (at the beginning, when Liz Franz could still talk) to comment on passersby while sitting on the balcony, to laugh (although laughing caused her pain) and make fun of the amusing ones; to think up stories and tell them to each other.

I suddenly felt great pain at that remark (well, yes—I don't actually know what **great** pain is like): again, always, ever was there someone else. Even Liz Franz had someone else, with whom she was happier, by whom she preferred to die, with whom she chatted and flirted (I assume) in a way that she never chatted or flirted with me. Because there wasn't anything serious between them. Damn that "something serious"! I grasped that ultimately, *I* hadn't been the one who pushed her hand off of my chest, but rather she pushed away my hand, which never even rested upon her own. I even teared up out of jealousy, pain, and self-pity; I turned my face away towards the window, the city, but Heinrich nevertheless noticed that I was crying, took my hand, squeezed it, and I was thankful to him for that.

That is generally everything that I found out. Umberto and Marco and I said goodbye downstairs in front of the building; I was supposed to fly out the next day. Heinrich and I walked together for a while; I would have liked to ask him further about Jüri Katz, but I didn't. As I remained silent, he was soon the one to say that he was going, that he would probably go and check out a few more bars. Apparently, he certainly did not want to live with anyone anymore, but from time to time (quite often, to tell the truth), he needed *someone* all the same. "Just for the sex." He apparently isn't especially selective. And life goes on. He embraced me, we exchanged the traditional cheek-kisses, to which I have become quite accustomed by living in France, but which will probably never become really natural for me. Heinrich gave me his card, just in case.

I meandered along the streets of Upper East Side: the night was hot, outright stifling. I bought a bottle of fresh orange juice from some outdoor Deli counter—I wanted to sober up completely. I reached Second Avenue. I started to walk down it. The night was certainly stifling, but it didn't make me sweat outright anymore, either. I looked at the time and confirmed that it was now already full morning in Livonia, in Estonia. I inspected the bus schedule at the stop, but the bus had just left; I continued on foot. I like nights when the air is so warm that you don't even feel it. The river of taillights flowed in bursts in the same direction—downwards—in sync with the way it was released from behind the weir of traffic lights. I didn't think about anything definable. I wasn't sad. I was in some midway state, where in truth, there isn't anything. Maybe that *is* freedom. It's so rare in life. I watched intently as an enormous cricket scurried across the sidewalk before my feet, disappearing into some sewage opening. He lives here in this city, I mused. I passed a large pile of transparent plastic bags full of food leftovers—that is, scorned food. Is that truly the daily portion of one restaurant? Watermelon rinds, slices of white bread, squeezed orange halves were showing. I wonder whether those remains were also incinerated, burned up? Or were they buried, composted, made into dirt, as would be "more ecological"? I even stopped to inspect the remains and ruminate on the problem. It was then that I remembered what had come to mind on Brooklyn Bridge one day, but not quite. I realized what I must do. Yes, of course—it didn't even amaze me. What could be more natural? I have to make a film, and I knew exactly *what* film. How indeed had I not come up with it earlier? A film about Liz Franz. But not about *her*. Because I don't know anything about her. About myself. *That* is the only person I know, the only reality that I have. But that means it will be about Liz Franz as well, about all people. People are all so much the same, in the end. If you know yourself, you know everyone. Inspecting the large plastic bags filled with food remains, I was suddenly convinced of it, and not even that surprised me.

I don't know how many kilometers I walked that night—I made a few more circles, reached the banks of the Hudson in the meantime, smelled the aroma of lindens again, sat down beneath them, was already sketching out film scenes in my mind. I have all of them precisely in mind—now, the main thing is only to write them down, to formulate them; I don't doubt that I will make this film. Who could impede me?

Then, I went to the southern tip of Manhattan, where open water is already visible, Staten Island off in the distance. I observed that water, which was now dark, velvety; I tried to think about the ashes drowned in the water. Yet, I understood that it really has no importance—the ocean's chemical makeup might as well have stayed the same. I finally did reach Chinatown with my circles, although I didn't aim for it directly. The sun was already starting to rise. I abruptly noticed with astonishment that I was in front of my building. My legs had carried me there. The steel doors below were locked at that time, of course; the steel stairway and workshops were quiet. I wonder whether Liz Franz was really thinking about such stairways when she warned me that there are steel buildings in New York? Apparently, that warning belonged to the same category as her claim that the Devil lives in Tartu. I'll never find out what she was in fact thinking, nor would I have found out even if she had lived, if both of us were to have lived for centuries more. I stood at the window in the atelier and watched, entranced, how the glow of the city outside transformed into the glow of the day without being able to detect the moment, when one vanquished the other. Soon after the dawn, a pleasant fresh breeze began to blow in through the window, bringing even more of the smell of hay.

I forgot to say that I also received one thing from Umberto, which Liz Franz left me. It was a small, flat box tied up and sealed with tape; made from the same kind of red cardboard, in my mind, as had been that "shoebox" containing ashes. Upon receiving that little box, I thought again automatically: I wonder how much money is inside? When I opened up the package after taking leave of Heinrich, however, I found only two things inside. One was that icon in a silver frame—Konstantin's inheritance. It is on the table in front of me here right now. Since the Madonna's face has been damaged, is scratched, she appears to be grinning mischievously; but the babe in her lap is serious, so they form a humorously contradictory pair.

It was because of that mischievous expression caused by the defect that I even kept the icon: it should now be the only of Liz Franz's "little things" that I have. The second item in the box I received from Umberto was a CD, unmarked, apparently self-recorded. I had stuffed both the icon and the disc in the breast pocket of my white jacket, and hadn't thought about them further. Now, at dawn, I remembered the disc. I also remembered that Carl Frederick had a CD-player there. I put the CD on. I immediately realized it was the same record that I had. The one with a white and pink sleeve. Its re-recording with the scratching and all. The sun rose and shone in through the studio's large windows—not golden this time, but apricot-colored. I hadn't listened to that record in so long. At first, I wanted to turn it off. But then, I listened through to the end, as if hypnotized. I put it back to the beginning. Then, I had an idea. I opened all of the windows in the studio, turned the volume all the way up; let them wake up (the Chinese), I thought—it's already time! I knew that even in the relative morning quiet, the volume of that little CD player wouldn't sound all that far onto the street. But I felt as if it sounded across the entire city. In any case, it sounded across the building. I was gripped by some kind of wild intoxication, desire. I undressed myself, touched myself, danced—I almost didn't need to do anything for it to come. After that, I danced more slowly; then came the song, which I had sung in my car once long ago, centuries ago, two months ago, "to my own tune," while driving from Tallinn to Tartu. Now, I bellowed along at the top of my lungs; so what that our voices probably didn't harmonize at all—I can't sing, but I know regardless, better than anyone else on Earth, what song it is, what it means. I bellowed like a lunatic, without any kind of melody. I turned off the CD-player, took the CD out of the device, and threw it out the window. The silver disc fluttered while glinting in the sun, fell to the street. I didn't look to see what became of it further. Now, I sang alone, at the top of my lungs (*à tue-tête*), crying and not crying: I long for the bosom of the rowan tree, to bury my head in its branches, I long for the bosom of the rowan tree, to rest there would be good. The rains wash its berries, I press my mouth upon them. Take me into the shade of the leaves, the blazing autumn tree. To you I sing, and you understand, you are so simple and good. To you I sing, and you understand. I rest my head on your trunk. I long—for the bosom of the rowan tree . . . To bury my head—in its branches . . . I long—for the bosom of the rowan tree . . . To rest there—would be good . . .

TRANSLATOR'S NOTES

p. 42   *pkui hüiad wimati keik surnud töuske üles, siis olgo sino käsi ka mino haua küles:* When thou finally call for all the dead to rise, then may thy hand also be upon my grave.

p. 42   *Jehowa, ma ootan so õnnistust:* Jehova, I await thy blessing.

p. 53   Verst: A Russian measure of length. 1 verst = 0.66 miles.

p. 69   *Wastne Testament:* Old Testament

p. 76   *Le Printemps adorable a perdu son odeur!:* "Adorable spring has lost its fragrance!"—from the poem "The Desire for Annihilation" ("*Le goût du néant*").

p. 83   "*Tuu om üits uuperitiiva*": "That is an opera diva." (Spoken in Mulgi language, a South Estonian dialect.)

p. 83   "*Mina saa tiivass.*": "I'm going to be a diva." (Mulgi.)

p. 99   "*Kas saate välla!*": "Are you coming out!" (Mulgi.)

p. 100   "*Näeh, tuu laits ju laksuta kui üits ööpik! Vii ta linna kuuli, tule tõisest viil uuperipriimadonna.*": "What do you know, that kid warbles like a nightingale! Take her to the school in town, they'll make an opera prima donna out of her." (Mulgi.)

p. 109   "*Mis ta siin võta' või . . . tulli' niisama, et pruuvi . . .*": "What's there here to bite . . . I come just the same, to try . . ." (Spoken in Võro language, a South Estonian dialect.)

p. 110 "*Eks see särg, särg jah, näe sõi ussi är'. Aga mul om iks mitu
ääd ussi üten.*": Guess that roach, a roach—yeah, ate up
the worm, see. But I've still got lots of good worms with
me." (Võro.)

p. 136 "*Isand Jesus Christus / mina ey ole ni auwus / et sina tules
mino kattusse alla änne ütle ütz sena sis saâb terwes mino
heng...*": "Lord Jesus Christ / I am not worthy / to have
you come under my roof, but only say the word, and my
soul will be healed..."

p. 174 "*kas siis selle maa keel laulo tules ei voi taevani toustes ülles
iggavust ommale otsida.*": "might this land's language
rising to the sky in the winds of song then not search for
boredom unto itself."

p. 195 "*Pahwli I. Rahmat Korintileistille, XIII. Pähtük,*": "Paul's
First Epistle to the Corinthians, Chapter Thirteen."

p. 195 "*Arm om pikkämeelelinne / nink helde* [...] etc.: 1 Corinthians 13: 4–13

p. 200 "*Kas tiaatrin ka?*": "To the theater, too?"

p. 201 "*Ikka, tiaatrin ka, uuperin. Riia uuperin omma' ilusa'
verevä' vaheteki'.*": "Sure, to the theater, too; to the opera.
Riga's opera has pretty red curtains."

p. 240 "*Lämmi päiväkene om. Kogre matsutava tiigin.*": "It's a hot
one. Carp are smacking in the pond."

p. 295 *Who fanned my brow with fronds of palms / And whose sole
task it was to fathom / The dolorous secret that made me pine*

away. Translation from William Aggeler (*The Flowers of Evil,* Fresno, CA: Academy Library Guild, 1954).

p. 301   "I can't live without you,": "you" is spoken in the formal tone.

Tõnu Õnnepalu is one of the best-known authors in Estonia. Born in 1962 in Tallinn, he studied biology at the University of Tartu. Publishing under his own name as well as a variety of pseudonyms, including Emil Tode and Anton Nigov, he began his writing career as a poet in 1985. Õnnepalu's real breakthrough came in 1993 when he (or "Emil Tode") published the novel *Border State*, for which he received the annual literary award given by the Baltic Assembly.

Adam Cullen originates from Minneapolis, Minnesota. He currently resides in Tallinn, where he moved in 2007 to become fluent in Estonian through complete immersion.

MICHAL AJVAZ, *The Golden Age.*
The Other City.
PIERRE ALBERT-BIROT, *Grabinoulor.*
YUZ ALESHKOVSKY, *Kangaroo.*
FELIPE ALFAU, *Chromos.*
Locos.
IVAN ÂNGELO, *The Celebration.*
The Tower of Glass.
ANTÓNIO LOBO ANTUNES, *Knowledge of Hell.*
The Splendor of Portugal.
ALAIN ARIAS-MISSON, *Theatre of Incest.*
JOHN ASHBERY AND JAMES SCHUYLER, *A Nest of Ninnies.*
ROBERT ASHLEY, *Perfect Lives.*
GABRIELA AVIGUR-ROTEM, *Heatwave and Crazy Birds.*
DJUNA BARNES, *Ladies Almanack.*
Ryder.
JOHN BARTH, *LETTERS.*
Sabbatical.
DONALD BARTHELME, *The King.*
Paradise.
SVETISLAV BASARA, *Chinese Letter.*
MIQUEL BAUÇÀ, *The Siege in the Room.*
RENÉ BELLETTO, *Dying.*
MAREK BIEŃCZYK, *Transparency.*
ANDREI BITOV, *Pushkin House.*
ANDREJ BLATNIK, *You Do Understand.*
LOUIS PAUL BOON, *Chapel Road.*
My Little War.
Summer in Termuren.
ROGER BOYLAN, *Killoyle.*
IGNÁCIO DE LOYOLA BRANDÃO, *Anonymous Celebrity.*
Zero.
BONNIE BREMSER, *Troia: Mexican Memoirs.*
CHRISTINE BROOKE-ROSE, *Amalgamemnon.*
BRIGID BROPHY, *In Transit.*
GERALD L. BRUNS, *Modern Poetry and the Idea of Language.*
GABRIELLE BURTON, *Heartbreak Hotel.*
MICHEL BUTOR, *Degrees.*
Mobile.
G. CABRERA INFANTE, *Infante's Inferno.*
Three Trapped Tigers.
JULIETA CAMPOS, *The Fear of Losing Eurydice.*
ANNE CARSON, *Eros the Bittersweet.*
ORLY CASTEL-BLOOM, *Dolly City.*
LOUIS-FERDINAND CÉLINE, *Castle to Castle.*
Conversations with Professor Y.
London Bridge.
Normance.
North.
Rigadoon.
MARIE CHAIX, *The Laurels of Lake Constance.*
HUGO CHARTERIS, *The Tide Is Right.*
ERIC CHEVILLARD, *Demolishing Nisard.*

MARC CHOLODENKO, *Mordechai Schamz.*
JOSHUA COHEN, *Witz.*
EMILY HOLMES COLEMAN, *The Shutter of Snow.*
ROBERT COOVER, *A Night at the Movies.*
STANLEY CRAWFORD, *Log of the S.S. The Mrs Unguentine.*
Some Instructions to My Wife.
RENÉ CREVEL, *Putting My Foot in It.*
RALPH CUSACK, *Cadenza.*
NICHOLAS DELBANCO, *The Count of Concord.*
Sherbrookes.
NIGEL DENNIS, *Cards of Identity.*
PETER DIMOCK, *A Short Rhetoric for Leaving the Family.*
ARIEL DORFMAN, *Konfidenz.*
COLEMAN DOWELL, *Island People.*
Too Much Flesh and Jabez.
ARKADII DRAGOMOSHCHENKO, *Dust.*
RIKKI DUCORNET, *The Complete Butcher's Tales.*
The Fountains of Neptune.
The Jade Cabinet.
Phosphor in Dreamland.
WILLIAM EASTLAKE, *The Bamboo Bed.*
Castle Keep.
Lyric of the Circle Heart.
JEAN ECHENOZ, *Chopin's Move.*
STANLEY ELKIN, *A Bad Man.*
Criers and Kibitzers, Kibitzers and Criers.
The Dick Gibson Show.
The Franchiser.
The Living End.
Mrs. Ted Bliss.
FRANÇOIS EMMANUEL, *Invitation to a Voyage.*
SALVADOR ESPRIU, *Ariadne in the Grotesque Labyrinth.*
LESLIE A. FIEDLER, *Love and Death in the American Novel.*
JUAN FILLOY, *Op Oloop.*
ANDY FITCH, *Pop Poetics.*
GUSTAVE FLAUBERT, *Bouvard and Pécuchet.*
KASS FLEISHER, *Talking out of School.*
FORD MADOX FORD, *The March of Literature.*
JON FOSSE, *Aliss at the Fire.*
Melancholy.
MAX FRISCH, *I'm Not Stiller.*
Man in the Holocene.
CARLOS FUENTES, *Christopher Unborn.*
Distant Relations.
Terra Nostra.
Where the Air Is Clear.
TAKEHIKO FUKUNAGA, *Flowers of Grass.*
WILLIAM GADDIS, *J R.*
The Recognitions.

SELECTED DALKEY ARCHIVE TITLES

SELECTED DALKEY ARCHIVE TITLES

JOSEPH MCELROY,
Night Soul and Other Stories.
ABDELWAHAB MEDDEB, *Talismano.*
GERHARD MEIER, *Isle of the Dead.*
HERMAN MELVILLE, *The Confidence-Man.*
AMANDA MICHALOPOULOU, *I'd Like.*
STEVEN MILLHAUSER, *The Barnum Museum.*
In the Penny Arcade.
RALPH J. MILLS, JR., *Essays on Poetry.*
MOMUS, *The Book of Jokes.*
CHRISTINE MONTALBETTI, *The Origin of Man.*
Western.
OLIVE MOORE, *Spleen.*
NICHOLAS MOSLEY, *Accident.*
Assassins.
Catastrophe Practice.
Experience and Religion.
A Garden of Trees.
Hopeful Monsters.
Imago Bird.
Impossible Object.
Inventing God.
Judith.
Look at the Dark.
Natalie Natalia.
Serpent.
Time at War.
WARREN MOTTE,
*Fables of the Novel: French Fiction
since 1990.*
*Fiction Now: The French Novel in
the 21st Century.*
*Oulipo: A Primer of Potential
Literature.*
GERALD MURNANE, *Barley Patch.*
Inland.
YVES NAVARRE, *Our Share of Time.*
Sweet Tooth.
DOROTHY NELSON, *In Night's City.*
Tar and Feathers.
ESHKOL NEVO, *Homesick.*
WILFRIDO D. NOLLEDO, *But for the Lovers.*
FLANN O'BRIEN, *At Swim-Two-Birds.*
The Best of Myles.
The Dalkey Archive.
The Hard Life.
The Poor Mouth.
The Third Policeman.
CLAUDE OLLIER, *The Mise-en-Scène.*
Wert and the Life Without End.
GIOVANNI ORELLI, *Walaschek's Dream.*
PATRIK OUŘEDNÍK, *Europeana.*
The Opportune Moment, 1855.
BORIS PAHOR, *Necropolis.*
FERNANDO DEL PASO, *News from the
Empire.*
Palinuro of Mexico.
ROBERT PINGET, *The Inquisitory.*
Mahu or The Material.
Trio.
MANUEL PUIG, *Betrayed by Rita Hayworth.*

The Buenos Aires Affair.
Heartbreak Tango.
RAYMOND QUENEAU, *The Last Days.*
Odile.
Pierrot Mon Ami.
Saint Glinglin.
ANN QUIN, *Berg.*
Passages.
Three.
Tripticks.
ISHMAEL REED, *The Free-Lance Pallbearers.*
The Last Days of Louisiana Red.
Ishmael Reed: The Plays.
Juice!
Reckless Eyeballing.
The Terrible Threes.
The Terrible Twos.
Yellow Back Radio Broke-Down.
JASIA REICHARDT, *15 Journeys Warsaw
to London.*
NOËLLE REVAZ, *With the Animals.*
JOÃO UBALDO RIBEIRO, *House of the
Fortunate Buddhas.*
JEAN RICARDOU, *Place Names.*
RAINER MARIA RILKE, *The Notebooks of
Malte Laurids Brigge.*
JULIÁN RÍOS, *The House of Ulysses.*
Larva: A Midsummer Night's Babel.
Poundemonium.
Procession of Shadows.
AUGUSTO ROA BASTOS, *I the Supreme.*
DANIËL ROBBERECHTS, *Arriving in Avignon.*
JEAN ROLIN, *The Explosion of the
Radiator Hose.*
OLIVIER ROLIN, *Hotel Crystal.*
ALIX CLEO ROUBAUD, *Alix's Journal.*
JACQUES ROUBAUD, *The Form of a
City Changes Faster, Alas, Than
the Human Heart.*
The Great Fire of London.
Hortense in Exile.
Hortense Is Abducted.
The Loop.
Mathematics:
The Plurality of Worlds of Lewis.
The Princess Hoppy.
Some Thing Black.
RAYMOND ROUSSEL, *Impressions of Africa.*
VEDRANA RUDAN, *Night.*
STIG SÆTERBAKKEN, *Siamese.*
Self Control.
LYDIE SALVAYRE, *The Company of Ghosts.*
The Lecture.
The Power of Flies.
LUIS RAFAEL SÁNCHEZ,
Macho Camacho's Beat.
SEVERO SARDUY, *Cobra & Maitreya.*
NATHALIE SARRAUTE,
Do You Hear Them?
Martereau.
The Planetarium.

FOR A FULL LIST OF PUBLICATIONS, VISIT:
www.dalkeyarchive.com

ARNO SCHMIDT, *Collected Novellas.*
Collected Stories.
Nobodaddy's Children.
Two Novels.
ASAF SCHURR, *Motti.*
GAIL SCOTT, *My Paris.*
DAMION SEARLS, *What We Were Doing
and Where We Were Going.*
JUNE AKERS SEESE,
Is This What Other Women Feel Too?
What Waiting Really Means.
BERNARD SHARE, *Inish.*
Transit.
VIKTOR SHKLOVSKY, *Bowstring.*
Knight's Move.
*A Sentimental Journey:
Memoirs 1917–1922.*
Energy of Delusion: A Book on Plot.
Literature and Cinematography.
Theory of Prose.
Third Factory.
Zoo, or Letters Not about Love.
PIERRE SINIAC, *The Collaborators.*
KJERSTI A. SKOMSVOLD, *The Faster I Walk,
the Smaller I Am.*
JOSEF ŠKVORECKÝ, *The Engineer of
Human Souls.*
GILBERT SORRENTINO,
Aberration of Starlight.
Blue Pastoral.
Crystal Vision.
*Imaginative Qualities of Actual
Things.*
Mulligan Stew.
Pack of Lies.
Red the Fiend.
The Sky Changes.
Something Said.
Splendide-Hôtel.
Steelwork.
Under the Shadow.
W. M. SPACKMAN, *The Complete Fiction.*
ANDRZEJ STASIUK, *Dukla.*
Fado.
GERTRUDE STEIN, *The Making of Americans.*
A Novel of Thank You.
LARS SVENDSEN, *A Philosophy of Evil.*
PIOTR SZEWC, *Annihilation.*
GONÇALO M. TAVARES, *Jerusalem.*
Joseph Walser's Machine.
*Learning to Pray in the Age of
Technique.*
LUCIAN DAN TEODOROVICI,
Our Circus Presents . . .
NIKANOR TERATOLOGEN, *Assisted Living.*
STEFAN THEMERSON, *Hobson's Island.*
The Mystery of the Sardine.
Tom Harris.
TAEKO TOMIOKA, *Building Waves.*

JOHN TOOMEY, *Sleepwalker.*
JEAN-PHILIPPE TOUSSAINT, *The Bathroom.*
Camera.
Monsieur.
Reticence.
Running Away.
Self-Portrait Abroad.
Television.
The Truth about Marie.
DUMITRU TSEPENEAG, *Hotel Europa.*
The Necessary Marriage.
Pigeon Post.
Vain Art of the Fugue.
ESTHER TUSQUETS, *Stranded.*
DUBRAVKA UGRESIC, *Lend Me Your
Character.*
Thank You for Not Reading.
TOR ULVEN, *Replacement.*
MATI UNT, *Brecht at Night.*
Diary of a Blood Donor.
Things in the Night.
ÁLVARO URIBE AND OLIVIA SEARS, EDS.,
Best of Contemporary Mexican Fiction.
ELOY URROZ, *Friction.*
The Obstacles.
LUISA VALENZUELA, *Dark Desires and
the Others.*
He Who Searches.
PAUL VERHAEGHEN, *Omega Minor.*
AGLAJA VETERANYI, *Why the Child Is
Cooking in the Polenta.*
BORIS VIAN, *Heartsnatcher.*
LLORENÇ VILLALONGA, *The Dolls' Room.*
TOOMAS VINT, *An Unending Landscape.*
ORNELA VORPSI, *The Country Where No
One Ever Dies.*
AUSTRYN WAINHOUSE, *Hedyphagetica.*
CURTIS WHITE, *America's Magic Mountain.*
The Idea of Home.
Memories of My Father Watching TV.
Requiem.
DIANE WILLIAMS, *Excitability:
Selected Stories.*
Romancer Erector.
DOUGLAS WOOLF, *Wall to Wall.*
Ya! & John-Juan.
JAY WRIGHT, *Polynomials and Pollen.*
*The Presentable Art of Reading
Absence.*
PHILIP WYLIE, *Generation of Vipers.*
MARGUERITE YOUNG, *Angel in the Forest.*
Miss MacIntosh, My Darling.
REYOUNG, *Unbabbling.*
VLADO ŽABOT, *The Succubus.*
ZORAN ŽIVKOVIĆ, *Hidden Camera.*
LOUIS ZUKOFSKY, *Collected Fiction.*
VITOMIL ZUPAN, *Minuet for Guitar.*
SCOTT ZWIREN, *God Head.*